KING DAVID:
WAR AND ECSTASY

KING DAVID: WAR AND ECSTASY

COLIN PRITCHARD

JANUS PUBLISHING COMPANY
London, England

First published in Great Britain 2000
by Janus Publishing Company Limited,
76 Great Titchfield Street,
London W1P 7AF

www.januspublishing.co.uk

**A CIP catalogue record for this book
is available from the British Library.**

ISBN 1 85756 414 6

Typeset in 10pt Baskerville

Cover design Hamish Cooper

Printed and bound in Great Britain

DEDICATION

This book is dedicated to my wonderful women,
Rebecca Anne, Claire Elizabeth and Beryl Anne.

Rebecca and Claire have given me love and inspiration,way beyond my deserts.
Beryl Anne has sustained, supported and cherished me, and lived with David in patient good humour and never failing invaluable advice.

In appreciation and love

I am grateful for yesterday,
Thankful for today,
And hopeful for the morrow,
For I am content.

Margrit Petrick

DRAMATIS PERSONAE BOOK 1

Biblical names given in brackets. Fictional character [f].

Aaron   [f] Friend from David's boyhood, part of the trio.

Abashi   [Abishia] Brother of Joab and a firebrand.

Abathar   [Abiathar] Son of Amelech his ultimate successor as Chief Priest.

Abibadab   Second older brother of David.

Abigail   Wife and then widow of Nabal, a wise women and David's third wife, who bore his second son, Kilab.

Abita   David's sixth wife.

Abner   Cousin of King Saul and second man in Israel sought to block David's Kingship.

Absalom   David's third son, born to Macha, daughter of Talmai, King of Geshur; seeks to usurp the crown.

Achish   King of Gath, one of the kings of the Philistines who befriended David in his exile.

Acrah   [f] Lover of Achish.

Adonijah   David's fourth son, also seeks to usurp the kingdom.

Amlech   [Amhilech] Priest of Israel murdered by Saul.

Amnon   David's eldest son, born to his second wife, Annah.
Annan   [Ahinoam] of Jezreel.

Ashael   Youngest brother of Joab and a brave officer in his army.

Beniah   Friend, counsellor and captain of David's guard.

Boaz   An older brother of David.

Canan   [f] Benjaminite solider, and member of Jonathan's guard.

David   Youngest son of Jesse of Bethlehem of the clan of Judia, shepherd, poet, musician,warrior, outlaw and King of Judah and Israel, the subject of his history.

Eli   [f] Friend of David's boyhood along with Aaron and Josh.

Eliab   Eldest son of Jesse and brother to David.

Elim   The armour bearer to Jonathan, though the Bible did not give his name.

Gad   A prophet, David's adviser.

Goliath   A giant of a man from Gath, champion of the Philistines.

Ganz   [f] A cousin of Goliath.

Hitophel   [Ahitophel] David's friend, who later deserts him for Absalom.

Horah   [f] David, Eli, Aaron and Josh's trainer.

Hushai   David's friend. Another companion, like Beniah.

Ishoboth   [Ish-Bosheth] A surviving son of Saul, made King by Abner.

Jesse   David's Father and youngest grandson of Boaz who married Ruth the Moabite.

Joab   Son of David's sister, Zeruiah, becomes 'Second Man' in Israel.

Jonathan   Son of King Saul, a brave soldier and leader and lover of David.

Josh   [Joseph] A boyhood friend of David and one of the Three Great Men of Israel.

Kiliab	David's second son, born to the wise Abigail.
Kish	A candidate for Saul's Kingship.
Leah	[f] David's first love, a prototype of Ruth who was David's Great Grandmother and was married into Israel.
Mephib	[Mephibosheth] A physically handicapped son of Jonathan and grandson of King Saul.
Merab	Eldest daughter of Saul, promised to David after the death of Goliath.
Michal	Second daughter of King Saul, David's first wife.
Nathan	Prophet and spiritual adviser to David.
Samuel	A prophet and the last of the line of the judges who ruled Israel.
Saul	First king of the nation of Israel, son of Kish of the tribe of Benjamin.
Shammah	Third son of Jesse and brother to David.
Uriah	A Hittite, one of David's Companions, husband to Bathsheba. David arranges his murder.
Ura	[f] A Hittite older brother of Uriah, friend of Jonathan.
Uzza	Soldier of David "brother" of Ura, died for "sacrilege" of touching Ark.
Zadok	Joint priest with - and eventual successor to Abathar.
Zeruiah	David's sister, mother of Joab, and also name of his Mother.

ACKNOWLEDGEMENTS

I am indebted to generations of students, who have asked searching questions about the human state from the Universities of Bath, Leeds, Manchester and Southampton; on the continent, Bucharest, Budapest, and Skopje; in Australia, at the Universities of Curtain, Flinders, Monash, New South Wales, Queensland and Sydney, and the Hong Kong Polytechnic University. I have drawn upon a wide range of sources, King James' revised version of the books of Samuel I and II, Kings I and II was my raw material, whilst the psalms of David were an inspiration. Although eschewing theology, Sir Fred Catherwood's text was helpful and Charles Pellegrino's histrico-archaeological *Return to Sodom and Gomorrah* was seminal. A significant part of the writing was by Mahler's Toblacher see in the South Tirol, and I am very grateful for the friendship and hospitality of Werner and Heide Petrick. Finally, my thanks, to Rod Spreadbury for his invaluable support and friendship.

CONTENTS

PART FIVE - THE FIRST COMMAND

PART SIX - THE EXILE

PART SEVEN - CATASTROPHE AND KINGSHIP

PREFACE

David: slayer of Goliath, Conqueror and King of Israel, lover of Jonathan, and murderer of his friend Uriah, whose wife, Bathsheba, he ravished. David's many exploits have echoed down the ages. It was believed that he walked with God and heard His voice. David was a sensualist, an idealist, a protector of the poor and a great poet. He was a controversial figure, certainly, for he was a man of mighty passions and God's warrior bard.

Over the passing years, lesser men turned him into a religious icon and his essential humanity has almost been lost. This book allows David to tell his own story as it happened, not with the benefit of hindsight, nor the sanitised version that turned him into a saint, but the story of the real man. There is little virtue in sainthood if there is no fear, hate, passion or uncertainty to demonstrate a life's worth.

David was inextricably caught up in the struggle between the Prophet Samuel and King Saul. Hence, his story includes the titanic clash between Israel's High Priest and Israel's first King.

David's life was also greatly influenced by Saul's son, Jonathan, the noblest prince of all time. David's love of Jonathan has always been contentious, but I believe that the essential spiritual and physical aspect of their love transcends others' insistence that it was platonic in nature.

The story takes us to his coronation, when, as the result of many brutal struggles, David reunites Israel after it had been shattered by the tragic and tormented Saul. Historical honesty concedes that it was the Philistines, not the Israelites, who were relatively civilised 1,000 years before Christ. Indeed, part of David's divine task was to educate the semi-nomadic tribes of Israel and to illuminate his deity through his psalms of matchless beauty. His poetry demonstrates that David was a believer for whom the divine was a real experience, despite his occasional confusion at the actions sanctioned by his God.

David's core humanity illuminates the lives of the other characters in this psychobiography. It allows us to look more deeply into the traditional Biblical narratives and see people authentically - neither as saints nor demons. David was a man of understanding and had compassion for others. Nevertheless, he too was flawed and speaks for all when he says, "Judge me, Oh Lord, for I have walked in mine own integrity."

Some brief explanatory points are necessary. All names have been modernised. Only one main character, Leah, is fictional - the rest may be found in the Biblical narrative. I have also resolved a number of Biblical inconsistencies in David's story. I have aimed for psychological authenticity and thus, I have presented the most likely explanation of what happened during those brutal and confusing times.

Colin Pritchard
University of Southampton
and Toblach   June 2000

PART ONE

THE YOUNG
DAVID

Chapter One

The Dream and the Promise

"DAVID! DAVID! LION OF JUDAH! DAVID, KING OF ISRAEL! HALLELUJAH! HALLELUJAH!" The sound was deafening as the people of Israel acclaimed my coronation.

My senses reeled and I was overwhelmed by the crowd's excitement. The sun glinting off the ranks of upraised swords dazzled me. I felt giddy from staring at the mass of palm leaves as they were waved from side to side like giant flags. The glorious colours on the clothing of the Twelve Tribes filled the valley as far as the eye could see.

The assembled multitude chanted in unison, "DAVID, KING OF THE JEWS. HALLELUJAH, DAVID. KING DAVID, LION OF JUDAH. DAVID, KING OF ISRAEL!"

The rolling waves of sound and colour crashed against the hillsides, and cascaded back again, each cry building upon the previous as the Israelites celebrated their renewed nationhood.

Yes, all the Twelve Tribes were there. All could see that I led a united people and that every face reflected back my delight. Forgotten or forgiven was the blood that had been spilt. The years in the wilderness, when Jew had hunted Jew, were finally at an end. When these self-inflicted wounds threatened to shatter our people for ever, I had staunched the bleeding. I had been victorious against our enemies and I had turned our weapons against the foes of the Living God.

I was almost in a delirium, yet I could look around and make sense of what was happening. This had been God's special gift to me: even in the turmoil of the stomach-wrenching fear amidst fight or desperate flight, I could still see clearly. Others were overwhelmed by events but I rode through them, even though I shared the emotion. Oh yes – I too feared the spear thrust. I dreaded the slash of the sharp iron biting deep, deep into my limbs, as I, in return, slashed, hacked and cut into the limbs of him who would kill me. I too felt the exhilaration when my sword crashed through his defence and pierced his quivering body. Then the tired dread as another warrior stood before me, and the kill-or-be-killed began again.

"DAVID, KING OF ISRAEL. DAVID KING OF ISRAEL," had become a driving rhythm and the Horns of the Rams of the priests blared in unison with the cries of the people. Each man and woman was as one; they acclaimed their king, affirmed that they were One People and that his Triumph belonged to them. Even Joab was smiling. Our eyes met. He looked at me with unusual warmth. My dour second in command, though a nephew, was only two years my junior. He liked to style himself "The Second Man in Israel". He was taller than I was – a big man with his dark hair showing beneath his armour.

I walked over and embraced him. I could feel his excitement, smell his perspiration. I looked into his eyes, and perhaps for the last and only time, I could see total joy and loyalty. I kissed him and if possible the shouts grew even louder.

He returned my embrace in a huge bear hug, "David, David, you've done it, you are King. The Tribes are yours, we are one people, you are the Lord's anointed."

He stood close, giving recognition that it was my triumph. Oh yes he had helped, but here was his admission that I was the chosen one, and through all the doubts and trials, I was the rightful King. I kissed him again and then raised my hand to salute him. The crowd went wild as he kneeled before me.

I walked over to Joab's brother who was standing amongst the Band of Thirty, my brothers in arms, my Captains over the thousands.

I turned to Abishi. Ever dauntless, ever true, his face told it all as he kneeled before me; his delight was for me. He had never doubted, he shared unquestioningly the goal of freeing the people. He looked up, "David my King, my general, Chosen of the Living God. David, I am so proud and so humble."

I put my hand gently to his mouth, and raised him up, "No, no Abishi, my Captain, companion, friend and from this day, brother. You and your brothers, along with the Captains and the Six Hundred, you have made this day. You have accomplished all that the Lord of Hosts demanded of us. Your wounds are marks of honour in God's and the people's service. I am the privileged one. Although God chose me, it was your right arm that slew God's enemies and set the people free."

I had to shout this to make Abishi hear even though I was close to him. The other Captains, Uriah the Hittite – the bravest of them all, Ahitofel the cunning, Hushi the Edomite, Beniah the wise and captain of my guard, heard what I had said and repeated it to those around as I went and saluted each of them in turn. Unbelievably the noise increased to new heights.

The Thirty were my bravest captains and my earliest Companions. They had first served with me under Jonathan, son of Saul. They shared my exile when Saul's madness drove me out, as he followed his own tortured way, which made Israel so vulnerable to the nations surrounding us. They led the Six Hundred, men who had formed the elite of our army. Who taught the tribes of Israel how to use the iron swords; to face and win against the odds – against the cruel Amalekites – the fierce Ammonites but most of all, our most dangerous foe that sought to enslave all, the Philistines. From their cities with their cunning organisation and advanced weapons, the Philistines had enjoyed tribute from Israel. They had undermined our unity by buying some of the Tribes with their wealth. Yet we had beaten them all.

The Thirty as one man, kneeled and began to sing our battle song. "Hosanna to the God of Israel, Hosanna to David the Lord's anointed."

The Six Hundred followed, as did the crowd. The only people standing were the priests surrounding the Ark of the Covenant.

The people's voices swelled into a glorious choir. The valley echoed with the melody that reminded them of our journey together.

I walked towards the Ark, symbol of God's promise to the seed of Abraham, the first father of all Israel. I was smiling but saw clearly what had to be done.

My smiles were returned as I walked towards the singing priests. Abathar, who I had made High Priest, loyal because he had no where else to turn, sleek and lethargic with an over indulgence of the sacrificial meats. His father Amlech had been priest before him. Saul who had slaughtered the rest of his family, even though they were of the seed of Moses. Gad, a prophet and aesthetic, whose only ambition was for the people of Israel. Zadok, young but very able, tall and watchful and Nathan. Dear Nathan who was both support and spur, willing to share his communications with God, ever ready to be critical if he thought it would help.

I turned first to Abathar, who had led the re-anointing and who could administer the rites and enter the Ark of the Covenant without it being sacrilege. I looked into his eyes and gently placed my hands upon his shoulders and, as if I were about to kiss him, I gently pressed him downwards. He knew what I wanted. At first there was tension in his body, whilst he could not look me in the eyes, he was aware of the moment. We were fixed in time. The King of Israel stood with his hands upon the High Priest of Israel. Who would kneel to whom? Each subtle movement seemed to take an age.

I was conscious of the smell of the holy oil on Abathar's hands, of his woollen cloak coloured scarlet, of his blue headband holding fast his hair, which drooped in long curls. His skin was moist and at the corner of his mouth the light caught the spittle lying upon his lips from his singing.

Would he never kneel, or would I have to bow and give way? My arms grew tense. Though my face still held its smile, there was no pretence in my grip as my fingers dug into his flabby shoulders. Suddenly, the tension eased as Abathar slowly bent his knees. He lowered his head, kneeled upon the ground, threw wide his arms and cried, "Blessed be David, King of Israel, the Lord's Anointed, Hosanna."

I looked around and saw Gad already on his knees; he wanted this as much as I did. The people needed to see that it was the King who led in Israel. Nathan followed and joined in Abathar's rhythmic chant, " Blessed be David, King of Israel, the Lord's anointed."

It was Zadok, who I might have known, was last on his knees but he too gave his voice to the priestly descant that rose above the Choir of Israel.

Now I was King indeed. Amidst the peoples of Israel no one stood except I. It was the King who was the Lord's Anointed; he led God's people because he was chosen. Though it was the priest and Prophets who confirmed the Lord's anointed, it was the King who ruled the peoples of Israel.

Now it was the time for me to prophesy. With a gesture, I caught the people's attention and suddenly all was silent. This was almost more awe-inspiring than the earlier hallelujahs. All had become as one person. There was a catching of the breath; the moment was an island of silence, as the tension became palpable, unbearable.

I was inspired. I knew that God was about to speak through me in a way He had never done before. But as before, I felt an emptying of myself, everything fell from me.

There was stillness inside me, as I became part of everything – a blade of grass, a stone, a cloud. I was nothing but belonged to everything. For that brief and eternal moment I was at one with the One.

"People of Israel," I cried. "People of Israel, your Lord's Anointed speaks to you from the Lord of Hosts. I am commanded to say His words, from the mouth of the Ever Living God. You are My chosen people. Through you I will reach the ends of the world. You are My people who will fulfil My purpose for all mankind. As I spoke to your father Abraham and to Moses who brought you out of the land of Egypt, I am still with you."

I paused. There was utter stillness. Even the breeze was still. I circled, with my hands raised high. Every eye was upon me. I was possessed with the Spirit.

"Hear what the Lord your God says to you. This day is a day of renewal of My covenant. You Are My people and I am Your God. I will make you great in the face of all peoples.

"The King shall rejoice in the strength of Lord. I will bless the Lord at all times; in Him do I put my trust. Oh clap your hands you people of God, shout unto Him with the voice of triumph for He is a Great King over all the earth."

I was overcome; I sank to the ground, my arms out held in supplication. Weakly I spoke the words, "Hosanna to the Lord."

Abathar, Nathan and Gad took up the words, so did the Captains and the Six Hundred and so did the peoples of Israel, as once more they united in a glorious choir.

Slowly I rose, dazed and drained by the power that had possessed me.

Abigail – sweet, sweet Abigail – my wife had come to me in my faint. She was one of the greatest loves of my life, and though a woman she was wiser than many a man. She shared my counsel as no other. She was gentle, knew me better than myself and, moreover, she was forgiving.

She drew me up and as she did so I saluted her. "Daughter of Judah, my succour. I acknowledge you and all the daughters of Judah who gave so much." This was unprecedented. A warrior and King giving public praise to a woman – even though she was his favourite wife!

Next to Abigail stood another wife, Annah, whom I also saluted. She was from the tribe of Issachar, and my words clearly pleased her and the Issacharites.

I sensed a step behind me and there was Michal, the daughter of Saul of the tribe of Benjamin, my first wife. She was queenly. This was the high point of her life and our marriage. She loved me in her way, but never allowed me to forget that she was the daughter of a King. She had been given to me as sop instead of her elder sister Merab whom Saul had married elsewhere, despite promising her to me after I had slain Goliath.

"To you Michal, royal daughter of Benjamin," I said, "for your loyalty and devotion to Israel's cause I salute you also." This reminded the Benjaminites of my direct link with their tribe and Israel's first Royal Family.

Looking at Michal there could be no doubt that she was indeed royal. She bowed rather than kneeled. She proclaimed, "Oh King My Husband, I am your maid servant, and the daughter of Saul." There his name was out in the open.

"I salute you in obedience, as the Lord's anointed and ask for the people's prayer that I may give you a son."

Poor Michal, despite her beauty, her bearing, she always said the right thing in the wrong way. Her mentioning her father reminded us of his failure. How he had turned away from God. How he had divided the people and despite his many earlier victories, had laid the country open to our enemies.

She, who longed to continue a royal line, reminded everyone that despite having had two husbands, she remained childless. Whereas Abigail had already given me Kileab, Annah a son Amnon, and my other wives had given me my sons Absalom, Adonijah, Sheph, and Ithream.

This gave me the opportunity to fulfil my obligation to Abigail and all the women of Israel.

"Men of Israel," I commanded, "salute your wives, mothers, sisters who have also borne all our tribulations. Hosanna to the women of Israel."

There was a great answering shout of "hosanna" from every man present and then the women's ululating cry, which we warriors heard only when we went to battle. My hair rose on end, as did every man's. It reminded us that the line between being a worker in the fields, a shepherd, and being a solider that goes to kill or be killed, is very thin.

As the women's cry faded, Joab came forward, ever the practical man, and said, "David, our King, let us begin the sacrifices to the Lord and then the feast."

The priest came forward led by Abathar, supported by the others, and then sheer revelation from Gad the prophet and priest. "David, King of Israel, you have given us the word of God, now give us your word."

I was stunned for a moment. I could hardly think and then signalled to the Thirty Captains. They strung out into the tribes, a hundred paces each so that they could hear my voice and then pass on my message, the way we spoke to the army in battle. This would be my message, my recollection of how it was.

"The Lord is My shepherd, I shall not want, he maketh me to lie down in green pastures."

As long as it takes to say it, all the people took up the psalm – which I had written at another time, for another cause – but in which the Six Hundred had found an inspiration. When we came to the point where we all recalled our inner dread;

"Yea though I walk through the valley of the shadow of death I will fear no evil."

After a silent pause there was a roar and the chant broke out again

"DAVID, DAVID, LION OF JUDAH. DAVID, KING OF ISRAEL. HALLELUJAH. HALLELUJAH."

I awoke with a start. Where was I?

Was that a dream or a precious memory? I looked around; the lamp had ceased to burn and a thin curl of smoke moved towards the door under which grey daylight seeped.

My re-anointing was both memory and dream for which, as an old man, I was grateful. My hip ached, how many years had passed since that time? How many now slept in the bosom of Abraham? Their faces merged into my memory, tumbling over each other. Leah, Jonathan, Abigail; all whom I loved. Saul – yes I once loved Saul even though he tried to kill me. Samuel the prophet, Achish, though a King of Philistine was my friend. Acrah, another friend, but who died from wounds I gave him. Then stark, the face of the first man I ever slew – his face almost above all others is burned into my brain. Where are they all now?

How had I, the youngest of my father Jesse's house become the Lord's Anointed and undisputed King of Israel?

I am old, and though just awakening from sleep I am already tired. I ache inside my head. What was it all for, I who am waiting to die? I wonder why I did not die sooner and save myself so much misery.

If I had died within ten years of becoming King, I would have been spared the crime of becoming old and the compromises and sins that are inevitable to men burdened with power. For the sins of men in authority, unlike the sins of ordinary men, lie heavy by seeming inescapable. Moreover, they have consequences far beyond what was intended. Yet I tried to make my life a service for a greater purpose. Or was it?

I thought I wanted to die after Leah, even now I can not think beyond our beginning. She was the first love of my life. She taught me that the fusion of two minds, two spirits and two bodies could reach the ecstasy of God. Yet even in my sorrow for the loss of her and other terrible grief's I endured, I did not seek that ultimate oblivion but await my end in hope.

This dream, a memory of my coronation, has returned so often that I begin to see it has a meaning.

I must face my past because there is so little future. For those who come after me, they too must solve the inevitable clash of duty, which brings power, promises of pleasure and freedom. But with that power there are repercussions, which are compounded as the small flaws of the humble man are magnified in the mighty.

I understand. I must correct those myths, which makes me sound miraculous and perfect.

9

I remember the flattering, corrupting cry, "Saul has slain his thousands but David his tens of thousands" and I was not then   eighteen!

To those detractors, who mire everything, suggesting all I sought was domination and the fulfilment of my carnal desires, I answer, "though I have loved many women, yes, and gloried in many concubines – indeed, loved two men – the idea that my power was only the pursuit of pleasures of the flesh, that I was a hypocrite, that I abused my gifts and communion with God, shows they understand nothing."

My life was the story of a search for a better communion with the Ever Living God and communion with the essential beauty of the world. Communion to understand one's own mind and intellect. Communion with the merging of two bodies into one. Communion with the people to fulfil the greater purpose of God.

I shall write my story, not as history but as how I experienced it at the time. Not with the benefits of hindsight and not as a mature warrior and King, so that both triumphs and disasters become understandable, but how it felt as a young man.

Now I understand, I must tell my story without excusing myself. How I responded to each situation but with the weight of being God's chosen upon me.

Oh yes, you might well think being Chosen would be splendid. Though God sometime spoke and clearly guided me, most of the time I felt the agony of not knowing when it was his voice, or no voice at all!

I was a musician, a poet, who would have been happy to serve by praising God, and our beautiful land. Instead I had to become a warrior and, yes, a killer of men – living a story whose end I did not know.

When first I met a Philistine warrior face to face, I was just sixteen; he was a full man. He tried to kill me and I thought he was going to. He might well have slain me had his spear not glanced against the rock face. My story was only at its beginning but it might have been the end had it not been for God defending me. For how could it have been anything other than God's hand, for in all my battles, I was never wounded?

Yet could all of this have been mere chance and I am simply   justifying events? Such doubts and questions were once asked by a friend and enemy – terrible thoughts, which I reject utterly.

I killed Goliath of the Philistines, but not effortlessly as the myth tells for I was so close to death. Though I was confident that God would be with me, I had to endure terror in my soul. The mind-bending fear was still there and I had to withstand not knowing the outcome of that terrible battle.

My songs, called psalms, tell all. Often I felt desolate the loneliness of him with responsibility. I was twenty when I began an exile in which not a month passed but I might die. I could only hope, think, struggle, and throughout I did not know how the story would end.

I was not thirty and felt the full weight of God's demands. A people's needs were heavy upon me from a nation who had a covenant with God. They had been broken, beaten, paying tribute and splintered, but I reunited them against all odds. Though I knew I was doing what God required, his ways were often inscrutable. I was tortured by the uncertainty, was I but a symbol, a necessary sacrifice: preparing the way for another?

Now is the time for me to tell my story, because one end I do know. Soon I will be in Abraham's bosom, becoming one with God's Oneness. That is certain despite the doubts I once had.

It has been prophesied that my seed would be "a light to lighten the gentiles", so I will try to make my story explicable to strangers who are to come after me and who may not be familiar with the story of God's covenant with Israel.

I pray that the Lord of Hosts will give me the strength to tell all. How a man's life has to bring everything together. How a man is not whole unless he is at one with his people, his God, his world, his mind, spirit – aye, and body too. For ecstasies abound for him who brings together the joys of his body in union with another's – whose mind and spirit are at one with God. Thus his life is fulfilled in the service, so that God's purpose, so fleetingly seen, can be achieved.

My story is here for *you* to determine. And before God and man I ask forgiveness for my weaknesses. Above all, I seek your understanding and hope that when you face your challenge; there may be comfort in a benediction from one long since gone.

Here is the story of David, a shepherd, poet, soldier, prince, prophet and king. But above all, a weak and frail man who played his part as best he could, and asks of God and You to

"Judge me oh Lord for I have walked in mine integrity."

Chapter Two

The First Kill

What kind of boy was I? Before I let the young David tell his story in his own words, I must describe him who, for many years, has become a beautiful stranger to me.

At first there was little to distinguish this young Judean from other youth of Bethlehem. He was not very tall; he had shoulder- length hair, typical of young men, bound by a white headband indicating his post bar mitzvah status, which when coming of age would be woven with his tribal colour of white and gold. A red stripe would be added when he became a full warrior at 20, or when he killed his first man.

He had a sturdy athletic build, with broad shoulders and tapering waist typical of athletes and long distance runners. He had a fine upright head with a broad forehead, which sometimes he would hold to one side in a questioning, quizzical, look.

He had a ready smile, and two dimples that embarrassed him when young. Olive skinned and, though his manhood had arrived, as yet there was only slight evidence of an emerging beard.

A firm regular nose and rather full curved lips, which many a girl would envy and secretly sigh after, balanced his open face. Most unusual were his dark blue eyes, which possibly reflected his Moabite inheritance.

His eyes and smile were his best features, which would part explain his apparent easy popularity, not just with his friends Josh, Aaron and Eli but with many adults. However, on closer inspection, one could recognise that his eyes were those of a dreamer, as when unobserved, they would mellow, so that even then, you could sense his intuitive mysticism. At other times his eyes would shine with excitement and intelligence. His friend Eli had a half understanding of why, when his teacher overcame the clowning with his classmates, the Rabbi's soul was uplifted by David unconsciously teaching the master, by asking questions to which he had no answer.

On rare occasions, however those eyes could be palest blue-black in

12

anger. They pierced with a fierce concentration, which explained why there was no real threat from older youths, as even the bully Boaz approached him wearily.

In short he was a youth entering the first flush of manhood. Bandied up and down by love and anger, not too good or wise, but having the reck-lessness of youth; he would risk all for a friend, an idea, and the moment. He might be hurt for a little while but the smart would soon be forgotten amidst tumbling smiles, as a new hour, a new day opened and life with all its excitement beckoned. His friendship with Josh, Aaron and Eli was enviable as they had all the exuberance and energy of adolescence, with its charm and excitement, which makes old men smile in envious memory. But let my young self tell his own story and live again in those far, far off days.

My story begins after I was fourteen and I had completed my bar mitzvah, and became part of Israel, as a thinking being. Not that our childhood is unimportant, but our worlds are bound by such immediacies as getting through the day, avoiding the bully, and there are always bullies in childhood. Sadly they can lurk even in the family, my brother Boaz being a case in point. He was only four years older than I was, but had resented me from the day I was born. A tyrant in the house is far worse than one outside. It means that home instead of being a refuge has its dark corners. It would have been unthinkable to take my troubles to Father. Nor could I appeal to our mother, Zeruiah, for that would have been very unmanly. However from my fifteenth birthday, whilst still having to be obedient to Boaz, I was strong enough to easily out run him, so life began to be a little freer.

Childhood leaves its mark, but probably the person whom one becomes is shaped by those teenage years, whose memory has a special luminosity. Unlike childhood where a day seems an eternity, in youth its seasons, which last for ever, though one has the experience to know that they change. It is a time of turbulent ups and downs, but many ups. The burning embar-rassment of not knowing how to address an elder or, the first time one is pinned in a public wrestling match. Of not knowing how to respond to the look of a girl, or failing to meet your target in the sling shot. We all feel so vulnerable yet take delight if another fails. We laugh to hear the Rabbi or the instructor Horah suggest they take up women's work – as long as the barb is not aimed at us. Yes the scars we gain at the beginning stay with us for ever.

This is also the time when one first really begins to think. Not just about girls, but understanding something of the world, war, God, and yes and death too. Despite the mental turmoil, who would be without the allure of new knowledge and new meaning? Oh if I had known at ten what I knew at fifteen, life could have been so much easier.

I was no different from others of my age in Bethlehem, though I was one of the best long distance runners. Though I could not sprint as well as Eli, Aaron or Josh, but after a mile no one could keep up with me, whilst I could hold my own amongst the best wrestlers in my age group.

Perhaps the only thing different about me was my music. My music had always been part of me. It came to me naturally, almost without effort, so if I heard a tune two or three times, I could repeat it on the harp. Rabbi Aaron gave me much encouragement, and taught me in such a gentle way that it was always fun to try new tunes and I would sometimes make rude verses about Elders or Rabbi's whom no one liked. This caused a lot of mirth but my father also beat me for it. I was never teased about my music, because unlike Deon, who also played, I always made it clear that I was going to be a warrior. Though when elders came to visit I played and was given shekels by appreciative visitors.

Bull Horns

In the winter after we had brought down the sheep into the family pens we spent much of our time with the Rabbi. He took special care with we four and taught us to read and write. I admit I thoroughly enjoyed this, as Rabbi Aaron was unusual, unlike the majority of crabby and restricted teachers, he encouraged us to use our imagination.

We trained intensively with our instructor Horah. He was not very old, but had been badly wounded in the wars and had a marked limp. We were loyal to him and learned much, though his sharp sarcasm was not always necessary.

We were experts with the sling from when we could first walk, which was vital in looking after the sheep, and all were excellent marksmen.

We had wrestling and I soon learned that being a little closer to the ground allowed me to use the weight and power of my opponent against him. Josh, his real name was Joseph, and I, were the leaders of our group. Josh was a little older and taller than I was, though we had some great bouts, and were more or less even.

We learned to use a sword, in preparation for becoming a full warrior. This meant that Horah's lessons were serious affairs. Our skill could mean life and death when facing a Philistine or an Amalekite who would try to kill us, so we had every intention of getting in first. Consequently, no time was wasted as we were being schooled for life and not to learn would result in a swift and bloody end.

From the spring until early autumn we would spend weeks away by ourselves looking after the sheep in the green hills of Judea. You may think that our land of Israel is always brown and dry, but this is not so. In summer of course, in the wide valleys the sun can skin you, but in spring and early summer the land is a riot of colour.

Josh, Aaron, Eli and I took turns with our family herds. Not everyone liked this duty as some found it boring to be alone, but how could you be alone amongst the mountains?

I enjoyed the responsibility. The excitement of dealing with lurking wolves or the fierce mountain cat whom could be deadly, and with such potential adversaries, life was anything but boring.

I had my dog, Sep, with me. He was so intelligent and would listen to my musing with such earnestness that I had no doubts that he understood. He was brave, and if the nights grew cold, he would snuggle up under my cloak – who could ask for anything more?

Rabbi Aaron said that dogs do not have souls, but he can never have had a dog like Sep. Responsive to your every mood. He would fly like the wind and turn in a flash, hurtle back at your call, eager and willing for the next command. He taught me what soldiers should be like.

With Sep by my side, when it was my turn I could not wait to go. It wasn't that I did not like my friends Eli, Josh or Aaron, even young Joab with his persistence, but none of them wanted to talk about the things I was interested in. I could also practise my music without interruptions or scorn from Boaz and I could try composing new music, as there was inspiration everywhere.

It lay in the silence.

This may be a little surprising, but high in the hills there was so many different kinds of silence. Each was filled with a sound that lay just below the surface. I would cry out or sing into the silences, sometimes this was in harmony, at other times it created a harsh discord. I would try to tune and pitch my harp to project the right note to harmonise with the silence. This was wonderful as the note filled the blue white silence, reverberating into nothingness, like water filling an empty pool, the silence flooded back to refill the space my note had made. Whilst beyond the silence, the note winged its way and echoed back into the stillness of my mind.

I must describe my valley because it plays an important part in my story.

It was a sharp wedge shape, high up in the mountains, beneath a wide plateau, which was green most of the year. It was our very best grazing land and we returned every week or second week after the grass had re-grown.

It was called Bull Horns because the shape of the cliff side looked like the front of a bull's head with peaks on either side like horns. High up on the final ledge, which ran across Bull Horns, lay a cave. This was virtually secret because it could not be easily seen from the valley below.

After ascending 4,000 feet, you would arrive at a V-shaped grassy plateau, with the grass running right up the narrowing gully, ending at the cliff face. The top end of the gully was surrounded by a light ridge, making the land a shallow dish, so that the grass was protected from the wind and frost that could sweep along the hills. This also gave a partial protection against the sun, so it was a particularly lush pasture.

There was the range of Mount Atta on three sides and at the centre was my clough, with its cliff face Bull Horns, from out of which ran a thin stream for most of the year. I had discovered the mystery of the clough by following the stream and as I climbed upwards, the sides of the hills drew closer and closer to being barely 30 yards across. But the sheep could walk up here easily. Driving onwards for about another 40 yards, the stream ran through a little gorge barely 20 yards wide. Then sharply turning left, scrambling up three or four yards, the gorge widened out again into a flat plateau about 50 yards wide, with the walls shaped like a bull's horns. It was a perfect fort.

I could take the sheep down into the lower slopes during the day and herd them back upward through the gorge, which was narrow enough to make a fence so they could graze peacefully at night.

Bull Horns had two sharp ascending ledges, with natural ridge paths so I could get close to the rock face from out of which trickled a thin waterfall. The waterfall came out of the rock face, and on the highest level there was a wide buttress in front of the cave, which was at the centre of Bull Horns. There was even a fringe like hair, made up by the growth of scraggily trees growing out of small nooks and crannies in the rock face.

The trees were amazing. The twisted roots extracting every ounce of moisture. Josh, Eli and I swung hand over hand amongst them, much to the alarm of Aaron who pointed out that if we slipped and didn't kill ourselves we would be badly injured. The trouble was he was right. Once Eli had been too daring and the out-jutting bough had broken – he had to hang on for dear life until we could drag him back. It had scared us all, so we left the boughs to the roosting birds and swirling wind.

Bull Horns was just perfect. Sep and I could watch the sheep and see beyond into the valley below. More wonderful, was the pool, which had been carved out by flowing water, which never dried out. It was deep enough to swim in at the centre.

I had worked on my cave for the last two years. I had cleaned the cave floor, collected rushes to make a comfortable bed and could leave my harp and staff safely. Moreover, I had cleared the rocks and stones in the pool floor and used them to build low walls across the ridge path of both horns.

More important were its practical advantages, as anyone trying to get to the cave had to climb one of the steep ledges on either side. This would give me time to scramble out of danger, up a narrow cleft in the rock, which took you out to the top and then over the hill back to Bethlehem.

One thing Father told me when looking after the sheep was that, if there were marauders, to give the alarm as quickly as possible and not fool around thinking that I was able to deal with them. This was sensible advice because if I saw any enemy, I was fast enough to get back to Bethlehem, which was less than six miles away.

Safe in Bull Horns I could play and dream away the time – it was a marvellous life.

Eli, Josh and Aaron thought it a great place and we had played warrior games there, but I think they came mainly for the swimming.

Aaron was a little reluctant to swim first because he was a little anxious about being naked. Josh somewhat cruelly suggested that it was because he was small in the phallus: "If you were as good as me and David you wouldn't be so modest," which was a bit hard on him, but Aaron took it in good part.

It was good to have one's friends, and after a swim in water we had an exhilarating run down to the first plateau, drying ourselves in the warm sun. With whoops of delight we ran and waved our arms in the freedom, fun and the warmth of companionship that we knew would last our lifetimes.

The only other person I showed Bull Horns to was Leah.

The Kiss

Leah was just a year older than I. She was a bond maiden of my mother Zeruiah and I have much to tell about Leah.

She was a Philistine who had been taken captive when she was eight years old. I was not sure of the circumstances, but I think she was already an orphan and had been captured in a raid on a caravan in which she had been travelling.

My mother had taken a strong liking to her. In many ways she was almost part of the family, and like most bond men and women, accepted their lot, especially if they had a good master.

Leah was beautiful.

She was as tall as I was. Slender, with light brown hair, eyes that were green. And when I looked into them, my heart knew there was something very wonderful about her.

I would pretend to be doing something else but I would watch her secretly. If she were working she would peer intently. At other times there was softness in her eyes, matched with her part open lips, as if she were humming a tune in a way that I had never seen in a woman before. Moreover, most unusually, she had learned to play the harp when with the Philistines.

She was so graceful. She had a lithe body, which swayed, under her burden; her skin seemed to shine. My brother Boaz was always around her, but as she belonged to my Mother, she was safe from him.

I cannot remember when I first noticed Leah as a person; she had been with us so many years. She had always treated me well and when I went alone to practise if she was free, we would play together.

Last year I asked her whether she could remember her life amongst the Philistines. Rather crassly I said how much better it must be here because, after all, the Philistines are uncircumcised and do not follow the Living God.

Later I realised I was somewhat naive because, of course, no one would volunteer to be a slave. She told me many interesting things about the Philistines, and was very patient with me and explained their customs in such an intelligent and interesting way that I   forgot she was a woman and treated her as a friend and equal.

"Oh David," she would say. "No, I am happy here with lady Zeruiah and the family of Jesse. Yes, and even with you, impudent and cocky David, who thinks he alone has discovered the world, but truly, whilst I am content to be with you, you are wrong about my people."

I would retort somewhat warmly, "Your people, the Philistines, are uncircumcised and unclean. They worship an animal god, Dagon. They think only of destroying Israel and taking our Promised Land."

"But David, what about the people who were living in your 'Promised Land' before you came?" she would reply calmly and so infuriatingly logically. "Are you surprised that they resented your intrusion. After all, our bards tell us that even we Philistines were invaders, and drove the Canaanites and Jubiuzites into the hills. I can not help but feel sorry for them because, after being driven from the lands close to the Great Sea, your people appeared out of the desert robbing, pillaging and claiming their land as your own."

What could I say to such nonsense, only explain that land can only belong to people strong enough to hold it? That Israel are God's chosen people and that someday the world would see the greatness of our God, whose rule would be just, righteous and of peace.

She would look at me, her green eyes opened wide, looking into mine and sadly murmur, "David, how can conquest be righteous, just and peaceful?"

I would get angry with her, and then get even angrier because I knew that what she was saying had some truth. But then that's why women are subject to men; they would not fight and be victims of those stronger.

"Let's not quarrel, Leah – it hurts." Then I would blush. "No, let's talk of other things. Sing to me."

Her voice was exquisite, soft, low and melodic. We would walk together in the evening and find a quite spot and sing and talk the evenings away.

Then I began to realise that I was thinking of her not only as a friend but also as a woman. Her image would haunt me at night, which caused me some embarrassment. I was of course in love with her, but I did not quite know what that meant. Amazingly, and this was truly miraculous, I later learned that she had begun to love me.

She always agreed that the idea of the Living God, who sought justice, righteousness, and mercy, was different than Dagon, her god. He was only concerned about a warrior's behaviour, conquest and bloody sacrifice. This made me uncomfortable because sometimes in Leviticus and the other holy books, our God had also been concerned with such things.

"David, I have to thank you for this, but Moses taught that your God shows interest in the afflicted, the leper, the blind, the poor. And in your songs, you sing of the spirit of wisdom." Then she would get very excited. "Without wisdom, without knowledge, without thought, we are little better than animals."

She would explain something, which at first filled me with surprise. Her people used to have a god similar to ours, who was concerned with justice and beauty. Though there is little in our holy scrolls about beauty because we are worried about slipping into the folly of idolatry, but justice and beauty do seem to go together.

Her people had left their original lands following a great earthquake. Their old gods were interested in learning, and, cleanliness was as important amongst them as it is amongst Israel. Indeed they had a god of knowledge and their men and women of good families would be educated and both could read and write.

I was at first shocked, but I was not sorry when she told me of the history of her people. Though the Philistines are our enemies, I came to understand from her that although wrong, and living in cities, sailing on the Great Sea, having kings, and smiths who smelted the new iron not just bronze, they can be quite honourable. She told me of the different customs the Philistines and I realised that the more one knew about your enemy the better. One strange custom was that some warriors had a special bond between them, called philian. They were closer than brothers, which inspired a special bravery, but I did not quite understand.

She also told me of a time when she had visited the Great Sea during a storm.

"Can you imagine the noise of the water and the roar of the wind with waves that crashed against the sands," she said. She described, "Waves rolling as high as a man, coming from the sea which stretches out to the end of the world."

I had heard of but never seen the Great Sea but it sounded wonderful. One day I became bold enough to ask Leah if she would like to see my secret castle?

"Secret castle, David – what are you talking about?" she responded. Then, seeing my hurt look, "I am sorry. That was thoughtless. I am speaking without understanding. Tell me about it."

Was there any wonder that I was in love? Here was this marvellous person who seemed to understand what I was thinking and feeling even before I was aware of the thoughts myself. Hard as it is to believe, she seemed to enjoy being with me, and asked Mother's permission to visit me at Bull horns: I could hardly wait.

Sure enough three days later, just before I was to return to Bull Horns she left a little flat stone with the message, "Expect me early on the third day."

I do not know how she arranged it for at first Mother was uncertain, saying, "Leah, my child, you are very dear to me, but my husband Jesse may have other ideas about David, though he is the youngest." She went on "However, what the men don't know they won't grieve about. But be back before nightfall without fail."

Barely an hour into the day, I was watching from my cave at Bull Horns and there coming out of the early heat haze was a slight shimmering figure. I peered intently.

"Can you see who it is, Sep?" I whispered.

Sep was alert at once. He sniffed at the scent on the breeze and instead of growling, he invariably growled when people approached, his tail wagged. It had to be Leah because, after me, Leah was Sep's favourite.

Yes, I could see it was a girl, with her long veil and cloak. My heart pounded, Leah was coming here to see me. My thoughts whirled, my mind filled by thoughts frightening and wonderful. My mouth felt dry. I put behind me the dreams and fantasies that I had. This was my friend, the person most dear to me in the whole world. I must not think of anything but how to welcome her and keep her safe.

Within minutes I had traversed the steep side of the ledge and was running towards her. I didn't shout; I didn't need to. My whole body was resonant with joy. I did not feel the earth beneath my feet. I did not even notice whether or not I drew breath but I covered the distance so quickly that I caught up with her at the entrance to the gorge.

There she was. At first she had not seen me and was delicately stepping over the stones in the stream. Then she heard me, looked up, and – oh, my heart stopped.

The smile on her face, her cheeks slightly flushed with the exertion of the climb, but her eyes, oh her eyes melted me in their welcome. She did not say anything but stood quietly and looked at me.

Then it happened, in a flash, but in my memory, I recall everything as if it took a lifetime. I was within three feet of her. I could hear my heart pounding.

My eye took in every nuance of her being. Her head veil had fallen over and bared her shoulder. I could see every pore of her smooth, smooth skin. Her slight bosom rose with her breathing, she half opened her lips to speak but did not, but revealed her white teeth lapped by the softness of her tongue.

She held out her hand. This seemed to be a delicate jewel, as I touched her. My fingers flowed along her fingers till my hand encased hers. I had never felt such a touch before.

The world stood still. Her touch inflamed me.

Was this just a hand, whose warmth held my warmth? Her fingers explored my hand. I drew her towards me, our eyes bonded in amazement, as if we were seeing each other for the first time. We were so close; I could sense the warmth of her skin. I took in her gentle fragrance, so different from my own. I wanted to enfold, possess her. My body longed to thrust into hers. Yet I was overwhelmed by the need to protect and cherish her, fearing that my roughness would shatter this delicate butterfly into a thousand fragments.

As in a rhythm that yielded to its own time, we drew together. Her arms entwined in mine. I drew her towards me, reverently. Her head lying upon my shoulder, her upturned face looked at me with total trust as our lips gently came together. We kissed.

Oh, that kiss! My whole being was centred upon my lips as I traced the outline of her lips upon mine. Her mouth held mine as our lips opened together and for the first time my tongue's tip touched another's.

My tight embrace answered hers, as we clung, tightly, tightly to each other. My now rigid body lay hard against her; my senses reeled, as we both sunk to the ground.

I lay above her, her eyes closed, the sunlight flowed over her precious face, and her mouth opened in answer to mine as our tongues became entwined. In a counterpoint to my body, she seemed utterly, utterly soft, as I lay against her. My phallus yearned to enter her. I was close to explosion. My thoughts scattered.

I breathed her name in a plea, a prayer, "Leah, Leah, Leah..."

She held me tight, as we lay there. She in complete trust, so that I dared not move.

Suddenly, Sep had decided to join us and the spell was broken, as he thrust his shaggy head between us.

Leah laughed in delight, "Oh, Sep, you are a dear!"

I asked, "But what about me?"

"Ah you, sweet David, are my love." Then she said gravely, "If you are my love – truly my love – then I am yours, now and for ever."

My heart thrilled. I was loved and cherished by this wondrous creature, this was beyond belief.

"Oh, my Leah! You have my vow – for now, for the future and for ever."

We embraced again, but differently this time as if we both knew that the journey we had travelled could not end here, though a time would come soon when that journey, which is always a mystery, would be fulfilled.

We rose in complete harmony, our hands entwined as I showed her Bull Horns which was now hers for all time.

We did not speak much but sat close together, arms about each other as she sang to me an old lullaby, which overwhelmed me with love and longing for her again.

I let her go and lay back upon the bank in total surrender. My mind, soul and body were at one; at that moment I lived only for her.

I opened my eyes to find her kneeling at my side looking down upon me. She kissed me gently, moved away from my imploring arms which caressed her bosom whose firmness filled me with inexpressible longing.

She smiled and said, "We must not forget that I told your mother I would be back well before sunset."

"Hey – wait!" I spluttered. "Mother won't mind. You can't go now. I...I..." and tailed off lamely.

"David, it's better this way. I will be able to come again. We must not spoil it. Soon you'll be sixteen and..." She didn't say anything further, but blushed delightfully.

I knew what she meant. We Judean men can marry at sixteen – though seventeen was more common. By eighteen or nineteen most young people were married. I remembered that she was a year older than I was.

She was right, of course. So I got up and helped her prepare for her return, but we both knew that our lives had reached a turning point and that we would never be the same again.

I escorted Leah to the edge of the valley. She turned frequently to wave to me, and as she went from view I felt desolate.

What had Leah experienced? She had pondered hard and long. Her secret was safe with her mistress, but what would David think if he knew that she was not one, but more than two years older than him?

She had explained to Zeruiah how, when she was captured by the Israelites, she realised that it was safer to appear as a young child, than risk being seen by those cruel men as a maiden. The longer she could delay that realisation, the better.

She knew she had been lucky in being part of Jesse's family, and especially in finding a mistress who had almost become a mother to her. A woman's lot was hard, but a slave's was even harsher. Her mind clouded over the early days – after being brutally dragged away from what little security she had following the deaths of her parents. Intuitively she sought to avoid the hard stares of men who were not constrained by family and tribal obligations and she needed her sharpest wits to elude them.

She had first been attracted to David because of his curiosity. She was ever grateful that he had shown some interest in her as a person and not a thing. That he had the imagination to ask questions about her people, and though he was prejudiced as the others about Philistia, he was willing to listen to her and had the intelligence to perceive that these hill people had much to learn.

Of course, the music was a special bond and, with his open looks and occasional gentleness, she began to hope that, despite the gaps in their age, he might be interested in her. Her feelings for him excited her and she prayed and prayed that he would notice her.

Being close to her mistress she sometimes heard things that she knew David did not know about. She felt intensely jealous when Zeruiah had casually mentioned that a recent visitor, Asher, might be betrothed to David, as she was the daughter of Jesse's cousin.

Mother had said, "It would be a good match, Leah. She's quite comely and she could do worse than a younger son because he would be a kind husband. It would also strengthen the bond between our families."

Leah was relieved to learn that as yet there had been no active discussion of David's marital future.

Leah's earnest agreement with her mistress that David would be a "kind husband" was the first clue to Zeruiah of Leah's growing feeling for David. She had been slightly irritated because it meant that she had to decide what, if anything, she would do about Leah and a possible man for her.

Union between bondmen and women was allowed, though their children remained bonded. Whereas if a bond's woman was taken as a concubine or, much more rarely, married to an Israelite, her children were absorbed into Israel and she, too, became a free woman.

As Leah's hopes and feelings for David grew, she took every opportunity to make contact with him. However this coincided with the growing interest that Boaz had shown in her.

If David was her dream, then Boaz was her nightmare. All the qualities she loved in David were somehow cruelly distorted in Boaz. His obvious family resemblance was subtly marred: David's intelligence appeared as cunning in Boaz; David's respect of her as a person became a leering, groping gauntlet she had to run whenever she met Boaz.

She was overjoyed when she perceived that David's enthusiasms, mixed with blushes, mirrored her feelings for him. She knew she loved him, and when she saw him looking at her she felt a warmth and excitement that she dared not contemplate.

In their talks together his search for meaning fascinated her: his utter acceptance of his God, his insistence that his God cared. She prayed and prayed that, as she loved David and he loved his God, He might accept her worship too.

Sometimes she felt violently angry at the injustice of her situation. Why could she not dream of personal happiness with a man who loved her? But life in bondage had taught her not to expect much, because the gap between hope and fulfilment was often bridged by bitter disappointment.

When she had reached David, she knew that, no matter what, she would always love him. That, amazingly, her prayers had been answered and this wonderful young man cared for her. She wanted him so much, and she threw caution to the wind as she felt the pure joy and exhilaration of his arms about her. At that moment her bondage slipped from her, she was whole and she longed to be filled by his body. She was aflame. His touch so gentle, so firm, she was ready to merge with his body. Yet his reverence for her made her love him even more, as it seemed that God had listened to her prayer, for he wanted her as much as she wanted him. She left David more determined than ever that they would be together.

She was frank with herself and dared to hope. She knew she was vulnerable to the bitterest disappointment, by her throwing away the only protection slaves have: of not thinking of the morrow, of not having ambitions, of not risking an even worse fate than that which had befallen them. No, she would no longer cocoon herself in defensive apathy; she was a human being, reborn in the acceptance and love of another. She would dare thinking of happiness.

She hurried homewards suddenly realising that this had been the happiest day of her life and, yes, she could now hope for even better tomorrows.

The First Kill

I could not think or do anything as the thoughts of Leah overwhelmed me. I was ecstatic and despondent, elated and despairing, on fire and chilled, as my brain battled to comprehend the thoughts that my body conjured.

I knew what I wanted: to meld my yearnings for her kindness, joy, fun and wit with the deep desire to fill her body with mine.

That night I spent in turbulence. A succession of wild thoughts and half dreams became entangled with considerations of the practicalities of our situation. Though I was the youngest, and therefore in the scheme of things less important to the family, I was of Judah and Israel. Though I was almost sixteen, few married until they were seventeen. Whilst Leah, for all her beauty and Mother's support, was both in bondage and not of Israel.

How could I fulfil my destiny without Leah – for surely God had brought us together? What I felt for her was not just the lust, which we boys sometimes boasted about, but this was a true union of souls, minds and bodies, which sought pure harmony.

I looked at the darkening sky and watched the stars peep shyly through the haze of moistened clouds. The brightening stars seemed to have a message for me. Over towards the far west, between the hills, now plumb black, the silver orb of the moon rose majestically, giving a silver sheen to the growing conglomerate of clouds.

Sep nuzzled up to me. He sensed my turmoil but was a calming influence. His soft eyes looked into mine, and his low, sighing whine seemed to be in sympathy and to bid me to be of good cheer.

Of course, it would be well. Leah had offered me her love. She was immaculate and we could wait. Together we would bring Mother and Father to agree. I did not even consider asking to take Leah as my bond maiden – or, for that matter, my concubine – which would have caused little comment. No, she was close to God; her reverence to the ideals of justice reflected the spirit of God working in her. Ruth, my great-grandmother, had converted to Judaism, why not Leah?

My senses still burned, but I could seek no relief in the usual fantasy response, because my love was pure. Without her presence there was no relief, only an animal reflex that belittled what we shared.

Josh, Aaron, Eli and I sometimes talked about women – Josh especially – and once, when we had wrestled, I could feel him stiff beneath me. We

25

had exchanged looks at our aroused members and he first showed me how to "spill your seed", which we had both laughed at.

I understood about our bodies, but by themselves they are nothing more than reflexes: no better than beasts in the field. We are part of something higher, and the love of a man and women is more than just a coupling. What I felt for Leah comprised the whole of my being and I worshipped the whole of her.

I looked out at the now black, inky sky, filled with wondrous jewels of the stars.

"Sep, oh Sep, I can reach out and clasp a star easier than I can Leah."

The warm evening breeze flowed back across the valley and I flung off my clothes. Clad only in my loincloth, I called out into the night.

"Leah! Leah!" Her blessed name echoed back between the twin rock faces.

I stared hard into the dark and saw the wonders of the Lord's handiwork.

Now I was praying and sharing my soul with God who had blessed me with Leah. I took up my harp as my soul was filled with awe and worship. I sang:

"The heavens are the Lord's and his handiwork, the moon and the stars which thou hast ordained, oh what is man that Thou should'st mind him."

How wondrous that God should think on us. I repeated the refrain as my mind fingered out an accompaniment.

"The heavens are the Lord's and he made them, see his handiwork, oh what is man that Thou should'st mind him."

I was on fire with love for her and the knowledge, intense and undoubting, that my love for God was understood and accepted. That He held me in the cradle of His wondrous world.

I stood, arms outstretched, in reverence at the star-filled heavens, my passion and devotion to Leah. Suddenly the words came, as in a benediction.

"On this now sacred spot stood my glorious Queen.
My arms, a poor altar I entwined about her waist,
My eyes, blinded by the vision seen –
Of the rose in her cheek.
With fingers unholy I traced the beauty for ever mine,

26

Whilst my lips did seek to raise that veil of rapturous mystery."

Then I slept soundly and had not the whisper of a disturbing dream.

Next morning saw a complete change in the weather. It was dark and overcast as the brown-grey clouds of heaven began to blow a harsh dry breath across the land.

There was going to be a storm, not as in the winter with torrents that restored the land, but a sandstorm that would scour man, tree and beast.

Worst, mountain cats, which I kept at bay with sling shot and fire, would take advantage of the changed terrain and seek to steal into the valley and take my sheep.

I had learned to deal with the cunning wolf that hunted in pairs or bands of four or five. With Sep's alertness I could rely on him to find their scent and warn me, and the well-placed fires behind my fence should keep them at bay. On occasions I would go out and meet them with sling shot, giving many a wound on hind or eye. This made them very wary of troubling David bar Jesse.

But mountain cats were another matter. They seemed less afraid of fire, and when desperate for their young, would dare all and this was the time of suckling their litter.

"Sep, Sep, we must be careful, we have to keep the sheep penned in, even if they get restive, but in this light, if the storm breaks we won't be able to see and the sand will skin us."

Sep seemed to know my mind as we went down to the lower slope. He drove back the silly sheep, which on seeing me thought they were about to be freed to go into the valley.

I gave Sep his instructions. He herded the sheep into the side of the hill, whilst I saw to my fencing, making extra ties to resist the sheep pushing down the barrier and strengthening the defence against the possible onset of a hungry mountain cat.

Some called our mountain cats lions, and though they were often a yard and a half long, and a yard high, they were not the lions which the Egyptians and Assyrians hunted.

These cats were so fierce they had often killed guard dogs and there had been times when they had been known to kill a grown man.

It was now blowing a gale and the sand and dust was whipped up into spiralling heights and I could barely see ten yards ahead.

Now I thought, Stop and think. Where might the danger be and is it a cat that is stalking the herd, or is it just your imagination?

I stood, took a deep breath and thought about the situation.

Because of the time of the year and the storm, I was quite certain that a hungry mountain cat must be interested in the sheep, especially the lambs that they could so swiftly carry away. The mindless sheep were disturbed by the storm and were very resistive and making an enormous din.

I understood what I had to do. I needed to know when or where the stalker was lying and I needed height to ensure that my answer, a sharp sling shot, would be able to do the most damage.

"Sep, Sep, here boy, guard the front," I commanded and led him down to behind the fence. "If you smell him, let me know, now stay, stay."

I gave him hug and my heart warmed to him. He clearly understood but whined a little because he hated being separated from me. But boldly, he did as he was bid.

He sat with his back to the sheep, looking out over the fence into the howling wind. He eyes were screwed up against the sharp blast, but his snout was held into the flow to catch any hint of danger. As I raced off, I suddenly felt a cold chill as I realised that whilst I climbed up to the first or second ridge, Sep was both guard and target, and despite his bravery, he was no match for a mountain cat.

I reached the ledge, at this height and an angle, I could look into the raging tempest.

The storm carried sand, dust and debris and seemed to throw it with special venom at my wattle fence. The fence caught the flying debris, which began to collect and grow into a pile, quickly building up against the middle struts as the weight of loose dirt began to make it lean inwards.

Yes, I thought, you will sense this and this is where you'll attack.

I moved towards the edge of the ledge, not quite losing the half protection of the buttressing rock, but beginning to be scoured by the flying rubble.

Suddenly I heard a low growl and then angry barking from Sep. I peered hard into the grey brown swirling mist; the sun now lost amidst the sandstorm. There was something down there with a firm outline. Was it moving, or was it my eyes making images that I feared?

Sep's barks became more urgent. Though I could barely make him out, I was sure that the long shadowy length was not a figment of my fancy. It was moving closer to the centre of the fence, which was beginning to lean over at a crazy angle and would soon be nothing more than a mound of rubble.

What should I do? Oh God, what should I do?

If I fired a sling shot how effective would that be? He could easily bypass the fence and be amongst the sheep and could move far faster than I.

If I went down to the centre he could come around me. My heart chilled, the shape was moving in a determined way. I fired a shot, but it was into the wind. "You fool. You fool!" I cried to myself. I had forgotten the effect of the wind; my stone, if it found the target, would be like a baby's pat.

I concentrated. Did I pray or had God already heard me, or would he expose me for the idiot I was to foolishly rely on my own skill?

I knew what I had to do. This was going to be a fight to the death and my only ally was Sep, but he was in danger and I needed to be there with him.

I might lose a sheep but I could not lose Sep!

As I started to run toward Sep I heard him scream in anger and pain. As swift as it takes to tell, I was close to him. There in the whirling fog was the nightmare come to life. The mountain cat had struck Sep and caught him a blow from which he was bleeding profusely. Though Sep had retreated, he still stood his ground with fangs barred.

I knew what I had to do. I saw it all. No thought for the consequence if it went wrong. It all depended on Sep being an effective decoy. Emotion was denied by what was to come.

I pulled out my knife. There was nothing left to do. Leaving Sep to be the object of the mountain cat's attack, I relied upon the density and manic noise of the storm, and his preoccupation with Sep.

The monster was going in for the kill. Sep stood or half crouched, snarling in angry defiance, I was within a yard of my enemy.

The mountain cat was about to spring at Sep. I flung myself at him in a wrestling tackle. My whole body hurtled into him as I charged, clung desperately to his side, as my left arm plunged into his body. It was like hitting a muscular rock. My blade had bounced from a rib. I was hurled to the ground, half smothered, but still holding on. I was almost suffocated by the stink of cat. I felt my grip slipping. The chill of death was upon me as I tried to protect my head from his snarling maw.

As best I would had been clawed badly or died then, but Sep threw himself at the mountain cat, catching him at the side of his head. This was my opportunity, as he tossed Sep off with a sledging blow, I used my knife as a dagger and thrust fast into his unguarded front. The mountain cat's body went into frenzy, but I did not make the mistake of trying for another blow. But with the knife deep inside, I dug deeper, pressing, carving ever deeper into him.

I was rolled over, and over, as I clung in a desperate wrestling hold with his snarls deafening my ears. I was drowning in his stink, as he released his piss in a shower over me. I could not breathe as I felt a flood of sticky ooze over our rolling bodies. I was losing my hold, but I sensed his frenzy lessening, so I let go and threw myself away from this threshing body.

My legs were as water; I could not stand or sit upright. I was consumed by an exhaustion I had never felt before. I half raised my head, my chest heaving for clean, clear air, as I raised myself tremblingly upon one arm. The mountain cat's body was still twitching and clawing feebly at nothing, but I knew I was going to live and he was dying.

The storm still roared on but I felt calm, although exhausted. I lay there lifeless, I don't know for how long, whilst my senses came back, and as they did so my body began to tell me that I was hurt and bruised everywhere. Until now I had felt no pain. Amidst the battle I had no knowledge of my hurts or the efforts I had made. Now I was weaker than any newborn babe. I was utterly defenceless and had no energy to feel any sense of triumph.

I sat up, still gulping for air as the storm lessened but still continued fierce.

I could see my enemy, dead – utterly still.

I almost sobbed. Gone was my terror and anger. Gone was my rage and fear. I crawled over to the lifeless form and ran my hand along its still sides. Its soft fur was still warm. I kneeled at its side, peering at the face of my foe. It eyes closed, but with a claw across its chest as it sought to pluck out my deep buried dagger.

With difficulty I rolled its body over and drew out the knife, now rapidly congealing with his life's blood. I felt a wave of sadness and pity for this magnificent creature.

Oh my God – Sep, Sep! What happened to Sep? In my weariness, I had forgotten about Sep.

I staggered to my feet and a few yards away, I saw him, still – so, so still.

I cried out in anguish, "Sep! Sep, what have I done? Sep! Sep, I've killed you."

I was consumed with anguish. I knew I was responsible, I had used him as a decoy. My mind tried to suppress what I knew to be the truth. My whole plan had been built on Sep, and I tried to keep this from my consciousness.

I was at his side now, and oh the relief, joy and fear together. He was still breathing; he was still alive, but terribly wounded. The last clawing blow had torn him and had broken his leg. His first wound was covered in dirt and debris but was not bleeding. What should I do?

I leaned over him and held his head and kissed him, and blubbered amidst tears. "Sep, Sep, please don't die. Please don't die."

He opened his eyes. His tail moved feebly as I held his shattered leg. He licked my hand as it moved over him.

I had to splint his leg, for if he could not run or walk properly, he would be done for. I pulled at the fence, and drew out a stick, measured the length and broke it with enormous effort. I was still very, very weak. I had to bind it. My shirt had been lost in the fight; I tore at my loincloth, which too was in tatters.

With stiffening fingers I made strips of bandage and fixed the splint against Sep's leg. It pained him. But as I murmured to comfort him, he knew I was trying to help. He whined and continued to lick my ministering hand though his body shuddered with the pain of my efforts.

The storm was near its end, and began to die out almost as quickly has it had sprang up so now I could see clearly. The sheep were frantically milling around the foot of Bull Horns, making a dreadful noise. Fortunately in their panic they moved away from the dead mountain cat and were milling beneath the cliff face. I was so relieved that they had not stampeded. Nothing could be more humiliating that being run over by one's own sheep! They were all right. I think I swore at their stupidity. If only they had stampeded, with purpose, they could have trampled the mountain cat to death. Why had God made them so witless?

I found what was left of my shirt, picking it up and tore it into bandages. When Sep began to recover, he might start to bleed again and I would need the cloth to stem any blood flow. I dressed his second wound as best I could but decided not to do any more for if I tried to move him, I feared it might disturb his wounds.

I whispered gently to him, "Stay Sep, stay. I'll make you comfortable."

I dragged myself up to the cave. Sep and I needed water. As I got close to the sheep they became very agitated. Then I realised that I was covered in the blood, piss and stink of the mountain cat. So I moved away from them. The last thing I needed now was for the wretched beasts to panic.

I went toward the west ridge and with almost as much effort as fighting the cat; I climbed upwards, never slower. I really was weak. I needed food, water and rest. My body cried out for ease. I have had beatings before, from my brother Eliab and especially from Boaz. I had lost wrestling matches and knew the exhaustion of defeat, but this was beyond anything I had experienced.

I reached the cave, found some loaves and dried mutton and with an effort started to eat. I went to the pool and collected water. I felt a little easier and I went to the edge of the pool and eased my body into its waters. It was wonderful, awakening me with its chill as the blood and debris floated from me.

I took water down to Sep and he drank thirstily, but at first would take no food.

I sat with him for the next two days, hardly moving from his side, as slowly his strength returned. Into the third day he improved fast, though I was still stiff from the bruises which were now showing through. Yet it was clear that God had showed his grace to me, as I had avoided both the claws and fangs. Though I have had wrestling bruises, these were something extra-ordinary. I went cold when I thought what might have happened.

My last problem was rather silly. As I had used my shirt for Sep's wounds and most of my skirt and loincloth for his splint, and my cloak had blown away, I was practically naked. I decided that as it was the mountain cat's fault, I would have to have his pelt to clothe me. I had never skinned such a big animal before. I turned to the task with some distaste and a sense of remorse. But then thought, I am really honouring you, taking your skin as my trophy as you would have taken my sheep as your trophy. His body was five feet long, but with his tail he tipped seven feet.

Sep looked interested in the carcass but I could not bring myself to cook and feed him to Sep. Instead I dragged him to the end of the gorge and covered him with stones. Perhaps it was irrational, but somehow I felt that burial was right.

I must admit I looked rather wild and splendid with the skin draped over my shoulders. With the front paws tied under my chin and the cat's face lying in front of my breast, it made the sheep very nervous.

Two days later Josh came to relieve me. When he saw me he said, "David, what in the name of...?" He was silenced. His face looked in amazement. I had not quite appreciated how I might look.

"You look like a mad hermit from the desert, and who gave you that bruised face." He came closer to and examined my bruised body. "David I don't know what the other fellow looks like but you look as if you've been beaten up. And why have you no clothes on?" Then he laughed. "David bar Jesse," he said very formally, "you always were a show off. You're not really decent, you know?"

"Doesn't my skin cover me properly?" I asked.

"Well only as far as it goes. But come tell me, what's been going on here?"

I told him the main details, and tried not to feel too pleased with his first wondering and then frank admiring response.

"You mean you killed a mountain lion?" he said, unable to conceal his amazement.

"Mountain cat," I corrected. "It was a big one, I admit, but it was a mountain cat, not a lion." I ended somewhat smugly. I was becoming conceited.

Josh retorted, "Cat, shmat! David, but with only Sep to help," and pointing to him, "and look at the poor creature. He's obviously been in the wars, and yet" he said slowly incredulously, "you, killed him with your bare hands?" His voice tailed off and his face showed awe, excitement and a respect that began to make me feel uncomfortable.

I could not really answer any more so said, "Let's change the subject. Have you any spare cheese? I'm famished."

He grinned at me in delight. "Oh boy! I know someone whose not going to like this." He began to giggle as we both knew who he meant, and I started to laugh with him. "Poor old Boaz. He'll be furious – he won't believe you."

Then he stopped laughing and said, "And if you weren't my best friend I might not believe you either, but ..." He then gestured towards the skin, my lack of clothes, Sep and his splinted leg"... I suppose there's nothing else for it. Seriously, David, it may take some crediting, but don't shock people even more by looking like a desert loon. You'd better borrow my cloak, because if you go back to Bethlehem like that they'll call the Rabbi."

I knew he was right but refused to take his cloak but agreed to take his shirt and loincloth, leaving him my tattered remains.

We embraced. He half went to go into a wrestling mode, but seeing me wince he stopped. "Sorry, David. That was careless of me – sorry. Off you go and don't forget to tell me everything when I see you next."

As I left Josh I realised I had not thought about my return. So as Sep and I limped along with me I said, "I'd better keep a cool head, Sep, and not show off." But I confess I began to feel pleased with myself as I started off for Bethlehem with a growing sense of warm anticipation, especially about the impression I might have upon Leah.

At the stream before entering the town, I cleaned my face and did my best to tidy up my hair. I took the opportunity to see my reflection. I adjusted Josh's skirt and pulled down my shirt and carefully arranged the mountain cat pelt, fastening it with a thorn pin. I tried not to grin but I thought I looked very grand. Sep seemed to think so too, because he began to bark and prance up and down, so that I think his leg must have healed. Though Sep did not like it, I thought he ought to keep the splint on, so that people could see how much of a hero he had been.

Chapter Three

David the Bard

The Harpist

As I walked down the dusty street there was no one about until I saw Ashi, one of my friends. He saw the skin and at once began asking me about it.

His father, Heban, came out of their house and immediately began to question me. "It's a fine pelt, my boy. Where did you get it?"

I told him and at first he showed doubt but noticing my bruises and the wounds on Sep, he looked suitably impressed.

"That brings you great credit, David, but weren't you foolhardy? You might just as easily been seriously hurt or, worse, lost your herd."

Wasn't that just typical of adults? They're always ready to be critical. But then he responded to my crestfallen face. "Nevertheless, lad, it's a great achievement and I am sure your father will be very proud of you."

I walked on with Ashi in attendance. He was doing a great job running ahead and calling our friends, so that within a hundred yards of my house there was quite a crowd. I walked as slowly as I could, because in many ways this was one of the greatest days in my life.

Sep too was getting a lot of attention from both the boys and some of the other dogs, who found his splint very interesting, and I saw that dogs can also be show-offs.

I was thinking of what I would say to my Father, but more importantly, how to show Leah my trophy.

Then, amidst the hubbub, I heard the name "Samuel the Prophet".

"He will be very interested in your adventure, David," said old Abraham. "The Prophet has called upon your father and some of the Elders are attending him. It is a day of double blessing for the house of Jesse."

By this time Aaron and Eli had arrived and, though I tried not to, I was grinning from ear to ear. Everybody seemed really pleased, though one or two of the other men agreed with Heban that I must have been lucky.

"Well, David. God smiles upon the lucky and perhaps you deserve it," said Eli's father as he clapped me on the back.

As I approached home who should come out but Boaz. He took one look at me and said, "What have you got there?" Without waiting for an answer, he continued "You are late. Father wants you to come in immediately and get your harp for the visitors."

He glared at me and went on, "Why anyone should want to hear your braying is beyond me!" He aimed a not-too-friendly swipe, which I easily ducked.

Eli spoke up for me, "Boaz, don't you see what David is carrying? He killed a mountain cat by himself." Seeing no proper reaction from the surly Boaz, he emphasised, "... and did not lose one single sheep."

Boaz was totally unresponsive.

"Just look at his bruises," went on Eli. "You can see he's been in a fight and a half – you ought to be proud of him."

Boaz did not like the last remark. "Proud of this dreamer?" he spluttered. "I very much doubt if he killed the cat. It looks very mangy to me – I bet it died of old age. He's making up the whole story."

I suppose this was possible but anyone looking at the pelt could see that, though it was a mature beast, it was not more than four years old.

Then it didn't matter, for out of our house came my eldest brother, Eliab, followed by Leah, Mother having sent her to see what had happened.

Leah did something remarkable: totally ignoring everyone around, even Eliab, she rushed towards me, "David, David! What has happened?" she cried anxiously.

I didn't even feel the clout given me by Boaz who was shouting for me to go on, and that she should, "be off about her business".

I didn't even take in what Eliab was saying; my complete attention was on Leah.

"All right, all right – I'm coming," I said dismissively to my brothers. But to Leah, I tried to tell what had happened. "Sep was marvellous."

But I was cut off. "What's this?" demanded Eliab, my eldest brother, who was never the quickest wit in the world. "What have you got there?"

Boaz would have interjected but Eliab stopped him, "No, David. Go on. What happened?"

This was my opportunity, and whilst apparently addressing Eliab, my words were entirely for Leah. I told about the storm, how Sep braved the mountain cat and that God had blessed me. Though I'd had the wind knocked out of me, I didn't feel the bruises and Sep's wounds were nearly healed.

35

Everybody, except Boaz, seemed suitably impressed and a murmur of appreciation went round while I beamed at Leah,

"I'm all right. I was only bruised," I reiterated. Then, instead of saying something or showing her pleasure, she gave me a withering look and stormed off without a backward glance.

"David, David! Never mind about Leah," said Eliab, but with a degree of respect I had never heard before. "Come – our house has been honoured by a visit from the Prophet Samuel and three tribal Elders. They have expressed interest in hearing you play."

I jerked to attention and followed him into the house, though my thoughts were still trying to interpret Leah's look. I could not understand it. I was hurt and confused No wonder women are difficult to comprehend.

Boaz, of course, behaved as usual. He shouted at the people, "What are you making such a noise about? What will the Prophet think of us?"

He angrily followed us in, though a number of voices indignantly asked, "Who in Israel do you think you are, Boaz bar Jesse? Stop giving yourself airs." One from Eli was so crude and rude that I thought his father would correct him, but he seemed to agree.

As I entered the cool shadow of our house, I paused a little and gave extra prayerful thanks as I slowly caressed the mezuzah on the door lintel. The mezuzah is a reminder of God's protection at the Passover. It suddenly struck me quite forcibly that I really had benefited from God's protection. Often, even Father could be somewhat casual in his oblation to the mezuzah though, if I was ever flippant, I was quickly corrected. On this occasion, however, my thanks had never been more sincere. I began to appreciate just how much help I had received.

I followed Eliab who crossed the open hall and went into the large eating room. In honour of the visitors Mother had arranged oil lamps and, with the light from the small unshuttered window, I could see them sitting on Mother's best rugs.

I quietly sat with my back to the wall and bowed towards Father, who had hardly looked up. Discreetly, I took the pelt from off my shoulders and quietly folded it over my arm.

Father was addressing a man who had his back to me, and to whom he showed great deference. It was obvious that he was Samuel the Prophet.

Down his broad back fell long, white locks of braided hair. His white sacred ephod was picked out with the colourings of all the tribes of Israel.

Just thinking of who he was thrilled and chilled me. Here was a man to whom God had spoken. Who spoke to God? My mouth went dry in awe. I hardly noticed the three Elders who were adding their comments to Father.

Samuel answered. His voice was pure delight, with both allure and threat. It was soft, but with so many levels, like a quiet chord of some deep-based harp; he held everyone's attention.

"Then we are agreed, friend Jesse. You will speak to King Saul and tell him of our concerns." My father nodded respectfully. Then Samuel swung around and looked directly at me. "And this is the youngest of the house of Jesse?"

He had the most magnificent head one could ever see on a man. He was old, but his eyes saw everything. They sparkled and gave out their own message. As he spoke to me his face was as gentle as a woman's, filling you with complete confidence, but you knew that behind this kind look was a countenance that could freeze mind, heart and body.

I could not answer, nor even nod, but just stared at him.

He went on, "I have heard much of your skill with psalm and harp." Then, pausing, looked hard at me. Almost in a whisper that made me think that no one else could hear him he said, "And you have had an adventure?" As I nodded agreement, he went on. "In which the Living God blessed you and kept you from harm, even though you were in great peril?"

I did not know what to say. He seemed to be seeking a response from me. How did he know? Could he read my thoughts? My mind flew back to the mezuzah where I had prayed. Did he hear? Did he know?

I threw myself before him, raising an arm in salute and obedience. "Oh Samuel, what am I that you should think of me?" I rushed on, not even wondering whether what I was saying would sound silly because, at that moment, there seemed no one else in the room but we two.

"You who speak with the Lord of Hosts know that I escaped the hand of death and that God heard my prayer. He held me safe in the storm and I am humbled by his mercy." With that I kneeled before him and offered him the pelt. I said,

"Take this trophy as a witness that your care of Judah brings blessings, for we know that your prayers intercede for all Israel. Bless me for I am nothing." I bowed upon the ground.

There was a murmur of approval around the room. I could see Father was pleased. But it did not matter, for all I could see was Samuel, who could read my heart and knew me for what I was. He smiled and held out a hand and drew me up.

"Come, my boy. Play for us and praise the Lord," he said softly.

I walked over to where my harp was, but Father had got there first and he handed it to me. That was unusual. I thought about what I should play. I could not think of anything at first, but then inspiration came, or did Samuel guide me, as I sang from the Book of Moses.

I plucked at the strings; developed the note; alternated an oscillating chord; and then pitched my voice against the melody and rhythm of the harp.

"And I will raise me up a faithful priest,"

I sang and repeated the line. Then,

"He shall do that which is in mine heart and in my mind,"

and again a repetition linking both verses.

"This day will I magnify Thee in the sight of all Israel that they may know that, as I was with Moses, so I will be with Thee."

I had them spellbound – even Samuel – as I came to the end.

"And I will build him a sure house and he shall walk before mine anointed for ever."

As the sweet, high note of the harp drifted off into silence, I again bowed before Samuel.

There was applause from all around, but I was riveted upon Samuel whose response was seen in a great sighing smile.

"David bar Jesse," he said formally, "you are twice blessed. First in your daring and music, and second by the gift of sharing that music." Then turning to my father, "Jesse, old friend, it's true what they say about the boy. You must be very proud. He must come to me and later he should visit Saul." With that he gave me his blessing and my cup ran over.

Then Shammah, the nicest of my brothers, interjected, "Pardon me, Samuel the Prophet, distinguished Elders and my Father, but David has songs not just from the holy scrolls but of his own invention."

My heart stopped. I wished that he had not said this. How could words of mine match what had gone before? I stood blushing with head bowed down and just wished to escape, but it was too late.

Samuel turned to Shammah and said, "It is pleasing when an older brother has respect for a younger. So, David – you have more for us?"

It was a question but also a command. I could see out of the corner of my eye that Father was now looking somewhat vexed, though whether it was with me or Shammah I did not know. I didn't blame him. It had all gone so well and now I had to continue. What would I give them?

Then I thought of Leah. I loved her not just for her beauty but also for her soul, which was pure and true. She had heard a few of my verses: some she encouraged, others she gently advised to put on one side.

Making every effort to control my nerves, I sought to explain. "At night, looking after the sheep, one sees the heavens littered with stars and – well – this made me try to capture it..." I just stopped and dried up.

I could sense their embarrassment, but struggled on concentrating, emptying my mind. I gave three ascending trills on the harp, closed my eyes and sang with the undulating chords.

"The heavens declare the glory of God,"

This was repeated, quietly, and then, rising on a crescendo,

"The heavens declare the glory of God and the firmament shewest his handiwork."

I stole a quick glance around. There was no sense of embarrassment now: I had their attention. I repeated the melody with my voice and then brought harp, rhythm, melody and words together in a slow unified movement.

"And the firmament shewest His handiwork, day unto to day uttereth speech, and the night sheweth knowledge, and the heavens declare the Glory of God."

I had my eyes closed. I dare not open them. I felt so exposed.

There was total silence. Then I felt his touch. I opened my eyes to see Samuel close beside me.

He raised his hands above me and declared, "From out of Judah comes God's warrior bard. Amen."

There was loud applause at this. I looked at Father, who looked at me quizzically, as if I was a stranger, but he came forward   smiling.

"David," he said, "you should thank Shammah for his kindness and the Prophet for his blessing."

I knew then that it was all right.

Father turned to Samuel and asked, "Shall I serve the supper Samuel?" The Great Prophet nodded. I was about to leave the room to my betters, but my father said, "Samuel, if it please you, the lad may sit quietly and eat with us?"

"Of course. Sit, sit my boy – you have earned it."

I withdrew to the back of the room. There, sitting with my back to the wall, I smiled thankfully at Shammah and just got my legs out of the way from a vicious kick aimed by Boaz, who snarlingly whispered, "Show off!"

as out he went.

At Father's signal the women came in and began to serve the meats. Mother looked glorious; she was so proud as she served Samuel, whose graciousness quite turned her head. My eldest sister, Zeruiah, the mother of Joab, had come in to help Mother and was serving Father.

Mina, my father's concubine, was attending the Elders. I was a little surprised because she and Mother did not get on well, but Mother was probably glad of the help. Mina was tall and as old as Shammah and handsome in a way, but I was surprised that Father still wanted a concubine. I sometimes thought that he might want to impress the neighbours with the fact that he could afford her.

Then in came Leah behind my mother. She was brutal. She totally ignored me! Despite my gaze following her around the room, she deliberately, quite deliberately, looked the other way. She looked stern, proud and aloof. Whilst full of dignity and very courteous to our visitors, but to me, it was as if I might never have existed. I was desolate.

I was served last by Una, Leah's friend, who was also a bond maiden. Una, though we all called her "Mouse" because she was so tiny, had the widest big brown eyes and a nervous smile that was quite delightful. She was younger than I was and I quite liked her, not least because she was completely devoted to Leah.

As the men began to eat the talk and noise grew so I could speak to Una without being overheard, "Mouse, Mouse, what have I done to Leah? Why is she so angry with me," I said plaintively.

She smiled and quietly answered, "Oh, you are silly. Of course she's angry with you. You might have been seriously hurt and she said no sheep is worth that. We could all hear your singing, and the last one, wasn't that a song you made with Leah?" she asked.

"She told you, Mouse," I sighed. "Oh, little Mouse, tell her not to be so dreadful to me. It's difficult enough with the Prophet but if she's..." I didn't know how to finish what I felt and just shrugged helplessly.

Mouse's eyes twinkled. "David, I have saved a special piece of lamb for you, and..." she paused for effect "... and a sweet kebab made by Leah – just for you."

I took it gratefully: it was my favourite. Perhaps all was still well with Leah and I.

"Mouse, I must speak with her. When the Prophet has gone, can you arrange it? I'll be in the usual place." By that I meant in the small tree grove, behind our house. "After dusk – please Mouse – please ask her to come."

As I said this I was close to despair. Gone was my pleasure in my return if Leah did not look kindly on me. I felt a sense of panic, loneliness and longing. I could not bear the thought of us being at odds.

Out of the corner of my eye I could see Mother gesture towards Mouse and she tripped away. The women were so attentive with food, wine and water, but Leah did not give me so much as a glance. I began to feel angry, lost and resentful.

"Why have a love," I thought miserably, "if she is so callous? Damned Bloody Hell! I swore. "I won't go to meet her. I won't turn up to be humiliated. Josh, Aaron and Eli will be dying to know what has gone on. Why should I worry about her?"

But I knew that whilst I may well go and see my friends, I would be at the grove no matter what and, though my heart fell at the thought of her not being there, I knew I would wait for ever.

The women were clearing away. I looked with longing at Leah's retreating back. Perhaps she might relent a little and acknowledge my existence, but – no! "Bloody, bloody, bloody hell" I swore to my self. "Oh, Leah. Leah? Why?"

Samuel and David

I was quite cast down; my thoughts were miles away so at first I did not realise that I as being spoken to.

"David? David, young poet and dreamer." It was Samuel. "Where were you?" He did not wait for an answer, but standing above me, he drew me to my feet and said, "Come, walk with me and be my staff."

With that, after saluting the company, he steered me out of the room, out of the house and into the evening sunshine.

We walked along without speaking. I could not help notice the people giving way in respectful silence until old Abraham cried out, "Blessings be upon you, Samuel, Prophet and guide of Israel." The people clapped as Samuel gestured in acknowledgement but continued to walk on at a surprisingly brisk pace.

He did not really need me as his staff, as his touch upon my shoulder was very light. We must have gone almost a mile and he had not said a word, so, of course, I waited until I was spoken to.

He guided me towards some trees in front of a small hill. Still without speaking, he was obviously looking for somewhere to sit. I ventured, "Over there, Rabbi?"

"Yes," he answered and we went over and sat upon a convenient rock.

He then asked to tell him in detail about the fight with the mountain cat. I was taken aback as he probed everything. Suddenly he knew all and so did I. I was shocked to realise that I had been willing to sacrifice Sep.

I looked at him pleadingly. Had I been so callous and calculating? Did that really happen, or was I making it up after the event?

As if he knew my thoughts he said gently, "I can see it troubles you, David. That's good. But did you think or see what might happen? Or were your feelings such that fear and anxiety turned to anger and rage, so that your emotions overwhelmed you? When looking back, is your memory more of an explanation for what happened, rather than what occurred?"

I thought hard. Then I knew – apart from forgetting about the direction of the wind. "No, Rabbi. That's how it happened. Was I wrong?"

Suddenly, to my utter amazement, he slapped me across the face, quite hard. He didn't say anything. Then he slapped me once more, this time saying, "Now think – don't feel. What is happening?" and slapped me again, sharply twice across the face.

I stood up. I was burning. I was angry. Had he gone mad? Was he possessed? Should I call for help?

Then I heard him say again, "Don't feel – think! What is happening?" This was followed by another sharp slap.

My brain whirled. Then I knew.

I said between gritted teeth, "I see an old man who has surprised a boy." In my anger I did not bother to correct myself and say a young man. "It's a test. It's a game to discover whether the young man was telling the truth. To see whether he can think and not be confused by the unexpected." I just glared at him, half expecting another slap.

Without a word of apology, he beamed, "David, that's excellent! You really can think when most others would be overwhelmed with feelings. Yes, it has been a test and you have shown something special that merits nurturing."

He stopped smiling, held my hand and looked into my face, "It's a gift my boy, but not without pain. Kings would give half their kingdoms to be able to think in the midst of battle and not be bowled over by emotions. I called you a warrior bard – that is even rarer." He could see my disbelieving look. "Oh, tis true, David – I assure you. Tell me – and this is another test – do you think you hear God?"

I was flabbergasted at this question. What did he know? I half thought of not answering, but his look held me as a snake holds a rabbit. I could not do or say anything other then tell this man the truth.

"I don't know," I said very slowly as I thought through his question. "I don't think I've heard a voice. But sometimes I think I have felt His presence when I'm amongst the mountains and amidst the silences. Sometimes, He's in my music when the words come effortlessly unbidden.

He seems to be the echo in everything I feel, touch and see."

I had never said anything like this to anyone before: not to Leah, nor, even, to myself in such words.

He did not say anything but waited for me to go on. I knew I was describing something I could not possibly explain, but on rare moments had experienced with complete certainty and clarity.

"Sometimes," I continued, "when I am alone, words come to me that I did not know before. My songs seem to come from nothing – but nothing can come from nothing. It's not me that gives the words, they simply pour out of me." As I spoke I began to understand something of the creativity that had been given to me. The Prophet sat silent.

I faltered on. "I have never thought of this but the words are given to me. I am a vehicle – for what I don't know. I have never heard God's voice with my ears, but somehow my mind, body and soul knows his presence." I spoke these last words in a whisper as the revelation was made clear for me.

Samuel still did not respond and then I felt bold enough to ask the question that all Israel wanted to ask, "When God speaks to you, how does he sound? Is it His voice in your head, or in the burning bush like Moses? What did God say to you when he first called you?" Then I said in wonder, "You were younger than me when he first spoke to you."

He answered, very slowly. "God's voice is always a mystery. Sometimes it comes in the stillness of the still. Sometimes I hear Him in the storm or amongst the cascading rocks and waters and in the tumult of the sea. But most of all, it is a still clear voice inside of me. It is quite unlike anything else, yet I know it for certain when He calls."

He went on and I appreciated that I was sharing something very special. "Often, I yearn for Him to answer me. Often, I seek for His guidance, but nothing comes. Then I feel terribly alone – alone with the responsibility for Israel. I cannot command God. He is not my servant. The people imagine a vain thing if they believe that I, like you, am a vessel, into which, in His infinite wisdom, He sometimes pours Himself into."

Samuel's words became barely audible. "I am His servant. I am His potsherd, for Him to fill and discard. Frequently, He leaves me desolate." The old man visibly shook with both sorrow and anger. "Often, when I need Him most, there is no answer and I have to struggle by myself to find the solution. There are times when I could curse Him for His neglect of me. But there are times when I am inspired, possessed with the love and certainty of God; when I know I am filled with the Lord."

He drew himself up to his full height and stretched out his arms, his face now ecstatic. "And then, when He speaks, I know the power of His direction. I know the course of His will. Then I feel no ill, no fear, no uncertainty, no doubts, and no tiredness. My spirit soars as with wings of eagles."

He stopped, turned lovingly towards me and smiled. "Aye then, David my friend. Then I feel as if I could run as fast and as long as you! Yes – then even I could wrestle with a mountain lion." Then, in a matter of fact tone, he said, "We are going to be friends, aren't we?" It was such a simple question made in total humility. Here was Samuel, the Prophet of Israel, asking me to be his friend.

"I am not worthy, Rabbi," I answered, overcome with love for this noble, noble man.

"Oh, my friend David," he interrupted, "but you are, because you know something of the mystery of God. I have a duty to seek the Godhead in every man, but sometimes I have to dig very deep. For you, however, the privilege of knowing the presence of God makes you close to my heart."

He looked me straight in the eyes. "You asked about my call?" he said inquiringly. I was agog.

Then he looked away. "Perhaps, some day, I will tell you everything. I told Eli my master. It was a message that I wish I did not have to give." Sighing, he went on, "That revelation has helped me over the years. But," he said cheerfully, "now that I have found another friend, I won't feel so isolated. Tell me about the some of the words that have been given to you."

I did not have my harp with me so could not play. I explained that the inspiration came to me at a full moon, or at the dawn, or in the middle of the night when my spirit seemed to get lost in the world around me. I quietly sang the words.

"O Lord how excellent is Thy name in all the earth who has set Thy Glory above the heavens.

Out of the mouths of babes and sucklings thou hast ordained strength.

When I consider thy heavens, the work of thy fingers, the moon and the stars which Thou hast ordained.

What is man that Thou art mindful of him and the son of man that Thou visitest him? For Thou hast made him a little lower than the angels and hast crowned him with glory and honour."

As I ended I realised that I had added to the last two verses,

"What is man that Thou shouldst be mindful of him."

I now felt fully inspired and wanted to share this with my friend, my master, and my father. As I ended he had lowered his head but said nothing. I began to feel uncomfortable. The sun had gone down behind the hill and, whilst the evening was warm, there seemed to be a special stillness around us.

He raised his face to me and I saw that there were tears on his face. He embraced me and we sat quietly till there was no light left in the sky.

He was the first to break the silence as he stood up, "David, my friend – for so you always shall be – we shall not speak to others of our evening together."

I nodded, only half understanding.

He continued, "But we shall speak again, especially because I truly think you should go to the King. You have much to offer Saul, and he needs his spirit lightening."

Again, I did not follow the gist of the latter part of his remark but he interrupted my musing. He stopped, held me by the shoulder and looked straight into my face. "You are in love with religion, aren't you?"

I put aside the temptation to tell him about my love for Leah. "I don't know, Rabbi. I know I love my music, the Holy Scrolls, my land, my family and my friends in Bethlehem." I said shyly, "And now I love you as my Rabbi and father."

He smiled and said, "All those things, and I am honoured that you take me for your friend and that I am a father to you."

With that he gave me the father's blessing, "This is my beloved son in whom I am well pleased." He then warmly embraced me. "Now, David, I will lean a little. I am getting tired but it has been a good day. We have done the work of the Lord together."

I took him back to our house and handed him over to a wondering Eliab, who took him at once to Father.

I was obviously dismissed.

Betrothed

Suddenly I realised that I was late for Leah and now it was dark. Would she be there? I rushed off in despair, looking neither left nor right to see whether anyone was watching. I quickly arrived at the grove. The trees were as black shadows, outlined by the stars and half moonlight.

I peered into the trees. I wondered if I dare call out. Where was she? Had she come? Had she been waiting and then left because I wasn't there?

I was engulfed in misery and half moaned and half called, "Leah? Leah!"

There was no answer. Everything was quiet. From the town I could hear a dog bark, which was answered by another.

I heard a scuffle and the sudden cry of a bird who was being disturbed on his roost, but no sign or sound of Leah. I began to raise my voice, not caring who might hear me. "Leah? Leah! Please come out. I'm sorry – truly sorry. Please answer."

Then there was a slight movement at the far side of the grove and I heard the sound of quiet weeping. My heart stood still. I walked into the grove and there in the shadows was the shape that I would know anywhere.

I rushed towards her. I took her unresisting form into my arms and tried to kiss away her tears as they mingled with mine.

"Leah. Leah, my love. What is it? What have I done? Please – please, my darling, don't cry. Forgive me. I'm sorry."

She looked up at me. Her face, her eyes were wet with tears. I wanted to take them from her. I wanted to caress her. As she had not rebuffed me, I began to feel elated.

"Oh, my dearest!" I held her tightly and her answering arms made my senses reel. I knew it was all right as our bodies melded together. I was ablaze with longing. I held her tighter and tighter. My mouth sought hers as we sank to the floor.

My hands followed the taunt shape of her bosom. I was thrilled as my body, like an arrow, ached to find its mark. Her hands came to my face, holding me apart a little. She kissed my eyes, my mouth and then allowed her hands to flow down my body. I wanted to explode and to possess her.

I waited – not daring to breathe. I did not want the moment to go, but waited for the signal that did not come. My body pleaded with her. Her breaths came quickly and deeply, but still she gently moved me away.

"David, no! Oh, David, you might have been killed." And with this she began to cry again.

Out of her tears she said, "How could you risk so much when you know what you mean to me? I could not bear it if you had been hurt. I could not live if ... if ... if ...," and her words ended in soft weeping.

My spirits rose. She was crying for me. She loved me! She was not angry but afraid for me. Everything was clear.

"Leah, my dearest, don't fear. I was not really in any danger. Truly – it sounded worse than it was. Boaz was right – it was a mangy old cat, barely able to give a scratch. If Sep had not been so clumsy he would have chased the old beast himself. I was just showing off." I babbled on, casting away any pride so as to comfort my love.

She stopped crying, and smiled at me. "David, you're not a very good liar, but I love you for trying."

Our mouths met. I took her lips in mine and tasted her sweetness. I was afire again as I buried my head in her breast. I nuzzled and found a gap in her smock, my tongue laved her smooth silken skin. My hand followed my tongue as I traced inside following her contours as I caressed her round firm breasts, whose softness and warmth possessed me. I took a breast in my mouth and – oh! – I sank into her, my body a spear.

Her hand held my head to her breast as she murmured my name. My phallus was clear and pressed into her soft, smooth thigh as I leaned into her maidenhood. I was engorged and desperate for union as my hand went to her thigh. But then, with a sigh, she half drew away,

"Oh my love, please." She did not say anything else.

I lay at her side, my arms around her. She did not resist and I knew she would not. I yearned to enter her. My phallus quivered with longing. I was hard, hard, hard! My whole body was a spear. But there was no responding harmony and I sensed this was not the time.

I moved away a little and, curling up my knees, moved my phallus from her. I softly lay my head upon her breast. We remained still for many moments, neither speaking, as we tried to allay our passion. I loved her so much and wanted desperately to please her, to have her approval, yet I would do nothing that might break our harmony.

She caressed my head like a mother might a small child as she soothed me.

Minutes passed and then we began to speak of our betrothal: how we were now pledged to each other. After I received my colours, I would have my first man's headband of white and gold. Then we could marry.

She expressed doubts but I said very firmly, "Nonsense, my love. If Father objects, then we leave Bethlehem. I am sure Samuel the Prophet will help us. You will join our faith won't you?" This was the only question which might have proved an obstacle.

"Like your great-great-grandmother, Ruth," Leah laughingly answered. "Weren't they wonderful words she used:

...Where you go, I go. Your people are my people, and your God is my God...

I hugged her in delight, and sat up. "Leah, you remember! It's a great story and brings much honour to my ancestors. We can be like them."

Leah answered, "Be careful, that's what Boaz keeps saying to me."

I was brought up sharply. A fierce stab of jealousy went through me. "What do you mean, Leah? What's Boaz got to do with us? He may be my brother but I have no respect for him. He's a bully and worse."

She started to explain that Boaz had offered himself to her but then she felt my body's angry response. "Don't be silly. He means nothing to me. He reminded me that – how did he put it? 'Our family have a tradition of having non-Judean women'. He said he was named after your great, great grandfather Boaz, who was an elder of the tribe. He said he'd be an Elder some day and that I ought to be grateful that he treats me with respect. He reminded me that I am only a bond maiden and have no rights."

I was furious. With something of a shock, I realised that I actually hated Boaz, not just for his petty bullying and mean spitefulness, but for the cruelty and violence that lay hidden just beneath the surface. I suddenly remembered incidents over the years where he had taken delight in the pain of others and of animals. I had not thought about this for a long time.

I told Leah of the time, when I was very small, I had a puppy that had been hurt by a cart. Boaz, though he was not then my age, had seen my distress but, instead of taking the dog to Father, he killed it before my eyes.

"Leah, now I understand. He actually enjoyed what he did: not just picking the dog and bashing its head against a wall, but in watching my face. He enjoyed seeing me distressed. He revelled in it. I was crying and he mocked my tears. I was only four."

The intensity of the recalled memory made me feel cold and anxious. "Leah, oh Leah, be very careful of him. If there is any difficulty, go to Shammah – he'd always help. Even Eliab would not stand for Boaz's nonsense and I am sure he would listen to you."

It was her turn to reassure me that she was in no danger. She said that Boaz was just being boorish. Lady Zeruiah was always a tower of strength and, despite Boaz being near to being a full warrior, he still had respect for our Mother. Besides, she continued, my Father, Jesse, though he had a concubine, still honoured Zeruiah. So Leah was confident that Father would not tolerate any improper behaviour from Boaz.

Then, a thought struck me. "Is that why he has not married yet? He wants to marry you?" I was fraught with jealous anxiety.

"He did speak of it last year," Leah admitted. "I was never in the slightest interested and your lady mother was very kind, reminding him that I am her bond maiden – not the family's – and therefore he has no rights over me." She hesitated and then said, "I was not going to tell you. Your mother had asked, 'Why not marry Boaz?' as it would have given me freedom but I always had hopes of you. Now you have given me your pledge, I told your mother and, though she thinks there could be difficulties, she will try to help."

She looked anxiously at me, I smiled at her, and she blushed and asked in a small voice, "Did I do wrong?"

I laughed. "Darling, I gave you my pledge. True – I hadn't used the word marriage, but you don't think I would take you as a concubine, do you? Of course we are to marry. It was clever of you to get Mother on our side. She has always had a special place for me. I think that's why Boaz is so horrid." I paused as I realised that this was the core of his jealousy. I could almost feel sorry for him.

"And today has been quite something." I laughed again. "You know I can almost measure good days by how angry Boaz becomes; he was furious about Samuel's kindness to me."

Leah then wanted to know all about what had transpired. She told me that the women were listening and that she was very proud. Mother, too, was very pleased.

"While she accepts Mina," said Leah, "she is still obviously the chief woman, and so only a little jealous. She said to Mina, 'That's my boy! He gains merits from the Prophet. You heard him call David the warrior bard? Even if you ever have a son, that won't be said about him!' That's why I think it must be terrible to be a concubine – even with a kind master like your father."

I assured her that, "When I am awarded my colours we will marry whether or not Father approves."

"Never mind," said Leah. Changing the subject she said, "Now tell me what the Prophet said to you."

I told her of his wisdom and of his kindness. I confided in her that he had said he wanted to be my friend but I kept the secret of his revelation. I admit I was pleased by her response. She was definitely impressed.

"He really called you 'his friend'?" said Leah. "Him, the wisest man in Israel, who guides the King, and speaks to your God? David, I know I did not need the Prophet to tell me, but you are very special."

Could any man fail to love her?

"And you, dearest, dearest Leah, are ten, a hundred, a thousand times more special." We clung together and kissed with joy, even if not with our earlier passion.

"You said you had written a song for me. Can you remember it?" she said.

I laughed and said, "I thought you would never ask! Of course I remember it. Shall I wait till I have my harp?"

"No. Tell me it now."

So I gave her the verses inspired just by her – those that were not inspired by God or the Lord's wonderful land.

"On the now scared spot stood my glorious Queen
My arms, a poor altar I did entwine about her waist.
My eyes blinded by the Vision seen.

With fingers unholy I traced the beauty for ever mine,
Of the rose in her cheek.
Whilst my lips did seek to raise this vale of rapturous mystery."

She was very silent.

I asked tentatively, "Don't you like it? Have I said too much about us?"

She still did not answer. Then she raised her head and I could see that she was crying again.

"David, it was beautiful. You called me a Queen and said that we share a 'rapturous mystery'."

I said, desperately seeking confirmation, "And we are betrothed, Leah, aren't we?"

"Oh, yes!" she breathed and she looked truly happy.

We embraced and I could feel my senses rise again. She clung to me tightly as we sought each other's bodies: she my firm chest, I her wondrous bosom.

Our mouths fused together. We sank to the floor. There was no resistance – only a mutual urging and an indescribable joy. Her gentle hand slowly flowed along my hard, hard phallus. My head, heart and body were hers and as I sought to enter her.

Suddenly, there was a change in her response. She was pushing me away. Disappointment and confusion overwhelmed me. Then I heard what she heard.

Wandering around in the dark was a figure speaking in a hoarse and forced voice, as if trying to produce a loud whisper. "David! Leah! David ... your mother is calling for you."

It was Mouse. She was calling us.

I groaned a curse and rolled away from Leah. I lay on my back, eyes tight screwed up, face in a silent snarl. She had shattered our moment. Then I felt total concern for Leah, filled with remorse that I had marred her in any way.

I rose quickly, held her gently, brushed her down and answered in as controlled voice possible, "All right, Mouse. We can hear you. Just a moment. Stay there – we'll come to you."

Leah threw me a grateful look as we sought to tidy ourselves. Then she gave me a delightful smile, kissed me gently on the nose and said, "You're forgiven, but no more hunting mountain lions single handed – not even with dozy Sep."

We walked out of the grove towards the diminutive form of Mouse.

"I am sorry, Leah. Sorry, David. The lady Zeruiah wants to talk to you. She sent me to find you. I told her that I thought you would be walking around the tabernacle so that it would give you more time."

Cunning little Mouse. The tabernacle was where the town's copies of the holy scrolls are kept at the opposite side of Bethlehem – at least half an hour away.

I looked at Leah when I said this but she just smiled quietly, and then asked,

"I wonder what your mother wants?"

"Oh, I know," interjected Mouse. "She wants to talk about what the Prophet said about you going to King Saul. David, she was pleased – we all were. I know she realises you have feelings for Leah. I know as well, don't I, Leah?"

Leah nodded for, though Mouse was just fourteen, Mouse was Leah's closest friend and I realised then that they had shared everything together.

"Yes, she wants to ask you what you intend, because I think she would be happy for you to take Leah if the lord Jesse agrees."

That was great news. We all hurried over towards home because, no matter what might happen, I knew Leah and I were betrothed.

Who knows? Samuel might agree to marry us after Leah joins Israel.

Chapter Four

The Battle of Bull Horns

The Duel

I had expected that, having Mother's approval, Leah and I would be able see each other more openly. However, Mother counselled against this and Leah followed her advice. Reluctantly, I had little choice but to go along with them, so I spent my time with Aaron and Eli, as Josh was away.

I gave Eli strong hints that, once I had my colours, my status would be changing in other ways, too. Colours were only given half yearly and those who received theirs late could feel a little bit put upon. Eli already had his colours, as, like Josh, he was some months older than I was.

Eli was intrigued about the Prophet's visit but I was unforthcoming. I felt a little ashamed about this so, swearing him to absolute secrecy, I told him about Leah. He was pleased for me but asked what Josh would think? I could not see what he meant by this.

He explained, "Well, it breaks up our foursome. My father has already chosen Zena to be my bride. She's only thirteen so I'll have to wait three years. Josh is not interested in having a wife yet, despite all his joking. He may feel hurt that you are preferring a women to your old friends."

I wasn't sure whether this was Eli talking for Josh or for himself, but I assured him that, even though I hoped to marry sooner rather than later, we would always be friends and brothers.

I hardly saw Leah before I had to return to Bull Horns. Nevertheless, she was so sweet and encouraging that I returned reasonably happily, especially as she promised that she would visit soon.

On my arrival at Bull Horns, I told the waiting Josh about Samuel's visit, doing my best to avoid sounding as if I was boasting. On the other hand, I hardly mentioned Leah.

He wanted to have a wrestle. "I'm so bored. I don't know how you seem to enjoy it so much here. I need the exercise."

We came together but I wasn't all that enthusiastic because, frankly, I wanted to be alone and think about Leah. He threw me to the ground and pinned me quite quickly. He held me down, panting hard, and clearly had expected more resistance.

"What's the matter, David? Haven't you got over your fight with the mountain cat?"

This seemed to be a good get out so, after bashing my stomach with his head two or three times, honour was satisfied and he left without feeling that I had been unfriendly.

Sep, as usual, was pleased to see me. I checked out the herd and refurbished my den, which for some reason, Josh did not appear to have used much. To tell the truth, I think Josh was a little apprehensive about the cave. I don't know why, though Eli had talked about ghosts.

The time went well. I had so much to think about. Though Leah would not visit this time, hopefully it would not be too long before we were together.

I felt at peace and thought of the future when Leah would accept the God of Israel and then we could marry. We had spoken about this on a number of occasions, and I had talked lengthily about my "vision of God". She had the bizarre idea that perhaps the apparent differences between people's gods were more do to with how people described the one God. That, in reality, there was only one God but the various nations emphasised different aspects of the many manifestations of a single God. She insisted that there were elements in her people's religion that were not very different from the best to be found in the laws of Moses: reward for virtue; care for the distressed; the pursuit of justice; due honour of the warrior. She clearly had thought much about this and took a great interest in such things. I felt confident that, once she came into Israel, the Prophet would recognise her as a very spiritual person, even though a woman.

It was hot and the high sun, whose heat sculptured the air with mirages, surrounded all. The vale beyond was now a shimmering haze of gold, speckled by gentle dust shapes. Sometimes spiralling high, others seemed to shadow rolling balls of wind grass. In the stillness of the afternoon, I dozed, dreamed and relaxed. I was emptying my mind and letting myself go to be receptive, and, sure enough, new words emerged which I could share with Leah.

"I will bless the Lord at all times: His praise shall be continually in my mouth. My soul shall make her boast in the Lord and the humble shall hear and be glad."

I let the verses roll and felt them echo around my soul. Then, as a descant, newly-shaped sounds filled me with a wondrous elation. I sang loudly:

"O magnify the Lord with me and let us exalt His name together."

Yes, Leah and I would magnify and be magnified in the Lord; this would be our bridal song.

"Oh taste and see that the Lord is Good, blessed be the man that trusteth in Him. The young lions do lack and suffer hunger, but they that shall seek the Lord shall not want any good thing."

In her ecstatic kisses, we would ascend the heights. Together we would praise the Lord in our joy, our voice, our song, and love.

I imagined leading her to meet the Living God, her soul linked to mine, expectant and open to His presence.

"Come ye children, harken unto me I will teach you the fear of the Lord. The righteous cry and the Lord heareth and delivereth them out of their troubles."

The harp soared. As chord followed chord I was ecstatic. It was God who had led me to Leah. He was blessing our love. Therefore there could be no doubt that Father would approve what God had ordained.

I was afire with love of Him and yearned with my whole being for Leah. I was aroused, as my soul, mind and body was united in the search for God and my love of Leah.

Suddenly, I was aware that something was not right. My senses were drowned with the madness of my song that had possessed me. Dimly, I sensed rather than heard a warning growl from Sep. My ecstasies were shattered.

I felt very wanting, as I peered out into the haze of the mid afternoon sun to see where, if any, the threat was coming from.

My feelings of embarrassment increased when I realised that my song had been given to the whole world in the belief there was no one out there. What if Josh or Eli – or worse, Boaz – were stumbling up the path and had heard every word?

Then again, from the direction of Sep's clear growl, the intrusion was not coming from the direction of Bethlehem but from beyond the valley towards the west.

Then I felt it like a blow. Out of the haze – much, much closer than I had thought possible – I heard the harsh laughs and shouts of men. Just at the opening of my gorge were four figures, two mounted on horses, with an armed warrior running at the side of each. It could only mean one thing: a scouting party of Philistines. They must be either marauding warriors, out to test their skills, or scouts ahead of a larger body preparing for a major raid.

My stomach heaved in straight fear. I whimpered so, that Sep came to me in comfort. I was close to panic.

"Oh, God, God, God!" I prayed or cursed – I know don't which. "Help me. Help me!"

They were waving their spears towards me, as their mocking voices with their harsh Philistine accents floated across the plateau.

"Hello little Jew. Are you lonely?" said one in an exaggerated tone.

Another man's voice was clear and obscene, "Come, come, my pretty boy. Let Eglan tan your tight little ass."

Other such crudities were bandied between them. I learned their names from them as they spoke.

Eglan was the broad-fronted warrior who was especially crude and was making frightening gestures to me.

The other man was taller but thinner, and had alighted from his horse. He seemed to be the leader and was addressed as Achish by the younger of the four whose name had not yet been mentioned.

The man who had remained with the horses was called Ganz. He laughed at how Eglan was going to abuse the pretty Israelite.

I was devastated.

They were full warriors in light bronze armour and, typical of the Philistines, went bare-bodied expect for a small cloak, which they made into a thin band across their chests when travelling.

All were helmeted and fully armed. I could see bows and spears strapped to the horses.

Then, very deliberately, leaving the one called Ganz to stay with the horses to avoid the awkward scramble up the gorge, the other three came running lightly towards me.

I was close to abandoning everything and fleeing in blind confusion. My throat was constricted. I feared for my life. I cursed myself for a vain fool, as I felt the dread of never seeing Leah again.

I knew what was expected of me: I should flee. That was the instruction we boys had been given. Go and raise the alarm and prepare for the worst. This compounded my panic because I thought of my Father's fury at being alerted perhaps only minutes before the enemies arrived should they follow me home.

Sep was barking furiously. I half turned and then I heard ... or felt ... or became aware of Samuel's voice: "Don't feel – look! Don't react – think!"

I pulled myself together and took a deep breath to calm me.

What could I see? There were four raiders who had obviously travelled far. My singing had attracted them. I angrily suppressed blaming myself – I had to deal with the situation as it was, not why it had happened. It was no use worrying about what one could not alter. On reflection, I quickly realised that I could probably outpace any of them, despite them being full warriors. I had the advantage of height and was not tired. Moreover, I knew the ground and, in all likelihood, if they could not catch me before I escaped up the cut at the back of the cave, it would be they who would be in trouble because they had been discovered.

My mind flew on. All right you mockers, I thought. Before raising the alarm, let's see if we can cause you some embarrassment to pay you back.

I told Sep to stand and be quiet. I ran along the ridge and looked down the 150 feet or so.

"What a noisy lot you uncircumcised are," I shouted down at them. "And you," I cried pointing to the one called Eglan. "You'll not get near enough to anyone to tan their ass. If there's going to be any tanned ass, Philistine, it'll be yours."

The other two men were surprised at this and laughed. The warrior called Achish beckoned to me. "Well said, youngster. But come down, lad, and we won't hurt you – I promise."

Of course not, I thought. He knows he can't reach me quickly enough to prevent me sounding the alarm, so he's seeking an easy capture.

Achish went on, "We don't want to have to kill you – not after all the prayers we've heard!" and they all began to laugh again.

Their laughter was the last of that day and the beginning of a nightmare that still haunts me.

By this time, I was above and ahead of them. Even though I was 20 to 30 yards away, I loaded my sling.

In quick succession, *whiz, whiz,* went my missiles, followed almost immediately by a frightened neigh from the first horse, whose flank my sharp stone had struck squarely in the middle. He reared and, quicker than it takes to tell, he wrenched the bridle from the keeper's hand and plunged wildly back down into the valley.

The second stone had also hit its target: right on the other horse's head. To make matters worse for the attending Philistine, this horse bolted off in the opposite direction to the first. Both startled animals sped away from each other, cheered on by my shouts and Sep's excited barking.

The warrior who should have been controlling the horses had just made the first payment for my humiliation. The solider turned first one way then the other, confused.

Achish, the leader, barked an order – no humour evident in his voice this time.

"Ganz! Ganz! Get after them, man, or we're lost. Go! Go on, after them!"

He could see the man was flustered and ordered, "Catch one first, then you can round up the other. Get going. Move!" He gesticulated and yelled, even though Ganz still hesitated. "We'll deal with this little devil by ourselves."

Achish turned to me and called out, "You shouldn't have done that, Israelite. Now this is your last chance. Come down quietly and I promise you won't get hurt, but if you don't then your death is on your own head."

Seeing that I had not stirred a single muscle, he said sternly, with great command, "Now come down at once. At once! Or surely you will die."

It was obvious he meant this. The situation was turning serious. Perhaps I ought to run now, but then thought, I've just got enough time to get a little bit more of my own back.

They were very cautious now. At first, I could not see what they were doing as they ran close to the cliff side to avoid any of my sling shots coming after them.

I could sense that the group had split into two. The big Eglan was coming up the nearest, but steepest, horn on the left, whereas the other two were over to the right, on a route, which whilst not as steep until the last ledge, was 50 or more yards longer.

Fine, I thought. "I know where you are. By the time you've reached the top – any of you – I'll be away up the cut. You'll never catch me and you still have to round up your horses. Otherwise, you're trapped here.

My plan was simple: I would use my sling, targeting each one in turn, with Sep threatening and covering the other side.

"Sep! Heel, boy. Obey!" I pointed to my right flank. "Stay and guard."

He was superb. He did as he was bid, allowing me to engage with Eglan in some anticipation.

I looked over the ledge and saw he was approaching slowly. He carried a spear and a heavy skin shield, with his vicious-looking sword still sheathed at his side. He was taller than I had at first thought.

He came forward, crouching behind his buckler, with his helmeted head just above the shield. Even from this distance, I could see deadly intent in his eyes.

There was no mirth on his face – only total concentration: fierce, cold and steady as a rock.

I felt a stab of anxiety. I had to be careful not to let him get too close. I fired my sling very accurately. But he was watching as the stone sped towards him. With great dexterity, he flicked up his left arm, caught it on his buckler and parried it away, harmlessly. As he did this, he advanced cautiously another five yards nearer. Although still being very careful, he was edging closer and was giving the other two a chance to surround me.

I would have to be going soon. I turned to the right Horn, calling Sep to me to stay and guard the left approach.

Achish, their captain, was without a shield as his had been tied to a fleeing horse. His companion, the youngest of the four, was not much older than I was. He held a shield to cover Achish and himself from my missiles.

Then, the first great crisis arrived: they had reached only the third of the four ledges when Achish spotted the cut behind the cave and saw my escape route.

He called out, "Acrah, look above the cave, he'll bolt up there. You keep him occupied while I cut him off. Wait until I give the signal."

It was too late. I had run very quietly along the ledge and was far closer to them than they expected. I was barely fifteen yards away and, more crucially, just above them. The young one, Acrah, was standing at the edge and had lowered his shield as he turned towards Achish to receive his instructions. I swiftly took aim at an open target. With hardly a sound, the stone whizzed through the air and caught him on the side of the head beneath his helmet.

Stunned, he half-stumbled. Achish called out in warning as my second stone followed after him, catching him on the knee. That was great – I'd done what I wanted and I was just about to turn and run, but was then held spellbound.

The young warrior began to lose his balance, teetered like a drunkard and then, as if in slow motion, stepped off the platform below me. With a despairing cry, he slithered and slid down the cliff side. Faster and faster he fell, until coming to a crunching, stomach-churning halt, caught and held by a jutting tree branch.

Everything seemed to stop.

All was silent ... until we heard Acrah's groans. I could see the red blood beginning to ooze down the cliff: he was obviously very badly hurt.

Achish, filled with concern, wisely retreated to aid his companion. I turned to run, and was about to call Sep, when I saw, just below the last ledge, the head and shoulders of the Philistine Eglan.

I called to Sep and called again, but it was no use. In the excitement at seeing the enemy come closer, Sep disobeyed and had sprung at the ascending warrior. If I had been there with my sling I might have been able to halt when happened next.

It all began to unfold as if we were all in some slow ritual dance, like priests serving at the altar.

Sep, with fangs bared, had thrown himself at the advancing Philistine. He seemed to move so slowly that I had all the time in the world to see the colours of Sep's coat, the thickened left rear leg, his trophy from the mountain cat, his teeth exposed in an angry snarl as he hurtled through the air at the enemy.

Eglan, tall and muscular, had stood upright. I could see his light ring-plated body armour. I could see his bulging muscles and the sweat on his skin gleaming through his armour. I even had time to notice the bronze patterned grieves on his massive legs and almost pathetically, a hole at the side of his skirt, which he had clumsily tied together, through which his paler thigh shone.

He had laid down his spear and, balancing lightly with legs apart, had his shield half in front of him so as to offer as small a target as possible, as his sword slowly cleaved the air.

I saw, rather than heard, Sep's cry as the cruel iron travelled downward with remorseless force and lightening speed hit the flying Sep – deep, deep into his neck.

Sep fell at Eglan's feet.

The Philistine had snapped quickly back into a defensive position to await any following sling shot from me.

I was turned to stone. My eyes burned into Sep's still form, urging some sign of life that I knew would never come. There was no doubt: Sep was dead.

I could see his inert torso, as my enemy callously kicked away the body of my friend. The cursed Philistine advanced closer, closer to the cliff face, and towards the last ledge below me.

I was totally cold – not the chill of fear, but with the deep rage of hate, a cruel hate I had never experienced before.

Half my brain told me now was the time to go; now was the time to flee; I had done everything and more than could be expected of me. Run, run – before that terrible form should add me to his trophies. But instead I turned towards my attacker, the slayer of Sep and knew what I was going to risk.

Up to this point, I had been in control. Until now had carefully thought about each move. From now on I did not know how it would end. I was fuelled by a cold yet flaming anger that impelled me forward. I rapidly calculated how to kill, for murder was in my heart.

"You Philistine bastard! Bastard Philistine!" I snarled at him. "How well your Philistine women will sing of your exploits this day – four warriors against a mere boy and his dog. You who would tan ass, have a companion bleeding to death below, your horses are gone, and all you have to show is a dog's carcass."

I stood not ten yards above him and only ten yards away, in a show of total contempt and defiance.

Our eyes were locked together in a chilling stare. His hard grey eyes were flecked with red from his rage and exertion. They were merciless eyes and they held mine in the killer's snake-like stare.

Everything which happened next occurred so quickly that it was probably over in a moment, but my perception of the action seemed to last for ever.

He did as I expected. He knelt down, grasped his spear and in one movement hurled it at me. I was waiting. I ducked and it glanced off the rocks a little above my head, clattering to the ground a little behind me.

He next reached for his sword. I had time to either turn and run, or to fire another shot. That's what he expected, hence he was still on the defensive.

This gave me time to grab his spear and turning towards him cried out my challenge. "You bastard Philistine! Killer of dogs! What are you waiting for, dog killer?"

My shout stung him into action. He did not hear his captain's call of warning. He was filled with a rage and hate at this impudent Israelite and, roaring his defiance, he ran up the slope. He thrust himself up the last five paces of the ledge, his sword held in one hand and his shield in the other.

He clambered up to steady himself, and pushed himself upward and forward over the ledge. With a mighty effort, he levered himself up in a final spring to reach me.

In his crouched position, he was half kneeling and, though he had sword and shield in hand, they were on the ground as he prepared to launch himself up. He was thinking whether he could retrieve his spear and cast it at the fleeing enemy, or whether to use his sword to cut down the knees of the Israelite who had so insulted him. Now, he was attacking, charging after an enemy he was convinced was in flight, as he catapulted himself upright.

This was my chance. I was not retreating, fleeing or cowering in fear. I was attacking, too.

It seemed to take an age to accomplish. The scene has been chiselled into my consciousness. As if from a distance, I observed the brutal slow clash of our colliding bodies. It began and ended in a flash, but the dance of death unfolded with such slow deliberation.

His head was upright. His iron look was that of the victorious raging killer. I could see his face: his teeth wretched in a grimace of anger and effort as he lurched towards me, raising his sword arm to give the blow that would end it all.

I saw the droplets of sweat flung threw the air, the patterned bristles of his unshaven face, his hair tight at the back.

I charged, charged at the form hurrying to meet his doom. With his spear, I threw the whole weight of my body with unerring aim at his throat as he came hurtling to meet me.

Now he understood – too late, too late. He saw and his eyes went wide with astonishment. His enemy was advancing not running before him. His spear began to pierce his skin just above his breast bone: the spear that he had sharpened time and again with such affection: his spear over which he had prayed: his very own spear was now cruelly seeking his life.

He saw his own death.

Desperately, he tried to dive to one side, but I saw the way his body was falling and followed him.

He tried to cry out, but the spearhead was already cutting through his windpipe as we fell together in a grotesque grappling.

His threshing limbs bowled me over. I nearly lost the spear that was juddering in my hand as his body toppled onto to me. In some parody of wrestling contests, the vanquished lay above the victor.

His blood gushing over me overwhelmed me. I was choking in mine enemy's blood. I threw my ebbing strength against his twitching body, which even in death would have crushed me in his shuddering death throes. With a huge effort I got my knees up and I thrust him from me.

He rolled over ... dead.

My cold rage was ebbing fast. My mind was beginning to slip away, with the greatest difficulty I tried to concentrate whilst my thoughts moved as if in clinging mud.

I knew I had to do something else, but couldn't remember what it was. I half rose and suddenly I felt a debilitating tiredness, not of muscle and bone, but from an insidious weariness of soul.

My senses were reeling. What had I done? I had forgotten something. My mind was full of horrific scenes, of Sep being severed in two before my eyes. Of a young warrior crashing down the cliff. Was this a dream? Was it some nightmare sent to drive me into madness and despair?

I gulped the air. Slowly, my thoughts were coming together and I heard the shout of the other Philistine below coming nearer.

I stood up.

Before me lay the outstretched warrior, one hand clutched vainly around his spear, which had emerged from the back of his neck.

I stood there and, as if all that had just occurred was now forgotten, I began to think, That won't come out very easy. I'll borrow his sword.

The fallen warrior's sword lay pathetically on the ground a little ahead of him. It was still covered with Sep's blood, but as the rivulet of blood pooled along the path, a small line trickled and lapped against the sword's hilt. I picked it up in my left hand and took up the sling from the ground with my right, and turned to where the remaining Philistine enemy was advancing.

I reached the top of the ledge and was at the beginning of the sloping path, a little more than ten yards before me.

What he saw must have amazed and bewildered him.

What did Achish see? This was scheduled to be the last day of their intelligence-gathering patrol. He knew he had led his small party well, which he recalled grimly was not easy with someone of Eglan's temper. They were about to circumvent Bethlehem and add the final pieces of information, which would assist a probable raid later in the year. The knowledge of the whereabouts of villages, who could provide food when they lived off the land, was essential to a swift punitive attack. It had been very important not to be detected; hence they mainly travelled at night or early morning. With a few exceptions, this had been achieved, though there had been a number of Israelite casualties to ensure that no one knew of their mission.

They had come across Bull Horns when hearing the Israelite's song. The lilting sound had unnerved them at first, as the youth's voice rose through the haze in some mystical sounding chant. But they were amusingly shocked to see this handsome youth in such an obvious state of arousal and oblivious to the world. They had laughed and jeered, thoroughly enjoying the Israelite's discomfort. But when the sling began to fire, Achish realised that here was no easy capture as the lad had shown daring, and if he got away, this was potentially very dangerous to their mission.

Whilst he was not pleased to temporarily lose his horses, especially the one which carried his shield and spear, he was pleased with the speedy way he had responded to the minor crisis.

He gave Eglan firm warnings about letting the boy get away. "I'd prefer to capture him. It might well save us the trouble of going on to Bethlehem."

Eglan's crude answer about what he'd do to the youth slightly irritated Achish because he made a mockery of men's love. He put that behind him and quickly made his dispositions.

By keeping Acrah with himself, yet letting him carry the shield to protect them both, was a particularly good move: pleasing his friend and at the same time keeping him under unobtrusive supervision. He thought to himself, although Acrah has killed a man – two in fact – he has still has much to learn. The thought never crossed Achish's mind that he was protecting his lover from danger, because that would have been a dishonourable idea.

As they began to move forward, he saw with approval Eglan's skilled dismissal of the Israelites sling shot, but his sense of irritation at losing his shield and spear was growing, because with them he could have advanced immediately, cancelling out the ground advantage which made the sling shots effective. Oh why had he not simply taken them from his horse as he alighted? It was so recent. He felt he could have stretched out his hand and taken them up. "Dagon's curses on me!" he swore to himself, for without his shield he was only half armed. Despite the self-criticism, he knew that it would not be very helpful to dwell upon it, and focused his mind on the business ahead.

Suddenly he began to have doubts. Perhaps this was a diversion. Would not it be better to cut the youth off from his town? Then he saw the possibility of him escaping, he called to Acrah and almost before the words were out of his mouth he sensed the deadly danger. It was too late – Acrah was hit; hit again and was falling dreadfully. He felt numb. He retreated to see what had happened to Acrah and then decide his next move. He warned Eglan to keep close to the Israelite but watch whilst he either assisted Acrah or retrieved his shield and then deal with the Jew.

"Eglan! Eglan! Keep close to him but wait till I come," he shouted. Then he turned to Acrah. "Oh Dagon! Dagon!" he said as he realised that, without help, there would be no rescue for Acrah. And, as for the shield, it had rolled far below.

Then he heard a dreadful cry. He recognised that it was a death scream – nothing but death held that despairing agony. But whose?

There was nothing else for it: he had to advance and count the cost, even if it meant taking a blow from the stinging shot. Yes, that was the answer. Bounding forward, he reached the ledge. Oh Dagon, help us all! What had happened here?

He rushed up the last part of the ledge with sword in hand. He had hoped, or indeed expected, to see his warrior companion triumphant. Instead he saw a bloodied youth, panting, wild eyed, covered in gore that clearly was not his own, and now armed with a sword, the kind of which was only forged in Philistia.

Blood Brothers

The Philistine captain was within yards of me. We stood and looked at each other. I half advanced with sword in my left hand and my sling in my right, but I was dreadfully tired. I knew I could only get one shot in before turning and running for my life. I tried to prepare myself and took in deep breaths.

Neither of us spoke. Amazingly, I realised that the whole attack and repulse from beginning to end had lasted less than ten minutes, whilst my grappling with Eglan had been completed in seconds.

What would he do?

I was weary. I feared I might faint. To clear my head I tried to think of Leah, but could not recall her face.

We stood silently. An impasse – neither he nor I had the energy or the will to continue the battle. He could not attack and I could not run.

The Philistine, whose thin sweat-coated face looked at me, asked quietly, "Is that Eglan slain, lad?" His question was almost gentle as if he needed confirmation of a sight he could not believe. I nodded.

"How?"

"With his spear," I answered. Then, as if to excuse what I had done, I added, "He killed Sep. He killed my dog. He needn't have done that. I was going to run. I wasn't trying to kill anybody."

He looked as if he understood me and nodded, as if to himself, taking in what happened. "I'm sorry about your dog."

This was too much. I stood above him, not threatening or being threatened but his kindness unmanned me. I began to cry silently: dry tears, as if still being at the centre of danger, my eyes would not yield their tribute to Sep. I stood at bay, ready to try to repulse any attack.

I stood and dry sobbed in front of my enemy. I could feel no shame in my sorrow or any triumph in my victory. All my anger had gone.

He looked at me and then beyond me towards the prostrate Eglan. He half turned back as if he was going down the next ledge.

I was terrified, expecting a ruse that he would spring to attack. I held the sword and prepared my sling.

He didn't advance or seem to threaten me, but indicated his wounded colleague below.

"He needs help," he said.

I nodded.

Then he asked me, "Is this your first man? It's always hard the first time." His faced was filled with a sadness that suggested his memory had whirled back to his own first duel to the death.

We were silent again, but neither taking our eyes off each other. We heard below, the faint calls of his stricken comrade.

I was overcome with sorrow. I recalled the young man's face. "I'm sorry," I forced out and then stupidly said, "Can I help?"

He looked at me as if I had said the most obvious thing in the world. Then he seemed to collect himself and he addressed me in a matter-of-fact tone, but one in which there was respect, as if he were speaking to an equal.

"Hail, Israelite. This is your day of triumph. I am Achish, son of Achish, King of Gath, who honours a gallant enemy. Truly, the day is yours."

He paused, frowned and looked directly at me with no animosity, as if he too was very tired.

"Let us call a truce. I swear by all my Gods that, for three days and another day, I will be thy friend. In this time I will defend you. If you wish to leave to go home, you have my word: I will not treat you as my enemy. Do you agree?"

I was not sure how to answer. I had no doubts that he was sincere and felt no danger, and clearly, if he was going to get his friend down from the cliff, we would both have to work together.

So I answered, "I, too, swear by the Living God of Israel, that for three days and the next to be thy friend and to offer you no harm."

Then, after a little thought I said, "If you like, I will try to help your friend, or if you would rather, I shall return home but not tell anyone about you being here."

"How are you called Israelite?" he asked.

"David, bar Jesse of Bethlehem, of the tribe of Judah."

"Then, David bar Jesse, Judean," he said, pointing down to his friend, "now the battle is ended let us together aid a fellow warrior in distress, after which, we will do the rites for the dead." But he went on sternly, "Though you slew him, I cannot allow you to defile Eglan's body."

The thought of such a thing was unthinkable, but then I remembered we usually took their foreskins as trophies and they, in turn, ripped open the bowels of our dead in a defiling humiliation.

I nodded and muttered, "Of course. Yes, let me help. Would you like a drink first?" for as I said this I realised I had a raging thirst. He was advancing towards me, no weapon in his hand.

I had let my weapons fall and turned towards the cave, "I have a rope as well which might help."

He was now by me. For a moment I was overwhelmed by panic. Had I been fooled by his soft words, his easily-given oath? I was at his mercy! His "truce" could have been just a trick. I held my breath in fear of an attack, which I was in no position to resist. But he made no motion against me. I knew then that this battle had truly ended for the time being.

I looked at him. He was as tall as Eglan but not as bulky. He was a full warrior of about twenty-four years. I was in his power but understood with absolute certainty that he would never betray his oath.

As if the thought crossed his mind he said, "Rest easy, David bar Jesse. Both drink and rope would be welcome before starting the rescue."

I explained the water was pure but if he wished I also had some wine.

He took both eagerly. In the tradition of Judah, I offered my guest the first drink even though my tongue cleaved to the roof of my mouth.

He quickly gulped down some water and a little wine. He picked up the rope and offered me the wineskin, gesturing his thanks as he did so. I drank deeply. Never had wine tasted sweeter.

The drink refreshed me, though I also realised I was hungry, but we had no time for food as I followed Achish down the path to try and reach his friend.

He had stopped moaning and we both wondered whether he was dead.

"The only way is for one of us to go down with the rope and lift him from there," said Achish. "If you're still willing, it will have to be you because I would be too heavy for you to hold. Also, I doubt if the branch would hold my weight."

This made sense so, fastening the rope around my waist, I clambered down from the buttress in front of the cave where Acrah lay stretched out on the tree above the overhang.

The sun had moved and lost its worst power though the cliff side was still hot to touch in places.

With Achish's encouragement, I slowly reached his friend and almost began to laugh. Here I was, an Israelite of Judah, assisting a wounded Philistine, who if he had not killed me, would certainly have taken me into bondage. Then I recalled what Achish had said "a fellow warrior in distress". What an incredible idea: he sounded as if he accepted our common humanity and didn't regard the Israelites as aliens. Of course, the more I thought about it, the more it struck me as being true. When people are not fighting, we do share common courtesies. I remembered that Moses, who could be fierce about the uncircumcised, had taught; "if a stranger come amongst ye, treat him as ye would yourself, for ye also were strangers in the land of Egypt." So perhaps this idea of a "fellow warrior", a "human being", belonged to both Israel and Philistia. I quietly promised myself to ask Leah about this when I got home.

I struggled towards the still form of Acrah. Being so close to my recent enemy brought my sense of sadness back as I could see he was not yet a full warrior: probably barely eighteen. I guessed that this must have been his first mission.

I did not allow myself to dwell on this, not least because we were not far away in age and it might have been me hanging here had things gone wrong.

Straddling over him I loosed the rope and fastened it as secure as I could. As I did so I noticed his wound in his thigh was still oozing blood. I tore at my shirt and made a pad, tying it around him.

Then, after offering up a prayer to God, I called out to Achish below. "I've got him tied as best I can. I have one end of the rope around a rock as you told me and I will try to lower him slowly."

Achish asked was Acrah conscious, as if in answer, he murmured "I'll be all right Achish." He then looked at me through slit eyes and said feebly, "I'll try ... I'll try to help you."

This was the dangerous part. There was least a 20 yard drop to a small ledge below to which Achish had climbed. Below that, was another drop of 30 yards. I had to make certain that we could get him from his present position, hold him so he did not fall and injure him any further, and hope that Achish could make him secure on the ledge below, from where we could carry him down.

I held the rope around the tree and, using what was left of my shirt, covered my hands as Achish had advised.

"Here he comes," I called.

Acrah half rolled himself forward when I said I was ready as I slowly pushed him over the edge.

I was thrown violently against the cliff face. I thought I was going down too. The rope slipping from the tree through my hands, burning me. I did not seem able to control the falling body. I threw myself backwards and used all my weight to wedge the rope. As fast as the falling had started, I felt the weight eased from me. Achish had caught his friend below.

Achish called up to me, "I've got him, David. Well done. Take care, now. Careful – you're no help if you get here too quickly but the worst is over."

I had to smile at Achish's effort at humour and suddenly understood something of the qualities that make a good captain. Achish may have been a Philistine but he was brave and was worthy of obedience. He was a warrior from whom one could learn.

The hard part was completed. By the time I had reached Achish, he was holding Acrah in his arms, having freed the rope from him. I looked at my hands, which were bleeding and sore.

"David – just steady me as I climb down," said Achish.

He showed incredible strength as he carried his friend down the steep side along the very narrow ledge. He hardly needed me, but as I occasionally steadied his arm or his shoulder, he noticed the blood.

"We'll have to do something about that when we're down," he said with genuine concern in his voice.

Achish had thought of everything. He had brought the rest of the wine and water, as well as a rush bed, as he carefully laid Acrah down. As gently as any maiden, he applied a mixture of wine and water to the lips of Acrah.

He would have drunk everything, such was his thirst, but Achish slowed him down.

I could see that one leg was badly broken and, by its odd shape, probably in two or three places. His arm was badly gashed though, as it had been crushed, it had not bled like the wound in his thigh. I had no real knowledge but knew his wounds were serious and there would be no hope if he had to be moved too soon.

"Achish, will our truce be long enough for Acrah to travel?" I asked.

"In two days we'll know the worst. If that fool Ganz can find at least one of the horses we should be able to move on," answered Achish.

Acrah seemed to be sleeping now rather than being unconscious. Luckily, when he fell he had not hit his head or, if he had, his helmet may have saved him before it was knocked from him.

I organised some food. Achish and I ate ravenously without saying anything.

After some time, Achish left me with Acrah. When he returned he was carrying Eglan's sword and helmet.

"These are now yours, David bar Jesse," he said solemnly.

I did not know what to say so I just accepted them quietly.

Achish then spoke with resolve. "Now, David, comes the hard part. We must honour the dead."

The last thing I wanted to do was to return to the scene of my desperate battle with Eglan. Nor did I want to see Sep's mutilated body, but this was outweighed by Achish's concern that we must give them a proper farewell.

I began to cry. This time, real tears that would not stop.

Achish sat silently whilst I wept. As I began to recover he placed his arm upon me. "All warriors want to weep. The first battle is the worst. It is good you shed tears, this honours you and the fallen. Come we will send their bodies to the gods."

I followed Achish, still reluctantly, fearful as to what I would see. We climbed the ascending paths to the cave and passed poor Sep on the ledge below.

"We'll collect him when we return, David," Achish said gently.

We reached the top. Eglan lay there so still. Achish looked at him stonily. I did not know what to say or do. I sought some signal from Achish that I was forgiven and that I was not to blame. Then I realised I was behaving as if I were a delinquent who was afraid lest the Rabbi hear of my fault.

With difficulty, but with respect, we carried him to the bottom where we built a funeral pyre.

Achish spoke first. "We shall prepare his body, but better not wait for Ganz's return. He was Eglan's cousin."

I was so shocked by how quickly we learn to speak of people in the past tense.

Achish stripped the body of his armour and, as he prepared, I could not help noticing his phallus. It looked a little strange, as I had never seen an uncircumcised man before. It did not appear horrific and unclean as I had been led to believe; it just added to the pathos of the whole scene.

Achish had cleaned the body but could not cover the only blemish, which was the horrific gash made by the spear.

I could not have done what he did, but Achish cut the head of the spear off and drew it out of the wound.

He explained, "It is a mark of honour to show that the warrior's death blow was on his front, not his back as if he were fleeing."

I brought Sep's body down and laid it at the side of Eglan. I disgraced myself again. I suddenly felt exhausted, ashamed, disgusted and afraid, so that I began to cry again.

Achish put his arms around me and I sobbed uncontrollably for a few minutes.

I forgot that he was my enemy as I felt towards him what I might feel for my friends or a very close brother.

Achish kindled a flame and within minutes the bier was alight. The flames quickly consumed their tragic load. I was relieved when we returned to Acrah, as I could not bear to watch any longer.

At our approach Acrah came out of his light sleep. He was obviously suffering and we gave him more wine. Achish said he would go and look for an herb that he knew could ease the pain of wounds.

I was left alone with Acrah. He wanted to talk but I protested he should rest.

He nodded. "No, it will take my mind from ... well –" and indicated his wounds.

We had splinted his broken leg with the spear shaft and fastened both to his good leg. This eased him but one feared for him when he had to begin to travel.

He seemed to sense what I was thinking,

"David bar Jesse, I am not sure whether I will travel easily, but I am grateful for your help in bringing me down from the cliff. We two are now brothers in arms."

I felt very protective towards him. We were near in age. It was a terrifying thought but it might easily have been Eli or Josh lying here with these dreadful wounds.

To occupy him, I asked about Achish. "Is he your captain?" I asked.

He became quite animated. "Yes. Achish, son of Achish the King of

Gath, honours me as his friend, mentor and captain. He is my philia – we are philian blood brothers."

I knew what being a blood brother meant, though we in Israel did not cement special friendships this way, but I did not understand the other term. He explained how they had a special warrior bond, in which the older solider taught and guided the younger, but there was also some kind of physical bond. Then I remembered Leah had told me of the custom of philia – a special attachment.   When I tried to understand and asked her what do they do, she had laughed and said, "I don't know what you men do when you're together!" I was too embarrassed to press her any further.

I looked at Acrah. Perhaps I was a little shocked, for if I understood aright this was like the adultery and other abominations written about in our holy scrolls.

But Acrah, sensing my confusion, laughed. "But the love between men surpasses any bond with a women. Surely you who will be a great warrior must know this. Our love makes us braver because we would rather die than shame our friends by running away. The love we have is total and life long. I honour him and his family."

He went on to explain how in their country if one of the lovers died or was killed the remaining man would support his friend's family as if they were his own.

I asked him whether he had a wife.

"Not yet, though my father has chosen a girl of good family. I shall marry her when she is old enough," he said with absolute certainty.

As Achish had still not returned, and Acrah was looking uncomfortable, I told him a little of Leah. I explained why I was devoted to her and that I thought my love of her exceeded anything except God.

He was amazed. "Surely you would put your father and your friends before a mere women – and, of course, your God?" He went on. "Achish has a wife and he is fond of her – very fond of her – but she does not have the mind of a man. Though I cannot match Achish, if he only had his wife as a life companion it would be pretty barren for him."

It was becoming a very strange conversation. I decide not to tell him that Leah had been born a Philistine. Whilst he was respectful of her, he clearly could not understand my veneration. I began to realise that, although some of their customs were honourable, they were a very different people from us.

Acrah had not hinted at, or offered a word of reproach about what had happened, for which I was very thankful. I lapsed into silence and began to think of Leah.

What would she say to what had happened and, strangest of all, of how

I had made two new friends? Though I was responsible for Acrah's wounds, I now felt towards him as I might Josh or Eli. Certainly he and Achish were brave and upstanding men and, in different circumstances, I would be honoured to have their friendship.

I lit a fire to keep Acrah warm and then I heard a neighing of horses. In the distance I saw Achish with his companion returning with both horses.

The other Philistine I saw at once had the look of Eglan, though he was older, more coarse and heavily built. He rushed ahead of Achish and, to my alarm, had drawn his sword and was coming towards me.

I picked up Acrah's spear and held Eglan's sword in my hand. He may be a full warrior but I was not going to succumb easily. Seeing I was armed, he slowed down but began to mouth curses at me.

Achish came up and sharply ordered him to cease. "Ganz, that's enough. We have sworn a truce and this warrior is an honourable man. He has shown his worth, both as a solider and in the truce. Without him I could not have rescued Acrah in time."

Ganz would not be assuaged. "He's an Israelite dog. He killed my cousin. It can't have been a fair fight. He's only a boy – it must have been witchcraft."

This made Achish and Acrah look concerned. Ganz pressed his advantage whilst I stood on guard, though I still had confidence in the word of Achish.

He continued, "How else could a mere boy – a pretty youth – kill Eglan face to face? Eglan was one of the best spearmen in the company – unless he was bewitched? Don't forget we heard him praying and braying to his devil God when we fell into this accursed place."

He moved towards me, with sword at the ready. I retreated keeping my eyes on him as I called to Achish. "Achish, son of Achish, King of Gath, I have a truce with you. I have kept my word. Is that not true, Acrah?" I was confident that Acrah would back me.

Ganz interrupted. "Oh yes, Acrah. We must not forget Acrah: brave, youthful warrior, philia of Achish. On your first expedition to be worsted by a boy – a boy who is not yet old enough to carry a sword. Where's your manhood? He could only have overcome you by sorcery."

Despite his wounds I could see Acrah's now blushing face in the flicker of the firelight as the sun began to disappear into the night.

I began to think about turning and fleeing for, even though they had recovered their horses, in the dark and over rough ground, I doubted they could catch me if I had a start on them.

"I do not accept that, Ganz. He fought well. There was no witchcraft," said Acrah.

Ganz would have gone on, but Achish barked, "Ganz! I said enough. With your stupidity you might think it sorcery, but you're wrong. Yes, he is young but, as Acrah says, he fought his battle like a captain. He used the terrain against us. He knew his weapons and Eglan, may Dagon have him in his keeping, became angry and was over-confident."

Ganz was about to argue but Achish cut him off. "Yes, yes," he said impatiently, "in another hundred fights, Eglan, on neutral ground, would have slain David bar Jesse of Bethlehem. But to attribute his victory to witchcraft dishonours your cousin and my comrade. It is the excuse of the puerile when things go wrong."

This quietened Ganz. Achish went on. "He has a truce, aye, and will have more." He walked over to me. "No one will dishonour the word of Achish."

I still kept my gaze on the angry Ganz but had total trust in Achish. He took my left arm and, before I knew what was happening, had pricked first his own vein and then mine.

He held our arms up and apart, and asked, "Would you be my blood brother, David the Israelite, so that though our peoples make war, we can not make war on each other? That I defend yours and you defend mine till we die? Or if we break this oath, may Dagon curse us as your God will curse you?"

I was astonished. This was an incredible idea. I wanted to say yes, but how could an Israelite and a Philistine be friends?

Before I could answer, Acrah joined in. "Achish, my captain and philia, may I add my blood bond to yours, for he is an honourable foe and I would be his ally and friend. If he becomes your brother, how could he not be mine?"

This pleased Achish enormously, whilst all was being observed by the silent brooding, hostile Ganz.

"David bar Jesse," inquired Acrah, "how do you answer my captain?"

I knew this to be important. I had to make a decision, which I sensed would affect the rest of my life.

I looked at the two Philistines and said slowly, "I am deeply honoured, but this is a custom my people do not know." I was half thinking of refusing politely, but then remembered that the most precious person to me was born a Philistine. This had to mean something. I thought that God, who though a jealous God, could not have delivered me out of this danger without knowing that this would occur. I had no sense that God would be displeased.

I went on quickly. "But I swear by the Living God of Israel, the Lord of Hosts, that I am sensible to the gift of brotherhood you offer, and that I,

David bar Jesse, of Judah, take it gladly."

We three came together. I now knew I could turn my back on Ganz in complete safety because my new brothers had pledged their honour and Ganz would not dare to infringe it. But I saw at once that he would be my deadliest enemy until the day one of us died. Prophetically, I knew one of us would be the slayer of the other. But with Achish and Acrah as my warrior brothers, though they were Philistines, I knew they would guard me with their lives. Ganz would have to kill them first before he might do me harm.

The mood changed, though Ganz would not sit or eat with us and went away some hundred yards, off by himself. Achish had crushed the herb he had found and gave it in a drink to Acrah. We arranged ourselves by Acrah and shared meat, bread, salt and wine in comradeship, which rapidly increased because the herb seemed to have a surprisingly speedy effect. We had eaten well and we were pleasantly tired. I felt I could now relax after this dreadful day.

I wanted to sing my song for Leah, for truly "taste and see that the Lord is good", but knew that was too precious to share. Then I felt inspired and asked them if I might bring my harp.

Achish smilingly agreed. "David, you are full of surprises! Are you a minstrel as well as a warrior?"

The trip to my cave had given me time to think of what I might share with them. Hurrying back, I carefully tuned the harp strings.

They waited politely as I said, "Forgive my presumption, but I have learned much that I admire of Philistines." I could tell this pleased them by their encouraging nods. "May I offer a prayer for peace, or at least under-standing, for our peoples?"

Achish's face went serious. "Peace and war are matters for the Kings. Now you have a King in Israel – it will be what he decides, not what we may wish. While ever Israel looks jealously at our land, it will be hard, but," he said thoughtfully, "it is right on this night that we think of it." He gestured up into the sky. "See the works of God."

I was amazed. "Do you believe that God made the heavens?" I asked.

Achish answered without any hesitation. "Who else?" On reflection I caught the hint of a question as much as the inferred answer.

I had the chord. I strummed the melody and let the words come from whence they did.

"Pray for the peace of the peoples, they shall prosper that love thee."

I stood up excitedly. I knew the words I wanted and gesturing towards

Achish and Acrah, recited in descant with my harp:

> *"Peace be within thy walls and prosperity be within thy palaces. For my brethren and companions, sakes, I will now say, Peace be with Thee because of the house of the Lord our God, I will seek thy good."*

They applauded and we renewed our oaths of friendship. We knew that we were blessed in our companionship which, though beginning in strife, was growing into something different.

We drank and talked the night away. We, who had started as strangers and enemies, had become the strangest brothers, and ended a day that bonded us for ever.

I awoke with a start: I had not realised that I had fallen asleep.

Where was I? Then, the tumult of the day before came rushing over me. "Sep, oh Sep," I mourned. Then I tried to squeeze out from my mind the face of Eglan, hurtling towards me, his visage contorted with rage, and the dreadful scream of his death cry.

I sat up. It was well before dawn.

Ganz! I worried about the whereabouts of Ganz. Looking ahead, I saw with relief his still sleeping form.

I looked for Acrah, who lay close by, also asleep. It was not an easy sleep, constrained as he was by the spear to splint his broken limb.

Then with a jolt I was wide awake because I knew I was being observed. I spun round and there was Achish.

In the pre-light of the early dawn he looked a grey figure, taller, more like a ghost then a flesh and blood warrior, except his stare. His eyes looked at me unblinkingly, fixed, but had a light of their own, brightened by the dying embers of the campfire.

I suddenly realised that he had been awake the whole night. He had been our only sentinel, and his guard had been for me, to protect me from the still hostile Ganz. I did not know what to think but knew he was my friend and, despite the chill of the ebbing night, felt warm towards him.

I waited for him to speak. "Ah, my little Israelite. David – my brother," he said quietly, half mockingly, half in admonishment. "You forgot what a captain must never forget: the safety of the camp. Now you are alert we must think what next to do."

I felt ashamed of my thoughtlessness but knew I had learnt a lesson I would never forget. I answered, "Achish, captain and brother. Thank you for the lesson and chastisement. My captain at home would have beaten me: first for needing the lesson and then again for forgetting."

Achish laughed. "He seems a stern captain, but," he said teasingly, "I'm sure you do not forget many lessons?" Without waiting for my reply he continued, "However, we have to think how best to get Acrah home."

He said that he and Ganz would rest during the day and then begin the journey home, carrying Acrah between the horses. They would have to go to find the materials to make a stretcher, and it would be best to make a start before the heat of the day. I readily agreed to look after Acrah.

When they had gone, Acrah drifted in and out of consciousness. When he was awake, he seemed very alert and wanted to talk. I kept him comfortable by keeping the flies away from his wounds, which, though bound, could obviously still attract interest by the smell of blood.

I learned much from him about the way of life in Philistia. Much of what he said seemed attractive. I recognised, as Leah had said, that there was some similarity in their search for God, with the Living God.

He told me of his hopes and aspirations for Achish, whose many qualities might well lead him to be elected High King of all the cities of Philistia.

Foolishly, I asked what did he want for himself. He did not answer for a long time, until he saw my concern.

"I have a long journey ahead. Who knows its end?" He gazed straight at me, his eyes held mine. I saw there the confusion, anxiety, hope and despair.

He held out his hand. "If it has a bad end, I forgive you my death."

I couldn't answer him. I was choked with conflicting emotions as I took his outstretched hand. I knew it was fruitless to try to diminish the reality. He had to face a horrendous journey, which could only promise agonising pain, no matter how slowly the horses walked.

He smiled at me. "David, my friend. It was an honourable fight and, if we are to meet again, then we may seek that peace you sang about. And if not? Well, then my ancestors respect both victor and vanquished when honour was their cause. We both have gained much merit by this mission."

Amazingly, it was he who comforted me. I found myself in fervent prayer, that this noble man would come safe home.

When Achish and Ganz returned, Ganz accepted that I would keep watch whilst they slept.

Achish had more medicine for Acrah and this time his sleep seemed easier, so my hopes for him began to rise.

Late afternoon, as the shadows lengthened from Bull Horns, Achish awoke and began to prepare Acrah for the journey. He had made a kind of sling or hammock and, by walking alongside their horses, it was beginning to look feasible that even over rough ground, Acrah would be saved the worst of any jarring.

Acrah insisted that they ride, but Achish simply ordered him to be quiet. He said that he and Ganz would make sufficiently good time without causing him unnecessary distress.

Achish was very formal with me and saluted with his sword. He embraced and kissed me saying, "Hail, David bar Jesse, of Judah. I, Achish son of Gath, salute thee. We are now brothers in blood and never will I take up arms against you and yours. Nor you against mine even though our peoples are in conflict. Come therefore the day of battle, I will turn aside, as you will turn aside."

He gave me a hug and then bade me, "Go in peace. You have observed the truce. You have learned of Philistine honour and, in turn, I trust your honour and our new brotherhood. Farewell."

With that they began their journey. Acrah waved a last goodbye and closed his eyes.

I felt quite bereft. I ran to the top of the Bull Horns and watched them wend their slow way towards the descending dusk.

Our parting had lacked something. I wanted to say – I don't know what – that I valued their friendship as people and not just the opportunistic truce.

I ran for my harp. I thought for a moment to recall last night. Was it only one night ago? Then I shouted out our verses in the hope that my voice would carry.

"Peace be within thy walls and prosperity be within thy palaces, for my brethren and companions, sakes. I will now say,"
and I yelled as loud as I could,
"Peace be within Thee, because of the house of the Lord our God, I will seek thy good."

Did I imagine it? I thought I saw Achish turn around and wave a final farewell.

The Return

I was grateful when the next morning came as I had a night of troubled dreams, half remembered, half feared and I felt bruised and, very, very stiff.

To my surprise, I saw Josh running up the valley. I felt anxious; it was not the time for me to be relieved from my duty. What had happened? Was it Leah? My Father? The Prophet? But as he looked very jolly waving and shouting I felt there could be little wrong.

He reached me with a bound, bowled me over and began to wrestle, which I was certainly not inclined to do. He sensed my lack of resistance and disinterest.

He stopped, sitting on my chest, bashed my stomach with his head, got up and crossly said, "David bar Jesse, what's a matter with you? You're as much fun these days as a bucket of cold spit!"

He was clearly angry. As he continued I realised he had been feeling resentful for some time. "I know you think you're special – perhaps you are – but Aaron and Eli, who usually take your side, have said you've become too miserable."

He stood glaring at me. I was not expecting his outburst and, frankly, at that moment, I was not too bothered. I did not answer.

He grew even angrier at my lack of response. "Who do you think you are? So you killed a mountain cat – others have done it. So you can play a bit – Deon can too and just look at what we all think of him. You're a bloody pain! You're got so serious that you're boring. You're worse than Rabbi Aaron. That's it – you're going to be a bloody Rabbi and you think yourself so superior."

He went on, "We care for you – all of us – but you're so cold, distant. We don't know you any more. But don't forget that we knew you better than anyone else and, if you don't pull yourself together, you'll exhaust your friends."

For peace I apologised and said, "Yes, I've had things on my mind. I haven't been fair, especially to you Josh. I am truly sorry if I've been as useful as 'bucket of cold spit'." This reply including his own metaphor made a smile creep across his face.

He laughed. "You agree then – you've been a bloody misery. God Almighty!" He could see my slight look of admonishment at his oath. "See what I mean: you're turning into Rabbi Aaron! He hasn't had a hard-on for years."

I dissolved into laughter at the thought of Rabbi Aaron being aroused. Josh was marvellous fun.

"All right, all right," I said, "I admit I've let you all down."

But then I became very serious. "But, Josh, you, Eli and Aaron are more than brothers to me. I'd die if you cut me off."

He looked at me, held out his arms and we hugged each other. He held me tight and I couldn't help notice that his eyes were moist.

I gave him another big squeeze and said, "Right, when I'm fit I'm going give you a real thrashing, I've been thinking about a hip throw I've heard about and, now you mention it, just for you, I'll blaspheme and make a verse about a randy Rabbi."

With that we fell into laughter again.

I asked why he had returned so early.

"Ah, you see, I've come to protect you. Yes, it's true. Your Father was the senior Elder and, when he heard the news, he asked me to come earlier and warn you."

"About what?" I asked.

"Horah's brother, Israel, was visiting relatives when he found two farmhouses wrecked and all the people killed. It was those bastard Philistines – either a raiding or scouting party. They didn't burn the farms because that would have given them away, but they killed all they found – the swine! Your Father did not think they'd come this far, but wanted me to make sure you kept a good look out."

He paused to see the effect of his news. He was puzzled by my calm reaction.

"Have you've seen them, then?" he queried.

"Yes."

"You what? You've seen them! When? Why didn't you warn us?" he asked.

"Well, they came here, and," I felt stupid saying this, "I admit it, I was dreaming. Before I knew it there were four of them up the valley and, I, I…" I stopped.

Josh saw something was afoot. "Did they see you? David, what the hell's been happening here?" Suddenly he said, "And where's Sep?"

That did it. I had to tell him that Sep was dead and that there had been a fight.

"A fight, David? But you've not yet received your colours. What the hell were you doing getting into a fight with a party of Philistines?"

I suddenly felt very, very weary. No pride or any exultation as the memories came flooding back. So I said nothing but brought out of the cave Eglan's sword and helmet.

Josh just stared incredulously. He just about managed to get out, "I don't suppose they gave these to you because you're a pretty boy. What the hell went on here?"

I told him as simply as I could. He obviously was unsure how to respond, either to the death of Eglan or about the ensuing truce.

He simply stood open-mouthed. "Hell, David. But Hell!" With that he came and embraced me. "God, David. God! You might have been killed, but you got him and did for another one of the bastards."

"Josh, they're not all bastards." He was astounded but I went on. "I was with them. One was a King's son called Achish. Yes, I think it was the same

78

man who did for Kish the Reubanite. He called a truce because none of us could do anything else. We talked and I learned a lot about them – they were quite honourable."

Josh exploded. "How in God's name can they be honourable? You tell that to Israel, who saw the devastated families! You tell that to the widows of Israel whose men they have mutilated! You tell that to anybody but your friends and you'd be outcast at best – and bloody likely stoned!"

He was getting excited again. "Honourable? They're bloody killers! They tried to kill you. You're crazy! Just bloody crazy!" This was typical of Josh: quick to fire and even quicker to forgive.

He calmed down a little. "But it was bloody, bloody marvellous! You did for two of them. You took on four full warriors. Oh, brother! That's marvellous!"

I didn't feel marvellous. I realised that Josh's response would probably be typical and that I better keep my new perspective on the Philistines to myself.

Josh agreed that I should take the trophies to Bethlehem, report to Horah and the Elders, while he would take over at Bull Horns.

As he began to hustle me off, I saw that he was looking hard at me. "You know, David? I'm not jealous but I think that you are something special. And I'm pleased – no, proud – of you because you're my friend." Then, with great sadness in his voice with an awareness that surprised me, "It can't be easy being what you are. It must be dangerous and frightening. Anyway, away with you, but think what the news will do to a certain relative of yours."

He was now laughing. "Poor, miserable Boaz. First the cat – and it was a mangy cat, you know David bar Jesse – and now this. He'll choke. He'll bloody well choke!"

I arrived back in Bethlehem in a very confused mood. No matter how I tried to rehearse how to tell Father about the fight, it did not come out right.

I was aware that there would be so many questions about my behaviour. I should have given the alarm. I should not have stayed and fought. What could I say about the rescue of Acrah? I grew more anxious I held on tighter to the helmet and sword of Eglan.

Sure enough, the worst happened. Almost the first person I saw was Father, who was visiting a friend on the outskirts of the town. Whether it was my demeanour or the fact he noticed the trophies, he immediately went into an inquisition of "why?", "how?" and "why not?".

As his voice got louder and louder, we attracted attention and people began to gather. I felt as panicky as I did when facing the Philistines. Then to make matters worse, Boaz arrived.

Amidst the hub-hub, I suddenly realised that Father, instead of berating me for my stupidity, was saying in a loud voice, "See, neighbours. My youngest son brings home trophies of the accursed Philistines. Though not yet a warrior he has killed his man. I thank Thee Lord for such a son."

I was amazed. Before I knew it, people were crowding around and shaking my hand, admiring Eglan's sword and the fine helmet.

Rabbi Aaron arrived and, on learning what the commotion was about, added his voice, saying, "Jesse bar Obed, the Lord smiles upon thy house. Thy house and Bethlehem have found favour in the face of the Lord."

I began to feel some relief. Moreover, as Boaz, seeing that I was not getting into trouble, had sneaked away. Then, to be honest, I was beginning to enjoy the attention. I still felt confused about now celebrating victory over men who I had begun to think of as friends.

Rightly or wrongly, I had not told Father of my brotherhood with Achish, though he seemed to accept that the truce was a good stratagem. I did not elaborate any more. It was obvious to everyone that the patrol, which had done the raiding and killed twelve men, women and children, was likely to be the same as the one which had arrived at Bull Horns.

So Father emphasised how I had taken revenge for Israel. "Surely the accursed wounded will perish facing such a journey? To have exterminated two of those vermin will be great news to the families Esua and Horhab."

I was escorted back home. Again, I felt very grateful for my safe return and I knelt before the Rabbi.

"Rabbi Aaron, God held me in his hand. May I offer this trophy as a thanksgiving for my safe return and have it placed next to the tabernacle?" I handed him the helmet.

He took it and briefly examined it, his face wreathed in smiles. "Jesse bar Obed, here is a beloved son indeed. This trophy will remind the arrogant, who would decry the Living God, that he is so powerful. Even a shepherd boy can be an instrument of His chastisement."

This pleased both the crowd and Father, though I was not too sure about the "shepherd boy" bit.

Then I had an inspiration: I knelt dutifully in front of Father. "My Father, I am your obedient son. Take this sword in gratitude for God's grace and your guidance."

He took it and held it in front of him. He turned to the crowd of our neighbours in obvious delight. He didn't say a word. He simply showed them the workmanship. Many touched it and gave a blessing.

Then, everyone fell silent. Father responded in a loud voice so that everyone could hear. "This is my beloved son, in whom I am well pleased," he proclaimed, giving me his Father's blessing.

He continued, "Take thou this sword, David bar Jesse, and use it ever in defence of Judah and Israel." Everyone applauded. He went on, "And I invite each head of family to honour the house of Jesse. I invite them to attend a feast I shall hold for my son's safe return and his victory over the uncircumcised."

Eli and Aaron were so pleased as I let them take the sword. So, too, was Horah, our instructor, as I assured him that I had learned everything from him. We entered my home, where Mother called me to her. She gave me her blessing before bustling around with damp eyes to prepare the feast.

I was excused my usual work and, this time, Leah, although obviously very busy, smiled a radiant welcome.

The feast was a great success. I sat on my Father's left, with Rabbi Aaron on his right. There were lots of toasts, with the wine brought by the other fathers and Elders. I was desperate to see Leah so I admitted I was tired and that, after so much honour, I should retire in deference to the presence of the Elders.

Father was obviously pleased by this and gave me tremendous hope when he said, "Aye go, my son. Your mother tells me there is one who pleases you. You have our leave to greet her, but we will talk more of this later."

I could hardly get out quickly enough but still had to endure many of their congratulations as I left.

I hurried to the copse to find Leah already waiting for me. We flew into each other's arms. I was intoxicated by her scent and her soft smoothness. Our mouths closed and inflamed us, and I was aroused as our bodies clung together. I could feel my hardness seek out her secret place. My mouth went to her bosom as I nuzzled under her smock. My lips found her sweet nipples. As my tongue laved the mounds of her swelling breasts, her hands touched me along my hardness. I was dizzy with her, her bright eyes and her rapid breathing in tune to mine.

Then I sensed a slight tension as she held me back, gently at first, but as I leaned into her entertainingly, she moved me away, slowly but firmly.

She spoke. It was shattering. "David, my love. You are safe and I thank the Living God, but why did you have to kill? There was no need for you to fight. You had every reason to escape. No one would have thought the worse of you."

I was confused and angry. What was she talking about? My head spun. I was still full of the praise from my townsfolk, yet here she was, my love, who should have been proudest for me, talking nonsense.

I was furious with her. "What do you mean? You don't know what you say! You would make a woman of me. Would you shame me? I had to fight." Then the thought flashed across my mind, "It is because you are still a Philistine? Is your allegiance still to them? Don't forget they killed the families of Esau and Horab. It was right that they should die." I got angrier and angrier, and just glared at her, my passion fast ebbing.

"David, you are my love and I would be yours – in every way – but doesn't more killing mean another turn of the screw."

She knew she was talking nonsense. I tried to explain to myself that she was a woman and did not understand, though she had talked like this before.

"Leah, I am going to be a warrior. I want to defend my people and our God. Don't you understand? The world is as it is. If we don't defend ourselves, can you imagine what would happen?"

She sighed. "But I heard you had a truce with them?" I nodded and she continued. "Well then? If you were honourable, might not such a truce be extended into peace, so that the peoples can live like neighbours? And if there is a dispute, they ask, like neighbours do, the wise man to arbitrate the justice of the cause."

It was an incredible idea: peace with the Philistine – with the Amalekites!

"Leah, you just don't understand. There can be no peace because there are oceans of blood between us."

She looked at me gravely and asked, "But there is not always war. You do have truces, or it seems to me that both sides get tired and avoid fighting. When there's peace you all prosper and increase your herds and crops. Would not peace be better than perpetual strife?"

I could not manage this. "What you're asking for is a dream. We took this land at God's instruction by war, and we shall hold it only as long as our right arms are strong enough."

She was silent. I did not know what to say or do.

I was still hurt and angry. "Leah, we shall quarrel if you persist," I warned her.

She stood stock still. "David, you are not answering me with logic. Instead, you threaten me. Perhaps I was wrong to think you could reason things through. The justice and mercy you say your God represents is beyond you."

She stood there, proud, and to my astonishment, she too looked hurt and angry. I was about to turn and walk away because I could not trust myself. I half moved and heard her begin to cry. I was bereft. I could not cope with her tears.

"Leah, please stop. I don't understand you. I've tried to explain how and why I feel what I do. Ideas of peace are dreams – fantasies."

I found my effort to be reasonable had angered me again. She moved away and sat down without saying anything. I sat near but did not touch her or say anything. It was the longest silence of my life, but I was determined not to be the first to break it.

She raised her head and finally spoke. "David, I am sorry that I have offended you. I am proud of what you have achieved, who you are, but it was you who taught me about how God loves. I just developed the idea."

She went on, calmly. "The fact that you fought Philistines is not the issue. Though, as you have said, they have better arms so it makes them more dangerous. But now I belong to the family of Jesse, and I owe you obedience. True, part of my response was my fear for you. I can see, even though I'm 'only a woman', that you will be a great warrior, but as I love you, I fear that if not next year, the next decade, there will come a time when your arm, your eye, will not be at its best. I could not bear life without you." She now wept torrents.

I melted. Of course, I forgave her. By this time I was by her side and so relieved that her ideas were inspired by her concern for me. I put my arms around her and she dissolved into them with gentle sobs, clinging to me tightly.

I felt myself physically moved by her body but knew this was not the time.

I sought to comfort her by saying, "Leah, darling Leah. That was our first quarrel. Let's not hurt each other again. Let's forgive each other."

She nodded agreement and then asked about the men I had met. I was not sure whether to tell her I how I felt about Achish and Acrah. Though the hatred I felt for Ganz seemed as natural as the lamb for the wolf.

Her questions, however, cleverly came to the nub of the matter. "When Achish asked you for a truce, you believed him without question. Why?"

I explained and she interpreted what I'd said. "So you recognised him as an honourable man. You were both willing to trust each other, yet moments before you both had tried to kill each other."

"All right, but the man I killed was a bully – crude and brutal. Of the other, called Ganz, there will never be a truce between us. Even Achish hardly trusted him. I certainly didn't."

Infuriatingly, she reasoned on. "So in a way you relied upon a Philistine to protect you from another Philistine. So you both behaved with great honour?"

"Yes and I'll tell you more – but only you. Achish explained their custom of blood brothers. I realised that if I accepted his offer he would defend me and mine and I his until we die."

She asked quickly, "Did you become his philia?"

"No," I quickly assured her, and was grateful for the dark so she could not see my blush. "That's not possible in Israel, though I can see that those who become philian become even braver for each other. Acrah was amazing. It was obvious, despite his ghastly wounds, he was not going to let Achish down – every warrior would admire that."

But then I changed the subject. "Father was pleased. He hinted he knew about us."

"Yes," said Leah. "Your lady mother has spoken about us, but still we need to be careful."

She smiled and, taking my head in her hands, kissed me gently.

"Oh my brave, brave love," she purred. "Yesterday you were only a youngest son; today your Father is so proud of you. You may have increased your marriage portion in his eyes."

I moaned. "Oh, no. I'm sure not. That's why I offered him the sword."

She gently admonished me. "Perhaps, my love, you've been too clever. The lady Zeruiah is still on our side. So let her speak to him when she feels the time is ripe."

But the fact that Mother had let her leave before clearing up the feast showed that she was sympathetic and, besides, there seemed to be so much wine that the old men might go on drinking till morn.

Laughingly, Leah agreed, but said very firmly, "But we can't go on till morn." Then, seeing my hurt look, added, "But I will come to you very soon – I promise."

What else could I do? So we returned home slowly, arm in arm. I was filled with even more love for her as we sang our goodbyes, leaving me to dream and hope for tomorrows.

"Oh taste and see that the Lord is good - they that shall seek the Lord shall not want any good thing."

Chapter Five

Leah

The Love Feast

I had returned to Bull Horns. Josh left me quite quickly, sensing that I needed to be alone. I understood that something had changed between us. Being a little younger than him had not mattered before the fight. Now I had killed my man I felt that this troubled him.

He said, "You're clearly the captain now." There was sadness in his voice. He was not jealous, for who could be envious of the cruel duty of the warrior, only it had happened to me sooner than either of us had expected.

He left without his usual exuberance. No challenge, no wrestling. Uneasily we both felt, not so much a distance between us, but that a line had been crossed from which there was no turning back. I think we had lost an innocence that we only dimly perceived. I spurned any further reflection but understood that battle changes a man's spirit forever.

When Josh had gone, I returned alone to the familiar landscape around me but it, too, had been changed forever.

Was it the spirit of Eglan? No, it was something in me. In many ways it was the absence of Sep. This made Bull Horns seem less friendly, less familiar, less secure. I found myself looking across the valley so as to catch a glimpse of him as he gathered the sheep. I listened for his bark of command to some dilatory ram – but everything was silent. Empty.

Josh knew about Leah. I had wanted to tell him more, how she had changed me. The joy, the excitement and the closeness I felt. For even though he was my best friend, I had never had such a feeling of union with another human being, but I knew it would hurt him.

It was an amazing revelation: that she was more precious to me than any in all the world. And that she felt similarly about *me* – no wonder my spirits soared.

Josh had Miriam, who he would marry next year, and he sometimes spoke about her, but only in the half joking matter of young men's physical fantasies. I had no feeling that, as yet, she was a real person to him – with a mind as well as a body.

As I wandered around I fell to thinking about Leah. I became excited at the thought that she had promised to join me, and had mysteriously promised to "bring a present".

When I had pressed her to explain, she laughingly touched the tip of my nose with her finger. I dissolved in love for her as she treated me as if I was a little boy. "Soon. Soon, you'll see," she whispered as she had returned to the women's quarter, leaving me to ponder what she was planning.

As I mooned around, I finally reached the spot that I knew I was avoiding.

There had been a little rain and the wind had already begun to erase the marks of Sep and Eglan's funeral pyre. There were still some charred embers of wood remaining and, as I stared at the black grey scar of the blackened ground, I was shocked at the transitory nature of our bodies – at the shortness of human life. Its stark brutality overwhelmed me: it was all so recent. Eglan had been like me, in the fullness of his manhood. No thoughts of death. Not really, because even when training for war, despite the fear, we all think it will be the other man, not you. But he was gone, gone for ever. In another week, a month, or so, the wind would have blown over the plain and any trace of Sep and Eglan would be erased for eternity.

But what did Achish say? That Eglan was "in Dagon's bosom". Did their God sustain their spirit after their life's end? Surely the Living God, at my end, will take my soul unto Himself, which is the divine in all men?

I pondered hard on this. Some Rabbis taught that, though we were part of God's plan, it was as one of his chosen people, not as an independent, separate soul. If this were so, we would be little more than sheep – nothing but a part of a crowd. Surely, a man's soul was God given and is what surely makes him an individual, and God, like a father who nourishes his son, would care for the soul of his son?

I wanted to be at one with the place, but my mind was held back by my part in the creation of the blackened scar and drifting embers. Even as I watched a gentle breeze teased a little more of the dark dross and scattered their remembrances away.

Time passed and my mind stilled. There was a special stillness that had descended upon the valley, and I knew, in that distinct silence, I was in the presence of the mind of God.

I knew it, utterly and completely, as the words came. God does not despair; God cannot be mocked by the emptiness of a man's denial.

A man must live his life as he must: even Philistines like Achish and Acrah. And as my mind shrank into stillness, the question came "... and even men like Ganz, my enemy?"

The abundance of life all around was no accident. He with half a eye can see its beauty and its plenty.

"Oh taste and see that the Lord is Good,"

That's what my love for Leah had taught me. God's care had taught my people that we could be part of him. Why, it would be like denying the Living God to deny one's soul.

Now the words came, I could repudiate the depressing misery associated with death and decay. I could reject with confidence those that see no help in God, no continuity.

"Many there be which say of my soul there in no help for him in God."

I laughed aloud at the nonsensical idea:
"The fool in his heart had said there is no God..."

I felt delirious: I laughed, I shouted, I wanted to dance. My mind, body and soul were all in tune with God.

"The fool in his heart had said there is no God,
Consider the heavens the work of his fingers."

I did not need my harp. My head was filled with the sound of strings of music echoing through my mind. I was His instrument and He led me forward as I shouted to the hills, heavens and all the people.

"I cried unto the Lord with my voice and He heard me out of his Holy hill,"

The words ran together in a gentle admonishment of any that might doubt.

"Many there be which say of my soul there in no help for him in God. But Thou oh Lord art a shield for me."

It was true. He had turned the spear away from my head. Without Him I was nothing, He was the shield.

"Thou oh Lord art a shield for me, my glory and the lifter up of my head. I cried unto

the Lord with my voice and He heard me out of his Holy hill. I laid me down and slept; I awaked for the Lord sustained me."

I walked slowly away, utterly drained but content. I whispered a prayer for Sep and, yes, for Eglan also. I returned to my cave and, even though it was but early evening, I slept soundly.

I awoke. It was not yet day. I was refreshed. There had been no dreams, no yearnings for Leah, only a sense of calm.

I stared out into the night sky, which held the promise of an early dawn.

Time passed as I waited for a new beginning. What it would be I did not know I was certain that God had begun to prepare me for a task still before me.

I looked out into the burgeoning sky as the stars merged and diffused into a silvery sheen. I thought of Leah, her face was in my mind. The stillness was so complete that I could hear my heart beat, pulsing to her image, as my body began to yearn for her.

In synchrony, a shaft of light oozed out from behind a cloud, signalling the coming dawn. I rose and, with prayer and yearning, my body and mind was on fire for Leah. I marvelled at a sky filled with merging colours. No lines showed the transformation from one hue to another in a beauteous calm.

I prayed without words. My imagination was filled with the love of Leah, of God and of life. As my blood raced, a silent music within my mind conjured a wondrous dance. Then, suddenly, the sun broke through and cast its early silken beams over me. I was clothed all in God's gold.

"Oh taste and see that the Lord is good, they that shall seek the Lord shall not want any good thing."

I sang out loud. This was our song. This was our anthem, ready for a union of minds, bodies and spirits that could not be long delayed. Then wonder.

I heard, not in my head, but a melodic answering from around the hillside:

"Oh taste and see that the Lord is good..."

It was her voice – she was here!

Her voice had caught the echo, so I was unsure where she was. Was she here, or, in my yearning, had I imagined her?

"David! David!" I heard her gently call. I saw her elfin figure ascending the ridge. Then she walked in harmony to our song, her body swaying purposefully upward towards me. I was transfixed with the vision of her. My breath was stopped by her beauty.

She approached me. I did not dare move lest I shatter the moment. In a gesture that dissolved me, she knelt and uttered the confirmation of our love and her offer of herself. "Wherever you go, I will go. Your people are my people. Your God is my God."

I was by her side. I knelt with her, my arms around her. Our lips gently caressed, our kneeling bodies hard against each other. I was about to speak but her kisses closed my mouth, as she murmuring whispered, "David. Oh, David!" In framing my name, her lips opened mine. Her tongue sought mine and I was filled with her sweetness.

We held each other tight, as my body answered hers.

She lay back, I at her side. Her smiling face and eyes glowed with love and complete trust. My hand traced its contours and kissed her deeply. Her hands were to my breast as her firm hands explored me. My hands cupped her breasts in an answering rhythm. My mind was overwhelmed by her firm softness, her smoothness, in a quickening, quickening dance that sped our passion.

I was hard, so hard that it hurt. I craved to bury myself in her. Her beauty, her smell, her smoothness drugged my senses. Yet I held back lest I shatter the delicacy. As my phallus urged me forward she opened herself to me. Her fingers explored me and wondrously caressed my hard, hard smoothness.

I was near to exploding. I was above her. As I followed the contours of her thighs, her body answered mine.

I could feel her. With an agony of restraint I gently leaned into her, our bodies' heat creating its own sweet friction. There was a tension. I heard her catch her breath. My rigid phallus could feel her soft sweetness. I tenderly answered her rhythm.

"Leah! Leah!" I breathed and bore downwards into her. Slowly, seemingly for ever, I was engulfed by her hot, moist tightness. I thrust deeper, deeper, and deeper in one long, long tight-sweet plunge.

I dissolved into her. Her up-thrusting body held me completely. Our tongues melded as I was engulfed by her sweetness and our flesh became one. From my feet, thighs, chest, my breath, heart, my hard spear phallus became me, moulded by her moist flowing sweetness.

I thrust down. Her hard body answered my plunging as waves of delightful sweet pain engorged my whole being. In, in, in, into her I exploded and poured my sweet-sharp seed into her. She cradled my love's torrent as I drained myself in adoration. She took and gave in perfect harmony.

We were one.

We lay quietly, but close. Bound together in the total stillness of our bodies. It was like a benediction. We breathed quietly together, in harmony. I could feel the warmth of her limbs. Her heartbeats, like mine, paced down from our ecstasy.

She was mine: I was hers. There was no doubt. As my mind struggled to comprehend what had happened, I was flooded by an emotion of love for her, which was as overwhelming as our bodies, climatic union.

"Leah, Leah, Leah!" my thoughts sang. Her name was a prayer, a benediction, a war cry and an assertion of life. "Leah, Leah, Leah!" She was the beauty of the world, the ecstasy of God: no longer the echo, but now the holder of my soul.

My thoughts beat out her name, "Leah, Leah, Leah!" in time with my pulse. She is my body. Her breath is mine and mine is hers.

I felt myself beginning to be newly aroused, and was conscious of Leah's body answering my movement, feeling the soft friction of her touch.

Her fingers were gently running through my hair. We still had not spoken. We were still joined together.

Her eyes widened as she smiled and as she felt my growing arousal. Her lips sought mine in a new union and a new dance. Slowly, but quickening, I grew inside her, as her sweet secret flower moved in a delicious harmonic rhythm. Her honeyed self rippled over my now hard phallus as I leaned over thrusting deeper and deeper into her.

Our bodies were cloned together as she responded to my gentle but speeding movements, as I followed her body beneath me.

Our breaths accelerated. She was a flowing silken stream. As her current took me along, we clung in a sinewy embrace. Moving, ever moving, her honeyed cavity, now less tense, moulded around me. She took me into her, answering me, urged me along, quicker and quicker. With a delicate sharp sweetness that made my senses reel. My phallus and her body resonated faster and faster. I was lost as I erupted into her, with a burning torrential draining as I thrust down, down, into her enveloping sweetness. We cried out together in a melding of our bodies and spirits in an emptying that defies description.

Surely we could not get closer until we both were absorbed into the bosom of God?

I was hers to the uttermost. There was a satiated tingling between our now limp, exhausted torsos.

No mind, no thoughts, but an exhaustion that merged our beings into a rapturous oblivion.

We lay for a long time. Did we sleep? Slowly, my thoughts were freed from the enchantment of our forged mind, body and spirit, where no words dwell but a delirious euphoria.

I answered God's gift in a wordless prayer, which was beginning to take shape.

I was so blessed. I was so unworthy of her – even thinking of her sent a wave of music in my head, which was unsingable in its thankfulness.

I knew I did not merit her. Yet, He had brought us together. I began to see a dim plan: no shepherd had ever cared for his flock as He was caring for me.

"The Lord is My shepherd..."

I knew it.

Leah broke into my reverie. "David, David," she breathed, "you are my lord and I am your bond maiden." I was about to protest, but putting her hand to my mouth she went on. "Dearest David, I am yours. I have sworn that wherever you go, I will go. Your people are my people and your God is my God."

She uttered the words of my forebears with such total simplicity. This was our marriage bond.

"There can be no forbidding obstacle that has any meaning, because I am yours, as your bond maiden, concubine – it matters not. I am yours." As she said these words, she was looking deeply into my eyes.

I sat up and, looking down at her shining eyes, gave her my vow. My offer to her was of myself: not to a bond maiden or a concubine, but as man to his wife.

"I, David bar Jesse, of Judah, declare to you, God and the world, that I am your husband. Nay, I proclaim to the world that God has made us one. We belong to one people, one flesh and are joined in worship. Nothing but death can ever sever this oath witnessed by God."

We kissed, chastely, and stood together. In a spontaneity that showed our souls were one, we rose and hand-in-hand, raised our arms and sang in glorious harmony our prayer:

"I will bless the Lord at all times; his praise shall be continually in my mouth."

This was our anthem. We would share it later with the people. Her voice soared like doves, as mine followed willingly after her in a shared reverence.

"My soul shall make her boast in the Lord, the humble shall hear and be glad."

And then in a wondrous climatic duet, we sang:

"We will bless the Lord at all times; His praise shall be continually in our mouths.

Our souls shall make her boast in the Lord,
The humble shall hear and be glad.
Oh Magnify the Lord with us let us exalt His name together."

This was our wedding day, this was our blessing and this was our time. We had no need of rabbis. We had dedicated ourselves to God: our vows, hearts, minds and bodies were one. We were man and wife.

We were happier than any humans could be. We both knew that today had blessed our union – a union that would stand until the end of time.

We sat down beside each other and let our gaze wonder across the panorama, which perfectly reflected our happiness.

The sheep beneath grazed in a sea of rippled green as the wind gently crossed the valley. Above, the wheeling birds were put to rout with the upsurge of the warm breeze catching the mountainside. The sky's blue was dappled with graceful clouds that softened, not masked, the sun, so that its warmth was a benison that did not burn.

Suddenly, Leah pointed out almost wondrous sight. Two pure white doves began to circle and rise beneath us. They seemed to caress and dance in the air – their whiteness etched out against the blue of the sky. We both held our breaths. Our thoughts were one. Here our love was mirrored in God's own birds.

Leah closed her eyes and quietly murmured to me:

"Oh that I had wings like a dove, for then I would fly away – "

"No, my darling. Not without you – but with you." She gave me a look of total bliss, closed her eyes and again conjured the spirit of those wheeling free doves.

"For then I would fly away and be at rest."

"David, I would change the world so that we could be as we should: no war; no hate; no bondage; only love. Oh, I can see you think me a silly woman, but I can dream. No – more than dream, I have sought your God. Now He is my God and in Him I have found freedom like His doves." She sang:

"Give ear to my prayer O God and hide not thyself from my supplication."

I was amazed and overjoyed. With such a spirit God could not deny her. I sang the words after her, for would we not make the world in the image the purity and gentleness of doves?

"Give ear to my prayer, O God, and hide not thyself from my supplication."
We sang it together as if a vision had been granted. This would inspire us but also reminded us that we were earth-bound. Yet, now we had found each other, we sang to confirm our union and hope in our time.

"Give ear to my prayer, O God, and hide not thy self from my supplication. Oh that I had wings like a dove for then I would fly away and be at rest. Lo then would I wander far off and remain in the wilderness."

I sought to serve her and I brought us some bread, wine and water. We made a sacrifice, offering each other bread as confirmation, and drank together from the same cup.

We ate quietly, offering each other the food.

"David, let us remember this day every day, so that at each day's beginning, we will take bread and wine in remembrance."

"Yes," I said, "it's a lovely idea. We'll celebrate our marriage daily, not just the once. In our daily prayer we will commemorate today."

We were completely happy but then the thought struck us in perfect union. We both thought of Sep and Eglan.

Leah said, "Let us offer the dead a blessing." She turned down the cup in a libation to the wondrous earth, and the gentle red wine and water sprinkled the ground beneath.

After pledging ourselves again and asking God to bless the libation, I silently prayed for forgiveness. I offered the upturned cup of wine in memory: the blood-red drops to quench their thirst.

His Colours

Leah told me how she had persuaded Mother to allow her to come and how Mother had begun to speak to Father, who had more on his mind than his youngest son's marriage, so was relieved of the need to take a decision.

"I have a surprise for you – it's time for your present," she said, chirpily.

I was puzzled. What gift could she have brought?

She had dropped a small bag a little earlier and now ran to retrieve it.

"This comes from my hand but with the blessing of both your father and mother," she said.

She opened the cloth and there lay a newly embroidered head- band with the white and gold of Judah. But this was not just a young man's band as, woven into the colours, was the red of the full warrior – of he who had killed his man.

I immediately gasped with pleasure at the honour and then suddenly appreciated what it meant.

"Father really permitted this? He was happy for you to weave it?"

She nodded assent. We hugged each other. The weaving of a warrior's headband was the special duty of his wife or betrothed. It confirmed our betrothal. There would be no suggestion of Leah being bonded or merely a concubine. We would marry and she would be entered into the people of Israel.

There were no more obstacles.

I got up, shouted, ran around, and danced and whooped with joy, to the amused delight of Leah.

Leah laughingly left me for a while and I sat alone. I was still. No thought, just being. I felt the breeze play upon me. I was so totally content.

"My cup runneth over."

I heard a splashing of water and heard Leah call from the pool. I stood up and walked over towards her but was halted in my tracks by the vision before me. Leah had bathed and now stood before me in all the beauty of her nakedness. I had never seen a naked woman's body before, and the shape before me dazzled my eyes.

She stood, modestly, her hair over her pale smooth shoulder making a canopy for her breast. Oh, her breasts: hillocks of sweetness that were my bliss, so white against her paleness above her bronzed arms which had no protection from the sun. Her torso, a smooth curve carved by the hand of God, so perfectly flowed into her hips, was a delight of alabaster. My hands, cradled in adoration, were bewitched by the sensation of her.

No sense of shame, but wonder and delight. Surely when Adam first looked at Eve he tasted the divine.

Water droplets stood upon her, and rivulets ran between her thighs making a pattern of dark tendrils. I held her gently, tenderly, not wishing to obscure the picture of her loveliness. I held her from me, drinking in my joy, as my body sang with the excitement.

Without a word, she led me to the pool and gently lifted my shirt from me, bearing my chest. Her hand plunged into the water and bathed my warmth from me. I stood motionless before her magic. She drew me into the pool, eased my skirt from me and untied my loincloth – from which she pulled me rampant.

I half drew away. Few had ever seen me naked; no one had ever seen me aroused and longing for love.

But then I shared her laughing joy, as she splashed me. She took pleasure in the sight of me as I took delight in the sight of her.

We came from the pool, letting the wind gently dry us, marvelling at God's creation, feasting our eyes on each other. With a sigh, she traced the water from my chest to my stomach and down to my manhood in total acceptance.

My hands followed her motions and my hand rippled over her breast. My hand progressed to her tender midriff and caressed her downy secret place, opening its sweetness to me.

I was on fire again. She drew me into her. My mouth took in her breast and we joined our love, with limbs together, in a perfect pulsating curve.

Eagerly, our hands were about each other. Gone was any tiredness as we reached new heights of ecstasy too intimate and sacred to be spoken of.

We lay there, locked again in the divine union. No words were needed, as passion spent our eyes and hands brushed each other in soft caresses, marvelling at each other's firm smoothness.

Time passed and we relaxed. We talked about organising our marriage ceremony with the rabbi and even the possibility of getting the Prophet Samuel to come.

She told me about what she considered to be her "secret". That, to protect herself from men, she had hidden her real age; in fact she was two years, not one year, older than I. I laughed at her anxious looks. What did that matter? We loved each other!

"You don't mind me being so much older than you?" she asked, anxiously.

"Of course not, and two years is hardly 'so much older'." Then I began to truly understand what being bondage must be like.

I frowned at the thought. "No, it was very sensible of you. You needed to be protected. It can't be right, can it? Yes, of course, in war it is better to take captives than kill wantonly, and slaves do help the tribe, but that does not stop them from being human, does it?"

Bondage was something I had previously just accepted as an inevitable part of either victory or defeat. I had given no thought to those people as people.

"Dearest David, that's one of the reasons why I love you so much. You can see another's point of view. Of course we in bondage are human, though sometimes some of your neighbours – or even your family – would never acknowledge that."

She refused to enlarge on that any further. She told me how Mother had persuaded Father that, as she had given Leah little gifts over the years, she probably had as good a dowry as many youngest sons might expect. This had been the final argument for my Father, as it would save him shekels when I joined the army.

"Leah, you're marvellous. You have a dowry. Sweetest, you don't need it, but it will help to equip me when I go as a warrior. Without your help Father would have had to find the money. Of course, I already have a sword."

"Don't spoil our day. Don't talk of war." She shushed my protests, "No, no, no, no. No bad thoughts. Let's not think of war, or battles, or other such stupidities that you men get embroiled in."

So we talked about how we would help to farm the family land, shyly about the children we would have, and about our music.

"Leah, this is what is so special. How many men have such a clever wife with whom they can make music?"

She reminded me that she could cook sufficiently competently to please my father, the sternest critic, and she could weave as well as Mother.

I told her, "You are the most beautiful, kindest, cleverest women in the world."

She laughed. "I'm hardly that clever to chose and be chosen by a youngest son!"

So we sang and played together, and, between our singing, we made love again and again until the night fell.

We went to sleep in each other's arms and awoke, aroused by one another. The front of our cave was brilliantly lit, with the full moon at a wonderful angle.

We drew apart and went out onto the ledge. There was a marvellous stillness that was holy. The moon threw a beam of shimmering light onto Bull Horns, clothing our nakedness in wondrous silver.

Above us was a bowl of stars. Leah pointed to a shooting star and holding my hand she whispered, "When I was a child I asked what happened to people when they died. I still cry because I cannot remember whether it was my father who answered me, but I was told that good people join the stars and shine kindly light upon those below."

Her voice became even quieter as if the stars were bending low to eavesdrop upon us. "David, if I should die, I will be a star for you, and we will become stars together."

It seemed a promise and a new bond. Even though we looked with separate eyes, we saw that we were one, bathed in a mist of starlight. We could feel the pulse of eternity.

We were overwhelmed with the moment. The still, echoing silence masked our beating hearts. We were no longer separate people, no longer separate from all around us. In that moment we were at one with time and all creation. We were part of the rocks, the flowing grass, the sinewy trees, and the stars. There was no distinct existence: our souls, bodies and minds had merged for ever and ever ... and ever.

The stillness was all. We had become nothing ... and everything. We were in the presence of God.

I don't know how long that moment of transcendent union lasted. If one can measure eternity, it was eternity. The look of astonished amazement on the face of Leah matched what I felt.

In confirmation of our oneness Leah was the first to speak. "David, we were in the presence of God!"

There followed a delicious languor which led us to sleep and we did not wake again until the sun was high in the sky.

We bathed together, as naturally as if we had been born to it. Because our bathing aroused us again, we completed the morning by making love.

We realised that we were ravenously hungry and had a perfect feast. Re-commemorating our wedding day by taking the bread and wine in remembrance of our first day.

"I do this in remembrance of you," Leah said.

"And I of you," I answered.

Leah gave me my harp and I began to strum. Our eyes met and the words came as each line flowed effortlessly. She repeated them with perfect harmony.

It was obvious.

"The Lord is My Shepherd, I shall not want,
He maketh me to lie down in green pastures,
He leadeth me beside the still waters,"

Of course, as a shepherd I looked after my sheep. God was my shepherd. He had brought us together, giving us the perfection of pasture and our still waters.

"He restoreth my soul;
He leadeth me in the paths of righteousness for his name's sake."

Of course God sought to bring his people to righteousness. The best in our people's history taught us that.

Then I thought of the violent perils that God had brought me through:

"Yea though I walk through the valley of the shadow of death I will fear no evil, for thou art with me, thy rod and staff comfort me. Thou preparest a table before me in the presence of mine enemies."

After these lines Leah did not play or sing after me, but let the words drift in the air to have a special consecration.

My love for Leah and her love for me had transformed me. She made my life complete. Her love demanded only my best. Her love had made me a king. I was anointed by her love.

"Thou anointest my head with oil,"

God's gift to me was greater than His when he presented Adam with Eve. That God had created her mind, her spirit and the joy of her body meant there was no shame in the blissful harmony that we offered to him.

" My cup runneth over."

Of this there was no doubt. We were the happiest people in the world. Our joy was overflowing. God bringing us together meant that we could look forward to the future.

"Surely goodness and mercy shall follow me all the days of my life and I will dwell in the house of the Lord for ever."

We looked at each other. Where had the words come from? I knew she was the inspiration but the words were given to me by God. I knew He had never given me a more perfect psalm.

Then, Leah sang it for me, without hesitation. Her voice rang out pure and perfect over the valley. The echo took up and magnified her voice. I marvelled at the creation. The psalm filled out the silence as if a thousand instruments were in harmony and her voice brought into being a wondrous choir.

"The Lord is My Shepherd, I shall not want, he maketh me to lay down in green pastures, he leadeth me beside the still waters.

He restoreth my soul; he leadeth me in the paths of righteousness for his name's sake.

Yea though I walk through the valley of the shadow of death I will fear no evil, for thou art with me, thy rod and staff comfort me. Thou preparest a table before me in the presence of mine enemies.

Thou anointest my head with oil; my cup runneth over.

Surely goodness and mercy shall follow me all the days of my life and I will dwell in the house of the Lord for ever."

What else was there to do? We quietly, reverently, blissfully made gentle love together and thus brought an end to our momentous wedding day.

For Leah, the day had begun when, with growing excitement, she had prevailed upon Zeruiah to get Jesse to agree that it was right for David to have his colours early. This would please David enormously and agreeing to her weaving his colours was an acceptance that they were willing for them to marry.

She had left the house well before dawn, weak with excitement and hope. She still did her best not to think about how well matters were going, because she was so afraid of disappointment. But even if David's family changed their minds, they would certainly not object to her becoming his concubine, as she loved him more than she dare acknowledge.

She had no doubts about David. Though the issue of her hiding her age made her a little anxious, but when she reached him at dawn and saw his unfeigned delight – the way in which he took her in his arms – all doubts and anxieties melted away.

She looked into his eyes and saw nothing but love. Her lips burned to take his lips into her mouth. Her breasts, her secret place, all glowed with pulsating warmth that only his arms and body around her could ease. She was afraid that her yearning for him would offend him. He might be repulsed by her immodesty and her choking desire to be filled by him.

Then they were in each other's arms. She felt his body caressing hers. She was dizzy with his warmth, which further inflamed her own as she felt her body dissolve into a liquid centre.

His member was wonderful and frightening. His obvious restraint simply added to her wish for him to melt into her. As his fingers caressed hers, she felt her moistness flood before his hard manhood. He so sensitively eased himself into her. With hardly a moment's tension she felt the tight, hot tearing membrane give way before him. It caught her breath, but with a delicious fire as he filled her in a moment of expanding ecstasy.

He was inside her. She was full but wanted to yield even more. He slowly took up his rhythm and her body answered his. Waves of pleasure flooded over her. Her breath and heart beat in unison with his. His taste, his fragrance filled her mouth, and then the unbearable tension gushed as she felt his eruption. She rhythmically milked him as every fibre in her body drained itself of his throbbing fire.

She could not let him go. If she died now, it did not matter. His love for her and hers for him gave meaning to her life. The purity of his accepting love cleansed away the years of servitude and humiliation. This wonderful, wonderful man was hers. He, the best in his family, clan and people, loved her. No princess could be more honoured by his adoration.

Their lovemaking was beyond anything she had imagined. When they emerged from the pool together, she had never thought that man could be so beautiful. But his laughing face, his curved lips, his broad chest, his smooth hardness, the miracle of his rippled sinewy muscles, his narrow hips from which stood erect her elation, were all a wondrous surprise. His obvious delight in her was further confirmation of the jubilation they both found in the mad exploration of each other.

As she told him of her need to hide her age, despite her confidence, she was so relieved to be reassured. But, best of all was their union of minds as each sensed what the other was thinking.

She had thought carefully about how she would offer herself: freely and utterly. There was no shame in surrender when it was mutual. This was their wedding day, no matter what was before them. Their music completed the betrothal and the mystery of the moment in the moonlight when she felt his God's presence in a blessing that no words could express.

Now, she had few anxieties that her mistress would chastise her late return for she had shared something of their Living God. Perhaps this was the beginning of her belonging to the people of Israel. For the first time, she allowed herself to think that her new people were worthier than her own. With such men as her David, they were destined to establish themselves in the land of Canaan.

She wanted to stay. Leaving him was hard but she was uplifted by her excitement of the forthcoming preparations. She knew it best to go. She thought warmly of Zeruiah, who had been a mother in place of the one she had no memory of. She smiled at the dour importance of Jesse and Eliab. She could almost feel sorry for Boaz and his importuning. She realised that he was going to be her brother-in-law. She felt delight at the pleasure Mouse would feel for her and permitted herself a slight feeling of smugness at how some of the other women would feel – knowing she was marrying for love. She was marrying David, whom she had heard other women admire.

This slave, this bond maiden, was going to be free of all their slights, because whilst she had known she was their superior in mind, she daily had to bear the degradation of captivity. She would no longer have to hide what she felt or how she could think. With David beside her, the shame of the yesteryears would slip away. No more would she be a potential target for some drunken lout. No longer the butt of cruel remarks from freeborn women.

As she ran homewards towards Bethlehem, her heart sang the words of her love.

"Oh taste and see that the Lord is good – the Lord is My shepherd I shall not want – surely goodness and mercy shall follow me all the length of my days."

Leah drew close to Bethlehem and knew there was no happier woman in the whole world.

The Tragedy

Though we were married in the sight of God and, therefore, Leah now belonged to me, we had not yet had formal confirmation from my family. We both appreciated that the betrothal would not be complete until we went to the Rabbi.

Reluctantly, we made our sad farewells because I would not return for almost another week. We both wondered whether we could live this long apart now we had found each other.

I watched her go, turning every so often and waving back to me, until even the little dot on the horizon was lost as she returned to Bethlehem.

The days dragged. I could not even find conciliation in my music. My thoughts were full of Leah.

We had agreed that, in view of the interest Samuel had taken in my music, she would put it to my mother that the Prophet might respond to an invitation. This, of course, would delight my father, but she would only ask this if it seemed likely to have their approval. Otherwise, Rabbi Aaron would be asked to marry us so as to avoid giving offence.

As she had no family, and Mouse did not count because she was a woman, we would ask my brother Shammah to be her sponsor. He always treated her with courtesy. She annoyed me when she said that if her heart had not been given to me, then Shammah was someone whom she could have thought of as a husband. I reminded her that Shammah already had a wife, but I soon saw that she was just teasing me, though I did not like the new feeling that her words drew from me. I suddenly knew for the first time that I could feel jealousy – and very quickly where Leah was concerned.

It was Eli who relieved me this time. He told me the news that the Prophet had arrived the day before. I dared not hope. I casually asked whether Eli knew the reason for the visit.

"No, it's some Elders business – as usual – but he spoke to me and said to remind you that he would welcome a word with you when you returned."

Eli was obviously impressed that the Prophet had deigned to speak to him and even more so that he had asked about me.

Then Eli noticed my headband. "You've got your colours," he said, "and red for the warrior."

He studied me hard. "David, you must be one of the youngest ever to have killed his man."

There it was out again – this barrier between my friends.

"Eli, you too will soon have your full colours. I was just lucky: in the right place at the right time."

I told him that Leah had woven it and that father approved.

He was surprised and impressed. "You're going to marry her then, not just take her as a concubine?"

I hesitated at first to tell him that we were already married but then thought better of it – after all, he was a good friend.

"Eli, I know you won't tell anyone until after the wedding ceremony, but Leah and I are already married."

He was astounded. "But how? Did the Rabbi come over here?"

"No," I answered slowly. "We were married in the sight of God."

He thought for a moment and then grinned a delighted grin. "You mean you did it? You made love together?"

I blushed. I was confused. I was angry and annoyed. He just stood there with his eyes alight. I knew he wanted me to tell him about it – after all, for the last year we did not speak of much else.

"Oh, come on David. Tell me was it good." Then he saw my face and said, "Good God! You really do love her, don't you? After all, you didn't *need* to marry her?"

Then with his generous spirit he said, "I didn't mean to sound crude, of course. I can see it was good. Only, I wanted to be the best man, though I suppose you'd have had Josh. But if I'm the first to know, then I'm honoured. I can see that something special's happened, hasn't it?"

I knew what he meant. Both Leah and I had something special. I tried to explain how at the end of my morning prayers, Leah had arrived "almost in answer". I explained that she and I had exchanged vows, and that we had made love only after making those vows of marriage.

"Yes, we made love. Eli, there is nothing bad, or crude or ugly in that. I can't explain, but we love each other and it's just as simple as that."

And then, hesitatingly, I told him how emerging from our time together, in the moonlight, we awoke to see everything illuminated.

"What was so marvellous was that we didn't need words. We saw everything anew but not by ourselves. Because, Eli, for that short moment that seemed to last for ever, we were different. We were no longer separate people, but felt part of everything around us. We were at one with being."

As I had told him so much, I now trusted him completely. "When the moment passed, Leah said it for us both: we felt we had been in the presence of God."

We looked at each other. There was apprehension – almost a fear – in our eyes as both of us grasped the enormity of what I had just said.

It was Eli who spoke first. "I'm not sure I fully understand, because nothing like that has ever happened to me. It sounds ... wonderful!"

And with that dear Eli gave me a big hug and said "Now clear off! Go to that delightful wife of yours – only make it official before we can all see the fruits of what's been going on here." He was so warm-hearted.

Though I was anxious to go, I knew that if I got back by midday it would probably be the earliest I could see Leah because of her work. So I did not leave straightaway and whiled away the time.

When I left, I ran at my best rate. I quite forgot the long, dreary week of lonely nights as I flew homewards and to my love.

As I approached the town, my sprits rose. I began to sing aloud our new psalm.

"The Lord is my shepherd, I shall not want – my cup runneth over."

I saw a female figure at the end of the town. At first my heart sprang; was this Leah coming to meet me? Perhaps the Prophet was coming to our wedding. Then I saw that the person was too small; it was dear Mouse.

I ran towards her, shouting with glee. "Mouse, dear Mouse. My cup runneth over. We are to be married."

I was upon her before I had time to take in what my eyes did not at first see. I grabbed her arms and whirled her around. "We're going to be married – we're going to be married – and you will be a maid of honour."

I stopped. She had said not a word. Her little face, often anxious, now wore a look of misery and all down along one side of her face was a nasty abrasion that was beginning to form into an ugly bruise.

"Mouse, what has happened? Have you fallen? Have you had an accident?"

She didn't answer but just looked at me.

"Surely," I said, "nobody can have struck you?"

Whilst bond maidens have few rights and could be beaten, it did not happen often. I could not imagine anyone ever wanting to beat little Mouse.

She still did not answer. I began to feel a sense of fear.

"Mouse! Mouse! What is it?"

She began to cry, silently.

I was in desperate anxiety. "Mouse! What is it? Is it Mother? Father? What is it? For Hell's sake, tell me!"

She stood dumbly, trying to speak.

I stood very still, not daring to think. "Is it Leah? Is Leah ill?"

At these words Mouse broke down and wailed bitterly. Her cries were the sound of a mortally wounded animal. My blood froze.

"It is Leah, isn't it? Is she ill?" I whispered.

Mouse fought for control and tried to mouth the words, then she fell into my arms and forced herself to speak.

"Oh, David. She's dead. David, she's ... she's ... dead!"

The world stopped.

"But that's ... not possible. We're going to be married."

Mouse didn't answer but just looked straight at me in a way I could not bare.

"It can't be true. I don't believe it. She can't be dead – she can't!" I said, hardly aware that it was me speaking.

"David, she *is*." The words fell from her lips with such flat certainty that I began to believe her.

I was wood.

I heard myself ask to know more, as if some one else was speaking my part.

"Was it the plague?"

She shook her head.

"An accident?"

"No, not an accident." Her face dropped.

I was now full of fury. "Then tell me for God's sake! How did she die?"

Mouse pushed me away, looked me straight in the face and answered, "You won't want to know."

I tried desperately to control myself. This could not be true. Leah could not be dead. My Leah? My darling wife? No! This was some horrid test.

Yet I could see it was no test that something terrible had indeed happened to my love.

I swallowed hard and said gently, "Mouse, please ..., please ... tell me or I shall go mad. Take your time. Just tell me what happened."

She nodded and cried a little. I understood that I would get nothing from her until the spasm of tears was past.

"It was Boaz," she said at last.

I stood transfixed, not daring to move but found my hand going to the sword which hung at my side.

"You mean ... it was Boaz who hit you?" Knowing his temper I could believe that he might be capable of hitting even someone as fragile as Mouse.

"Yes," she answered. "Boaz hit me because I saw what he did. He hit Leah too."

I could not believe this. I knew that Boaz was interested in Leah, but she had always skilfully avoided him.

I heard myself harshly say, "Tell me it all, Mouse. Don't hesitate. Tell me quickly. JUST TELL ME!"

Then she gave me a story that destroyed me.

"It happened this morning. We were at the river washing. Boaz had followed us. He had heard that the Prophet was coming and that you and she were to be married. He started saying dreadful things to her. She tried to answer gently, not wanting to offend him. She told him that your parents had agreed that you could marry. He was furious and started again saying horrible things about how she was an infidel Philistine; that she was not good enough for his family; that she had betrayed him; that she was a witch who had tried to cast a spell on him; and how she had lusted after him. All the time he was getting angrier. Leah tried to calm him and kept saying how sorry she was."

As she paused, I looked at her in disbelief but her simple words brought the horror to life.

"Go on, Mouse. Take your time but please tell me everything."

"Everything?" she asked, suddenly afraid. I nodded gravely.

"Her grabbed her and threw her to the ground. Leah tried to fight him off. I tried to help and," pointing to her bruised face, "that was when I got this."

Mouse took a deep breath and continued. "He dragged her down and ... and ... Oh, David, I'm so sorry. He ... he ... raped her!"

She stopped and I was totally numb.

I saw the scene in my mind's eye but at another level refused to believe it.

Mouse went on. "He abused her – not just with his ... thing. He was calling her terrible names and, as he raped her, he beat her until she was half senseless. He got up from her and gave me another blow. Then, David, he wiped himself on me saying, 'that's all you Philistine bitches are good for', and went off."

I knew that Mouse was crying again, but I had to find out the last terrible detail.

"Mouse, when did this happen?" I breathed.

"Less than two hours ago." Her answer was devastating.

Less than two hours ago! I might have been here. My thoughts reeled – I should have been here. Oh, God, help me! I could have prevented this nightmare. My agony of spirit nearly choked me. Less than two hours ago? Oh, dear God, how could you look on and not take her part? She who had found and revered you. Oh Hell – Hell – Hell! Why, oh why, did I not come home directly? Why, oh why, was I not here for her?

But there was more, for Mouse had only told me of Boaz's blasphemy: she had not told me how Leah had died.

"Mouse, was she hurt so badly that she died? Mouse – for pity's sake – how did she die?"

Mouse's distress worsened and then she told me in words that clamoured doom in my brain.

"She told me that Boaz had defiled her love and she could not live with knowing that she had dishonoured you. So ... so ... she killed herself! Oh, David. She killed herself!" Mouse sank to the floor and wailed.

I could feel nothing. Killed herself? My thoughts were sluggish. Killed herself!

I knelt beside Mouse and held her close. "Tell me, Mouse. Tell me the end."

After a while she recovered and, as if she was describing something far off, she answered, "When Boaz left, she lay there. I went to her. She wasn't crying – indeed, she comforted me. She said to give you a message: that she loved you and that she would always be grateful for your love. She said that she had brought shame on you and could not bear to have your name besmirched. She kissed me and told me to come and wait for you. I am to ask you not to forget her, but to find it in your heart to forgive her."

I was aghast at this. How could she feel that *she* had let me down? How could she feel guilty? It was that swine, Boaz. I nodded for Mouse to go on.

"She insisted that I repeat her message to you to make sure I had got it right. I pleaded with her not to do anything, but to come to you herself. She saw I was upset and she tried to calm me down. She told me that I was her best friend and that she was sure you would look after me. She said that, after you, she loved me the most." Here Mouse broke down again. I waited silently.

She recovered herself and went on. "She insisted that I do as she said and assured me that it would be all right when she had finished what she had to do. Then, what Boaz did to her would not matter. David, she went into the house ..." she paused and then said quickly, "she took a kitchen knife and ... pierced her heart."

I did not think it possible to be alive and yet feel dead. The words were unreal: "and pierced her heart"? She had killed herself – this was the ultimate rejection. Why blame herself? Why hurt herself and me? She had done nothing wrong. I knew I could not let myself think about Boaz's abomination – his defilement of her. I knew this agony would come later. But why? Why take to herself the disgrace when the abomination was Boaz?

I calmly asked in a frozen way, "Where is she now, Mouse?"

She got up and, holding her hand in mine, led me home. People stood in the street and watched silently as we trod our way to our house. Now I could hear the keening wail of the mourning women.

I went in and there, on a bed, lay my Leah. Oh, that memory is burned for ever in mine brain. She lay so still, pale, with harsh bruises on her face and shoulders, with the deadly mark of the knife which had made the fatal ruin of our love.

My mother came to embrace me. I held her gently and then led her to her seat.

The other women continued their chilling cries as they prepared Leah for her funeral.

Funeral? The thought was like an iron flame. We had been preparing our wedding ceremony – now it was to be her funeral! My mind ran apace. Since she was not yet my wife, in law, as a bond maiden, she would be interred in common ground.

"Mother," I said, "will she be buried in our family grave?"

Mother looked at me in some confusion. Then nodded and crying said, "Of course. She was already a daughter to me and would have been my dearest daughter-in-law."

"Thank you," I replied politely.

I knelt down and caressed for the last time my darling's face. I kissed the lips that were now so cold, which proved beyond doubt that my love had fled and hid her face amidst a crowd of stars.

"Goodbye, my darling. Goodbye and good night." I got up and strode out.

Standing in the sunlight, I looked around and then my rage hit me.

"BOAZ! BOAZ! BOAZ!" I screamed "YOU DOG BOAZ. WHERE ARE YOU?"

I ran around into the next courtyard and there he stood, arrogantly laughing.

"What's all the noise about? You'll wake the dead," he said.

Though he is my brother, at that moment I hated no man more than Boaz. I just had sufficient control to throw my sword from me before my blood red rage overcame me.

I hurled myself upon him. He was ready for me and kicked out, hitting me in the groin. The pain pierced my rage but still I went on. I reached him and grappled him to the ground.

His hateful face was contorted in a fury that matched my own. He brought his knee up, again and again, taking my wind and filling me with pain. But my hands were about his throat. I sank them, like talons, into his neck and banged my forehead into his face. I felt the exhilaration as I heard the bone crash and felt his blood and gore spurt.

We rolled along the ground. He was on top of me trying to crash my head into the ground. I sought the strength to tear into him but I could not breathe. He let go his hold and pulled away from me.

I staggered to my feet to go after him but he had snatched up a heavy stool and was using it as a club against me. Vainly, I raised my arms to hold him off while still trying to close with him, but his blows came quicker. I felt the searing pain as the bone snapped and my arm fell useless at my side.

He swung the stool at my head. The blow rocked me. I was choking with my own blood. The dizziness and pain blinded me. He hit me again and, despite my rage, I felt myself sinking, sinking, sinking.

I threw a last feeble blow. He kicked me under the heart felling me senseless and I knew nothing more. He went on kicking and kicking, until restrained by Shammah and the other men.

Mourning

It was thought that I would also die. For nearly a week I lay close to death. Amidst the painful haze of those days, I was hardly aware of the pain but only the agony and misery of knowing that my Leah was no more.

Mouse had painted the scene so well that it had become a recurring nightmare. I was standing by and could only watch as my love was defiled. I was just a frozen observer while she, overwhelmed with shame, pierced her heart.

As the numbness of the pain eased, my mental hurt became more. I dully accepted the ministrations of Mother and Mouse. There was a half-memory of Father coming to say that he had banished Boaz. I was indifferent to that memory or the dream that Samuel had come to my bedside and prayed. I felt nothing, save a deep, deep nausea and total emptiness, as I silently wept for Leah.

Weeks went by before they could sufficiently rouse me to sit weakly in the sunshine outside. No one spoke of the dreadful events, though Father came and told me how he had confronted Boaz with his crime.

He had at first tried to deny any guilt arguing that, as Leah was only a bond maiden, the law gave her no rights. Father called Boaz a bully who had disgraced the family and himself, and that if he had killed Leah his punishment would have been worse. So he was sent away for two years to live amongst the Moabites.

If Father thought that this would please me, then he was disappointed. He told me that I was a fool to attack Boaz like that. I should have gone straight to him and he would have punished Boaz.

Father did not understand. Leah was dead. She died because Boaz had defiled her. Boaz was an abomination and nothing that Father could say or do would bring Leah back to me.

With Leah's death, something had died in me and I felt that I would never feel anything again.

The months passed. Winter came and I passed another birthday, but life seemed to hold little purpose and the idea of my music was repugnant to me.

The only positive action I was able to muster was in response to Mouse. She told me that she had nightmares and was so afraid, especially if any men were near. I remembered from Leah's message, that she had asked me to look after Mouse: how like Leah to think of others. Yet that thought gave me pain, because in her death she had not thought of my suffering when she deserted me.

Mother saw that Mouse was frightened and that she was making herself ill through constant anxiety. Mother had tried to reassure her but, apparently, Mouse felt that her only comfort would be if Mother gave her to me. As I now had my colours Mouse could become a part of my household. I agreed and she became my bond maiden, although she continued to live and work for Mother. I was totally indifferent.

It was Josh who started my recovery – though it nearly wrecked our friendship. He, with Aaron, Eli and the Rabbi Aaron, had been talking about me. The Rabbi had said, "He has a melancholy sickness. If it is not ended soon, it will sap his reason. He will sink into madness."

Josh came to see me. I sat numbly but he refused to accept my inertia.

"David?" he began hesitantly. "David, we've got to talk about Leah."

I felt fury. No one, no one had mentioned her name since that fateful day.

"Josh, shut it! You don't know what you are talking about. You have no right to interfere. Now leave!" I snapped at him.

He tried to go on about how badly Boaz had acted but I angrily interrupted him. "What would you know, Josh? You have never loved. Now, shut it! Hell, Hell, Hell – I don't want to talk about it. Go!"

He was angry now. "How dare you say that. Don't you realise, you bloody fool – we love you!"

I was startled by his words.

"Yes, it may surprise you," he continued, regaining some of his composure. "It hasn't been easy for us either, coming here every day to see our best friend just lying there and weakly giving up. It's only because we love you that we here."

I looked at him blankly, but he went on. "We were shattered by what happened. Leah was terrific and you were lucky to have her. I was jealous in all sorts of ways."

And then he showed a sensitively that broke me. "Leah's death must have felt like a betrayal – not the rape. If Boaz, the bastard, had killed her, it might have been easier to bear, but in her nobility – David, what she did was noble – she cut you off too."

I could not take any more and fell into his arms and cried. I was crying real tears for the first time since it happened.

"Oh, Josh. Josh. She left me – she left me behind. She didn't give me a chance for me to show that it didn't matter. I would never have blamed her – never. But she didn't let me show her how much I loved her."

I knew then I that would feel again because I knew the sadness of the hurtful anger I felt for Leah. For the first time, I had allowed myself to own up to the painful, embittered feeling that I had been rejected.

I asked Josh's forgiveness.

Josh placed his hand on my shoulder. "David, there's nothing to forgive. All we ask is that you don't reject your true friends and that you'll come back to us."

I felt ashamed. That afternoon we went together to join Eli at Bull Horns and stayed a week.

With my friend's help my strength began to return. I started to train with Horah and the troop.

I often thought of Leah and often dreamed of her. Sometimes, however, I forgot and panicked when I tried to recall how she looked but momentarily could not bring her face to mind.

More than a year had passed when I was called to see the Prophet, who had come to Bethlehem. I did not want to see him because there were thoughts that I dared not confront. I tried to make excuses.

Aaron brought the message. "'Samuel the Prophet would speak with his friend and loyal Israelite.' David, I didn't know he was your friend?" ended

Aaron, questioningly.

"Oh, some nonsense when I was younger and he wanted me to play for him. As I don't play any more I can't think what he wants," I said, nonchalantly.

If Aaron thought I was being pretentious, I did not care. I knew I did not want to meet the man who walked and talked with a God who could let innocent women be foully raped.

As I began to think about a God who could allow such injustice and misery, I could not tell whom I was angriest with: God or Samuel. Reluctantly, I returned to Bethlehem.

I was ushered into Samuel's presence to find my father standing with him. Father had adopted an air of importance, which he basked in whenever he was seen with Samuel. I felt a stirring of contempt at his being so easily flattered.

I had a strong sense that they had been talking about me. Why else call for me?

The seated Samuel began quietly. "It is good to see you, David, my friend. I am sorry to hear that times have been bad for you. Come, ease your mind and ours. Will you play for us?"

I replied shortly, "I don't play any more. I have put away such childish things."

I could see that my answer infuriated Father, but I didn't care whether Samuel was pleased or no.

"Is David angry with his friend?" the Prophet asked in his softest, low voice.

I did not answer.

"I am saddened that you no longer consider me to be your friend," he said simply.

My father responded immediately and began to expostulate with me about impertinence. He said that he had been too indulgent with me just because I had been ill.

Samuel let this go. I just stood there with complete indifference. I suppose I must have looked surly and mutinous – almost inviting a blow from my Father.

Samuel sensed this and gently calmed matters down. "Yes, yes, friend Jesse. Your son has been ill. Life had dealt him his first real blow and he has suffered a great loss – truly, a great loss. He does not understand that we who bear responsibilities for our families and people have to bear many such affronts."

This may have calmed Father but it incensed me. What did this old, old man know? Surely, he had never loved as I? And if he had, his blood was now so thin that he would have forgotten that which I had just lost.

Father left quietly but cast me an angry look, which meant I could be sure that chastisement would follow later. But what did I care? He was too old for his blows to hurt anyway.

Samuel motioned for me to sit but, stubbornly, I remained standing. He sighed and said nothing more before entering into a reverie. I was determined not to be the first to break the silence between us.

Eventually, it was Samuel who spoke first. "David, would you be so proud if you were angry with your friends, Eli, Josh or Aaron?"

I did not answer. He went on. "I thought friends shared bad as well as good things."

As he still had no answer from me he mused, "I remember that if I, or my friends, did something to annoy each other, I would either apologise for my behaviour, or try to get them to see what they had done that had hurt me. So in telling each other, because we loved each other, that anger ended."

He then stood up and in a gesture of simple dignity he stretched out his arms in an appeal. "David bar Jesse, you once gave me your friendship. I believed you would always honour that friendship with truth. I say, therefore: David, my friend, how have I injured you? How have I made you angry?"

How could I answer him? "Samuel, you honour me too much. You expect too much. I am not angry with you. You have not done me an injury. I have suffered, as you say, a great loss. So, forgive me but I am not ..." I stopped. I had nothing more to say.

He nodded. "David, I am an old man. Please sit with me. Your troubled spirit troubles me, too. I am your friend and your Rabbi – but most of all your friend."

I sat down beside him, reluctantly. I knew he meant well but I really did not want to talk about it.

He said, "Your friends, Eli, Josh and Aaron, have been very concerned for you." I looked at him in surprise. "David, you are very fortunate in your friends – and they in you. Josh loves you especially well but Eli, I think, understands something of the hard road that you and I must travel."

What did he mean? Had Eli told him of our conversation? If not, from where had Samuel found that incredible intuitive awareness – as if he was hearing what I was thinking?

"Yes," he continued, "Eli has some perception that God sometimes comes close to you. He is already a good man. He does not envy because he has learned that such blessing brings terrible responsibility."

Puzzled, I said, "I don't know what you mean."

"David, in every man there is the touch of the divine. But some of us, like you and I, are more aware and sometimes this awareness burns."

He then spoke with great sadness – almost with regret. "This awareness is terrible. When the Godhead comes close, the ecstasy of the Oneness, the fire of that extreme infuses, illuminates our lives but it also almost consumes us."

He paused to let me consider this. "It is not given to many; nay, few, few receive such a double-edged gift. But it has been given to you, as it was to me."

He let the words fall between us. "David, I do not know what your destiny will be. My calling was early and straightforward: yours is yet to come. But that you have been called, I have no doubt."

I felt myself being trapped. What did he mean about calls?

I was now a little fearful. "I don't want your call – what ever it is. If this divinity in man only burns, destroys," I said with venom, "then I want none of it!"

"David, you are angry with God?" It was half question, half statement of fact.

I replied harshly as my anger flowed out. "You once said I was in love with religion – well, no longer! I was in love with a wonderful human being. She was kind. She had never hurt anyone in her life. She was orphaned. Then, as a child, she was cruelly dragged from her family after watching people who cared for her killed. She was made a slave and lived her life at everyone's whim. Yes, she was lucky: my mother was a good mistress. But can you imagine the slights and humiliations she must have suffered?"

I was in full fury. I was speaking for Leah. "She was a child who had to hide herself from men because of their grossness. She had spirit and intelligence, which she had to hide lest others envy her. But despite this she was kind, caring and took thought for others. She sought to understand life, unlike many men who would think themselves superior. She lived amongst us for ten years, yet you, and others, would call her a stranger. She loved me. She declared, as did Ruth, that my people were her people and that my God was her God."

The angry tears flowed. The half-formed thoughts poured out in a rush. I would tell this old man the truth which all were too afraid to own.

"She was blessed with that divine fire. She experienced the presence of God. Yet she, who was far closer to the Living God than anyone I have known, was cruelly defiled, spoiled, raped by her own brother in-law. Left alone, desolate and deserted by me, who could have saved her if I had come sooner. IT NEED NOT HAVE HAPPENED," I screamed at Samuel.

I swiftly drew breath and continued. "But she who had earned no man's enmity, no man's scorn, had been deserted. Angry with God? I curse Him! How could He stand by and let such a vile thing happen? You say He has a destiny for me – I spurn Him. I spit upon the idea. He is not a gift but a curse. How else can He be described who can betray someone who dedicated her life to his service, yet who died so shortly after her wedding day?"

I stood there, looking defiantly at Samuel. Let him answer that charge if he could.

Samuel asked quietly, "I did not know you were married. Had another Rabbi brought you together? I thought I was to have that honour?"

"We were married in the sight of God. We made our vows together. They were binding upon us whether or not a hundred rabbis be present."

He looked at me keenly. "So, you are a priest or a rabbi now?" There was almost a threat in his voice.

"We knew we were married," I said, defiantly. "We used the words of Ruth. God blessed our union. It was an experience too holy to tell even you. Do you dare to suggest that our love was unseemly?" I was ready to walk out: from him, from my family, from Israel.

He spoke in an even but authoritative voice. "I will ignore your arrogance. You are not thinking what you are saying because you are in grief. But Moses himself laid down God's commandments on how His people should live. The people's guide is the priesthood. Can you deny this? Would you in your pride create anarchy so that each man can make his own laws and measure his own way? Without the Law there is only turmoil. God abhors such a chaos."

This was all wrong. Somehow, he had changed the focus. I was being accused. I, the victim, was made to feel the wrongdoer.

"David, that you loved Leah and she you, I have no doubt. That your love was seemly and sincere, I doubt not. But such unions have to be within the law. Without the law the people perish. I, as well as you, am subject to that law. Yes, sometimes it hurts, bridles, chaffs, because of its apparent restriction. But, David, I prophesy that when you or I set aside the law, no matter how we may justify it, it is for our will, pleasure, and ultimate self-gratification. It becomes a tyranny of the soul. If you have power, it becomes an oppression for others."

I felt resentful at his words and answered, "But that does not answer what God allowed to happen to Leah. He betrayed her trust."

Samuel stood up and began to pace around in increasing agitation. "Did He give us free will or not? If intent and wishes were all, then there would be no problem with effect. Would there be no ill in the world, think you?

But would all men's wishes be the same? Men and God can only be judged by their actions. Yes, risk the supreme arrogance: dare to judge God."

There was a terrible silence at the enormity of his words. His voice had risen in a crescendo. There was a quiet fury in his words, which were truly dreadful.

"Yes," he repeated, "dare to judge God by His actions."

He approached me and hissed, his face right up in front of mine. "Was it God who struck Leah? Was it God who defiled her? Was it God who came too late? No! It was the grossness, the stupidity, the evil – of man."

Then, all fury spent, he imploringly took my arm and said softly, "God forgave you both because He had smiled upon you, He saw the aspiration in your heart. David, my dear, dear friend. Believe me: I am so very, very sorry."

He put he mouth next to my ear and whispered, "But was it God who took Leah's life?"

I was shattered. He had asked the question that I dared not. I froze. Suddenly, all the hurt and pain of Leah's death washed over me. I had no tears left, just unutterable sadness that she could not stay for me. In leaving me, she had not trusted my love to cleanse her defilement.

I had no words left, no anger. I was held in Samuel's gentle embrace as he began to pray over me, asking God to bring peace to my soul.

We sat for a long while. Samuel was the first to speak and told me how he had arrived, not for a marriage, but for a funeral, only to find me close to death. He had permitted Rabbi Aaron to say the prayers for the dead over Leah, as if she had been part of our family.

I asked him, "Do you think she is in Abraham's bosom?"

He smiled gently. "Who am I to know the mind of God in all things? Suffice that Rabbi Aaron is a good man, and God is merciful and compassionate. How else would he tolerate His people's backsliding. Yes – and His priests who cannot always live up to His ideals."

I felt a sense of some contentment, for I had confidence that He saw into our hearts. God already knew there had been no grossness between Leah and I.

"Would you play now?" Samuel asked plaintively. "We must set the seal on our re-bound friendship."

I did not want to but I could not refuse. Especially when, getting up and going to the back of the room, he brought out a new harp, which he offered to me without speaking.

I took it, still reluctantly, and slowly strummed the strings. I could feel its tone and its pitch' its range. It was a wonderful instrument. I played a few practice scales as my hand sought to become accustomed to its vibrant tone.

I said in awe, "Thank you, it is magnificent."

He asked, very considerately, "Would you play for me the last song you wrote for Leah?"

No, this was too much. I would never play that again. I did not answer.

Then, as if he read my mind, he added, "It will be painful but I can not doubt that you were given a special psalm. In sharing it with me, you will honour her. As you described her, she must have been a truly wonderful person. Few are blessed to have had a love like yours – even when they have a lifetime together. Play it in remembrance of her."

I remembered our troth to break bread together to commemorate our marriage day.

"You know not what you ask," I replied.

He nodded. "But for her, let her memory live in her psalm – as she was." Then, in a commanding voice, he said, "Think no more of her end, of her passing, but recall who she was. Remember only your love."

I fought back the tears. Yes, that is the way forward. Samuel was right that I should keep her memory fresh and not the tragic ultimate rejection.

My fingers ran over the strings, slowly finding the key and the rhythm to her melody. It was indeed her psalm that I shared with Samuel in a shaking voice.

"The Lord is my shepherd I shall not want.

He maketh me to lie down in green pastures; he leadeth me besides the still waters.

He restoreth my soul, he leadeth me in the paths of righteousness for His name's sake."

My voice lost its tremor. For the first time since her death I could think of her as she was. I sang for her.

"Yea though I walk through the valley of the shadow of death, I will fear no evil; for thou art with me; thy rod and thy staff comfort me.

Thou preparest a table before me in the presence of mine enemies; thou anointest my head with oil; my cup runneth over.

Surely goodness and mercy shall follow me all the days of my life and I will dwell in the house of the Lord for ever."

As the words and music drifted away into silence, all that could be heard was the sound of Samuel weeping.

The day after my meeting with Samuel, my Father called me to him. Samuel was again with him.

Father addressed me in a very matter-of-fact way. "The Prophet has been very gracious to you David and has forgiven you your impertinence. He has asked my permission – and I have agreed – that you be sent to Saul the King to be his bard."

Samuel then spoke – but as the High Priest, not the friend of yesterday. "David bar Jesse, though you have your colours, and God has been good to you and protected you in your first battle, you are still not the age of a full warrior."

He continued in explanation. "Saul the King has plenty of warriors, but his spirit has been low and I have spoken to him of you and your music. I think that you could be a good service to him as his bard."

Samuel could see my reluctance. "Young man, there will be warrior duties enough before long. But at this time your best service will be to serve him as bard."

Still I was unconvinced so he ordered, "Your father agrees it. No more! Prepare yourself to journey to the King."

Here was the masterful High Priest of Israel, the anointer of kings, speaking, issuing me with his commands, and bestowing me with my first mission. "Give Saul the King your Father's and my greeting. Say in my name that you are he whom I spoke of. Tell him that you are to serve with him for a year and, if you please him, for as long as he wishes. Is that not so, Jesse my friend?"

That was it. There was nothing more to be said. I bowed obediently to Samuel. I also received what I could not help but feel was a somewhat reluctant blessing from my father. I suspected that he still harboured his irritation from yesterday and he'd not had the opportunity to give me the beating he had obviously promised himself.

I have already spoken about Samuel and, now again, the King's name has been mentioned. You may think it strange that a youth from Bethlehem should be so free and familiar with the names of Israel's greatest men. In very different ways they both made such an impact upon what happened to me that I need to tell their stories to show how they influenced my life – even beyond the grave.

Their lives were a pattern interwoven with triumph and tragedy. They show that even those who would serve God and His people can still allow their envy of each other's greatness to erode and destroy what was best in them.

The rivalry of Samuel and Saul still reverberates in Israel. Much of my life has been spent trying to unite these competing themes.

PART TWO

SAMUEL AND SAUL

Chapter Six

The Story of Israel

All realities begin with history and my story is no exception. How a youngest son from little-regarded Bethlehem became King of Israel can only be understood in the story of the people. Much of it you may already know but I will briefly outline the story of Israel for those for whom it is unfamiliar. For it is a history which inevitably influenced my behaviour when I became King.

Like all peoples, it grew out of conflicts and betrayals, often masquerading as divine intervention, but proved that, in spite of the deviousness of powerful men, God fulfilled his promise against all the odds. Though the hidden animosities still find echoes in today's great issues.

As I said, I will tell the whole truth as I saw it at the time, not with the benefits of hindsight, as each event unfolded I was drawn into these antagonisms whose results I never sought. Out of this struggle were laid the foundations of my own kingship, but not before a tragic civil war, which God knows I did not seek. Indeed, I wish that it had never happened and believe it would have been unnecessary but for Saul's moon-struck jealousy.

Was it madness or pride that made Saul reject all that was good in his kingship? He denied his son, his friends and, though Samuel was not without fault, for he too had the frailties of a human being, Saul repudiated the man who had made him king.

Some will say that Saul was eaten up by his own evil soul. I, who knew him better than most – and who loved him – deny such an explanation, though he sought my life.

Now I am King, flatterers tell me that it was God's mission for my house and that Saul's madness was ordained to ensure my succession. Yet Saul's son, my dearest and best friend, was, as you shall judge, a prince above all princes. No, God would have to be playing a bizarre game for such an explanation to be tenable. God would not demean himself to play petty human political games. No, I became king in order to reunite Israel after

Saul's errors had put God's chosen people in jeopardy. My anointing was not a cause of Saul's fall but a consequence.

You may judge why Saul, Israel's first King, went from triumph to bitter defeat. But as you judge him – and me – consider how you might have acted and whether you would have avoided our mistakes.

It all began with the Patriarch of our people, Abraham, who died some 600 hundred years ago. The Living God made a covenant with Abraham that he would be the father of many nations, and that his people would be established until the end of time. God called us "His Chosen People". Though sometimes God appeared terrible when they strayed from the strict path, which was just tender fatherly care for His people.

God made tremendous demands upon Abraham's fidelity. Once he went as far as to test whether Abraham would be willing to sacrifice his son, Isaac. Amazingly, despite terrible anguish Abraham was willing to do this, but God relented at the last minute. So, instead of sacrificing Isaac, Abraham was permitted to offer a ram instead. Thus, Isaac lived to lead Israel.

The first conflict was when Isaac's younger son, Jacob, was preferred to the older Esau, and though the change in succession was accepted, the rivalries could still be felt.

At this time, we were a nomadic people and had not yet learned to use iron. We lived by following our herds across the hills as the seasons unfolded.

A great crisis arose when yet another younger son, Joseph, was sold into slavery by his older brothers. With God's help, Joseph earned the favour of the great Pharaoh of Egypt, then the greatest power the world has ever seen.

The story of Joseph itself is a miracle, as he became one the most powerful men in Egypt. Eventually, there was reconciliation between Joseph and his family, and the tribe of Israel entered Egypt under the protection of Joseph, the Pharaoh's favourite.

Over the years, the people forgot that they had a covenant with God, whilst the Egyptians began to resent the successful "foreigners". The people of Egypt, forgetting their former king's promises, condemned all the Israelites to slavery. Through the miraculous leadership of Moses, the people were led out of bondage and ready to fulfil the covenant to be the People of God.

Our rabbis still debate why Moses did not take his people directly to the Promised Land. The time in the wilderness lasted more than forty years before Moses could point to the land of Canaan, Israel's Promised Land. Moses' task was to lead and to be a lawgiver, to prepare the people for their inheritance as they lacked the discipline and cohesion to take the land pledged to them. In reality, they must have been little more than a rabble wandering in the desert. Having no experience of war during the years in captivity, they had to re-build themselves into a nation.

Most wonderfully, God spoke to Moses and gave him The Ten Commandments, which are the basis of all law between man and man. I admit such laws are difficult to live up to and are the envy of lesser peoples. I have sometimes fallen short of their ideals, especially those of the flesh. But there can be little doubt that the Israelites were the Chosen People. The evidence lies in what they achieved and endured. It would be unbelievable for the Israelites to have survived without God's active help, as other nations would easily have destroyed us.

The people of Israel had been divided into the Twelve Tribes, who were descended from Joseph's twelve sons, which still form the base of the army of today. So it can be seen that the original "seed of Abraham", despite everything, had prospered.

There were – and still are – other peoples who would seek our destruction and take our land for themselves. East of the Jordan are the tribes of Ammon, Moab and Edom. To the far North are the Assyrians but they, like the Babylonians far to the East and the Egyptians away in the South of the world, have not troubled us because of the distances involved. Between Egypt and us is the land of the Amalekites, who are the cruellest people.

By far the fiercest and most dangerous foes are the Philistines. They live in cities along the Western shores of the Great Sea (or the Mediterranean, as it was later to be known). They were the earliest users of iron and had settled the plains for many generations before us. Like the Egyptians, they made use of chariots in their armies.

They considered the nomadic hill peoples, such as the Amakelites and we Israelites, as uncivilised. Consequently, they periodically sent armies into our lands to ravage and pillage. Worse, they often encouraged the rivalries between the Tribes, skilfully creating dissent, and, as you will hear, they nearly succeeded in destroying our unity and our religion. Thus, whilst there were occasional wars against the Ammonites and the Moabites, it was the Amakelites and the Philistines who caused – and still do give us – most distress.

The Law of Moses governed Israel. Though warriors were important, the Priesthood, many of them being the descendants of Moses' half-brother, Aaron, the first Chief Priest, ruled the nation.

Each of the Tribes had a number of Priests who, as elders, ruled their tribe as Judges. While this was acceptable in ensuring the Law of Moses, it was not very effective when responding to threats from nations who were governed by kings who could take quick decisions. The Philistines, though having a number of kings of cities, could come together quickly under their elected High King and act decisively.

The Laws kept us healthy by avoiding unclean food. Moses established a system of supporting the Priesthood by taking a tenth of the harvest and the beasts, to maintain our worship of God through proper sacrifices to keep the covenant. However, the Covenant could never be safe if our unity was threatened. The big question was should we keep separate from non-Jews or not?

This was a rather delicate matter for my family because my great-grandfather, Boaz, had spent time living in the land of Moab and had married a Moabite, Ruth. Though she became a Jew, we still have distant relatives amongst the Moabites. My grandfather was Obed, Boaz's eldest son, but my father, Jesse, was yet another younger son, as indeed I am.

Samuel the Prophet

Central to my story is Israel's greatest prophet, Samuel. With him I bring Israel's story up-to-date. He is one of the great heroes of Israel as he was Chief Priest for more than 60 years.

Of course, this was some 50 years before I was born. He was a remarkable man: he conversed with God and yet was willing teach me, a young shepherd of Judah. Whilst some say he had his own objectives, I never found him but true to his ideals.

Samuel was very young when called to God's service – even younger than I. He was an assistant to Eli, the Chief Priest, who, although very old, led Israel at that time.

Eli knew he had to prepare Samuel to become Chief Priest, even though he was only a nephew, not a son. But Eli knew that Samuel would become a great prophet one day.

One of the biggest disasters ever to overtake Israel occurred when the Israelites responded to a major attack by the Philistines. Eli had completely misunderstood God's message. Leaving the hills, the Israelites descended impetuously into the plains where the Philistines used their chariots to great effect and we were almost annihilated at the Battle of Ebenezer.

Worse for the nation, was the loss of the Ark of the Covenant, which was captured by the Philistines.

I have not yet mentioned the Ark. The Law of Moses prohibited any graven images because God understands that such imagery eventually itself becomes the object of worship. People stop seeking the Godhead in themselves and turn to sacred images, which becomes simple idolatry.

Moses built the Ark to commemorate the Covenant. It was placed in a tabernacle – a tented dwelling place. The Ark contains the scrolls of the Laws of Mosses and the Commandments.

Only the Chief Priests can enter the Ark, and then only after special cleansing ceremonies. Such is the holiness of the Ark; any one touching dies because of their sacrilege.

The loss of the Ark shattered the nation: we had believed that it was the Ark that made us invincible. People asked: how could this be? Is our God dead? Has He deserted us?

I mentioned earlier that Moses laid great stress on cleanliness, which, in the desert, was very important. As part of this approach, he marked every male Jew sharing the Covenant by circumcising all boys shortly after birth. For us, the uncircumcised are an abomination: it is obviously unclean. We, however, bear our circumcision as a remembrance of whom we are, and we are clean for our women and ourselves.

Yet the uncircumcised Philistines were able to handle God's own Ark of the Covenant! They called upon their God, Dagon, to deride the Living God as impotent. They degraded the Ark, parading before it a huge phallus, smeared with the fat of unclean swine, and threw before it decapitated heads.

Israel was devastated. Yet the young priest Samuel rallied the nation.

Samuel showed the people that the reason for our defeat was our failure to honour God properly. He assembled the remains of the people and made a great sacrifice. Some protested. Indeed, some northern tribes were seriously considering going under the protection of the Philistines and worshipping their devil gods, Dagon, Molach and Ashtoreth, but Samuel held them together.

Samuel defiantly prophesied that the Philistines would rue their sacrilege and would beg us to take back the Ark. Whether people believed him or not, it kept them together in those terrible days after the rout at Ebenezer.

Then news began to filter out from Philistia. The Ark had first been taken to their great city of Ashod, not far from the Great Sea. When the Ark was placed in front of a statue of their god, Dagon, the next morning their god's image was found smashed to bits on the ground. Some, who lacked faith, thought that Israelite raiders had sabotaged the heathen statue, but this was very unlikely, for how would they have travelled all the way to Ashod in time? No, it was as Samuel had prophesied: God's revenge. Then a plague hit Ashod and, within weeks, carried off almost a quarter of their people. The Ark was sent to the city of Gath, the plague followed the Ark and almost a third of those inhabitants died. The Ark was next passed on to Ekron, much against the wishes of its people, and, sure enough, Ekron's plague was even more fatal: half the population of the city died.

The Philistines had had enough. They paid tribute to us for the first time ever – to take back the Ark.

Samuel gained considerable prestige and renewed the Israelites' faith in their priesthood and in the Living God.

Samuel was not yet finished with the Philistines. A year after the plague, the Philistines returned in a punitive attack. The Philistines' generals were excellent. They had trapped the Israelites and began to starve them out, and it was doubtful whether the army could have offered any serious resistance. That could have been the end of Israel.

The Philistines were encamped below the hills, in the Valley of Mizpeh. To get as close to the Israelites as possible, their main body lay along a dry riverbed that only has water in the winter.

Being the middle of summer, it was extremely hot. The Philistines thought themselves totally safe. They were confident that they had the Israelites in an iron trap: there was no way out other than a suicidal frontal attack or complete surrender into bondage. The situation was desperate.

Yet Samuel went down to the Philistines and, in the name of God, warned them that they would be destroyed if that did not obey him and retreat. He was laughed at and some of the demoralised Israelites complained that he was making matters worse by his rantings.

All appeared to be lost as the army realised they had less than a day's water left and not much more food. Yet, Samuel insisted upon making a sacrifice using what little food remained. The men, more in desperation than hope, went with him up to Mount Zion and sacrificed their precious supplies.

Suddenly, out of the harsh haze of the broiling sun, a small cloud appeared, and grew darker and darker. Samuel raised his rod high and prophesied the destruction of the Philistines.

Almost at once there was a miraculous thunderstorm. Roaring torrents hurtling down the mountainside. At first, the Israelites thought that this had merely solved their water shortage but, such was the storm, with lightning and thunderbolts, that waves of water were hurled down upon the Philistines encamped below.

Too late, the enemy realised their danger and thousands were drowned in the middle of summer – in the middle of summer! This was a miracle indeed. The Israelites, seeing the Philistine enemy being routed by God's storm, charged and added to the thousands of mourning Philistine women following the defeat at the Battle of Mizpeh. God did indeed fight for Israel.

It was the apogee of Samuel's priesthood. Virtually single-handed, he had held the nation together and, with the carnage at Mizpeh, had thrown back the Philistines. He ruled Israel for the next 30 years.

The Kingship

Samuel ruled Israel but complaints began to arise that Samuel's sons ruled Samuel. He had sent them to be priests and judges amongst the Tribes. However, instead of being shepherds of the people, Samuel's sons were said to be more like wolves.

My father, Jesse, was one of the Elders of Judah and was known for his closeness to Samuel. He began to find himself invited to meetings with other Elders to discuss how to check Samuel's rapacious sons. This was not a conspiracy against Samuel, who was still revered, but how to maintain respect for the priesthood. Yet the only bond that held the tribes together was their heritage in the Covenant. If the priesthood was diminished, our unity was undermined. The message was clear: only in unity could Israel survive and the best way to keep Israel together was for Israel to have a king. But how is a king chosen? It would need to have the approval of God – and this would have to be through the intercession of Samuel.

There were a number of possible candidates, but all these men belonged to especially rich families. It was feared that, instead of helping to bind the tribes together, there might be even greater competition amongst these powerful men.

The one name that began to surface, following the repulse of recent attacks by marauding Philistines and Amakelites, was Saul, a Benjaminite. He had earned a name for himself by being a very successful commander. He was tall and very handsome. He had shown he was willing to travel into other tribal areas to assist them if asked. His family was not rich, though long established, and his marriage to an Emphraimite woman, a niece of Samuel's, helped to spread his reputation. If, as some elders believed, Israel needed a king, then perhaps here was someone who had none of the disadvantages of the others.

There was a hurrying and a bustling. Great excitement was felt by all. I was not yet born, but later learned that my father was prominent in the subtle negotiations with Samuel.

Samuel was older than my father and had great presence. He had an enormous flowing white beard and kept his hair uncut because of his mother's vow. The effect was to give Samuel the appearance of being surrounded by a numen of shimmering light, half reflected in his streaming hair. However, his charisma lay in his eyes and voice.

His eyes were piercingly black. They seemed to have hold on people, penetrating their minds and souls. Yet, at other times, it was obvious that his eyes looked upon non-earthly things.

Samuel was a Priest and a Prophet; that is "He walked and spoke with God". When the prophecy was upon him we heard the mind of the Living God. This did not happen often, but any that were present when he was so inspired never forgot the experience. No one could ever doubt that Samuel was beloved of God.

At first Samuel was adamant; Israel had no need of a king. It had never had a king and there was no acknowledgement in the Covenant about a king. It was a foreign idea and custom. If the people had needed such an office, would not God have made Moses the nation's king?

What could my father say? He assured Samuel that no criticism of him was intended he said, "Sometimes, Rabbi, your sons have not shown the same wisdom as you have always demonstrated."

Samuel just sat and glowered, but my father noted that he was no longer protesting. Father continued, "Beloved Rabbi, Prophet of God and Leader of the Israel, consider what the Elders have put to you. Seek God's guidance, for we have every confidence that you, above all, will keep the unity of Israel before you. I am more than confident that the Elders would accept your choice of king."

Samuel refused to commit himself any further but agreed to "take the matter to God. If the Living God accedes to the people's request, and it is the wish of all the people, then the man would have to be chosen by God."

There was a long pause before the Prophet continued, "Yes, such a person would have to be God's anointed, as only God could choose one worthy enough to serve and to fulfil the Covenant."

Samuel now looked weary and tired. He seemed to drift off into either slumber or to another world. The interview was over. The lines had been drawn and my father knew that Israel would have a king. The questions now were: who should the king be and how would he be chosen?

The Choosing of Saul

As if to give urgency to the problem of choosing a King, two of the candidates, Jeph the Ephraimite and Josuah of Judah, were killed in battle. Saul, on the other hand, had effected a clever retreat against the Amalekites. He brought back the fallen, giving them proper funeral rites thus avoiding the barbarous defiling of the bodies.

Things went quiet until a very strange event which, even today, is not fully understood.

Saul's father, Nish, had lost a herd of sheep and ordered Saul to go and find them. Strangely, Nish told Saul not come back without them.

Saul and three companions went after the strays. Weeks passed as different sightings always found themselves arriving a day late. With hindsight, it seemed that Saul was being led beyond the land of the Benjaminites and into the land of the Ephraimites. In a village they were told that a man of God was waiting in the city of Shiloh. As Saul journeyed towards Shiloh, a messenger came from Samuel.

The servant said to him, "My master sends you greetings in the name of the Living God. Come no further, as that which you seek you will find in three days, near the hill of Shiloh."

Saul was taken aback, but there was another message for him. "My master said that God knows your heart, as does the Prophet of the Lord. You are to go alone to the hill but be totally clean. Therefore, do not lie with any women, fast, and be prepared for the sacrifice."

Whatever misgivings Saul had, he did as he was instructed. He arrived at Mount Shiloh and found a small gully and there his father's sheep were grazing peacefully.

Under the shadow of an out-jutting rock, however, he noticed smoke seemingly coming from inside the cliff face. Suddenly, he felt very cold and, for someone in his prime and who had never felt fear, he now had a sense of deep dread.

Peering from the bright sunlight into the shadow of the cliff, he could now see that the smoke was coming from a tall pyre of burning cedar trees. There stood a lone figure of a man. But what kind of a man? His very form seemed to blend into the swirling smoke. He was clad in the sacred ephod, pure white, whilst his eyes were wide open and his face upturned to the skies. The man's voice was so quiet that Saul thought he heard the words inside his own head.

"Thou art Saul, son of Nish the Benjaminite. That which you sought you have found. Come close to this altar if thou art prepared for the sacrifice. Beware, this is holy ground for the Living God has visited here," the man said.

Saul was overwhelmed and threw himself to the ground, saying, "Surely you must be Samuel, the Prophet of the Lord. I am not worthy to be in your presence."

Everything was still, even the breeze. Saul felt weak, not just because of his three-day fast, but he felt weak and helpless. This superb athlete, who had faced the stark trial of battle without flinching, now felt in the grip of a terrible controlling power.

"Rabbi, speak. Say what I should do," implored Saul.

129

The answering words seeped into his brain. "Pray unto the Lord. Make a sacrifice unto him. Come before his Prophet in full obedience."

Saul did not know whether Samuel had spoken or if the words came from elsewhere. This added to his fear. He felt a bottomless chill, despite it being mid-day with the sun at its highest.

He crawled towards the burning pyre. His limbs were weighted down with an exhaustion he had never known before. He moved forward as a man half-drowned might have dragged himself from the sea. He drew closer and could hear the roaring flames of the burning altar. But there was no heat!

Suddenly, Samuel was standing behind him and said, "Arise. Seek ye the Lord's Blessing." This time, there was no doubt; this was the voice of Samuel.

His utterances now had a deep but gentle cadence to them. "God will restore you. If you follow the Word of the Lord you shall prosper. Here upon your head I pour the oil of anointment and cry unto you and all Israel, 'here is the Lord's Anointed, the King of Israel'." Samuel's voice echoed around the small clough. But instead of dying away, the words become louder and louder as if some choir had replied in descant. Each echo rose in an ascending crescendo as the words reverberated amongst the hills.

Saul felt uplifted. His strength returned and, in an ecstasy of certainty, he knew he had been chosen. He had never felt so tall, so strong, so full of vibrant energy. His mind was clear, his thoughts raced, he knew he was possessed of the Spirit of the Lord. He stood without fear – the dread had fallen away from him. He saw what he had to do. He was part of the Covenant along with Isaac, Jacob, Moses, and Josuah. He was the chosen: the King of Israel to be.

"Rabbi ... master ... guide me in the ways of the Lord. I accept the anointment of the yoke of God."

Suddenly Saul felt that he too could prophesy. For the first time, he was able to look Samuel directly in the eye without flinching.

Samuel's gaze was steady but waiting, as if to say, "So?"

Saul raised his arms above his head, reached out to the heavens. "I, who am so unworthy, dedicate myself, my soul, my all, to Him. I prophesy that I shall lead and unite His people. I will serve and honour the Lord at all times. May my right hand lose its cunning if ever I stray from the Way of the Lord. Amen."

It was over. The fire burned low. It was now an ordinary day once again. Samuel began to explain what he wanted Saul to do. "So far, no one else knows of God's choice." He said this in a matter of fact way, explaining the situation as he might to a student of the Laws. "Take your sheep home, collect your companions and return to your father. I will call a meeting of the Elders of the Twelve tribes in Gigal." He could see Saul was surprised at the venue. "Yes, it is next to the land of the Philistines, but it is important for the people to know that you will be a warrior king: this is their wish. Frankly, I thought it too soon but, after much prayer, God has accepted their desire. You must prepare to lead Israel so that no uncircumcised will dare defile our land or be arrogant in the face of the Living God."

Saul was about to seek further advice, especially now Samuel seemed an ordinary mortal. He had so many questions.

But, with a slight, peremptory wave of his hand, Samuel said, "No more. Go. We shall have counsel later. But I command you: you must not tell anyone what has happened here or that you are the chosen one. When the time is ready, I will declare it."

Suddenly, Samuel seemed frail, as if his years had caught up with him. He nodded kindly to Saul. "Now go, my boy; go with God. You will be restored. You will not need to break your fast until the sun has gone down and you are reunited with your servants."

Saul turned to walk away then he spun around. Where had Samuel gone? Saul could not see or hear anything. He was alone.

Lord, what kind of man is this? he thought.

He again felt the chill of the unknown. He thought of calling out, but then thought better of it. Quietly, he said a prayer to himself. "Help me, oh Lord, to deserve thy trust. Help me, oh Lord, in my ignorance to know. Help. Help me, oh Lord."

With what was to come, one could already begin to feel sorry for him.

When Saul met his companions they sensed something different about him. His life-long friend, Eban, said, "Saul, what has happened? How ...?"

Saul cut his short. "Say nothing. You have seen nothing," he barked, but in such a way as they knew he had been close to God.

Not one of them dared tell him that, amidst his black hair, was now a white strip that had not been there that morning.

There was great excitement throughout Israel. The message had been quite explicit. Samuel's sons had visited every Tribe and told them to send the Elders, along with exactly one hundred of the best warriors, and to have supplies for three days. All must be ritually clean; that is, they must not have lain with a woman for three days. They must sacrifice before setting out and that they must fast for two days before meeting with God's prophet to hear His decision about the kingship.

Not a hint of whom would be chosen King. There was no doubt, however, that, whoever it was, Samuel, the Living God's representative, would anoint that man.

The venue of the meeting caused some surprise: Mount Zion was at the extreme of our land. Indeed, the nearest town, Jerusalem, was one of the very few still in the hands of the Jebuzites, one of the earlier settlers. There had been for many years an uneasy truce between them and us. They posed no threat but the town's citadel was impregnable and had withstood every effort to take it. It was a brilliant choice: heavy with symbolism as Jerusalem was at the very centre of all the roads of Israel.

Samuel, dressed in a magnificent pure white sacred ephod, came riding on a bedecked mule in a glorious procession. He did not travel direct but journeyed through the Tribal Lands before arriving at the great assembly of the Tribes of Israel. It was a magnificent cavalcade and Samuel's journey was an opportunity for him to show himself to the people. Indeed, it was a kind of coronation – only the Chief Priest of Israel did not need mere human affirmation of God's approval.

The delight and reverence of the people was unfeigned and it must have been very obvious to the future King the respect in which Samuel was held.

Saul was in a lather of anxiety and anticipation about the Assembly. He had not told his father of the anointing – nor anyone else. He had been very severe with his friend, Eban, emphasising that there had to be total secrecy. Even though, people could not help but notice his changed appearance.

Then, the summons came. One of the priests, a Zubulunite named Zacheus, slowly approached Saul. Zacheus was tall, thin, gaunt and unsmiling.

Full of his own self-importance, he spoke to Saul very formally. "Saul, son of Nish the Benjaminite, hear this: I, Zacheus, Priest and emissary of the most holy Chief Priest Samuel, am sent to give you this."

Zacheus handed a scroll to Saul. "Here, you will find your instructions, which you must obey to the letter."

Saul eyed him steadfastly, showing no emotion and no overt sign of the irritation that he must have felt with this strutting peacock.

"I, like all Israel, am ever ready to answer to the voice of the Prophet of God," Saul said evenly.

"And obey, Saul, son of Nish," Zacheus retorted.

With complete calm Saul said, "Obey Samuel ..." He paused, then continued, "... as the voice of the Living God. Who of Israel would not be honoured?"

Saul now looked the priest straight in the eye. "But Zacheus, you are not

He. You are but his messenger. Therefore, take care that you do not give offence by taking onto yourself powers that belong to the Prophet alone."

Before Zacheus could reply, Saul went on, "I have already met the Chief Priest of Israel. We have sacrificed together. He has prophesied for me. He has called me his son. I knew to await your coming."

As if to give further emphasis to his words, Saul strolled around the now disconcerted priest and tapped him gently on the shoulder with the scroll from Samuel. "This message is for me ... and for me alone!"

Then, suddenly, from being the stern warrior, Saul flashed him a charming smile. "Please, dear Zacheus, be seated. Be my guest and record how well you are received and welcomed. Later, recall to me your kindness in bringing me the Lord's message from Samuel so that I may be a friend to you in the days to come."

Zacheus probably realised he had gone too far, yet he also took the hint of future favours. So he bowed, smiled and sat at Saul's feet.

"Zacheus, you know what is in the scroll?" Saul asked.

"Yes, and I am to help prepare you for the Assembly." Gone now was the arrogance of the Priest, who guessed, though it was not yet completely certain, that Samuel's instructions could only mean one thing: this proud, superb figure of a man, whose voice already had the tenor of command, was going to be the King of Israel.

Saul read through the scroll; quickly at first, desperately seeking what he wanted to read: that all would now know he was the King elect. At first he did not find it and his heart froze. Was the old man playing with me? he thought. Then he read the scroll a second time, slowly, carefully, weighing up each word.

It read: "Saul, greeting from Samuel the Chief Priest of Israel. You are to come, after making sacrifice and making yourself ritually clean, to Mount Zion. You are to speak to nobody and must not arrive until the day after the Elders are assembled. My messenger will tell you where to stay. He will begin the preparations that I will complete when I present you to the people."

There it was: "when I present you to the people". What else could it mean but that Samuel was going to complete this mystery and that he was going to be announced as the King of Israel? Whatever was to happen, it was certainly no hole-in-the corner event. No, in front of the Elders and People of Israel he was going to be declared King.

He read on. "When you are told to come forth, do so humbly but be prepared to answer my call to the letter. Be prepared to prophesy so that all may know that you are who I say you shall be. Do what I shall instruct you. Go in God's name, Samuel."

What did this mean? Saul was a solider, not a priest. Was there nothing more? He looked up from the scroll.

In a very matter of fact voice, he said, "Right, Zacheus. It seems we are all going on a journey. But we shall set ourselves aside, for Samuel, our friend, has some special purpose for us. Let us make sure we do all that is required. Come, let me show to where you shall sleep and then I will explain to my father that I have other tasks to perform."

The interview was over. Saul's life was about to change beyond anything he could imagine. He was preparing for a journey to a kingly crown – and into history.

The Elders had arrived, accompanied by their Tribes' hundred great men. The tension was almost palpable. Abner the Benjaminite, the son of one of Israel's richest men, was an obvious candidate. Tall, handsome and rich, he spent a considerable amount of time going between the senior Elders, reminding them of his experience, old favours and his success in war. He certainly attracted much comment for he was a man of conspicuous talents. Though, perhaps, too obviously the politician, he sought to create alliances by inferred offers of influence. However, when anyone asked Abner when had he last seen Samuel, his calm, usually attentive face lost its blandness. With some irritation he had to answer that he had not spoken with Samuel for half a year. But he reminded his interrogator that neither had Kish or Jephra the Ephraimite. And, therefore, unless Samuel was going to deny the people their demand for a king, who but he, Kish or Jephra had such good credentials?

Kish, the Reubenite, was very blunt. "It's either me or Abner from Benjamin, because can anybody see Samuel electing either Jephra or Saul the Benjaminite, whose father, Nish, can hardly clothe his family properly?" At least Saul's name had been mentioned.

Samuel arrived in great pomp. Loud hosannas and hallelujahs were raised. "Hosanna in the highest. Hail, Samuel, Priest and Prophet of the Living God." But, instead of calling a council as expected, he retired into the tent provided for him to pray and fast.

Samuel called for my father, as our tribe's Chief Elder, Judah, was sick and, therefore, ritually unclean and could not come into Samuel's presence.

Samuel instructed my father formally. "Jesse bar Obed, Bethlehemite of Judah, go and call the Chief Elders so that we shall pray and make sacrifice together and talk one time more."

There was consternation. Did this mean that Samuel was going to refuse, or prevaricate, or perhaps ask their views as to which he should choose? Though this latter idea was hardly given much credit, as Samuel never asked advice of others.

Ziba of the Zebulinites, supported by Elders of the other Northerly tribes, was very forthright. "This cannot go on. We in the North are tired of the wars and tribulations that you in the South bring upon us." There was outcry at this, but he went on. "Brothers, hear me! We are agreed we need a king, but we must have a decision soon, because I have heard that the young men of Abner and Kish have begun to threaten each other. They have large following and if we are not careful this assembly of Israel could descend into faction."

That silenced everybody. The idea of a split between the Tribes was fearful. Not to have a king would guarantee – soon if not now – the gradual diaspora of the Tribes into separate and independent groups.

My father stood up. "Brothers! I, Jesse the Bethlehemite, although one of the least in Judah, today I speak for our people. I think we should have no more counsel but ask the Prophet to come and speak directly to us."

Here he showed great skill. "But, though I am second to none in my total trust in Samuel, beloved of God, I am with the party who knows that only with a king can Israel survive."

This was well received, as Jesse was seen as an honest intermediary.

In due course, Samuel was brought in on a litter. His showed great presence. His flowing, vibrant white hair, piecing eyes and immaculate ephod gown gave him enormous dignity. They set his litter down. He sat there, as if on a throne. There was utter silence.

He raised his staff; every Elder, even though they were Chief Elders, as one man, threw themselves upon the floor. He spoke quietly: this they had not expected, for some thought he would castigate them with his fearsome roar. Instead, he spoke quietly, almost in a conversational voice as if to each of them, though they did not like the message.

"Brothers," he breathed quietly. "Brothers, I come before you after communing with the Living God." After every phrase he halted.

"He has heard your request that you would have a king to rule over you. I am charged with asking, for the final time, do you know what you ask? If you make me choose a king, he will have power and dominion over you. A king will demand taxes and tribute from you, and extend the influence of his family over you." He paused to let this sink in.

"A king will expect you to give him your daughters in marriage, even though you do not wish to do this. A king will take from you the best of your sons for his army, his service, and his glory. A king will seek to retain power over you – for ever. 'Yes,' said the Lord, 'a king can be glorious but a king can also be a tyrant. Think well before you proceed further.'"

These were powerful arguments, but many thought that Israel already had all these disadvantages from the old man's sons, with none of the advantages. No one spoke.

Aaron, the Benjaminite, the father of Abner, was furious for he was sure that Samuel was trying to wriggle out of an implicit agreement that he strongly believed he had for his son. "Great Samuel, Prophet, we have heard your words. Give the Elders leave to speak alone and then answer you so that you can answer us in the name of the Lord."

Samuel looked at Aaron in the kindest way. "Aye, I will leave you, and you, good Aaron, think first upon the Lord's Covenant and his people Israel. When you have debated amongst yourselves I shall return."

With that he left the tent.

Almost before the tent flap closed behind Samuel and his departing sons, there was uproar. Above the shouting was Rueben the Reubenite, the grandfather of Kish. "You fool! He has outwitted you. How can your Abner be even considered a candidate with such a fool as a father?"

Aaron's hand flew to his dagger and there could have been bloodshed if other Elders had not wrestled him to the ground. It was an incredible sight. There are no young Chief Elders, many indeed were very elderly, but here they were jostling and fighting like a party of unruly schoolboys.

My father, Jesse, walked up to the litter seat of Samuel. He stood upon it and drew out from behind the chair a horn, with which he blew three sharp blasts.

The struggling group of old men came to order and looked at him in both irritation and expectation.

"Brothers," my father whispered. He had learned much from Samuel, speaking quietly, almost too quietly so they had to be still to hear what was being said.

"Brothers, we have talked much. We have talked long. We know the arguments. I propose that there is no more talk, no more argument, because, if we cannot agree today, we shall never agree. Therefore, let us vote: 'Yes', to have a king chosen by the Lord's Prophet; or 'No', to remain as we are. But if only three tribes say 'no', they shall accept the majority. But if four tribes say 'no', then Israel shall have no king and we shall return to our homes with no further argument. Whatever the result, I suggest we ask brother Aaron of Benjamin and brother Rueben of Rueben to go and tell our decision to Samuel."

Joad of Asher cried out, "Yea, Jesse the Judean, you have it! Let each Elder draw lots to give his voice in order."

This was a very good move because it meant that no one could claim precedence over the others. Quickly, they cast their rings into a bowl from which the order of drawing out went to Joad.

The first ring was that of the Tribe of Gad. The Elder said, "Yes, for a king for Israel."

The second was that of the Tribe of Naphatali. "Yes, for a king of Israel."

Then, the ring of Rueben was drawn. The Chief Elder of the Ruebenites stood forward. He looked around and paused. Would he break ranks? Would he, fearing Abner's election, try to stop a king being chosen if he thought it would not be a Reubenite king?

"I, Rueben the Chief Elder of Rueben, affirm ..." He took a deep breath. "Yea, for a king of Israel." An audible sigh went around.

Joad pulled out another ring, and called, "Of Benjamin. What says Aaron for the Tribe of Benjamin?"

This was the crucial vote. Aaron did not appear to pause. "Believing in God's Covenant, believing in the unity of His people, I say ... Yea, to a king for Israel."

There were cheers, which grew louder when Aaron walked over to Rueben and took his hand. They embraced. The die was now cast. As each subsequent ring was drawn, each Chief elder confirmed the unanimous vote: "Yea, for a king for Israel."

There was silence. Each man knew that they had set the nation upon a new course, yet none knew where it would lead. My father signalled to Aaron and Rueben, and they walked together to bring back Samuel.

Within a few minutes, he had returned. He had that ability to appear before people as a terrible manifestation – as if God Himself would speak the next moment. At other times, he could lay his greatness down and speak gently as the most kindly grandfather.

He responded in the latter mood. "Chief Elders of Israel, you have chosen! You should know that I had doubts, but ..." He paused, smiled and went on '... have I ever been anything to you but a Father?' said your Living God? 'Have I ever wanted anything less than your fulfilment of My Covenant?' Thus said your God!"

He then spoke with such authority. "'I will set up amongst you a king over all Israel, whom you must obey. I will anoint him with My holy Covenant. He whosoever follows in My footsteps, I will be his God and he my king. I will use him to fulfil My Covenant with My people. But should he err from My ways, he will become a rod for the people. I will spurn him and deliver him into the hands of his enemies. I will scatter his seed amongst the gentiles, and he and his kind shall no longer be king in Israel.'"

What a burden and a curse! thought many an Elder: the threat of being spurned by God and their seed cut off for ever! Samuel paused to let the enormity of the warning sink in. The King of Israel would rule, but with an enormous threat over him.

Samuel went on. "'Pray therefore that your king attends My words and My way.'"

Samuel was silent. His hand still raised but then said in his conversational voice, "Now my brothers let us go and find him who you would have as King of Israel."

He turned on his heel and walked out, followed by stunned Chief Elders who heard the voice of the warriors raised in welcoming shouts. They were about to learn whom God wished to anoint their King.

Saul, accompanied only by the Priest Zacheus, had quietly left the main party of the Benjaminites, as dusk was closing in.

This was Zacheus's great moment. He proclaimed, "Come this way. The Prophet Samuel has arranged for you to prepare yourself. I found this cave, which has marks from the early people upon its walls. Locals from Jerusalem fear the power of the paintings and never come here." He hurried ahead, anxious neither to be seen nor to attract attention. He stumbled, fell with a shout and muttered an oath.

"Zacheus," said Saul. "Stop, stay, less noise, less haste. You will alert every sentry in Israel. Let us go gently and if anyone notices, they will think we are off to relieve ourselves. So, steady – otherwise, in your rush you are bound to attract attention."

Zacheus appreciated the sense in what Saul had said. He stood, regained his balance and quickly brushed himself down. He was anxious not to lose the little light left to find his way to the cave. His heart gave a wrench at the thought of not finding the opening, which was partly concealed so that, if one did not know it was there, it would be very easy to miss it.

Zacheus said in a worried tone, "All right, but we must not miss the place. I fear what Samuel might do, as he was very exact about what must happen."

The two men moved on. They were now but moving shades in the darkening gloom. The small rocks lying around made it not easy.

Saul saw that there was a level area of about 60 yards before the side of the mountain began to form a pillar of rock clawing into the sky. A small V-shaped plateau lay ahead and was covered in small shrubs, which made walking difficult, but it also told the experienced solider that water could not be far away.

By now, stars were beginning to be seen in the evening sky. The walls of the mountain began to close into an inky darkness.

Zacheus began to mutter, "Oh, dear God. Oh, dear God!"

Saul was irritated, for whether or not he was afraid of Samuel, to show such fear was cowardice and typical of priests. "Zacheus," Saul whispered. "A little less 'taking in vain'."

"We're not going to find it, Saul," said the increasingly panicky Zacheus. "You won't be ready. It will all go wrong. I don't know. Samuel may cancel!"

This made Saul think very hard. He issued a sharp word of command. "Stop. I said stop! Now tell me, where is this cave?"

Zacheus tried to expostulate, but Saul curtly stopped him. "No, don't try to show me. Describe where is it. Of course we can't see it, you fool! But if you're in the right place we can work it out."

What Saul meant finally got through to Zacheus. "Ah, yes – I see what you mean. Yes, of course. This is the right spot. If we go to the edge of the cliff face, the cave is cut back at an angle. The opening is actually facing up the cut towards' the mountain. That's why it can not be seen from lower down."

Within twenty minutes of reaching the cliff face they squeezed behind a bush growing close the cliff face. There, was an opening, barely a yard wide. They had found it.

Zacheus said, excitedly, "Yes! Yes! I knew I could find it. Here it is!"

They both went inside. It was pitch black. After a long, thin tunnel, hardly two yards high, it opened up into a cave, whose height could only be guessed. It was as if God had thrust a monstrous spear into the side of the cliff.

In the tunnel part of the cave, the air had seemed stale but here there was a sense of movement and the air was much, much cooler.

"I put it here – I know I did," said Zacheus, crawling on the ground, looking for something.

Saul stood still and waited. A gasp from Zacheus told Saul that, whatever he had been looking for, he had now found it.

He heard a flint being struck, saw a spark or two and then the torch, which had been hidden earlier by Zacheus, spluttered into light.

At first Saul was dazzled. He could not make out what was around him except the feeling that the cavern was vast, far wider than might be expected from the narrow opening. As Saul gradually became accustomed to the light, he saw the lank features of Zacheus in the flickering light.

The priest's eyes were wide with excitement. "This is where we prepare you and then await the coming of Samuel!"

He went on to explain that Saul must ritually cleanse himself and, apart from water, fast. He must purify and bathe himself. He should throw away any clothing and dress only in a new lioncloth, and don the sacred ephod that had been made ready for his coming.

Before beginning the preparations, Saul looked with amazement at the walls. They were covered with images, the like of which he had never seen before.

Of course, we are forbidden to have graven images, so we seldom see what others call pictures. At first Saul could not make out the stark lines slashed onto the flat rock face in blues, greens, reds and yellows. Then he understood it was a hunting party. Despite his lack of familiarity at looking at such things, he could see that there was a kind of rhythm and a fearful beauty in the images. The pictures told a story. He turned to take the torch from Zacheus and walked along the ancient images. He could see a group of men, assisted by dogs, confronting a lion, a bear, and a monster he could not recognise.

The images gave him a graphic feel of the chase. One man had been too bold and had been caught by the claws of a beast. Another was being gored into the ground by a huge bull-like creature and the red, red streams coming from the man's wounds reminded Saul of the thrill and fear of both chase and war.

He began to feel their power and the hairs on his neck began to rise. "Are you sure the Prophet of God wishes us to remain here, Zacheus? Is this not a place of demons, of unhallowed spirits – whose very walls mock the Commandments of Moses?"

Zacheus smiled grimly. "Yes, Saul who would be King." Saul took a sharp breath. There it was – out in the open!

Zacheus continued, "This is indeed a terrible place for we who follow the Lord. But, in the service of God and His Prophet, we must brave many things."

The word "brave" on the lips of Zacheus, inferring that he, Saul, was somehow less brave, caused Saul's gore to rise and he answered harshly, "Priest, anything you may dare I may dare ten – aye, a hundred times. Yes, I well know that, in the service of the Living God, I must be willing to face many things that ordinary men need not consider. If necessary, I may need to set aside the Laws of Moses if it were in the service of the people. But these images are from an ancient time, by people who knew not the Living God. They tell of bravery" said Saul, pointing towards a figure advancing with a spear against a bear "... and cowardice," indicating another figure running away from the following beast. "Come. No more. Let us rid ourselves of these images that frighten small minds and let us prepare for tomorrow."

Zacheus showed Saul a pool that lay at the far side of the cavern. Its water was sweet tasting but icy cold. "You are to bathe," instructed Zacheus, who was then embarrassed as Saul stripped off all his clothes and entered the pool. It was so deep that he had to swim.

I should explain that we Jews have difficulty about looking at the human body. It comes from the Book of Leviticus, where Moses explains who it is clean and rightful to lie with. There is much talk of nakedness, which we tend to avoid. Soldiers, of course, live so close together they cannot help but see each other. Both as boys and as men, if we find a river we usually all bathe together with no shame. Some devout men, however, still wear their loincloth whilst bathing. Though it is often a cause for laughter when a particularly modest swimmer's manhood slips out from under his loincloth.

Some priests seem particularly concerned with nakedness and one suspects that they have an unhealthy obsession. They will remind you that when Father Adam was tempted by Mother Eve and God came to them, they were "ashamed" because they were naked. When God asked them how they knew they were naked, they had to confess they had disobeyed and had eaten of the Forbidden Fruit. Priests will argue that their nakedness was an affront to God. But surely, God's wrath was because of their disobedience, not that they were aware of their bodies.

I think we have misunderstood Moses' instructions because the body is beautiful. It is God's creation. More so, we are created in the image of God. How therefore can the human body be ugly? Surely, only by misusing the body or doing ugly and profane things with our bodies, can this be wrong.

Some priests maintain that, as God to drove Adam and Eve out from the Garden because of man's sexuality, this was the "fall", and, thus, sexuality is evil. Surely it was their disobedience that was the crime? Yet, as God knew all, it was all part of His plan for humankind. There would be little to gain if Adam and Eve had stayed in the Garden for ever. Furthermore, our bodies were formed and made ready by God to people the world. How could any part of God's creation be basically bad? It is how we use those attributes – of mind, of spirit and of the body – that mar the plan that God has for us. But Zacheus, being a priest who attended the altars, would have little experience of seeing men together and probably forgot his boyhood days. He was to have a sharp reminder.

Saul arose out of the pool and shook himself like some great dog. The water flew making patterns of light amidst the torch flames. He was exhilarated by the change of temperature caused by the water upon his body. He was excited by the venue and, now, by the feeling of the drying air, which against the chill of the water seemed warm.

He had a magnificent physique: taller than most by a good head. His muscled body reflected the light and the flowing water made patterns down his hairy chest and legs. He took the towel offered by Zacheus, who had turned his head away.

"What's the matter, Priest? Are you not like other men?" Saul laughed, his humour fully restored. He dressed in a new loincloth and slipped over his head the square ephod, from which his burly arms were half-sleeved.

Around the edges of the white ephod were woven beautiful patterns of blue, gold and red thread. It was the most beautiful thing he had ever worn. He looked superb – even Zacheus could not help but admire him as he saw that he was every inch a king.

With real respect in his voice for the first time, Zacheus asked, "Is Saul, the Chosen of the Lord, ready for the prayers? I have the holy water, which we shall drink. We will fast together and await the summons of Samuel, the Prophet of God, who will come at first light. So, watch and pray, Saul, son of Nish, and I will watch with you."

Typical of the man, Saul forgot his irritation and stretched out his hand to Zacheus, who gladly and humbly took it. Saul, the soldier and leader, had gained another adherent.

Samuel commanded that the Horns of the Lord should be blown.

It was barely morning and the sky still had its dark mauve sheen of night upon it. Samuel came out from his tent robed in a splendid ephod and was surrounded by other priests swinging bowls of fragrant incense.

Samuel led the Song of Moses:

"Thou Art Holy oh Lord of Israel, Harken to Thy People, remember Thy Covenant and let Thy Chosen People be Joyful."

The priests took up the refrain and, then, all around into a wondrous controlled choir. Each man sang quietly, but each in his part felt held by the whole. The Song of Moses, rhythmically and in step, swelled above the host, as words and incense rose to God.

Samuel set out at a remarkable pace. People wondered where he was going. Leaving the camp, he began to ascend a steep track toward the cliff face of the mountain. He did not seem to falter or hesitate, despite his white hair. People remembered later the look on his face: ecstasy – he saw nothing but what was in his inner eye. He was communing with God and had the energy of eagles. Even the Chosen Hundreds of the Tribes felt a little breathless.

He came to a plateau and motioned the following crowd to form a half circle around him as he went closer to the rock face, stopping about a hundred yards away. He singled for all to kneel, which they immediately did as one man.

His voice carried clear and strong above their heads as he prayed for them and all Israel. "Oh, Lord of Hosts! Thy People seek Your Word. The Chief Elders are before You. They seek Your Blessing. Hosanna! Hosanna! Blessed be the Name of the Living God!"

Those around answered again in a terrible unison that went to the heart of each man as all felt starkly exposed to God. "Hosanna! Hosanna! Blessed be the Name of the Living God!"

The sun began to break out above the edge of the Mountain. The light grew and seemed to suffuse them all. As Samuel's hands were raised, the sunlight struck the edge of his rod.

He cried out in a voice that no human could use. "'People of Israel, would you choose a King?'" This was God speaking. All froze.

The silence gripped each man's mind and they heard Samuel's reply to the words but in a voice that was now his. "Oh, Lord of Hosts! God of Gods! Truly as Thou livest, Thy People seek Your Word. They would have You choose them a King."

With his rod held high, it caught the light and made a circle above their heads. It seemed to fill the rapidly lightening sky emerging between the cliff sides of the mountain.

Again That Voice. "'Samuel, my Prophet. Choose you a king above all Israel. Anoint him with holy oils in My name: that he may follow My path for ever.'"

The silence that followed was like an echo in each man's soul. Neither Abner nor Kish now considered or wanted this terrible burden. Not one man amongst all the greatest of Israel now wanted to feel the warmth of the holy oil upon them. Truly, all knew that such a yoke would destroy any but the chosen of God.

Out of the stillness, they heard Samuel call in a thin human cry, "Come forth, You who are Chosen."

His arm stretched out towards the rock face and they began to look in the direction he was pointing.

His voice became stronger and stronger as he repeated the cry, "Come forth, You who are Chosen."

And then, in a sound of command that no mortal could have ignored, he cried, "Chosen of God to be King of Israel, come forth. I call you in the Name of the Lord of Hosts. Saul!"

As the name was issued, no one had time to think what this meant because, a hundred yards away, a solitary man appeared. Slowly, almost stiffly, he turned towards the kneeling people. Had he appeared from out of the air? People could not believe their eyes. Had he emerged from out of the living rock face, from out of the ground?

The figure moved sluggishly towards them. He was a very tall, well built

143

man, dressed in a sacred ephod and clad only in sandals. Despite his strength, for all could see he was a powerful man, he walked as if in chains – as if his limbs were held in weights that would crush him.

Not a word had been said. Like a tableau, Samuel stood upright. His priestly staff aimed in a straight line at the advancing man's heart. The people knelt in wonder and amazement.

Now fifty yards away, they could see the Chosen One's face. His eyes were stark open, but they saw nothing. His irises were pinpricks. He neither looked left nor right. He didn't blink or move his face.

Then, in a piercing scream, he cried, "What is it that You would have of me, oh God? What is it You demand of me, People of Israel? Help me, oh Living God. Aid me, Samuel, Prophet of the Lord."

Saul appeared to be wrestled to the ground as he struggled with powers round him.

Samuel answered, "Saul, thou art called by me as God's chosen of Israel. Today thou hast no Tribe but Israel. Today thou hast no father but God's Prophet."

Saul half rose to his feet. His head was pounding, his eyes gyrating, his tongue protruding. He frothed blood and spittle. He lurched upwards. He felt on fire and the light span around his head. He tore off the sacred ephod, bearing his body to all. He reached out pitifully in a gesture of surrender and help, and began to prophesy. He fell to the ground in a writhing mass of limbs and words that tumbled over themselves as if in some great struggle and argument.

"My God. Prophet. The Dark One. Spirit. My soul's on fire!" could be distinguished amongst his wild babbling flow.

This lasted – how long? No one could be sure. For a moment – a life time?

Suddenly, with an echoing, piercing cry, "My God! Help me!"

He ended with the scream of a soul in desperate torment.

Then ... stillness.

Samuel moved forward towards the now still form upon the ground. Many a heart wondered whether the chosen of God would ever rise again.

Samuel moved gently, with a tenderness of a maiden, stretched out his hand and, in a sweet voice that whispered in the ear of all around, said, "Saul, God has heard your cry. God has heard your prophecy. You are forgiven and you are the Chosen one for Israel. Now arise! Come! We will sing unto the Lord a cheerful song and rejoice in God's anointed."

Saul slowly rose as the people answered the great refrain:

"Sing Unto the Lord a Cheerful Song, Let us Rejoice in God's Anointed."

As the singing slowly died away, Saul knew this was his moment. There was an expectant hush as the Elders pushed forward respectfully to hear the first words of their new King.

"I am Saul, son of Nish. Once of the tribe of Benjamin but now I know only Israel."

His voice was now firm, clear and carried far. There was no hesitation; all the doubts had gone. He turned to Samuel who was watching him intently.

Raising his arms in supplication he spoke so all could hear. "Samuel, Prophet of God, you have laid a heavy burden upon me. I accept. With your guidance and" pointing dramatically to the warrior Hundreds standing beyond the clustering Elders, "... with the help of my Brothers, we will preserve Israel. I will seek to be worthy of the Living God's choice and lead His people in unity. I call upon the Chief Elders to give me their counsel, but most of all I seek your steady hand, Prophet of God and High Priest of Israel."

There was loud applause; no one had ever been called High Priest before. Here was an innovation and they liked what they heard. The Hundreds appreciated being called his brother and the Chief Elders welcomed being asked for their counsel.

Saul had not taken his eyes from the face of Samuel. He stood impassively, his eyes half-lidded as if in he was in meditation or his thoughts were elsewhere. Saul looked for some signal, some indication, of even greater commitment from the Prophet. Saul suddenly fell to his knees and bowed low, giving unquestioned homage.

"Samuel! Samuel! The Lord called you to be His Prophet. You answered His call. The people call you to be their High Priest. You answer their call. Anointed by you, I am the Chosen of God. I call upon you to be my guide but, most of all, my Father. Answer my call."

Saul now bowed to the ground. What a tribute – to be asked to be another man's father.

Some took up the cry, "Samuel, Father of the Lord's Anointed."

Samuel was one of the oldest present but was filled with vitality. His whole body seemed like a burnished spear.

In his most prophetic voice he spoke. "I hear your call and I shall be thy Father."

Then, in a sublime gesture that each man recalled from his barmitzvah on becoming part of the congregation of Israel, Samuel gave the kneeling Saul the benediction of the Father to the Son.

Laying his hands upon his head, he recited the words of acknowledgement, of adoption, "Thou art my beloved son in whom I am well pleased."

He then raised Saul up and embraced him as a Father, enfolding him in his arms. It was deeply moving.

Samuel, gently releasing Saul, stretched out his hand to indicate to Eli, his son, to carry over a bundle wrapped in a pure white cloth.

Everyone's attention was fixed as Samuel slowly unwound the covering and revealed a superb bronze helmet. Around it was a wonderful filigree of soft woven gold. There was a gasp – such a wonder! Samuel held aloft the engirded helmet and placed it on the head of Saul.

"Saul, anointed of God, wear His helmet. Follow always in His ways."

The throng answered with a great cry, but then stilled again at a gesture from Samuel.

His motioned his second son, Ephraim, who also carried a long white wrapped bundle. Undoing the fastenings, Samuel drew out a wonderfully burnished iron sword, worthy of the Pharaoh himself. Who could make such a marvellous weapon? Sharpened on both sides to a fierce point, the handle and hilt were bound in gold.

"Saul, King of Israel, the Lord's anointed, take His sword. Fight only in His name. Defend His people."

Saul took the weapon, his eyes ablaze with excitement. He was soldier enough to appreciate that here was a marvellous, wondrous weapon. He held it aloft, saluted all around and offered it to Samuel, who blessed it.

"Father Samuel, for God's helmet I thank you. For God's sword I am in homage. I pray that it will always cut a sway through the people's enemies."

Samuel acknowledged the salute and Saul knew he had to complete the coronation.

He turned to address the throng. All hearing him recognised the voice of authority, of command, of a man who knew he was to be obeyed.

"Chosen by God, anointed by the Lord's Prophet, I am to lead Israel against the uncircumcised – the unclean – who would mock the Living God by their temerity to invade the lands of Israel."

Saul, although already tall, seemed to grow in stature. He seemed to lean over the assembled Elders and spoke directly to the Hundreds, the fighting men of the tribes.

"I appeal, I doubt not in vain, to you, the Hundreds of the Tribes, to join with me to repel the invaders and avenge our God."

A wild cry and whoop was heard, as the Tribes' Hundreds raised their war cries.

Then Saul went amongst the Tribes. First to the Chief Elder of the Ephraimites. Taking his right hand in his double clasp, the Chief Elder knelt in homage and repeated, "I, Mishra, swear loyalty and homage to

Saul, the Lord's anointed, King of Israel for all the Ephraimites."

Saul, wearing the helmet, held his sword aloft and saluted each Chief Elder and the Elders in turn, and said, "I welcome the fealty of the Tribe of Ephraim of the people of Israel in the name of God."

This was repeated with each of the tribes.

The moment was nearly over; the people were replete with the emotion and excitement of the day. The sun was high. Soon must come the feast and they would return home to tell their people of the marvels they had seen: of their new king, Saul, and the wonder of Samuel.

Saul realised there needed to be a proper end, and called out, "I would speak with the Chiefs of the Hundreds."

This was intriguing. What did Saul mean, another innovation? It was assumed that he wanted the leading solider from each of the tribes.

He acknowledged them as they came forward and they saluted him. "I choose you as my Captains of the Tribes. You shall wait upon me and we shall together decide what the Army of Israel will do."

This was very pleasing, and many a heart beat faster. In effect, it was a declaration of war. But against whom? This did not matter in the excitement and surge of enthusiasm at the idea of all the tribes contributing to an Army in unity of purpose.

Saul walked towards Abner, his fellow Benjaminite, and, taking him by the arm, went over to towards Kish of Rueben.

Saul spoke in a conversational voice but he knew he was being listened to intently by the other Captains. "Abner, Kish, you have great reputations as warriors. Abner, you are known for your sagacity and cunning in war. I heard how at the battle of the Valley of Edon you surrounded the Philistines, even though they had more men then you." Abner smiled with pleasure and looked Saul straight in the eye. Saul continued. "Yes, strong arms are essential but good thinking and intelligence even more so."

Saul turned to Kish. "Your bravery and daring are a by word."

Kish simply beamed, puffed himself up and said, "Abner's 'intelligence' is all very well but unless you get close to the foe you don't kill many." Kish was a big man, fleshy, and something of a bully – though brave – but only someone with his conceit and stupidity might think he would ever be chosen as king.

Saul smiled and did not enter into the tacit invitation to choose between them. A point Abner noted and admired.

"Whatever, my friends," said Saul, "when the Army of Israel goes forward we need to go in three columns and I want you two to be my army leaders."

Both men were pleased with the compliment.

Kish was very excited. "Yes, my King – just say the word."

Saul nodded, smiled at him and said, "You are my general of the Eastern arm." Kish's face broke into a delighted acceptance.

Saul turned to the other. "And you Abner?" Abner was not as tall as Saul was, and younger, but belonged to a more exalted family having rich estates.

He mused awhile before answering. "That is an interesting proposal and you seem to have thought about it. Do you see Israel dividing its forces to attack either the Philistines or the Endomites?"

"Abner," said Saul very directly, "I made you an offer. Do you accept?"

Abner smiled, holding Saul's glance, "My King, we have all sworn to obey the Lord's Anointed. How can I refuse? I await your orders."

Saul was very satisfied and with a gesture that gained him such following, his face filled with smiles, his eyes shone and he spontaneously hugged both men in turn.

Laughing like a schoolboy, he said, "Abner, Kish – Generals of the East and Western arms – we are going to have fun."

The coronation was over. Each group of Elders and their men gathered together for a feast before preparing to return home. Saul quickly went round the Captains and arranged their next meeting.

While all this was happening, Samuel had gone off into one of his reveries. He awoke, and called Saul to him. He invited him to his tent so that they might eat together.

Saul followed Samuel into the cool tent, which was very welcome after the heat and the emotion. He suddenly felt exhausted.

Samuel gave instructions and indicated that Saul should sit and await the food and wine. Neither man spoke. Saul waited, wondering about so many things. He welcomed the silence. He too let his thought drift and felt that he would need to learn patience from this remarkable man.

He quietly looked at the relaxed Samuel, who now sat like any aged Elder. He seemed much frailer than he appeared when standing as High Priest.

He smiled to himself: High Priest.

As if Samuel could read his mind, the old man spoke. "Saul, you did very well." His voice was pleasant and relaxed. "Thank you for your first appointment, High Priest. It has a good sound. However, I am not sure that I needed any more acknowledgements. But I accept."

A servant came in with the food and wine and then men fell silent again. They began to eat. Saul realised he was famished and ate rapidly and took great gulps of wine.

He said with real feeling, "This meat is marvellous. I have never enjoyed the sacrificial food before. The wine, too, is superb."

Samuel laughed. "It is something, King Saul, that you will quickly become accustomed to. By the way, I thought your handling of Abner and Kish quite excellent. Kish, of course, is a rash fool, but no threat because no one but he and his rich relatives takes him seriously. Abner – now, he's a very different sort of fish. He really is very able but he has accepted the role of third man in the Kingdom."

Saul thought: third man – what did he mean?

"Yes, Abner is very able. Some might have thought he would be first choice?" Saul said, inquiringly.

Samuel paused before answering. "You want to know why I chose you?" He could see Saul's acknowledgement. "It is a reasonable question and I suppose you deserve to know."

He took a deep breath and spoke almost sadly. "The new king will have much to do. I cannot be everywhere. You might not believe this now, but at times the people of Israel can be very stupid. So stupid that you too may despair and wonder why God should ever choose such stiff-necked, cantankerous folk. He did, and patience, guile, as well as all your military courage, will be needed."

He went on. "Yes, Abner was a real contender. But he would have been too independent and would have aroused far more opposition than you will."

He saw Saul's look of surprise. "Oh yes, my boy! There will be opposition! You may not have any real enemies yet. You may not intend to hurt anyone and therefore feel you don't deserve their enmity, but your success will be enough for others to envy you. Therefore, they will become your enemy."

Saul was about to say something but thought better of it. Samuel went on. "You have made a good start and, providing you follow my lead ..." Here was the real message. Now Saul understood about Abner being the third man in Israel: he, Saul, was the second and, obviously, Samuel still considered himself the first.

"... you won't have too much trouble from the others. Only if you follow and we keep the people together will the triumphs you are dreaming of be accomplished. What do you think?"

He fixed Saul with a stare. Saul took a deep breath and said, "I follow you in every way. I have said you are my Father. I will obey like a son." He then paused and asked, "But what about the army? Do you want to command the army?"

Samuel smiled. "No, no, my boy. That is your province. What I will decide is when, where and against whom you are to use the army. Of course, I will seek your views, but you have much to learn." Then, inquiringly, added, "Well, haven't you?"

Saul nodded. "Aye, much to learn." He closed his inner eyes and said, "Tell me, when, where and against whom – for I am your man." It was the first half-lie between them.

"Good!" said Samuel, rising. The first meeting of the High Priest of Israel with his King and General was over. Now Saul's task had really begun.

Saul wanted to know more, but he knew he had enough to do and would need all of Samuel's help to do it. And later? Well, Samuel was an old man ... that could wait.

Chapter Seven

Saul's Triumph

The Battle of Jabesh Gilead

After the anointing, Saul called together the Hundreds of the Twelve Tribes. They chose ten warriors to be their Captains. Thus, there were a hundred and twenty Captains who went to meet with Abner, Kish and Saul.

It was clear that Saul sought to establish his rule on as broad a front as possible and appeared happy to involve his erstwhile rivals. So Abner commanded the west wing of the Army, Kish the east whilst the King would direct the centre.

From the beginning, Saul showed that he saw the kingship as being in trust for the house of Saul. He appointed his eldest son, Jonathan, then just eighteen, as his deputy commander. This might have seemed too quick a promotion but Jonathan was known as a fine solider, having already been a successful company leader. Moreover, he had the charm of his Father and reflected the very best in this remarkable man. Although Jonathan was young, his appointment was well received, especially by the younger warriors, who saw that merit, not dead men's shoes, could lead to promotion.

Saul took great pains to consult Samuel and made sure everyone knew this. The Prophet was happy to leave military matters to Saul but made it plain that he would have the final say on any political issues.

One problem facing Israel was that, unlike the Philistines, whose weapons were all iron, we did not yet have sufficient iron-making capacity. This was one of a number of disadvantages that Saul had inherited.

He was very frank. He told the Captains and Samuel that the only mistake worse than underestimating your enemy was to overestimate one's own power. Therefore, by examining our weaknesses, we could overcome them.

The second problem was that the "Army of Israel" was a thing in name only. Whilst the tribes would come together for a particular battle, there had been no structure of command. Saul hoped that by making Captains responsible for their own tribes, they could also be Captains for all of Israel, learning to both give and obey orders from himself and his generals.

Again, he made it clear that he hoped to make other generals, beside Abner and Kish, who would eventually command regiments consisting of ten or more Hundreds.

Finally, battle tactics. Our warriors were as brave as anyone, but we fought as if each battle was a single duel between two men or, at most, a troop. We did not fight as a whole. The Philistines, however, who Saul sought first to emulate and then to surpass, practised war by regular manoeuvres. This was one reason why he later agreed that Jonathan spend some months with the Philistines, ostensibly as an ambassador, but really to try to get to know more about their methods.

Saul made great play on the strength of our men, as hill people. We were accustomed to travelling over difficult terrain quickly and he sought to maintain this speed of movement by having training competitions of men, fully equipped to travel six or seven miles in an hour.

This was faster than the Philistines could go in our territory, even though they had horses and chariots. Saul saw that when they left their plains, their cavalry slowed them down. He estimated that, at their quickest, the Philistines' army could barely manage three miles an hour.

The value of these preparations were quickly seen when Kish took five Hundreds from his tribe and, without consulting Saul, had gone raiding upon the Philistines. He had attacked the town of Gath and, after the initial success, our troops had begun to plunder, allowing the Philistines to re-form. Led by their king's son, Achish (whom you have already met), the Philistine warriors were regrouped and virtually surrounded the disorganised Ruebenites, who suffered great slaughter. Achish personally slew the brave but foolhardy Kish. The defeat hardly seemed an auspicious start for Saul's reign.

Saul, however, grasped the opportunity that Kish's death gave him. He decreed, on pain of death, no one without his express approval would initiate war. He emphasised that the Army of Israel would fight the battles of the people of Israel. It was appreciated that each tribe could now depend upon the whole of Israel for its defence. However, some did not like the "on pain of death" decree as they were unaccustomed to such authority.

There was great excitement when it became known that Samuel and Saul were to seek God's advice upon where the new Army of Israel should fight. The time for drilling was over: for only in war, the ultimate arbiter, could the army prove itself.

The question was where?

Samuel would have preferred to advance against the Philistines. Saul, however, convinced him they were still too strong to attack, though he was confident that the Army could resist any Philistine incursions.

The debate was eventually decided by a very fortunate accident.

The Ammonites, to the east, bordering the River Jordan, unexpectedly had raided our people in Jabesh Gilead. This was the opportunity Saul wanted. He could reassert our claim to the River Jordan by crossing into the land of Ammon, and demonstrate the strength and unity of Israel.

Saul divided the army into three. Abner crossed the Jordan over a northern ford while Jonathan took a southern route to create a dual flanking movement. Saul would lead his army directly into the land of Ammon, hoping to draw upon himself the bulk of the enemy forces.

Samuel, despite his age, had travelled with the Army and had officiated at the sacrifices the day before the force divided. He reminded them that they were God's chosen; that, as their forefathers had found, if they obeyed the word of the Lord, they would continue to receive God's blessing.

Samuel called them his children. He was superb. His voice reached every man. None had any doubt that the Lord was with the Army of Israel and that they were being personally spoken to by the Prophet.

Saul's tactics proved to be brilliant.

The Ammonites had no idea that Abner was to the north and Jonathan to the south of them. Saul, with great fanfares, had ensured that the Ammonite army knew of Saul's attack and they disputed the ground directly in front of him.

The King of the Ammonites, Nahash, fell into the trap: he advanced to attack what he thought was the main army of Israel.

Saul advanced two miles over the Jordan and then built a defensive wall of trees. Twenty thousand men worked with a will to build the encampment.

The Ammonite hoard must have numbered more than 60,000. On seeing us, they came forward in a furious wild charge.

Saul, tallest of all the men of Israel, was magnificent. He wore his kingly helmet of bronze and gold, so that the enemy could see him and so he could also be an inspiration to his men.

The warriors of Israel stood shoulder to shoulder, as they had learned to do. They resisted the assault and boldly fought for almost an hour.

Saul had to rally his men because, with the sheer weight of numbers, our line was beginning to buckle. Part of the line was pushed from the barricade, but this became an obstacle to the Ammonites, who had to clamber over their own dead.

Then, suddenly, the Ammonites heard a sound that sent fear and confusion amongst them. The battle horns of a new Israelite army to their north. As Abner's men came charging forward, King Nahash tried to get his men to face around. He took his personal bodyguard, who were acting as a reserve, to face the new threat. At first, he felt relieved because he saw that the attacking force was not as large as he had feared and, initially, his men were holding the new threat.

He urged them on, crying out, "The battle is nearly won. The dogs are fleeing over the Jordan. Hold, brothers. Hold and the day is ours."

Then, total destruction appeared as Jonathan's wing came up at their rear, outflanking their line. This meant the Israelite warriors were attacking enemies who were already occupied fighting men in front and to the side of them.

Jonathan was magnificent and led the charge aiming at the centre of King Nahash's bodyguard. He slew King Nahash himself. Jonathan charged over the fallen body, knowing better than to stop to take booty and short-lived gains. Keeping up the momentum, the men of Israel slew – and slew – and slew.

The battle of Jabesh Gilead was becoming a rout as the enemy realised that their King Nahash had been killed by Jonathan. Their cry went up, "King Nahash is dead!"

This was followed by that most dreadful event on a battlefield: that strange moment when an army becomes nothing but thousands of individual panicstricken men. The Ammonite army became a fleeing mob.

There were more than 30,000 slain and 10,000 captives, who would be taken into bondage. Saul advanced into Ammon and took thousands of women and children into bondage, and many of our men took concubines, which gave the women a little protection. About the fate of others less fortunate ... it is better not to speak.

At the battle of Jabesh Gilead, Saul continued the tradition of the "count". He collected the foreskins of the dead foe as a sacrifice to be burned on the altars to God. After the battle, the scribes let it be known that more than 32,000 foreskins had been offered up to God as a thanksgiving for Saul's great victory.

This pleased Samuel as it emphasised the religious aspect of the war, seen in the destruction of the uncircumcised idolaters.

Saul was splendid in victory. At first, he refused to accept the salutations of the Army. He called the Captains of the three armies together, along with the Generals, Abner and Jonathan, and Saul saluted all of them.

Both Abner and Jonathan bowed the knee to Saul and proclaimed "Saul,

King of the Jews. Hosanna to the Victor, beloved of God. Saul, slayer of thousands, destroyer of the enemies of Israel. Hallelujah! Hallelujah to the King!"

This roused the men into paroxysms of adulation. They cheered and cheered Saul to the heavens. The men of Ammon would never be a threat to Israel again.

The army had acquitted itself well and Saul was able to judge the Captains and created new Senior Captains and new Generals. There were decorations for valour with silver and golden chains.

He was, however, very keen to show that General Abner was second in the kingdom by insisting on serving Abner at the feast.

His personal daring in battle and his impressive ability to control his wing of the army also strengthened Jonathan's position. Furthermore, he helped his father, the King, to serve the Captains, which aroused great enthusiasm.

Strategically, Saul had achieved much by his victory at Jabesh Gilead. He had effectively obliterated any threat from the east. He could now concentrate against the most formidable foes: the Amalekites to the south and the Philistines in the east. His plans were developed accordingly.

To bind himself further as King of all Israel, Saul decided to extend the number of his wives, taking women from the tribes of Rueben, Judah and Gad. This extended his kinship and, after the battle, no one begrudged him taking his pick of the new concubines.

Saul strengthened his role as judge and, though confirming the Elders in their role as judges, he insisted that they did so as his lieutenants. More importantly, he encouraged the use of scribes so that decisions only had force if they were written down and carried the royal seal.

There was a rumour that Samuel did not entirely approve of these developments. Saul said his measures were to assist the priests who were so heavily burdened that sometimes people had to wait long for a judgement. However, Saul did not attempt to interfere with the priesthood acting as judges in cases that required adjudication of religious law. However, many found it easier to approach a scribe or Elder for judgement, rather than seek a decision from the priests.

Whatever Saul seemed to touch was successful. He was wise and fair in judgement. He held the Tribes together and showed none favour, emphasising that the King had, "No Tribe but that of Israel".

He was readily and easily available to all and the land of Israel prospered. It was said that he burned the midnight oil, toiling for the people of Israel.

Saul enjoyed the boast that, "Though I am King of Israel, I am the servant of Israel."

He even solved the problem that Samuel had first hinted at when admonishing Israel for wanting a king. That a king would take their own from them inform of tribute or taxes.

The people already paid a tenth of their harvest to the priesthood. He got Samuel to agree that two parts would go to pay for the King's expenses. As Saul was more successful, and with greater security there was less banditry and incursions from external enemies. The people felt more prosperous, so the Elders agreed that a further five parts would be granted to the King. Though, of course, these fifteen parts were only bearable while ever the people prospered. The question would arise in difficult times about the number of parts that should be given to the service of God and the King.

Saul astonished many by sending Jonathan under truce to visit the Philistines. Saul's reasoning was simple: he recognised that they had the best weapons, that their cities were impregnable to us and he was not too proud to learn.

What was surprising was that the Philistines were willing to accept a visit from Jonathan. In part, it was a tribute to Saul's achievements. They were willing to treat with Israel in a way they had never done before. In another part, it also reflected an age long debate in Philistia, which had echoes in Israel. Whether or not they would live in an alliance with their neighbours or in perpetual war, and seek to eradicate or at least neutralise bordering peoples.

Jonathan found much to admire and abhor amongst the Philistines. He was wise enough to share what he admired, and kept his own counsel about what he disliked.

He was interested in their military training, their tactics and anything he thought would improve our fighting ability. To lessen his conspicuousness, he adopted the Philistine tradition of shaving. He continued this on returning to Israel and it became a fashion amongst his immediate guard and young captains.

This was quite shocking to some of the Elders, including Saul, who, though not forbidding it, called it womanish. Some saw this as a badge of the "Prince's Party" and inadvertently it began to damage his relationship between him and his father. But, at the time, Jonathan did not appreciate this.

Samuel, whose beard was legendary, refused to condemn. Some suggested that Samuel was secretly pleased that there was a mild division between King and Prince.

Saul sought alliance rather than conquest as the most secure way forward for Israel and made allies whenever he could. This was directly in opposition to the priesthood. They feared that Israel would lose its separateness and, as in the days of the exodus, it would be in danger of being absorbed by other peoples and then worship other Gods. This was also Samuel's great anxiety.

Samuel was also concerned about diluting the purity of the priestly function. On two occasions, Saul had gone into a trance and had prophesied, which suggested that the role of King and Prophet were closer than anyone had considered before. Saul's friends made the logical link: if God chose the King, might he not also endow him with some prophetic powers? At the time it seemed but a slight adjustment in the balance between King and Prophet. Few thought it would grow into a serious rivalry.

The peace between the Philistines and us, of course, could not last. Samuel urged Saul to make the borders of Judah more secure by advancing to the west, especially as a plague had done great damage to the Philistines and there was conflict between some of their Kings for the High Kingship.

Saul reluctantly agreed. None the less, God seemed to be aiding us with the pestilence they had suffered and the internal division that had erupted – a disunited people can never be victorious. Saul accepted the argument that this was Israel's opportunity.

He decided upon a major raid to test our new tactics. He gave Jonathan the command and he was very successful, besieging and destroying the town Geba. Saul was so pleased he sent trumpets throughout Israel telling them that he, Saul, had destroyed Geba. This was the first victory of Israel over a fortified Philistine town.

Further to show his pride in the success of Israel's Army, he built an altar to God and dedicated it himself. Regrettably, he had forgotten that Moses had lain down expressly that this was the role of the priesthood. Heated words followed between Samuel and Saul, with Samuel making it quite clear he had exceeded his authority. For many people, however, they could not help but see that they had never been so prosperous. Their army was successful, so they were happy with Saul. Nevertheless, the hidden rift between King and Prophet was disturbing to the people, who still revered the Prophet as the Father of the Nation.

Samuel called a meeting of the Elders and, to their surprise, asked them whether he had ever been anything but a good shepherd. He reminded them that of the source of Israel's success was not him – nor Saul – but God. Samuel's desperate search for reassurance was readily given. However, it evoked great sadness amongst those who heard it. Here was the Prophet of God, who had been such a tower of strength, showing such fragility.

The Elders recognised Samuel's legitimate concerns and tried to mollify him. However, Samuel's overt weakness was counterproductive because he had unintentionally reinforced Saul's power. It seemed that Samuel's great years were beginning to bear him down. Many in their hearts turned closer to Saul as the rising sun and began to distance themselves from the Prophet's loosening grip on power.

Jonathan and Elim

The war between the Philistines and us had recommenced because, despite the after-effects of the plague, Saul's incursion had one very unfortunate impact: he had inadvertently provided them with an external challenge around which the peoples of Philistia could unite. Their Kings agreed to bring together all their powers and attack us.

Saul heard of their plans and divided the army into three. On this occasion, though, he kept the large bulk of the troops with himself in the centre.

He encamped in the area around Michmash, halfway up into the mountain area. He ordered Abner and Jonathan to take defensive mountain positions on two nearby mountains and await developments. He hoped that the Philistines would divide their army accordingly and then, with the speed of our troops, converge on one of their wings and use our local superiority to destroy it.

It did not work out that way. The Philistine army was so enormous that it spread over three valleys. Saul was concerned because he had not thought that they could assemble all their fighting men. He had thought that the divisions created in electing their High King would reduce their ability to unite. The consequence was that it was we who were on the defensive. In effect, we were surrounded and cut off from each other.

Saul had tried to get messages to Abner and Jonathan. On each occasion, however, the Philistines saw the scouts and derisively returned their heads to Saul's camp.

Well away from the centre of Saul's story, Aaron, Eli, Josh and I, as young warriors, were utilised either for messenger or guard duties. We found ourselves responsible for rounding up our livestock and then herding them into the mountains along with the women and children. This was very demoralising because it hardly suggested that Saul was confident of the outcome.

Samuel was asked to come urgently and give the army God's message and to prepare the men for battle. Never had Israel needed effective prayer more.

There is still some dispute about what happened. Some say that Samuel refused to go saying that he was too ill. Others that he admonished Saul's messengers saying that their master had led Israel into a trap and God had turned his back on him.

It was all rumour, but it disheartened everyone because whatever the truth, this was a terrible indictment that God was not with Israel.

Saul was furious. He told his generals to tell the men that Samuel was ill but that he was praying for God to help us. Some commanders worried whether this was taking God's name in vain. As for Abner and Jonathan, they had heard nothing from the King; nor could they communicate with each other.

The situation was beginning to become desperate.

Abner was totally immobilised. Saul, however, showed nothing but outward confidence, telling the men that the longer the Philistines stayed where they were, the weaker they would become. He was waiting for a sign for the right time to strike. He was magnificent. The men did not know about the rift between him and the Prophet, so their morale was still quite high.

Jonathan, however, understood all. He appreciated that the longer the stand-off lasted, it would be against the Israelite situation, which would worsen. Supplies were easier for the enemy but, more important, they had enough men to hold and contain two wings of our army and turn the remainder against our centre. In discussing the situation with his captains, he said that it was only a matter of time before the Philistine kings realised just how great an advantage they had.

Jonathan was convinced that it was only the rivalry between the kings competing for the High Kingship that had stopped them seeing just how weak we were. He was sure this could not last much longer. This gave him his brilliant idea of turning the suspicion between the Kings to Israel's advantage.

He proposed a desperate plan, which was so breathtaking that it just might work.

He asked for volunteers to undertake night raids against the two Philistine armies camped on either side of their mountain. Elim, Jonathan's closest friend and armour bearer, immediately claimed the "right to be by your side, my Prince".

Elim, tall but slender, whilst only nineteen, was a veteran of many fights at Jonathan's side. His example ensured that every one of Jonathan's captains volunteered.

The plan was simple: whilst seeking to kill as many of the sleeping enemy as possible, his main aim was to find and slay the city kings in the hope of exploiting the recent rivalries in electing a High King.

Jonathan would not risk a night attack with his whole army. He doubted whether this could be successful and, in the dark, friend might injure friend rather than foe. They would go, therefore, two by two in total silence and, when possible, kill the sentries and any sleeping men. If they were discovered, they were to pretend to be Philistines and tell them that they belonged to another king. The captains were very enthusiastic. Asser caused tremendous amusement when he asked for help with his beard, as he was the only captain whom had not followed Jonathan and become clean-shaven. So, with much joking and laughter, Jonathan's 50 captains all wanted to help poor Asser to get rid of his beard.

Night fell. After posting sentries, Jonathan led his desperate band down the hillside. For the last 50 yards they crept on their stomachs taking only their knives –they left their swords behind as would have made too much noise. As Jonathan grimly told them, he expected they would find swords enough to complete their work.

Jonathan, with Elim ten yards away, was the model for everyone else.

Because they each knew their comrades were there and they knew what to look for, they could just dimly see each other: it was important that they stayed in touch. They were a net of widespread marauders, sweeping through the Philistine battle lines. Crucially, Jonathan had told them that he wanted no casualties for the Philistines to discover in the morning and hence find out that it was an Israelite raid. So, if someone was wounded, they had to return because whatever happened they must not leave behind any evidence that it was an Israelite incursion.

They stole quietly into the Philistine lines. An occasional gurgling noise might be heard, like a bird, as Jonathan and his men crept up behind an unsuspecting guard and cut his throat. They then got to work on the sleeping men, using a heavy cloth to suppress any cries of agony.

This went on throughout the night. Occasionally, some of the captains were not always successful in being undetected and had to pretend they were Philistine warriors who had become lost looking for the latrines.

The few Philistines who were awake did not suspect them. Why should they? Why should the Philistines have been on their guard for pairs of lightly armed Israelites wandering about the camp? It just did not cross their minds that their enemies would dare a night-time incursion: that was the beauty of Jonathan's plan.

The task of moving around and silently killing the slumbering

Philistines was the job for the captains, but Jonathan and Elim had a special mission.

Jonathan, you will remember, had spent time amongst the Philistines and he decided to walk openly around the camp asking the way to the different kings' tents, pretending he had messages. On being told where the sleeping kings were, they were accompanied to a king's tent. These were easily distinguishable, even in the dark, because of the standard fixed outside. Jonathan and Elim would turn upon their erstwhile escorts. Then, carefully entering the tents, they slew the sleeping king and any of his companions. They did this safely on five occasions, though, on the last attack, Jonathan received a slight wound.

Jonathan kept careful watch on the night sky, waiting for the first hint of the dawn. After three hours of their bloody work, he asked Elim to imitate a nightjar – the signal for the others to withdraw.

Jonathan and Elim quietly returned back through the sleeping Philistine lines. Weary, exhausted and reeking of blood, they thankfully staggered back into their mountain retreat.

When they re-assembled, the sight that met their eyes was marvellous, yet horrible. All the 50 captains all had returned bathed in blood, but for eight of them it was with their own vital juices, as they had been wounded in fights before silencing their adversaries. All the injured had been brought back by their partners, obeying Jonathan's strict orders to leave no evidence for the Philistines. Three of the wounded died later that morning.

The captains looked ghastly. They had been effective: between them they slaughtered more than a thousand of the enemy. Whilst Jonathan and Elim had accounted for five city kings, one of whom was Gazara of Eskalon, a major claimant for the High Kingship. This death was especially important as Jonathan hoped that when Gazara was found, they would believe it was a revenge killing by Gazara's rivals.

Despite the limited water reserves, Jonathan ordered them all to wash and get some sleep, because he planned to return to the other valley the next night.

As the day began to dawn, Jonathan – and Elim, who refused to leave him – did not obey his own order. They crept down close to the awakening Philistine army and were very pleased by the extraordinary sounds that came from below.

There were shouts, the noise of men running around, cries of amazement and anger. Some Philistine warriors could be seen arming themselves as if for battle and then running around in confusion.

Jonathan smiled with grim satisfaction, "Elim, my brother, I think we are seeing the writhings of a snake with his head chopped off."

During the day, Saul's lookouts also noticed the movement amongst the Philistines.

Saul brought the men to battle stations because he thought the Philistines might be preparing to attack but, throughout the day, though there was considerable activity below, they showed no hostile advance against the Israelites. Saul pondered as to what this could mean.

Jonathan, who had finally got some sleep, heard from his scouts about the confusion in the valley below. Jonathan brought the remaining 42 captains together and asked them were they willing to repeat the night attack in the eastern valley – but perhaps stay less long this time, lest they risk breaking their good luck. Without hesitation, all volunteered, such was their metal and their confidence in Jonathan's leadership.

The Philistines were much more alert. Jonathan noticed that there were numerous campfires, still very bright, in the northern valley, but less so in the west to where the attack was now directed.

What Jonathan and his men did not know was that Saul had taken a decision that he would attack next morning, because, whilst he did not know what had happened, he suspected that there was some confusion amongst the Philistines. Saul reasoned that the Philistines would not expect him to make the first move, so he hoped to have surprise on his side for an attack early on the morrow.

He meditated on how he could boost his men's fighting spirit. He fervently wished that Samuel were present, because no one could pray and inspire the troops as he. So he decided that, if the Prophet could not come to him, he would have to be the Prophet.

He let the men have their midday meal and cunningly ordered extra portions, which, after the recent half-rations, the men accepted eagerly. Then, late in the evening, he called the men to him.

He had worked out good systems of communication. He would speak and every twenty yards or so a captain was stationed who would then repeat the King's word. This was then passed on to the next captain, so that the King's message could spread quickly among the host. The men maintained the strictest silence. This could be very disturbing to the enemy: to be faced with a silent foe.

Saul put on his best kingly gown and, in his gold helmet, he looked every inch a monarch.

His powerful voice began to cry out. Though the men furthest away could not hear him directly and had to rely on their captains, they could nevertheless see him and take pride in his magnificent presence. What they heard was inspiring.

"Men of Israel – brothers – I, your King, have a message from God." The men murmured. Had Samuel arrived?

Saul continued. "Samuel has sent his greetings and I, as the Lords anointed, have a vision."

The men wondered what this could be. Was Saul going to prophesy?

"As God told Abraham to prepare a sacrifice – yea, even his own son – to show his obedience to the Living God, I call upon you for such a sacrifice."

He waited till his words had travelled and could see their effect. There was an excited hubbub; they were expectant, but fearful. Was there to be a human sacrifice? This happened with some of the infidels and uncircumcised, but it had not been the custom of Israel since before Moses' time.

"Early tomorrow we shall smite the foe. God wants us to sweep the valley clean of their blasphemous arrogance, to scatter the dirt and stink of the uncircumcised. Therefore, to demonstrate our confidence in our God, like Abraham we must place our absolute trust in Him and His anointed. Though we are to advance against the enemy, we will fast totally from today until tomorrow nightfall. This will show that we have complete confidence in His aid to destroy His enemies."

There was amazement. Normally, if there was to be a battle, men ate and drank well, not weaken themselves with fasting. But the idea was novel and – yes – they could see the logic. God would be on their side because of their devotion. They began to cheer Saul the King. He was very satisfied.

He held his hand for silence. "Men of Israel! Brothers! Fellow warriors! Such is our confidence, I declare that any that break the fast will have broken their covenant with God, and will be cast out from the people. Such fast-breakers will be an abomination and will merit death."

Everyone was completely spellbound. Here was prophecy indeed.

"Hear the word of the Lord. Hear the word of your King. We fast for God until tomorrow nightfall. In the morrow's day, filled by His food of faith, we will have the strength of eagles and slay our enemies. Hallelujah! Hallelujah!"

The men were exhilarated and cheered him to the echo.

Saul sent scouts to both Abner and Jonathan, telling them of his plans: that they were to fast also but be prepared to support Saul's attack when they saw him move. The scout reached Abner safely and, when they heard the joyful shouts from Saul's army, they too became enthusiastic. Unfortunately, the messenger to Jonathan was caught and killed by Philistine lookouts. This time the enemy wisely decided not to let Saul know that his message was unsuccessful and carted off the messenger's body back through their lines.

Though Jonathan's men heard the noise from Saul's army, no one thought to tell the sleeping Jonathan. Neither did anyone seek to discover what it might mean.

As it came close to midnight, Jonathan, Elim and his companions again went out to wreak havoc amongst the Philistines.

As they had expected, they were more sentries about and they had to be more careful, but the plan worked well.

Jonathan and Elim went boldly to find where the different kings were tented. They found two kings early and quickly despatched the escort. They went into the tents and slew the sleeping kings and the men around them.

Jonathan came across a small group of guards who were sitting around a campfire and asked where King Issicah, the second major candidate for the High Kingship, might lie. At first, the men were suspicious. Where had they come from?

"From Achish, son of the King of Gath, who had a message for his cousin," proclaimed Jonathan, confidently.

This reassured the men somewhat. One said, "There's been some talk about a vendetta against King Issicah because of the death of King Gazara. Our King would not stoop so low. I told one of his captains that there must have been an Israelite raid, and it was their fault if they could not guard their king properly."

Jonathan gravely agreed, but could not shake off four of the men who insisted they would escort Jonathan and Elim to King Issicah.

Here was the crisis: if they could slay Issicah, after Gazara, Jonathan was confident that few Philistines would doubt that this was a revenge killing. Therefore, though he and Elm were outnumbered, he decided that, having the advantage of surprise, it was worth the risk.

They had walked about twenty yards and out of the glare of the fire. Jonathan silently drew his knife, put his arm around his guard in a friendly way and said quietly, "Now Elim."

As he said this, he plunged his knife into the side of the Philistine. As the victim sank to the floor, Jonathan plunged the reeking blade into the other guard's side.

Elim threw his arm around the man on his outside and cut his throat, but remaining warrior saw and, quick as a flash, slashed across the undefended head of Elim, who sank to the floor without a sound. Then the Philistine had made his fatal mistake: instead of calling out or attacking Jonathan, who was encumbered by his second victim, he turned to finish Elim off. Too late: Jonathan threw himself at the man, one hand over the Philistine's mouth while the other hand stabbed upwards into his chest.

They fell rolling to the ground. All that could be heard were the choking sounds of the grappling men as the Philistine's body curled up in death throws.

Jonathan made sure that all four Philistines were silent before turning to Elim.

He whispered, "Elim. Elim, my brother. How goes it with you?"

Elim still lay upon the ground and answered, "Give me a moment, my Prince. Help me to stem the flow of blood because I can't see. But, as you know, my head is hard and the fool struck me there."

Jonathan was almost overcome by the bravery of his friend. Elim's hand went to his head wound and found half his scalp cut from his head. But Elim was right: it was bloody but it should not be mortal.

Jonathan tore part of his shirt to make a bandage and stem the flow. He was for returning to the camp there and then, but Elim, who understood as well as Jonathan the prize that was so close by, refused.

"My Prince, give me a few moments to recover and then let's finish this business. Then I'll sound the nightjar signal."

Jonathan knew he was right and waited patiently until Elim rose. Elim then opened the tent flap for Jonathan to enter and do his bloody work.

Jonathan calculated that two hours had elapsed. He thought that, with Issicah dead after Gazara, the confusion they had created should be enough. Far better now to withdraw undetected than garner a few more hundred Philistines by staying longer.

Elim gave out his call. It was softly answered and slowly they returned. They had to be more careful to avoid alerting the guards but as they passed they accounted for the occasional sleeping Philistine.

They returned to their camp. Jonathan had to carry Elim the last half-mile because he was so weak from the loss of blood. Despite his exertions, Jonathan was fired with concern and love for Elim, and drove himself almost beyond human endurance.

When he and Elim re-joined the captains, it was less joyful. Eleven men were seriously wounded and, though all had returned, like Jonathan and Elim, each partner had brought his friend home. In the short term, some were despondent that they had accounted for far less than a thousand of their foes.

Jonathan could sense their disappointment. "Brothers," he said, "we are not mere foot soldiers. We have struck a terrible blow against the enemy. Tomorrow, when he wakes, he will find another of the claimants to the High Kingship dead. Only Nanez of the three claimants still remains. I foretell – not prophesy because I'm no priest..." They all laughed – priests were not popular with Jonathan's friends "... I foretell that they will begin to turn their swords against each other. Or at least, their confederacy will break up or be scattered because they will no longer trust each other."

He stood and embraced each and every one. Kissing farewell the five brave captains who would not see the dawn, he urged the rest to sleep for tomorrow they would learn just how successful they had been.

Jonathan stayed with Elim all night, refusing to let anyone else minister to his needs. In the early morning he was exhausted.

Jonathan did not need to go to spy on the Philistines in the valley: the noise they made was tremendous and anyone could see that there was total confusion in the Philistine armies.

The Battle of Michmash

In the camp of the Philistines, with so many kings dead, there was no one to take control. King Nanez of Eskalon, the last major candidate, was desperate not to appear to be taking advantage of the deaths of his rivals. Though an able man who saw what was needed, he feared that, if he tried to take command, at best he would not be obeyed, at worst there might be conflict amongst them.

The Philistine army had become paralysed.

Saul from his outposts realised that, for whatever reason, there was confusion and disarray in the ranks below.

He called his generals and captains to him. "I have seen the hand of God sow dissension amongst our enemies. I have heard the voice of God declare, 'Go down and fall upon the Philistines. I have delivered them into your hands.'"

The men were ecstatic. They cheered him as he went forward like the glorious King he was.

He drew his sword and cried, "The Lord of Hosts is with us. Follow for Israel; for God; and for your King!"

He turned and led the charge down the hill.

No man with a heart could have resisted such a call and the whole army followed and overtook him, crashing into the disordered Philistine below.

Neither Saul nor his men had any idea why there was such disorder before them. It did not matter, for it was obvious that God had created panic amongst His enemies. The Philistines fought back half-heartedly and suddenly began to melt away so quickly that it became a race. The Israelites tried to reach and kill the fleeing men, who had become a rabble as the would-be-victims fled.

Abner had heard the turmoil in the enemy ranks, appreciated what was happening and led the headlong charge down the mountainside, plunging into the flank of the discomforted Philistines.

Jonathan was awakened by his men and, seeing the other two armies of Israel attacking, cried out his war cry, "For the God of Israel and Saul, His anointed!" Despite his exertions of the last two nights, he was in the vanguard of the attack.

The Philistines in front of Jonathan's charge were confused, though some held their ground. It was at the pockets of resistance that Jonathan led his charge. To his amazement, he found Elim running at his side.

No time for a long greeting, but Jonathan's eyes gleamed with pride at the bravery of his friend. "Guard my back, Elim – over there."

Jonathan, with renewed spirit, moved his company towards a cluster of a few well-ordered bands of Philistines.

It was Achish, son of the King of Gath, whose men were resolutely fighting a rear guard action. Jonathan formed up his men and headed straight for Achish himself. The two princes came out ahead of their men and their swords clashed as they hewed at each other in a deadly duel.

A spear was thrown over the shoulder of Achish, which would have pierced Jonathan, but Elim, who saw what was happening, parried it. But the spear tore through his buckler and wounded him in the side. He fell to his knees but the press of men created a mêlée where no one knew friend from foe.

Jonathan had taken a gash on his arm from Achish though he, too, had given him an injury in reply. Then, like the way a wind on a mountaintop sometimes whisks away the mist, Achish's men saw that they were alone as all their support had fled. They began to weaken. Jonathan urged one more charge and, even before his men had time to react, the enemy in front broke and tried to make for safety.

Jonathan could see that his part of the battle was won. He now turned to help Elim, who was even paler than before.

Everywhere, as far as the eye could see, were desperate men racing for their lives. No longer warriors, but runners. Suddenly, this vast host became a mob pursued by the Israelites, who slew everyone before them creating a terrible carnage.

The battle of Michmash was over: the Philistines had gone. Saul was acclaimed a "Great King" and the men set up an altar to God in their celebration.

Saul did not know what he owed to Jonathan. Though he knew and had the foresight to realise that, whatever had caused the Philistines' disarray, like the great solider he was, he did not ask why but took his advantage when he saw it.

He had angry thoughts about Samuel, but "who needed Samuel?" he asked himself.

He was the victor of Michmash. He was the Lord's anointed. When deserted, betrayed by the priests, he had the inspiration and invention to do God's work. This was a mighty sign. In his secret heart, Saul yearned for the assurance that God was with him. He longed to be like Samuel and the Prophets of old: to hear the unmistakable voice of God.

Whilst there had been no voice and there had been no vision, he exalted in the fact that he had the intelligence to do what was necessary. Surely, turning undoubted defeat into glorious triumph was the sign he had been long waiting for. He felt so grateful, so humbled by God's grace. This was a new anointing, direct from God – not a politically derived, calculated decision by the "Old Man", the Prophet who would control all. No, such deliverance could only be the hand of God. Nothing could take this from him. He could banish all his doubts and uncertainties.

Michmash showed the world that he was truly the Chosen of God.

Chapter Eight

Corrosion

The Oath Breakers

S aul went around his cheering host, glorying in their approbation. His whole demeanour showed that now he felt truly King of Israel. He was the Slayer of God's enemies, the Lord's anointed and the beloved of God, whom he was convinced had fought for him. All could see that he was God's instrument.

This was his greatest moment of his life. He thought this was truly the first day of his kingship.

Abner came to him and bowed low. "Oh Great King, the Lord's anointed, has there ever been a greater scourge of God's enemies? Greater art thou even than Joshua."

The men took up the cry, "King Saul, greater than Joshua. Hosanna! Hosanna!"

The "count" was announced: 25,000 foreskins.

"Not as many as the Ammonites," laughed the King, "because the Philistines run faster." A joke that the now weary men of Israel enjoyed.

Abner saw the elated mood of Saul. Who knows whether what happened next was Abner's fault? He continued to praise Saul excessively, perceptively sensing something of Saul's over-elated feelings.

"Great King. To you God declared His voice. For you He moved His hand amongst the uncircumcised. This day God has re-anointed you. This day shows that you are beloved of God. Only to you and God does Israel owe its salvation. Hosanna! Hosanna to Saul, the Lord's anointed and Great King of all Israel."

The men cheered till they could cheer no more. In a calmer moment Saul would have realised that Abner had gone too far, but Saul could not contain his pride.

Then – disaster!

The moment came which, at the very heart of King Saul's great triumph, began his decline and eventual downfall.

"Aye, Abner, my general. God has shown through me that He cares for His people. I, His King, am His instrument. Those who doubted are an abomination. Did I not say that the fast of faith would inspire our right arms and that God would scatter our enemies?"

He was full of the excitement of the moment. If only he had turned or paused a little he would have seen Jonathan approaching, aiding his friend Elim, using a spear as a crutch. Wounded, weak and weary, they consumed a little bread to fuel them in their struggle to attend the celebrations. But Saul was blinded by the enormity of his pride and did not see his loyal and valiant warriors.

Saul went on, "Tonight, to fulfil my vow, after the fast is over we shall have a great feast. We shall build us an altar of thanksgiving to our God that, by the covenant I made with Him being fulfilled, we have triumphed."

Too late! He had reminded the men about the fast and there was Jonathan brushing the crumbs from his mouth before saluting his father.

"Hail, King, my Father," cried Jonathan with delight and joy on his face.

Saul cut him short with a dreadful roar.

"Dog! How dare you approach me with no shame that you have broken my covenant with God?"

Jonathan was totally confused by this unexpected riposte. He tried to discover what had angered his father, but to no avail.

Saul's face was contorted with anger. "I promised God and He promised me that, if Israel showed a faith as great as Abraham and trust Him, I would be His instrument of destruction."

There was great consternation. When Jonathan realised what their crime was, he humbly asked for forgiveness. He explained that neither he nor his men knew of Saul's orders, which, if he had known, would have been immediately obeyed.

"Great King, my Father. All men can see from all around that you have been God's instrument. We were yours to follow and obey."

Turning around the anxious generals, captains and men who could hear, Jonathan said, "Doubt not this my brothers, that after God, this day belongs to the King – my Father."

This caused some relaxation of the tension.

Saul looked as if he would be mollified until Abner asked, "Saul, my King. Of course, Jonathan, your son, may not have known of your decree, but God did! Is it not dangerous that the King's word can be flouted with impunity? Can we be sure that God would forgive? Pardon in your royal mercy, Great King, your son, Prince Jonathan."

Abner pointed to Elim. "But, what about him? He also broke your covenant. Let him be an example – a sacrifice – lest God and men think that there is no power in the King's word."

Saul was not pleased with this intervention because he was beginning to calm down.

Jonathan fell into the trap set by Abner. "Great King, my Father, Elim was with me. Pardon me: pardon Elim – condemn Elim: condemn me. We meant no disrespect. Banish us for a month from your sight so that all men may know and see your justice and wisdom."

If only Jonathan had been allowed the last word, all might have been well – but Elim intervened. "Sir King, I have these wounds in your service. What Abner suggests is unjust. We knew nothing of your decree. How could we? But, King Saul, you should know what feats your son did in your name. You should know how it was that the enemy was beaten. If you knew how much Prince Jonathan had been God's instrument in giving you your victory, you would never listen to Abner's mischief."

There was absolute silence. Fatally he had everyone's attention.

Elim's taught body, stood proud. "Hear what Prince Jonathan did." He explained how Jonathan had gone amongst the Philistines on two nights. "With his own hands, he killed seven kings of the Philistines. They, without their heads, were as wheat before your swords."

There was total amazement. Everyone understood immediately that the real hero of the field of Michmash had been Jonathan.

"Therefore, King Saul," went on Elim, whose admiration for Jonathan got the better of him, "show that you are a Great King, indeed. Show your gratitude and bounty him he who made your victory possible."

That was fatal. Saul roared in anger to this impudent young fool. He would snatch the garlands from his head even before they had been given. Elim's words struck at the very being of Saul – they challenged his view of his Kingship. They undermined his greatest achievement, which seemingly far outweighed Samuel's victory against the Philistines at Mizpah.

He threw himself at Elim and struck him a great blow. If Saul had grabbed a sword or knife, he would have ended Elim there and then. Instead, Elim was hurled to the ground and, falling heavily, his wound broke open and began to bleed profusely again.

Jonathan fell to the side of his friend, doing his best to contain his anger at Saul's folly. He imploringly said, "Father, that was unjust. Especially on this day of your great victory. He is a young man. He does not understand. That was unkind."

Saul was now beside himself. If anyone had looked at Abner they might have seen him hiding a look of satisfaction as Saul worked himself into a terrible rage.

The King called out, "Bring forward Magra, the executioner. These two abominations have broken my covenant with God. They are filled with pride, hate and lies. Let my word be fulfilled. Let God see that a King's oath is sacred. Like Abraham before me, I am willing to sacrifice my son!"

There was pandemonium. Two soldiers very reluctantly took Jonathan and Elim by the arms.

Jonathan just stared at his father. He could not believe what was happening.

Elim was almost senseless, but cried out, "Mercy, great King. I am the one who offended. To slay me would be just, but not Jonathan, your son. Let me be an example of your wrath, but not him who loves you above all other men."

Saul would not be appeased. When Magra, a Benjaminite, arrived, he knelt before the King and asked pardon for Jonathan. "I cannot slay the King's son – not even for the King."

Everyone took up the cry and it was clear that no one would lift the sword against Jonathan or Elim.

Saul felt impotent fury. So he ordered the delinquents to be taken away and held and that he would decide their fate tomorrow. "But no one – no one on pain of death must plead or intercede for them," he added through clenched teeth.

That satisfied the crowd. They were convinced that another day gave time for wiser counsel to be heard. As Jonathan and Elim were led away, the cheers that followed them burned deep into the mind of Saul.

He proclaimed that there would be a feast, but the soldiers' cool response told Saul everything – his triumph had been irreparably marred.

The men then drifted off and began to carry out the weary soul-jarring task that is almost as terrible as the actual battle itself: the duty of clearing and burying the dead. Their demeanour was now as if they had been defeated. Every man present now understood that, because of Jonathan's daring, they had been able to rout an army more than twice their own.

Oddly enough, no one seemed to appreciate that Jonathan's captains were also there and killed even more. But the men realised that, by killing the Philistine kings, they had totally demoralised and confused their enemy. This is how the legend grew that the Prince and his armour bearer alone had together slaughtered the enemy and sewn dissension in the ranks of the Philistines. It is easy to see how the myth grew and, of course, it makes such a great story.

All spent a turbulent night.

Saul kept alone. He would not even allow Abner to come near. He refused to see two priests who had come from Samuel and his night was very dark.

Jonathan was made comfortable by the men who were guarding him. They sought to reassure him that they were confident that Saul would relent in the morning. Elim, however, was very weak and Jonathan was more concerned about his friend than for his own situation. He feared that Elim's wound had become infected and he was beginning to burn with fever.

Nothing happened for three days. Saul kept himself apart and the two young men stayed under arrest. Most hoped that the longer nothing happened, the easier it would be to quietly resolve the situation. The army was very keen to avoid any sense of censure of Saul, who they admired greatly. However, the more that was known about what Jonathan and his captains had achieved, the more of a hero he became.

At last Samuel arrived and everyone felt renewed hope. At first, Saul refused to see him but Samuel would broker no dismissal. He simply walked into Saul's tent. No one had the temerity to try to stop him as Samuel imperiously ordered the attendants out.

"God's Prophet would speak with God's anointed," Samuel said in his all-commanding voice. They were left alone.

No one knew what passed between them but, next day, the word went out that Saul, with Samuel's help, would dedicate an altar to God on the site of the battle. No mention was made of the case of Jonathan and Elim.

Preparations were made and the army drew together. On seeing Saul and Samuel walk side by side, they gave vent to their enthusiasm at seeing them in apparent harmony.

Samuel spoke first. "People of Israel. God has given you a great victory. The Lord's anointed has done great things and the Lord of Hosts is pleased."

This statement drew considerable applause.

"The King will dedicate an altar to God in thanks for His great bounty," said Samuel.

Saul began to serve at the newly built altar, which had been decked out with garlands and the prepared sacrifice.

Saul then spoke. "People of Israel. I, your King, made a covenant with God – a fast of faith. Not all men knew of my vow, but the word of a King is like a rock and binds all."

There was a dread silence at this. Would Saul not relent, after all?

"Jonathan, my son, and Elim bar Ebenezer broke my word, even though they knew not. The oath was made to God, who, through me, gave us victory."

At this a few men took up cheers, but there was little enthusiasm because, clearly, there was more to come.

Saul asked, "Can I forgive them their sacrilege? Should I banish them for ever from the People of Israel? Or should they die because they broke my covenant with God, which imperils the people."

There was absolute silence as the alternatives were spelt out.

"But, People of Israel, if I either forgive or banish them, can you risk God's wrath because we did not fulfil our covenant? If I forgive Jonathan, men will say that the King favours only his own – and we know how hateful that it to the people."

This was a nasty cut at Samuel. All knew that the people had been tired of the favouritism and nepotism surrounding the Prophet's family.

Saul continued. "So if I forgive Jonathan, I must perforce show mercy to Elim and no one is punished. Will God accept this and will you dare his anger?"

There were mutterings around the crowd but it quickly fell silent.

"If I banish them, they are cut off from Israel for ever - and some may say it is more cruel as it would be a living death - but ..." He paused dramatically. "... there has been an offence: there should be some punishment. Aye, in justice, even against the King's son. For I am a just King and, though I am the King of Israel, I am the servant of Israel."

The men waited expectantly. What would Saul do?

"I think they should die!" he said in a loud clear deliberate voice.

There was an immediate response: shouts and cries of, "No – forgive them – don't do it, Saul!' The men began to crowd round kneeling, pleading with Saul, and raising their hands to his clothes and casting dust upon their heads. The pleas and shouts went on and on, growing louder and more insistent, Saul stood unmoved.

Then at last he held his hand for silence and their pleadings drifted away. All held their breath. "As your servant and King, bearing in mind the warnings that I give that God may not be satisfied without a sacrifice, I would counsel the law, even though he is my son."

The cries broke out again, Saul roared for silence.

"I seek to serve Israel and, for this time only, I will let the people decide. Each man will take a stone and cast his lot for the law, for banishment or for forgiveness."

This was a novel approach – a great idea! There were excited murmurings until Saul gained silence again.

"Let three great jars be placed before the host – one for each decision. But if one in ten cast their lot for the law, then the law shall carry and I will execute the law."

This seemed harsh but the novelty of the idea of a collective decision appealed to the men and Abner led the cry, "Blessed be the King who shows great wisdom."

The men lined up and it took hours for them to all pass by the jars. Five other jars were needed for acquittal and when the tellers came to break the jar for death, amazingly, there were just three stones in the bottom.

A great roar erupted. There were cheers for the King but most of all for Jonathan. Without waiting for Saul's permission, some of his captains rushed towards the tent where the captives lay. They seized them and brought them in triumph, carrying them on their shoulders.

Elim had to be lowered quickly for he was obviously ill, but Jonathan allowed himself to be cheered and then asked for silence.

He was lowered to the ground and said, "Thank you, my brothers, for your confidence."

Then, turning to his Father, he knelt. "Thank you, my King, my Father, for your great justice and mercy." He did not look at Samuel, who had stood quiet all the time as if he was not there.

Jonathan jumped up and cried, "Men of Israel, blessed are we in our King, who shows wisdom. Who shows mercy on the field of Michmash where Saul, the Lord's anointed, scattered our enemies. Hail Saul! Hallelujah! Hallelujah!"

The peace was made, but the corrosion that ate at the heart of the Kingship of Saul had begun.

The King's Psalm

I, David, am about to enter the story of King Saul and Prince Jonathan – now the greatest hero of Israel.

When the news reached Bethlehem of our triumph at Michmash we were delirious with joy. Part of the happiness was a sense of relief, though we young warriors had very mixed feelings about missing the battle. We escorted the herds, women and children back to our towns as the trip became a celebration.

Led by Josh, Aaron, Eli and I became very drunk. I awoke with a sickening headache and a mouth like a dry gully. However, I realised that I had not thought about Leah for days. This saddened me and, to my surprise, when Josh came around, looking very groggy, he mentioned her.

"David, I was glad you let your hair down last night. It was a good night, wasn't it? I don't think I've seen you laugh like that since Leah died." He went on,

"It's all right, you know. Though she was very special, I'm sure she wouldn't want you to mourn for ever."

He was right, but I couldn't help feel guilty and it was also a sharp reminder just how lonely I sometimes felt.

A message came from Father: I was to go to the King, as Father and Samuel had decided. I was to leave at once to take his greetings to Saul and congratulate him on his victory.

I said a hurried goodbye to my friends, who were frank in their envy of my role but not nastily so.

I travelled with a very dour man called Job. It took us three days' hard journeying to reach the King's semi-permanent camp at Gilbeah. On arrival, Job, without a word, pointed me in the direction of the King's tent and walked off and left me.

I was amazed at the noise, the bustle, and the colours. I had never seen so many people in my life.

The King, of course, would in times of peace travel in his tent around the different tribes, so he never had a proper home. This was to ensure that none of the tribes would become too proud and make the others jealous. However, it also meant that the King's men were always either preparing for the next move, or settling down in a site at which they had just arrived.

I tried to ask various people for some help but everybody was in a rush. What I did not expect was the coarse language.

No warrior seemed to speak without either an oath or some crudity. I was also surprised to find so many women camp followers. Some were respectably dressed wives and concubines, but many seemed to be overt prostitutes.

As I was trying to ask the way to the King, one of the young prostitutes came up to me and smilingly put her arms around me. I was flabbergasted,

"Oh, lovely boy! Where have you been? I bet you would like a good time! Do you like your Mera?"

She was actually very pretty and not much older than I was. I tried politely to stammer my "no thanks" to her, but her hands were all over me.

I did not know what to do. Her face was near mine. Her tongue kept tickling my face. She held my arm fast and then put her other hand up my skirt. I know that I was not thinking too clearly but, as her hand found my phallus, I found myself growing hard. I blushed and felt embarrassed.

I pushed her away. But she pursued me. "Come on, love. You've got a lovely one there. Let Mera suck it better for you."

I was totally confused. More so when I realised we had attracted attention of others, who called out, "Go on, Mera, you've got a pretty one! Give it him free – he looks like he doesn't know what to do with it!"

I fled like a lost schoolboy in panic. I got away and calmed down but felt an absolute fool.

I decided the only way to accomplish my mission was to find the King's tent and tell who ever was on duty that I had been sent by the Prophet.

I eventually found it. It was enormous with lots of warriors milling around. So, despite being more anxious than I can ever remember, I walked up and, seeing a man who looked important enough to know what to do, I asked, "Excuse me, general, sir. I am David bar Jesse of Bethlehem and I have been sent by the Prophet with a message for the King."

He was a tall, well-made man and wore some badge of distinction and a chain around his neck. His head was large, with grey-green eyes that struck me as very unfriendly.

"Do you know to whom you are speaking, boy?" he roared. Before awaiting my answer he spat out, "I am Abner, General to the King. Go away!" With that, he turned his back upon me. I was taken aback at his rudeness.

"Sir General, all in Israel has heard of the great Abner. I was also taught that he was a great warrior. I cannot believe the Great Abner would be so rude to a messenger for the King. Are you sure you are General Abner?"

He swung around. "Don't be impudent with me, puppy!" I could see from the slight smile of his companion that my comment had gone home to the annoyance of the great Abner. He barked at me, "State your business to this gentleman and if he doesn't think you should be whipped for your impertinence I'd be surprised!" He saluted the warrior and almost walked over me as if I was not there.

"Well, young man!" said the official with a smirk. "Prophet's messenger or no, you've not begun your time in the King's camp well, my boy. Tell me again who and what your errand is."

Despite his words I saw that he was being helpful and suddenly had a flash that my remark about Abner might have pleased him a little. Though I might at that moment have made a friend, how was I to know that I had also made an enemy – an enemy for life?

I explained and he told me to wait awhile until he came back, but as he left, another guard took his place. I nodded to him but he just ignored me and motioned me to sit down.

After about half an hour the first officer came and said, "The King will see you. Come."

I followed him with some trepidation. I was going to meet the King of Israel, the Lord's anointed and the victor of Michmash – and many other battles.

I went into the inner tent and saw King Saul for the first time. He was sitting, reading some documents. At first he did not acknowledge my presence. That gave me a little time to study him and to look around.

He was a magnificent man. In his middle years, he had two striking white flashes in his otherwise still dark hair, with a strong, square head. His beard was a mixture of dark and white and was cut pointedly, which gave him a very regal look. He was very handsome and dressed in clothes whose richness I had not imagined possible.

A robe, which fell to his feet, was slashed with silver and scarlet and had long, flowing sleeves that gave emphasis to his every movement. His inner shirt was open at the neck and I could see his still powerful frame, firm muscled, edged with dark hair touched with grey.

His headband was a wonderful colour of silver and gold; so cleverly woven I could not tell whether it was some soft metal or some marvellous fabric.

I could not take my eyes from him.

Then, he looked up and I was amazed. His dark eyes flashed me a warm smile as if I was his closest friend. His seemingly total acceptance completely unnerved me. I fell to the floor and made my obeisance and began. "Great King..."

"No, no, David bar Jesse, youngest son of my friend, Jesse of Judah. Welcome, welcome. You bring greetings from the Prophet, I'm told."

I answered yes and that I had been told to bring my harp.

"How kind of Samuel to think that the Lord's anointed should require the consolation of music," he said, raising an eyebrow.

I did not know what to say. Was there a note of sarcasm in his voice?

I stammered a reply. "Great King, my music is but that of a shepherd boy who loves the Lord and His King."

He surveyed me and waited for me to go on.

I continued. "Who am I that could bring consolation to the Lion of Israel, victor of Mishmash, slayer of the enemies of the Living God."

He smiled at me with his eyes, but his voice was grave as he asked, "Are you sincere, David bar Jesse?"

I was feeling confused again. This interview was not going in any direction I could ever have imagined.

"Oh, King. I have never been to camp before. I always say what is in my heart so I hope I am sincere. If I have offended, I am truly sorry. I would serve you and Israel – more as a warrior than a bard – though Samuel told me that you would welcome my music first. You already have many warriors far more able than I, though perhaps not so many harpists."

I knew I was blushing and, despite his kind look, was feeling very disconcerted.

"Do you have any enemies?" he asked, out of the blue, but then went on without my reply. "You are young. I see you are wearing your colours that say you have killed your man. So young! So, so young! Perhaps you are a doughty warrior after all, but are you still too young to have enemies?"

I did not know what to say.

Saul waved a hand at me. "I have enemies. I, who seek to be the servant, not the master, of Israel, have enemies. Not the Philistines and the Amalekites as you would expect, but some here in Israel. I did not seek their enmity but some envious souls hate because I am successful. So, without intent, the effect of my success for Israel is an enmity directed against me here – in Israel!"

I was astounded by his comments and forgot my shyness.

"King Saul, but that is dreadful," I said impulsively. "If you were not successful, Israel would be destroyed. If you did not rule justly there would be confusion and dissension in the land. He who resents you is a, a traitor! Against, not only Israel, but also against God, because you are His chosen one. You carry the Lord's burden..."

"David bar Jesse," he said, but this time without apparent deeper meaning, "you have it. You are wise beyond your years. The Lord Abner almost alone grasps the dilemma. It is the King who must curb the over-weaning subject who would oppress and confuse the people. You are right: such a man is a traitor, and he and his like disturbs my sleep."

He suddenly looked hard at me and asked, "Do you sleep?"

I had not thought about it. Then, remembering Leah, answered, "Ordinarily, King Saul, my sleep is such I do not even notice. Once, however, I had a great trouble and sleep left me as if it would never return."

Saul nodded at me. "David bar Jesse, you have it again. The King and servant of Israel must watch the day and long night to ensure his people sleep easily – I tell you this without pride or blasphemy. As the Living God never sleeps, His King seldom has an untroubled repose."

"King Saul, the Prophet told me that my music might be pleasing to you. When I was troubled, my music brought me some peace. Samuel, too, has found it soothing."

He told me to play. I began very quietly. He sat, looking at me, drinking deep from a wine goblet as I sang:

"O Lord how excellent is thy name in all the earth who has set thy glory above the heavens."

As I strummed softly, he closed his eyes. He moved his arm gently in time to the verses.

"When I consider thy heavens the work of thy fingers, the moon and the stars which thou hast ordained.

What is man that thou art mindful of him, and the son of man that thou visitest him. Thou hast made him a little lower than the angels and hast crowned him with honour and glory."

The chords quietly ebbed away into silence as we both remained motionless.

He suddenly sat up with a start. "Truly, that reached the heart. David bar Jesse, you have more gifts?"

Again, I was not sure if was he teasing me. He gestured to my harp and took it from me.

Then, to my astonishment, he began to trill it and sang back to me in a deep bass voice that quivered with emotion.

"When I consider thy heavens the work of thy fingers, the moon and the stars which thou hast ordained.

What is man that thou art mindful of him, and the son of man that thou visitest him. Thou hast made him a little lower than the angels and hast crowned him with honour and glory."

His rendering re-framed the psalm. It was full of longing and mixed with sadness, even though his voice rose almost ecstatically when he sang about honour and glory.

I forgot myself and applauded. "Sir, that was wonderful! You have made my song live. I had no idea that it could sound like that."

He was obviously very pleased and said, "Samuel was right. Perhaps he did not know, though there is little the Prophet does not know, that, when I was your age, I, too, was a warrior bard. Your song brings great consolation. Have you any more?"

I hesitated because, again, I felt there was another meaning beneath his words. Also, I suspected that he was probably a better musician than I was.

"Come, David bar Jesse. Do not be afraid – you're not afraid of your King, are you?" He flashed me a smile that melted all my half-hidden anxieties.

"No, Great King. Your kindness is overwhelming and I could never fear you."

He smiled broadly. "David bar Jesse, I think that it is possible we might become good friends. But I asked, have you any more songs?"

"I have one, sir, which I composed after hearing of your victory at

Michmash. I have not had time to practise it and Samuel has not had an opportunity to hear it, so it may not please you but –"

He broke in, "A new song? In my honour? Am I the first to hear?" I nodded. "Then play, David bar Jesse, my warrior bard – play on!"

With such encouragement, I closed my eyes and found the key through a series of chords. I recalled the words:

"The King shall joy in thy strength O Lord and in thy salvation how greatly shall he rejoice.

Thou hast given him his hearts delight – thou settest a crown of pure gold upon his head."

He stood up in apparent excitement. His eyes were shining and fixed on me with an almost hypnotic hold – but I knew I had to sing on.

"He asked life of thee and thou gavest it him even length of days for ever.

His glory is great in thy salvation honour and majesty hast thou laid upon him.

For thou hast made him most blessed for ever; thou hast made him exceedingly glad with thy countenance.

For the King trusteth in the Lord and through the mercy of the Most High he shall not be moved."

He repeated the last phrase and we sang it together:

"For the King trusteth in the Lord and through the mercy of the Most High he shall not be moved."

We both fell silent. There were tears in his eyes.

He asked, "Are you really what you seem? How did you, though a warrior bard, find the echo of my heart? What inspiration told you of my hopes and fears?"

Then, suddenly, he looked fierce and held me so tight that I knew he was bruising my arms. "Is it inspiration or ... something else?" he demanded.

"Great King, my music and my words are not always mine own. The Prophet tells me that is inspiration. When I began your song I did not know how the words would fall out – they just appeared. I hope they pleased you."

He released me. "David bar Jesse, you shall be my friend. David, my friend, my Warrior Bard, for I believe you were inspired – perhaps by God."

Then, with a sadness that was palpable, he said softly, "I, too, seek to hear the voice of God. In your words, I think I catch His meaning. David, you have a great gift. You have been sent to me. It is appropriate that the Lord's anointed should have such music – it was a benediction to my heart."

With that, he kissed me on both cheeks. "You shall stay with the camp and we must make music together!" he said, jubilantly.

Then, once again with a look of desperation, his voice faltered. "You shall ease my soul of its troubles. With such words coming from Him I feel you can ease my burden. Come, let us drink in friendship."

He took a second goblet and filled it with wine. His words troubled me. One could not help but feel sad for his discordant words hinted at dark thoughts.

"Oh, Great King. I am not worthy. Samuel the Prophet – he calls me his friend – but you are King of all Israel. For me to serve you as you would is more than I deserve."

He suddenly looked at me coldly. "Do you not wish to be my friend, David bar Jesse? You, who counts amongst his friends Samuel, the Prophet who speaks to and hears the voice of God, would turn me down?"

I hastened to correct his misinterpretation. "Great King, I spoke clumsily. I know my music has some power. I humbly believe that sometimes it serves the Lord. If you should call me friend and your bard, then I am amongst the greatest in all Israel. But I would not presume."

He was now relaxed once more. "Come, come, David. You said that well!" He linked our arms. He toasted me and I him.

"In friendship and for ever – do you swear, David?"

What could I say to this wonderful, magnificent but troubled man? Who could resist such an appeal? I would have done anything for him.

"King Saul, I swear until my dying day to be nothing but your friend. To serve you and yours, but, most of all, you in friendship."

He kissed me and embraced me. "David, you have done well. Leave me now. Tell Eban to admit no one. I would sleep. Farewell ... my friend."

I went out. My head and my mind were spinning.

When Saul looked up, he saw a handsome youth, whose eyes, despite the natural nervousness expected of a youth in the presence of his King, shone with intelligence.

Saul was intrigued. Why had the old fox been so keen to send this boy to him?

Samuel had stressed in his letter that he thought so highly of David bar Jesse that he considered him his friend.

God, the man's presumption! Did he think that this would be a recommendation to Saul, especially as Samuel had the impudence to suggest that he might also find merit in the boy who was wise beyond his years?

Well, thought Saul, that's true. The lad was obviously innocent. Clearly a lamb amongst wolves, yet he was so responsive.

His voice was passable, quite pleasant, but his words were magnificent.

Saul pondered: where was the catch? Why did Samuel want him to share in this very gifted young man. He mused: was he another spy? Then he dashed the idea from him, angrily. No – he, Saul, was a great judge of men! The youth was sincere and, for his song, Saul almost prayed in thankfulness: "If I cannot hear your voice direct, oh Lord, you have given me your bard."

Yes, thought Saul, David bar Jesse is my bard sent by God. Saul was confident that after a month he would win over David's loyalty and he would be unquestioningly his. He thought further: the boy was so accurate – he understood the burden on the King. He saw the importance of the pre-eminence of the King – without which Israel would suffer.

Saul nodded in deep satisfaction. He had found a friend and a bard – one who he was sure would be a lifelong "King's man".

The King's Camp

I walked slowly down the inner tent to try to gather my thoughts. As I reached the outer tent a tall man in armour stood in front. I moved to the left and he moved to the same side. I moved to the right and we again faced each other.

I had not time to take him all in as he tapped first my harp and then my head,

"Boy," he said, "set that to music and we shall have a new dance."

I was confused, "I'm sorry, sir," I answered, "but I've been to see the King and he said he did not want anyone else to enter."

The warrior, clearly important, looked a little amusedly. "Really, young man? I can see that you are a man, as displayed by your colours. Assuming, that is, you have not found them and are falsely claiming to have killed your man. Frankly, young sir, apart from your obvious dancing ability, you look too young to be so far from home, and hardly seem suited to be a King's messenger."

After such a day, I was tired and irked by his attitude – although I could see his teasing was half-friendly. I felt very foolish because I suddenly realised that I had no idea what I was next to do and said, "Sir, you are being presumptuous. My colours were earned. I have been both a messenger to the Prophet and now bring the King's instruction. Are you Eban, for I am to tell you that the King would not be disturbed?"

He laughed. "I think our boy harpist has a temper. Do you think he might challenge me to a duel?"

I suddenly realised that his remarks had also been directed at the guard who had earlier shown me to the King. It was the guard who I now realised was Eban.

Then turning back to me, the warrior said, "Where are you from boy? Which troop are you assigned to?"

Now I felt a real idiot. I did not know and my ignorance showed as I could not answer him.

"Well then, my fiery cockerel," he said, mockingly. Turning over his shoulder, he called to a dark-faced warrior, "Ura, look after our new King's messenger, will you?" Putting his hands on my shoulders, he spun me around and out of the tent. With me out of his way, he walked inside.

Eban also took hold of me and pushed me towards the laughing Ura, saying,

"Well, young man! First you offend Abner the second man in Israel. Now you offend Jonathan, the Prince. You have a real gift, young fellow! Ura, for God's sake, get this idiot out of here before he makes an even bigger fool of himself."

Ura come towards me, his long cloak and helmet showing he was not an Israelite. To my surprise, I realised he was a Hittite. He was tall, broad and looked very strong. Despite my confused embarrassment, I was relieved that his eyes were smiling at me rather than being a threat.

"Come lad. Yes, I'm a Hittite – proud of it, too. Even prouder that we serve our good ally, King Saul. My greatest joy is that I call my captain, Jonathan, my friend. You'll come to see, lad, that my only weakness is my modesty. What do you think?"

"Well, sir," I answered, grateful for his humour, "without having anything to be proud of, no wonder you are such a humble man."

This was a mistake. He grabbed me in a bear hug but I knew this was still in jest.

"Young man, I can make jokes because I am a full warrior in the troop of Jonathan. I am a captain of the senior line. You, on the other hand, why – you are a worm! A nothing! Worse than nothing! A king's messenger with a harp upon his back and in danger of being eaten alive by the camp's mice – let alone some others I could think of."

He released me, for which I was thankful as I could now breathe freely. He continued. "So lad, as my captain, prince and friend has said to look after you, I shall do so. Therefore, only I will be allowed to flay you alive if you continue your folly, which I shall do if necessary. No one will notice the disappearance of a crushed worm. What are you boy?"

I understood and dutifully answered, "A worm, oh noble Ura the Hittite, modest friend of the Prince."

He had let me go but I had to duck quickly to avoid his friendly blow that followed my sally. I jumped back out of range and bowed to him, saying, "Ura, sir, my apologies. I am truly very thankful that you are taking this trouble over this worm for I must confess I feel quite lost."

This candour seemed to win him completely over. He came to me in the friendliest way and asked my name.

"Right then, David the Bethlehemite. What do you need first? A piss, the latrines, a drink or something to eat?"

I must have looked a little shocked for I was still unused to the open crudity of soldiers.

"Well speak up lad: latrines or kitchens?" Ura persisted.

I then appreciated that it was the latrines and murmured so.

Ura gave me a sideways look. "Always remember, little Bethlehemite. Men are like animals. You either have to feed, water or muck them out. So come."

I followed him and then my heart sank. Who should be coming up between the row of tents than Mera, the girl prostitute.

She greeted Ura, "Hi, Ura. When are you going to come and see me?" She stopped suddenly upon seeing me. Ura noticed the interaction and she looked back at him. "Ura, who's your pretty friend?"

Then she spoke to me. "I didn't know you knew Ura."

Ura interjected, "So, little Bethlehemite! You've already found our pretty Mera. You'll know that she is the best bit of fun in the camp."

I was blushing again. They both stood either side of me. Mera began to put her hand inside my skirt. I did not know what to do. I could not run. She put her face to mine and I could not help but notice she had a beautiful little pink mouth.

"I like virgins, little Bethlehemite," she whispered, her face so close to mine that I could feel the warmth of her skin. Her hand grasped my rising member, slowly milking me. My mouth went dry. My eyes were glued to hers as I only dimly heard Ura's laughter. I still stood motionless with my arms at my side but longing to take her in my arms and join my mouth to hers.

Suddenly, thwack ... thwack. Two sharp smacks to my face as Mera screamed at me, "Rabbinical virgin! You would have me serve you free! Run away from me, would you."

She began to berate me and, without Ura's intervention, I don't know what I would have done. He promised to give her a shekel and come to her later that evening himself.

I did not say a word but miserably followed him to the latrines. As I stood there I noticed he was looking at me. I looked at his phallus. With a start I saw that he was uncircumcised. I could not help myself, I had never seen an uncircumcised living man before. As I stared at him I saw that it was lengthening and thickening, with its foreskin rolling back.

He laughed. "You're not the first Hebrew to be curious and, without giving offence, I like mine the way it is." He stood there boasting about his erect member.

His hand came to mine, which totally confused me. I backed away from him.

He grinned at me, not in the least offended. "You know, little David, you're not all that little. Mera is right: you'll have to be more relaxed. A camp is not a rabbi's school."

Then covering himself up and turning to leave, he added, "Look, I think you and I should visit Mera tonight. What about it?" A host of emotions filled me, but he saw my misery and said "What is it, lad? Have you a disease or something?"

"Ura, please forgive me, but I had a wife and I had only known her two days before she died in a ..., a ..., terrible accident."

He looked at me, not in jest, but with gentle sympathy.

"Ah, I see. I'm sorry, lad. Well, I think I understand. But, you know, life goes on. Give yourself a chance to feel again. I'm sorry if I went too far. Come, we'll go to eat and I'll let you buy me a flask of wine."

He was as good as his word. I had to use one of my ten shekels, but at least I did not have to pay for the meal that I ate ravenously.

Ura took me over to his troop and began introducing me to the other men. They were all older than I was.

One, a long lean man, called out, "Ura, are we so desperate that we are now recruiting boys? We are the Prince's troop. We are an elite, and you bring a womanish boy musician?"

Ura replied for me. "Canan, the Prince said to bring him – and bring him I have. Are you questioning the Prince?"

Canan quickly answered, "Nay, Ura, but come, look at him. Surely the Prince cannot have meant him for a warrior but as a camp boy – a musician."

Perhaps unwisely, I spoke for myself. "Sir, I have trained as a warrior. Though I have some skill with the harp, that is only in the service of the King and, therefore, it is an honourable duty. I am first a warrior, though I admit I have little experience. Yet you too, sir, must have started sometime. I am very willing to learn."

As I was speaking, I could see in his arrogance that he was trying to stare me down. I knew at once that I had unintentionally made an enemy.

Ura interjected, "That's a fair answer, Canan. Leave the lad be. After all, you have some skills with pipe and harp, so there's nothing wrong with being a musician, is there?"

Canan retorted, "I make no claims about being the King's harpist, but," and his voice dripped sarcasm, "the pretty boy shows modesty if he is truly willing to learn. Well, I will teach him, if he dare. I'll test how good his swordsmanship is. Dare you, pretty boy?"

I could feel all the men's eyes on me and my face stung.

Ura jumped in again. "Canan, leave it. You are the troop's best swordsmen, no doubt, but the boy doesn't know that. Wait until he has learned more before taking him on. Anyway, there'd be little honour in it for you – it would be far too easy."

I should have left it there, because I could see Canan was satisfied by Ura's praise. He was nodding in agreement at the comment of "no honour" in it for him. But his dark eyes were drilling into me with a venom I couldn't understand. I had always been taught never to back away from a bully because, otherwise, they always return. Undoubtedly, Canan was a bully.

So I replied, "Truly, Ura, there would be little honour for the noble Canan to use his sword on me. But," and I turned and walked towards Canan, "if, sir, you would be so kind, I would welcome a bout as I have much to learn. It would bring much honour to me to have learned from the best sword in the Prince's troop."

Soldiers are strange men: they can be cruel sometimes while, other times, they can be as gentle as women – but they always love a fight. Whilst they knew I would get a good thrashing, they appreciated that I had to stand up to Canan or lose their respect, so they cheered and clapped as someone went to fetch the practice swords.

They were heavy wooden swords with rounded blunt points. Yet we all have many a bruise from a lost bout. Horah, my old captain, reminded us that it was better to learn now and bear the pain, when the blow would not be fatal, than later against some enemy whose blow would leave you dead.

There was little light left in the sky. Some of the men built up the fire and lit more torches to give us light.

I watched Canan carefully. I could see he was angry. He preened himself as he stripped off his shirt, revealing an athlete's body at its very peak.

I slowly peeled off my shirt. I must have looked a poor match because, at seventeen, I must have looked thin against a warrior in his mid-twenties.

They marked out a square and the men lined up around the perimeter. I felt very alone.

Ura looked rather irritated and snapped at me, "Well, little Bethlehemite, don't say I didn't warn you. I told you the camp mice would eat you."

Then, as if he was sorry to be so unsympathetic, he whispered in my ear, "You did right to stand up for yourself, lad. But, for God's sake, look to your head. I don't want the Prince blaming me if he spoils your pretty looks."

I tried to grin reassuringly, but I didn't feel it. My mouth went dry as I nervously tried the weight of the practice sword. The shield, which was of the type we used at home, consisted of a wooden base covered in waxed skin, but it was almost as heavy as the sword. I tried to calm myself by repeating Samuel's dictum, "think don't feel". I tried to concentrate upon what Canan might be feeling. Pushing my anxieties down I observed him whirl the heavy sword and shield around as he warmed up.

I quickly saw that, in his hands, both shield and sword were weapons of attack. I just stood and waited.

"Right then!" Ura called us to the centre. "Best of three hits. Is that all right with you, Canan?"

"Only best of three? Why, it's hardly worth while me getting warm – but, yes, let's say best of three. I know you are trying to protect your pretty boy," he sneered.

I was stupidly about to say "best of five", but Ura gave me such a vicious look that I sensibly kept my mouth shut. After all, if I was going to be thrashed, it was better to have only two blows rather than three.

We were called to order. I kept my gaze on Canan.

Just before we began, Ura whispered to me, "Don't follow his blade – follow his eyes!"

Then it began. I felt the blow of Canan's sword slash to the right. I parried. The blow sent a shudder down my arms. He slashed to the left. I parried with my shield, but only just. I had to quickly jump aside as a looping blow narrowly missed my head.

His blows were fast and furious. I had never felt anything like this. I parried and skipped out of the way of a sword that seemed to follow me every where. I had not yet struck a blow of my own as I could barely keep my feet and body co-ordinated.

He came at me. Using his shield as a battering ram to push me back, his sword was slashing everywhere – especially at my head.

I knew I had to back off from him and not let him use his superior weight. Twice our shields clashed together and I was almost thrown off my feet. If this had been a wrestling match we would not have been allowed to fight.

I kept skipping away as fast as I could, but, as I backed away to the edge of the square, the men formed a wall that I could not cross.

Dimly, I could hear the men shouting, Canan had manoeuvred me into a corner of the square. His eyes looked deadly. I held my blade out in front, trying to aim it at his eyes. No good: easily, contemptuously, he flicked it away. Tap, tap, slash. Tap, tap, slash. I knew I couldn't keep up my defence much longer. My heart pounded, not just in fear, but with the physical effort of keeping him at bay and staying upright. I felt exhausted. I did not know which felt heaviest, my sword or shield arm.

I wiped away the sweat from my eyes. I could see that he, too, was sweating. He shook his head and the sweat flew from his brow. With a shudder of dread, I saw that he had not taken his eyes from me for a moment.

The flickering firelight illuminated our sweating bodies. I felt a new kind of exhaustion. Suddenly, he whirled away from me. I half went forward. It was a mistake – too late. His heavy sword flashed upward and downwards, and crashed through my attempted parry. The blow came crashing down on to my shoulder. It was agony. I jumped backwards into the centre of the square. My sword arm was useless as I could barely hold my weapon. I was totally open to him.

He advanced, his face drawn into a snarl. I staggered back. He raised his weapon above me. I cringed as I waited to take the blow that would finish me off.

"Hold!" Ura stepped in, his sword warding off Canan's sweeping slash that would have smashed my heaving ribs.

"That's a clear hit. Honour is satisfied. That's enough."

Canan stood there, his chest puffed out as he held sword and shield wide in triumph.

His face was still angry. "We said the best of three. He hasn't had all his lesson yet." Then, he turned to me. "You want to have all your lesson, don't you, pretty boy?"

My shoulder was still in agony. I wasn't sure whether I could still hold my sword. I moved it around, still not answering, as I needed to concentrate hard so as not to feel the pain.

I rubbed my shoulder painfully. Surprisingly, it was not broken. I felt the contusion burst and I was bleeding.

Everyone waited for me to answer. I could feel the tension grow. I deliberately refused to look in the direction of Ura, who I sensed wanted me to end it there.

I looked and smiled my warmest smile at Canan. "It was a valuable lesson, sir. I am grateful."

I could sense the tension reaching a peak. Everyone obviously thought I was going to do the sensible thing. I thought I was too.

"But you keep alluding to me as a pretty boy. Well, sir, you are a handsome man, but it is a little demeaning to be called a boy – even by such a warrior as yourself. And, after all, I think I lasted longer than you expected."

I could hear the gasps. Canan looked furious.

I wanted to make him angrier so I turned the screw further. "If you're too tired to continue the lesson – as you are a much older man and I can see you're sweating profusely – so be it and thanks for the lesson. Otherwise, I'm ready."

There was a shout all around: whether of approval, surprise or laughter at my stupidity I don't know.

Why did I say that? I stood there, trying to look unconcerned as the blood trickled down my arm.

The atmosphere grew dark. Canan hissed, "You impudent brat! Defend yourself!"

He raised his sword and charged at me.

What happened next was not entirely intentional on my part. I knew that I had to do something very different – to try and shape the fight the way I wanted because, clearly, I could not continue much longer.

As he charged forward, I rushed towards him instead of away, which totally surprised him. What I intended to do was to get close to him, get under his sword arm and give him a wrestling throw, thus using his greater weight against him.

Instead, as my forward movement catapulted me into him, he tried to adjust to my new position. I spun round and aimed at his midriff, but, as I did so, I half slipped. I was propelled forward, falling, with my stroke sweeping below his defending blade and shield.

He was too late: I caught him an almighty crack across his ankle. I tumbled away from him and went into a wrestling roll – rolling and turning away, as I scrambled to regain my feet before he could attack.

There was an almighty shout. When I looked up, Canan was on his knees. I could see the torn flesh where the heavy wooded sword had caught his ankle.

"You bastard! Bastard! Bastard Judean!" shouted Canan and mouthed more obscenities. "That was a foul blow. Now, I am going to kill you, you bastard! BASTARD!"

I realised, even if he didn't, that he probably wouldn't be able to stand on his ankle for some time.

"Sir. Canan. I am not a bastard. I am sorry if the blow was low. I did not intend it – I slipped. But the move would have been legitimate if I had not slipped."

I took a deep breath and cried out so that I could be heard above the din. "Still sir, I cry your mercy. I offer you my hand in gratitude for a lesson I shall never forget." I pointed to my bloody arm. "My arm won't let me forget this day for some time."

Canan's look was poisonous. He tried to rise and come on at me again, but, as I guessed, he could not stand properly.

He swore as he slowly shrunk back down on one knee. "Bloody bastard, Judean! Come on! Come on!" he cried. He was incensed. "We said best of three. I can still stand if you dare come within my sword length. We can finish it now, for good."

Ura decided to intervene. "No, this has gone far enough." He then tried to placate Canan. "He has done you honour, Canan. He has apologised and cried mercy. Come, take his hand. He has accepted he has had a lesson."

The men around shouted approval. Whilst they were loyal to their comrade, they seemed to have some sympathy for me and urged Canan to desist.

He saw that they were with Ura and glared at me. "You accept, Judean, that you have had a lesson from the better man?" he said, stressing the word "better".

I was about to respond but caught Ura's look. If Canan was expecting me to dispute the point he about to be disappointed. "Of course, Canan. You must be the better warrior. I have learned much from you. Truly, if that had been in battle, I would have been finished after your first hit. I would have had no chance to get in my lucky blow."

I said all this in the forlorn hope of turning an enemy into a friend. I offered him my hand.

He stood there for what seemed ages. I could sense rather than hear the murmurs of the men say, "Take his hand, Canan. It's a fair gesture, take his hand – well done, lad – take his hand, Canan."

He thrust out his hand and clasped mine in a bone-crushing grip, but his look of hate, and pleasure at my wincing face, told me I had an enemy for life.

He still held me, crushing as hard as he could, but by this time I had tightened my grip against him.

I had the advantage of standing above him. Whilst I may not have had the strongest grip in Judah, I had very flexible and broad hands and could move my hand within his grip. As he tightened so did I. And he, not having my flexibility, found that it was his hand, which was having the bones rubbed together. As the pain got to him, I thought he was about to strike me. We remained there, frozen like statues set in a bizarre pose. It was an endless impasse.

Ura moved to come between us, laughing. "A draw – comrades – a draw!" He deftly crashed his burly arms across us, forcing us to break our grip on each other.

Canan turned and hobbled away, followed by others from his tribe. To my surprise and delight, at least ten of the men crowded round me, pressing my hand, clapping me on the back. Two I recognised as fellow Judeans, so I might have expected their support, but the others were from different tribes.

One, Beniah, said, "Thanks for that, little Judean. Canan has often given us a beating. He's a bully and he won't forget you in a hurry. Welcome to our troop."

At that, the others clapped and welcomed me. Ura just stood beaming. It warmed my heart to see his obvious delight in his protégé.

Beniah, smiling broadly, was perhaps only four years older than I was. "What's your name, Judean? Yes, you are a pretty boy! That's why Canan was so rough with you." This was a remark that I then did not understand. He went on. "You're a pretty good fighter, too. I am Beniah bar Izra, a Reubenite, and would know you better."

He took my hand and congratulated Ura on gaining a new member to the troop.

Ura laughed. "No, it was not I. You know that the Prince has an eye for excellence, though I admit, in my usual Hittite modesty, I told David how to do it."

We all laughed together.

Ura, with tears of mirth in his eyes, cried out, "Lads, the drinks are on me! Though our new comrade, David bar Jesse, will pay."

Sure enough, as by magic, the wine flasks appeared and we all drank deeply.

Later, Ura kindly settled the bill himself, otherwise I would have been penniless.

Because of the fight, Ura did nor press me any further to go and seek out Mera – though I think he went alone.

I now forgot my earlier misery. I wasn't sure how it had happened but I was now a member of the Prince's troop. I seemed to be accepted by most of my new comrades and, for the moment, life couldn't be better.

Later, I was shown where I was to sleep. At first sleep didn't come easily as I tried to collect all the whirling events of the day. Then, my thoughts turned to Ura's likely visit to Mera. I realised that, since Leah, I had not thought at all about women – but I did now.

My fantasy raced and it was Mera's face I saw, not Leah's. I recalled Mera's hand inside my skirt. I found myself profoundly aroused. I thought of her open mouth and her pink tongue. I brought myself to a gushing relief and slept the deep, tired sleep of one whose day had been full indeed.

And that is how I first came into the camp of the King: gauche, awkward and foolish. All in one day, I had met the greatest, best and worst of Israel.

It set me on an adventure that few have had to endure.

PART THREE

THE KING'S BARD

Chapter Nine

Saul's Dark Mood

For days, my arm and shoulder ached from Canan's blow. Fortunately, to Ura's and my surprise there was no scarring. Beniah came to me and wanted to be my friend. Ura, to my delight, however, was unwilling to release me as his protégé, so I had the benefit of two mentors.

Late on the third day, a message came from the King: I was to attend him.

I went into the King's tent and, as I passed, Eban said, "I hear, little Bethlehemite, that you have another enemy. Well, young sir, don't say I said it but, if that bastard, Canan, is against you, then you can count me as a friend. He's always trying to ingratiate himself with the Prince – he can't kiss ass enough with the King. But there is something about his crawling that really gets to me. Anyway, be careful: don't go out by yourself at night. But don't say I said anything."

I was amazed at this. I appreciated that Canan did not like me and, indeed, to be fair, I disliked him also. Yet Eban was implying that Canan bore more than just dislike for me. It is odd: one can meet a total stranger and feel totally at one with him; or, from the first look, it is clear that there will always be animosity between you.

I went down the tunnel of tents. When I reached the King, I was shocked to see what a state he was in. At first sight, he was still magnificent. His robes and other accoutrements declared that this was the King.

As I approached more closely, I could see that his eyes seemed dead and lifeless. His skin looked dry and papery, and hung loosely as if he were famished. There was a general loss of vitality, which was made more dreadful by my recent memory of him being such a very inspirational man.

At first, he did not speak. He just sat.

This went on for some time, so I decided I would break the ice. "Great King, shall I play for you?"

He peered at me as if seeing me for the first time. With a sigh that came from his soul, he spoke very slowly. "Are you honest? Have you ever felt

197

that God has deserted you?"

What could I say?

He broke the silence again but spoke so haltingly with long pauses, as if each word carried the weight of his anguished soul. Sometimes, I was not sure whether he was murmuring to himself or addressing me. I had to strain to hear.

In a tiny voice, he said, "I would to God that He would speak to me. I hear nothing – nothing but silence. I look for his face in the stars, but I see nothing. I feel nothing. Everything is stale. My thoughts lie heavy upon me. Every moment is a struggle: the next thought, the next breath – everything. Why is this being done to me? Who is doing this? Oh my God, I do not deserve this."

He looked at me so pityingly that my heart went out to him.

"Great King, the Lord's anointed, your burdens are great. You hold the life of Israel in your hand. Your care is legendary. More has been put upon you than any man before – yes, even more than the Prophet. For though God speaks to him, it is you who must rule Israel. It is you who must place yourself in danger in the field. Without you, Israel would lose heart."

He looked at me dully, almost doubtfully, as I tried to find words of comfort.

"Oh King, how can you doubt? You were chosen above all other men. You were chosen to lead God's people. God does not need to speak because, in His actions, He has already shown that He loves you and Israel. He, through your valiant arms, has smitten all His enemies."

I did not stop for a moment to think, Who on earth was I, a youth from Bethlehem, telling the King of Israel that he was God's chosen instrument? At the time, it just seemed the most natural thing to say.

Saul sighed a deep sigh and then, with a wan smile, said, "David, my friend, you see so clearly. It is true that my burden is great. No one else but you sees or feels this burden: you are near to understanding. Is this is why I feel so weary with my spirit and energy all gone?"

I nodded encouragingly.

Saul continued, with a little more strength in his voice, "But why do I have those who whisper against me? Why do I have those who spy upon me? Why can't I feel the certainty of what you are saying? Why is God so far from me?"

I was at a complete loss but stumbled on, "I don't know. Samuel taught me that God is a mystery. Perhaps I should not say this, but I know that Samuel, too, sometimes waits in vain for God's voice."

This seemed to make a big impact on Saul, who instantly looked almost alert.

I went on, "He has said that God comes to him at His timing, not Samuel's." I paused, not sure how much to say. "Samuel once asked me if I heard God and I had to say no. But Samuel thinks, and sometimes I think so too, that the words of my psalms somehow come from God. Truly, when I begin to sing I do not know which words I shall use – sometimes not even the first line."

I had never even admitted this to myself before, let alone anyone else – not even to Leah.

I felt emboldened to take his hand and look him directly in the face. "My King, I know so little but I have also seen the great Samuel yearn to hear the voice of God. Just as you are now, but so often God is silent. I believe that Samuel thinks this is because God would have us understand for ourselves. That way we can grow and learn how to improve our skills. Nevertheless, Samuel said that it does not make it any easier."

His look encouraged me to go on. I did not think I was breaking Samuel's confidence, for I was speaking to God's anointed.

"When I asked Samuel about how could God be so disregarding of His Prophet, he smiled at me and said, No man, nor bard, nor Prophet, nor King can command our God – He moves in a mysterious way'. I think this must be so. Perhaps – and I don't know quite how to say this – perhaps, each man will hear or experience God in a different way. But your victories, your anointment: these are the greatest signs. There can be no doubt that God is with you."

He seemed reassured at this. "Yes. Yes, that is a good phrase," he mused. "Neither man, nor bard, nor Prophet, nor King can command God. Yes ... yes, that must be it." Then, he looked anxious. "Am I showing too little faith not to accept the many signs that the Lord of Hosts has given?"

Then I risked a lot. "Yes. Though I am lowly, you asked me to always speak to you as a friend. I think you do make too many demands upon God. Your faith should be boundless, because the blessings he has given you are boundless. You have no reason to doubt Him – no reason to doubt him at all."

He smiled slowly. He obviously wanted to be convinced. He took me in his arms and kissed me on both cheeks, "David, my young friend, my bard from God, I'd say that God is speaking through you now."

I was startled at this idea and he saw my remonstrating look. He shook his head. "Truly he is. Yes. Yes! God has sent you to me. You are a sign. Perhaps you are the voice of God but you do not know it. Come, play for me whilst I rest."

With that he lay back on his couch, closed his eyes and motioned me on to play.

I was confused, anxious even, at his words. Was I a messenger of God? How could that be? I truly felt fear at the thought. My mind raced as I had a feeling of dread. I could not bear the idea or the responsibility.

I looked at the reclining Saul, took a deep breath and I trilled my harp. The chords quietly flowed. What came seemed just right as I sang him my Mother's lullaby. It had no words but the soothing sound of a voice in accord with the gentle flow of the melody was just right.

I could see him smile as he recognised it. Within minutes he had fallen asleep. I played on quietly for a few more minutes, then stilled and let him sleep.

I stayed by him, marvelling that this wonderful man was still so oppressed by all that was before him. His magnificent frame lay back on his couch, but his whole demeanour was one of exhaustion – not of the body, but of the spirit.

Who could not have sympathy for Saul, who truly was the servant, not the master, of Israel? I sat quietly, keeping watch over the sleeping Lord's anointed.

I watched the King relax and then drift off into either meditation or sleep. I sat there and let my thoughts drift. Almost simultaneously, Saul awoke as his eldest son, Prince Jonathan, entered his apartments.

Saul looked at me and gave me a warm smile. With a slight bow, he said, "Thank you, David my friend, thank you."

Then, turning to the Prince, the smile rapidly left his face. The contrast could not have been starker.

"To what do we owe the honour of your visit, Prince?" The way he said "Prince" was so cutting. "I trust it is important. I well remember that I told Eban that I did not want to be disturbed, unless it was of vital importance to me."

Jonathan looked uncomfortable and indicated my presence.

I stood up to go but Saul intervened, "Stay, David. Stay."

Then, fixing his son with a very hard look, he said "David bar Jesse is my friend. My friend. Our dear friend, Samuel the Prophet, sent him to me." The way he said "dear friend" dripped irony.

Saul continued, "David is a skilled bard – indeed, he is my warrior bard. Let me introduce you. David, my friend – Jonathan, the Prince. But whether the Prince is my friend is difficult to judge."

I did not know what to say. I wished the ground would open up. Though I had seen Jonathan only a few times before, everything I knew about him showed that he did not deserve the humiliation I was being forced to witness.

Jonathan showed his magnanimity as he turned to me. He held out his hand and said, "Yes, Great King, my Father, I have already met this remarkable young man. I am truly pleased – truly – that you find him acceptable. Ura the Hittite has enrolled him in my troop. He has told me that David bar Jesse, despite his youth, has already made a big impression and that he is devoted to you. I am pleased to know you, David bar Jesse. May you long serve the King, my Father."

This could not have been said in a more kindly or conciliatory manner, but the King seemed to want to quarrel. "Sir, I need not your commendation for my friends. It is good that he is in your troop: he can be an extra pair of my eyes."

"Oh King, my Father, I lead the troop at your will. I command the army at your will. My only task is to serve you and Israel. As you are the servant of Israel, I am your most loyal and obedient servant – as well as your loving son."

With that, he made a low bow. What man could fail to be pleased by such an obvious demonstration of filial affection by a son who was the mirror image of his father? Jonathan seemed to exceed all men in grandeur of carriage and nobility of mind.

I dimly perceived that this mirror-image might lie at the root of Saul's irritation and the tension between them.

The King answered curtly, "I know that. You are nothing but what I made you. But why have you interrupted me when I distinctly said not to?"

Jonathan was clearly uneasy but did his best to contain himself. He paused, swallowed hard, "Oh King, my Father. Your servant, my friend and armour bearer, Elim is, I believe dying."

Saul simply glared at his son and did not answer.

So the Prince continued, "The wounds that he received in the service of Israel and his King he has born uncomplainingly. But now there is an infection." Here Jonathan was obviously moved and distressed by his thoughts. "I think ... no, I know he is dying. Elim loves you and would clasp your hand in loyal allegiance to beg your forgiveness for any misunderstanding."

I could not understand why but Saul's reaction was one of grinding fury. He almost spluttered in his rage and seemed to quite forget himself and that there was another present.

"Elim is dying? Let him rot! Your paramour! What is he to me, he that dared break my oath? His whole demeanour is that of a rebel or a traitor. His fawning affection for you is an abomination. He besmirches the House of Saul. You are a disgrace. You still protect him and call him your friend, knowing that I disapprove. Pah! His death might save your honour."

Jonathan went white. He knelt down before his father. "Father, do not say so. Elim puts you above all other men – as I do. It is the flatterers who wish to become between us. It is Abner and the rest who would separate us. My heart, hand and life are yours. It is the lying whisperers who would sunder us to hurt you in their jealousy."

Saul was not moved by any of this. He just stared coldly at his son.

Jonathan's voice was now trembling. "Oh King, my Father, how have I knowingly offended you? You are right to say that without you I am nothing. But I am your son: my enemies are your enemies because they would weaken you for their ends."

Saul's response was to continue to look at Jonathan angrily, as Jonathan tried to reason with his Father, "They know that you are loved and revered above all in Israel. They know you are the Lord's anointed. They know that you are invincible in war, in state craft, so, to hurt you, they try to blacken my name."

Saul either could not or would not answer but ground his teeth. Not one of Jonathan's words appeared to have made an impression upon him.

Then, seemingly in desperation, Jonathan tried to change tack and asked his father, "You are pleased then with your warrior bard? Is it permitted to say how he has pleased you, oh King, my Father?"

Saul frowned and then looked at me as if he had only just seen me. I was glad of the diversion from this painful interchange as he said, "Yes, David has many gifts. He can soothe because he is dutiful. He has an understanding beyond his years of the burdens I carry."

Then he gestured to me. "David, play for the Prince the psalm inspired by God which tells of my throne."

I felt uncomfortable again at having a psalm of mine directly described as being inspired by God, but I was very eager to calm things down and leave this distressing scene.

"Oh King, my master," I answered, "my verse is but a poor shadow of your glory. But, if you wish, I am willing share it with your son, the Prince."

Saul nodded assent, sat down and indicated for me to play. Jonathan gave me a quick look, which seemed to express his thanks. He sat down and bowed his head in submission, deliberately avoiding the eyes of his father.

I sang the psalm.

"The King shall joy in thy strength O Lord and in thy salvation how greatly shall he rejoice.

Thou hast given him his heart's delight – thou settest a crown of pure gold upon his head.

He asked life of thee and thou gavest it him even length of days for ever."

I could see that it was calming the situation. Both Saul and Jonathan looked intently at me as I sang on.

"His glory is great, in thy salvation, honour and majesty hast thou laid upon him.
For thou hast made him most blessed for ever; thou hast made him exceedingly glad with thy countenance.
For the King trusteth in the Lord and through the mercy of the Most High he shall not be moved."

Saul relaxed and smiled at me. Jonathan raised his head and made eye contact with his Father. The animosity that was there earlier was now much lessened. Then, Saul took up the last refrain. Quickly, Jonathan joined in. This was incredible because he had only heard it once. We all three repeated the acknowledgement of Saul's splendour.

"His glory is great in thy salvation honour and majesty hast thou laid upon him.
For thou hast made him most blessed for ever; thou hast made him exceedingly glad with thy countenance.
For the King trusteth in the Lord and through the mercy of the Most High he shall not be moved."

The words and the chords held the moment as they melted away in time and space. I did not dare say a word, but I hoped that their accord would hold.

Saul was the first to speak. "See, Jonathan, how David, sent by God, shares with me God's blessing. Can you doubt that he is God's warrior bard? Is he not a sign to me, to you and all Israel, that I trust in the Lord and am not moved?"

"Truly, oh King, my Father, he is a blessing. I praise the Lord for His words to you through your messenger," answered Jonathan.

As Saul did not answer, but still seemed calm, Jonathan continued, "It is marvellous and it is a sign: one who is so young and yet has an understanding of the burdens that the King carries. Yes, your strength cometh from the Lord and He guides you and Israel. Indeed, Father, David is God's messenger and I am privileged that you let him serve you in my troop."

Saul seemed to have forgotten his rage. "Yes, Jonathan, let the boy serve," and, turning to me, said, "you are happy to serve in my son's troop, David?"

I bowed low. "Wherever I can serve you best, my King. My troop commander Ura has, as Jonathan has said, been very kind to me. Ura has already taught me much and, most of all, of his pride that he serves you, the King of Israel."

I realised that this was getting close to flattery, even though it was the truth. I took my cue from Jonathan for, like him, I was keen that the King should be at peace.

Saul now seemed to be in an almost light-hearted mood. "Good. Good. So be it. You have my permission. Tell Ura that I am pleased. He is a fine warrior and will be a good example for you."

Then he addressed Jonathan. With only a trace of a hard look he said, "I am sorry to hear that Elim is dying. He was a worthy solider. Tell him I send my forgiveness. Say to him that, as he fought for his King and Israel, I will ask God to take his soul into Abraham's bosom."

Jonathan and I both stood. Jonathan took his Father's hand and kissed it. Saul responded and laid his hand upon Jonathan's head in a gentle blessing.

This positive end was also my dismissal. As the King acknowledged our salutes, he turned towards some parchments and began to study them.

We made our bows and left.

Jonathan – the First Meeting

"Well done, youngster. You did well!" said Jonathan, but as he spoke he looked inquiringly at me. "Did you understand what was happening in there?"

I thought quickly and decided that I could trust him. Indeed, I wanted to confide in him.

I answered, "I think so, Prince – I think so. The King is an incredible man and I can see a great resemblance of you in him." Then, I looked straight at him. "But I can understand something of the fear that must be in the heart of the King – perhaps a prince's too – because they carry such a responsibility."

I now spoke very hesitantly. "Pardon me, but when the King is so, as he ... is ...," I paused, "then he is not in command of himself, is he?"

Jonathan did not say a word but gestured for me to continue.

"His soul is heavy and it is cruel to see him so torn between his fear or anxiety. What seems to trouble him most is that he cannot trust people. He thinks there are those who plot against him."

I waited for Jonathan to speak but he remained silent.

"So, Prince Jonathan, as I cannot think that you are against him – everything that was said ran counter to such an idea – then his fears are fantastic and he turns against those who have most concern for him."

Jonathan nodded slowly. "Yes, David. I think you have it." Then, holding me hard by the shoulders, he said, "You are to say nothing – absolutely nothing – about what you have witnessed between us. The safety of Israel depends upon it." Seeing my response was one of indignation and that I was about to protest my total loyalty, he lightened up and smiled. "Aye, lad. I don't doubt you – not a jot. What we both experienced this evening tells me that you have a very cool head, and that you love your King and would die for Israel if necessary. But you must understand, even if you do not know – I'm sure that you must have worked it out in that pretty head of yours – there are those who still see themselves as an alternative King. Whilst they have been silenced by my father's victories, some are manoeuvring to be second or third man in Israel. If they could create the right situation, they might even be able to claim the crown for themselves."

This was an incredible thought, but Jonathan was right: I had worked that out for myself.

Impulsively, I reached for his hand. "You have my word. I am the King's bard and, as you are the first of the King's men, I am your man to command." I realised this was a little too earnest as I saw Jonathan smile slightly.

"David, I don't doubt it. Yes, you are a man, and I apologise if I seemed to be belittling your years, for few in Israel could have managed to be as balanced in such circumstances. I'm glad you are in my troop."

Then, moving away from the dangerous ground of the politics of the great, he sighed and changed the subject. " I gather from Ura that you show great promise. You lasted for more than ten minutes against the swordplay of Canan. That's no mean feat. I also learned that Beniah would be your friend. That, too, is good. Beniah has great judgement and he is one of my most loyal comrades. If he offers you his hand, take it in honour, for there a few better than he." By now he was smiling.

What he did not know was that his smile, with its openness and charm, was the same as that of his father – only with none of the haunted looks I had already begun to fear. No wonder every one in Israel would brave anything to gain both Saul's and Jonathan's approval.

"David, we have a secret between us. I do not need to ask for your promise – it has been given already. Tell me: your psalm, where did it come from?" But without waiting for my reply, he continued, "It was so perfect. It was inspired. Would you come and see my friend Elim to tell him what happened? Or, rather, would you confirm that the King has sent his greetings?"

His face seemed to fall with misery. "I fear that he will not see many more days." Then, almost to himself, he breathed, "Then I shall be alone again."

I did not know what to make of this, so I said nothing and followed him out towards the tent where Elim lay dying.

It was with a start that I saw Elim. He could not be more than two or three years older than I was, yet had been chosen by Jonathan to undertake such a daring and dangerous feat. Despite his youth and sparse body, he was a daring warrior.

I am no doctor, but I could see in his once handsome, delicate face that the high colour in his cheeks was not of health but of a fever. His eyes shone brightly and were so tightly constricted, that one wondered what he actually saw at all. He looked close to delirium.

When he saw Jonathan enter, he grasped his hand and kissed it as if he would never let go. Then he raised his arms upward and took Jonathan's head in his hands. Jonathan allowed himself to be drawn close to Elim's feverish brow and to be kissed on the lips.

They clung to each other in a quiet desperation, each seeming to try to stifle the sobs that would not be denied. I felt that I should not be here and would have left had I not realised that I had a message to bring. I also partly understood that I was privileged to be seeing something so extraordinary.

Elim spoke low. "Oh my dear, dear love. I do not wish to leave you. Yet you know I am close to my end." Elim quietly silenced Jonathan's attempted protestations. "You know it. I know it. There can be no untruths between us. There never was, so why now?"

He paused for breath as his face glowed with a disquieting urgency. "I do not regret a moment. Jonathan, the Prince, loved me. I have fought at his side. If I were to live a thousand years, what more could I achieve?"

I saw that this was a farewell. Again, I wondered whether I should be here but awaited my cue from Jonathan.

Elim went on, "I am the friend of the greatest solider Israel has ever had."

Jonathan would have demurred but Elim waved away his denials. "True. True! Joshua was nothing more than a daring brigand but you – you devised your father's victory. You saw what could be achieved from out of that dreadful trap that his pride and folly had driven us into. You were the instrument of his victory."

He breathed quickly and paused. The passionate words had exhausted him. He looked into Jonathan's eyes and smiled. "Now, have you been reconciled with your father? Has he forgiven me? I would not come between you – even at my... death."

Jonathan tried to speak calmly to match the bravery of his dying friend. "Yes, Elim. I saw him. He was with David the bard. He was angry with me at first – you know how on occasions he gets suspicious – but the bard calmed him with music. So, when he spoke, he spoke as the King he is, not tortured by the thoughts that distort his dignity. He understood and was grateful for your message. He fully accepts your allegiance and sends his greetings."

Only then did Elim notice me. In answer to his inquiring look, Jonathan said,

"This is David bar Jesse, a Bethlehemite. The Prophet sent him and, I believe, inspired him to bring peace to my father's heart. He will vouch for the King, whose messenger he is." Then, seeing Elim's look, he added, "Yes, he is young – but then so were you when we smote the kings of Philistia."

Their eyes meet in a look of secret delight and they laughed at the memory.

Elim turned towards me. He looked long at me and gave me a slow smile filled with so many emotions: sadness, a wistful longing – yes, even envy and urgency.

"Welcome, David bar Jesse. Elim, the friend of Jonathan the Prince, thanks you for your pains."

Then he said something very strange, which at the time I did not comprehend.

"David, I would know you better but that is not possible. Be a friend to Jonathan as I was. He is a noble Prince but, more so, he is a wonderful man. Though he is a prince, he, like all men, needs love. It is hard for a prince or a king to receive true friendship. But I think, looking at you, that you could be such a true companion. I envy you, for I can see he trusts you already. Offer him the hand of friendship, even though he is so far above you. In his friendship and love, you will see how steadfast he can be," and then, addressing Jonathan, "and he to you, my Prince."

Elim painfully turned his head to me once more. "Hail, David, friend of Jonathan the Prince. God is with you. Leave us now, I would be selfish and have my last hours with him."

I could not say a word. I took Elim's proffered hand, which was so desperately hot to touch that I almost gasped at its dry feverishness.

I turned away and left them alone.

I did not see Jonathan for over a week, but learned that he had stayed with Elim until the next morning, when Elim had died.

Over the next weeks, Jonathan was not seen much and seemed to shun me whenever our paths crossed.

Saul had me play for him three times a week and I began to appreciate that, whatever the mood or fit was, his misery and suspicion seemed to have lifted and he was more like his old energetic self.

He had me play "the King's Psalm" to all his generals. All applauded it, though Abner somehow tried to belittle it. That was the only time I saw Saul angry with Abner.

"Abner, David is my friend. God, not the Prophet, sent David to ease my soul. He is inspired by God who, through David, answers my call."

Abner at first had tried to argue in a way that I actually agreed with.

"King Saul, my Master," started Abner. "I am no priest lover. We both know how they can bleed, rather than feed, the people. Can this boy really be a messenger from God? Surely the Patriarch Moses taught us that this is a priestly function – perhaps even, oh King, a kingly function? So, would God choose a shepherd youth from Bethlehem?"

Saul would not be contradicted. "Abner, though you are second in Israel, I tell you: David is a messenger with an understanding beyond his years. This is itself a sign. I know what I know."

Abner was much too wise to pursue the matter. I then experienced his false friendship: if ever he saw me with Saul, his praise for me was dripping but his eyes, when he looked at me, were as stone.

I was uncomfortable because, if it became known that I had access to the King, many might feign to be my friend. I had to work hard in the troop to show that I only wanted to be a warrior amongst them. However, the fight with Canan was before anyone knew of my link with the King, so I knew my friends there to be true.

Through Beniah the Reubenite, I became a friend of Hushai, a Simeonite, who reminded me so much of Josh that I warmed to him at once. He, like Beniah, was four years older than I was, but that did not seem to matter as they both accepted me.

Beniah was not unlike me: dark haired, not very tall and he had a kind of stillness that others responded to. He, too, was a runner and sometimes we would train together.

When there was a quiet time, he liked to hear me play. I told him a little about Leah, and sometimes we would speak of serious things. He was absolutely devoted to Jonathan, but was generous in his spirit. Sometimes, when you have a friend, it is easy to become jealous if they share you. Not so with Beniah: he always had a warm spirit and told me how he had wept for Elim, for whom he showed not a jot of jealousy.

Hushai was a little overweight. He had an enormous appetite and was always willing to eat any scraps you might leave. He also had a great sense of humour. Like Josh, he was fierce in the wrestling ring, and was surprisingly quick for one of his build. I lost against Beniah and him most of the time, but if I did win a fall against Hushai, he told everyone about my victory in such a way, that I thought he was more pleased than I was.

Hitophel was another Judean. Naturally, he was very friendly but mainly I thought because he wanted to be close to Ura. Although he tried hard not to show it, Beniah and Hushai were Ura's favourites.

Ura was a delight. I did not realise just how lucky I had been to have him as my troop commander. I learned to laugh at his occasional crudities because he never meant ill. Always he saw the best in everyone – even Canan. Whilst he admitted to me once that I should be careful about Canan, he never let the opportunity pass to be positive about him.

Towards me, however, Canan behaved as if I did not exist. If he was in charge he usually ordered me to take the most menial duties but he never used my name. When Beniah and Ura became aware of Canan's attitude towards me, they urged patience and I took his pettiness as well as I could. I reasoned that to have only one awkward man was nothing to the joy of having friends like Ura, Beniah, Hushai and Hitophel. They were all full warriors, members of the Prince's troop, which, apart from the King's guard, was the one of greatest honours. As none was yet thirty, we were a wonderful band of comrade warriors.

We trained hard every day. It was hardest for me, not just because I was the youngest, but because they were the best and I had a lot to learn to reach their standards.

After some weeks, Jonathan came to command the troop in one of our training exercises. He seemed to ignore me. He was polite if he had to speak, but hardly ever addressed a word to me. I felt a little hurt by this, but reasoned that perhaps he was a little embarrassed because of things I should not have seen.

There was one occasion when I managed to surprise him. He was explaining how, when he had been with the Philistines, he had learned that they sent scouts into enemy country who were able to write things down and pass instructions that others that could read. This meant that a number of different troops or divisions could move into enemy territory without needing to rely upon people who knew the area.

Canan asked a very intelligent question: "Is this not difficult, Prince Jonathan, for I suppose they have to write down detailed instructions. That must take many scrolls – I would have thought."

There was a murmur of agreement.

"Yes," said Jonathan, "that's what I thought at first. But, no, there is only one piece of parchment. I was not allowed to see one, so I don't know how they do it."

"I do," I called out but, in my nervousness at speaking in front of the whole troop, my voice came out rather squeaky.

Canan cut in sharply. "Speak when you're spoken to. How dare you interrupt the Prince! Did they not teach you manners in dirty Bethlehem?"

I paused, cleared my throat and said, "Excuse me, Prince Jonathan, but I know how it's done."

Jonathan spun round, gave me a very searching look and, very smoothly, said "Really?"

I already knew that tone. When he was particularly displeased at somebody's slowness or stupidity, he used what we all called his "ice tone".

"Really?" he repeated.

"Yes, it's called a map. There's no need to write a lot of words as they use a series of symbols to mean different things."

Jonathan did not say a word, so Canan rushed in. I was not sorry that he did so, "Do you know their codes? I don't suppose you do. How can they know the direction? Boy, you really should not presume upon the Prince's good nature." He gave Jonathan what he thought was a dashing and ingratiating smile.

"Youngster, if you're wasting my time, you will do twenty punishment runs!" Jonathan looked stern as he said this but there was just a twinkle in his eye when he added, "Though I get the feeling you may know the answers to Canan's penetrating questions."

Canan looked smug but I knew I was going to get a little of my own back.

"It's really quite simple," I began. "May I demonstrate rather than explain?" Without waiting for an answer, I stood up, moved some of my companions aside and, scraping the sand flat, said, "Right – this is the parchment. We'll describe the camp." As I spoke I drew a diagram on the ground with the point of my sword.   "X is the King's tent. From where I am standing it is to the north. So mark where the North Star would be, decide that the width of my finger is equal to 10, or 100 or 1,000 metres, whatever. We are sitting east of the King – say, two fingers." I raised my fingers in Canan's direction and got a laugh.

"Let's mark our position with this Z. The latrines are due south of where we are – about two fingers, again – and mark here, Y. As long as everyone knows what the symbols mean – a hill, a river, a wood, an outcrop – the map can be as detailed or as simple as one wants. Moreover, wherever the North Star is, it can be used to indicate all other directions."

By this time everyone was looking. Of course it was so obvious, everyone understood it at once. There was quite a bit of excitement, and I wouldn't be human if I didn't admit feeling rather pleased at Canan's glowering looks.

"Where did you learn this?" asked Jonathan.

This was a little tricky. "Well, I met a raiding led by a man called Achish."

Jonathan interrupted sharply. "You know Achish, son of the King of Gath?"

"Er ... yes. Do you?" I asked.

Jonathan nodded gravely. He held out his arm and pointed to a scar. "He gave me this, though I gave him two in return."

I felt confused. I revered Jonathan. He had already become my idol but though I had only known Achish a short time, the idea of them in conflict was distressing.

"Is he dead?" I inquired, fearing the worst.

"Why should that concern you, youngster? Not to my knowledge – I wounded him badly but not fatally. Anyway, what's he to you?"

"Well, after the raid was over there was a truce. This was when I learned about the map. Achish's friend, Acrah, showed me his map, which annoyed Achish, but I pretended not to understand what it meant."

Jonathan gave me a long look. "Hmmm, that was clever. You're are quite right: once the principle is explained, it's quite easy. All right, young man, make me a map of the camp, and another from here to Bethlehem, using your symbols and we'll see how we can use it."

Even after that, Jonathan was not particularly friendly. Invariably he called me "youngster" or "young man" in front of the others. Only rarely did he call me by my name.

Whenever he was exercising with us, he always seemed to throw me down harder than anyone else. If he was testing our swordplay, it was I who seemed to have to take an extra blow.

I half-heartedly complained to Beniah, who agreed that Jonathan was hard with me. "But David, even though you lasted so long with Canan, you were right when you said in a battle you would have been finished. So Jonathan may be tough with you – he was just the same with Elim. He is like that because he cares."

This cheered me, so I strove every moment to be worthy of my troop, my friends and my captain.

Then, without explanation, Jonathan and Ura simply disappeared. No one knew where they had gone. Canan now took over the troop and intimated that he knew of their whereabouts but would not say.

For two weeks, my life was hell. I cleaned the latrines at least daily – even when it wasn't my turn. I had many punishment runs. I was sent away from the mess on the slightest excuse and, worse, he never once addressed me as a person. The only good thing was that his behaviour was so obviously prejudiced, most of the men showed me some sympathy. Beniah, Hushai and Hitophel were very supportive and either brought me the food I'd missed or, unbeknown to Canan, helped me with the latrine duties. Now that's friendship!

None the less, I was very pleased when Jonathan and Ura returned, looking somewhat physically tired. We all guessed it must have been a mission but they did not share where they had been. However, Ura came to me and quietly said that my ideas had been very helpful. The Prince was pleased and that they were going to give the Amalekites a great surprise but, infuriatingly, he would not say any more.

The Inspiration

Saul called me to play when he had visitors from Elders of the tribes. In particular, to a conference of Elders to discuss strategy, to which he had also invited representatives from the Moabites. Samuel was to come too, but he had been delayed.

Saul was on the top of his form. He went around his guests showing them every courtesy.

I met his daughters for the first time. Merab, his eldest, was so beautiful, and Michal, whose beauty was different but alluring. They did not pay me much attention, but their soft diaphanous veils filled me with exquisite delight as they moved around serving the King's important guests. Sometimes, Merab might offer me a little smile, which filled me with all sorts of thoughts. I realised that I was so far beneath them that I was wasting my time. On one occasion, Jonathan had noticed my longing looks at Merab and he teased me about it.

I tried to laugh it off. I said that I was too young, too insignificant, but he said, "How old are you – nearly eighteen? Well, I was married by then and it's good to start a family. Sorob, my wife, and the little ones are a great joy."

He went on. "Why shouldn't you look, David? Though they are my sisters, they are beautiful, and I can see that Merab charms, though Michal with her intelligence pleases me most. Who knows? You are the King's bard: they could do worse."

I did not know whether he was joking or not. Then I saw his calm but serious face, so I let myself look more. Not in real hope but – well, I was young – and without being vain, was not entirely ugly. This was the first confidence that Jonathan had shown me since the death of Elim. However, the more I thought realistically about it, the more I realised that I was a dreamer.

I sat quietly at the back until the feast was completed, hearing the talk about the coming of war against the Amalekites.

Saul told his audience that in consultation with the Prophet, he thought it time to deal with the southern threat once and for all. The Moabites were very interested because two years ago they had been badly beaten by the Amalekites, who had cruelly ravaged their lands. It was obvious that the King was hoping they might join in an alliance, and I could not help but feel excited at the thought of the coming war.

Would all my training be enough? Would I stand the test? Suddenly my thoughts crashed about me. I had yet to be in a battle. What if I let my comrades down? The thought of being unworthy made me go cold. Then, through my reverie, I heard the voice of Saul call out.

"My friends and dear allies, we will take counsel tomorrow when the Prophet comes and test whether God would bless our endeavours. Till then, drink deep and hear my bard. David bar Jesse, come, give us your message."

I played for them what the King called the Psalm of Saul. It gained great applause and had to play it twice more. What also pleased everyone was to see Jonathan sitting close to the King. Though the Moabites sat on his right, of course, Jonathan was amongst the Elders, whilst Abner sat on the right of the Moabites. To an outsider, the picture was one of total unity. Whereas, I knew there were deep tensions beneath that calm exterior, which clever men took great pains to hide.

Then Jonathan spoke. "Oh King, my Father, David, your bard, has pleased us well. He has reminded us that you are the Lord's anointed and 'shall not be moved'."

Then, turning to face me, he asked me directly, "Have you anything further for the King?"

I don't know whether it was my imagination but there was total silence. I wished I could have shrunk into nothingness. What was Jonathan asking of me? I tried to rehearse some psalms in my head that might be suitable, and silently cursed Jonathan for placing me in such a situation.

Then, the King spoke. "Yes, David, my bard, Jonathan the Prince invites your further inspiration."

It was a command. I could do no other. I looked over at Jonathan whose gaze held mine and, as I looked at him, I had a sense that he was urging me to play a part in a mission that I did not fully understand.

I bowed. My fingers strummed the instrument as my mind drifted away. I could feel a silence of expectation grow around me.

I followed some chords as I let the harp take me where it would. I had a sense of excitement as I closed my eyes. The words came, but this time with a sound in my head that was fearful. I had an appalling feeling of a sense of vastness, yet my breath and voice sang as if I was at total peace. I was filled with a sense of joy and dread in equal parts. For the first time, I truly knew the words were given.

"The earth is the Lord's and the fullness thereof – for he hath founded it upon the seas and established it upon the floods."

I knew the words would flow. I was conscious of nothing: my body, my mind not even my spirit existed. I was nothing but an instrument as I was taken over by the inspiration.

"Who shall ascend unto the hill of the Lord or who shall stand in his holy place. He that hath clean hands - who hath not lifted up his soul in vanity.
Lift up your heads oh ye gates and be ye lifted up ye everlasting doors and the King of glory shall come in."

I felt every man breathed with me. I repeated the line as my spirit soared to catch what it would.

"Lift up your heads oh ye gates and be ye lift up ye everlasting doors and the King of glory shall come in.
Who is this King of Glory, the Lord, strong and mighty the Lord, mighty in battle."

My voice took on a force of its own. I found a strength that I did not know I had as I sang the last phrase again.

"Who is this King of Glory, the lord strong and mighty, the Lord, mighty in battle."

There was not a sound as the chords fell away.
The stillness was almost painful. I was exhausted. I felt myself sway. My head span. I felt a vortex of dizziness. I feared I would faint.
I knew I had been close to something truly terrible. I slowly opened my eyes to see a look of wonder on everyone's face.
Suddenly, they erupted. "Hallelujah! Hallelujah! Hosanna! Hosanna! Who is this King of Glory? The Lord, strong and mighty. The Lord, mighty in battle."
I was, utterly, utterly drained. Empty, like a cast away potsherd.
Jonathan was embracing his father. The King embraced him in turn. Each man seemed to be clasping the hand of his neighbour. Even Abner

looked moved.

Saul came across to me and amidst the cries of "Hosanna! Saul, King of Israel, mighty in battle."

He raised his arms for silence. "Hear, oh Israel. If the Lord God is with us, who can be against us?" They cheered him to the echo.

Saul came to me putting both his arms around me to shield my waxen face from the gaze of others and quietly said, "You did not know, did you, what your song would be?"

I nodded, still drained, part with elation but more with dread. I knew something awesome had happened which I was desperate not to accept.

"These were not your words, were they?" Saul continued. "As you sang, were you inspired?"

I looked pleadingly at him. He would force upon me a responsibility that I did not own, that I could not control and that I was not worthy of. I knew that the words were given. What chilled my soul was the realisation that they were an inspiration. That, out of the silence high above, beyond the dreams of each man's soul, the words had been directed as sure as if a messenger had carried them on scrolls.

My soul whispered and my mind heard in dread, God help me. I am that messenger.

Saul smiled at me. "You too, David. You too are beginning to know the burden of His yoke upon you." He gave me a sad, almost pitying, look. "It is no more easy to be the bard of God, than to be God's anointed." He embraced me and kissed my tears. My soul wept with the affliction from the awareness of the trials that were before me.

"No, no, my friend David. You yourself said it: God speaks to men in different ways. It is better that you know the weight of God's hand upon you. Could you imagine that being God's bard would be without sacrifice?"

I looked at him in alarm. I knew what he was saying. I never felt closer to him, but I was almost dizzy with the apprehension. It was as if I was standing on a great height.

I had not sought this. I thought of Leah and her inspiration. I recalled Samuel's words, which I now realised were not a prophecy, but a warning.

Without waiting for his leave, I turned and rushed out into the night as if I could flee the curse of God's gift.

I ran, and ran, and ran for miles. My tears flew behind me. I knew I would never be free again. I felt terror, awe, panic, as I fell exhausted to the ground, filled with a lowliness that was overwhelming. I did not want this power.

My tears were choking me. The blinding illumination in my head was worse than death. What had I become? I was consumed by a power that was

215

blind to me. It engulfed me as the sea casts a grain of sand. I was possessed with a dreadful ecstasy.

I would never, never, be free! Through the whole aeons of time, I would be a messenger of God. I could not stop.

I cried out so loud that the mountains threw back my words. "I am not worthy. My God, my God, why hast thou chosen me?"

I collapsed and knew nothing but oblivion.

Chapter Ten

Saul's Victory

Jonathan – Friendship

I returned to my companions a day later, though I ached. My mind could hardly put a thought together. The journey back was agony as my limbs were filled with a weariness too absolute to describe. Beniah was waiting outside the camp. He told me that Jonathan had seen me flee and that he had come to see if I needed any assistance.

I was angry with Jonathan, as if what had happened was his fault.

I asked petulantly, "Why should I need assistance?"

Beniah looked grave. "You cannot see yourself," and said no more. I was grateful to him for his silence, but as we came close to a stream he stopped and said, "Let's drink. You first."

I knelt down and fell back with a start. The face that was reflected in front of me was my own. Yes, it was my face but it was changed as if it had been aged in some way. On my left temple, amidst the strong and youthful black, was a streak of pure white hair.

I stood up and fell into his arms crying.

Beniah was such a good friend. He was so sensible. He did not ask anything or press me. He suggested that we find shelter and rest for another night before going back. I wearily agreed, when he said, "I'm sure you wouldn't want to hear what Ura said last night. He said he was proud of you for leading such a merry singsong that the whole camp was alive with the talk of it. He said that he had encouraged you and, indeed, taught you some less solemn camp songs."

Despite my misery, I could not fail to smile at the thought.

We arrived back at the camp early the next morning. We joined our companions as they were beginning to wake. I did not know it but Jonathan had warned them that I might be a little distressed and that they were to treat me as usual.

So, to my relief, no one said a word about my absence, though Ura said it was time I was putting on weight.

"David, lad, to be fair, you have improved. I'll not say it's only because I am teaching you. But if you come up against an Amalekite as big as Hushai, he'll squash you before you can do any of your tricks."

The only person to hint at anything amiss was Canan – of course! He came to the sword practice and looked startled. "Your hair, it's... it's..." Then, being quickly silenced by the others, he sneered a cold smile and said, "Age seems to be getting the better of you."

The training went on but now it was my turn to avoid Jonathan. I played once a week for Saul, who was far too wise to say anything about our last conversation, and I always played safe psalms.

I began to think about my weight and what Ura had said, so I went into special training to try to build up my muscles, as well as going for a run very early most mornings. It was as if I wanted to punish my mind and body. I occasionally had thoughts about Merab or Michal when I saw them. I felt somewhat angry at their allure, though I knew that it was not their fault they irritated me.

I would not let myself think any further about the night of what I began to call in my mind the "Night of the Curse". Though some might think it a gift, I knew better. I had been close to the mind of God. My soul had felt the flame and terror of God.

The training and extra eating served to build me up and, as my wrestling and swordsmanship improved, I began to hold my own more often – though I still lost most times.

About two months later I was returning from one of my pre-dawn runs. I felt good – my running was so smooth. Athletes know the feeling when their training is just right. I had travelled ten miles and was aiming to go to the Pool of Joshua, about three miles from the camp, where I could bathe alone. When I arrived there, it was hardly light. I stripped off and luxuriated in the cool, cool water, watching the dust of the road lift from me.

I suddenly realised that I was not alone. A tall warrior figure stood at the side of the bank. It was Jonathan.

He looked as if he had also been running. He stripped off and kicked away his skirt.

He had a magnificent physique. He raised his arms high and then hurled himself into an upward dive into the water. He thrashed around with great swimming strokes as quickly he swam towards me. I did not know what to do.

He came up to me. He did not smile but asked quietly, "Why have you been ignoring me David?"

I could not answer.

"David, I asked you a civil question. Do I not deserve at least a civil answer?"

"I'm sorry, Prince. I have needed more training to catch up with the others. Ura rightly demands much from me. Perhaps I should not be in your troop." Then I said bitterly, "After all, everyone else is a full warrior. I'm one of the lightest. I'm easily the youngest. There is so much I don't know. Living in the camp is hard if you're..." I trailed off.

He answered for me. "Different? Yes, you are different, David. You have a gift – no, many gifts – but that's why more is expected of you. Though I must confess I never thought I'd hear self-pity coming from you."

I just glared at him and swam a little way off. He let the slow current bring him nearer to me.

"Sorry. Perhaps I was harsh. Yes, it's true that it must be difficult for you and for the rest of the troop, too. Though you have your colours, they weren't sure how to deal with you being the King's bard. But I'll say this, David, though it must be tough, you've earned their respect. So no more self-pity please, it doesn't become you. Come, let us go back together."

He put his hand out to me and it was like a shock. I felt confused and drew back.

"Come," he directed. "My father will announce the beginning of the war today. You should be there – especially as Samuel is expected tomorrow."

He swam back and I followed him. He stood up out of the water, his body open to the breeze. He shook his head and the water flew. As he turned towards me I could see his full nakedness. He held out his hand to me. I too stood up and half-turned as if to hide myself. I had never before been ashamed of my nakedness.

"David, come."

I took his proffered hand. I could not take my eyes from him, nor could I avoid noticing his body. Broad, firm-chested, with scars upon both his arms, showing up white against the sun-bleached skin. One ugly gash at the side of his ribs told how close he had been to death.

The rising sun picked out his soft, light brown hair, turning it golden on his chest. My eyes were drawn downwards along his hard ribbed stomach, to the sun tinted hair around his phallus, which was long and well shaped. He drew me out of the water and we stood close together. I was spellbound.

I don't know what I felt, but here was a man I knew I loved and admired above all others. I held my breath but could not help but wonder whether he could hear my pounding heart?

We lay resting upon the bank, letting the rising sun warm us dry – it seemed the most natural thing in the world.

"You must be pleased with your progress," he said. "I realise that I have not been too encouraging but, as I said, you're doing well."

This was high praise indeed because he was normally so sparing with such words.

"It may be the last quiet time we'll get for some months." Then he spoke more slowly. "Perhaps I should not ask – I only do so as a friend, not your captain – how well did you know Achish?"

Then, abruptly, he changed the subject. "Because of you, we can make maps like the Philistines. This is a great contribution to the war. The Amalekites will be surprised."

I suddenly realised that this was where he and Ura had been.

"Have you been on a scouting raid with Ura?" I asked.

"Yes, and we got some very useful information. But tell me," changing the subject again, "you never said how you came to know Achish."

I thought it best to tell him everything and explained briefly how we had come to an impasse and how I had helped with Acrah.

"You may think I did wrong but to seal the truce Achish offered to make me his blood brother."

Jonathan started. "Really! That is remarkable! Although he's our enemy," and pointed to his scarred arm, "he is a fine warrior. Blood brother is a rare honour." Then, sharply, he inquired, "Were you his philia?"

I flushed and answered, "No, of course not. He and Acrah were philian."

In part to cover my confusion, I asked him directly, "Were you and Elim philian?"

He took a deep breath and turned on his side towards me. "Yes – and only you know. Our love was something wonderful, but we in Israel do not understand that men can love each other. Does that shock you?"

"No," I hesitated. "Not that I fully understand, though I know that I admired Achish more than anyone I had ever met – until I knew you." I blushed when I said this.

"I know in my heart that though he is a Philistine, neither he nor you could do anything dishonourable," Jonathan said in measured tones.

Suddenly, I wanted to share everything with him: to tell him about Leah and how I still grieved for her. He showed concern, but what was I saying: Leah's death was almost a year ago but his loss was still green.

"Jonathan, I'm sorry. I was being selfish. Your loss is so recent. How do you manage now that Elim is gone?"

He lay back upon the grass and looked up to the now clear blue sky. He closed his eyes but then turned his head towards me. His eyes said everything. I was shocked at the depth of his distress. I realised that he had carried this burden without any apparent difficulty, whilst all the time he must have been devastated.

Impulsively, I stretched my hand out to him.

He took it and, as he held me, he said, "Thanks, gentle David. Elim is still a wound in my heart, I... I..." he struggled with the words "... I felt so desolate. I thought I would die with grief – especially as I felt so alone."

He sat up and we faced each other. "Have you any comfort, David?"

I thought. What could I say? Then I lay back, closed my eyes and sang what I knew was a benediction. I felt sure that Leah would not mind me sharing it.

"The Lord is my shepherd, I shall not want.
He maketh me to lie down in green pastures, he leadeth me beside the still waters."

I sensed Jonathan's response and prayed that it would heal him as it had healed me.

"He restoreth my soul, he leads me in the paths of righteousness of his name's sake.
Yea though I walk in the valley of the shadow of death I will fear no evil for thou art with me thy rod and thy staff comfort me.
Thou preparest a table in the presence of mine enemies, thou anointest my head with oil my cup runneth over – I will dwell in the house of the Lord for ever."

I opened my eyes as I felt Jonathan's tears fall upon my face. He laid his head upon my chest and I held him in my arms as we lay silent together.

He withdrew himself. "I'm sorry. I should not be weak but that was inspired. Thank you."

At his request, I taught it him and we sang it quietly together. Then he asked me about my "inspiration".

I felt and looked troubled so he did not press me but I needed to understand better myself.

I said, "It is hard to explain since I don't fully understand it. I have always enjoyed music and putting words to music but, over the past year or so, almost without effort, I have been composing psalms which I recognise move people."

I looked at him hesitatingly but his quiet look encouraged me to go on. "Samuel told me I was in love with religion – perhaps I was then. I'm not sure I am now. No, I love God – as I understand Him. But this power I fear. And the struggle I sense between the Prophet and your father, and you and he, is frightening."

"Yes, David. It is a heavy burden. My father spoke to me of you, of how he knew you had been called. I can only guess at the burden the King takes, even though some day I expect to carry the load. But I am serving an apprenticeship, whilst he has been alone from the very first. He is the King who must act now and there is no one – save the Prophet – to guide him. And you, David. He believes in you. You seem to understand the weight of the crown. This gives him much solace, which he takes as a sign from God. I try to help, but somehow he knows that he has to protect me. That's why when the dark mood is upon him I know he is ill. Fundamentally, he is a good man."

He said this fiercely, which made me understand how hurtful it must have been for a loving son to be so decried and mistrusted. With a generosity that was typical of him, he held no animosity for his father.

"It must be worse for you, Jonathan. The strangeness of it all – the situation has become too complex for me to grasp. As I let my mind drift, the psalms became surer, more focused, more certain. And the last time..."

My voice fell to a whisper as I faced him in wonder. "I knew they were not my words, but given. That the voice was not my voice, but had a force that I have not. Jonathan! Oh God, Jonathan! I am possessed! Am I mad, do you think?"

"You poor boy. You have coped with much that would frighten many an experienced warrior. I know also my father suffers from his gift of anointment and has on two occasions said that he wished he had never been chosen. It can seem more like curse than a gift."

I nodded. " Yes! Yes! That's how I feel – I don't want this 'inspiration'. I never asked for it. It is too great a burden." Then, almost desperately, I cried. "I can't cope, Jonathan. I am paralysed with fear. Nothing could be more terrible. It's choking me."

He held me in his arms and rocked me gently. "David, I am grateful that I do not have your inspiration – nor that of Samuel's, nor my father's. Gift or curse, it weighs heavy upon you all. But David, I cannot but think that God would not demand of you that which you cannot achieve. It would be against His purpose. I am confident that He will give you the strength and courage – aye – and wisdom too, to be His instrument. That at the end you will be blessed and He magnified."

I was overwhelmed by his kindness, protection and friendship.

His words smoothed my distressed spirit, as he repeated:

"...though I walk in the valley of the shadow of death I will fear no evil, for thou art with me thy rod and thy staff they comfort me."

Then he kissed me gently on the lips. Our eyes looked into each other's. I returned the kiss and felt a flush and warmth of my arousal, hard against his. He could see my confusion as I lay in his arms, totally trusting.

He smiled, kissed me again and breathed, "There will be a time, David – if you wish it, but not now. Come, let's dress and see whether the war of Israel has waited for Israel's Prince and bard."

Then, in the way I had become accustomed to, in his comradely manner he gave an order – not like some soldiers: barkingly harsh – but a firm direction as if he was asking you to do a favour.

"Come, you'll catch cold. We should return."

As we rose he suddenly looked sad again. "It is strange but Elim – dear Elim – urged me to speak to you. He saw not just your gifts, but your soul. He grasped before I did, though not before my father, that you were blessed of God. That your inspiration would lighten other men's road to God, though it may seem a burden to you."

Then the mood passed from him. He helped me dress without another word.

I did not know what I wanted, but meekly followed his lead and turned towards the camp.

We both realised that we did not need words. We had crossed a boundary and begun a journey whose destination neither of us knew. For me it was enough that this wonderful man was my friend and that I felt for him a love that was beyond my imagination. I would die rather than fail him. I would willingly lose my soul than cause him any dishonour as we ran together and re-entered the world.

Battle Plans

Samuel arrived in great state. He was met equally by the King, who was robed in his magnificence, and for whom all doubts seemed to have disappeared.

Samuel greeted me very formally and expressed pleasure that I had been of "Great service to Saul, the King. This pleases me more than you can appreciate, David bar Jesse."

The talk was of war.

The Moabites had agreed to provide a small army to march with Israel against the Amalekites. Samuel was not pleased. He argued that, as God had promised the land to Israel, only Israel should cleanse it.

Saul argued back, roundly supported by Abner and Jonathan, that there was nothing intrinsically wrong in Israel having allies – providing they were not disrespectful of God.

"Would you be dependent upon the uncircumcised?" countered Samuel.

Saul patiently tried to get Samuel to see that God's mark upon his chosen people was acknowledgement of the covenant. Providing others did not practise abominations, they too might turn to the living God. Would God reject people when they could not have known of the Lord of Hosts?

Samuel's argument was that of Moses: that the people were fickle, that in the wilderness they were too easily tempted to follow idolatry, human sacrifice – therefore, we should be absolutely separate.

Jonathan was to the fore in these discussions, partly because it avoided his father being seen too obviously at odds with the Prophet, which would not be good for morale. Abner on this occasion was happy for Jonathan to lead.

"Sir Prophet" argued Jonathan. "You yourself have taught that in seeking God, we seek justice, truth and light. Yes sir, human sacrifice is an abomination, but the Moabites do not behave so. The people were fickle, but that was many, many years ago, and now they have you as their Prophet, as their guide and as their father. They also have the King as their shield. This will ensure that the Lord's commandments are kept. You also taught us that God gave us our intelligence to understand for ourselves. Therefore, he does not speak everyday as a father might to a child. He is rather as a caring father to a young man: to guide him only when necessary, lest the son does not learn for himself. Also, Great Prophet, you taught us that God moves in a mysterious way and that God uses many instruments for his purpose. I cannot but see that the Moabites, being willing to fight alongside Israel, are fighting in God's cause as an instrument in His hands."

The priests, of course, argued with Samuel and more extremely, with piercing shouts and threats of excommunication and spiritual exile. They even suggested that Jonathan had gone too far. Who was he to say what was God's cause? They were not an attractive sight. They argued that God's covenant was with Israel alone and they they we are a special people, set aside by and for God. Jonathan was reasonableness itself and many I feel saw this as a good omen for when his time came to be king.

"Who can doubt that Israel is God's chosen people?" answered Jonathan. "He has given us so many signs. The time in the wilderness; Moses, the Patriarch; Joshua – you, our Prophet, and my father, his victories. But surely, God does not want a world in which only we know him? Is not our great task to show God to the other peoples of the world and, when we find men of good will, proclaim to them God's majesty, and lead them into a knowledge of the love of God?"

There was applause amongst many of the listeners.

Samuel smiled somewhat scornfully. "King Saul, did you know you had a philosopher for a son? See what happens when you allow him to live amongst the uncircumcised. He argues with a false logic, he does not grasp the mystery of God. He would put God in his puny likeness and finite intelligence. Remember our Father Adam's great sin was disobedience. In his effort to get knowledge, he would be like God himself. No, no, Jonathan the Prince, the Covenant is for God's people alone and the seed of Abraham will cover the earth. That is His promise. That must be the conclusion!"

I was torn in two. I revered Samuel and, though I knew I loved Jonathan, it was not my regard for him that made me side with him. Everything I knew about God had to mean that he would somehow include all the peoples. For the idea that he would simply destroy them in their ignorance, people like Leah, Acrah, Achish, was too harsh to contemplate.

The argument went on. Finally, whilst there was still some disagreement, they hammered out what seemed to be a compromise, which Saul accepted.

Samuel was fierce. I had never seen him more awesome. "Hear what the Lord says to you, Saul the King." His voice became like thunder as it rolled around the valley so that not a man present could not but hear him. "I have suffered many insults from the accursed, vile, uncircumcised Amalekites. Now is the time for you to go down upon them and scatter them from the face of the earth for ever. I will deliver them into your hands. But they are to be destroyed to the uttermost. Take no prisoners, destroy them utterly: men, women, children; their oxen, sheep and asses. Let nothing remain on the earth to show that the Amalekites despoiled this Holy Land."

This caused some consternation, not only amongst the Generals, but also with the Elders who were present. A "no prisoner" campaign would make the enemy more desperate if they knew the doom they were facing. Their resistance would become even fiercer and more men of Israel would have to die before they were overcome. Not that anyone felt pity for this most pitiless race, but there were many that quietly doubted the wisdom of total annihilation. After all, why destroy all that booty? The men would expect some spoils: at least the women and children, the former for their concubines and handmaidens, the children to take or sell into bondage. Yet I could not help but recall how Leah had shown me how cruel and unjust bondage can be.

To my amazement my reverie was broken as Samuel called out to me, "David bar Jesse, bard of God, what think you?"

I stammered and tried to say that I had no right to speak in this company.

"If Samuel the Prophet ask of you," he roared in his most dangerous voice, "who dare gainsay you?"

I was trapped. I looked to Saul, Jonathan and Samuel, and then around at the Elders. I realised some did not know who I was. Others were very surprised that the voice of a youth was being sought.

"Oh Saul, my King, the Lord's anointed. Samuel, God's and Israel's Prophet, that the Amalekites have to be destroyed so that they can never again be a threat to Israel seems right."

Samuel's eyes glowed in approval.

"But," I continued and he looked astonished, "the King is the father of his army and he would not lose a single one, though all know that some must make the ultimate sacrifice for Israel. If the enemy know there will be no prisoners, then in their desperation they will fight to the end. In their desperation the King may lose many of his children. Whereas, when they are delivered into our hands as you and God has promised, we could take them into bondage and scatter them around the world – even to the ends of the Great Sea and into the land of Egypt. As for killing the women, bondage is hard enough. I recall that Moses reminded us that 'we too were strangers in the land of Egypt'."

Samuel was not pleased. "Would you quote the word of the Lord to me!"

Without waiting for any answer, he turned and raised his staff high into the air. Everyone went silent. You could feel the collective cold shiver down every man's spine.

"I, Samuel, Prophet of God, give you God's word, Saul the King. Do not disobey, for if thou dost, then thy house will be scattered from the face of Israel and you and your seed shall be barren. This is the word of God. You will smite the heathen Amalekites utterly, so that even where the wind bloweth there will be no trace of this accursed race who have been a trouble to the people of Israel and the face of God."

Clearly, there was to be no more argument: the die had been cast. Despite the doubts in many hearts, we had heard the doom of the Amalekites.

Then, as if the rift was nothing, Samuel turned smilingly to the King in his most pleasing manner. "I hear that David the bard hath been a great inspiration to you and that he has made a great song of Saul. Shall we hear it?"

Saul was still somewhat struck by the overwhelming order he had just received, but eagerly took up the sign of some reconciliation. "Yes, but I have heard that David the bard had a song for thee, too, oh Prophet, my Father. Let us hear first your praise and the worship of God."

I came forward, knowing that I was part of some covert struggle. All I wanted to do was to bring some peace.

I played as instructed, calling out the Psalm of Samuel.

"Rejoice in the Lord oh ye Righteous for praise is comely for the upright."

I pointed to Samuel.

"He loveth righteousness and judgement, the earth is full of the goodness of the Lord. By the word of the Lord were the heavens made and all the host of them by the breath of his mouth.
Blessed is the nation whose God is the Lord and people whom he hath chosen for his own inheritance."

Samuel stood with his head bowed. Yet I could see that he was deeply pleased at the shout that went up from the congregation of the most important men in Israel.

Samuel said, "Blessed indeed is the nation whose God is the Lord. David, you have it aright. Now sing for us the psalm of Saul the King, so all shall know that he, next to God, is our most beloved."

This drew immediate applause as men breathed easier that the rift was not as deep as was feared.

I found the key and sang Saul's psalm, trying hard to be as even in the psalm's praise of the King as I was for Samuel.

"The earth is the Lord's and the fullness thereof - for he hath founded it upon the seas and established it upon the floods, Who shall ascend unto the hill of the Lord or who shall stand in his holy place. He that hath clean hands – who hath not lifted up his soul in vanity.
Who is this King of Glory, the Lord, strong and mighty, the Lord mighty in battle."

The acclamations reached the skies. The generals and captains gave out their hosannas, drew they swords in a great salute and, like a wondrous choir, rolled back the words in praise of their King.

"Who is this King of Glory, the Lord, strong and mighty the Lord, mighty in battle."

Saul could not keep the smile from his face. I glanced at Jonathan whose look said volumes, which encouraged me to move between King and Prophet. Without a word, I went towards Samuel, bowed low, and took his hand, drawing him on towards Saul. I drew him before Saul to whom I bowed low.

Their eyes met. I took up Saul's hand and placed it into Samuel's. They clasped each other's hand firmly and, to a great shout of rejoicing, they fell into each other's arms and embraced.

The cry went up, started by Jonathan, "The Lord is with us! Who then can be against us?"

That night, I was called by Jonathan to attend the King and Prophet. He made no intimation about our friendship, so I said nothing further to him.

Only Azrah, one of Samuel's younger sons, was present. He was a burly man, quick minded and less surly than some of his other brothers, who had never forgiven the House of Saul for what they still thought of as usurping the rights of the priesthood.

Abner was there and, though he said not a word to me, I could see he was not pleased at my inclusion.

I would have willingly stayed with my friends. I had no taste for these high politics, which cleaved friends and demanded choices that cut across companionship and loyalties. The atmosphere seemed relaxed though and Samuel was everything a gentle father could be, to both Saul and myself.

As we supped, Samuel took me aside a little and asked, "How like you your service with the King?"

I told him I was honoured and hoped that the strife between them was now ended.

He expressed amazement that he thought there was anything untoward. "After all, Israel's covenant is with God. I am God's prophet and I chose the Lord's anointed."

I relaxed even more as he said quietly, "You are still my friend, David, are you not? More so now that I know you know that you have been called."

I looked at him. He nodded. "My boy, did I not prophesy that whether or not you wished it, God had a plan for you and that he had marked you out for a great gift and blessing?"

Perhaps I was too blunt as I blurted out, "I did not ask for this gift. It does not feel like either a gift or a blessing."

He looked at me with understanding and some sympathy. "But now you know, do you not, David, that God has chosen you?" Then with a look of infinite sweetness which explained why I loved him, he said, "I too wept, and still weep sometimes when God speaks, and cry when He does not. We are all bound together: he, thou and I. And I tell you frankly, David, my son and friend, I do not know this story's end."

His words were curiously reassuring. When I thought about things later, if I'd been told that the Prophet did not know what was to happen, I would have been terrified. Yet now, I could see, albeit unclearly, that there was a purpose. God only allowed us to see a little at a time, lest His vision, His power, scald us.

I also saw, perhaps for the first time, that Samuel was similarly awed by the fellowship of God. Despite having this great privilege and nearness to God, he was still human – still fallible. In the hand of a power, and as he said, "whose story's end he did not know".

Then he asked, "And how do you deal with the King's fit when the mood comes upon him? Can you banish his dark thoughts?"

I was startled by his directness and stumbled out something that the King had been free of his passion for weeks now.

"So he still has them? Be careful my boy!" he hissed.

Then I heard Saul call. "Samuel, what do you speak of with David my bard, eh? What do you speak of? Come, come, tell me, David."

My blood froze. I recognised the tone, the suspicion. "Oh King, my master, I am telling Samuel how you have shown great goodness to me. That I, like the rest of Israel, am grateful to our King and Father."

"Well, Samuel? Is that so? Is that so? What do you think of the Psalm of Saul? He has your gift of divination, don't you think?"

I was beginning to feel very uncomfortable and could almost have hugged Abner when he intervened. "King Saul, Samuel, David plays the harp well but he is still a youth. He is but an instrument in the hands of his King and perhaps his Prophet. You both make too much of the boy. What do you say Prince Jonathan – are we making too much of this singer?"

Jonathan smiled. "Who can doubt the wisdom of Abner? I salute you," and, with that, he raised his goblet. "We should ask you and the King to share with the Prophet your great deliberations against the Amalekites."

I shot him a grateful glance as the conversation now focused upon the strategy and tactics for the coming war.

Saul was himself again as he, Abner and Jonathan sketched out the plan. The King and Abner would take command of almost half the army each, leaving Jonathan with but a division.

Jonathan's task was to take his column of 5,000 men, drive deep into the land of the Amalekites and do as much damage as possible. The idea being that he would attract the whole of the Amalekite army towards his column. With the recently introduced maps of their territory, he should be able to move quickly and keep just out of their reach. He had to ensure they did not catch him this side of the River Paran. Jonathan's main task was to draw the Amalekites over the water to our side and draw the enemy into the trap of the narrowing Valley of Havilah. With the river behind them, it was Saul and Abner's intention that once Amalekites were broken there would be no place for them to flee.

Saul turned to Samuel. "There, my Prophet. How like you our deliberations? You see I have every intention of eradicating the Amalekite threat for ever."

It was superbly simple.

My heart raced – I would be with Jonathan. Oh, I prayed that I would not disgrace him. Thinking quickly about the rapid marches we would have to make, I was thankful that my training had gone so well. Indeed, I thought I might be able to volunteer for a special mission because he knew that I was one of our best long distance runners. I let my fancy take me and began to imagine that he might make me his armour bearer – as he had Elim.

I was still with my thoughts when I realised that the conference was breaking up to shouts of "The army marches tomorrow! Hosanna!"

The King and Prophet were again embracing, each saluting the other.

Jonathan beckoned me over, not as my friend but as my captain. "The army marches tomorrow and we in the vanguard expect the troop to be at least two days' march ahead within the first day."

I grinned idiotically. I began to feel very excited. I knew I would not let him down. He must know it too. I would rather die ten times that bring any breath of dishonour upon him. My look seemed to irritate him as he snapped.

"You can take that silly grin off your face now, boy!" Then came the stunning blow. "You are not going."

I was totally flabbergasted. Was he afraid that I would fail him?

I opened my mouth to argue, protest, plead – anything to accompany him.

"Shut up and listen," he said sternly. "The King has important messages he wants to go to the northern tribes."

My heart sank – the northern tribes were weeks away.

Jonathan continued. "He wants you to take dispatches to Judah and find men there to take them on up north. At the same time, Samuel, who will follow the army a few days afterwards, also has dispatches that must go to Judah and to Gad. Again, you are to pass them on to messengers in Judah and come back here to escort the Prophet."

I was furious. They were making me a messenger boy – was not I now a full warrior?

I was so angry that I could barely speak. "I'm not going. I'm coming with you. I am going to be your armour bearer, as Elim was. He was young for his first campaign – remember?"

His look was as stone. "You will obey orders. Because you are a good runner and will do as you're told, instead of taking six days, the messages will take only five days. The messages will get to the northern tribes, who are to move south, not to attack the Philistines but to make sure that they are concerned with watching their borders rather than getting involved in our push against the Amalekites."

Then he glared at me. "I don't know why I am bothering to explain myself to you, David bar Jesse. I should slap you for your impertinence."

I pulled myself up. I, who understood the need for discipline, obeyed, though my flaming face showed my sense of shame. "I am sorry, Prince. Give me my instructions and I will obey", I said coldly.

His look softened, "David, I know what you are thinking – that perhaps I am fearful for you being in danger. No, no, I would not insult you. No, it makes sense that you are best used by ensuring that our people know what to do as quickly as possible."

He slowly led me out of the tent. "Now listen, go to Bethlehem. We have already sent earlier messengers so there should be new messages awaiting you to bring back here. These are to be handed over to your father, who knows where to send them on."

He thrust some scrolls into my hands. "Wait until you have the parchments from the northerners and the Gadites. If they are not there by the sixth day, then you are to return here and lead the escort of the Prophet. Surely, David, such a position of honour should even satisfy you, my young cockerel?"

I was not pleased but saw that it had to be so and was partly mollified.

Then, as he spoke, he melted my resentment away totally. He asked me softly,

"Have you thought about your feelings for me? You know that I want nothing more than your good. If you still feel about me the way I hope you might, when you arrive at your eighteenth year, you can decide."

I did not understand. "Why should we wait?" I asked, though what I was asking for I did not fully comprehend.

"Because, David, you may feel differently. Think about it. We are friends and our love can wait. Now, go with God!" He drew me towards him and kissed me warmly, but then saluted formally and returned inside.

I admit I was still disappointed but I thought that if he wanted the messages to get there in five instead of six days, I would start now and ensure that they arrived in a mere four.

It was night-time but I knew most of the way and could navigate by the stars. This was one of many things that Jonathan had taught me: how some stars were fixed and, therefore, how one could pilot the way in the right general direction.

I reported to Ura what was happening. If he thought anything, he did not say. "I'll tell Beniah and the others about your mission. Don't worry – we'll save an Amalekite or two for you!"

He embraced me and sent me on my way.

Una the Mouse

I arrived in Bethlehem just before sunset, less than three and a half days later. I was exhausted. I was kept going by the thought that if the northerners' and Gadites' messages had arrived, then I could get back in time to catch up with the main body of the army. Of course, they weren't there. I could do little more than accept the blessings of my father and tell him all the news.

Father called in Josh, Aaron and Eli, and we embraced. They were to carry on my messages north and east tomorrow, so we all felt very involved.

I told them about the camp life. Perhaps I exaggerated just a little about how fierce Ura could be, how heavy Hushai was to throw and how tough the drill was. However, I said nothing about Mera, Canan or the latrines. They were wide-eyed.

Then Aaron, of all people, flummoxed me. "And what about the women, David? Tell us about the women."

I laughed in amazement. "Aaron, my friend, I think you must have grown a lot in the last few months."

Eli assured me that Aaron did nothing now but talk about women and that Josh and he were sure that he only wanted to go to the army to meet those famous female "warriors".

I told him a little about Mera – but I did not say what she did or whom she did it to. Aaron was almost drooling, though both Josh and Eli were equally bright eyed.

Then I caught sight of a slight women's figure, bringing forth the meats. It took me a moment to recognise her.

"Mouse! Dear Mouse!" I cried.

She ran in, bowed to my father and threw herself into my arms. "Oh David. David, my master, I am so glad you're back."

She too had grown. I could not help but see she had developed a glorious firm round bosom. But she did not look well.

"Are you not well, Mouse?" I inquired.

"Well enough, master – and better for seeing you. I have had some slight pains here," pointing to her right side, "which sometimes makes me feel sick. But what am I saying? My master is back and I am glad!"

I suddenly felt guilty. I had forgotten that I was now her master. I felt sure that Mother would look after her, but not having a master around did make things a little difficult – especially if she took the fancy of some of the men. It would be different if she was my concubine: all would know that she was my woman and would not press themselves upon her.

"I will speak with you before I go to bed, Mouse," and dismissed her.

At the thought of bed, what with the run, the wine and my friends, I suddenly felt very tired.

Josh saw at once. "David, you must get to your bed. Why not take your little Mouse with you? But you look so done in you probably couldn't rise to the occasion."

Now if he had said that before I had been to camp I would have been blushing by now, even though I did not think of Mouse as a woman.

"I promise, Josh, that all is in good working order and just needs to be given the word. But you're right, I am tired. Let us meet at dawn before you go off and I'll happily tell you more about army life." They left and I went to the men's sleeping quarters, where each man had a space marked out with hangings to give him some privacy. The married men, of course, had their own small compartments with wooden barriers. As we all rose to go, I heard a step behind me: it was Mouse.

She did not hesitate. "David, take me as your concubine – please. I am not safe unless you do."

I was startled. I had not really thought of her as a woman. She was still slight – except for her breasts, which pressed through her dress in a delightful way. I could see why some of the men would notice her. I held her, not closely, but as a brother would.

"Mouse, you cannot be my concubine. That would not be right. You are like a sister to Leah and to me. You know that I could love only Leah."

"David, you don't understand. There are many that keep importuning me. I am not safe. Nor am I 'little Mouse' any more, but Una – I have been a women for more than a year and am now your age. Of course, I do not think to take the place of Leah. How could I? But think of how she asked you to protect me. At least, take me into your bed so that men will think you have made me your concubine."

I apologised for using her childhood name. "I was not thinking, Una. Now I look at you, I can see that you are a woman."

I could see the strength of her case. Yet I was uneasy because I dimly perceived that she might be comely and I did not want to dishonour her. However, her pleading look overcame me.

I nodded and was taken aback at the loud noise she was making, ensuring everyone could hear, "I come to your bed at your command, master."

She snuggled down beside me beneath the bed coverings. At first, nothing happened. I did not want anything to happen. I thought a ruse would be sufficient and closed my eyes, but I was so exhausted that I was soon asleep.

I don't know how long I slept, but I awoke to feel that the covering had been drawn back and there was a warmth beside me.

It was Mouse – or, rather, the new Una – with her hands around my phallus that now stood proud.

"This is not right, Mouse." I groaned a little and then whispered, "Sorry, Una. This is not right. My love is still for Leah."

She did not answer but I could feel her head upon my chest being wetted by her tears.

I tried to comfort her. But my whispers close to her ears became entangled with her mouth. Her tongue sought mine. Her hand was gently caressing my engorged member and I groaned – but in pleasure this time.

My mouth left hers and found her breasts. I felt as if I would explode all over her. Her breasts were firm and tasted of womanly sweetness as I breathed in her fragrance. Her mouth was on my chest, her tongue licked my nipples and I felt an urgency that I had to quench. I took her in my arms – she was as light as a feather. I easily drew her up over my body, letting my striving phallus rest up against her secret treasure.

Her hands went around my buttocks as she began to lift herself on to me. She pulled aside each lip as her moistness laved my hard member. I could feel her tense. I held back from her – she was so slight that I feared I might split her in two. She opened her legs wide, my hands caressing her silk, smooth flanks. I longed to thrust her onto me, but waited for her. Her mouth found mine, our tongues entwined and, with an exquisite slowness, she skewered herself on to me. I could feel her tightness. Suddenly, it gave way as she plunged down upon me as I thrust up. Her passion became more urgent as she engulfed me. We rode to a rapid climax. From my toes, feet, head, hands came the sweet and hurtful ecstasy as I gushed out a fountain that I felt would never end.

I fell back exhausted and submissively took her gentle kisses that seemed to go everywhere.

I slept – minutes or hours, I know not – but was aroused once more, as her sweet slender body merged into mine. I half kneeled above her, drawing out her full length to feast my eyes on her nakedness. In the dim gloom I could see her slight pale body, with the sun-burnished arms and legs emphasising her ivory skin. She was beautiful. Her beasts mounded sweetly, aching to be kissed, caressed and suckled. Her body was no longer that of a girl but held the allure of a light but curvaceous woman. Her

234

uplifted arms showed the wondrous transformation from Mouse to my Una.

This time I rode. I plunged deep, deep down into her. Her open mouth gasped for air that I covered with mine. I could feel her shape beneath me. I wanted nothing but to feel her possess the whole of me as my bursting juice shot into her. We reached a climax together. There was no need of subterfuge now – anyone in the house could not fail to know that we were lovers.

I lay still and we smiled into each other's eyes. I grew inside and we made love again. Waves of joy ran down my shaft in a speed and harmony that made me cry out as I gave my final exploding thrust deep into her. I collapsed and she lay still. Then her hands gently soothed my brow as she began to hum a mother's lullaby.

I entered a blissful sleep.

When Una had seen David she thought she would faint, firstly with excitement, secondly with amazement.

It was clearly David but there had been a transformation. He no longer looked like a youth but his whole demeanour reflected some great change that had come over him. The white slash in his hair had not been there when he had gone to the camp. His body was more full and, with her awareness of what she sought, more beautiful.

Whilst she had been aware of some of the youths looking at her, being close to the lady Zeruiah had meant that they knew their place. But Una knew that she wanted David and – with a start – she realised that she had always wanted him.

Despite her previous timidity, she now had a fierce determination. She knew why Leah loved David. Who wouldn't? She now knew that she loved him also. Since David's departure, she had thought about nothing but how to get him to take her as his concubine, though she had no expectation that he would marry her. Being his concubine would be enough. She dourly acknowledged to herself that one way of coping with this life was to expect as little as possible, then one would not be disappointed.

She was worried that the pain in her side might make her too ill to want to come to David. But once he had agreed that she could come to his bed, she was confident that he would love her. She took an extra draught of the herbs that eased the pain.

She smiled at his subterfuge when he pretended to be asleep, and felt nothing but warm protection when in his tiredness he did sleep.

Slowly, she drew back the cover and stared intently at his slumbering naked form.

In the dim light, she could just see that his head was on his arm as he lay turned towards her. His skin almost glowed in the dark as she could feel the warmth of his blood pump beneath his skin.

Gently, so gently, she ran her fingers on to his chest, which was so firm but smooth – as yet, there was no down on his chest.

She gave a gasp as she made out his firm stomach and could feel the line of his muscles that gave her fingers such great pleasure. She could feel her own warmth begin to flow and her breasts yearned to feel his bow lips around her hard nipples.

She grew more excited as she saw the dark mound of his hair cradle his soft, lush phallus that lay so innocent and soft. It was almost as long as her small hand. She quivered with excitement at the thought of it expanding.

Her fingers slowly, tenderly felt its size and weight. His bag and phallus lay heavily in her hand. Her breath quickened as she felt rather than saw it begin to stiffen and grow.

David groaned a little in his sleep. His arm went back as he lay on his back. The miracle of his phallus took away her breath as it grew erect, sprouting out hard, but with a silken sheen at its hard head.

Her mouth was dry. Her skin had never been more acutely aware of her own and another's body. She lowered her head to kiss David's half-open mouth as her hand could barely caress around his smooth but hard manhood.

He groaned and moved, and she began to milk him in the rite of love.

Suddenly, he was awake! He didn't reject her and, oh, her heart sang, he found her comely.

She banished all thought of her anxiety, of the pain in her side. She let her body lead her as she impaled herself upon him. As she felt his member push against her hymen, he was so big, so hard, she almost recoiled in fear that he would impose pain upon her. But with his eyes fixed upon her, he let her find her own rhythm. He was so gentle as she levered herself on to him. She yearned the consummation, longed to be filled by his beauty as the tearing sharp pain washed over her as his phallus filled her and triggered rhythmic waves of delight that she had not dreamt of.

His movements so sensitively followed hers: as she became more urgent, so did he. As her mouth opened for breath, so did his and, oh, the ecstasy of their mouths together. His whole body possessed her and she knew love.

After their early passions she saw him above her. His silky arms were like knotted branches of some young tree. His chest hard against hers and with his shaft inside her, she felt wholeness. Her hands went to his neck, then down his back and finally to his buttocks. His hands followed hers as he thrust deep into her and parted her cheeks. She did the same to him and felt his exquisite explosion.

Una felt that she had come home. She was one with Leah. Life had become worthwhile.

She did not mind his complete exhaustion. He fell quickly into a deep sleep and, from being the lover, her love now swathed him in a mother's lullaby.

She was at peace.

Next morning as I awoke, I found Una – I knew that I would never think of her as Mouse again – intent upon my face. A shadow crossed her countenance as I think she saw my response. I felt guilty.

What I felt for Leah could never be surpassed. What I felt for Jonathan was a love that had no parallel with Leah but complemented another side of my being. But, as I looked at Una, I knew that my body had been hers in friendship and, a little, in pity. But was it love?

At one with my thoughts she spoke, "David, my master, you have honoured me. I love you but that does not mean that you have to love me. I am grateful that you find me comely. I am grateful for your friendship. Because of that I am confident, but I cannot – nor would not – take Leah's place."

Then, with a delightful giggle, and a naughty piquancy I never thought she possessed, she added, "But, master David, I am your concubine now. Did we not ride well? I doubt others can do better."

I felt an upsurge of warmth for this dear, dear creature. I did not want to hurt her. I did not want her to feel used. She was my friend and she had comforted me greatly.

I felt myself become re-aroused. She smiled delightedly. She took me into her once more and we quickly came to a gushing conclusion. The thin fire burst out along my stomach, thighs, feet, and, like a hot wire, seemed to melt and explode into her.

We lay still.

She was the first to speak. "I am yours, David, my master. My friend, I am yours alone. I ask nothing else but that you think of your little Una as your friend. Go safely, dear David, but please return soon."

Our tears were mixed with each others as I dissolved in gratitude.

I knew that though our bodies had tasted a great harmony, our souls were not entwined. I also knew that the desires and fantasies I had for Mera were outside of what I felt for Una.

And the feelings I had for Jonathan? I did not seek to measure those but would wait to see if ever there would be ... a time.

Chapter Eleven

Annihilation

The Battle of Havilah

I was half sorry when the messages came from the North and Gad, as it would not have been a great burden to stay another night with Una.

Instead, after wishing my three friends well and with the promise that they would join me in the Prince's troop, I gave one last farewell to Una, had my Father's blessing and set off to the King and Prophet hoping that I would be back there in time.

I arrived, shattered after doing the journey in less than four days. My eyes burned in their sockets, my mouth was dry and congealed. My lungs seemed to be full of gravel.

It was already dark when I reached the tent of the Prophet and, of course, the army had gone. Worse, I was intensively irritated. Agar, Samuel's son, met me and insisted there was no way I could interrupt the Prophet's sleep.

I tried to tell him that I was to escort his father to the army and felt a shock when he said, "Presumptuous you are indeed. That is neither necessary nor proper. The Prophet has decided, and the King agrees, that the Prophet, my father, is to have his own guard – commanded by me. The King has supplied us with fifty experienced warriors, all sworn to my father, the Prophet. Now get out of here you Bethlehemite upstart."

There was no arguing as, after taking the messages, he turned his back. I did not know why, but I knew I had another enemy.

Tired and dispirited, I found scraps of food and curled up in my cloak. I slept the sleep of the exhausted, falling into oblivion.

There was no news, though the camp was being struck and moved southward. I took stock and realised that I had drained myself so much that, for at least a day or so, I would be better tagging along with the

Prophet's contingent. However, I felt distinctly unwelcome!

I was completely surprised, therefore, when Izark, who I slightly knew from the camp, found me and commanded me to attend the Prophet.

Izark was a little morose as he had hoped to be with the army. "There'll be a lot of spoil and I've missed it – but at least the Prophet gives good maintenance." This attitude shocked me. Jonathan had once touched upon it: how some men had become full-time warriors for spoil or pay. He was uncomfortable with the idea that men might fight mainly for plunder and not for Israel. I could understand that even Israelites might become like the mercenaries, who sometimes were found attached to Philistine armies or the Assyrians, in the far north. Men whose allegiance was only to their paymaster!

The Prophet greeted me kindly enough from his litter. I walked by his side and he commented that I had been speedy, "You must have been desperate to see your old friend," he teased me. "Is God's warrior bard so keen to flesh out his sword against God's enemies?"

He waved away anything I might say. "You can do me a great service if you can be as speedy in reaching the King as you have been to return to me."

I nodded. Here was appreciation. I was to serve.

"Remember, David, you have been chosen. King Saul considers you his bard, but you and I know that you are God's bard. Is that not so?"

I felt uncomfortable. Here were echoes of the tension between the twin arms of Israel that I wished to see in harmony.

"Well, David? Why do you hesitate?" demanded Samuel.

"Prophet, forgive me. Though you and the King have honoured me with such a description, I wish to be a warrior who serves God. My music is secondary to –"

He interrupted me. "Nonsense, David. You have special gifts. It is extreme arrogance to deny it. You know you have been called. I am sorry to have to say this but I have noticed a tendency in you of being almost arrogant and self-willed. Do you, or do you not, serve the Lord above all other services?"

The answer was obvious. "I serve the Lord. I can do no other. I am an obedient and humble son to the Prophet, and am ashamed that I have given offence."

He seemed mollified. "Good, that's better! You should never forget that it was God, through my direction, that sent you to Saul. That the King thinks of you as his bard is, and I mean him no injustice, a misunderstanding. Your inspiration comes from God and, therefore, you shall always remain the bard of God."

This was not an easy conversation, partly owing to the bumpy ground and Samuel swaying above me in his litter, and also from my uneasiness at realising that the litter bearers could hear every word.

"Now, David, go as quickly as you can to the King. Greet him in my name. I must tell you I have sent the same message daily."

He saw my look of puzzlement and explained, "I am mindful that the King must understand God's message – nay, instruction. The Amalekites are to be annihilated from the face of the earth. He must obey! I'm sure he will – he would not dare to defy the word that came from the mouth of God. It is vital that he knows that I mean that God's instruction must be carried out to the letter. Hence, I am sending you with the same message to ensure there will be no ... *misunderstanding*."

I sought a little clarification but he said, "Nothing – I repeat, nothing – is to remain of the Amalekites. You are to relay this to the King. God has decreed that nothing of the Amalekites must exist. I am but God's instrument. Saul, too, must obey God's word or risk all. You understand?"

I nodded. It was to be a total annihilation! At that moment, I could not appreciate what this meant but I did know that God was going to deliver the Amalekites into our hands. This would end their cruel threat to Israel for ever. So, I had no doubts.

After saluting him and receiving his blessing, I began another journey.

Though a little stiff at first, as the day warmed and I got into my stride, I quickly left the Prophet's train behind and headed due south.

The King's plans worked superbly. Jonathan's division moved as planned. With our troop at their head, they had cut deep into Amalekites' territory, inflicting enormous damage. What confused the leaders of the Amalekites was that, unlike most big raids, which they, and sometime we, carried out, this was not for plunder. It was larger than usual, but the division stayed and waited until relieving forces appeared before swinging away – not back north to Israel but even deeper into the land of the Amalekites.

What bewildered them was that Jonathan's men seemed to know where to go. Different captains of the Amalekites sent forces to cut off what was expected to be the retreating Israelites. Yet they often found themselves outnumbered locally as Jonathan swung back to inflict another defeat before turning around and cutting even further southward, imposing terrible carnage wherever they went.

After more that a week of this the Amalekites were aroused. King Agag, once a fierce warrior whom we had feared, was now so old that some of his nobles felt he had lived too long for the good of his people. King Agag called out all his people, as at last he grasped that the whole army of Israel was descending upon him. He sent his speediest troops to try to catch up with Jonathan, who was now fighting a running rearguard action against desperate odds. Staying just long enough to draw out the best of King Agag's men, after a skirmish, he wheeled away back across the River Paran and seemingly towards safety.

There the Amalekite army crossed over, bent on a bitter revenge for all their losses. They were now so incensed they too were declaring a no prisoners policy.

Jonathan withdrew slowly but kept his and the enemy's skirmishers in contact as Saul had planned: it was brilliant.

Across from the River Paran were an old riverbed and a narrow, but long, Valley of Havilah, down which Jonathan retreated. It narrowed down to about a hundred yards wide, tapering to about sixty yards along its whole length of about a mile, before widening out again into a flat plain. The valley sides were awkwardly rather than impossibly steep and afforded some protection for a smaller force from a larger attacking army.

Jonathan drew up all of his men at the beginning of the narrowing valley and took up defensive positions. We had been practising a new tactic of a two-line defence. The front line would kneel down and have their shields up. Fixing the butt of their spears firmly into the ground and using the ground as a lever, made the weapon very firm indeed. The second line stood just behind the first and held their spears out, adding to the hedge of spears, and could use either their shields or swords to defend the man in front. In practice, we found that, whilst it did not let you attack much, it was an almost impenetrable obstacle – especially if the ground was favourable.

On came the Amalekites, furiously dashing themselves against this wall of iron, many skewering themselves on our spears in their desperation to get at us.

We lost men, of course, but for every one of ours it must have been three or four of theirs. Jonathan kept the line together by slowly retreating down the Havilah Valley, which as it became narrower meant that our shrinking line could be kept intact.

Oh, I wish I had been there! I was so proud. They were outnumbered more than ten to one but, of course, the Amalekites could not get at us because of the narrowness of the ground.

Our troop was at the centre where Jonathan stood controlling every-thing. He used us as his reserve to fill up and hold the line.

The enemy's archers were not very good and could not fire because their own men were so close to our line. When the Amalekites drew back a little to let their archers fire, the second line simply put up their shields so they were very ineffective.

What the Amalekites did not know was that on our side of the valley, up the awkward slopes, the ground rose about 400 feet to a low hill. Out of sight at the other side of that hill, Abner was waiting with his army. Whilst Saul's section was around the other side of that hill, needing a six-mile dash to come around the ridge and enter the Havilah Valley at the rear of the Amalekites.

Jonathan knew he had to hold on for at least another hour. The fighting was bloody and we were getting tired because, though retreating, most of our men had to be in one of the lines all the time, whereas the Amalekites could rest whilst their place could be taken by fresh warriors.

Jonathan had retreated to the narrowest part of the valley. All he could see ahead of him was a sea of vengeful Amalekites. He bawled out the order, "No retreat. No retreat." Here they had to stand ... or die.

He sent Beniah, who at first was loath to leave him, up the eastern hillside to alert Abner and get him to start his downward attack to take the Amalekites in the flank. Beniah flew to the top of the hill where he found Abner was being very cautious. Abner wanted to know exactly how Jonathan's division was doing. Was the Prince wounded? Was it not too soon to attack because there was no news yet of King Saul's army?

Beniah fixed him with a stare. "Lord Abner, you must attack now. We cannot retreat any further. Unless you come at once, the enemy will break through. The trap will be destroyed and the battle be lost."

Abner was for more delay but, untypically, Beniah was brutally blunt. "Lord Abner, if you don't come now, it will look like treason – as if you want the Prince's army to be sacrificed."

Abner was furious but Beniah had turned on his heel, drew his sword and cried out, "Hail the Lord Abner! He says attack! We are to attack, save Jonathan and destroy the Amalekites for ever. Lord Abner says forward! God has delivered them into our hands."

The men, already expecting such an order, needed no second urging. Whilst Abner had no choice but to appear to be leading the charge, he knew he had been out-manoeuvred by Beniah.

Abner's army of 20,000 men streamed over the top of the hill and down the sides, crashing mightily into the flank of the Amalekites. The fighting was bloody, as the first charge had made terrible inroads into the enemy, but they were not cowardly. King Agag quickly re-organised, formed his army into an arrowhead shape and they began to fight back.

Though Abner's men had the advantage of the ground, there were enough Amalekites to be able to re-form their line and meet Abner's attack, yet still keep pressure on Jonathan.

The fighting was getting even more bitter. Slowly, Abner's men realised that they were no longer the attackers but confronting a more numerous and determined enemy who, having held their ground, were now counter-attacking. We began to lose men quickly and Abner had to get his men into a defensive line. He did this very well but the day was still doubtful, not least because Jonathan's men were so exhausted that all they could do was hold their line.

King Agag, realising that he still vastly out numbered his foes, began to concentrate against Abner, while slowing pushing back Jonathan, whose line was beginning to bend.

Then it happened: like a tidal wave! Saul arrived with the larger part of the Army of Israel and hurled himself at the rear of the Amalekites. This was too much for the enemy and, almost quicker than it takes to tell, the disciplined ranks of the Amalekites collapsed. At best, there were clusters of men huddled together, back to back, trying to defend themselves from the Israelites, who now knew that their cruel enemy had been delivered into their hands.

There is nothing so dreadful as when an army becomes a mob. The Amalekites fled in terror. This was fatal for they had nowhere to go. It is usually the case that more men die in a rout than in the fighting that led up to it.

Some threw their weapons down but they were given no quarter. They quickly realised this and some fought on in utter desperation, but their ranks were all broken and the battlefield was now a slaughterhouse.

The killing went on while there was light.

At dawn the next day, Saul renewed the pursuit of the few who had escaped. It was obvious that the Amalekites would never be a threat to Israel again. God had given Saul and Jonathan – yes, and Abner too – a magnificent victory, which I still feel ashamed that I was not part of.

As I came close the River Paran, I was amazed to find the bitter evidence of the battle still present nearly three and a half days later. Not just in the Valley of Havilah but for miles inside the Amalekite territory. There were bodies everywhere. No evidence that they had been collected, counted and either buried or burned to guard against pestilence. The stink was dreadful as the bodies were beginning to rot. I did not really know where to go but simply followed the trail of death over the river and into the land of the Amalekites.

As I entered villages, to my amazement, there were more bodies – only this time there were women and children amongst them. This did not seem right. I came upon small parties of Israelite soldiers – some wounded, some whole – but all were totally exhausted.

I asked where the King was and was wearily told that he was further south, so I hurried onwards.

By the afternoon, I saw in the distance a cavalcade. As I neared I was thankful to realise that I had at last caught up with the King.

As I approached I could not help but see that every man looked like death. They were so drained. Some obviously had wounds but all had a forlorn sickened look that at first I feared some plague might have struck them.

I advanced to the King, who hardly responded to my salute,

"Great King, again you are victorious. Truly your victory was absolute."

The King just stared at me. To my discomfort, I noticed that he was caked in blood.

It was Abner who spoke wearily, but with his usual sneer. "And what does the King's bard want? You have come a little late, singer."

I replied politely, "I did as I was ordered. I delivered the King's messages and then I escorted the Prophet into the land of the Amalekites. I bring a greeting and a message from the Prophet."

"Well?" said Saul tersely. "What does the old man want now?" There was no disguising his bitterness.

"He greets you, oh King, as victor. God has delivered your enemies into your hands. But the Prophet says to remind you that nothing of the Amalekites shall remain on the face of the earth."

There was a cold silence.

"Is this your message as well, David?" asked Saul.

"King, I have no message from myself. I am but the messenger. I do not truly know what the Prophet means because I have not found an Amalekite alive."

There was harsh laughter at this comment.

"Oh! Oh!" mocked Abner. "The Prophet's messenger has found nothing alive because we've slaughtered every living thing in sight. And I, for one, am sick, sick, sickened of the blood and gore. I tell you, oh King, I want no more killing."

Saul nodded. He spoke to nobody in particular and said in a very deadened voice,

"No more killing. No more. We have slaughtered enough. The men won't do it any longer. We are human beings. We can't kill in cold blood. Samuel does not know what he asks. With all this death around, even vengeance can pall."

Then, turning to Abner, Saul said in amazement, "Abner, you know Iphraim the Gideonite? He lost all his family from an Amalekite raiding party. For two days he could not kill enough. In the battle he was terrible.

244

Yesterday he was still killing, but you know what he said to me, not an hour ago?"

The King did not wait for an answer. "Iphraim, who lost his parents, his wife and his children, said, 'King Saul, I can't do it. I can't go in saying "take this for my wife, take this for my children, take this for my mother". King Saul, I have killed a city of wives and mothers.' Do you know what he did, Abner? He threw his sword away and wept."

There was complete silence at this but every man except me nodded understandingly. Everybody ignored me and they seemed to be drifting away aimlessly.

With trepidation, I followed the King and quietly said, "Oh King, I have to give my full message." I waited but he did not say anything. "The Prophet said that nothing, but nothing, must remain – and that you are to obey. If not you will suffer the consequences."

Saul just looked at me. I hurried on. "I think he must have meant destroying the army. I can't think he meant killing all the women and children, but I had to give you the message in case there is another meaning."

Saul nodded vacantly. "Hmm," he muttered "Yes. I think you had better go to find Jonathan and tell him to do what he thinks is best. Oh yes, and tell him that I am proud of him. He'll like that, especially as he will know, you know. Yes, I'm very proud of him." With that he just wandered off.

I went south, asking the way when I met any Israelites. They all looked so washed out that you might have thought that they had lost the battle, not won a great war!

I asked a couple of captains about whether the count was going to be taken. They just looked at me in disbelief and called me "a blood-thirsty little bastard!" and asked if I was a priest.

I came to the outskirts of a village that I could see had been totally devastated. Women's and children's bodies were being ravaged by the dogs and the kites. I drove them away but as I left they returned to their hideous feast.

I was passing a small copse when I heard a brief rustling. Oh, I wished I had gone on! Instead I walked over to see what was the cause and peered amongst the bushes.

Suddenly, I was confronted by a big, burly, but slightly wounded, Amalekite brandishing a spear. At his side, hissing curses at me, was a woman who looked possessed and was wildly waving a sword.

"There's only one Jewish bastard. Kill him! Kill him!" she screamed. At her heels ran two distraught children, adding to the nightmarish scene.

It was a nightmare. I retreated rapidly out of their range, my tiredness having left me very quickly as I drew my sword. I did not know whether to advance or leave them, for they were no real threat to me as I was sure I could outrun them.

Unfortunately, the woman, screaming obscenities, had circled around behind me and had cut off my escape route, whilst the warrior was advancing purposely towards me. I had to either run away, taking a long diversion, or I deal with them.

I had intended to say that I meant them no harm, but no opportunity presented itself.

First, their children, aged about seven and nine, began to throw rocks. The man and his wife began to close in on me. I ought to have run. I suppose my guilt at not being in the battle got the better of me. Instead of thinking, I began to feel angry.

I decided that he was the real threat so I gave my war cry and charged at him. His care worn face was convulsed by an agonised cry of hate as he charged towards me, thrusting his spear at me. I parried with my sword and walked inside his thrust, as Jonathan had taught me, and I plunged my knife into his chest.

As our bodies crashed together, the knife stuck in his rib cage and the weight of his falling body snatched it from my grasp. He went down as I half-rolled and jumped away, waving my sword towards the children, who scattered.

The wife was a demon possessed. She howled with a hurt and rage that chilled my blood. She threw herself upon me, hacking, hacking, hacking at me with the sword. She was no warrior but her desperation and rage meant that I had to parry and retreat, parry and retreat. As her strength began to fail she took one more swinging blow at me. This was what I was waiting for. With a parry and flick, I turned my blade over hers and disarmed her as away flew her sword. She stood incredulous and motionless. I went and picked up the sword, which I could see was smeared with blood.

"Stay your hand, woman!" I cried, desperately trying to take control of the situation.

She ignored me and stumbled back to the fallen man, whose last gasps had ended. My knife stood proud in his motionless chest, its handle pointing hideously towards the sky.

"Husband! Husband! Don't go! Don't go! Oh no, don't go! Oh God, don't leave us. There's nothing left. Nothing! Nothing! Nothing left." Her cries were piteous as she embraced the body of her man, whose face was contorted in the rictus of death.

I was horrified and just stood there, helplessly. The children ran towards their mother, crying. She stood up. I thought she was going to speak, instead her look became even more crazed and dazed.

She half-cried, half-muttered, "There's nothing left. It's all gone. There's nothing, nothing ... nothing."

Then she knelt again at the body. The mad look went from her face as she called to her children. "Paran, come here sweetheart. Amil, my darling, come to Mama."

She said this with such sweetness that the children stopped crying and, holding out their hands to her, they went to her for comfort. At this moment she was transformed. She looked beautiful – was beautiful – personifying motherhood. I was staggered at the contrast.

With such gentleness she first drew the older boy to her and kissed him, embracing him in both her arms and then laid him gently upon the ground. She then took the little one and soothed him in a warm embrace. Then I heard his voice choke as she withdrew my knife, which she had plucked from the heart of her husband, from his throat. She lay the second boy tenderly upon the ground.

Both looked so peaceful. They were not asleep – but dead!

I could not even cry out. Then she rose to her full height and, crying to her gods, drove my knife deep into her bosom. Not once, but again and again, before collapsing and crashing to the ground.

I shall never forget – nor forgive – myself. I turned and fled. I prayed that I might not dream of their agony.

I knew with gathering horror that this scene would haunt me for ever.

I found Jonathan and the troop a few hours later. I was eager to see and tell him all but, on seeing his face, I knew my revulsion paled into insignificance at what he and the others had experienced. From our troop of a hundred, I realised that we had lost thirty-seven good comrades. This hurt everyone. Their ashen, waxed looks were not because of the many wounds they carried, but because, on the anvil of this unrelenting war, their hearts had been broken.

Beniah was first to greet me, but with some difficulty. "David! Good, you've found us. I'll take you to the Prince."

I followed him, looking at my comrades who, in their indifference, treated me as if I was a stranger.

Beniah, looking haggard, said slowly, "David, it will be hard for you to understand, but .., but ..., well, there's no other way of saying it: you were lucky you weren't there. After the battle, the murder – oh God, David – it was murder! I ..."

Then he stopped and looked at me imploringly. "Oh David! Afterwards ..., afterwards, it was so ..., so ..." He went silent as he tried to recover himself.

"You won't understand, so please don't ask. I tell you about the battle later. That was what you'd expect but don't ask me – or him," as he pointed towards Jonathan, who was sitting wearily on a rock.

My heart thrilled to see him but I appreciated what Beniah had said. Jonathan looked gaunt. It was not the four days' growth of beard on all of them, nor even the blood-soaked bandage on his shoulder, nor even a vicious, ugly contusion at the side of his face. It was the way his haunted eyes chilled any greeting on my lips.

He tried to make an effort to greet me but I demurred. "Jonathan, my Prince! Please don't trouble yourself. Is there any way in which I can serve you or the troop?"

He thanked me but gave no indication of what that might be. So I just sat with him and the others, quietly, until I intuitively understood that, whilst they were exhausted, shocked, they were also hungry. So, with no more ado, I found two stray cattle, slaughtered them, and began to roast them.

The smell of food stirred the men and, as I cut off huge lumps of flesh, they began to devour the meat hungrily. The latecomers were queuing. The smell of the food made them relax a little and they talked quietly amongst themselves. By nightfall everyone had eaten. We had found some wine. Many became tearful, and sung sad songs.

Jonathan surprised me by asking me to teach the men The Good Shepherd psalm. I would have preferred not to, but I could refuse him and them nothing.

I went to the fire, which was now burning low, as the men gathered round at Jonathan's suggestion.

I strummed the chords of the harp and, in the night air, the sound seemed to drift as I slowly and sadly sang.

"The Lord is my shepherd, I shall not want.
He maketh me to lie down in green pastures, he leadeth me beside the still waters.
He restoreth my soul, he leads me in the paths of righteousness of his name's sake.
Yea though I walk in the valley of the shadow of death I will fear no evil for thou art with me thy rod and thy staff comfort me.
Thou preparest a table in the presence of mine enemies, thou anointest my head with oil my cup runneth over – I will dwell in the house of the Lord for ever."

As the chords and words ebbed away into that silence that is the beginning and end of every prayer, I felt a new, deeper silence. This held a tension that reverberated amongst the men. I waited and Beniah, who had a soft tenor voice repeated the lines:

"The Lord is my shepherd, I shall not want.
He maketh me to lie down in green pastures, he leadeth me beside the still waters.
He restoreth my soul, he leads me in the paths of righteousness of his name's sake."

Then, Jonathan joined him.

"Yea though I walk in the valley of the shadow of death I will fear no evil for thou
art with me thy rod and thy staff comfort me."

But they did not complete it. Beniah's voice cracked and he fell into
Jonathan's arms crying. Some whispered the line, whilst others wept
unashamedly. Jonathan released Beniah and went round the troop shaking
their hands and embracing his men. All fell together seeking comfort in the
release of tears. Jonathan turned to me and, with choking voice, urged us
all to join him.

"Thou preparest a table in the presence of mine enemies, thou anointest my head
with oil my cup runneth over – I will dwell in the house of the Lord for ever –
Yea, I will dwell in the house of the Lord for ever."

Hushai came to me. "David, when I saw you I did not want to know you
because you were not there at the battle. I did not want to share what I had
done – because I am ashamed. But through your psalm, God has given me
His forgiveness and, perhaps, I will sleep tonight. I will talk with you
tomorrow." He ran off in overt distress.

As the men began to prepare for sleep, many came over, most without a
word, took my hand and just nodded or murmured "thanks". I could not
say anything but felt an overwhelming sense of sadness that I had not been
with my comrades. I had let them down, yet they had forgiven me.

Jonathan walked over. "Thank you, David. We shall all rest now and,
tomorrow, you can rejoin the troop."

I wanted to say more, to apologise, to explain, but I realised that this
had cost him a tremendous effort so I quietly answered, "Thank you, my
Prince. God give you His rest."

The next day Jonathan sent scouts out to bring in all the survivors, men
as well as women and children. We heard terrible things. Many of the
Amalekite women and old men had killed themselves and their children.

By midday we must have collected over 3,000 stunned and silent
Amalekites, mainly women and children but a few old men. After the battle,
all had been rampage and slaughter but as the killing continued, the men

had neither the appetite, energy or will, as self-disgust began to take over. Some of the men suggested giving the women protection by taking them as concubines. This happened with hundreds and, of course, those women's children received a degree of protection too – or at least they would not be sold into bondage away from their mothers. Other Amalekite women, I have to say, refused the offers and killed themselves in front of the men who would have helped them – cursing them as they died. Indeed, one woman killed one of our men. The men were so exhausted with bloodletting that they merely slew her and did not take revenge on anyone else.

When we returned to the King, we found that many other groups had also collected women and children. Amidst these and the livestock, there was confusion. After the silences of a battle's end, there was now quite a din.

The King welcomed Jonathan and announced to all who were near, "This is my beloved son Jonathan, in whom we are well pleased."

The men slowly cheered Saul and our spirits began to revive.

Then the Prophet arrived. At first the men cheered him and his guard who, like me, had obviously not been in the fight.

Samuel looked magnificent. He strode up to Saul, totally in command, and raised his staff high.

In that marvellous voice, he boomed out, "Hail, Saul, King of Israel, the Lord's anointed. This day, as He promised, He has delivered the uncircumcised heathen dogs into our hands. You have wiped them from the face of the earth, those who would mock the Lord of Host. You are His instrument, the very hands of God's vengeance."

Saul looked uncomfortable but came forward bravely. "Thanks, Samuel, Prophet of God. Truly God is avenged. There is no longer an Amalekite army. They are scattered and slain by God's soldiers. Surely these men of Israel who shared the glory of Havilah are God's warriors. The fierce enemy are smitten into the dust for ever." The men liked this and started cheering again.

How did Samuel do it? Suddenly, his body seemed to freeze as he whirled around with hand and staff outstretched.

There was total silence. All that could be heard was the soft sounds of women's voices, the faint crying of infants and the low bleating of some sheep.

Samuel uttered not a word, but those sounds became magnified by his and our attention. Every man caught his breath, as the sounds of women and children were unmistakable.

Samuel seemed to crouch, to shrink and then grow tall. Was it a trick of the eyes? Was this figure, consumed with a choking dread, human?

Almost in conversational voice, Samuel said, "King Saul, you had God's

250

message? Nothing, absolutely nothing, of the Amalekites was to remain."

Saul did not answer. No one dared utter a word but all were filled with dread.

"Saul, I anointed you in God's name. I brought you God's instructions. I know you have been presumptuous in the past, behaving like a priest at Michmash. God forgave though warned you. Surely, I cannot believe my ears, but are those sounds of women? Amalekite women? Amalekite children, and their herds?"

His voice had now risen in a crescendo. This was not an accusation, it was a sentence!

"You have disobeyed! You have not annihilated the Amalekites. How dare you set yourself up above God?"

No one had ever seen Samuel like this before: he was incensed – possessed almost.

"Well Saul, Benjaminite. Give orders now – at once, at once – and slay everything of the accursed Amalekites. If not, be accursed and rejected of God." From the stunned silence there emerged a growl from the men. They had had enough of killing. Samuel clearly did not understand what he was asking of them. He swung round. "Who dares murmur against God's Prophet?" he challenged. No man looked him in the eye but as his gaze passed over them, the mutterings returned.

Saul stepped close to the Prophet. "Samuel, no one is disobeying God. We truly have smitten the Amalekites, so much so that we did not have time to do the count before their heathen bodies rotted. They can never be a threat again." Samuel just glared at him.

So Saul went on in his reasonable tone. "The women and children are into bondage and will be a great boost for the coffers of the priesthood. Why kill perfectly good sheep and cattle, which again the army will share with all of Israel and its priests?"

"Saul! God said to annihilate everything. Do you put yourself forward as someone who knows better than God?"

Saul looked desperate and made a direct appeal – not in his usual formal reverent way, but as man to man. "Samuel, for God's sake! You don't know what you ask of us. We have no reason to kill any more. Man, look around you. You can't imagine what 'destroy' everything means. Babies? Girls? Old women?"

"Are you saying you know the mind of God better than God's Prophet?" roared Samuel.

Saul was getting angry but still made one last effort to persuade Samuel. "No, but I think you may be mistaken this time. After all, God's word is not always so precise."

"God's Prophet never makes a mistake and you have disobeyed again. Twice you have set yourself up in the priestly and prophetic function. You were warned: your guilt, your pride, your disobedience has washed away the sacred oil. You are no longer the Lord's anointed. You and your seed will perish from the land of Israel."

There was a deadly silence. Saul looked as if he had been struck in the face.

Jonathan came forward and knelt before Samuel. "Oh, Great Prophet. None doubts that you are God's messenger – that it is the Lord of Hosts who commands you to instruct us. But after four days of killing, we have no enemy left but frail mothers, orphans, old men and widows. You have taught us God is merciful. You have taught us God is just. You have taught us the word of the Prophet Moses to succour the poor and the widow. When passions are spent, warriors cannot kill defenceless people."

This gained the approval of the men who could no longer consider killing women again.

To my amazement, Samuel called out, "David bar Jesse, bard of God, are you here?".

I stepped forward.

"What say you? Do I not bring the word of God?" As I nodded, he went on, "I see that you confirm my view, you who have the gift of inspiration."

My spirits began to soar. Was Samuel going to draw back?

Instead, his voice roared again, "Even the bard of God, who you, Saul, claim to be your bard, knows that I speak the word of God. He will punish you for your disobedience."

My thoughts raced. There must be a way out. This schism between Samuel and Saul would not just end here.

I knelt in supplication to Samuel, "Samuel, God's Prophet, Father and Guide of all Israel, Maker of Kings, and mover of the winds and floods. Let me plead not for the King or the Prince, they have no need of my supplication, but let me plead for the glory of Israel."

He looked at me and gestured for me to continue. I could see Saul and Jonathan's intent look and, in the tension of the moment, I forgot my natural anxiety and remembered Samuel's words, "don't feel, think".

"I am David bar Jesse. My father is Jesse bar Obediah whose father was Boaz, who took to wife Ruth the Moabite. She and her people came into Israel and found God, who was pleased to accept her."

I waited. No one moved. Samuel still paused.

"With such a precedent, we can extend the glories of Israel by offering those who would accept conversion. If they refuse, then they doom themselves and should be driven into the wilderness for denying God. Those that accept can be instructed to learn of the love of God, and His people will be extended."

There was a shout – cheers even. The choice for life or death was now with the Amalekite women and few doubted that they would accept. Everyone felt relieved. Saul knelt before Samuel. "Great Prophet! In your wisdom you called upon God's bard, your 'son', who learned his inspiration from you. Take unto Israel new converts for God and His glory, and those who refuse then they deserve banishment into the wilderness. Such recreants will have spurned the mercy of our God."

The tension was unbearable. Surely Samuel could take this olive branch?

Samuel looked at him coldly. "If some women come for instruction so be it, but wholesale conversion to circumscribe the Word of God, never. Thou art damning yourself even further. God is not mocked!"

Samuel pointed over towards the women. "Their doom has been pronounced." He would not bend in the slightest.

Saul looked shattered and bitterly disappointed. A break had occurred between Israel's Prophet and King: there could be no going back.

Saul drew himself up to his full height. He, too, could fill an occasion. "Warriors of Israel, we have heard the Prophet. You know we disagree. Samuel says he alone can speak for God. But, Samuel, did not God speak to us also?"

The King waved his arm to include all. "He put into my head the plan of placing Prince Jonathan in the Valley of Havilah. My beloved son facing the might of King Agag, then having the brave Abner prepare a surprise for the enemy. Was it not God who showed me how to seal that trap which destroyed for ever the threat of the Amalekites?"

His voice rose in a competing roar. "So, men of Israel, God delivered them into our hands. King Agag, himself, is my prisoner as a demonstration that Saul, the King of Israel, is beloved of God."

Samuel was furious. "You have dared to spare the King of the uncircumcised? Your pride and vanity has – "

Saul silenced him, no holds barred. "God delivered him into my hands. It was the army, these warriors before you, these heroes of Israel, who faced the foe. It was the King of Israel who had to fight the battle against the odds. If God doubted us, if God thought we were disobedient, would he have given us victory? He might have given His people victory but I, the King, was on the battlefield. If I were accursed, I would have fallen at the hands of God's foes. No Samuel, you brought the message that God wanted us to destroy their army, but you are wrong when you would make the victors of Havilah butchers and slayers of women and children."

The men cheered him in their relief.

Saul raised his hand for silence and was immediately obeyed. "Samuel, God's Prophet. Go in peace, but let not one of your men, priest or guards touch a hair of the captives. Go with honour and gladness. We will send after you the meats of the sacrifice and, later, the women for instruction. Go and say to all Israel that God has delivered her out of the hand of the Amalekites for ever and that Saul, Jonathan and Abner, read the mind of God and were His instruments of vengeance at the battle of Havilah. But God is satisfied. He would not have His honour and ours soiled by brutal acts of meaningless vengeance."

Samuel turned on his heel, followed by his very chastened guards and priests. He left Saul whom he was never to see in friendship again.

Samuel had badly misjudged the mood of the army. Whilst some realised that there was a dangerous split in Israel, all were very happy that the killing was over and went off to congratulate the women. As expected, most of the women accepted entry into Israel, for where else could they go?

Jonathan came over. "It seems that you have made a choice, David?"

I was very unhappy about this. "I trust, pray, that the King and Samuel can be reconciled."

Abner moved towards us. "Ah, young man, you did well. But you cannot hunt with both hare and hounds. The die is cast and you will have to choose between your King and those churlish priests. But be happy in the knowledge that the Old Man can not live for ever. No, not even he – and, when he's gone, the rest will be like headless chickens."

He gave me no chance to reply but walked on to where the women were crowded as he went to choose some for himself.

Jonathan looked at me inquisitively as Saul joined us. "Jonathan, my son, I was pleased!"

Then, looking at me, he said, "David, you gave him every opportunity to avoid the rift. We all did. He's a stubborn and unintentionally cruel old man, who is consumed by his own vanity."

He shook his head. "Why did he have to drive it to the bitter end? Why? I never wanted this. But, David, you know things will never be the same again and it's entirely his fault. How stupid can he be? Did he have to reject the way out you and I gave him?"

He frowned and looked worried and desperate. "This is bad for Israel. While I am victorious, there's no problem. But there is always someone who feels they would make a better King. Who would be anointed if they got that old fool to commit such an act of treachery?"

Jonathan interjected. "Surely, Father, there's no one who could make any claim against you. They might fancy their chances against me, but can you imagine anyone challenging you, Abner and me?"

I added my voice. "Oh King, I am sure Samuel would not wish to cause civil strife. You are the most successful victor for Israel ever – even greater than Joshua. After the battle of Havilah, it would be both a fool and a madman who would traitorously consider themselves as an alternative to you, the Lord's anointed." I said this with total sincerity and conviction.

I believed it then and for a long time afterwards. Whatever happened, I never went into active rebellion against the Lord's anointed.

Nor did I ever think that I was a traitor to the House of Saul and Jonathan.

Bitter Aftermath

The army slowly returned to Telaim, where we assembled when there was a campaign in the south. I had little chance to converse with either the King or Jonathan. Everyone spoke of the rift with the Prophet but all hoped that reconciliation would soon follow. Certainly Saul worked for that, though perhaps more in hope than expectation.

The battle of Havilah, however, had two more unhappy consequences, the first involved only me.

The night after Samuel left, I was restless. I had listened to Hitophel and Beniah tell of their experiences until they went off to their new concubines to enjoy their just deserts. I felt out of sorts and vaguely angry. I wandered aimlessly to the edge of our lines.

Suddenly, I heard a women's voice, imperatively calling, "David bar Jesse, David bar Jesse. Don't you dare ignore me!" Out of the gloom and into the half moonlight stepped Mera. I was not pleased.

Her slender frame was silhouetted against the moonlit sky. Her face half illuminated showed her beauty and angry scorn. "It's your fault, I hear. Do you know, you've ruined my trade?" She spat out the words.

What did she mean? I was not in the mood for her coquettishness, so I did not answer.

"You heard what I said," she hissed angrily. "It was your idea that brought these bloody moping Amalekites into the camp. Now there's no trade for me. It's your fault with your high and mighty ideas. Why couldn't you do as the Prophet commanded?"

It slowly dawned on me what she was on about. "Is that all you think about, your trade?" I angrily retorted. "You'd have innocent women and children die because it interferes with your sordid commerce?"

I flung my purse at her. "Here, take what I've got and leave me in peace."

I went to move away from her.

Instead, she caught hold of my shirt, pulled me close and coldly said, "Who do you think you are? Isn't my meat good enough for you? Do you think you've got something that other men don't have? You're a hypocrite – a hypocrite! Don't pretend I didn't turn you on. I bet you brought yourself off thinking of me."

She laughed as I flushed. She could see she had hit the mark. "I've known men like you before – they're all hypocrites. You give yourself airs, like all those priests, but underneath you'd love to fill my quim."

I was getting angry. I'd had enough but, as she spoke, her hand was under my skirt and skilfully found my hardening phallus.

She challenged me. "Ho, ho! I can feel that my argument is getting to you. Come on, you've paid for me. Show me what kind of a man you are – if you dare!"

Her last words had dropped soft and her hand was slowly milking me. No matter what my mind thought, I was feeling – not thinking. I admit she had riled and yet had managed to arouse me.

"All right then, Mera. Where?"

She smiled, beckoned me along and we moved between some bushes with good pasture where she had obviously been before. I began to have second thoughts, but she threw off her dress and raised her arms in the air as if she was bathing in the moonlight. The light and shadows played across her body, highlighting her firm, round breasts whose nipples were showing their excitement. Her movements led my eyes down to her navel and her mound – I was lost.

She came up to me, quite naked, and slowly began to undress me. I stood motionless but felt aroused and angry, both with her and with myself. As she dragged my skirt from me, I, too, stood naked in the moonlight, so hard and ready to strike.

"Come on then, show me!" she taunted. I went up to her, crushed my mouth against hers, inhaled her fragrance and, half wrestling her to the ground, pushed my hardness between her yielding legs. There was no hesitation: she opened to me as I plunged hard in and was met by her counter-attack as she thrust upwards. I felt no love – only lust – as I drove into her as if I would split her in two. She clung to me savagely and her nails ran down my back. I exploded inside her in an angry, burning explosion. I lay on top of her, my arms pinning her to the floor, glaring angrily at her.

"Was that man enough for you?" I stupidly asked.

She pushed me aside and laughed at me. I was humiliated.

"Why, it was so brief! I took you for a man, I have to say you've got a good body, but you're really only a boy, after all. No stamina, no technique.

Pardon the pun dear, but you were boring."

I stood up, looking for my clothes. She rose with me and, as she did so, she gently placed her arms about me, ran her lips along my chest. Softly teasing my nipples, with her other hand she gently stroked life back into me.

I was aroused again. As I rose hard, I entered her, dragging her light, lithe body on to me. She grunted with pleasure and curled her legs around me as I slowly knelt. This time I concentrated upon pleasuring her. Still together, I lay on my back and, cupping my hands upon her delicious buttocks, pulled her on to me and thrust up, not violently, but with a long slow stroke. She purred with pleasure. I continued to focus upon serving her. She, rhythmically, held me in a mind-bending embrace: hot, sinewy and taut. I was close to an exploding climax but I concentrated hard, shut my mind from the waves of delicious sweetness and focused alone on her. I shut from my mind the explosive thought of my phallus near to eruption.

My thrust became deeper and deeper, but I refused to be rushed by her urging hands along my back. My hands pulled at her cheeks, almost splitting her on my thrusting member.

This was now a duel to a sweet oblivion. My senses were close to reeling but, in my controlled anger, I used my phallus as a plunging instrument to overcome her jibes. I fastened on her breathing, which began to be a racking moan, as her throat tightened. Her arm clung to me in ecstatic frenzy. She let out a deep growl as she sought to split herself upon me. I felt no sweetness – only anger. No softness – only seeking to possess utterly.

Suddenly, in an arching thrust, her voice cut off in a guttural cry. She went into a frenzied, undulating crisis. She tightened, rippled ecstatically up and down on my hard, hard anger and then ... collapsed on top of me.

I held my crisis back. I held her up in one enormous thrust as she seemed to melt and collapse over me in a moaning complete submission. As my senses spun, I yanked her under me. I rolled on top of her and took delight in her cries of total surrender. In a burning flood, my phallus exploded with sharp, exquisite climax like liquid metal as I exploded into her.

We lay utterly exhausted – I know not how long. Her gentle caressing simply revived my anger. I pushed her angrily from me. Too late, I felt ashamed of myself. I saw her defenceless. Her eyes had been filled with total acceptance, but now she felt betrayed by her own vulnerability.

She angrily rolled away. I would have given a fortune to have been able to take back my bitter exploitation of her. Too late, too late. Her sobs choked in her throat, hers eyes lost their focus and became dull, dead orbs.

She sat up, refused to look at me and, before I could express my regret, said, "No, no! Don't say a word. You won! You reduced me to utter oblivion. No man will ever, ever, ever do that to me again!"

I tried to touch her in apology, amidst her scolding tears, she screamed, "Shut up! I don't want your fucking pity."

Her harshness appalled me. She, too, knew how to hurt.

"Yes, you can tell your friends that Mera was fucked into submission. I'll never forgive you. You bastard ..., bastard! But my revenge – oh yes, I'll be revenged. You'll never forget me and what you've done to me will be a cancer in your mind." She stood up. I was too shocked to ask for her forgiveness. Then, with a harsh crudity which I recognised as bravery, she dragged her skirt back on to her. Angrily wiping away the stains of our ecstasy, she stood up, laughing and crying at the same time.

"David, you're a prig. That's a pity but what you don't know is that I could have given you joys that would have made today seem like a prayer meeting."

She tossed her head angrily at the tears that flowed. "Don't you dare give me your fucking pity," she snarled.

Then, angrily laughing again, she added, "But, David bloody bar Jesse, you'll never forget this fuck!"

I winced at her crudity and she seemed to gain strength.

"Aye, it was the best you'll likely ever have, because, David-bloody-bar-Jesse, you're a great fucker but such a cold-hearted bastard. With all that airy fairy religion, you'll never release your talent if you can't make your mind up between being a priest or a soldier – that's your curse!"

She drew herself up with great dignity. "Mine is that we met at the wrong time! Someday, you will make a woman deeply happy – but only when you've found yourself!"

With tears streaming down her face, she walked away and called behind her, "I never want to see you again. You callous religious hypocritical bastard!"

She walked into the night leaving me with many lessons to digest – not least for a cruelty I did not know I possessed.

I took no pride in my conquest. I was consumed with a sadness at a memory that I knew would be doubled-edged. I would relive these moments that were both an ecstatic triumph and a bitter defeat. I knew with certainty that I would never see her again: thus, I would never be absolved from my abuse of another human being.

The next two nights, I ached for her. During the day I had tried to find her, suddenly realising that I needed her forgiveness. Each night, I relived and ejaculated to my double triumph and defeat, as I cursed the discovery of dissecting lust from love.

On the third night, the moon was full and I wandered off from my sleeping comrades. Without being sure why, I took my harp with me.

As I wandered alone in the bright moonlight, I realised that, in the last few weeks, I had lost touch with my soul. Then I reasoned how could I seek God when blood was my argument as I thought back on what I had witnessed and what I had done.

I must have wandered for an hour when I heard the sweet melancholy of a harp, accompanying a soft, deep, bass voice.

The player had his back to me and was engrossed in exquisite chords of great sadness. The full moon picked out the player who, to my surprise, was a very elderly man, all in white.

Kneeling upon bare ground, with piteous words I would never forget, he cried out, "My God! My God! Why hast thou forsaken me? Why art thou so far from my roaring?"

He threw himself down on his knees and, holding aloft his harp in one hand, he stretched out his other ancient arm in supplication to the heavens.

. I stood still at his intense devotion, suddenly feeling ashamed at seeing this ancient man in such utter degradation and sorrow.

With a start, he seemed to sense my presence and spun around.

He asked eagerly, "Are you he that is chosen to give me my death?"

I was shocked. "Sir, pardon me, I did not wish to intrude, but why should I, or any, want to give a reverent sir his death?"

He laughed a short, hard laugh. "Young sir, pardon me. When you know what I have lost, who I was, what I have become, you would understand that my death would be a boon. I am Agag, King that was. King of the Amalekites, that was." With these words his tears flowed again.

I was amazed. This was King Agag, a man of monstrous cruelty. He had ravaged Israel's people for more than three decades. Was he now reduced to this skinny wraith whose face, bleached by the moonlight, seemed so insubstantial as if already fit for the funeral pyre?

"Ah you know me, my boy. Yes. Yes. I am Agag – come to this." He piteously stretched out his skinny arm. "Where are all my troops now, my slaves, wives, concubines, servants, sons? Oh, my sons: where are they now? You know they wanted to rule before my death. They were so eager for the 'old man to go' – their father! I tried to tell them we needed to advance only when we knew where Saul's main army was. But no, they knew better and ran round after that accursed Jonathan – oh clever ... clever." He began to cry again.

Despite who he was, no one could fail to feel pity for this utterly downcast man. I took my harp and began to repeat the chords I had heard.

He sat up attentively. "That's good, boy. Yes, that's good!"

He sang in a half-crazed voice, words that would haunt me.

"My God, my God, why hast thou forsaken me – my God, my God, why hast thou forsaken me – why art thou so far from helping me and from the words of my roaring?

My God, my God why hast thou forsaken me – O my God I cry in the daytime and Thou hearest not, and in the night season I am not silent – My God, my God why hast thou forsaken me?"

I tried to comfort him and distract him, for I feared he might do himself a mischief.

As if he half read my mind, he responded, "No, no, my boy. I cannot die by my own hand. That is the final blasphemy. If you are not my executioner, I must bear the misery of these days a little longer. Saul, you know, would be kind ... kind. Would that he had given me my death. It's vanity really: he wants to show his people King Agag who frightened the pusillanimous Israelites for thirty years."

As he said this, he looked every inch a King but, guessing my thoughts, he continued, "All is gone. Vanity. I serve King Saul's vanity. Well, that's the way with kings. True, my boy. If you should ever be king, you, too, will become vain."

I was intrigued in spite of myself. "Nay, sir. I can never be king, not least because, though I am humble, I can call Jonathan, the King's son, my friend."

He looked alert. "Jonathan? Cursed be that name! If my sons had not been so foolhardy, I would never, never have entered that trap at Havilah. Ah, I see I please you. You know Jonathan. Yes, yes, it was a brilliant battle plan, without which the battle might have gone either way. Instead, we were drawn into that slaughter with no escape." His tears flowed again.

I rather stupidly tried to comfort him, telling him that it was God's will.

"God's will? What are you talking about, boy?"

I was rather nettled by this. "Well, sir King, it is well known that you worship the godhead of a bull, Nebalis."

"Fool," he said rudely. "There is only one God. Peoples try to define him and simple minds need symbols, but it is always the same divine shape we are seeking."

He laughed at my shocked reaction to his blasphemous idea, for our God was unique and our people were specially chosen and, therefore, different from all the other peoples of the world.

"I'll tell you something else – a terrible secret," he said, conspiratorially. "There is no difference between peoples – we are all the same: all desperately stumbling in the dark trying to make sense of what is around us."

I tried to say that we were God's only people.

"Boy, you have only listened to your own priests. They would separate people from each other." Seeing my look, he said, "Aye, and Kings and Princes too. They would keep the people distinct, or pretend they are distinct, to raise themselves on thrones of pride. Oh, I have done this too. But I know your people's story. Don't you see – we share it! Abraham is your great patriarch, but where did Abraham come from? Was he so different from my people, or those we call the Moabites? Would God cut himself from all other peoples by choosing only Abraham?"

I tried to reason with him but he cut me off rudely. "Boy, there is only one God. It is men's stupidity that shapes Him differently. All can catch a glimpse of the divine – but I think you know that."

He fixed me with a harsh stare and slowly said, "Yes, you know that don't you? Who are you that would bring the doomed comfort?"

I told him. He mused. "Ah, David bar Jesse. You may be the only one left to close my eyes. I pray you, in pity, do me that small service when the time comes. When you come to your great trial, think on me – on what I was and on what I became."

With that, he waved me away imperiously so that I could do nothing but obey.

Two days later, the King sent for me as he wanted me to take messages to Samuel. As I was waiting, a messenger came from the Prophet. I could see that the King was pleased. Was this the hoped for reconciliation?

In came Ariz, second in command of Samuel's guard. "Hail King. Have I your pardon and leave to give you a message and greeting from God's Prophet?"

This did not sound too optimistic. The King nodded his assent gravely.

"Then hear, King Saul, the word of God's Prophet, He who anointed you. The abomination must end."

There was a growl of anger from the men standing around Saul.

Ariz continued. "To prove that God's hand reaches further and more swiftly than the King's, here is a gift for thee to remind you of your disobedience and that God is not mocked."

With that, he signalled to the man just behind him, who handed him a travel bag. Ariz yanked it open and upturned the contents upon the floor.

There was a terrible exclamation. It was the severed head of Agag rolling along the floor. His white locks now bathed deep in the crimson of his blood. I was nearly sick.

"My master says this was a task for you, but God is not mocked. So end all who would set themselves against the Lord."

Saul slowly rose to his feet. He was ashen but, with great control, said,

"We thank the Prophet for his gift. We note his words."

Then his voice rose. "We also forgive him his own zealousness. For this was a prisoner of the state, which we could have used for Israel against the remnants of the Amalekites. Now we have no lever to use against any survivors. Samuel's hasty concern for his dignity will have driven the rest of any friends of the Amalekites towards our enemies, making God's people's task more difficult."

By this time, he had stood up and looked every inch a King. Every man's eye was upon him.

"Tell the Prophet that this day has placed an extra burden upon Israel. But, no matter, God gave us the victory of Havilah." Here, the men roared their approval.

Saul carried on. "God gave us the skill and foresight to plan the utter destruction and our men the power in their arms to smite the uncircumcised to the bone." Again, great acclamations from the surrounding men.

Saul spat out the following words, one at a time. "Tell Samuel that the sin of impatience is not excused in one so old. Now, before we smite the Philistines, we have allies of the Moabites, the Ammonites and the Kenenites. We could have had the remnants of the Amalekites, too. Samuel's rash action ill befits his whitened hairs, but we still honour him. However, tell him no more will he give us council until we ask for it. He is to remain at Rammah and pray for our people Israel.

"You, Ariz, are to return and guard the old man with dignity. But, if ever you or yours exceed your authority again, you die."

The King flung out a hand. "Now go and deliver our message."

Saul looked majestic. But my heart was melancholy for here I saw the beginning of the schism in the people of Israel and of the ruin of the House of Saul. All acclaimed the King but everyone ignored the grisly ball at the King's feet.

With great sadness, I recovered the bag and quietly replaced the head. I felt disgust at the still moist object that stained my hands. Sadly, I left having fulfilled King Agag's strange request and prophecy as I closed that poor head's eyes and then buried the last King of the Amalekites.

To my surprise, I shed tears.

PART FOUR

GOD'S WARRIOR

Chapter Twelve

Samuel's Plea

The army were disbanding and returning home. I was given messages from the King to take to my father. I had spoken little with either Saul or Jonathan. Indeed, when I last spoke with Jonathan I was not too pleased. The issue was about who would be his new armour bearer ahead of the spring campaign. With hindsight I rather stupidly raised it on one of the rare occasions we were alone. Normally, when by ourselves, we never spoke about Jonathan's command.

When he told me it was going to be Canan, I suppose I showed my disappointment and surprise.

Tersely, he said, "David, you are being presumptuous. Consider a moment. If you were thinking of volunteering – don't. Never take a public decision on personal preference. Act only on merit so that all men can see your decision is based on good grounds, not favouritism. The men know that I don't particularly like Canan, but he volunteered. He is undoubtedly the best swordsman in the troop, he is four years older than you and has faced three battles. He is brave, reliable and has much to commend him."

I opened my mouth to say something not very wise but Jonathan's face stopped me.

He was cold, formal and very distant. "David bar Jesse, you have much in your favour. The King, my father, regards you highly as his bard – albeit a warrior bard. I esteem you more highly than you can ever know. But – and this is the issue – you are still young, inexperienced and there are others in the troop who have greater claims to this onerous task. In their honour, it would be an affront to them to advance you to Elim's position."

I felt squashed, resentful and, with rather bad grace, coldly accepted his embrace. He gave me a chaste kiss and asked me to pass on his greetings to my father.

My farewells to Ura, Beniah, Hushai and Hitophel were much warmer. Ura, in particular, was very encouraging and assured me that I was now part of the troop even though I had not fought at Havilah. The men appreciated that, because of the map making, I had made an important contribution that had saved lives – all comrades and warriors appreciate such skills.

To my delight, Ura said that, if I recommended them, he would be willing for Josh, Eli and Aaron to join the troop. "If you think they are good enough, knowing that you are barely good enough, then I'll tell the Prince. We'll have three more Bethlehemites for me to have to break my back upon. I can but try to turn them into decent soldiers."

He gave me his big bear hug as Hitophel and I returned together towards Judah.

When I turned off for Bethlehem, I must confess my thoughts began to turn to Una and our lovemaking. I did not feel too guilty: after all, she needed my protection and she was not a threat to Leah's memory. She would be safer sharing my bed. As I ran the last five miles I was looking forward to her warm welcome and feeling her slender, pliant body next to mine.

I was immediately called into Father, who wanted all the news. To my surprise he was somewhat critical of the King because of his "disobedience". Apparently, he and the other Elders agreed with the Prophet that the Amalekites should have been annihilated.

"But Father," I protested, "there had been so much killing. The army would not stand for it. After four days the men were sick of it. It did them honour not to kill defenceless women and children."

"So," he roared, "you too are demonstrating rebellion. Samuel anointed Saul in God's name. Samuel knows the mind of God. How dare you, young man? 'The army would not stand for it'? Pah! Do you think you know better than your fathers and the Elders? Have you no respect? Were you not trained in obedience, as I was obedient to my father and he to his? Can you doubt that Samuel, knowing the mind of God and being loaded with years, should not receive total, unquestioning obedience?"

In a flash I saw what this was about and did not like it. If the army ruled in Israel, this would undermine the authority of the Elders, who, of course, were too old for battle. That was why they were backing Samuel in his quarrel with Saul. His authority was similar to theirs.

For the first time in my life, I consciously prevaricated with him. "Father, after you, I honour the Prophet above all other men."

I knew it to be a lie. With a sharp stab of awareness I realised that, whilst I respected and obeyed my father, I revered both Saul and Samuel more – and loved and respected Jonathan even more than them. So, I made my peace and kept my counsel, listening to views with which I was increasingly at odds. Like every Hebrew, I took the word of the father before everything else so I listened politely and did not argue.

He appeared mollified and told me he was pleased. The Prophet had expressed many positive things about me. I seemed to be favoured by "Saul", whom I noticed he did not call "King". Then, to my amazement, he asked me about marriage.

I told him that since Leah's death I had not given it a thought. "Father, perhaps, I am being presumptuous, but my eye is greatly pleased by Merab, the King's eldest daughter."

He laughed. "You have great ideas for yourself! But you are not thinking in the right direction. I believe, though there have been no nego-tiations, that Mera, the Prophet's great granddaughter – the daughter of his eldest grandson, Abrahe – might be a very great alliance for our family."

When he said Mera my mind immediately thought of Mera, the camp follower, and my blood sang a little. So I let my mind pleasantly dwell on Una again. Then, the impact of my Father's words suddenly drove home.

"Father, do you think an alliance with the daughter of the King of Israel, as unlikely as it is to happen, is surpassed by Mera? She is only the great granddaughter of the Prophet?"

"Ah, you're not as slow as I thought you were. After all, Saul has disobeyed God. Will he always be King?"

I was shocked. "But Father, the King has four sons and the eldest, Jonathan, is a great commander."

He looked at me as old men do when they think you have been espe-cially stupid. "David, my boy, kings are anointed by the Prophet of God. There is no rule, law or any experience that says that the sons of kings become kings just because their fathers were. That's a preposterous idea. It's a blasphemous idea – stupid. For though a man may be both a good solider and a wise king, his sons could be witless and unfit to rule. Would you seriously make a man king simply because he was the son of a previous king?"

Then he began to get angry again, saying this kind of thought showed how corrupting it was to send young men to the army too soon. Again I kept my counsel, but was saddened by realising that my father's support of the Prophet was more to do with Father's pride and desire for influence, than the good of Israel.

After telling me not to think further of Merab but look to the future with the possibility of an alliance with the Prophet's family, he dismissed me.

I went eagerly to seek Mother. After receiving her blessing, in which her tears wet my face, filling my heart with gladness at her obvious concern for me, she began to tell me how happy she was.

"God has not seen fit to take any of my children from me," she said. "I pray every day to the Lord of Hosts for the safety of all my little ones – especially yours."

What son could resist such an admission?

I let her babble on happily. "I am so glad that this terrible war is over. I felt so afraid. I am comforted, however, by the thought that, every day, somewhere a mother is raising her hands in supplication to bring her son home."

"Mother, that is a nice idea but what about the Philistines or the Amalekites? If their prayers were answered, we would not be home."

She snapped at me. "I always thought you cleverer than the rest, but sometimes you're just as big a fool. Don't you see if all the sons came home then we would have no wars? No wars – no widows, no orphans and no famines. That's what your Leah said. She taught me to think for myself."

Then, looking very concerned, she asked in a soft voice, "Is it true that they killed all the families? Did they really slaughter the old men, the women and the children?"

"Mother, you know you ought not to ask questions like these – but, yes, it was terrible."

As I answered her, the memory of the suicidal mother flashed across my mind. In similar circumstances could my Mother be such a woman?

"But, Mother, it was not quite as bad as that because the men would not go on killing and the King let the women join Israel. Most of the women, being widows, were glad to come under our men's protection. Israel is increased and the rabbis are busy giving them instructions. But, Mother, be careful: Father did not approve of what the King did, so I wouldn't say any more about this."

After asking and receiving her blessing again, I cheerfully asked, "I'm tired as I have come a long way. Will you send for Una so she can prepare my bed?"

As I spoke, her face seemed to collapse and her eyes took on a deadened look.

I grew alarmed. "Mother, what is it? What has happened?"

"Oh David, my son." She began to wring her hands and her tears flowed. "David, Una is dead."

Before the words were out my heart froze.

Calmly and coldly I said, "Tell me what happened." Then, with a sense of overwhelming rage, I shouted, "It was not Boaz again, was it?"

"No, no, no – of course not. Boaz has not been home since ... since ... well, you know. No, she suddenly died a week after you left. She had been having hard pains in her side for two weeks before you came home. She did not tell you because she wanted to please you." She hesitated but I waited for her to tell me all. She went on with a sigh, "Why am I fated to lose my best bond-maidens? She was as close as Leah – like another daughter and without Leah's pride."

She saw my look. "You might not like me saying this but, though Leah was good to me, she had her pride and she would not have been an easy wife."

I did not respond to this but said quietly, "Tell me about Una, Mother. Please."

"Well, she was happy when you made her your concubine, because some of the men had begun to find her attractive. After you left her, her sickness became much worse. She was very brave because she had what we call the board sickness, when the belly becomes hard all over. You may remember your young cousin, Isaac, died of it when you were ten. She had so much pain and a fever that set her on fire, I knew she could not live."

She tried to comfort me. "David, she was very fond of you. It must be a disappointment but you don't want to be getting involved with women outside the tribe – and certainly not from outside Israel. Perhaps it's for the best. She was happy with the short time she had with you."

She hesitated. "I don't know whether I should tell you this but she said that she loved you above all other men. She was sorry she could not serve you longer but she would be in Abraham's bosom with Leah to watch over you."

I could hardly restrain my anger and grief at her words, but I knew she meant no harm. So I bowed to her, asked for her blessing and ran from the house.

With each pounding footstep, the words were hammered into my head: 'Una is Dead, Una is Dead, Una is Dead'. My tears flowed.

I ran as hard as I could, trying to flee the thoughts in my head, but they came all the same. Why, why, why?

What curse did I have that those I loved died? True, I loved Una out of pity rather than from the heart, but I could have loved her in time – even if not like Leah. But it did not matter: both were gone.

I breasted the hill and ran on into the gathering gloom. To my surprise, I found that I had arrived almost at Bull Horns. I saw that the sheep had been brought down so there would be no one there.

I slowed down to a crawling pace, exhausted with grief and anger. Why, why I thought. I wanted to curse and raised my head to shout my anger, hurt and defiance and saw above me a cloud of stars.

I stood stock still. When had I last seen stars like this?

Then I thought, somewhat guiltily, when had I stood and looked at anything for a moment? Since going to the camp I had thought of little other than kings, princes and war. I mused, a little ruefully: I could not expect to have peace of mind if all I thought about was battle and power.

I sat down on a rock and fixed my face upward towards the star-littered sky.

Even in the sky's darkness there were patterns of deeper darkness and ripples of shimmering light. The stars were an accompaniment to the dark bowl stretching overhead.

I recalled what Leah and I had spoken of. "When we die," she had said, "I think we hide amidst a cloud of stars, which are the eyes of God. I think that is the real home of those who rest in the bosom of Abraham."

I cried silently to the stars, hoping that, somehow, my silent call would reach Leah and little Una – sweet Mouse – amidst their cloud of stars. I slowly walked on. In the starlight I could see the dark silhouette of the mountain etched, inky black, against the paler dark of the night sky. I mourned again for Leah till I was exhausted. I was drained and empty but I recognised the shape of my hills, which gave their own peace even in the stillness of night.

Then the words came, halting at first, as my soul tried to suppress its sorrow in its search for meaning and peace in the words of God.

"I will lift up mine eyes unto the hills from whence cometh my help. My help cometh from the Lord which made heaven and earth."

Yes, I thought the hills are where God's strength is. His strength to me and to Israel. This is where Leah and Una can find peace, amidst the sleeping eternity of the mountains, which are a balm and refuge.

"I will lift up mine eyes unto the hills from whence cometh my help. My help cometh from the Lord which made heaven and earth."

In amazement, I realised that He had cared for me all along the dangerous road I had travelled. Oh, what sublime surety and confidence – all totally unearned for I was unworthy to live when others died. Now, out of the blackness came words of comfort and hope.

"He will not suffer my foot to be moved, he that keepeth thee shall not slumber. Behold he that keepeth Israel shall neither slumber nor sleep."

My loves are with the Lord of Hosts. Leah, dear Leah, and sweet Una: both are with Him who never sleeps. Again I had that sense of total confidence:

whilst evil may challenge and seek to oppress, God holds us all in his hand. With a sense of surety for Leah, for Una, as well as for the poor self-killing Amalekite woman, I knew – and knew with a certainty that was unmistakable – that they were safe. I prayed for them, confident that they rested in God's mercy. I mouthed the words given to console Leah and the others:

"The Lord is thy keeper, the Lord is thy shade upon thy right hand.
The sun shall not smite thee by day or the moon by night. The Lord preserve thee from all evil and he shall preserve thy soul. The Lord shall preserve thy going out and thy coming in from this time forth and even for evermore."

I returned home just as dawn was breaking and the house was beginning to stir. I was seen and told to go immediately to father.

A message had come from the Prophet and I was to take the answer back. Was this the reconciliation?

But when I found Father, my hopes were dashed. To start with, he was angry.

"Where have you been? The Prophet has sent for you."

As I began to speak he said, with great irritation, "David, listen, you are the message."

As if he had an idea what I was thinking, he added, "It's nothing to do with the House of Saul. Frankly, my lad, its time you started to think of the House of Jesse. The Prophet has said he intends to advance our house. Naturally, I mentioned my hopes for your brothers, Eliab, as eldest, Abibadab and Shamma. But he says Abibadab is too lazy. Yes, that's true. But he refused to say how he would raise our house. All he said was that he wants you to go to him at once. Actually, now I remember he did say that Shamma shows great promise – so don't start getting too big ideas of yourself. Don't forget you are the youngest. Why the Prophet should see merit in you when I cannot is beyond me! But that he does, is enough."

After dutifully receiving his blessings, I hurried off to Rammah, two days away, wondering what Samuel wanted.

I reached the Prophet in the early evening. I had made excellent time but was now exhausted. To my surprise, and despite saying that I was still filthy from the road, I was ushered immediately into Samuel.

On seeing me, his face flooded with smiles and I felt so guilty that I had doubts about him. He refused to let me make my obeisance to him. Ignoring my protestations that I was sweaty, he hugged me in a surprising tight embrace.

"David, my friend! David, you are still my friend, are you not?"

He paused, holding me and looking deep into my face as I held his gaze.

This wonderful old man overwhelmed me.

"Yes, I can see. Despite all the allure, the pomp, the majesty of the royal camp" – words which were clearly barbed – "you are still the Lord's Bard. Your inspiration and your allegiance are still to the Lord of Hosts. You make an old man happy by being his friend."

Laughing, he pretended to first notice my stink. "Come. First drink and then let us walk, for I would share my counsel with you."

What could I say?

We walked some way without speaking. When we reached a tree-shaded spot he smiled and said, "Do you know this is holy ground. I usually come alone or only with those who have a special bond with God. Do you know why?"

He went on, smiling at my puzzlement, "This is the sacred spot where we buried my master, Eli, so many, many decades ago. I come and bring wine or water and make a libation in his memory."

I was awed as Samuel wistfully recalled his old master. "It's appropriate for us to talk about Eli. He walked with God and he too knew what a rocky way it often is. Lonely, oh so often very lonely, though there are moments that, even to you, I cannot tell of the sacred transforming joy. But those are so infrequent and others do not understand one's burden. They scorn, criticise – indeed, in their ignorance, they blaspheme because they do not know any better. I do not chastise them."

He stopped and, in the semi-gloom, asked, "David, tell me – on your word – do you think I'm cruel? Do you really think I could misunderstand the words of God?"

I was startled. Firstly, by his absolute simplicity and the conversational tone he was using, as if we were two friends discussing an unimportant matter. Secondly, because, with his great powers, he saw the hurt and fear I had in my heart. His honesty demanded my total openness in return.

I spoke carefully but forthrightly. "Master, though you call me friend, I am not fit to tie your shoe. I will try to share with you what is in my heart."

I took a deep breath and began. "I am so saddened at the strife between you and the King. What you have achieved is greater than both Moses and Joshua." He was about to protest, but I would not allow it. "Truly, Master, Moses was a great Prophet and leader but he could not enter the Promised Land. Joshua was a great soldier, but he was not up against the might of the Amalekites and the Philistines. You alone have scattered the Philistines and Saul has destroyed the Amalekites for ever."

He accepted my words up to this point but then came to the difficult part. "But, Master, did we really have to exterminate them all? Saul was right: the men were sick and tired of killing – especially the women and children. It seemed wanton cruelty. We could not understand."

I had not criticised him, but laid out the problem as I saw it.

He rubbed his chin. "I am grateful, David. The issue is not how many died, or did not die, but one of obedience. Twice, Saul directly disobeyed God's instructions. There have been many little things that I forgave and God winked at. I understand men's pride – am I not a man, too?"

Samuel placed his hand on my shoulder. "But let me tell you, here in this sacred place of my master, that Eli received instructions that he did not understand and which, at first, appeared cruel, callous and hard."

I looked puzzled again as I did not know of this story.

His face was filled with a sense of a distant sadness as he whispered, "I was five when they sent me to serve this old and fierce man. Five – can you imagine what that meant? True, I learned to love and revere him, but my mother's vow to give her son to God's service did not mean much to the son who was sent. I did not understand the words, other than I was to be parted from my mother, father and all familiar things that, up till then, had surrounded me. Suddenly to be wrenched away to live alone from everything I'd known. What a cruelty that was! I was not an orphan! I was not with parents who had too many children that were grateful to pass on to others who had none or few. I was their only son – I was so loved, so cherished. Yet I was banished, banished and never saw them again."

He fell silent. I was filled with a sense of pity and wonderment as I saw this ancient man sit and grieve for a mother lost aeons ago.

His eyes shone in the starlight. "I did not receive my call from God for another five years. I served like a bondsman though I was only in bondage to God's service. I remember the nightly tears that I shed for my lost home."

I felt for him. I immediately thought of Leah's great sadness, at the years the locusts had eaten from her brief life. I recognised the injustice and I understood how this gentle old man, who had such responsibility, had felt hurt, outcast and lonely all those years ago.

He continued. "Now, what I am to tell you has been told to no man. Eli told me that he had not heard the voice of God for over a decade, though he had been told of my coming. He was told that I would carry the torch, which meant that it would be another, rather than his sons, who would be the prime servant of God. Many wish for the call – except those who receive it. Though it hurt him, he obeyed."

Samuel became excited. "Every day, as I waxed stronger and more knowledgeable in the Lord, it became more obvious that it was I who would succeed – not his sons or grandsons. Nevertheless, Eli obeyed because he did what God told him. He understood that, though he would not live to see it, God's purpose was being worked out. We mortals have neither the wisdom, the grace, the inspiration nor the years to see the unfolding of God's plan for His people. My call, when it came, was marvellous and, at the same time, terrifying. It gave me joy – as, perhaps, some day it may give you. A joy that is unspeakable – but it also gave me knowledge that felt like a curse."

He looked hard at me but said with pity and understanding in his voice, "When you cursed your inspiration, you were wise. The responsibility is onerous, truly terrible, but you were a young man, whereas I was barely ten years old.

"And what did I learn? That my master, who I had now come to regard as Father, the only person in the world to show me personal affection, was going to die! Eli in his years had not been the stern Father that is sometimes necessary, so Israel was going to suffer because the people had strayed from God's word. When I heard this message, I cried and cried, yet Eli knew that I could not tell him and I had to carry the burden of knowledge alone. I had to do my duty. I did not understand. I could not see and it felt like wanton cruelty to me also."

As he spoke, his voice rose with the anger. The frustration of the remembrance of the isolation and burden placed upon the child he once was. "I did not, nor dare not, question God's purpose. I realised then, as I know now, we are all instruments in His hands. We must play our part and, when our task is done, to be laid aside as I shall be laid aside – and you, too, even though you are just at the beginning of your strength."

He calmed down and continued. "Since the time I was dragged, crying, from my mother to the time I received my call, I felt a dread and isolation. Until this day, I have never shared this hurt with another soul. Later, when I was directed to go into the mountain and lead the people against the over mighty odds of the Philistines, I did not question. I did not tell God how afraid I was. He knew. But I knew that though I could not see the purpose, if God had directed it He would give me the strength, the knowledge, wisdom to achieve His purpose. So I walked amongst the people seemingly serene. Though I tell you in all humility, I did not know what my next words would be, or what would ensue."

As if making the final argument he went on, "Sometimes, my friend and son, sometimes God seems to be making inhuman demands upon us, because He is so holy, we cannot get close to Him. He demanded obedience from Father Abraham and demanded from Abraham that, if necessary, he would have to sacrifice his own son – his own son – for God's purpose. Even though Abraham could not understand this apparently 'wantonly cruel' gesture, he was willing to obey. Why, even Saul in his pride, even he knew

that the burden of the battle would have to be carried by his son Jonathan
– whom he loves – even though Saul is jealous and tortured by the pride
that has destroyed him. I am not unaware of how great a soldier Saul was.
It was a brilliant plan, but it depended upon him being willing to sacrifice
Jonathan, in whom he has his highest hopes."

Yet again, the old man had amazed me by the depth of his intuition. He
smiled at me. "You looked surprised that I know these things, David. I have
watched men for more than three score years and I know. Yes, the proud
and ambitious Abner might have hesitated, but even he knew his duty and
that Havilah would take his chance away of ever being King in Israel. Saul
has played his purpose out. God warned him, gave him a second chance,
but he blasphemed when, in his arrogance and blindness, he dared to
question what God wanted."

He could see that though I was not totally convinced by the argument,
I understood more, but I had a sense of dread at the implications of what
he was saying.

"David, as someone who has experienced hurt, bitterness, danger, scorn
and isolation, do you think I am cruel? Of course not! I am the wind that
God directs. I am the flame that He conjures from the thunder. I am
nothing. You are nothing. Saul and his pride are nothing before the might
and purpose of God."

I was chastened and, haltingly, asked, "Perhaps I understand. Saul has
sinned, so when will Jonathan be King?"

He was angry. "Have you not understood? The House of Saul is disin-
herited. The Kingship of Israel is not the gift of the King, but whom God
chooses," he said with great emphasis.

I was confused. "Will it be Abner? Who else is there of the great of
Israel?"

He smiled. "I do not know my boy. I am old and sometimes I am very
tired with a weariness you will not know for many years. But I do know that
I will be told and will anoint him – and then I shall die and be in the bosom
of Abraham."

He said this so matter-of-factly. He was prophesying his own death.
"What I can tell you, my friend David, is that God has a purpose for you
even more than he has already shown you. What it is, or when you will be
called, I don't know, but it will come: tomorrow, or next year, or in ten
years. Who can know the mind of God?"

He laughed and clapped me on the back. "Come, sing me my psalm. Oh
yes, I have something more to ask rather than tell you."

I wondered what it could be.

"Before you return home, I want you to speak to my son, Agar. He will have a scribe with him and I want you to give him all the words of your psalms. You do know that your verses are inspired, don't you?"

I nodded, though this was the first total acceptance that I was sometimes the mouthpiece of a power outside myself.

Samuel continued. "I think it will be good for the people to know that the inspiration has continued in their times."

Then, quite abruptly with a complete change of mood, he said, "I feel we shall meet only twice more before you hear that my eyes are closed. No, don't say anything. I am looking forward to it – truly. But if would be good to have the words for the people and I feel that you have had a recent blessing that will be a benediction for me."

He knew everything so I shared with him a benediction for all that would dwell in the Lord.

"I will lift up mine eyes unto the hills from whence cometh my help. My help cometh from the Lord which made heaven and earth.

He will not suffer thy foot to be moved, he that keepeth thee shall not slumber. Behold he that keepeth Israel shall neither slumber nor sleep.

The Lord is thy keeper, the Lord is thy shade upon thy right hand.

The sun shall not smite thee by day or the moon by nights. The Lord preserve thee from all evil and he shall preserve thy soul. The Lord shall preserve thy going out and thy coming in from this time forth and even for evermore."

As the words died away to echoes, Samuel had a look of ecstasy on his face.

Saul's Agony

I returned home a little slower then when I set out, for my time with Samuel had troubled me deeply. The implications were horrendous. I had given my service to the King and to Jonathan. Yet Samuel was prophesying their downfall! I could not face that. It seemed to me that, whatever happened, I had given my allegiance to serve the King and I would honour my word. Providing – and, oh I prayed – providing it was not in obvious opposition to the Prophet. If that should come then I would not know what to do.

As I approached Bethlehem, it was virtually dark but I saw the outlines of Josh, who obviously was waiting for me. I hailed him in delight and rushed towards him. He was grinning from ear to ear. He gave me a big bear hug and wanted to know all my news.

I told him that, once I had reported to Father, I would be all his and that we had so much time to catch up upon.

276

I could not help but say, "Josh, you have grown so much. You look terrific!"

He seemed pleased. "Aye, David, but I have not changed as much as you. Your hair, your face, you have a ..., a ..." He stumbled as he sought for the word. "... a presence. It seems that meeting all the mighty in Israel has made you even more different."

I felt hurt by this, as I saw he was very serious. "Josh, oh Josh, don't you know I will always be your friend till the day I die? There are few whom I love more."

He was quick to seize upon this. "So, there are a few more then, David?"

I felt slighted again. It seemed as if he wanted to quarrel. "The Prophet and the King like my playing. I am nothing more than a servant and a youngest son. All right, I never played for them the 'Farting Rabbi'."

We both laughed at what now seemed a distant memory. "Yes, Josh. I have a few new friends, Ura, Beniah, Hitophel and Hushai, in my troop. They are great warriors and truly want to meet you for I have told them that you are the best wrestler and the most honest friend a man could have. And one of the best runners – after me." We both laughed as I said this. "Moreover, Ura the captain of the Prince's troop, has said that you, Eli and Aaron are welcome to join the Prince's troop."

Josh seemed pleased but then said, "But who else have you not mentioned?"

I flushed at this for I realised he meant Jonathan. "Josh, I admit: I admire Prince Jonathan more than any man I have known. But he is the King's son. He is a great general and is much older than the men in his troop – well, perhaps ten years older – and we all love him."

"And ... does he love you?" Josh asked.

I blushed at the question because I did not know how to answer this. I held out my hand to Josh. "Josh, I love you! I always have and always will. You know me better than any. I am just a funny loon from Bethlehem who makes up poems, but we are brothers. Look, Achish the Philistine made me his blood brother. Why don't we do the same ..., here ..., now."

Josh's eyes shone. He drew his knife. Without thinking, I scratched my wrist. He did the same. We mingled our blood together.

"Brotherhood!" I said as we embraced and kissed. But his lips held mine in a new way. His lips seemed to be seeking mine as I might have sought Leah's. In his embrace, I could feel him hard against me. I did not know what to do. Josh had declared himself to me. Oh my God, how could I tell him? How could I show him that I loved him – but not in that way?

I half-pushed him away and tried to make a joke. "Josh, we are brothers now but not like the Philistines, as philia. We Hebrew boys don't do that.

Come, let's go and find Eli and Aaron."

His fingers dug into my shoulders. He choked the words out. "David! David, I do love you in 'that' way, as you put it. I don't want to. I don't understand it. I'm not even sure how to. Don't make me beg. Don't despise me."

I put my hand on his chest and stood a little apart. "Josh, I think you are wonderful. I've always admired you. But don't rush me. We are blood brothers – we are bonded for ever, on that you have my word. I could never despise you. I am proud, so proud to be your friend. Look at all the times you got me out of trouble, stuck up for me against Boaz. Let us take things quietly and see what happens. But because you are my brother, I have to tell you that I don't feel to you as you seem to feel me. I do know that amongst the Philistines men who are more than blood brothers are greatly honoured and are considered the best warriors. One such is Achish, who might well be the Philistine High King someday."

Josh stood quietly, his face a mystery. "All right, I'll be satisfied for now. You've been very decent about things, David, but whether I'll join your troop, I'm not sure. I'll need to think about it. Eli, Aaron and me: we wouldn't want to let you down in front of your new friends – "

I interjected. "Josh, you're being a bore. Don't be silly! I want you to come. For God's sake, didn't you realise that, though I was at the army, I was not at the battle. They gave me other duties. I'm still a novice. Please, don't say no. Promise me we can all go up together, exactly as we'd always planned."

To my relief, Josh allowed himself to be pacified so we parted on reasonably good terms.

Father was agitated, "Saul is calling for you. The Prince is calling for you. Apparently, the King is ill and they need you to play for him. Frankly, it seems obvious to me that this is God's answer for his disobedience."

He saw my face and replied irritably, "Of course, you've got to go, but don't forget what I told you: the Prophet has said he has high hopes for our house."

Then, suddenly realising that I had just returned from Samuel, he asked,

"Well? What did he want? Has he promised you anything? Did you ask for your brothers? You know you have an obligation to Eliab and Shamma especially. Don't look at me like that, young man. All this gadding around talking with the great of Israel is going to your head. I don't expect you to tell me everything but, don't forget, I've known the old fox for years. Whatever, be careful and go with my blessing."

Incidentally this was how the myth arose that Samuel chose me after inspecting and rejecting all my older brothers, but waited for the absent shepherd boy whom he had never met. It makes a very good story. I have even had it told to my face.

I went as quickly as I could and realised that my father had said far more than he intended. "Old fox" indeed – I could not help grinning to myself. My father was an antidote to the anxiety I was beginning to feel, for I knew that the next time I was in Bethlehem things would never be the same.

I arrived back in Gilbeah at around midday.

Eban greeted me with alacrity, but looked very serious and distressed.

He said, "I'll tell the Prince that you're here – he'll be relieved. Oh David, my master is very low."

To my surprise there were tears in his eyes. Then I remember that Saul had the power to inspire his men as he inspired me, and that Eban had been his armour bearer and friend for a long time.

Eban, almost choking, said, "I think you ought to wait for Jonathan – though the King did say to send you in as soon as he arrived."

He looked at me intensely. "He's got great faith in you being able to help him. He's already thrown out two priest doctors and ..., well – you'll see for yourself."

He sent a man after Jonathan who came quickly. He looked very grave and, nodding kindly to Eban, said, "Thanks, old friend. I'll explain every-thing to David."

Jonathan took me on one side. I could not help but notice that, in his preoccupation, he had not greeted me.

"He's very ill, David. His spirits are very low. You know, those black moods? Well, they are back and they are much worse. He's talking about conspiracies again. He's been cursing Samuel and – yes – even God. He says he is being deserted and that it's unfair. Oh, incidentally, there is almost certainly going to be a campaign against the Philistines next spring. Thanks to your friend Samuel, they are really alarmed at what we did to the Amalekites. Doesn't that old fool realise what he's done?"

Jonathan spoke with real bitterness. "We've virtually told the world that we will annihilate anybody who is not of our people. Father had hopes of some kind of gradual alliance with them. A kind of arrangement which would ensure that they would not poach our northern tribes and we could be a bulwark for them for any threat from either the south or east. All that's gone now."

He saw my troubled look. "I know you like the Old Man – I do too. He is a great man and has served Israel wonderfully, but times are changing: we are no longer a nomadic people. Father and I think that there will come a time when we will truly settle down and learn to live in peace and agreement with our neighbours. Of course, we must always remain strong but we can't fight the whole world for ever."

Needless to say, this did not make me feel any easier. I felt confused. Here was the man whom I admired above all others, being disloyal to the Prophet, yet I could see the right in both of them. Jonathan took me in to greet the King and what I saw shocked me.

The King lay slumped along a couch. He was unkempt and his beard ragged. Piles of untouched food lay around. I suddenly realised that the debris on the floor was other food that the King had thrown about.

His eyes, when they eventually opened looked pained, and full of trouble. His speech was slow and ponderous, as if every word had a weight attached.

I made my bow and greeted him. "I am honoured, oh King, to bring Bethlehem's greeting to the victor of Havilah."

He didn't answer for a long time. Then he snarled at Jonathan, "Leave us. Leave us!" and waited till he left.

There was another long pause but then the words came, slowly, filled with such anguish that his mental pain was almost physical.

"David? David? Why does God persecute me? Why does he not speak directly to me? Why does he not give me a sign? I am destroyed!"

His face was ashen. "I, Saul, who feared no man, feared and honoured the God who chose me. But he has gone from me. I can trust no one – no one."

Then, staring at me in a frightening way, he said, "Can I trust you? Can I?"

"Great King, I am your warrior, your bard, your servant. I have sworn to honour and follow the House of Saul and I shall do so until the day I die," I answered.

He did not reply, but seem to have drifted off into a harsh muse.

I tried to get through to him. "King Saul, Father, you once called me friend. I do not know why these dark thoughts fill you so. You are truly beloved of your people, your sons, your generals and your captains. It is the burden you carry, virtually beyond an ordinary man's ability, that troubles you so. You must learn to rest and take comfort in what you have achieved."

I then took a risk. "I believe that my psalms are from God and, if that is so, they are for all time. Remember the psalm they now call the Song of Saul?"

I began to play.

"The King shall joy in thy strength O Lord and in thy salvation how greatly shall he rejoice.

Thou hast given him his heart's delight – thou settest a crown of pure gold upon his head.

He asked life of thee and thou gavest it him even length of days for ever.

His glory is great in thy salvation, honour, and majesty hast thou laid upon him.

For thou hast made him most blessed for ever; thou hast made him exceedingly glad with thy countenance.

For the King trusteth in the Lord and through the mercy of the Most High he shall not be moved."

He rested quietly for some time. The music seemed to have soothed him, so we sat quietly together.

Then I had an idea. I called for a servant for bathwater and wine, saying that I would be honoured if I might help him prepare. Standing close to him, I knew he had not washed for days. Without giving him the chance to say yes or no, I took off his shirt and began to sponge him down. I took off his skirt and had to hold back my surprise at his physical disarray. I called for more water and finished cleansing him. Finally, on my knee, I offered him wine and bread.

He took them but then, suddenly, grasped my hand urgently. "David! David! You'll never betray me, will you? You are my sign that God has forgiven me many things."

He clearly did not want an answer but held me in an iron grip all the same, which was both painful and worrying. Was I going to provoke a rage in him?

He gasped, "I trust you, you know? If you let me down, I could trust no one.

"You are my lucky omen. I know you came from Him. The Prophet thinks he sent you, but I know that God sent you to me. How else could you know my pain? David, ask of God that you shall bring me comfort. Bring me a sign that the Lord is with me. Give me a sign that I shall regain my strength?"

He said this with such desperation that no one could have refused him succour, so I said, "King, my Master, Father and friend, I have a new psalm, which perhaps was made for you. It brought great comfort to me in my puny sadness. But first, let us go to the hills together where we can better share a new psalm for God's anointed."

He hesitated at first and then nodded. He slowly rose, releasing me to my great relief, and allowed me to lead him. As we left his tent, he walked, as I thought he might, more upright. As his men saw him, they cheered and hailed him.

Eban rushed towards him, crying, "Hail Saul, the Lords anointed, Great

281

King of Israel! Hosanna! Hosanna!"

All the men took up the cry. Saul did not speak, but responded magnificently – as I hoped he would. His back straightened and he walked purposefully, acknowledging their greetings with a majestic wave as he passed
them. I could see Jonathan who, like the rest of the soldiers, knelt as his
father went by. The look he gave me told me that if there was anything
amiss between us, all was forgiven.

We walked towards the hills in silence. The early evening twilight was
beginning to gather. As we climbed the rise, the sun had burnished the sky
but was now going quickly down the heavens, filling the whole horizon with
magnificent red glow and gilding the clouds at the summit of the hills. We
both stood in awe at a wonderful sunset.

"A sign, Great King, that God's beauty is over all your lands. We are
blessed indeed."

As the sun's glow began to ebb, I took up my harp and sang:

"I will lift up mine eyes unto the hills from whence cometh my help."

He must see, feel, that the hills blend with the heavens and this is the place
of God.

My help cometh from the Lord which made heaven and earth.
He will not suffer my foot to be moved, he that keepeth thee shall not slumber.
Behold he that keepeth Israel shall neither slumber nor sleep.

He must know that amidst his battles, the Lord has preserved him.
The Lord is thy keeper, the Lord is thy shade upon thy right hand.
The sun shall not smite thee by day or the moon by night.
The Lord preserve thee from all evil and he shall preserve thy soul."

This is the psalm for Saul. Here is God's promise not to condemn him to
madness. God's care will soothe his frenzy and, through all, the Lord holds
him in His hand.

"The Lord shall preserve thy going out and thy coming in from this time forth and
even for evermore."

At first, the King made no response but slowly tears ran down his face. He
repeated the words:

"The sun shall not smite thee by day nor the moon by night.

The Lord preserve thee from all evil and he shall preserve thy soul.
My help cometh from the Lord which made heaven and earth.
He will not suffer my foot to be moved, he that keepeth thee shall not slumber.
Behold he that keepeth Israel shall neither slumber nor sleep."

"David, yes! This is a sign. My soul is restored, you have planted me anew by the waters."

He embraced me and I him, as his tears broke my heart. I felt him riven with sobs and saw the King of Israel weep like a girl.

Happily, the worst of the mood had left him and, within days, the King was himself again.

I visited the King daily. Sometimes I did not play for him; on others that's all I did. There was an atmosphere of expectation around the King, tinged with some anxiety.

Jonathan, on his own responsibility, recalled his troop and the kings.

Saul's guard was fixed at a thousand mature warriors but he agreed that Jonathan's troop might rise to a quarter of a thousand men.

I was delighted when Ura called to me. "Call your Bethlehemite friends. It's my burden for being too soft with you in the first place."

There was very little time to see Jonathan alone and I wondered whether he was avoiding me. On the one occasion we were together he went out of his way to tell me of the many tasks the King had placed upon him. Not least, going to the northern tribes, who were receiving blandishments from the Philistines. Apparently, the northerners were against a war. They did not seem to realise that Israel had no choice, because the Philistine High King, Eglon, had decided upon an invasion that we had to answer.

Jonathan expressed his appreciation at my contribution in reducing his father's dark mood. However, though the King was recovered, there was a new fragility to his mood. A man previously noted for his decisiveness, he now found decisions almost impossible to take.

We heard nothing from the Prophet, despite two messages to him, other than a polite greeting. Crucially, and I know it distressed the King, no endorsement was sent for the coming war other than a cryptic remark, "God will show his power through the lowly and Israel and the world shall marvel."

When Josh, Eli and Aaron arrived, I was delighted and I have to admit feeling rather smug that I knew my way about the camp. Ura drilled the troop daily, morn and noon, which, at Jonathan's urging, had never been harder. So every night we crawled back to our tents exhausted.

Aaron in particular seemed to be suffering most, not least because

Canan seemed to make him a special target. Canan had become insufferable now he was Jonathan's armour bearer. He spoke of the Prince at every opportunity as if he was his closest brother.

Canan had a tilt with Josh, who had quickly become popular with everybody by his high spirits. During wrestling practice, which Jonathan said was as important as sword and line drills, Aaron was not doing very well. Canan came up and began to berate him. Everyone could see that Aaron was getting very distressed.

"I didn't know Bethlehem sent its women to war," Canan sneered. "Look, you woman, grab hold of your opponent firmly, as if you mean it. If you can't hold Ezra, who's hardly a giant, then at the first foray you'll have your throat cut. Now, come here, woman, and try to throw me."

Poor Aaron, who was never the best wrestler, found himself facing Canan, who stripped off and showed he was so much bigger. This cowed Aaron, although he had a fairly good physique. Aaron might have done better, but he was so demoralised and humiliated by Canan's bullying that he forgot everything he had ever learnt.

Canan came up to him. They locked arms but Canan thrust his leg between Aaron's, drew him towards his chest and, in a novice turn, threw him across his thigh, hard into the ground.

There was silence as Aaron lay there but Josh came to the rescue. "Bravo, sir Canan. Now I can see why you are the Prince's armour bearer. I, too, am from Bethlehem and would be honoured if you would show your excellence upon my unworthy self."

Some of the men laughed because they could see that Josh was no slender violet. Without giving Canan time to riposte, Josh had stripped off and advanced towards him.

Canan was no fool. He knew that Josh was a different metal to Aaron. Without wasting words, hoping to take Josh by surprise, he launched himself at Josh in a waist-high charge. It almost worked. Canan's bulk charged into Josh, who rapidly had to give ground and just barely held himself upright.

Their two bodies were now locked in a trial of strength. Though Canan was older and slightly heavier, he had lost his initial advantage.

They each grappled, trying to gain a decisive hold. Their muscles cracked as they strained against each other, neither daring to let go of the other. Each rapidly tried to unbalance the other by twisting and turning. They raised furious clouds of dust that caked their sweating forms.

At first, the men had shouted encouragement to each in a light-hearted way, but we all saw that this had become a bitter bout and we all fell silent.

Suddenly it looked like Josh's strength had given out for he let go of

Canan and fell back a pace. Canan, with a shout of triumph, went forward to get a head hold, but Josh, in a vicious trick that I'd learned to fear, quickly fell to one knee and, in a flash, threw a pile-driving punch at Canan's midriff.

Thwack! The wind was knocked out of Canan as the pain doubled him up. Even more quickly Josh stood up and drove his knee into the writhing Canan's groin.

It was all over. Canan crashed his full length to the ground, half unconscious with the pain. For good measure, Josh dropped like a sack full of rocks on top of him, pinning him down.

The men gave a shout of applause, whilst Eli and I looked at each other in mixed delight. We felt joy for the triumph of our friend and of the face-saving for Aaron, but we both knew that here was someone who had even more cause to loathe the Bethlehemites.

The army reassembled and, as the orders came to march over the next few weeks, the men began to realise that the situation was grave. The Philistines had entered our lands and seemed to be everywhere. The marching seemed aimless and the uncertainty that I heard Saul express in counsel was getting to the men. Worse, we found that the northerners had not sent a full contingent and the men of Benjamin, Judah, Rueben and Simeon, found themselves the only effective fighting force.

Slowly, worrying whispers arose. Half-rumours were heard asking the question, "Why did the Prophet not come? Why did the Prophet not send God's message?"

After two months of uncertainty and seemingly fruitless marches, taking up positions against an enemy who always seemed to be more numerous, holding better ground, we were becoming demoralised. The question was out in the open. If neither the Prophet nor the priests were here, had God deserted us? Were we to avoid battle, for how could Israel go to war without the sanction and support of the Lord of Hosts?

The third month was even worse. The heat grew and anxiety began to spread on the faces of the captains and generals. The word got around that the King was paralysed with uncertainty. There was beginning to be a trickle of deserters.

In my one conversation with Jonathan, I asked, "How can it be that men who hailed the King as victor at Havilah, now have no trust in him? Jonathan, they seem beaten even before a battle."

He agreed and talked about the secret of morale. "David, for God's sake, don't even think of this, but the King has no confidence in either his judgement or in the strength of the army. It's as if, after a long run, his spirit and his legs have just gone to sand. I've tried everything I know. He listens to everyone, but no one. I can see Abner is as worried as I am."

Then he said angrily, "Yet you know, if your friend Samuel came out for us, the mood would change in an instant. This schism can't last. The men are not fools and they fear that if God's Prophet is not with the King, how can God be with the King's army. I know you want to defend the Old Man but without faith an army's nothing. The Philistines can almost feel our defeatism."

With only a few skirmishes, in all of which we were worsted, nothing happened for another month except ceaseless marching, whilst our lands were burnt. We began to feel our retreats were already defeats.

The council meetings were now openly critical of the King, who simply sat and said nothing, but glared as captain and general argued. Whilst Abner, to be fair, tried to be loyal to Saul, he ended up saying either: disband the army, let the men go back to their tribal lands and defend themselves by retreating; or lead the army against the Philistines before our morale evaporates away to nothing.

The Voice

Then the blow came. We had been manoeuvred into a cul-de-sac in the Valley of Eilah. At our rear were high hills that cut off our retreat. We had very little water and the whole of the Philistine army covered the entrance to the valley, which was five miles wide. When the captains reckoned up the numbers needed to hold this space, they were devastated. We were still about 50,000 strong, but they must have been more than a 100,000.

Worse was to come. We took up our line about a mile from the Philistines. We could do nothing but go on the defensive. The argument now had become not how to fight but how to achieve a breakout from what increasingly was seen as a trap.

Heralds arrived in a most dreadful form. With trumpets blaring their brazenly arrogant call, three heralds called forth marching in front of a giant warrior.

We could not believe it. He was enormous. He must have been more than seven feet tall. Huge arms like tree trunks and legs like stone pillars.

His voice roared his challenge in the name of his god. "In the name of Dagon, the All Mighty God of Philistia, I pour scorn on the puny God of Israel. Lay down your arms and become bondsmen of Philistia – and your lives will be spared. If you do not surrender, assuredly Dagon will destroy every last man of you and the dogs shall eat your flesh. But Dagon is merciful. Send forth your champion to fight with me, and he who is victor will decide the field."

With a terrible laugh he concluded, "When I win, I will eat his flesh and watch as you all enter under our yoke."

We were expected to produce a champion at noon. Oh, the Philistines were clever!

Could we dare pit a mortal against this giant? Yet, the longer we stayed in this accursed valley, the worse our position became. Either way, it was as if someone was turning the screw of our despair.

At noon, we had no answer.

The Philistine heralds promised to come again the next day but warned, "But only one more day after that, Israelites. If after the third challenge you produce no champion to exchange blows with Goliath, Dragon's true champion, then we shall destroy you."

We had heard the name of our doom: Goliath. He was a giant warrior in superb bronze armour, fitted head-to-toe like a King, with a flashing helmet which revealed only his mouth and eyes. He possessed a great breastplate that covered back and front, armlets that secured up to his elbow and iron grieves almost up to his knees. If one could get close enough to land a blow, there would be no target. Yet, with arms that seemed to stretch for ever, with shield, spear and sword, who could get near him?

It was a brilliant tactic: drawing out our agony. We had little food, we were already on water rations and we were utterly demoralised.

The council meeting was a disaster. As I expected, Jonathan immediately offered to fight Goliath, but Saul would not hear of it, arguing that no man could fight this giant alone. He angrily silenced Jonathan, adding, for good measure,

"It shows arrogance, Prince Jonathan."

No one else came forward and there was real confusion. There was a hint that perhaps the King as the Lord's anointed might go forth, for who would dare strike God's anointed? But that just reminded people that the Prophet had not responded to the King's earlier requests. His silence was a judgement, confirmed by this blasphemous Goliath scorning God before all the people.

The following day, the Philistine heralds repeated their ritual and, though now having seen Goliath twice and the shock was reduced a little, the effect was even more daunting. Someone, who in the heat of the moment might have volunteered, would think again after seeing him twice. Everyone could see just how strong he was. After the jeering challenge and an insult to God was heard, there was a dreadful moan of despair from our men, which boded ill when, if at all, battle was joined.

The council meeting was even more tumultuous. When I returned to the troop, even Josh was silent.

Ura had a word with the Prince as he thought he might volunteer, "I owe the King much. He has been kind to the Hittites. If my death would take away this shame and restore the King to strength, I would do it willingly."

Jonathan was very moved but argued that such a sacrifice would be in vain. After the duel, the Philistines would obviously attack anyway and he doubted if we would stand.

It was out: even Jonathan was despairing. He had acknowledged that the King had lost his strength. Worse, he said we ought to begin to prepare the break out. That meant that we and the King's guard would have to become a rearguard to try to hold the Philistines and so give our men chance to break out of the trap.

The men took such news quietly. To their honour, no one protested that it was a vain gesture. Without needing to say it, we knew that we must restore the honour of Israel in the hope that God would re-gather His people.

I felt a dreadful unease. I contemplated seeking out Jonathan for a last farewell, or perhaps joining Eli, Josh and poor Aaron, who was looking very afraid, but I could not settle. I knew I would not know what to say.

On impulse, I went out alone into the night. Without knowing where I was going, I began to climb the hill. My thoughts were in turmoil at Israel's peril and likely humiliation. A fear of disaster had sapped all our energies.

I walked on and began to be angry with Samuel. How could the defeat of Israel forward God's purpose? I then committed the gravest blasphemy as I asked myself how could God let His Prophet remain silent while his people were destroyed and his worship be lost for ever under a Philistine bondage?

I was angry, confused, despairing. Had I imagined that God inspired my muse? On the morrow I knew I was to die for nothing, nothing would stop me being at Jonathan's side in the desperate rearguard. As I my thoughts dwelt on this, I felt the chill of fear about whether I would stand and or run at the sight of such overwhelming odds.

I felt the nerve-sapping fear of fear itself.

I was desolate, alone. I looked to the skies but there was no encouragement there: heaven's lights were covered by a blanket of cloud. The empty darkness reflected my mood. There was no hope – it was all going to end!

I knelt and raised my arms in supplication but I was so empty, cold and despairing that I had no expectation of an answer. It was habit, ritual, instinct, to call to Him who was about to desert Israel and let her best be slain.

I had no emotion left for tears or anger. I was a dry empty vessel. I had no words. My soul cried out in silence yet there was no answering inspiration in my mind.

My spirit called again, silently into the barren blackness. Nothing.

I was as nothing. I was no person. I was utterly insignificant.

Suddenly, I began to feel a new cold, as if the residue of my being was being frozen and shrivelled. What consciousness remained was being turned into stone.

Then came a dread – like nothing in life had prepared me for. A fear that was all consuming and I wanted to flee far from this terror of confronting an unimaginable force.

My soul was being crushed, obliterated, choked. There was no place left to flee, my panic was blinding. Panic, terror and dread.

Slowly, I sensed a beginning warmth. I saw, etched in a golden haze, a young man stretched in terror on the ground below.

Hazily, I thought that the gaunt, terrified figure was familiar. My soul tried to recognise the form as it became slowly became clearer.

Like a punch to the face, the realisation hit me: the young man I could see was ... me!

I was looking down upon myself!

The warmth brought an all-enveloping calm: a peace that was beyond understanding.

I was safe. I had always been safe. I was with God.

This knowledge filled my soul with an ecstasy, an elation, that only my love for Leah had come close to. I was renewed. There was a joy and balm that obliterated doubt, fear and anxiety. I felt deliriously happy.

How could I ever doubt? How could I ever be afraid? My soul chuckled with joy. It sang.

I was at ONE with God.

It was obvious: it was God who held my soul in His hand as He did all mankind. Not to be happy was foolishness and my soul laughed and filled the sky.

Then I heard it. No mistaking what or who it was.

Quiet.

Gentle, but commanding: a Voice.

DAVID?

The Voice said my name.

The Voice possessed me and spoke to into my head.

DAVID?

I answered, "Speak, Lord, for Thy servant heareth."
The Voice breathed.

YOU HAVE LEARNED WELL. IT IS GOOD THAT YOU FEEL NO FEAR.

How could I ever be fearful again? The Voice was all around me. It filled me and I was a part of It.

DAVID, IN YOU AM I WELL PLEASED.
YOU ARE MY MESSENGER AND THROUGH YOU I WILL SHOW ISRAEL AND THE WORLD NOW AND FOR ALL TIME THAT I AM NOT MOCKED.
TOMORROW YOU WILL BE MY CHAMPION.
TOMORROW I WILL DELIVER GOLIATH INTO THY HAND.

I had the temerity to wordlessly ask: how? Not in surprise, nor fear, nor doubt, because I was filled by His certainty.
Did the Voice chuckle as well?

DAVID, THINK!

I thought but with a rapidity of thought that was impossible to comprehend. In a blinding flash, I saw it all. It was terrible, it was fearful but with such a certainty that my soul felt a snatch of compassion for Goliath.

DAVID IN YOU I AM WELL PLEASED.
GO UNTO ISRAEL AND PROCLAIM MY NAME AND MY SALVATION.

The Voice had gone but I still had its warmth and security. The golden haze was sucked up by the new dawn and I was suddenly alone, cold on the ground. I called aloud to return to Him and His certainty. I wept to remould my soul with Him but there was no answering voice.
Wherever my soul had journeyed, I was back on the stark earth.
With a shudder of dread, I recalled my vision of the battle that was to come.

Chapter Thirteen

Goliath

The Challenge

I returned to the camp and saw at once that, in the intervening hours, the despondency had deepened. I avoided my troop and companions, as I wanted no diversion to stop me carrying out my task.

As noon grew close, I could see the heralds and Goliath stride out for the third and final time. But before they reached our lines, I snatched up a trumpet and, blowing hard, I ran out to meet them.

"Goliath, you uncircumcised dog that dared to flaunt the Lord of Hosts, I call upon you to repent or assuredly you shall die," I shouted.

There was absolute chaos.

I was within twenty yards of the heralds and could see Goliath towering above them. I dimly perceived our men shout for me to return.

Instead, I called, "I am sent to chastise your arrogance, Goliath. I shall smite you for your blasphemy. I shall show you, Israel and the whole world that the Almighty God liveth and will not be mocked."

Goliath found his voice and boomed out, "Who are you, you impudent puppy that dares Dagon's champion? I am Goliath! You are unworthy to stand before me."

Then, turning towards our lines, he sneered, "Are you not ashamed that you allow this mere boy to usurp a warrior's place? Will no other come against me?"

I blew hard and long into my trumpet. "Goliath, yet again you mock the Living God. Do you not know that I and I alone am sent against you? Surely as the Lord liveth, I shall slay you as I did the wolf, the mountain lion and those who came against me."

Whatever our men thought of these words, they cheered, enjoying the disconcerted Philistine heralds and their champion.

I called out, "Goliath! At noon tomorrow, come alone and armed to meet me, David bar Jesse of the tribe of Judah. Hearken unto that name for it is thy doom, promised to me by the Lord of Hosts. Now go. Return tomorrow for you are an affront in the sight of God."

With that, I cheekily turned on my heel and sent him a crude gesture that made our men roar with laughter.

As I rejoined their welcoming embrace, I heard Goliath call, "So be it, David bar Jesse. I will return and give your puny flesh to the dogs and the fowl of the air."

Of course, I knew I was in big trouble, despite the cheers of the men whose spirits had enjoyed our wordplay.

Jonathan was the first to reach me. He was absolutely furious. "What in God's name possessed you to do that, you fool? You arrogant fool! Do you know you'll have to go to your death tomorrow?"

I was virtually dragged along to the King with a continuation of such phrases ringing in my ears. I finally stood before him.

Saul looked every inch a King. "How dare you beard our enemies in God's name and proclaim yourself champion? I tell you, David, though I love you, this presumption is such that it may earn you your death even before you face the Philistine."

I threw myself before him. "Great King, the Lord's anointed, I meant no presumption but feel keenly the disgrace to you and to God that this mocking Philistine offers. Truly, I am your champion if you will accept me. You asked for a sign, Great King. In all humility, I ask you for your permission to stand forth tomorrow and slay the infidel for you and for God – I am the sign you sought."

One side of me felt totally confident because I was still moved by my vision and my experience of the Voice. But on the other hand, as reality began to set in, I could not help but be impressed – no, over-awed would be more accurate – at just how gigantic Goliath really was. With my modest height he was a yard taller and, close up, his body was even more massive. I began to wonder whether I was to be the sacrifice to save Israel, rather than Jonathan's planned rearguard.

The King accepted my championship. What else could he do? Whether any of us liked it or not, I had been publicly declared champion of the King and Israel – on this there was no going back.

Giving me a hard look, Saul breathed, "David bar Jesse, we are pleased to appoint you this day our champion and that of Israel. I believe that you have been sent by God as His sign and that He has not deserted Israel – or His anointed."

There was a shout of encouragement at this announcement. Whatever the morrow brings, I thought, at least there is a change in our morale.

However, this remarkable day had not yet been emptied of all its surprises. Late that evening, there was another Philistine herald who wished to parley with Prince Jonathan and me.

The messenger explained, "It is Achish, son of the King of Gath, who would speak in truce with Prince Jonathan and your champion."

I was astounded and excited. What on earth could Achish want? I could see that Jonathan was equally intrigued.

He looked at me and said, "Well, it's no good wondering. We had better hear what he wants."

Jonathan turned to the messenger and instructed him to bring Achish to his tent – an arrangement that the King had little choice but to agree with.

I stood nervously behind Jonathan, waiting for Achish to appear.

He entered. He had not changed much, though looked as severe as when I had first met him at Bull Horns.

He saluted Jonathan gravely, "Hail, Prince Jonathan. We know each other well and will know each other again."

Achish then looked at me. "David bar Jesse! Brother! Hail!" He held out his arms and I went willingly to take his embrace.

He held me close, then, holding me back, said, "You have grown, little brother. I can see you are now a man."

Turning back to Jonathan, he said, "You have made him a fine warrior, I can see. You must take great pride in him."

Jonathan flushed and answered rather churlishly, "He is an average member of my troop and, like all the others, he is valiant, brave and will bring much rue to the homes of the Philistines."

Achish laughed easily and they exchanged looks that I did not understand.

"David, what have you done? I suppose I should not be surprised but Goliath is truly terrible and despite his bulk, he is fine warrior. Is this one of your stratagems?" Achish asked, with concern in his voice.

I answered his friendly smile with warmth. "No, Achish. Tomorrow, I intend to go against Goliath and one of us won't walk away from the encounter. But tell me, how fares Acrah? Has he recovered from his wounds?"

As I spoke I could see the answer. Achish's face hardened as he frowned at a sad memory. "Acrah greets you from the shade. He is in the bosom of Dagon after dying the death of a warrior. He asked me to greet you and said that he forgave you his death. Otherwise, I, as his philia, would not be here but would be challenging Goliath's place."

Then he smiled. "But you are my brother. Acrah, who was wise beyond his years, prophesied great things for you. Amongst our people, we take great store of the words of the dying and, sure enough, you are the champion of Israel."

He suddenly became very animated. "But what in Dagon's name do you think you are about? Prince Jonathan, frankly, I expected you to face Goliath. I doubt not your courage but no man can match Goliath in single combat."

He now looked very serious. "David, don't think you can outwit Goliath. He may not be the fastest thinker in the world, or the fastest warrior, but one to one he is deadly – invincible. I've had bouts with him and come off worst. Moreover, can you remember Ganz? Well, he is Goliath's cousin and he's told him about your sling shots, so he will come prepared."

We all fell silent at this and Achish went on, "I have asked myself whether I should be concerned for you. You are my brother, although an Israelite, and you have proved to be an honourable adversary. So, in brotherhood and at the will of Acrah, I bring his gift to you from beyond the grave to give you some protection and hope for tomorrow."

With that he clapped his hands. In came his single guard, carrying a huge bundle that he placed on the ground and opened up.

Jonathan and I gasped. It was a wonderful suit of armour. Superb bronze, not the light brass like much of our best. It was a kingly gift. I was much moved and I could tell that Jonathan was very impressed.

I stuttered my thanks. Achish came forward said, "Come, let me help you to arm. It may need some adjustment, for Acrah was a little taller than you."

With that he and Jonathan stripped me off and helped to put on the armour.

It was magnificent. I must have looked very impressive and, of course, I could not tell Achish that the weight was overbearing. I thanked him profusely and embraced him freely, not understanding the looks that Jonathan gave him.

I wondered. Was Jonathan a little jealous? After all, they both were great Princes amongst their peoples and already knew each other's worth.

I said my farewell to Achish, who had saluted Jonathan again.

Achish looked so gloomy that I felt I had to cheer him up. "Don't worry, Achish. Come the worst, I can always run faster than that man mountain. He won't catch me."

Achish said sombrely, "Unfortunately, the rules of battle will mean that you cannot leave the battleground until one be dead. There will be no refuge, no place to run to tomorrow."

He gave me a warm embrace and left. I had the very uncomfortable feeling that there were tears in his eyes.

Jonathan insisted that I show myself to the King in my new armour. "It will help you get used to it. I suppose you've never had anything more than a helmet, have you?"

The King was very impressed. I could see from Jonathan's look that the armour was splendid. It felt really fine, slightly long in the calf and perhaps a little tight on the breastplate, but that could be eased by having the straps a little looser. I must have looked like a King. But it was heavy.

"David, it is a very good fit. I doubt whether my father's armour is as good."

The King agreed.

I slowly began to strip off the armour. They were astounded.

"Is it not a magnificent suit, David my son? Why are you removing it?"

"It's no good – I have not proved it." I grinned at their surprised looks.

Then Jonathan slowly said, "You know something that we don't? You have a plan?"

I nodded.

There was a long pause and Jonathan hesitantly suggested, "Father, I think we should allow David to fight Goliath the way he wants to. It seems that he has a stratagem, which we might best leave to him. We'll just have to trust him."

I smiled my thanks, and answered, "The armour is far too heavy and much it's too late for me to learn to fight in this. Of course, it would be great if I could use it in the troop." I laughed. "I'd be everybody's target – they'd think I was you. Can you imagine what Canan would say if I assembled in this. There was no way I'd want to hurt Achish's feelings by refusing his gift. He has already helped me tremendously."

Jonathan gave an anxious, rueful smile and said, "Well, there's no way out now. Don't forget what Achish said, Goliath's cousin – Ganz, wasn't it – has told him all about your mobility, so he won't be an easy target."

Jonathan's words brought me up sharply. I had to keep my mind clear and concentrate upon what the Voice had said and what I had seen – or thought I had seen, as I began to realise the imminence of what was ahead. I answered him slowly, "You are my Prince. There is no one in the world I admire more than you."

We both flushed at my words. He waited for me to continue as the King listened intently.

"You, along with the King and the Prophet, know that sometimes I have an inspiration. It's something I did not look for and, who knows, it may never happen again, though my songs are clearly something beyond me."

I paused, thinking how much I could or should say. "Last night, I went alone to the mountain and had an – I don't know how to describe it – an experience. I had a vision – an idea. The Prophet taught me, and you have confirmed it, 'don't feel, think', so tomorrow I'll meet Goliath. I think I'll kill him, but my way."

Then the doubt began to set in. "If I'm wrong and didn't understand the message properly ... well – I won't. Whatever the outcome will be, I know, really know, that it will turn out well for Israel."

The thought suddenly came to me: the Voice had said 'This day will I deliver Goliath into your hand'. Oh God – that meant today!

Perhaps I should have taken the challenge today? By tomorrow, a whole day would have passed!

I immediately felt quite weak and very frightened.

Jonathan came over to me. "I can see you believe in what you are going to do, but I see, as everyone can see, that the risks are enormous."

Then he said with a fierce, hard look that frightened me, "But I promise you, David, if you should fall, nothing in the world, nothing will stop me trying to avenge you."

With that, he and the King embraced and kissed me. They bade me to rest for I must be as best prepared as possible for the morrow.

I was alone, protected from any intrusion but I did not sleep. I was moved by what Jonathan had said, especially about trying to avenge me. I began to think perhaps that's what might happen. I was going to be God's sacrifice for Israel. After all, we have a tradition of being willing to sacrifice sons for God's plan. If Goliath made short work of me, Jonathan in his anger could – if anyone could – slay the giant. If he did, the morale of our army would be sky high and I would have been justifiably expendable. Well, I mused, that's the kind of decision kings and generals have to take – so why not God?

I tried to pray and tried to think of a psalm that might bring me comfort, but I could not. Slowly, the night and early morning passed by as I dozed intermittently between sharp bursts of anxiety as I tried to keep my mind free from the coming noon.

Suddenly, I was awake. I had a visitor, standing at the door of the tent. At first I could not see who it was. I hoped it might be Samuel, telling me I need not go through with my great gesture, but it wasn't him. It was Saul, the King.

He spoke in as warm a voice as I had heard from him in months. "David, my warrior bard, I have come to prepare you. I implore you to take my sword and use it against he who would mock God. Whatever happens, I know that what you are doing is for Israel. I, too, have an inspiration: a certainly that has banished the dark thoughts from me.

Through you this day, Israel and I will triumph."

His voice trembled with emotion. "Do you realise that you have made every man a giant. There were no desertions last night – not one. Indeed, there must have been over a hundred returning, for they have heard about you being the Lord's champion. You have inspired us all and I have no doubts."

His voice went up in ecstasy and excitement. "Oh David, I have no doubts! The dark thoughts are scattered. We shall be victorious today. Through you, I am restored. If you live, you shall have Merab my eldest daughter as wife and you shall be my son indeed."

He was totally transformed. Despite my circumstances, I could not help feeling some pleasure at his promise of Merab. I was already half in love with her and Jonathan had implied that she might not be indifferent to me.

I knelt down and thanked him. "Great King, your bounty and goodness to me is that of a Father. I hope to claim your promise. Now I can confess to you that Merab is already very dear in my sight."

He embraced me and I could feel his whole body shouted out at his sense of revival.

But what about me? Suddenly, I felt fear at the pit of my stomach. I was about to die. This was what I was to achieve for Israel. I was to re-light the fire in Saul and the army. I was to be their inspiring sacrifice.

I could not help recall the words of King Agag: 'My God. My God, why hast thou forsaken me, why art thou so far from my roaring?'

Then, Saul began to chant:

"The King shall joy in thy strength O Lord and in thy salvation how greatly shall he rejoice. Thou hast given him his heart's delight – thou settest a crown of pure gold upon his head.

He asked life of thee and thou gavest it him even length of days for ever.

His glory is great in thy salvation, honour and majesty hast thou laid upon him.

For thou hast made him most blessed for ever; thou hast made him exceedingly glad with thy countenance.

For the King trusteth in the Lord and through the mercy of the Most High he shall not be moved."

The chant in his warm baritone voice became infectious and I found myself joining with him. Though the psalm was for the King, it was for me also. God has seen me through dark days and we repeated together God's promise for us both.

"For the King trusteth in the Lord and through the mercy of the Most High he shall not be moved."

I shall not be moved and then I recalled my joy in the Voice and knew as I sang alone.

> *"The Lord is my shepherd, I shall not want.*
> *Yea though I walk in the valley of the shadow of death I will fear no evil for thou art with me thy rod and thy staff comfort me.*
> *Thou preparest a table in the presence of mine enemies, thou anointest my head with oil my cup runneth over – I will dwell in the house of the Lord for ever."*

Taking up Saul's sword, I walked out into the day believing that He, even in the presence of such an enemy, would prepare a table for me.

Goliath – the Making of a Legend

As I emerged into the light, the whole army was there. The cheering reverberated across the hellish valley of Eilah.

There, too, were the joint heralds with Jonathan amongst them. He explained that a space had been marked out between the two armies and that no one would be allowed to enter on the pain of death. Nor would either of us leave it until the fight was over! Jonathan came to escort me towards the battleground.

He quietly whispered, "We've made the ground as broad as possible. They wanted twenty paces. With Achish's help, we've got you fifty, though the ground is rocky."

I nodded. The shouts were deafening. As noon grew close, I drew to the end of our lines. Our men saw Goliath approach and they, as well as the Philistines, grew silent.

Jonathan and the heralds fell back.

I stood alone.

I had to walk the quarter of a mile to the ground marked out with lines of white stones.

Goliath was already striding forth, armed, as he wanted, with spear, sword and shield. He was warming up, stretching and whirling his monstrous sword over his head, which caught the rays of the sun, sending warning flashes across the plain.

The Philistines roared with approval and our men sent back a counter cry in encouragement.

As we both drew near the battleground, everything became silent – other than Goliath's heavy tramp upon the ground. I was sure I could sense the vibrations in the ground of his huge confident strides.

Ten yards from the stones, I looked back in anguish from a fearful lone-liness, but hurriedly turned my head forward again towards my foe.

My mouth was dry. He was truly enormous. I was awed!

He had not said a word. I was close to running, running, running from this dreadful place.

What was I doing here? I was close to crying. I began to fear that I might disgrace myself and loose my bowels, as my stomach churned over in a sickening dread.

I struggled to concentrate, desperately trying to press down the choking bile in the throat and the bone-dissolving fear.

Goliath had reached the battleground, deliberately took a huge stride over it, shook his sword at me and turned towards his own lines and roared, "I will kill this puny Israelite that dares to enter the ground in an affront to Dagon. I, Goliath, have sworn to crush his bones and give his flesh to the dogs."

The Philistines cheered him wildly, with the accompaniment of blaring of war horns and trumpets.

I fought to gain a deep breath as my heart was pounding at a pace that made me almost dizzy. My arms seemed like twine, as a cold sweat, despite the heat, dripped from me. I was so afraid that I was almost petrified. Oh, I was so close, so very close to running – anywhere!

Instead, I knelt down, closed my eyes, laid down the sword of Saul and my sling on the ground, and prayed aloud.

"Into Thy hands oh Lord, I commend my spirit."

As I looked up at my advancing enemy, my thoughts began to clear: "don't feel, think", that's what the Voice had said, that's what the Prophet had said and that's what Jonathan had taught. With a last a great effort, I became cool as my thoughts closed down on the task in hand. I excluded all those fearsome diversions as I watched with a sense of detached interest.

Goliath, now in the middle of the ground, was urging me to enter.

Now was the time for the plan to be put into operation.

I laughingly called out, "You bag of lard! You fat stink! You pitiful mon-strosity! The Almighty Living God has delivered you into my hands."

I walked boldly into the arena. "Your parents must had fainted when they saw the monster they had given birth to. Yet you have the arrogance to mock the Lord of Israel? Goliath, I will relieve your parents of their disgrace when I cut off your disfigured head."

The barbs had reached home. He rushed at me, angrily waving his sword. Of course, I simply danced away from him.

He rushed again trying to trap me in a corner, but I ran lightly around him, keeping at least two spear lengths from his pounding bulk as we circled around each other.

This time, there was no doubt – I really could feel his weight shuddering through the ground. He towered over me. He easily blotted out the sun and I knew I was too close to him.

I decided it was time to sting the beast. I took one of the many round pebbles I had collected and loaded my sling. I ran up to him, within just ten yards, and, taking aim, hurled it at his head.

To my great consternation, he moved his shield expertly and simply diverted it away. He then came forward in a gallop towards me so I had to retreat very, very rapidly.

I tried again, coming in at an angle and flinging another missile. Had he had not used his shield, it would have hit in the middle of his mouth.

Again – clang! – the pebble glanced harmlessly away. He laughed, really laughed! It was horrible.

"Is that all you have, prick-mutilated Israelite? A child's toy? A bee sting?" He sheathed his sword and drew out his spear. In an incredible feat of strength, he held it right at the end and charged me.

Oh God! Have I left it too late?

I had no shield and no buckler.

I half-stumbled on the uneven ground and slipped to one knee. He let out a roar of triumph and, with a terrible speed, he was on me. He waved the cruel point of his spear within a hand's breadth of my throat.

Desperately, I threw up my sword in a right parry and hurled myself to the left as he charged passed me. He brought himself to a violent halt, used the spear as a club and whirled it around to crush my head.

I was just able to duck under it. With quaking relief, I regained my feet and danced away as fast as I could to the other side of the ground.

I dimly perceived that there was shouting. I'm not sure whether it was from our lines or his. I paid no attention but reminded myself, "think not feel".

I took up a stance at the Philistine side of the ground so that he had the sun in his eyes. He was clever and seeing this, came at me at an angle, but at least he was still facing the sun.

Again I fired at him, loosing three, four, five missiles in quick succession. All but one would have found their target, except for the quick movements of his shield that deflected them away. Worse, on two occasions, he just stood there and swayed out of the way of the whizzing stones that would have crippled a wolf, a fox, or a man.

I felt another grip of bile-creating fear. Ganz had taught him well. He was much more sure of his movements than I had anticipated. After the first rush of anger at my taunts, he had kept his head and was countering everything I threw against him.

For at least a further ten minutes, I kept well away from him. I kept as close to the boundary of the battleground as possible, though for both of us it was so real a boundary that it might have been a wall.

He followed me like some huge bull, trotting after me, calling upon me to,

"Stand and fight! This is boring, little man. You are bringing disgrace upon yourself – listen to the laughter."

I could not hear it other than merely as background noise. I watched him so intently.

Then, the end nearly came. I was skipping round him, trying to tire him and make him hot beneath his iron armour. He was about ten yards away. I was in the eastern corner with him facing the sun. He manoeuvred as if he was going to throw his spear. I stood easily, weight evenly balanced on both feet and ready to push off in either direction. He held his spear high. I watched it, eagle-eyed.

He leaned back. Here comes the throw, I thought. Then – disaster!

I had failed to watch his left hand, which held his shield. Skilfully and with stealth, he had changed his grip. Suddenly, before I knew what was happening, with a snap of his wrist he'd caught the edge of the shield. In one movement, he crouched down, not to throw the spear, but to wing with great accuracy a spinning shield that had become a discus.

Too late, I saw the change. I had no time to jump out of its way and the spinning metal disc caught me a staggering blow on my left hip as I threw myself to one side.

With a cry he was upon me. The pain was intense: fire and cramp screamed in my leg as he followed up with his spear. He stabbed. I had nowhere to go but roll along the ground away from his lunging, stabbing, death-dealing spear.

I shrieked in fear and dread. Like a wriggling fish, I rolled amidst the dust and debris as his spear probed and stabbed – just missing my writhing body.

He was above me. I was on my back, open and exposed. His face, half-hidden behind his helmet, was jubilant in his triumph as he thrust down in a terrible stabbing motion. In my fear and extreme terror, I threw myself sideways as the plunging spear caught my tunic and I felt its hot blade touch my side.

In total desperation, I hurled myself in the opposite direction. God was on my side because, in Goliath's triumph, so sure was he that he had me, he had thrust his spear so fiercely into the ground that he needed two efforts to pull it free – and that gave me a vital second. I rolled away with the slope, now half-naked, with Goliath once again chasing me with his sharp spear. My flesh crept. I screeched out in despair as he strode towards my half-prostrate body.

I knew that the watching armies were screaming almost in unison with what my soul knew to be its death cry. I was now less than a spear length away from Goliath.

He rose to his full height. I was crouching, bloodied, bruised and only barely in control of myself, unable to muster a secure defence. With another cry of triumph he came forward and raised his spear to finish me off. Our eyes met. In slow, slow motion as each saw that death was riding on his spear.

I took in the fact that his helmet had been reinforced with extra bars to resist my slung missiles. As if I was reading a book, I understood that I had been aiming at the wrong target!

It did not matter: I was doomed. He stood over me with his spear. His eyes, red with exertion, were now filled with exhilaration as he was about to make the final plunge of that dread spear into my heaving, naked chest.

I could hardly breathe but my hand clasped a rock the size of my fist. With all my might, I hurled it – not at his head, not at his face – but at his knee, just above the grieves.

His spear was already accelerating towards me before its release when the jagged rock crashed into the side of his knee.

He gave a surprised cry of pain. His bulk swayed. In pain, he slowly sank on to one knee.

He still had his spear – but he now had no shield!

In that moment, we met and knew each other for the first time.

His look was one of hurt surprise and incredulity. I was now at his height and in my left hand was my sling.

Faster than it takes to tell, the first stone whizzed towards his face: it was not a well-directed missile but this time it got through, just above the eyes.

He roared in pain and anger. He struggled to his feet to tower over me once again, and, whirling his spear, it was clear he was not yet finished.

Another sling shot, this time aimed at his legs, caught him painfully on the inside of his groin. He swayed again.

In front of me was a rock half the size of a man's head. I swooped down and seized it. He cried out in an agonised anticipation. I crashed it on to his already wounded knee.

He fell forward, on all fours. I could sense his agony as my next stone caught him above the eye. Blood and sweat blinded him.

I threw myself forward as I attacked for the first time.

Bravely, he had turned himself upright, with one hand on the ground to steady himself and, in the other, he held his great sword that he had wrenched out of the dust.

Too late! As I spun at him from his blind side, I hacked downwards with my sword at his exposed arm.

I felt a juddering blow as my sword bit into his shoulder.

His roars became even more enraged as I found the energy and speed to spin off at an angle, so quickly that I was behind him before he could turn and defend himself.

Here was my opportunity. I slashed my sword at the back of his helmeted head. The blow nearly broke my grip. His cries were now high, piercing screams. He had turned to me but blood was all over him – he could not see.

With a brutal deliberation, I did the last thing he expected. I walked towards him. We stood there, chest to chest and foot to foot. I dropped my sling. I could see the amazement on his face.

In a flash, I drew out my dagger and thrust it deep into his upturned throat. The blade sank in deep. His throat hissed out his final breath as if he had been punctured.

In his death throws, he flailed his arms around, caught my waist and crashed over on top of me. I was being crushed and could feel his gore cover me. I thrashed, almost in vain, against his clinging, oppressive weight. Kicking upwards with my knees, I was just able to lever myself out from under his dreadful fall.

He lay there. His gurgling, choking sobs filled my ears. He was on his back, stranded like a terrible beached whale.

I was dizzy with exhaustion. I swayed.

With the final energy in that immense body, he was trying to crawl crab-like away from me and vengeance. I was half-blinded by sweat but there, I could just see, lay the King's sword.

Goliath and I looked for the last time into each other's eyes. Neither of us could believe it. I staggered over to him and pushed the blade inside his breastplate, cutting his clawing hands that sought to deflect my final thrust. I threw myself on to the blade and plunged it deep into him, almost suffocated by the stink of his sweat and body fluids.

I leaned on the sword. Beneath me, the expiring Goliath had no breath left, no time left and no life left. I just leaned on to him, as would a boy on a farm gate, and skewered him beneath me.

It was over.

I had a sensation of cries of thousands of men but I was so exhausted they sounded a hundred miles away – a hundred lifetimes away.

I could not think. I could barely stand. I could hardly see.

I had no emotion left. The knowledge that I was still alive left me disinterested.

The blood all around me belonged to Goliath yet, in my confusion, it seemed that it could so easily be mine.

All I wanted to do was to leave this dreadful place, to sleep and be free of this nightmare.

Out of the confusion came a cry, "David!"

How did I hear it amongst that bedlam? Was it because it was Achish's voice? I will never know, but amidst the tumult I saw an armed warrior break from the ranks of the Philistines.

He hurtled towards me and the marked battleground.

I dimly remember thinking he cannot enter unless I leave. Through my screwed-up, tired, sweat-blinded eyes I recognised the shape – it was Ganz!

Without a pause, for now I hated and, for the first time, I wanted to hurt. Now I felt not thought. I turned to meet this new threat, fuelled by the energy of primeval hate.

I could see his face, tortured in rage. I saw him extend his stride and in the classic pose prepare to launch his spear.

His voice was raised in a bloody war cry that both of us knew was the mark of one of our deaths. He paused slightly to take better aim. In that fleeting moment, I crouched and, with my sling, took a side shot at him that possessed an energy I did not believe possible.

The missile flew straight at him. Would it reach him in time to defeat his spear throw?

It did.

Crashing by his upraised arm, it caught him centrally, between the eyes. He did not cry out. He dropped like a sacrificial bull to the ground.

In a stride, I was up to him. My sword was in my hand. I stood over him.

He opened his eyes. He looked in disbelief and total loathing as our eyes bored into each other. His hands came up feebly to ward off my blow as I grasped his helmeted head, jerked it upward and slashed down, once ...,
twice ..., thrice... and pulled away the severed head.

I stood upright, swaying in utter exhaustion. My legs, my arms, my head, had all become sand.

I screamed as, with my ebbing strength, I threw the dreadful trophy of my enemy into the ranks of the demoralised Philistines.

I feebly croaked, "On men of Israel, for God and King Saul!"

I don't know whether I fainted or collapsed, but I was dimly aware of a stampede of bodies hurtling passed me.

Our army attacked as one man, recognising the sign of God defending Israel. The Philistines were rocked by the deaths of Ganz and of their champion, Goliath.

They broke and fled, hotly pursued by the exultant army of Israel.

I took no more part in the fight.

I think I sat down, trying to find breath and some energy.

I had one more task to do. I know I did. But what was it? I could not remember.

My head ached. My arms and legs had become lead.

My breath was short and painful. My body reeked. I had nothing left to give.

I don't know how long it took me but I dragged myself back towards our lines and then I saw what I had to do.

Stretched out like some hideous sacrifice, lay the body of Goliath.

As our men had passed him, some had struck at his now defenceless form. The death wound I had given him was obliterated by the multitude of avenging stabs of the passing warriors. I could only recognise him by his armour and his size.

Ah, yes. I knew what my final task was. I dragged myself towards him. I looked around and found the King's sword in my hand. Yes, that's the job. I returned to the corpse of Goliath and hacked, with difficulty, through that thick neck for the trophy I had promised the King.

I freed my spoil from its helmet because it was already so heavy. I half-carried, half-dragged the bloody trophy towards our lines.

Out of the bustle and mist emerged the King.

I croaked, "Great King, before you is God's and your enemy."

I could not throw the head down but, in my exhaustion, I let it fall at his feet. As the head fell like a bloody football, it soiled the King's embroidered shoes.

I collapsed in a swoon and knew nothing more.

When Achish had heard that an Israelite had accepted Goliath's challenge he was convinced that it would be Jonathan who would be forced to retrieve the honour of Israel. He was at first astonished and then filled with pride, that it was David, his blood brother. His emotions were confused: fear for his young friend and pride in his courage. It was not rational but he recognised the glorious gesture and the faint hope that the sacrifice might bring Israel some relief.

Then, Ganz approached him. He challenged him as to where his allegiance lay, to his "would-be-philia or Philistia".

Achish was so angry at doubts about his loyalty that Ganz realised that he had gone too far.

Ganz grudgingly agreed that, whilst Achish could not directly fight David, "Goliath will do that well enough". Achish would feed his sword on Israelite flesh and "might finish off their Prince in the style of the heroes of old."

Achish grimly confirmed that he and Jonathan would meet someday and he would avenge Jonathan's depredations against their people.

Ganz, however, would not be silenced as he boasted how he was going to prepare Goliath and tell him all about "the boy's tricks with that sling". But "you can only play that trick once, and man against man, there'll be no mistakes this time".

When Achish was finally free of Ganz, he felt troubled. This was the first time that his brotherhood with David had called into question his allegiance. On the one hand, he was bound to help his brother, on the other he would be King of Gath some day. Though he hardly dared let himself think the thought, perhaps High King of the Philistines, too. There was not a doubt that he would die for his people against all enemies, including David.

None the less, he knew he had to speak to David and warn him of Ganz's enmity. He also had to reluctantly admit to himself that he was keen to see David again. Ganz's taunt had not been too far from the mark.

He went out with the heralds and, with very mixed emotions, was brought into the presence of Jonathan and David.

His heart leaped. It was David as he had remembered him – yet very, very different.

David had become a marvellous youth and his face lit up with undoubted pleasure at seeing Achish. He reminded Achish of that heart-warming, open face with lips that yearned to be kissed. What was so appealing was that the boy did not know the charm he had.

Yet he saw also that David was different. It was hard to explain but the streak of white running through his dark hair looked like a wound. Furthermore, there was something in the eyes which, though smiling in delight at seeing his brother, seemed to show that he had witnessed new sights, strange vistas and incomprehensible visions. Such experiences had given his face a preternatural aura of seriousness as if he been in the presence of some incredible beauty.

In an instant, as Achish took in both Israelites, he recognised Jonathan's naked jealousy of himself, and realised that, whilst David and he were close, David had not yet understood the nature of Jonathan's feelings towards him.

Achish held Jonathan's eye grimly as, in that look, both confirmed their mutual admiration that, in another situation, would have bound them in the closest friendship. But they knew that fate would demand one to be the death of the other.

They were so alike. Achish noted with amusement how David tried to please them both as his affections were torn by their polite, but only partly concealed, animosity.

When David took the armour, Achish was warmed by his enthusiasm and overwhelmed by David's superb physique. He was not yet marred by war. Though just less than medium height, his muscles rippled under his satin skin, which still had the typical glow of youth.

Achish's heart went cold. He would back David against any of his own age – possibly against many an experienced warrior – because of the bright intelligence and enthusiasm that shone from him. But how could he survive one to one against the monstrous Goliath, who had never been worsted in single combat?

Achish told David everything he thought might somehow help him. As he took his leave, he felt sure that he would never speak to David again.

He returned back to his lines in great sadness. Musing how he seemed doomed to lose those he loved: first Acrah and now David.

Next day, Achish made sure he was stationed as close to the battle-ground as he could by volunteering to represent the Philistines and marking out the ground.

As Goliath marched out to great acclaim, Achish mouthed the words of encouragement and Dagon's blessing – but he could not speak them aloud. He was unsure why, but he decided to be near Ganz, even though he would have to endure his taunts at David's downfall.

The more he thought of this, the more he feared. Then the thought struck him. What if David fled? That would be sensible – no, of course not; not David. What if there was a miracle and David won? What kind of stratagem could the boy have against this giant in the open field?

He pondered hard. He knew David was no fool, so could there be a way out? Then he understood: David would be brave, but the odds were over-whelmingly against him; all would see that and his final sacrifice was futile but this would inspire the Israelites. Inspired by David's death, the Israelites would be at their most dangerous.

He called up his four captains and told them what he feared. "Warn the men to stay in company lines. Don't be diverted by the fight. When the Israelite is down is when they might attack. We must be prepared for the unexpected."

His captains were impressed by his soldierly caution but suggested, crudely, that after Goliath had split the little Israelite's arse they would have to move fast to catch up with the fleeing enemy.

The captains rued their words as Achish angrily said battles were lost just as easily by people who were overconfident. They were to obey orders, keep close watch and be ready to either attack or take up a defensive line when called upon.

Achish knew he was being hard on his captains. Yet he slightly amused himself with the thought that it would not do the men harm to know that their general was always prepared for any eventuality.

Goliath stepped into the battleground. Achish could barely make out David's face, though the whole of his body language showed fear as he knelt to make his prayer.

Then David's voice came across thin but clear and, again, Achish marvelled at his friend's brave sacrifice and his ability to disregard his plight.

Achish prepared himself for the butchery that was to come.

Ganz's warnings about David's ability with the sling shot were immediately obvious. Even at this distance, Achish could see that David's tactics had come to naught.

Efforts to tire out his giant opponent were obviously limited because David could not leave the field. It was just a question of time before he came into range of that terrible spear.

The dancing and prancing of David caused roars of amusement in the ranks and the crudities came thick and fast. "Nail his willy to the floor, Goliath, and you'll make a sling out of it!" The more David pranced away, the more derision he aroused from the Philistines.

Achish tried to keep his feelings in check by observing the affair as if it was an exercise. He paid particular attention to what was happening in the Israelite lines.

He was relieved to see that they had become almost silent. It did indeed look as if their champion was, as one of the men had said, "a dancer preparing herself for her captain's pranks".

Then there was a sudden roar from both camps. Goliath had cornered David, but he had just escaped. Achish's pulse raced. This could not go on much longer. Again the pause and laughter and then – oh Dagon, it was Goliath, not David, who had done the unexpected! The stratagem of using the shield as a discus was brilliant. David was bowled over.

The dust rose and partially obscured the flurry of movement. Goliath's spear rose and fell while the body of David seemed to be thrown about like a rag doll. Then, Goliath's spear clearly pierced through David's shirt.

As some of the dust settled, all could see that, despite rolling along the ground, David was still alive. Goliath tossed away the fragments of shirt from the blade of his spear.

The boy half crouched. His terrified screams still rang in Achish's brain as he saw the dust-stained body await the final stroke. Achish resisted the temptation to shut his eyes as sternly he awaited the doom of his friend.

Then it happened. The upraised spear faltered. There was an impression of a rock thrown at Goliath, but no one at this distance could say for sure. Goliath was almost bestride David but he swayed and half fell, sinking to his knees.

David was suddenly up!

Now it was Goliath who was defending himself. Another missile was clearly launched. The cries came not from David but from Goliath. There was pandemonium.

Then ... silence as the deadly duel came to a climax.

Achish could see that Goliath was still dangerous even though he was immobilised. Achish willed David to move and prayed that he was not wounded. David seemed to have sufficient energy to seize his advantage.

David whirled around the stricken giant with a speed that amazed all. He struck Goliath once ..., then twice. Not perfect blows, but Goliath was nevertheless reeling.

David went around, behind him. Then, Achish felt that David had made an error: he had gone too close in his excitement and now the giant's arms seemed to embrace his tormenting foe in a rib-crushing hug. But no: their bodies clashed and Achish saw a flashing blade.

The combatants fell over together and, from amidst the swirling dust, David arose and stood erect.

The death cries of Goliath filled the air.

Achish was exultant as he saw David stagger away from his victory, reeling in exhaustion.

Suddenly, Achish sensed a man dash past him – it was Ganz.

Achish cried out one word, "David!" as the new and more deadly enemy bore down on David.

The thought flashed through Achish's head that Ganz was behaving dishonourably. He prayed, "David, stay inside the battle- ground."

But David was risking all and renewed by the challenge had advanced towards Ganz. Achish screwed up his eyes to await the disaster that would surely follow.

Ganz prepared to hurl his spear at the seemingly defenceless boy.

Suddenly, Ganz threw up his arms and crashed to the ground as if smitten by some invisible hand. Achish knew that it must have been a sling shot.

David went forward with a sword, and hacked and hacked.

It was all over.

Achish could feel the shock ripple through the army.

His voice rang out loudly, "Men of Gath – in square formation. Prepare to resist the enemy."

After that, there was total confusion.

Achish could see the advancing hordes of exultant Israelites charging across the battleground. He saw the Philistine lines break and the men flee. In front of him was a tall Israelite, screaming madly and swinging his sword. Coldly, as if he was performing a sacrifice, with a parry and a thrust the Israelite fell to the ground, his eyes clouding over in surprised death.

The Philistines now felt the full attack of the Israelites, as men hacked and parried, thrust and stabbed. The air filled with death cries that drowned the roars of triumph.

Almost as suddenly as it began, the Israelite attack slackened as they picked off the easier targets.

Achish permitted himself one more glance towards the battle area. He saw David stagger up to where the prostrate Goliath must be.

In a harsh voice, cracking with emotion, Achish called his companies to attention and, in a square formation, they all retreated intact from that dreadful field.

Achish's one last thought was of David and his God. Yet there was nothing miraculous: one man, against all odds, had triumphed honourably over a more powerful adversary, who, in turn, had fought his fight well and, indeed, had so nearly slain his opponent.

Achish pondered. What kind of God or what kind of faith had led David into confronting such impossible odds? Achish felt a shiver of fear for his people. With such an adversary, how could they overcome?

Perhaps his friendship with David might have more meaning than he had first thought.

He and his troop were the only Philistines to retreat from that place without loss.

Chapter Fourteen

Jonathan

Saul's Challenge

I was hardly aware of what was said to me: the shouts, the cheers and the congratulations all passed me by. I dimly perceived the smiling face of Saul, exultant as he reminded me of his last encouraging words, "Surely, David, my friend, my son, that was a prophecy indeed."

He instructed me to go into his tent where attendants came and stripped off what was left of my blood-and dirt-soaked garments. They found water to bathe me and gentle unguents for my aching, bruised body.

My hip was especially blackened where Goliath's shield had brought me down. The upsurge of that memory filled me with a choking fear. I did my best to forget the nightmarish ordeal.

Ganz's death, I confess, gave me a satisfaction that surprised me. I knew him to be my foe whether he was a Philistine or an Israelite. There had been a mutual loathing between us. Somehow, I knew that his death would not cause grief to either the shade of Acrah or, hopefully, the still-living Achish.

With a start I thought, Will Achish have survived this day? I then thought of Jonathan, who I knew would be leading the charge. I silently prayed that they would not be brought face-to-face and that both would return safely.

I endured the painful ministrations of the attendants over my stiffening limbs as, slowly, my mind cleared.

They dressed me in new garments. As I sipped wine and water, my spirits began to revive.

Eban came in. His whole demeanour to me had changed. He had always previously been kind, but I knew I was always a lad to him. Now he showed

311

me a deference that I found almost alarming.

"David, if it please you, the King would have you join him. The army of the Philistines is scattered we have taken the body count: there are over 20,000 new Philistine widows. We lost only 400 men – a miraculous victory. The King would make a sacrifice and wishes you to attend, if you are recovered sufficiently."

I said I was ready and asked after Jonathan and his troop.

Eban smiled. "That's good that you should think of your comrades at such a time. Because of you, David, with God's help, they are victorious and pursuing a fleeing enemy, not fighting a desperate rearguard."

Eban then looked serious. "But, sadly, Prince Jonathan..."

My heart stopped. What was he going to say?

"... sadly ... Prince Jonathan's armour bearer, Canan, was slain by Achish of Gath. I know there was ill feeling between you and him, but he died for Israel, facing the King's enemy. That is a death none can quarrel with."

The relief I felt about it not being Jonathan was tremendous. Then I marvelled, whilst truly I could not feel grief for Canan, I did have respect for him. I pondered how many other good men died on the wrong side today?

As I followed Eban outside and into the light, there was more cheering. To my immense relief Jonathan greeted me. He was covered in blood and dust but, apart from a slight flesh wound, the blood was that of the enemy.

To my intense embarrassment, he saluted me, "Hail, David bar Jesse of Judah, lion of Judah, indeed. The King's and God's champion!"

The men took up the cry. I must say I was pleased that Jonathan, as a Benjaminite, had acknowledged Judah.

Jonathan looked resplendent in his warrior's glory, shining with sweat and exertion, covered in the gore of vanquished enemies, and surrounded by his admiring troops.

I saluted him and are eyes met and the light I saw there overwhelmed me.

He escorted me to the King.

Saul came forward and greeted me formally but in a ringing voice for all to hear. "Hail, my champion! You went forth in God's and my name. As I prophesied, you conquered against all the odds."

He began to take up his psalm, in which the men joined him.

"The King shall joy in thy strength O Lord and in thy salvation how greatly shall he rejoice. Thou hast given him his heart's delight – thou settest a crown of pure gold upon his head.

He asked life of thee and thou gavest it him even length of days for ever.

His glory is great in thy salvation, honour and majesty hast thou laid upon him.
For thou hast made him most blessed for ever; thou hast made him exceedingly glad with thy countenance.
For the King trusteth in the Lord and through the mercy of the Most High he shall not be moved."

He then called for silence.

"Warriors of Israel! Yet again, against all the doubters and the stay-at-homes," which was a clear jibe aimed at Samuel and the northern tribes, "God has given us the victory. Only this time, He has sent us a great champion, who though but young, inspired and directed by our prophecy, he went forth and slew the enemy who mocked the Lord and your King."

The men cheered loudly. They could not fail to remember how many had felt that, without the Prophet and the priests' blessings, to begin a battle was tantamount to expecting defeat. Yet here was Saul, not only King, but also claiming prophecy and inspiration.

I was a little uneasy in my mind but I had to be fair: I had been truly close to panic and without Saul's intervention reminding me of God's promise through the Voice, who knows what might have happened?

"This day," went on Saul, "has made David bar Jesse a captain of a hundred. When we return, he shall marry my daughter and be a Prince of Israel."

I was overcome: Merab was to be mine! I looked over to Jonathan, who smiled encouragingly. I asked the King if my troop could be part of Jonathan's command, which both he and Jonathan were happy to grant.

I knelt before the King, saluted him with Goliath's sword and said, "Great King, all was achieved for Israel in God's and your name, but the inspiration and strength came from the Lord."

I knew I had to give proper thanks. I took up my psalm with the verses that recalled the fight I had been through, yet was a balm to my troubled spirit.

"Yea though I walk in the valley of the shadow of death I will fear no evil for thou art with me thy rod and thy staff comfort me.
Thou preparest a table in the presence of mine enemies, thou anointest my head with oil my cup runneth over – I will dwell in the house of the Lord for ever."

I was tired again and would have wished to be alone, but the King wanted to feast. We now we had the camp of the Philistines for plunder, so we had food, wine and riches enough.

Jonathan had ordered two divisions to pursue the enemy back to

Philistia and had given strict instructions not to fight any more battles but to keep the momentum of their flight going.

As the feast was being prepared, I tried to go and find my friends, but I could make no headway.

Jonathan asked what I wanted. When I told him he laughed. "David, you are now a captain. Command and you shall be obeyed."

This was a novel idea. When I asked some men close by, they seemed delighted to serve and jumped up to seek out my friends.

First Beniah, then Hushai, followed by Aaron, Eli, Hitophel and, lastly, Josh arrived, covered in the debris of their terrible hunting. All but Aaron looked bloody, wearied but happy. I realised that all had now killed their man.

They came to me as if to a stranger, but as I embraced them all, they returned my greeting. When I asked it they would join my troop, stressing under Jonathan's command, they assented with one voice.

"Captain," said Josh. It sounded very odd to be called captain and in such a respectful way by Josh that I thought he was joking. "Captain, I speak for all of us – don't I, Beniah?" He realised that perhaps in his enthusiasm he should have waited for Beniah to speak first. "From this day, though our friendship was always yours, now you also have our obedience."

I was very moved and the emotion made me feel even more exhausted.

We proceeded to the feast. Everyone drank deep, except for me – for if I had anything else, I might disgrace myself by falling asleep. As the night went on, the exertions of the day rapidly began to affect everybody and soon we all sought to find a comfortable place to lay our heads.

Next morning we heard the news that the King's daughters, Merab and Michal, were leading a deputation to bring greetings from the people of Israel. The King smilingly agreed that I could accompany Jonathan to escort them.

We arrived after nightfall at their campsite, less than two days' journey from the King. Many women and attendants accompanied the two Princesses.

Jonathan allowed me to go first, where I was brought up sharply by Michal, the King's second daughter.

She was very beautiful but oh so haughty. Though more than two years younger than me, on the few occasions we had met she showed me that, in her eyes, I was no better than a servant – and an unimportant servant at that.

When I asked to see her sister she replied in her coldest most sneering tone,

"You wish to see the Princess Merab? What impudence! I don't know how you dare address me without showing proper respect, least of all asking to see the King's eldest daughter at such a time."

She seemed impervious to my new ephod, even though it was now travel stained, and totally ignored my captain's chain.

She brushed aside my attempts to explain. "How dare you! You are speaking to a king's daughter who, some day, will marry a king and beget a line of kings." A laughing Jonathan interrupted her tirade. He had heard all this. He greeted his sister in a way that quite melted her. For a brief moment, one could see her beauty and the hint of a potential charm, for she had all the grace of Jonathan and something of his looks.

He told her that she was a shrew. "Come now, Michal. Stop pretending you don't know David bar Jesse. He's not a servant, you know? Indeed, he is now a captain and the King's bard and champion – as well as my dearest friend."

She looked annoyed. "Hardly a champion! He killed his man with a sling shot – as any shepherd boy might chase away a fox."

This was the first time I had heard this version of my fight with Goliath. It became a popular myth as people got the fights with Ganz and Goliath mixed up. I was never able to correct the story, no matter how I tried. People seemed to prefer the simple account.

"Dear sister, it was not like that. David showed that he was a great warrior. Now come, bring Merab to us, for our father has decreed that he shall reward his champion's valour with the hand of his daughter."

She looked distinctly unpleased. The emotions on her face were indecipherable. "What? The King, our father, would bestow a princess upon this shepherd, this ..., this... nobody! This youngest son of a nobody."

Jonathan was not amused. "You go too far and –"

He was interrupted by the entrance of Merab's wondrous slight form.

She looked radiant, soft and diminutive. Though, as was proper, she went directly to Jonathan, she cast a quick look in my direction that told me she had heard the news and that she was happy with this. My heart quickened as I took in her loveliness. When Jonathan led her to me and gave her into my hands I was on fire.

She knelt before me and in her oft-remembered voice softly said, "The King's wish is my command. In duty, I am happy to greet David bar Jesse, the King's bard and champion, as my husband elect."

I knelt at her side, my eyes blinded by her vision. Our hands clasped. My blood raced at the answering look I saw in her eyes. I felt such a fervour that my aches disappeared and I longed to take in her my arms.

"Dearest Princess, your royal sister has it right. I am not worthy of you but I swear to serve and protect you from this day forth." Then, all my efforts at politeness were swept aside by my feelings for her, as I said, "I cannot wait until the moment we are married."

Jonathan gave a warning cough. "That may be, but up both of you. I can see that this is a love match and I am happy for the pair you." He was obviously as pleased to see the harmony between Merab and me as it displeased the frowning Michal.

Taking command of the situation, he said, "Come, Michal. You shall give me some wine. David and Merab will join us in fifteen minutes – precisely."

I was very grateful but could not help notice the word of command. Even so, it was still a gift of a quarter of an hour alone with my love!

We were by ourselves. At first, we both were extremely shy and stood without even looking at each other.

Then I blurted out, "You are happy with the idea, Merab? I would not force you to marry me, though you know I would die to be yours."

She turned to look at me. Without a word, she held out her arms to me as I embraced her.

Our lips were gentle against each other, but our bodies were locked firm into each other. She made no move to retreat from my erect hardness. My hands were about her. The touch of her delicate skin fired me even more, as my lips opened her mouth and our tongues glided over each other's. I was overwhelmed by her eagerness and my mouth sought out her breast. My nuzzling head pushed aside the thin covering of her dress as I took her erect nipple.

I thought I would explode as she clung to me even tighter. To my amazement, her hand explored my hard, hard member. My hand went in an answering search of her sacred moist parts. I knew I would either have to draw back or nothing could stop me from consummating my love there and then. With a great, great effort of control, I gently disengaged.

With a voice dried up by passion, I croaked, "Dearest Merab. I did not know but have always hoped. Dearest, tomorrow you shall be mine before all the world."

She answered, "David, David, you've made me so happy. I could not believe it. I have always dreamed of this. You must know I have always considered you ... well... er ..., er – " and she laughed.

She regained her control. "You know the King nearly married me off twice. Once, he thought of Abner. On another occasion, he might have given me to the King of Kir to bind them closer to our house. But, oh David, I don't have to – I can go where my heart is. God and Father are so kind."

Before she could go on, I stopped her mouth with mine and re-kindled the fires as, in our embrace, I yearned to join her body to mine.

Then Jonathan returned. He told me later he had coughed and sneezed but we had been oblivious to him. "If I had not broken you two up," he said, wide-eyed, "we would have had to have the marriage then and there."

I was not pleased at either the interruption or his later jibes, but consoled myself that, in three days at the most, Merab's promise to me would be fulfilled.

We returned to the King in a great procession. The warriors were all out in line, saluting and cheering the royal princesses.

The King came forward to greet them. He looked resplendent. No one could imagine that he could ever have doubts about himself. He exuded total confidence and was every inch a king.

He greeted his daughters. Then, he acknowledged Jonathan's and my salutes with a regal bow and a beaming smile.

Then, disaster! As the women approached, singing the King's praises – indeed, singing my psalm for Saul,

"The King shall joy in thy strength O Lord and in thy salvation how greatly shall he rejoice.
His glory is great in thy salvation, honour and majesty hast thou laid upon him.
For the King trusteth in the Lord and through the mercy of the Most High he shall not be moved."

some of them shouted, "Saul has killed his thousands, but David has killed his ten thousands."

In a flash, Saul's face changed like thunder as he threw me a look of venom that made my heart sink. I groaned. I could see that his old suspicions had re-erupted like some pustulant boil.

I cursed to myself, stupid, stupid, stupid – someone, in their efforts to please both Saul and me, had got it very wrong.

Jonathan and I exchanged glances, which were not lost on Saul. This interchange lasted for less than the blink of an eye, but I knew from that moment that my life with Saul had changed irrevocably.

Saul recovered his composure. I could see that, whilst he still looked very regal, his gestures lacked real warmth.

We went into the King's tent and began a feast. I was placed on the King's right hand, with Merab on his other side, but he barely spoke to me other than in a courteous, distant mode.

I exchanged looks with Abner who was intently taking in those subtle vibrations.

To my intense annoyance he spoke up. "Oh Great King. My master." Was there a subtle emphasis upon the "my"? "To give your champion even

317

greater glory, the women have sung of your trophies of slaying thousands. You, the victor of Michmash, Havilah, Eilah and others. Whilst your young champion is credited with tens of thousands. It is good to encourage merit, is it not? Though we should warn our 'slayer of ten thousands' that he has a long way to go, nonetheless, he has added to your glory." He stirred the pot as he smiled a false smile at my face. "Lord Abner, you do me wrong. I am King's servant. I am not worthy to lose his shoe. I was very lucky. Without God and the King's help I would have achieved nothing."

Abner replied, "Now, now Captain David, soon to be a prince of Israel, you are too modest. The slayer of giants and the uncircumcised has achieved nothing? Though the King slew the infidel King Nahash with his own hands, the women of Israel sing of victories to come."

Then, turning to address the King, he asked, "Great King, have you decided about his reward?" He laughed a cold laugh. "Your champion readily acknowledges the great help he received from you. That's good, but Saul, my King, we ought to return to other matters. What have you decided about King of Kir's request for an alliance bound by the hand of your daughter?"

"What was this," I thought. Merab and I looked at each other in desperate anxiety.

The King explained and, as he did so, my hopes evaporated. "The King of Kir, hearing further of my victory at Eilah, has again sought the hand of Merab to cement an alliance. I am mindful of the needs of Israel and have acceded to his request."

I was dumbfounded. Why, oh why had I not consummated my love with Merab yesterday and then she would have been mine? I dared not look at Merab for I sensed she was as close to tears as I was.

Jonathan interjected,

"Great King, my father, but have you not already given Merab to David, your bad and champion and – "

Saul rudely cut across him. "Prince Jonathan, do not interfere. Your partiality sometimes makes me think you consider your friends before your King. Your duty is to your father and Israel. I may have thought about giving David one of my daughters, but a King must weigh his people against his personal inclinations. On more mature thought, after the excitement of my victory at Eilah and my prophecy of David's triumph against Goliath, there is more time for reflection as to what would be the most benefit to Israel." He paused. "I agree with David – he really was very lucky. If you think about it, Goliath had defeated him but for a convenient rock with which he wounded his opponent – that was not really a warrior's way."

I grew cold with fury as he went on. "Yes, whilst Goliath was large – huge, even – he was a mindless ox. What we saw was a fight between schoolboys with stones. It was not a duel between warriors. On reflection, I think I was hasty in my generosity and liking for my little bard. Come, come, David, do not sulk – that hardly becomes a newly made captain."

As he laughed, worse, some lickspittles laughed with him – though thinking about it later, there were not many.

This re-writing of events before my eyes made me furious and, combined with the threat of losing Merab, I impulsively retorted, "Then, King Saul, how do I add balance to my lucky victory over Goliath that I might claim your daughter's hand?"

There was total silence, the feast had stopped as the tension and hostility were overt.

"David bar Jesse, you appear disconsolate. Despite your inspiration, there are those who say you are growing disproportionately proud. Perhaps I should begin to listen to them."

I would not be stopped. "King Saul, did you or did you not promise me Merab? Whether or not you gave your word in a fit of 'generosity'."

Then, I made a mistake. "I know that Merab would be happy with your gift."

He snapped back immediately, "What presumption! What have the girl's wishes to do with it? She will obey her father as any maid in Israel will obey the man of the house." His sarcasm was liquid. "What other new innovations would young men bring upon us? That we ask our women their approval of our actions. It is sufficient that we care and tender their safety. They, in gratitude and affection, do their duty."

There was a murmur of some approval.

I knew I had lost the argument so, lamely, I returned to his promise. "King Saul, I have spoken rashly. I am, after all, merely a youth, but one who for a day was privileged to be called your champion. I was sent forth to slay one who mocked God and you – no matter how I did it. In the end, the uncircumcised dog's head was made your football."

I could see I was back on firmer ground, but Saul was not yet finished.

He did not answer for some time. "Yes, for a day you wore my colours, as might any in Israel." Then, addressing the men around, he called out, "Is there any here who, if asked, would not take on the championship of their King and of Israel?"

Here, he spoke slowly to give his next words emphasis. "Especially if your King had prophesised your victory. Is this youth to be set over all your manhoods?"

Jonathan looked as if he were about to speak in my defence but I caught his eye and gestured not to – the situation was messy enough.

Then, Abner, my "friend", spoke. "Great King, slayer of King Nahash, victor of Michmash, Havilah and Eilah, in your greatness you sometimes err in generosity to share God's blessings amongst your followers. If David is really worthy of your daughter, then in the face of Israel gathered here, let him earn her in a proper feat of war, but slaying your Philistine enemies in a manner fitting his captaincy. Let him bring you 50 Philistines' foreskins as her dowry price to show you he really is deserving of your bounty."

There was some applause at this because it appeared a compromise. Saul had been clever. He had reminded the assembly that for three days no one but this youth had dared face Goliath and they felt a little ashamed of themselves. They were happy to have their pride mollified by this sanitised version of events.

Saul nodded sagely. "Lord Abner, as always you are my other self. Rightly second man in Israel. Fifty might be enough for the daughter of an elder, but I am a King – and the King of Israel too. No, 100 foreskins in 100 days. He may take his captain's band – if any will go with him – to demonstrate he has learned the skills of war."

There was a gasp. A 100 slain in a 100 days?

I was angry again and wanted to shame his ingratitude. I impulsively burst out, "Great King, one hundred? Pah! That does no honour to your daughter or your House. Make it two hundred Philistine foreskins to throw at your feet. Then, and only then, will I consider myself worthy to hold the hand of your daughter."

Whether there was laughter or a gasp of admiration at this foolhardy response, I don't know. My blood was up and I had forgotten to think – I only felt hurt, betrayed and humiliated.

Saul's response was cordiality itself. "My dear David bar Jesse, you have it right. I knew I could rely upon your sense of honour. So be it. Two hundred in a hundred days. You leave tomorrow. So that Israel may see I am considerate to my little bard, you may take ten followers with you. Now, enough of one man's vanity. There are hundreds who deserve chains of valour for what they added to my victory at Eilah."

I felt shattered, angry and hurt at his ingratitude. As I left the King, Beniah, along with Hushia, Aaron, Eli and Josh came out after me. Beniah looked very grim and I half expected him to tell me how stupid I had been.

Instead, he said, "Hail, David. We have spoken. We are yours to command. When do we start?"

I was overwhelmed with emotion.

Josh joined in. "You don't think we'd let you go off an adventure like this alone, do you – especially as the King behaved so badly? Pompous old fool! Without you – ”

I cut him short. “Dear, dear friend and brother Josh. Beniah, all of you do me too much honour. The King is the King and his words are our command. But what can I say? If you all come and win me a wife, we will gain so much glory!”

They laughed uproariously at this. I thought it best to join in, pretending I had intended the joke.

Up strode Jonathan, looking very serious. “I can see that your comrades have already shown you much honour. I have to tell you that the King refused my and Ura’s wish to volunteer to join you.”

There was a surprised and pleased response to this news. That the best captains in Israel should be willing to join us!

“However, you will have more glory to share on your return. I’m sure my sister will be for ever in your debt.”

Again, there was laughter, which Jonathan led. Then, he gave each of my supporters the Jonathan smile that made every man feel that he was concerned with them and them alone. “You have chosen a wonderful party, David. I promise you that there’s not a man in Israel who won’t envy your achievements when you return. So go with God, my comrades. I am proud of all of you! I will finalise the preparations with your captain. Each of you, go with God!”

He embraced them all in turn. Each went off with spirits soaring.

Jonathan was such a wonderful leader of men that, for a moment, I was almost jealous.

The Pool of Joshua

As my little company moved off to prepare themselves, Jonathan motioned me to one side and we began to walk to the outskirts of the camp.

He looked at me. His eyes betrayed his agony as his words sorrowfully berated me, “David! David! You bloody, bloody fool! You of all people know how vulnerable he is. That damned chant about you killing your ten thousands – it would have stung any warrior, let alone him with all his dark devils. I don’t suppose there’s any chance of you being sensible and calling this mad scheme off? God, David, at this minute, I don’t know who is maddest: you or him!”

Sadly, I had to say no. “Jonathan, I promised Merab. I love her. I want her for my wife and I told her that Saul had agreed. She showed me how much she wanted us to come together that...” I flushed for, after all, I was talking to her brother.

Jonathan answered, “I didn’t think you would withdraw. Frankly, I am not sure he'd let you back out now. God, David, sometimes I think we are all trapped in some great conspiracy. Turn as we might, we are moved by unseen powers that control us."

Then, he laughed ruefully. "Do I sound as if I think people are against us? Well – apart from Abner."

He went on. "Come, let's get away from here and this dreadful heat. Let's see if I can talk some sense into you. Now, you'll need horses."

Ever since Jonathan's stay with the Philistines he had argued that, as a mountain people, if ever we were to hold our own on the plains against the city people, we would have to master horses.

Not many in Israel rode but Jonathan had collected almost a hundred horses and had persuaded more to try riding. He, of course, was a superb rider. I had become quite good because I was keen to please him – and I could also see the strength of his argument.

Jonathan continued. "I've asked young Lev to take charge of the horses. I'll let you have six so that half can ride whilst the others walk. Lev seemed quite keen. Whether it's you he's coming for, or the chance to show what his horses can do, I don't know, but keep him in reserve. Also, keep one horse for equipment. You'll not need too may extra spears because you should be able to take all you need from the Philistines."

This was good news because Lev, though only a new full warrior this year, was that rarity: an Israelite who loved horses and could work with them. He was easily the best rider we had.

Jonathan's wise instructions went on. "Now, you'll have no trouble in getting access to Philistines. Knowing them, they'll have lots of patrols out in case we make an incursion after your victory at Eilah." He smiled a little at his emphasis, which I could not fail to notice.

"But this is where Lev comes in. You must take out every one of the men in the patrols. He should be held in reserve, ready to track down any fugitives. Nobody must escape from your attack. If one does, none of you will see the next week because they'll hunt you down. What they would do to you after Eilah does not bear thinking about – not even your friend, Achish, would have a chance of giving you a quick death."

His brutal assessment was, of course, accurate. The Philistines would hardly miss the opportunity of making a horrible example of the man who had slain their champion.

We walked on, now in almost complete silence. The heat was easing up a little but as we strode out, to put space between us and the camp below, we were still working up quite a sweat.

I did not know where he was leading. It did not matter. I felt secure. Here I was with Jonathan, the man I loved best in the entire world, who was showing his concern for me. This was especially soothing after the rejection I had received from Saul.

So whatever the morrow brought, I did not care. I do not think I even gave much thought to Merab, for whose sake I was putting my companions and myself in danger.

The night came quickly in the hills but there was a superb full moon, so bright that I could make out the growing stubble on Jonathan's chin. I was ascending the hills, "from whence cometh my strength".

The day was ahead of me, when I hoped to gain my love, but at this moment I was content. I could relax in the knowledge that I was safe in Jonathan's protection, even if I allowed myself the thought that perhaps Jonathan did not think he would ever see me again.

We left the track and began to ascend a sharp path that, even in the bright moonlight, was nothing to anyone other than one who knew where it led. At last, it came to a grassy plateau where lay the Pool of Joshua. I should have known he would have brought me here. It was a delight. A slender waterfall filled the pool, which shone silver in the reflected glory of the moon.

I didn't need to ask whether we were going to swim. With an audible sigh of delight, Jonathan raised above his shoulders his prince's ephod, slipped from his skirt and, without a backward glance, he plunged into the waters.

I stripped off and followed him.

At first, the chill of the water on hot sweating bodies was like a sharp slap but, as we grew accustomed to the change, the water took on the texture of liquid velvet.

For a time, we swam in unison. I could not help but admire his bold strokes. He created a wave in front of himself as he surged through the water, making it look sparkling and milky in the moonlight.

He stood up and looked at me without any emotion on his face. When he saw my delight, it surely told him that I would not be anywhere else in the world but here with him. He relaxed and, with a laugh, his face broke into smiles. I saw the man, the boy, not the prince.

We came together in a friendly wrestle in which I was no match for him. He whipped a leg underneath and, drawing me across his buttock, threw me over his shoulder, where I sank amidst laughing, gurgling splurts. I was moved by his comradeship and filled with admiration for him. He had thrown me as if I was a child.

I signalled my surrender and staggered to the bank, shaking myself like a dog. I was really enjoying the balm of the evening air upon my wet body, and delighting in the silver and black sheen of the bright moon.

Jonathan followed me out and, standing but a yard away, danced with his arms chopping the air in total abandonment. I could not help contrast the relaxed, unconcerned beauty of his face against its usual tense alert look that denoted the man in authority.

I lay prostrate looking up at him as I drank in his beauty. I have seen naked men before – my own body is familiar to me – but I had never looked as I looked at Jonathan that night.

With a gasp, I saw, as if for the first time, his magnificent chest with its taut muscles rippling under his silken skin. I took in the cruel scars on his arms and the jagged mark of an old spear thrust. The water streamed down in rivulets, arranging his hair in straight lines that took the eye to his swinging manhood.

My mouth went dry as I saw him in a new light. My mind dimly laughed at my priggishness with Josh, as I drank in his body. I did not know how but I wanted to feel its closeness as I used to long for Leah.

I began to feel aroused and I rolled on my side to hide it. He did not seem to notice. With a spat of disappointment, I saw his phallus lay long, heavy but limp.

He sat close beside me, so near that I could feel the heat of his body. I yearned to touch him. I thought about what might happen and realised that it would never happen if I did not begin now.

To my immense surprise, he looked at me and asked, "David do you like me?"

What a question! I was astounded. What could he be thinking about?

"Like you, Jonathan? But you're my Prince ..., my captain ..., you are more – "

He interrupted me. "No, not that Prince and captain stuff. No, I mean do you like me as a person ..., as simple Jonathan ..., as you see me? When I am here – naked, as you are – am I not a man like any other?"

Then he said very quietly, "Do you like me in the way I think you like Achish? Even though you are not his philia – and may not yet know what that means – I have seen you look at him with a warmth which ... Well, do you think of me like that?"

I could not believe it. I flushed a little at him putting into words the thoughts about Achish that, even in my dreams, I had never confessed to myself. I was suddenly aware that he was jealous. My love, Jonathan, was delightfully jealous.

I stood up, took his head in my hands and looked, perhaps for the first time, fully and deeply into his eyes. No pretence, nothing hidden, as frank a look as our naked bodies.

"My dear, dear Jonathan. I love you like I did not think it possible to love another human being. I love you as much as I loved Leah."

With that I put my lips to his upturned mouth and we kissed. At first, our lips were chaste but I grew bold. My lips opened his and, in a shared blissful homecoming, our tongues explored each other.

His arms came up to me and entwined about my waist as mine pulled him close to me. His hands moved down to my buttocks. From his kneeling position, he caressed me, pulling them apart in a new sweet tension.

I was fully aroused and my erect hardness was pushing into his face. I gave us both one more chance to stop what was unfolding. I slightly pulled back from him and had to laugh at the glorious sight: there was Jonathan, like some young god, not avoiding my hard phallus, but, with his eyes upon me, he teasingly let his lips explore my shaft. I nearly exploded at that image.

He stood, laughing, and now I saw him in all his might and glory. His full physique was carved in muscle and sinew. Like a magnificent sword, he was fully aroused. His phallus stood out proud and quivered with passion.

My hand went to him and, for the first time, I touched him as I had never touched another man before. I was overawed by the power of the demon that lay curled up in it, waiting like a rapturous snake to thrust out and take its prey.

I slowly moved my hand up and down in the age-old ritual. Jonathan moaned in quiet pleasure as his hand took me and, with quickening strokes, began to move up and down my shaft, imitating my thrusting with a woman. But this was different: he, as a man, seemed to sense how much I could take of this delightful torture. Twice, or maybe three times, I came near to firing but, on each occasion, he slowed down and held me back. We came close to each other. Our bodies pressed hard, hard against one other. With one arm behind the other's back, the other holding our erect members, our mouths were glued together.

If this had been Leah or Una, I would have entered them now, but this was wonderfully different – yet familiar. I felt weak with delight. I did not know how this sweet adventure could end but I wanted it to last for ever.

I sank to the ground in a languid passivity and Jonathan lay his fell length along mine.

My phallus seemed to want to reach the sky whilst Jonathan's superb weapon sank into my side. Our mouths came together. I held his head and lay back drawing him upon me. I was totally utterly defenceless. I had never given myself to another person like this.

I opened my mouth as he plunged his tongue into me as my thrusting buttocks began to answer the urgings of his hand upon my hardness. I could feel the gathering knot within my sack as his jerking motions became more pronounced, faster then slower. I thrust upwards to meet his final downward plunge on my quivering rampant self. My mouth was taken over by his and the sharp, sweet pain shot from my balls along my pipe and fired high into the air in an ecstatic explosion. I touched Jonathan's rearing phallus and he added his creamy seed to mine as it spattered upon my prostrate form.

Wonders! He then lay alongside me and massaged his seed with mine along our hard stomachs. He moistened our throbbing manhoods with our merged milky fluids.

We lay entwined for ages, each reluctant to break the spell.

Eventually, Jonathan breathed, "David bar Jesse, I love you until the end of time. Someday, you will tell our story. Truly, I know you will. Men will envy Jonathan for the love of his David."

I hugged him even closer. "Jonathan, I am the one to be envied, to be loved by you. Not just because you are our finest general, captain and soldier but inspire love and devotion in everyone. If ever I sing a song of our time, men will marvel at the generosity of the mighty Jonathan taking pity upon this poor urchin from Bethlehem."

We lay and laughed. Jonathan said, "How I wish the Almighty had not set his hand against mirroring his creation. I wish I could capture this moment for ever in a marvellous frieze, like those I saw in the houses of the Philistines. David, yes dear friend, still youthful David, with a body, lithe and firing sparks of life and vitality, with your wondrous prick, quiet at the moment, but with such sleek lines that all who see it would want to caress it."

With words like these it is no surprise that these sleek lines were beginning to lengthen again as I joined in the celebration of discovering each other. "And the world would see the beautiful, mighty Jonathan, prince, father, warrior, wearing his scars of war like delicate shafts of lightning. And with his phallus already standing to attention with such force and majesty that it would scare all the virgins with longing anxiety and excitement."

We both stood up in our excitement at the new sight of our bodies.

Jonathan plunged into the waters crying, "We've got to cool down, the world cannot take our love."

I happily followed him and trying to gain my revenge for the earlier throw by grabbing him from behind and trying a half buttock throw. He was too quick and powerful, as he rode the twist and carried me over him and down I went again. He left me choking in another inevitable defeat and returned to the bank offering me a helping hand to return.

I looked into his eyes again in total trust and we knew we were bound for ever and ever.

My senses were filled by his presence as my excitement showed in my re-arousal. Gone were my shyness, my priggishness, and my unease with the physical reality of love. Oh, why had our priest made us feel ashamed and unsure of our bodies. What could be more glorious?

Jonathan now lay in passive submission upon the green swards, with his insistent phallus so hard and erect it almost touched his flat ribbed stomach. I looked at the miracle of man. I had seen Leah naked and had swooned with joy and desire. I looked again but anew at Jonathan: the tautness of his stature, the rippling movements that followed his every gesture reminding one that here was an animal, sapient, but a creature of sinew, muscle, bone cast together in a miraculous mould. God Himself must look something like this for, after all, we are "made in his image". This chest, biceps, wondrous veined arms, flat stomach swooping down to his wondrous bush from out of which sprang his rampant manhood, this was God reflected in the flesh.

At first I did not do or say anything but kissed him chastely. I felt a new inspiration as my love, bonded pure, wondrous as that for Leah had been consummated, blessed by God, for here was virtuous man indeed who always sought to do God's will for Israel. I looked at him and knew that, though I prized him and he was mine, he also belonged to my comrades.

I gave way to my inspiration.

"Blessed be the Lord my strength which teacheth my hand to war and my fingers to fight."

Who better than Jonathan to teach me and all soldiers of Israel the arts of war?

"My goodness and my fortress, my high tower and deliverer, my shield."

Then, I remembered other words from Leah and our celebration of our sharing in God's plan that, despite our puny strengths, we were His chosen instruments.

"O Lord how excellent is Thy name in all the earth who has set thy glory above the heavens –
What is man that thou art mindful of him and the son of man that visitest him.
For you have made him a little lower than the angels and hast crowned him with honour and glory."

Who could doubt these words were meant for Jonathan. This son of man whose physical beauty cried out the perfection of the creator.

Jonathan was moved by my words but I explained, "That's why God wants no graven images. They are pale imitations of living human bodies that are perfection. Lesser peoples make pictures but they are dross in your presence and the reality of the living man. Jonathan, my Jonathan, you are only a little lower than God's angels and surely you will be crowned with honour and glory. I will be your bard and friend for ever."

He raised his arms to me and pulled me on top of him. Our hands explored and caressed each other, as mine followed his, finding new delights as he touched me in a way that sent my senses swooning.

He turned around as I, delirious with happiness, melted into a passive expectancy as his lips and tongue explored my chest, licking delicately my nipples which I did not know could respond as vibrantly as any women's. His mouth travelled down my chest bone and his tongue tickled my belly hole so that I curled up in delightful tension. We laughed in each other's joy and then ... oh ... then his mouth came near my bush. With his tongue, shyly at first and then bolder, he teased out my hard, hard length, as he laved the head of my phallus with his moist mouth. In one sweet rapturous movement his mouth was over the head of my phallus and he took my whole length into his mouth.

I was going to explode. The ecstasy was so great and he so gentle, that I avoided erupting for ever.

I sensed his longing, too. His body turned to me and my mouth followed the line of his stomach to his bush. I bathed the end of his vibrating member with my mouth. Our tongues in harmony swept fires up and down our shafts. Was it my phallus that had the tip of a tongue in its hole, or was it my tongue making Jonathan's phallus squirm with delight and harmony?

We were mouth to phallus, he on top of me as I followed his instructions and pulled hard at his buttocks as he pulled mine. He thrust his manhood deep into my mouth. I almost gagged but learned to relax. I thrust upward, upward, as his hands pulled hard on my shaft, lengthening it even beyond its limits into a sweet ecstatic tension as his fingers moulded my sack into a gentle ache. I did the same to him and I could feel his passion close to explosion.

He tried to pull away but I would not let him. Whilst his sweet mouth refused to leave my aching hardness, I would not let his go. I felt the tremble from the tips of his and my toes as waves of hot sweetness rushed through us. Our thrusting loins pumped out our seed, which gushed our love.

We exchanged a deep and lasting brotherhood. Falling into a complete exhaustion as our passion ebbed, we clung even closer together in love and complete friendship.

Whatever was to come, we were philia. I knew that whilst Leah had my heart for ever, I was bound to Jonathan in an eternal brotherhood.

I knew, somehow, that God had not brought me so far, or given me such joy, for nothing.

I was certain that I would succeed in my quest and that Jonathan would see me alive again.

PART FIVE

THE FIRST COMMAND

Chapter Fifteen

The Night Patrol

Jonathan and I returned to camp. Despite being emotionally drained I was grateful for the time to quiz him about military matters. He gave me a plethora of invaluable advice about being in command of men, ideas that I had hardly considered.

He said, "I don't doubt that you'll overcome and return in triumph."

I thought he was lying, but I loved him for it. He went on, "But after all, this is your first campaign as commander and it is a very different from the first battle where you only have to be afraid for yourself."

I expressed surprise at his talk of being afraid.

He almost snapped. "Of course I feel afraid. Only a fool does not fear a battle or a fight. It's how you deal with that fear that matters. I know you keep your head in tight situations, you 'think rather than feel' – or you did until you got yourself into this stupid venture."

I could sense that, with our special closeness, he was frightened for me, yet he did not want to mar with harsh words what might be our final time together.

We agreed I was a fool and there was little to be gained by going over it, other than as an example of what happens if I forget that golden rule.

"Especially when you're in command," he said. "You must always be thinking ahead, and not be afraid of recognising your company's weaknesses as well as their strengths. Crucially, you must always give the impression that, no matter what happens, it is all working out exactly as you planned. Even if it obviously weren't, your men would prefer to feel you're in control. Be ready to show that you'd already thought about what had happened and offer a 'solution'. Finally, show your men that you are thinking of their safety, so that even if you can gain an advantage over the enemy, it won't be at their cost. Remember, in one way, numbers don't matter but morale does. You should always hit the enemy with your largest force at his weakest point. Local advantage will give you victory and from

333

that position you can withdraw – one up, as it were."

I tried to take all this in. Then, Jonathan stopped and said, "David, in God's name, don't let pride ruin your venture. When you get a twenty body count, bring your troop home. It will be far, far better than getting fifty and only returning by yourself."

He held me by the shoulders and looked me in the eyes. "I love you so I am biased and afraid for your safety. I can understand why you will go ahead. But I would be failing my duties to you and your men if I did not tell you the truth as I see it. I don't think the task is achievable. No, not even with you. Therefore, take it as an opportunity to grasp the lessons of an independent command. Despite everything, my father still needs you and if you came back intact with just twenty, it would satisfy everyone's honour. He and I know you have much to give him and Israel. So, dear David, no unnecessary heroics: it's not fair to your men. Finally, I need you. Even if you don't marry Merab – well, if you so keen to be part of the House of Saul, you can always marry my Uncle Issach's daughter, Iscrah, and we can all escape that pride of yours."

He closed his lesson with smiles but I could not help but recognised the wisdom of what he was saying, especially about being "fair to my men".

So I told him my first lie, "You right, of course. I won't be over-zealous and just aim at fifty – which will please Abner, even if we don't get them!" We both laughed, he embraced me and I joined my band.

Little did I realise how quickly I would feel the fear and loneliness of command. Only Joab was younger than I was and yet here we were travelling in single file with me at the head worrying over the new maps that Jonathan had made. They were not as comprehensive as the ones he had undertaken for the Amalekite campaign, so I had to concentrate all the time.

We alternated between riding and trotting to avoid tiring out either the men or the horses. Yet it was amazing how much distance we covered with them.

As we came near the land of the Philistines I decided it best for all to walk so as to avoid giving our presence away. I hoped to locate a Philistine scouting party by the dust they might create. I thought, later when we have all proven ourselves, we might use the horses to attract the attention of a patrol and to lead them into a prepared ambush.

I recalled Ura's wise joke about men: feed, water and muck them out, but be careful not to leave any telltale trails for scouts.

I called the group together and they formed a circle round me: Lev, in charge of the horses, and Josh, Beniah, Hitophel, Hushia, Aaron, Eli. There were also Judah and Allot, fellow Judeans, and, despite his years, in a mad fit of Bethlehemite enthusiasm I had brought along Joab, who had been in camp the day before my confrontation with Saul. He claimed to know how to ride, so Jonathan, to whom he had appealed, had seconded him – so here he was.

I explained my general plan: how we would seek to repeat what Jonathan and Elim had done – namely, raid sleeping Philistine camps.

Joab, as I might have expected, said he thought this cowardly and Josh, who ought to have known better, supported him.

"David, my captain, if we steal up on them at night there is little honour, we are no more than bandits."

I kept my patience. "Josh, Joab, your enthusiasm does you credit but there'll be plenty of open fighting, no doubt. But remember we are out-numbered and whilst strong because we know what we are about, we have to use every stratagem to outwit and defeat a dangerous and much more numerous enemy."

The irrepressible Joab broke in. "Ah, we're going to bag another Goliath, then."

It seemed a good omen as the men laughed, so I left it at that.

Sure enough, in the next half hour in the gathering gloom at the end of the day, about three miles away we saw the dust cloud of a patrol that could only be Philistines.

Now we would find out just how good we were.

Until then I had not prayed to God because I felt that this was my campaign and to ask for myself did not seem right. But I must confess as my anxiety. Yes, I admit it: my fear began to descend upon me and I offered up a silent prayer.

I did not expect the Voice to answer but, as I breathed my psalm, I remembered the Voice reminding me to "think don't feel" as I closed down my emotions and coldly surveyed what had to be done.

The Philistine patrol consisted of fifteen or so warriors, noisy sentries, who were settling down for the night after having collected wood for their fires.

We had got within 200 yards of them and we could hear, rather than see, them. I could make out that they had not formed a square or set up any defensive barriers.

I held the men back. With Beniah and Josh 50 yards away to my left and right respectively, we crawled towards the enemy positions. We got within ten yards or so and saw clearly that, whilst there was more men than we had first thought, they had been careless as they clearly were not expecting anyone.

We waited. The time passed so slowly. My knees ached from the stony ground on which I was kneeling as the minutes dragged by. I hoped that Lev would make sure that their horses would not sense ours, hence my plan to attack against the wind, but would our horses make a noise if they sensed the Philistine horses?

As the time eked out I began to berate myself for a fool. What was I doing here? Worse, what was I doing risking my friends' lives? Then I pulled myself up with a jolt. I was here, I was in command and this was just one of the new testing innovations that Jonathan wanted. We were all warriors for the day. We would simply deal with each situation as it arose, so I coldly suppressed any more feelings of self-pity and fear.

They had set three sentries who did not appear all that alert. I gave my nightjar call and crawled back to the men to check out with Beniah and Josh what they had seen as well.

We all agreed. The enemy had both meat and drink and did not appear to be really expecting any incursions. After all, this was now some days after the battle of Eilah.

I gave my instructions but, as I was about to do so, I caught Aaron's eyes. He looked terrified. I suppressed my sense of irritation but appreciated that he had not much experience. I said that Beniah should take Hushia and Judah; Josh go with Hitophel and Eli, Allot and Joab come with me, and Lev would remain mounted in case any Philistines escaped.

"Aaron, I'd be very grateful if you would keep the horses together and, very important, keep them quiet."

Whether the others realised the state Aaron was in I don't know, though I suspected that they were all concerned with their own feelings.

The three parties crawled out, keeping about twenty yards apart. Each man was about five yards from his comrade as we set off to encircle the camp. Beniah, Josh and I had the task of dealing with the sentries.

By now it was quite dark but there was a slight moon and plenty of stars. As I moved forward, I occasionally carefully raised my head to check my direction by a star I had lined a sentry up against. I could not help but recall Leah's ideas about stars, and here I was about to add to their number. I regained control over my thoughts and moved on.

I was within five yards of my quarry – he had no idea he was in danger.

Stupidly, he had made a small fire in front of him because the nights can be cold but it meant that he would be dazzled and could not look out beyond the camp properly.

I drew my knife. My mouth went dry. My eyes were snake-like, not daring to blink.

The sentry turned in my direction. I froze. Had he heard me? No, he just sat there, a youth of about nineteen with a pleasant face. His thoughts anywhere but on what might be out in the darkness.

He sat there blankly, with a cloak lightly wrapped around him, huddled against the slight breeze that blew from the mountains across the plain.

I had aimed to come up behind him and had started my final crawl to him, but now he had moved around and I was in dead line of him. I could scarcely breathe. I felt sure he could hear my pounding heart, which was drumming in my ears.

There was a choking sound away to my left, which would be Beniah finishing his task.

God, the youth was more alert than I thought. He stood upright, letting go of his cloak to show that he was wearing no armour as the light from the fire illuminated his bare chest.

He was totally alert. He rose, picking up his sword. He took a half pace forward as if to go in Beniah's direction and thought better of it. Then I realised that he was about to give the alarm.

I sprang up within a yard of him. He turned towards me, his eyes wide open in horrified amazement. He half raised his sword as he opened his mouth.

Too late. I was up to him. I kneed him in the groin taking away his breath, at the same time plunging my knife beneath his ribs and clutching his throat to stifle any cry he might make. He slid to the ground and I with him, our faces not even inches apart as he looked into my eyes and I his. I saw his life glaze over as we clung together in a parody of a lover's embrace.

I kept my hands on his throat as I felt his blood spread over me. His body trembled in its final distress. I lay at his side for an eternity but, in truth, it was barely half a minute. He would know my face in some afterlife as surely as I would not forget his.

I felt a tap on my shoulder. I nearly screamed. It was Allot beaming his approval.

As I rose to look around I saw that Josh and Beniah had dealt with their sentries, so we could move forward, quietly, quickly, half-crouching in our darting runs.

I came across two sleeping figures. Fixing a grip on the first man's mouth, with my other hand I plunged the sentry's sword into his sleeping throat, doubly serving to finish him off and keeping him relatively quiet.

I did the same for the next one.

Ahead of me, I could see Allot dealing similar blows to two others. He nodded and, by the look on his face, he seemed to be enjoying himself.

Nearer the central camp fires were five men sleeping. We cut the throats of the first two with no sound but I was less fortunate with my third. As I grasped at his throat he had moved his head and was awake in an instant.

He cried out, biting my finger but I levered my sword into his side and that was his end.

But the others were now awake and the night was filled with shouts.

One huge man grabbed up his spear and went for Allot, who just jumped aside and slashed downwards on the undefended head as he passed him, bringing him crashing down.

The man in front of me cleverly got behind the fire so that he could see. He had armed himself with spear and sword. I whipped out my sling and – thwack! The stone took him at the side of his head. Now his guard was down and I rushed forward. From a kneeling position, I thrust up between his guard with such violence that my blade went completely through him. As he fell, his body weight dragged the weapon from my hand.

"Think, don't feel" I kept saying to myself as I surveyed what was going on around me.

There was pandemonium but I could see that we were clearly winning, though there were still six enemies on their feet. But they were now out-numbered and surrounded. There were to be no prisoners. When two raised their arms in surrender, Eli, with so cold a face that I hardly recog-nised him, slew the man before him as I had ordered, whilst Judah did the same for the other.

The shouts and curses of the Philistines were desperate as they faced their doom.

I looked around and saw a dark figure retreating.

I called out, "Lev, to your left. He's escaping."

I heard the sound of a galloping horse at the periphery of the camp. I saw Lev, the crouching hunter, ride off into the dark. I listened. There was a shout, a howl and a triumphant war cry.

"David and Judah!" said Lev as he returned into the light. He was limping slightly, leading his horse with one hand and in the other a blood-stained sword.

It was over. I was desperately tired and I wanted to cry. I wanted to escape this killing field, but I had my duty to respond to my elated comrades.

It was wonderful. Josh and Eli had slight scratches – no one else was hurt. When Aaron brought up our horses, I knew we were all safe and felt an overwhelming sense of relief.

I never wanted to go through that again. I decided that, tomorrow, I would release them. No man – least of all me – had a right to risk their lives for my personal happiness.

I ordered a harsh, "Quiet men! Quiet! You've done magnificently but we don't know where the next patrol is. They may be near enough to hear us."

That stopped their noise but they still grinned with delight. Josh, Hushia and Joab were clearly high with excitement. I embraced them first and then everyone else in turn, including Aaron.

I had a special word for Lev. "Lev, that was brilliant! It must have been especially difficult riding in the dark, but you got him before he got away."

Lev was elated. "Yes, isn't Mera wonderful?"

I found it a rather startling name for his favourite horse.

"She is so sure footed. As soon as you called I'd got him lined up and it worked like a charm."

Then he said something that I should have paid more attention to. "The silly thing was that, as I struck him, I fell off Mera and banged my blasted ankle. Still, I can ride – not like you poor infantry lot – but I'll make cavalry of you all before the venture's over."

I knew he had said something important, but I lacked the energy to concentrate and figure out was it was. Also, despite the excitement, we all began to feel a reaction set in and began to feel tired.

However, we still needed to do a body count, and then strip and get rid of the bodies before daybreak. No matter how tired we all felt, our work was not yet over.

I ordered that Lev would deal with all the horses, including those we had captured from the Philistines, and that Aaron would do the body count and soak the foreskins in wine before drying them later.

"Aaron, I also want you to be our sentry. I'm sorry, but we can't be too careful."   I did not say that I thought he had had the easiest job. As the others helped to drag the bodies in a pile, I could not help but notice they all averted their eyes from their handiwork as they sat down and took a well-earned rest.

To our surprise, we had accounted for twenty of them. There had been more than we had expected though, rather distastefully, it turned out that six were only youths, obviously in training and barely passed sixteen – but that's war.

I told the men to find food and wine, and suggested that, at first light, we would move out, sleep during most of the day and then we would start again under cover of darkness.

I went round the men expressing my thanks and admiration at their success. Aaron tugged at my sleeve. "David," he said anxiously, "can I have a word?"

He walked away from the men, obviously wanting a word in private. I thought that he might be going to complain about me giving him the position of least honour and began to think of how I might answer him. To my surprise and growing anger it was nothing of the sort.

"David, I'm sorry, but I can't do it."

I looked at him blankly. "Can't do what?" I asked uncomprehendingly.

"I can't mutilate the bodies. I've already done three but I've been sick each time. They're still warm and I have to cut off their... Oh God, David! I know you're my captain but I can't do it – I can't."

I snapped, "Pull yourself together, Aaron!"

He was almost hysterical and tears were flowing down his face. What could I do with him?

I thought quickly. "Look, Aaron. I think I understand. It is horrible but the foreskins of the enemy are the tribute we have always taken. You have had the slightly easier task. I can see that you're not enjoying this..." I trailed off.

What else could I say? He was my friend but his look of misery told me that he would be little use in a real fight. If I was not careful I would reduce him to nothing and then he would be a complete liability who could undermine the rest of the troop.

"You're thinking, why did I volunteer?" he said as he saw my expression. "Well, I don't blame you. But don't you see? You're my friend: you, Josh and Eli."

He had a smile on his face. "I thought coming to the King's camp... Well, there might be women." He saw my look and hurried on. "But it wasn't just the women. I really thought that, if I was with the four of us, I'd get over my fear – I could become like the rest of you."

Then, with total despair in his voice, "David, oh God, help me. I don't think I can ever be a warrior – not like Eli, Josh, young Joab or the others. They have no fear. They seem to enjoy it – well, once they've started. But ..., I'm sorry ..., I ..."

He stood looking utterly dejected. I did not know whether to comfort or beat him.

"All right, Aaron, so you're afraid. We're all afraid, only it gets to people differently. If you want, you can go back. I'll find some excuse."

He grabbed my arm. "David, I couldn't go back on my own! I couldn't. I'd kill myself! I couldn't live with their knowing my cowardice."

Nothing Jonathan had told me prepared me for this, but then I understood. Aaron had always been the most sensitive of we four and each of us had protected him in his own way – Josh, particularly. For example, when Josh stood up for him against Canan. We had carried him and now, in his mistaken loyalty, in his friendship, he had reached out to us and volunteered because he was too afraid not to do the sensible thing.

I thought that, although he might be a passable soldier in the troop, in this guerrilla kind of war, there was no place to hide. This thought started making me feel angry again, at the mess he'd placed us all in.

"All right, listen. I'll work something out. You did a good job with the horses, now come with me and I'll do the cutting for you – but you'll have to bring the bag."

At first, I thought he was going to refuse even this but, with a nervous smile, he wiped his mouth and nodded his assent.

Aaron was right, it was a dreadful thing to do in cold blood. In the fight I would not give it a thought. All that mattered then was that I got my blows in before my opponent got me. Yes, immediately afterwards whilst my blood was hot, I could take my trophies. But this? This was the stuff that nightmares are made of. I went to the first body and turned it on its back while studiously refusing to look at its face. I raised the phallus... Oh God! No wonder Aaron could not complete the task. Closing my eyes, I cut off the member and, not daring to look at Aaron, I moved on.

I felt sick. My hands were caked. I was disgusted and, with real relief, I turned to the last one. But, oh dear God, my eyes slipped and I saw his face – it was the boy sentry I slew. Worse, his eyes were still open, accusing me. I stood hypnotised – I couldn't move. For the first time, I looked at the body: he was virtually my age. He still looked beautiful until my eyes met the hideous rent in the side of his blood-drenched chest. I was completely immobilised. My rising gore nearly choked me with nausea and grief at the ruin of this young man.

Aaron looked at me and guessed. "You knew him, David?" he whispered.

I nodded.

He put his arm on my shoulder. "All right, I'll do this one now my stomach's eased."

I wrenched myself away from him in anger, disgust and self-loathing.

"I couldn't give a fuck about your stomach!" I screamed.

We both stared at each other, at my language, at my temper.

"Now, shut up being sorry for yourself and get on with it. Oh yes – and no wine, only water for you. If you fall asleep as sentry there'll be no excuse and you'll pay the penalty. Now get out of my sight and make yourself bloody useful."

He had never seen me this angry. Certainly, I had never been so crude to a friend before. It seemed to put some spine in him. He completed the task and joined the others.

I was shattered. That boy's eyes were still haunting me. I sensed someone behind me. I turned – it was Beniah. I didn't want to be troubled but his grave look was somehow comforting. He was carrying a skin of wine that his gesture insisted I drink.

As I took a mouthful, he said, "David, I can understand you want to be alone." He paused and went on slowly. "But you should know that was a brilliant piece of soldiering. You'd thought of everything. We're all amazed at how well it went. Despite our brave words, I suppose most of us weren't entirely sure – but we've no doubts now. But I have some idea how much it must have cost you."

That was so generous and typical of him. I had to turn away otherwise he would see my tears. It did not matter. He put his arms round my shoulders like an older brother. He comforted his weeping young protégé as he led me away to sleep amongst my comrades. Each, in turn, shook my hand in a bond we all knew would last our lives long.

The men slept well into midday with the sun almost at high noon. To my relief, Aaron showed he was still alert and, apparently, through the early hours he attended to different people as, without words, he had made himself our quartermaster.

I went to him and neither of us mentioned last night. We spoke evenly and I congratulated him on his vigil.

He smiled thinly. "I will be excellent at the things I can do, I assure you, my captain. I have to report that I had the impression that there was some movement way over to the northwest, behind that ridge. I thought I saw the outline of a horseman. As he, nor anyone else, came nearer, I thought it best not to rouse you unless they were coming within range."

I nodded approval. Now was the time to reframe the expedition.

I called the men together and spoke to them frankly. "Comrades, I speak as your friend, not your captain. I think last night was a great achievement and we all learned a lot. However, I think there is little to be gained by going on. I can't ask you to risk your lives against these odds for what is, after all, my personal quarrel with the King."

There was a murmur of disapproval.

"No, hear me out. I think we can risk one more venture then return whilst we are ahead – with no one really hurt. With one more ambush, we will have done enough to satisfy all our honours."

There was some consternation at this, followed by a hurried conference between Judah, Beniah and Hitophel, who were the eldest and most experienced. Beniah was going to be their spokesman. "David, your offer is very generous. You are our captain and you command. But we have engaged ourselves to your service. If it please you, we 'old ones'," and there was laugh at this, "we old ones would like to consult with the troop without your presence. We respectfully beg that you will consider the opinion of us all when we know it."

What could I say? I moved a little way away but, within minutes, Judah called me to rejoin them.

Beniah looked pleased with himself. "Captain, your troop are of unanimous opinion." He repeated the phrase unanimous as I darted a quick look at Aaron. "We should go on for at least two more attacks and review the situation then."

That was it – the die was cast.

Aaron had been right. As we slowly moved to the northwest, two days later we came across another enemy patrol.

We repeated the tactics to wait till nightfall and, after dealing with the sentries, crept up to the sleeping men and slew them – all twenty of them. This time, no one got away. Lev jocularly said that he felt cheated and we really should have left something for the "cavalry" to do. Lev had this great idea that he and Jonathan could create an Israelite cavalry to challenge the plain's people. Indeed, this venture was the first time any Israelite war party had used horses in this way. That is, if you don't count Jonathan's and Ura's mapping expedition. I was continuing to add to their initial maps, thus adding to our knowledge of the Philistine lands.

A third patrol was finished in the same way and, as there were again twenty in the body count, we had passed our fifty mark – which Abner had asked for. However, as we had had no real casualties ourselves, the men refused to even consider concluding the venture.

Nevertheless, our last success seemed to be the cause of our first setback. Suddenly, there was a great deal of activity, with large numbers of horses – fifty or more – and even as many as a hundred warriors. In a flash, instead of being the hunters, with a sense of dread, we realised that we were now the hunted.

Here, Aaron came into his own. He was meticulous in making sure we left nothing behind and suggested that, by moving closely in pairs, he, following up behind with brushwood, could sweep away any tracks which we and the horses might make.

To Lev's distress, we decided that as there was now a horse for each man, the spares would have to be let go – though we kept the best, of course.

Then I had the idea of travelling one whole night back towards our lands. We would make no secret of our retreat, making the enemy believe we had left, but, after resting up, we would reverse and cover our tracks back into the core of their land.

It worked. Their patrols lessened and, after two weeks, reduced in numbers.

On consecutive nights we were able to ambush two small units and, apart from Eli having a bad gash on his shoulder, we added twenty-four more trophies to our count without loss. Again the men did not want to discuss my offer to end our patrol, but I felt that they would be happy if we reached the King's original hundred and then return.

I must confess to a sense of selfishness as I began to get used to the strains of command. My thoughts turned again to Merab, and my mind and body yearned to be with her. I had almost given up any realistic chance of marrying her but thought, perhaps, if we reached a hundred then the King might relent.

I decided that our "departure" ruse would not work a second time, so I took the troop deeper into the lands of Philistia than we had ever gone before, skirting the cities of Gath and Escalon.

There we had an incredible piece of good luck in coming across a re-victualling party. Not only did we account for another ten, though they were mainly made up of older semi-retired warriors, but they were also carrying supplies to their archers of new bows and arrows.

We Israelites had archers but our bows were not very good. Nor were the arrows very true because we did not possess any yew trees, which the Philistines did have. Now we had these superb weapons. Such was their quality that, after a little practice, we became quite competent archers. I added two bows and three sets of arrows for each of us, which gave me far more options in any attack.

Success and Reverse

We came across a heavily marked track, which was obviously a well-used roadway. It ran east–west through the land of Philistia. After some miles it meandered through a small ravine which was an ideal place for an ambush.

I discussed my plan with Beniah, Judah and Hitophel, who all agreed that it gave us a great opportunity.

The question was: how a big a party could we take on after the impact of the surprise was over? In particular, we had to make sure that no one escaped because we were much too close to Philistine cities and a very long way from home.

We secreted ourselves on either side of the ravine, up on the slopes, about a hundred feet above the roadway. On the second day, a war party of at least a hundred and fifty warriors, plus a number of women and attendants, went slowly by. It was far too powerful and we just had to let it pass.

Another large body came through two days later and I again judged it too risky. Just two days on, as I was beginning to think that we had been here too long for safety, our luck changed in every way.

This time, a smaller party of about thirty-odd warriors came along. As it was nearly evening, they looked as if they were preparing to camp at the exit of the ravine. They had obviously travelled a long way and they were making a great noise in anticipation of settling down for the night after going through the ravine. The decision had to be taken. Did I wait and make a nightfall attack or should I strike now from where we were? I wish I had reasoned it all out, but I was impelled by the thought that this would break the hundred mark and then we could head for home.

I gave the signal.

Again, the dry excited fear of battle and the stomach-turning anxiety that made one afraid of soiling oneself. I had ordered all to make no noise by using only arrows and to take them silently for as long as possible. Once they knew we were there, then we would charge and, with extra surprise, expect to break them.

I aimed my bow at a warrior, barely ten yards away. He was half-sleeping on his horse. Thweee! The arrow sang and took him between the shoulder blades. Without a sound, he slid from his horse. Amidst the noise of the troop, his clatter to the ground was not heard.

Another was to his left. I fired and caught my target at his side but he cried out as he fell. All hell broke loose as the Philistines realised they were under attack.

As I had expected, they did not know where the attack was coming from and they were in utter confusion. I loosed another arrow and gave my war cry as we advanced against them on both sides. We were still using arrows but then got amongst them with our swords.

A tall, grizzled warrior stood before me. He was giving orders in a very loud but controlled way. "Form a line. Come to me. Form a line."

Some of his men were struggling towards him. He obviously was a captain. I lunged at him. He parried and, suddenly, with a sense of grinding fear, I knew I was in a real fight against an experienced swordsman.

He held his sword out, inviting me to thrust too early. As he kept me at bay, his commands were beginning to be obeyed and I knew I had no time. I had to finish him quickly or he would bring them to an order where their numbers would count.

I had a spear that I threatened to throw. As his shield arm went up, I lunged but from the ground upwards with my sweeping sword, just catching him before his backward jump had taken him out of reach. He cursed, swayed and, whilst off balance, there was a gap between his shield and sword. My right arm whirled downwards across and between his defence.

There was a shuddering jarring as my blade crashed across his neck. He sank down. I did not need to finish him – he was out of it. I did not delay and had just enough time to parry a blow from a young warrior who had come to the aid of his captain. On seeing his leader fall, he hesitated. That was all the time I needed as I did my favourite manoeuvre of a spiralling run and hacked with my sword as I turned by him. I caught him under the ribs and down he went.

I looked around. Josh had got his man down and was finishing him off with a spear thrust through his belly. Two warriors raised their arms to Allot and Beniah, but there was no time for prisoners.

To the rear, Aaron had joined us but was being beaten down by a big, burly, brute of a man, whose cries of triumph and rage was his undoing. Eli saw what was happening and, just before he could give Aaron his blow, Eli took him from behind and sent him crashing down. I had time to see Eli smilingly pull Aaron to his feet and take him down the track to seek out more enemies.

I had already turned that way. There was a new sound. Not just the moans from the dying and severely wounded, but that of crying women.

I had no time to think of what to do with any women, but shouts up ahead of the track demanded my attention.

There was the noise of a fight. Then, the strangled cry of the defeated. Then the stillness in which, again, I could hear women's sobs. Out of the gloom came Lev leading his horse.

Even in the poor light, I could see he was hurt.

As he saw me he tried to make light of his injury. "David, I got two of them who were getting away. I finished off the lot, but I fell off again as, after bringing down the first fugitive, I slipped from my horse and the other turned and got me here before my sword did its work." He pointed to an ugly gash under his hand which he had placed over his stomach.

He was out of breath and, even in the poor light, I could see the wound was mortal. The entire troop hurried towards us. I called for Judah and Aaron to keep guard whilst we attended to Lev.

When we came to him, it was obvious that we could do little for him. Indeed, we all marvelled how he was able to struggle back to us. His hand was literally holding in the slippery, shiny guts, which threatened to slip out of the hole that the Philistine spear had made. We laid him down so gently and brought water for him to moisten his mouth.

Everyone left it to me to say something. What could I say?

I thought of some cliché that he would be all right but instead he spoke, "David, my captain," His words brought on a fierce bout of coughing and, with each heave, there was more ooze.

I urged him to rest but he answered with a thin faint smile, "I shall rest soon and for ever in the bosom of Abraham."

We could not say anything. I think I heard Josh beginning to sob as he walked angrily away.

"David, promise me you'll try the cavalry."

I promised and held his hand.

He lay quietly for a while and then opened his eyes, which were fast losing their life gaze. "David, don't blame yourself. It was a great fight and I am privileged to be the first to die for you."

I was appalled. I wanted to remonstrate, but it was too late. My comrade was dead as the light left his face and eyes for ever.

I stood up, steeling myself to be completely in control my feelings.

"Right men. Lev's gone. Let's do what we have to do and then give him a proper burial. Now, did I hear woman?"

Beniah brought up four quaking young women and one old woman, who was obviously looking after them. The old women looked in real pain and then I realised that she had been shot through the chest. Most of the arrow was still inside her. We looked at each other,

"I am sorry, mother. We did not intend to make war on women but in the light ..." What else could I say?

Her hoarse voice croaked, "Young prince, I am doomed but, in Dagon's name, have mercy on my charges. They are young girls on their way to be married in Gath. Anna is bound to be the wife of Achish, the new King of Gath, and she will be a valuable hostage for you and your men."

She then grabbed me fiercely by the arm. "Don't – in your God's name and by the love you bear your mothers and sisters – defile them. If you do, I prophesy that our Philistine vengeance will never rest till you and yours are quartered on the altars of Dagon."

She fell back exhausted, near to death. She had resolved her charges.

Beniah asked, "What will you do, David?"

I almost angrily retorted that I had no idea what to do and that he had asked bloody fool question.

Instead I bit my tongue and said, "We shall see."

The men, with their blood high after the fight, showed much too much interest in the women. Aaron was unashamedly caressing the breasts of one of the crying maidens with anything but a soothing intent.

I barked out an order. "Stop that, Aaron. These women are under God's protection. Not one is to be ravaged. They can either be married to you here and now, or we take them with us as hostages. As the old woman said, they may well be our way out if it ever comes to bargaining."

The men looked at each other. I realised that, for the first time, they did not like the orders they were receiving. Custom was that the men could use the women as they willed. That the captives should be protected, they thought was a novel idea.

"Captain?" said Judah, slyly. "Captain, I think the idea of enjoying our good fortune later, away from all this mess, is a good one. I think I speak for all the men, no one would begrudge you of first choice and first go."

I flushed. They were all attractive girls – especially the one I knew to be Anna, who, if the old crone was right, was destined for Achish. If so, it was a strange story indeed.

"Judah, I don't think you understood me. There will be no interference, no rape and no concubinage – only marriage. Otherwise, they come with us until the campaign is over."

I said this quietly and coldly, in the best Jonathan manner when he wanted to show he really meant business.

There were looks between the men as Beniah said, "That's clear, Captain. Thank you. Right men, you heard the Captain. Let's clear up our mess and be ready to move on."

Then, cleverly, he helped me deal with the situation by saying, "Captain, you should know that Aaron got his first man today – nay, two – so now he too is a full warrior."

I led the congratulations of the band. I was relieved to see that the beaming Aaron was momentarily diverted from what he and some of the others saw as the spoils of war.

I went over to the women, who clung desperately to each other as I approached them. They appreciated that they were not going to face the worst so they all fell at my feet with sobs and cries of gratitude. I really did not how to deal with this.

I barked out in my harshest commander's voice, "Silence, you fools! You are not our guests. You will be bound and if one of you makes a wrong sound, you will all die instantly. You must make yourselves useful and at all times stay together and be quiet."

This quietened them as the full horror of their situation dawned on them.

I went on for good measure, "We men of Israel do not make war on women. I would that you were not here but remember, my men have been away from women for months and you know what that means."

The one called Anna answered or, rather, asked a question. "And have you also, brave Captain, been away from women for such a long time?" Her sally provoked an amazed ripple of stifled laughter, so I was grateful that in this light they couldn't see my blushes.

I answered, crossly, "That's a stupid statement. Look, you are in real danger. Frankly, if I thought you were a risk to the troop, I'd cut your throats myself."

This quietened them because they sensed I meant it.

I turned to Anna. "You will be their leader and be responsible for them. Equally, if they do anything stupid, you die. If you try to escape or warn any of your countrymen, you all die. Have you understood? Right, get on with it and make yourself useful."

Anna came up to me. "May I speak to you, Captain?"

At first, I was about to send her on her way, because I was not pleased at her witticism at my expense, but her demeanour seemed docile now. I nodded.

"Captain, I heard your man call you David. Are you perhaps David bar Jesse of Bethlehem?"

I was astounded and apprehensive as to what was coming next.

"We all have heard of you, the slayer of Goliath. But what my sisters do not know is that I know you to be the blood brother of my Lord Achish."

I inwardly groaned. This was getting worse by the minute.

She continued. "My Lord told me all about you and how some Israelites are honourable – indeed, he believes some of you may even become civilised. As you are his blood-brother I have the right to call upon you for your protection as a kins-woman."

What a situation! I asked, "Are you one of his wives?"

She hesitated. "I could lie but you deserve better. No, I have not yet had that honour but we are betrothed and, as such, I am part of his family."

I almost laughed in her face. "That may be, but in our country a betrothal means nothing until the marriage is consummated. Therefore, whilst I will protect you as a future kinsman, I cannot consider you as Achish's wife, for here the law of Israel, not Philistia, rules."

That disappointed her. Then, with a start, I realised we had been wasting time.

"We'll speak again. Now go!" and I returned to my duties as commander.

The bodies of the slain had been stripped and our trophies taken. Now, all shared the task, including Aaron, and I smiled grimly to myself appreciating how we were all getting hardened to the cruel realities of war – especially war in the lands of the enemy.

Eli came up. "Captain?"

I noticed that since my altercation with Judah, everyone was being very formal.

"Captain, we did not know how well we have done. There are forty-three more foreskins destined for your wedding dowry."

I looked hard at Eli. Was there a hint of sarcasm in his statement, as if I needed reminding that Lev had died because of my vanity?

"Good, Eli. We all mourn our comrade Lev. Truly, if ever I have the power, I will urge Prince Jonathan that we have cavalry. Come, let us leave as quickly as possible. Our victory cannot go unnoticed and soon they will be upon us. Instead of returning the direct way, where the enemy would expect, we head due west. We shall deviate neither north nor south until we reach the Great Sea – the last direction the Philistines would expect."

Trying to lighten matters, I added, "I've always wanted to see the Great Sea."

There was much excitement at the direction. At first, not all welcome, but then they saw the obvious. The Philistines might expect us to go a little further west but then turn either north or south before trying to get back to Israel. Heading on to the Great Sea would be the last destination they would think we would take. So, after giving due burial to Lev, we moved out. We tied two women on one horse, so they would be too laden to escape. Despite Lev's death, I was surprised that we left in fairly good spirits.

We found a place to hide for most of the day and then trekked onwards during the late afternoon and early evening.

Two days away from the ravine, I called the men together. Now was the time for straight talking.

I explained that I had been rash to aim at such a difficult target. I was not going to discuss the matter with them but simply to tell them of my decision.

"As far as I am concerned, my search for a 'dowry', as Eli put it, is over – finished! There's far more to lose than gain. Hear me out."

The beginning of their protest was stilled.

"What we have achieved together is marvellous. What is more important for Israel, however, is that we get back safely with all the maps intact. We have information showing that Israel can reach the Great Sea and return even though they would obstruct us. We may have fights on the way but only if they are forced upon us. From now on, our objective is to get back unscathed and avoid any unnecessary confrontations."

There was silence.

Beniah was first to speak. "Captain, I swore to serve you in your cause. Well, I do not break my oath. I think what you said is both sensible and honourable. More importantly, it shows your care and concern for us all. It would be churlish if we argued the opposite in false pride. You have not asked for a discussion but I, for one, commend you and await your further orders."

There was a growl of approval from the others.

Then Aaron, who was obviously feeling more confident since gaining his full colours asked, "What about the women?"

Suddenly the air was filled with tension.

Aaron gave me a piecing look. "Is it true that you have some kinship with Anna and that she is destined for Achish of Gath?"

Josh cried out, "You bastard, Aaron! I told you in secret." He strode angrily towards Aaron, who retreated behind me of all places.

Josh continued, angrily, "Captain, you told me of how you got your colours. I told Aaron how you had become a blood brother with Achish, as we are blood brothers. If I get my hands on that snivelling bastard there'll be no blood left in him to have kinship with anyone."

This was getting out of hand.

"Joseph!" I barked. I never called him his formal "Joseph" before. "Stand back. Aaron, you stand over there."

I waited till some sense of discipline had been restored and briefly told them of my pact with Achish. "He made me his blood-brother to keep me safe from my enemy, Ganz, whom I slew with Goliath."

There was surprise at this news.

"As a blood brother, Achish could not fight against me and gave me great help in my fight with Goliath. I am in his debt. Although Anna is not yet Achish's wife, I am duty bound to honour Achish and, therefore, to protect her."

I paused. "As she is betrothed, I will honour their laws which protected me. Israel has little tradition of blood brotherhood, though I am privileged to be blood brother to Josh. To answer Aaron's original question, Anna is under my personal protection as kin. Thus, any insult to her is an insult to me. But, I have told her and the others, if I thought for a moment they imperilled the troop I would cut their throats myself."

Then, I made my appeal to them. "Comrades, whilst my kinship with Achish gives some protection to Anna and hers, in turn, she has obligations to protect me and mine. Therefore, for better or worse, the women are with us till the end of our patrol."

This seemed to satisfy them. I was very pleased to see Eli spurn Aaron's efforts to get alongside him, despite him killing his man. Then I had another thought: this is a dangerous ground for a split. I would have to watch the situation careful and, hopefully, perhaps via Beniah and Eli, restore Aaron to the good opinions of the rest of the troop.

To everyone's relief, a week later, we came to the Great Sea – it was awe-inspiring.

I did not know what to expect but to see such a vast expanse of water, to beyond where the eye could see, was as humbling as when one is overawed by the mountains. The brilliant lights reflected back from the sky were exquisitely beautiful. The men were happy to traverse two half days southwards slowly. Yes, I had taken my decision. I was going to return the slightly longer route and go through the former lands of the Amalekites, before finally swinging east for home.

Just before we left the coast, Anna came to me. "Great Captain, brother of Achish, why not let us go here? You have reminded my sisters and me that, as you have honoured your kinship with Achish, we, too, are bound to aid you in your return. To avoid any further risk, release us here. We will say that you have gone north, the way you would be expected to go. Without us, you will probably travel faster."

She stood there, slender and beautiful, barely a year younger than me. Her dark, intelligent eyes had taken in everything and it gave me some satisfaction that she would be able to report well of me to Achish. I suddenly realised that we were alone and that the moon was beginning to rise, with stars and moon mirrored against the dark purple sea. I knew it to be beautiful and knew her to be very comely.

I tried to restore the situation. "You said it earlier, Princess. I, too, have not been near women for many days and it is not seemly that we should be alone like this."

Instead of being rebuked, she laughed delightedly. "Why, David bar Jesse! You sound afraid of a mere woman – you, the champion of Israel! Do I trouble you so much?"

She brazenly looked me in the eyes. What I saw there made me think of her with Achish. How sweet it would be to have my arms around her breasts and her mouth melting into mine.

She stepped close to me. I could feel my senses be aroused. She lowered her head, putting her arms to my shoulders, and buried her head on my breast.

Oh, I wanted her! She seemed to want me, as she pressed herself against my now rampant hardness. But this was wrong. Not just to Achish, but to the troop. With a snarl of frustration on my face, I gently levered her away from me. "Sister, that gesture was kind, but I cannot let you go on. When we reach the land of the Amalekites, I will arrange a truce so that you can be returned to your Lord, my blood brother Achish."

She stood alone for a moment. Then, drawing herself upright, she said, "Thank you, David bar Jesse, for showing me my duty."

She walked away sadly, but with dignity.

I was troubled. What was I thinking of? After all, I was in this dangerous situation because I loved Merab. Here I was, aroused by a beautiful woman who was going to be my blood brother's wife. I berated myself. What kind of man, warrior and commander did I account myself if I was so easily diverted from my main responsibilities?

That night I dreamed of Merab – and of Anna with Achish – which brought its own relief.

Israel's Cavalry

The next two weeks were tedious, soul-destroying journeys. Hiding most of the day, we could only travel in the dreariness of the night.

I used the time to muse over what I had learned and the mistakes I had made. In particular, I thought long and hard about the death of Lev. He had said something that I ought to have taken note of, but I could not quite remember what it was.

Then I had it: he had fallen from his horse when trying fight from horseback. The Philistines used a rope around the body of the horse and a raised cloth, which created a saddle. This, with the bridle, helped to steer the horse along, but it did not give much purchase from which to launch a blow. Lev had said that he slipped off because he lost his balance.

I had an idea. If we could stand and sit on the horse, we would be much more able to fight from horseback. So, I tied extra ropes around the horse, making rings through which you could place your feet – in effect, like the stirrups which we used to bring up water from a well. Thus, together with the stirrups and raising the saddle, it made a much more secure basis.

I experimented and found that it gave a much better seat when charging with your sword, or bending down to aim low without falling off. It was so obvious I was amazed that no one else had thought of it.

As we journeyed onwards, we practised horse wrestling. We also developed our archery and sling shots from on horseback. Although not yet as good as at ground level, both were effective enough. If the horse was stationary, however, then our slings and bows were as good as infantry on the ground. At a slow trot, they were still very effective.

So, we adapted every horse and had brief daily exercises. At first, the horses did not like their new bonds but within a week they grew accustomed to the extra bindings. Of course, the negative aspect was that they sweated more. We solved that problem by cleaning them down more often – especially after a gallop.

We made every effort to avoid enemy patrols, which often meant that we had to travel miles out of our way.

On the sixth week, we came face to face with one. I had made Aaron, who had become a very good rider, the forward scout.

He came hurtling back. As he had been circumventing a small hill, he had come face-to-face with a Philistine war party. He thought it was less than a mile behind him. Indeed, as he spoke, we could hear the thunder of their hooves.

I looked around. There was nothing for it.

I called the men together. "We've only a little time. Listen to my orders and be ready to meet them in a straight line. Fire when I give the word. Get the women to dismount. Now, damn it!" I snapped at their bemused looks.

I had reasoned to myself, with the women on the ground, it might attract some of their warriors' attention and could prove a useful decoy. The women did as they were bid but looked very frightened.

I called out, "Now wait for my word. Afterwards, reassemble at the foot of the hill, tonight. So follow your stars."

Trying to urge an enthusiasm I did not feel, I added, "Our war cry is: the Lord of Hosts and Lev's new cavalry!"

With that, I turned my horse towards the galloping Philistines. "Draw bows and, at my command, loose arrows."

We were but ten in our line, yet no one flinched. I was so proud. If we were going to die, then we would give a good account of ourselves.

The shouts and screams of the Philistines were horrendous.

As they got within thirty yards, I cried, "Fire!"

Our ten arrows whistled forward and brought five men crashing down. In their confusion, they brought down others. There was just time for a second salvo, which, being nearer, did more damage. Suddenly, there was a hole in their charging line. They began to slow down and look confused.

"Arrows again," I yelled, my voice screeched high in excitement.

Our arrows arced away from us and soon four more enemies were down.

The Philistines began to ride around us as their charge lost its impetus. Though we were still outnumbered something like four to one, our archery kept them at bay. I saw that the next strategy was to use our slings against their horses.

The enemy horses began to rear out of control. We were all firing like mad. They were now down to about fifteen mounted men. With confusion reigning amongst them, I was not now seeking to mount a rearguard action. I saw that I could go for all out victory.

"Charge!" I screamed. Drawing my sword, I urged my horse forward. Within five strides, I was close to a mounted warrior. He tried to parry my blow but, tensing myself for grim death in my stirrups, I swung at his head and down he crashed. I forced my horse forward to a wild looking man, who tried to turn. Leaning forward I struck him a savage blow on his spine, which was nearly my undoing as the force of the blow nearly unhorsed me.

I turned round and saw Aaron fighting desperately. He had got between two of the enemy. One aimed a blow at Aaron's mount to great effect, bringing both horse and rider to the ground. In a flash, Aaron was bravely on his feet, skewering the man who had brought him down, who had fallen also from his horse.

I shouted, "Aaron!"

Too late – another Philistine had reached him on horseback and rode Aaron down. The Philistine could do no more damage as I swung over my head a downward blow bringing him to the ground, where he too struggled amongst the trampling horses.

I looked around. The only enemies left alive were on the ground. Six men had formed a ring and Beniah, Josh and Judah were about to charge them.

I roared, "Josh, halt! Stay and use your slings." We kept well out of range and virtually stoned them to death.

I was exhausted.

I cried out, "Check the wounded." I wanted no hidden assailants and two had their throats cut.

When I found Aaron, I almost fell from my horse. My legs trembled with weakness as I dismounted.

At first, I thought he had suffered just superficial wounds, but then he turned his head. I could see a terrible injury to the side of his skull, which was caved in from the hooves of the threshing horses. He could only see out of one eye. I was amazed that he still lived.

I knelt beside him, crying his name, seeing only my childhood friend in agony.

"Aaron! Aaron!" I cried.

He could still speak. "David, am I forgiven? I tried so hard not to let you down."

Josh joined me. His distressed face said everything. My tears flowed unashamedly and I could not answer him other than to clasp his hand.

Josh spoke for the both of us. "Oh, little Aaron. Aaron, of course you haven't let us down. We're Ura's four Bethlehemite bad cases, aren't we?"

His voice faltered. "Oh, Aaron. I'm so sorry for doubting you. Can you forgive me?" He could speak no more as Aaron reached for his hand.

By this time, Eli, too, had joined us as we knelt around our dying comrade. Eli's tears, as he leaned over to kiss Aaron, washed the side of his head and balmed some of the blood.

Aaron suddenly had a desperate look on his face. "David, I didn't let you down, did I?"

Then, in great agony of spirit, Aaron said, "Josh, Josh, I'm frightened –

frightened. Oh God, God, God! I can't see. I can't see! Hold me."

He clung to us in desperation as we tried to comfort him in his agony.

Later, I recalled with gratitude Eli's words just before Aaron died. "Aaron, dear, dear friend. Aaron, there is no need to be frightened. We will hold you, for this day you are a warrior of Israel and will soon be in Abraham's bosom."

Aaron turned his face to Eli, mouthed the words "thank you" as his tears ended in choking sobs. With a hideous shudder, he gave up the ghost.

We three wept unashamedly. Gone were any thoughts about being manly in the face of adversity, gone were any ideas of the commander bearing up. I was first to stand and took in this piteous sight of a dead young man, surrounded by his grieving comrades. I hated myself, the Philistines, Saul and God, who let these terrible things happen – but most of all, I hated myself.

Aaron was my friend, yet I had dragged him through countless humiliations. Exposing him to ridicule, to tasks beyond reason, then, finally, to pain, mutilation and a hideous, terrifying death. All because of my vanity! I could not bear it, I walked away. I had to be alone.

My thoughts raced. Why had I let this happen? Oh Aaron, I'm sorry, so sorry. Forgive me. Forgive me, Aaron.

As if to punish me, memories of our boyhood came rushing at me. I knew I had lost my innocence. Innocence – what was I thinking? Innocence after these dreadful months of the slaughter and murder of sleeping men? I knew Aaron's death, even more than Lev's, was a watershed. I felt an urgent need to be with my friends and gain their forgiveness for what I'd done.

I turned towards them and took in the horrid sight of the battlefield. It was littered with bodies and frightened horses. The only standing figures were our men surrounding the kneeling Eli and Josh. A little way off were the Philistine women.

I stood stock still. The scene burned into my memory. No sense of triumph or achievement – only horror. I felt a sickened tiredness, as if my grief for Aaron was a grief for us all, the living as well as the dead.

Eli rose and came towards me. He held out his arms and we fell into each other's embrace. I tried to say that I was sorry.

"David, what are you saying, you have nothing to be sorry for? You saved our lives. Aaron died well – as a warrior. He wanted nothing else but to please you. He's at peace now. He sought our forgiveness and we asked for his. You have nothing to ask forgiveness for."

I did not answer Eli. These were the words I wanted to hear. Was it the beginning of the subtle poisonous balm of flattery, which was even sweeter because it came from friends? In my heart, I felt then and now that I was responsible for Aaron's death and for all the deaths around us. But I felt the bone-numbing tiredness that comes after battle and needed some absolution for my tired soul.

Anna and the other women came up to us. They kneeled before us.

"Great Captain," started Anna.

I was furious at this form of address.

She went on. "This was a great victory though it cost you your dear friend. To us it has renewed bitterness to see our kin slain."

Her simple words made me think for the first time about the situation they had just endured: when freedom beckoned and safety was so near, to be such close witnesses to such slaughter.

I waited for her to go on.

"David," she said with a great effort to control her feelings. "We understand you have things to do. Give us permission to prepare your friend's body for burial as our tribute to him and our gratitude for your continued protection."

I realised what she meant: after such a battle and Aaron's loss there was no knowing how the men might react. Her words reminded me that indeed there were "things to do" so I gave instructions as we tried to make some order on that bloody plain.

Beniah and Joab joined me.

Beniah, as always, had just the right words. "David, remember there is nothing for you to regret. Aaron, like us all, was proud to have been part of this victory. It would have pleased Lev as well. His "Israelite cavalry" beat the Philistines. David, do you know what we've achieved today? If I had not been here to see it myself, I would not have believed it."

Joab spoke excitedly. "David, we got fifty-five. It was a whole warrior party, all horsed – all horsed, mark you. Your tactics worked even better than in your fight against Goliath."

As he said this, the others joined us and began their congratulations. Although almost hideous to me, these few moments bound us and gave us some kind of absolution from the blood on our hands. It transformed us from being murderers of our fellow men, to being glorious heroes – even though I wanted to scream, "Rubbish! We've become killers!"

The hurtful thing was, despite this blinding flash of understanding; I colluded and allowed myself to smile as their mood changed from the post-battle inertia to a cheering celebration.

I continued to smile and enjoy myself until Josh led us in my psalm.

"The Lord is my shepherd, I shall not want.

He maketh me to lie down in green pastures, he leadeth me beside the still waters.
He restoreth my soul, he leads me in the paths of righteousness of his name's sake.
Yea though I walk in the valley of the shadow of death I will fear no evil for thou
art with me thy rod and thy staff comfort me.
Thou preparest a table in the presence of mine enemies, thou anointest my head
with oil my cup runneth over – I will dwell in the house of the Lord for ever."

At first, I could hardly join in. Then, as the words broke through my distress, I began to sing it with fervour, as we all sought a cleansing of the horrors we had just been a part of. I confess that the sharing of these words, which belonged to another time, another place and another psalmist, eased my heart. Yet I could see that its inspiration balmed our souls.

There was no need now of trying to hide our presence. After taking the useful booty and the trophies, we were all ready to join the women's ministrations for Aaron.

We laid him in the earth with his sword and bow. We covered his resting place, far from home, with stones and rocks ensure that his sleep would not be disturbed.

We rode away and left him behind for ever.

I realised that I was more silent than usual. I was grateful that no one unnecessarily troubled me. Beniah and I calculated that we might be only two days from the lands of the Amalekites if we rode openly, or four at the most if we went cautiously.

Then Judah spoilt the peace by asking the question I did not have the spirit to contemplate. "Shall we try for the last ten, David? It should be easy now."

I had to control myself. My feelings were so mixed. The thought of venturing into any more danger disgusted me. Yet, to be honest, I could see that a remarkable and unexpected success was possible – I knew I was tempted.

"Nay, Judah. Surely we have had enough? We have gained great honour. What if the King does not think that our trophies are sufficient for the hand of Merab? As much as I revere her, I would not risk any of us any further."

Beniah saw my ambivalence. "Come, David. We need not go looking for any enemy but I say that, if the opportunity arises, we should take it. Not in pursuit of your quest but if God puts them before our swords. We will not reject His offer."

I was somewhat unhappy at the idea that God placed enemies in front of us.

I answered, somewhat priggishly, "We ought not to tempt God any further, Beniah. We have tempted him much already."

Beniah laughed. "Then, my Captain, if He has carried us so far, let us fulfil His purpose as it unfolds."

So, it was agreed.

I had an idea and said, "If, and I stress if, we do meet any enemy patrols, providing it is not foolhardy, we will confront them. This time, though, I want to take some prisoners – two, I think."

This got them wondering but I simply grinned and refused to tell them what I was hoping for.

Of course, I ought not to have yielded to temptation, as there was more to lose than gain.

Later, perhaps two hours before sunset, we saw dust clouds in the distance – horsemen.

We prepared ourselves.

This time, Eli insisted on scouting ahead. Within half an hour he was back. He was so high with excitement that he was almost incoherent.

"There looks to be about twenty of them – all mounted. Well?" he asked, expectantly.

I quickly surveyed the scene. "How far ahead are they?" I asked.

"A little more than a mile," Eli replied

"Right, let's reach yonder small hill and claim the higher ground. When they see us, they'll charge. Await my signal but, again, first arrows and then sling shots at the horses. If the situation changes, we shall seek the summit of the hill and escape by darkness."

We released the women some hundred yards behind us, not only to ensure their safety, but also to avoid any treachery and use of them as a decoy.

The waiting was tedious. We had ridden a fair distance and we were tired. Suddenly, I thought, Are the horses all right? I cursed not having Lev to advise me.

Too late: the Philistines came round between the low-lying hills. At the sight of us, they sent up a piercing war whoop and charged us immediately.

When they were within range, I cried, "Fire!"

Our arrows flew to their targets. Six men came down and, as one fell, he brought another horse and rider crashing to the ground. Another volley of arrows brought four more down.

As previously, these tactics shocked the Philistines and their charge faltered.

"Forward! Use your slings," I yelled and rode my horse forward.

Our missiles were amongst them and, to my intense satisfaction, there was not a man still left mounted.

"I want prisoners, remember," I shouted. "Be careful!"

As we rode amongst the fallen men, some we finished off immediately, but we captured two of them. One was even a captain.

It had all seemed almost too easy. I began to feel proud. Fatal pride! Perhaps God relented.

Beniah, Eli and I had remained on our horses, feeling satisfied with our exploits. Suddenly, from around the corner, rode another party of Philistines. This time, all the confusion was on our side.

I shouted for our men to use their arrows but some had already laid down their bows, thinking it all was over.

Allot was the first to receive their charge. He saw what was happening and grabbed a spear from a dead Philistine. He took up the defensive position that Jonathan had taught. He brought down the first horseman and wounded a second but a third, with a cruel blow, almost took his head clean from his shoulders.

I fired three arrows but only one was successful. Beniah and Eli came to me and, as we showed a greater threat, the enemy turned to the easier task of our other men on the ground,

I screamed, "Josh, Hitophel, Hushai! Get together, back to back."

They had sufficient presence of mind to do so, but not before Judah, having just killed his man, was hacked down to lie in the dirt.

We were seven – they were fifteen. Now I realised that our horses were exhausted and hardly had any life left in them. As we tried to get to our mounts, a group of ten Philistines saw the three of us and made us their first priority. Our arrows suddenly made them appreciate they had chosen wrongly, as three of them went down immediately.

We quickly jumped up on to the backs of our horses. Eli's horse suddenly buckled under the strain and it collapsed, with Eli getting out from under it just in time.

"Eli! Eli, to me!" I screamed, my voice high with tension and fear.

Beniah brought down another and then we were hand to hand, five against three. Eli saved the day by running behind their posse. He hacked at the horses' legs, bringing down their riders. One he killed immediately but the another engaged him in a fierce duel.

The Philistine in front of me was a youth. He suddenly saw his predicament and turned to flee. Without hesitation, my sword was across the back of his neck. My horse was rapidly weakening and, to the astonishment of the second warrior in front of me, I sprang from my horse as it slowly rolled over on the ground kicking out its hooves. This caused his horse to rear up, throwing him crashing to the ground.

I held my sword at his throat. "Yield," I screamed. He looked as if he was about to make a grab for my leg. I was not going to be caught off-guard – my sword took his hand off at the wrist. I left him till later.

Beniah was clearly getting the better of his man, whom he called upon to yield. This freed me to rush to Eli's aid. He already had a dreadful arm wound.

I roared at the Philistine, "Dog! Try me, you uncircumcised dog!"

He span around but, from my half-crouched position, I was under his guard and my blade crashed into his knees, bringing him to the ground. I skewered him in a fury that was fuelled by my anxiety for Eli.

It was all over.

But, oh God, we were so nearly defeated.

I looked desperately for Josh, who, to my immense relief, was right behind me. I fell into his arms and we both rushed over to Eli.

I was crying with anxiety. "Eli! Eli, are you all right?"

Eli gave me one of his calmest looks, for which I will ever be grateful. "My dear David. Why shouldn't I be?"

Even amidst that tension Josh and I started giggling like the schoolboys we had all been what seemed like so little time ago.

Beniah had charge of my two prisoners, though whether the handless man would be able to do the task I had for them, I was unsure.

We bound them fast. We called to the women and then turned to look for Allot and Judah.

What a disaster! Allot and Judah were both dead.

I could not speak much as the realisation of how close we had come to failure because of my stupidity – and my lack of forethought. I should have known that a group of twenty was only a half-party. My ambush had nearly been our own trap. I should not have listened.

Oh, dear God! Aaron, Lev, and now, Judah and Allot – all gone.

I motioned to Beniah and half croaked, "Beniah, deal with things. I can't. I'll be back in a minute. I'll ..." I staggered away as the enormity of what had nearly happened bore down upon me. I grieved for my companions and for myself.

Beniah was superb. About an hour later he called me back for the ceremony to bury our fallen comrades.

I dreaded this moment.

They all waited for me. I was their captain yet, apart from Joab, I was the youngest and I had never felt so vulnerable. I pulled myself together and stopped feeling sorry for myself.

"Comrades, this is a sad day. I should not have listened. If I had taken proper care, we need not have fought this battle."

I paused – it was so difficult. I looked over their faces. Joab, though bruised, was looking tired but happy. Beniah looked grave and composed. Eli, waxen from the loss of blood, nevertheless looked reasonably alert. Hushia and Hitophel, amazingly, seemed to look fresh and answered my looks with gentle smiles. Young Joab, who had acquitted himself so well despite having a bad contusion across his face, still had the spirit to grin from ear to ear.

I had to speak slowly as I was filled with turbulent and conflicting emotions.

"My friends. What can I say? I shall never forget how we have served together.

"Each one of you is a hero and deserves to be a captain a thousand times over. I am privileged to be amongst you. Whatever the King may say about me, your many victories over the past months are something that the whole of Israel shall acclaim."

Then, Joab broke in. "Yes. David, we've got another forty-seven foreskins!"

I wanted to roar at him. What was he thinking of? As if that mattered now. But my anger choked me.

Beniah saved us all. "Be quiet, Joab. Sometimes you forget you are the youngest and should give way to your elders and betters."

Joab looked hurt and angry, but then seemed to understand.

He said, "Well, yes. You know, Old Beniah, I am only the one who is younger than the Captain. So there, Old Man."

We all smiled at this tension-relieving sally.

I had other work to do and it was my turn to be captain again,

"Joab, you are a presumptuous young puppy. If Beniah were to beat you, you would deserve it. I tell you, if you wish to be a leader of men, though truly you are already a doughty warrior, but if you wish to lead other men then study carefully Beniah. His thinking, his skill in battle, his consideration of others is an example for us all. So, if he does decide to beat you, you could not have a more honourable chastisement."

Joab beamed whilst even the usually unemotional Beniah looked happy.

"Now, I intend to question the prisoners to make sure we know where we are. Then, we'll send them under truce to the Philistines to come and retrieve the women. But only if they agree to an unchallenged safe passage."

At first, the Philistine prisoners were very surly and laughed in my face. "Do you think we would parley for damaged goods? Who wants ravished virgins for brides?"

Josh struck him in anger.

I called the women up. One, Phebe, was a distant kinsman of the prisoner. She berated him so much that we all felt sorry for the husband who would receive her. None the less, Phebe and Anna had a demeanour that no one could believe but that they were still maidens.

This changed the Philistines' attitude towards us considerably.

Achron, the oldest and whom Josh had struck said, "Sir, Captain. First I owe my sister and you an apology. It is not often in war that Israelite men behave with honour." Then, his voice cracked with bitterness. "Your valour is all around you. You and your men have shown you are mighty warriors, as mighty as your shepherd champion, David."

Joab could not contain himself. "Oh Philistine, do you not know you have been vanquished by David and his companions. This is the David who slew Goliath and we, his companions, bring a great trophy to our King Saul."

We all laughed at this and Eli said, "Young," and he emphasised young, "Joab has it right. We are all proud to be numbered amongst David's Companions."

That is how we earned the name and I have never found a reason to change it .

We arranged the truce and I gave them my instructions quickly. We found a deserted Amalekite village with good shade and water and awaited the return of Achron and the youth I had wounded.

Beniah asked whether I had any doubts about the Philistines keeping the truce.

I showed total confidence, "Beniah, despite their ignorance of God, I have learned in many ways they are honourable people. So, as Achron gave me his word and the young Moda also swore to defend us and ours until the truce is over, I think we can accept. Either way, we are only staying here two more days to allow our horses to recover and for Eli's arm to improve."

I must confess to being a little anxious on the morning of the third day. I thought that, perhaps, I had misjudged my man. As the day began to lengthen and we were preparing for the last leg home, we heard distant trumpets. Out of the morning gloom, rode, though dirty and dusty, a figure that I would know anywhere. Above his head, his armour bearer carried the white flag of truce.

Of course, it was Achish.

I advanced towards him, perhaps too eagerly, for Achish barked formally, "Hail, David, champion of Saul. You have done great damage to my people but you are an honourable warrior and therefore, in honour, I offer you a truce for a day and a night in return for our women, whom we learn you have protected as do civilised people."

I was not sure how to answer, and was irritated about the slur about not being civilised. But, as he alighted from his horse, I realised that I could show no fraternisation because, after all, our peoples were at war.

"King Achish, so now I must call you. We accept your honourable truce and I am happy that my Companions and I have been able to protect your ladies, whom we found lost on your highways." He gave me a grim smile at my attempted joke.

The sally over, I longed to embrace my friend but knew I could not.

Gravely I returned Anna and the other women to him.

Achron rode up and saluted all of us. "David and His Companions, I greet you as valiant foes and worthy of the praise of Dagon, who loves brave warriors. I thank you from my family that you protected our kinsmen and wish you farewell."

The parley was over. I shook first the hand of Achron, who was willing to return the embrace, thus allowing me to offer my hand to Achish, who in our embrace whispered, "Little brother, though I be a king, you are now a great commander and I am proud of you. Thank you for my new wife – she will remind me of you. Think well of your brother, Achish, and greet Prince Jonathan for me. Farewell."

I would have kept him longer but knew he had risked much already.

So, with formal salutes on both sides we turned our horses towards the east and home, while they swept away to the west and the Great Sea.

We were at Gilbeah within two days of hard riding. At our first sighting, the people who thought horsemen meant Philistines, fled. Lev would have been pleased.

We looked dreadful: unkempt and now all bearded. I was eager to return and lay down my command. My thoughts were so full of Merab that it helped to pull a veil over some of the horrors we had experienced.

We seven rode to the camp in a great gallop. I thought it best if Beniah did the honours. He walked up to Eban, who looked delighted to see us.

"I am Beniah, a Companion of David. I bring our Great King Saul 239 foreskins to burn on the altars of God and to celebrate another victory inspired by our Great King."

Men came running from everywhere.

Eban quickly went inside and returned in a short while, followed by the King, who looked surprised. Jonathan looked both amazed and delighted. Frankly, he, like the rest, had hardly expected us to return – let alone with so many trophies.

Beniah knelt before Saul and said, "Great King, I present to you the trophies of another great victory inspired by you, as David, your bard, led his Companions to achieve the dowry for your daughter."

I will never know what Saul really thought. I also wondered whether I ought to have given him more time to reassess our situation, but I was dreadfully tired and perhaps was not as careful as I might have been. Certainly the way the King, Jonathan and the men looked, they were still surprised and disbelieving at our more than twenty kills each. Of course we all felt proud.

"Is it truly you, my son?" said Saul, as I alighted from my horse and knelt before him.

"Great King, the Lord's Anointed. Your inspiration led my Companions and I to enter the land of your enemies at your instructions. We have slain more than 200 of your enemies. Great King, Father of Israel, I was made a captain by you and therefore must first report upon the valour of my Companions."

I couldn't keep the emotion from my voice. "Father, sadly four noble warriors of Israel now lie in the bosom of Abraham. Lev, Judah, Allot and Aaron are gone, but not before striking terrible blows for you and Israel. Great King, I am unworthy of this command because all these men have shown such valour that your Glory is enhanced before all peoples and especially in Philistia. If I had the power they would all be captains. If you grant me time to tell you of all their achievements, you will have as much pride in their valour and loyalty as I do."

This speech drew great applause and I meant every word of it. All had been heroic and had come through against terrible odds.

Saul drew me upright and declaimed, "this is My Bard and now, my Son, in whom I am well pleased. I stand here before all of Israel and call upon the Lord Almighty to witness that our inspiration transforms young warriors into veteran captains."

He threw out his arm towards my kneeling companions and declared, "Arise Captains, the Companions of David, my Bard and now my Son."

My heart leapt. I had no need to remind him of the reason behind this bizarre adventure. Now, I allowed myself to appreciate how crazy, how stupid I had been, and, surely without God's patience at my folly and His care, we should have all been in the bosom of Abraham.

I could not help myself. I know I was beaming, as my mind and my pulse beat in harmony. Merab, Merab, dearest Merab, you are to be mine.

As the King went to each of my Companions and embraced each in turn, I looked over to Jonathan, who was striding towards me.

I could not understand it: after his first delighted, welcoming look, he now appeared grave.

He embraced me and whispered, "What ever happens next, be grateful. Accept and say nothing."

I was confused what did he mean? I was soon to know.

The King called for silence. "Men of Israel, whilst I am King of Israel I am its servant, but a great joy is to reward loyal service to Israel and me. Be it known that David my bard is now a Prince of the House of Saul and will, tomorrow night, be joined in marriage to my daughter, Michal."

My mind froze. Saul was going on. I could not believe it. What did he mean? Michal? I loved Merab! I did not even like Michal and worse, she had never shown any liking for me. For God's sake, she was a shrew.

I dimly realised that Saul had stopped speaking. Whether he noticed my stunned look or not, it did not matter.

Jonathan proclaimed to me and the men around. "I, Jonathan, will this morrow eve lead my beloved sister, Michal, to the bed of my brother, David bar Jesse. We shall have a great feast at my expense and we will celebrate the marriage promised by the King, my father."

Everyone seemed to be cheering. From every corner, my companions and I were cheered, clapped and hugged as Jonathan moved again towards me.

Taking me in his arms, he whispered, "David, this is still a time of congratulations. You have a king's daughter. Merab was married to King of Kir last month."

He sensed my stiffening anger but he held me firm. "David, be grateful. Use your wisdom – a youngest son marrying the King's daughter? Michal is comely and intelligent. I congratulate you. I hope you will allow me the honour of sponsoring her."

The King again called for silence and asked me, "So, David my Son, how think you of our royal acknowledgement of your Companions achievements?"

I could say nothing except bow the knee and mutter something about not being worthy.

My heart was breaking.

Beniah had watched with growing fascination how David had grown into command. He marvelled at the apparently easy way he took on the role of captain. He politely, but firmly, indicated what he wanted, whilst at the same time, men older and more experienced, as well as boyhood friends, seemed to find it quite natural to be led by an eighteen-year-old. This was evidence of something Beniah had also recognised in Saul and Jonathan: David was a natural leader.

From the first, he had been attracted to David because of his sharp intelligence. More important was the speed of his thought, which enabled him to take in things so quickly. Initially, this lay at the root of his occasional impetuosity. This was not driven by mere youthful pride, but his quick ability to see things as they were. Even when, in his early innocence – for example, the feud with Canan – he had somehow turned it to his advantage. And, just as important, he learned from the experience.

Beniah smiled to himself when he acknowledged that one of David's most attractive features was the subtle sympathy that he had developed with himself. Not many grasped Beniah's quiet, perceptive gift of understanding people. Yet this showed up in a remarkable maturity in David finding just the right word or phrase to communicate sensitively, just as he always seemed able to find just the right word for the other person.

Beniah felt, like the rest of Israel, that David's challenge to Goliath was going to be a worthy inspiring sacrifice, though he half sensed that David had a special knowledge. Beniah's blood ran cold, as for the first time he understood that David felt he had a special mission, which he guessed that others sensed, for some had said that David walked with God. He wondered, "but at what cost to David's peace of mind?" This could be observed in David's eyes, which were already too far seeing.

Beniah shuddered for his Companion because, whilst he admired him beyond any other man of his generation, occasionally, David sometimes showed he was still a youth. Could he go on bearing these apparently self-inflicted strains without breaking?

Beniah was not especially religious, though liked to contemplate the world around him. He was far more intrigued by his fellow men and their motivations that were discernible and which he could assess for himself. However, he readily appreciated that many situations did not have rational explanations. Beniah almost begrudgingly recognised that he probably would never have a religious experience, but felt sympathy for those who did. Though he could not help but observe that the claims of those knowing God, often went hand-in-hand with particular, more-earthly interests.

Even so, Beniah knew that he was fascinated by politics, by the accretion and use of power – not that he would ever seek to lead: he lacked that certain ruthlessness, or the fierce inner individualism, which went with leadership. But he knew himself to be an ideal deputy.

He pondered over what he had learned from the campaign. Beniah realised that David would be a major power in the land. It seemed inevitable and obvious to many though, oddly enough, not yet to David himself.

Beniah was honest: he wanted to follow this new power to see where it led.

He was not an emotional man. He knew some thought him cold and too logical, but he was moved how, throughout the campaign, whilst David was obviously distressed at the realities of war, he had kept his control and helped others to keep theirs.

On at least three occasions, Beniah had expected David to crack – but he hadn't! No, not even at the greatest crisis of the last battle.

Certainly, David was emotionally and intellectually exhausted and, with his high nervous energy, this was not surprising. Yet David had avoided blaming Eli for not checking that there were no other enemy patrols about. It should have been obvious that the Philistines would have had a whole war party, but Eli allowed the excitement to get to him and that had imperilled them all. Yet David deflected any implied criticism on to himself and, though he was greatly distressed at their losses, he had not criticised Eli.

Interestingly, Beniah mused, Saul and Abner would have been the quickest to blame others – though not Jonathan, again parallels and differences struck him. Some might think that David was too emotional, too sensitive, but it was that nervous, sensitive, highly strung intelligence which made up a large part of his creativity. Strange – on reflection, Beniah saw similarities with Saul, though knew David would be amazed to think that they had anything in common. However, Beniah thought grimly that the once sensitive and youthful David had, like the rest of them, been tempered in the iron heat of war. David could now say "no prisoners" without an apparent qualm.

Then the greatest act of self-control: learning that his bride was not to be his beloved Merab but the scold Michal! Beniah saw an astute politician at work in David's submission to the King. It was as masterly as was his binding the Companions to him forever in his generous speech before the whole camp. Yet, Beniah was quite sure that David was not yet consciously 'political' but responded to the situation around him, especially to the emotions aroused.

Beniah mused, had the speech been disingenuous – or was it calculated? Perhaps David was simply a natural, yet he felt sure that David had matured because he had given himself impossible odds. The new David, after all the lessons he had learned on the campaign, would never again allow his heart to rule his head.

Beniah summed up the situation. David was still enthusiastic, but he had learned important lessons from his first command and from his experience of the mean-mindedness of the world, where great and not so great men showed themselves puny in their spite. How much had it scarred this young hero? Yes, Beniah thought, as yet they were just scars – not wounds, which would continue to fester and which men in power have to learn to bear. For as in war, one has to get in one's blow in first, so that others bear the hurt. He is not yet damaged enough to be cynical, but he is tougher than he was, and the change was there for all to see.

Then Beniah allowed himself a final thought. Who could have believed the entire venture was possible? He was a careful man, yet he had found himself being swept along by the spirit of David. Suddenly, Beniah felt cold. David had greatness, but the words of Lev came back to him. Lev was the "first to die for David". Beniah suddenly knew that, before the story was fulfilled, many others would die for David – and gladly, too. But would it be the same idealistic David of the fast-growing legend?

Grimly he told himself, for better or worse, he was bound to David for the rest of his days – and he knew there would not be many quiet ones.

Chapter Sixteen

The Outlaw

Michal

I was in a daze for the next day and a half. After all the strain of the campaign, I could hardly think straight. A later discussion with Jonathan explained Saul's rationale for giving Merab to King of Kir. It sounded fine if one thought of people – even women – as mere chattels to be bought and exchanged for policy, but Merab and I had feelings for each other. Jonathan listened but did not seem to grasp what I felt. I resented being used. That was what Saul was doing.

I did not quite understand the politics but, on the other hand, I was confident that Saul really liked me. I also realised that somehow I was useful to him in his subtle but still half-hidden struggle with Samuel.

I was cleaned and gowned. In other circumstances, I suppose I would have felt proud at how I looked. I tried to be cheerful with my Companions, who were to be second sponsors to Jonathan. The King had given them chains of victory. They were wearing their captain's insignia and, though not yet been given a troop of their own, that would only be a matter of time.

Joab, however, was a little cross because he would not be made a captain until next year because of his age. He wisely had allowed himself to be guided by Beniah and was being patient.

I had to endure the inevitable pre-marriage jokes and, as all the Companions except Joab already had wives, they claimed to be experts. Hushai and Hitophel went on about what to do with rebellious wives – though, looking at their marriages, it seemed they were not taking their own advice.

The trouble was all my friends remembered my earlier conversations when, in praising Merab, I foolishly had expressed sympathy for Michal's future husband. I'd said, "Only the Great Pharaoh would be good enough to satisfy her pride."

Inevitably, the evening came around and I stood, adorned as the bridegroom, waiting at the entrance to the canopy. Where, I thought bitterly, I was to join my beloved eager wife. My thoughts could not help but recall Michal's obvious dismay at the prospect of my union with her house. I tried to console myself that other men married wives whom they had not even seen. I confess to thinking of delaying matters by waiting to ask for my father's permission but Jonathan counselled against and his amused look did not make me feel any better.

The horns sounded, the music played and Saul led Michal by the hand towards me.

My heart stopped. She was ravishingly beautiful. She was clothed in pure white with magical silver braids through her dress that flashed light as she walked. She was magnificent! Every man's eyes were taken with her as she strode proudly with her father. She was every inch ... a princess!

Despite my previous glum thoughts, I would have had to be made of stone not to begin to feel excited at the prospects before me.

But, when the King handed her hand to mine, she flashed me a look of such superiority and contempt that made me think I had seen friendlier looks on the face of enemies. I wished I could be anywhere rather than where I was.

The ceremony went on, followed by interminable speeches from the King, the priests who waited upon Saul, the various elders and then, finally, Jonathan.

Michal, now my wife, sat as still as a rock next to me. As a friendly gesture I had moved my hand to hers. I might have been a scorpion as she snatched hers away.

What was I going to do? I really did not think a good beating would get us very far in the long run. If we were going to live together, having war in the hearth is hardly conducive to a lifetime of harmony.

So there we sat – miserable, the pair of us. I felt so despondent that I did not even drink much and Michal, I noticed, not at all. The result was the worst of all situations: you are cold sober but surrounded by people made happy and expansive by wine in your honour.

My thoughts were elsewhere when I sensed Michal's body stiffen sharply. I heard the words of Jonathan tell the company that now was the time to escort the Princess, his sister, and David, his brother, to the bridal chamber.

He held a brimming wine goblet up in the air. "May the seeds of our two families plant a tree that will be a support for Israel forever."

This toast gained great applause as I glumly thought, well I suppose I am willing, but is she?

It was terrible. We were alone at last but for ten minutes she remained silent. Finally, I said, "Michal, I know you – "

She interrupted me and snapped, "I am Princess Michal, daughter of the King. At the orders of my father, I obeyed and you are my husband but you are never to forget who I am and who you were."

We were at loggerheads. Her remark had made me very angry – so angry I did not say anything. We fell into a stony silence which endured almost an hour, making mockery of the loud celebrations coming from outside.

There was nothing else for it. "Princess," and I stressed the "Princess", "we are man and wife. This is our marriage night. You have to prove yourself in the morning so I think we should go to bed."

She gasped and looked at me in sheer terror. Then the thought struck me: of course, she is shy! I am her first lover. Recognising the first human trait in her, I felt a slight sympathy, appreciating that I would have to be very gentle with her.

So, with no more ado I blew out the lamp and began to undress.

At first she did not move. Then I sensed she was removing her dress and could just dimly see her lovely shape outlined in the darkness. By this time, I had completely stripped off. My senses led me and I moved towards her. Ever so gently, I touched her smooth, naked shoulders. She froze and I backed away.

"Princess, do not get cold. Let us rest upon the bed."

I passed in front of her. I was careful not to let my now erect member touch her. I simply lay quietly and awaited her.

She first sat down and then lay her full length upon the bed. I was so close to her, I could feel the warmth of her body. Her sweet fragrance began to please me and then infatuate me. I leaned towards her and she went rigid but allowed my hand to flow over her back. I realised that she was crying softly and would not be comforted. Her whole demeanour was such that she soon reduced my adoration to nothing!

We lay like that for ages and, to my intense irritation, not once did she relent. So, wondering whether I had done the right thing and that perhaps later she would relax, I said coldly, "Good night, Princess," and drew the coverlets over us. I turned my back to her and angrily sought escape in sleep, fighting down my feelings of bitterness at this mockery of a marriage.

I drifted off to sleep and wondered whether I dreaming of the warm, slender body curled up against mine. Was a delicate, small, smooth hand really at my phallus? Whatever, it quickly brought him erect. I moaned with pleasure in my dream until –

Suddenly, I was wide awake with Michal's warm body next to mine. I slowly turned to her and wisely said nothing to break the dream state as my lips sought hers. She accepted my touch, before slowly answering my gentle urgings to share our tongues. I had held myself back from her until this moment but now gently moved my body to hers. To my joy, her hand went to my hardness. I slowly let my fingers find her secret garden.

At first, she leaned away and I felt the tension return. Avoiding the temptation to take her by storm, with one hand I caressed her wondrous breasts, whose hard nipples triggered spasms of expectation in me. In harmony, I slowly caressed her moistening loveliness. I leaned into her and, to my increasing excitement, she lay back and stretched her legs. I entwined my limbs around hers and, leading with my finger, slowly eased into her in one movement, past the gasp of pain and tension. Then my phallus followed where my finger had been and I lay inside her, full but motionless.

I eased myself up and my lips found hers. As she opened her mouth, our tongues joined and I began to ride to a climax. Wondrously, as if a dam had given way, she engulfed me. Her arms clung to my back as if she would press me even deeper into her. Her hips thrust upward to meet my engorged, descending hardness. For a few moments, we were both captivated by our accelerating passions and then, with a cry, she reached a trembling climax as I let go my hot, sharp-sweet seed.

For a moment, we were as one.

Then, the delightful languor swept over us that has a completeness that makes us glimpse at immortality.

I lay inside her and began to think of a second climax. But, to my surprise and disappointment, she moved from me, making slight sounds of disgust.

She hissed, "Don't say a word. I have done my duty. They will have my proofs in the morning."

I was astonished. I felt used – besmirched. Was that all she was thinking of – to stain our bridal sheets with a virgin's blood? When, for a little while, I thought she might love me and that our early conflict had been a misunderstanding, had I been so completely wrong?

She turned over and moved as far from me as possible, leaving me feeling rejected.

This would surely undermine any willingness to forget how my love had been snatched from me and replaced by her shrewish changeling.

When Michal had heard that Merab was to marry King of Kir and not

David, she tried to contain her rising hopes. She despised the attraction she had long felt for him, whom she contemptuously called "the shepherd". She had always been jealous of Merab's ability to evoke kindness and tenderness from others. She knew that she was as beautiful as her sister was, but Michal always found fault with people and made it plain that she did not suffer fools gladly – and she considered most to be fools.

Michal had always felt out of things. Only with beloved Jonathan did she let her longings be seen. She idolised him as he refused to respond to her self-defeating sharpness. He made her laugh and brought out her gentleness, as well as her undoubted intelligence, which would have surprised all who knew her. She had always been conscious that she was a daughter of the King. The only slight flaw in her hero, Jonathan, was that he did not demand proper respect. Ruefully, she regretted not being a man. Not just because men commanded, but because she was more intelligent than most men were. Her perspicacity was seen as unwomanly and her interest in politics was considered shocking.

She would have willingly been married to the King of Kir – not because she was in love with him. He was far too old. She wanted to be the wife of a king and help to rule.

The daily prayer of the men of Israel was an affront to her: "I thank thee God for making me a man". No amount of gentle care and protection this gave women could erase the humiliation of being little higher than the best cattle.

Yet she was honest enough to admit to herself that she would rather marry David, as he was the only man, except Jonathan, who seemed to have any vision. Angrily, she fought the feeling that David was very comely.

When her father told her of his decision and, as he sometimes did, talked about his reasons, he gave tacit recognition to her natural understanding of politics. Her heart sang at Saul's hesitant suggestion that if David came back with only fifty trophies, there would be great merit in me being seen to be forgiving, for I value him greatly.

Her father believed David was bound for greatness and, since his slaying of Goliath, he had become an omen – a symbol for Israel and his Kingship.

Of course, in spite of her secret feelings, she expressed her proud disdain at the idea: the King's daughter marrying a "shepherd". Yet she was quick to interject that, whatever "the King, my father, thinks best, I am his to command".

None the less, she had worked herself up to feel that, publicly, she was being perceived as second best. No matter how hard David tried to hide his disappointment at her father's offer, she knew that, yet again, Merab had his love. The covert smirks of David's friends almost announced to the

374

world that she was considered a shrew. So be it, she angrily concluded.

The marriage ceremony was agony for her. She fought her excitement at the thought of being alone with David against the sense of being invaded, possessed, owned and belittled.

She breathed a sigh of relief that, when at last they were alone, he had not been savage as she knew men could often be.

When she saw his silhouetted nakedness, she ached for him. But her fearsome pride stifled any response to his tenderness, so that when he spurned her, which she knew she deserved, she felt doubly humiliated.

As David fell into a light sleep, her thoughts raced. How would she feel in the morning when there would be no virgin blood on the sheets to display? How would she face him in the daylight? She drew closer to his body. She could feel his warmth as she let her hand gently caress his smooth, frighteningly firm body, which both repelled and urgently attracted.

She cruelly suppressed the warmth she kept feeling, as her thoughts conjured up the delight of him exploring her body, of his tongue caressing her breasts and then ...

Oh joy! She knew he was aware of her. Her hand traced his manhood, which simultaneously thrilled and appalled her. How could she receive him –this! – into her, but oh, she longed to be filled by him.

When he turned to her, she almost choked with delight at his gentleness, which she knew covered a vibrant strength. Her downy softness yearned to be in harmony with his silken, sinewy vigour that caused feelings of fire to engulf her body.

The moment came. She could not help herself. The tension returned as he leaned into her.

Oh God, no one had told her of the sharp tearing.

Then, he slowly, exquisitely filled her moistness. All her body centred upon this flooding, engorged warmth. Her spirit cried out in ecstasy as she knew she loved this gentle, diffident, valiant, noble man, whose possession of her would make every maid in Israel jealous.

She rode with his passion. Could this be real? A glowing, exploding warmth filled her every fibre with delight, to be followed by a sweet exhaustion as if she dissolved in velvet water. In her wildest imagining, she had never thought it could be so good as this.

She lay motionless, thanking God. Then, in a gesture that she knew she would regret for ever, she tersely reminded her love of her "position". Oh yes, she loved him. Only she dare not, could not, must not show him, lest she lose herself for ever.

Poor, sad princess. She did not grasp that love is the abandonment of self in a delight of sacrifice, each to the other.

So she turned away, secreting the moment close to her soul that yearned to transform his seed into his child.

Yet her pride had declared, at best, an armed neutrality, which, hopelessly, she knew would cost them both dearly.

Saul's Attack

I never really understood Michal. There were times when I could have really loved her, for she was intelligent and, on rare moments, she could be charming and very loving. At these times, it was she who would be gentle. Yet, if I ever failed to be totally considerate, she became completely impossible.

I tried on a number of occasions to speak of the prospects for our love. Sometimes, in the deep of the night, her hands and lips would surprise me and we would have wonderful lovemaking. But she insisted on keeping this side of our marriage separate from any emotion. Yet, as we shall see, she gave me absolute proof that her thoughts were first for me, despite telling me almost daily that "she was the daughter of the King."

Later in the year, it was decided that Jonathan, with me as his second in command, would take a division of five thousand men and undertake month-long raids into Philistia. We recognised that the Philistines had not yet recovered from the battle at Elah, as there continued to be suspicion between their kings. This gave us an opportunity to remind them of the dignity of Israel and to train the men in our new tactics.

The Companions, Beniah, Hitophel, Hushai, Josh, Eli and Joab, each now had a company. Moreover, my other captains claimed the right to be known as my Companions, so there were now thirty of them. However, I still had much to learn and Jonathan gave me a gift beyond price: Ura the Hittite, his second in command, was to be my deputy.

At first, neither Ura nor I wanted this but Jonathan argued that, as the King's son-in-law, I would soon be commanding a division of the army. Ura was best placed to assist me to prepare for an independent command. Ura was wonderfully honest and said he would rather serve Jonathan as a body servant than be a deputy army commander to anyone else.

"Even to you, David, whom you know I love and respect, but Jonathan is my captain."

Of course, Jonathan had his way because his argument was overwhelming. Ura had experience of organising a large body of men – I had not.

So Jonathan pleaded with Ura. "Look after my brother, dear Ura. You brought him to me, you taught him the basics, without which he would have been crow's meat. Ura, he needs you. Please, my friend, become a Companion and make sure that they don't make too many mistakes."

Ura had to agree. "Well, I suppose these Bethlehemite hard cases still have a thing or two to learn, but I have a request for David."

Of course, I offered to grant him without knowing what it was: "if it's in my power."

Ura said, "I have a brother, only two years younger than you, Uriah, a bit serious like you. Can he join you? I'll guarantee to knock him into shape. After all, I haven't done such a bad job with you, now I think of it."

What could I say? After all, Uriah was no younger than Joab.

"Ura, I am honoured. I feel that having two Hittites amongst the Companions will make us invincible – I know you're too modest to declare that yourself!"

With laughter all round, it was settled and Uriah enrolled.

Uriah could not have been more different from Ura. He was a very handsome youth, taller than me, dark-skinned like most Hittites, with superb physique. But he was without an ounce of humour – serious way beyond his years. It was obvious even then, he was a young man for whom duty and honour were paramount. After Jonathan, he was perhaps the bravest warrior I ever fought with. But, oh, he was dour!

Over the next two years, Jonathan and I led either half or whole divisions into the land of the Philistines. We always came away victorious, despite their finally appointing Zera, King of Ashkelon, as their High King.

In many ways, these were the happiest two years of my life. I was learning from Israel's greatest commander, who was also my friend and lover, yet I did not have to carry that dread burden of overall command.

Jonathan was the soul of honour and integrity. Hence, when we were on duty in the field, he felt that one of us should always be available to our captains. Of course, he was right and I felt guilty on the rare occasions that I could argue that there would be benefit in allowing one of the Companions to be in command, with Ura as his deputy, to give them the necessary experience. Jonathan's smiling acceptance thrilled me because he knew that my arguments were a kind of seduction to which he was happy to succumb. Though, of course, I always considered the situation before making the offer, otherwise, no matter how much Jonathan loved me, he would never imperil his command.

So our stolen moments together were always exciting, sometimes characterised by the highest passionate climaxes. At other times, we enjoyed a gentle, mutual solace that gave balm to our souls and bodies.

Lev would have been thrilled because we began to extend our use of horses and, with the use of saddle and stirrups, our warriors quickly became good horsemen.

We did not have many horses, and the lack of good bows and arrows was still a problem. Nevertheless, we were able to trade with the Phoenicians and, of course, make up any shortfall from the Philistines. Thus, almost half our command, two and a half thousand men, were trained as horse archers and slingers.

Of course, the Philistines adapted and, on their terrain, we could not match their cavalry, not least because of their numbers. With our slings, though, our men had become highly mobile heavy infantry and could therefore do the job of both infantry and cavalry. Thus, we maintained our advantage whenever the numbers were fairly even.

Jonathan was thrilled by the birth of a son, Mephib, but, a year after his birth, he had an accident and it was realised that the boy would never walk properly. Jonathan took the news calmly but I could see it hurt him. Of course, he would have other sons in time.

He was too thoughtful to ask about Michal not yet giving me a child. He knew she and I made love frequently. Though, perhaps, not as often as I would have wished as she had some notion of improving my strength of seed, but of course I never forced myself upon her. Poor Michal, she was so desperate for a child, though I never blamed her for her barrenness, every time her month came round she was best avoided.

My relations with the King, whilst friendly on the surface, worried me. I felt that no matter how much I tried, we were drifting apart. Everything I did or said was perversely miscast and misunderstood. My successes against the Philistines were either sneeringly belittled or, in a convoluted piece of logic, made to sound disloyal. My playing, which would soothe him one day, would be transposed the next either as an inference of weakness or, worse, that my muse was somehow a cause of his occasional sharp melancholy.

Jonathan tried to ignore it.

Michal, shrewdly and loyally, blamed the influence of Abner. "He would have been King in my father's place. He calls himself the Second Man in Israel and my father is content to let him. You and Jonathan are fools not to know he is your enemy. All know that my brothers Isscanue, Malki and Ishboth should have been women. If ever something happened to Jonathan – please, the Living God, that it will not – but if it did, then Abner would seek an accommodation with Samuel and the priests."

I did not like Michal's analysis and I would remonstrate with her that these matters were not for women. At such times we were bitter towards each other and she called me a fool, which in many households would have led to a beating. I persevered because, though she invariably took a negative view of the motives of people, she was often very accurate.

Sadly, I learned that where there is power, there quickly follow jealousy, deceit and manoeuvrings in pursuit of personal ends. Some would even trample on the rights and needs of Israel for some slight advantage or trivial title.

The crisis broke when I played for Saul at his sixtieth birthday and my forthcoming twenty-first. I was called to him. We were by ourselves and I could see he was irritable and had a dark mood upon him.

"Have you enemies, son of Jesse, the King's bard?"

I was worried by this kind of question, which had become more frequent recently.

He went on. "I have enemies. I did not seek them, but my glory becomes an affront to them."

I offered to play but he curtly said "no".

"Are you jealous of my glories, David?" Before I could answer, he shook his hand angrily at me. He wanted no discussion.

"Whom do you serve? Oh, I know you will say, 'after the Lord, your King'. Is that so?"

I tried to interject, but he wouldn't let me.

"You will answer when I say so, young man. You are getting beyond yourself. Do you know, David bar Jesse, you are becoming quite conceited?"

He paused, frowned and looked very troubled. He kept turning his head as if he was looking for someone or could hear something.

"I know Jonathan loves you more than he should. He always takes your part and you his – no, don't interrupt: your honeyed words simply confuse me. Silence. I want to think straight."

Saul seemed to be struggling to express himself. "Your babbling ... Yes, your babbling breaks up my thoughts, so no words."

I was now afraid but did not dare disobey him, so I quietly knelt before him.

"Have you been speaking to the Old Man? I am surrounded by his priests. He sends them ostensibly as his messengers, but I know they are spies. I am spied upon everywhere."

There was a long silence.

"The kings of Philistia have great respect for me. There is some talk of an alliance, or at least, a long truce. The damned priests do not want it but they do no fighting. It is I who risk my body for the Lord. I, the King and servant of Israel, have no peace, no sleep. Do you sleep, David?"

Then he laughed and was quite crude. "I doubt not that my daughter, Michal, gives you little peace in the night until you have given her due. I have seen her looking at you. She would devour you if she could. What made you ever think of Merab? She was nothing to that fiery one. Ah, she is her father's daughter. Michal should have been a man. But even there your slyness has undermined her loyalty – as you have with Jonathan."

This was too much.

"Great King, my Father. You do Jonathan and Michal great wrong. They are devoted to you before all others. It has always been so and will always be so. Anyone saying otherwise is a traitor to you and yours."

He did not answer but glared at me.

I went to pick up my harp but he nodded his shaggy head, and muttered, "I do not sleep. I hear no comfortable words. My spirit is disturbed."

He stood up and walked around agitatedly. He kept turning his head as if anxiously he expected to see someone. Then, walking over to where his weapons were, he seized a spear and, with terrible deliberation, took aim at me.

My blood froze. My thoughts raced. He slowly drew back his arm ...

I did not wait but sprang to one side as the spear flew through the air. I parried it with my harp as I threw myself backwards and out of the door, rolling passed the startled Eban. I did not need to look back at the spear, shuddering in the ground where I had been sitting.

I ran to Jonathan and told him what had happened. He looked very grave at the news.

I pleaded with him not to go immediately to the King, but to wait as long as possible in the hope that the mood would pass. He saw the wisdom of this but decided to consult with Eban – not least to ensure that he was aware of what had happened and, hopefully, keep the King secure from anyone else.

I returned home and told Michal what had happened.

She was wonderfully cool and without wasting time asking for details said, "His black fit has returned. I've no doubt that is what is clouding his judgement – that and the poison that Abner slowly feeds him. Oh, he's clever that Abner. A word here and there does not seem too hostile. He knows that when my poor father's black mood returns, those planted weeds come to the surface."

I was amazed at her understanding and was moved at her sympathy for her father. Now my fear had passed, I realised that he was moon-smitten. Though madness in a king was very dangerous for all, especially me.

Then she totally surprised me. "I don't know how or why, but he fears ... no, he knows that you will be King some day. I know I was born to be the wife of a king – he knows that too. But David, my husband, we have to preserve you. Remember, the moods do pass. I think it's time for you to visit your family in Bethlehem – until you can return safely."

That seemed an eminently good suggestion but we were interrupted by Jonathan. He had come to tell us that the King had settled and, after drinking much, Eban thought Saul would not stir again for some time.

Jonathan counselled against my leaving Gilbeah. "That will make it look as if you have something to be guilty about. But Michal is right: the mood will pass. Wait till then. I will see him and have you reconciled."

It seemed we could do no more.

After four days, all could feel the tension in Gilbeah. Jonathan was called for and I learned that he had made a great appeal on my behalf.

Jonathan told me, "David, there was something very different about him. He looked sly – that's not my Father. He's not afraid to say what he feels, but he looked as if he is formulating a plan. However, he will see you tomorrow, but we'd better go together. I don't need to tell you: be very careful."

As Jonathan had said, I was escorted into the King.

I passed the anxious eyes of Eban, who whispered as I went by, "I do hope you can bring him to himself again, David. God give you the wisdom – but be careful."

Saul, at first glance, seemed to be himself but, as Jonathan had described, there was something very cagey about his behaviour. This created an atmosphere of caution that I realised would feed back into his suspicions because we all reacted to him in a circumspect way.

He did not refer to his assault upon me other than to say that he had forgiven my misunderstanding. In two nights' time he was going to arrange a feast to celebrate my twenty-first birthday. That seemed to please everyone but we all were relieved to be dismissed by him, although he did it pleasantly enough.

Less reassuringly was the presence of Abner at his side who said not a word throughout the fairly short interview.

As Michal prepared for my feast, she became involved in a series of events that were to save my life and change hers for ever. Late that night, she happened to be visiting her father's quarters when she overheard the King issuing instructions to Naan, the captain of his guard.

Saul was addressing Naan in an almost conspiratorial tone and was ordering him to make arrangements for my "execution as a traitor".

She had to endure the agony of waiting for Jonathan and me to return from a hunting trip.

She came to me looking serious and quietly excited. "David, he has planned to kill you! No, don't ask how I know – I know. There is very little

381

time. It is planned for either tonight or early dawn tomorrow. I don't know for certain but he may also have made plans to ensure you won't escape earlier, so do not go to Samuel at Rammah as he has probably posted guards in that direction."

She saw my look of surprise. She calmly explained she had thought it all out.

"Of course, where better might you get protection? Even the King would have to be careful there. No, don't go to Samuel but you do need some sanctuary. So go to the Ark at Nob – the priest, Amlech, is friendly to you. If you appeal to him, I am sure he will let you enter the outer tent and seek sanctuary. I will delay them by saying you have been taken sick."

She looked straight at me. "Now go! There's no time for delay."

Her calmness and the import of what she was saying overwhelmed me. Most women – and many men, too – would have collapsed in such a situation. For a moment my response to her was such that I almost forgot how difficult and dangerous my situation had become.

"Michal, I am amazed. You put me before your Father?"

She looked at me coldly and said, "Of course I do. I love you, you fool!"

Her eyes filled with tears that she had been striving to hold back. I melted before her. Overwhelmed by the fact that she had never expressed any sentiment towards me – let alone love.

I moved towards her and took her gently into my arms, "Michal. Dear Michal. I shall remember this moment for ever. You have done me great honour and I cherish your love." To seal the moment I closed her mouth with kisses.

She clung to me passionately – so tightly, that both our senses were aroused and I would have made love to her there and then.

She pushed me back. "Dearest David. No, that you know I love you is enough. I have always loved you and I always will."

As I tried to re-engage with her, she held me at bay. "No, we have no time for that – though you fill me with such delight." I saw that she was blushing but she went on. "I know I have not been easy, and could not hold it against you if you did not yet love me like you dreamed of loving Merab. But enough! Go now and grant me the peace to know that you will be safe. Soon we can try again to give you the son I long for."

We embraced and, snatching up the little food and the wineskin she had organised, I fled into the darkness of the night.

What happened then was remarkable. Michal let it be known that I was sick and had taken to my bed. She filled the bed with clothes, shaped into the form of man's body, and placed a melon at the top for my head. In the daytime it would not have fooled anyone but it was good enough in the dim lamplight. Whether Naan was deceived by the protesting Michal, we shall never know, but he returned to the King with the news, which gave me invaluable time.

Next morning, Naan and a file of guards returned to complete his instructions. He was now "to kill David the traitor wherever he lay".

Great was the confusion and rage when they found, not a sleeping David, but an ingenious dummy.

The bird had flown!

The Anointing

Michal was brought before a furious Saul, who berated her for her "treachery". Wisely, she protested her innocence, claiming that I had threatened to kill her and that I had planned the escape with her as an unwilling helper. As she had anticipated, Saul immediately ordered a patrol to be sent out to look for me towards Rammah. If they should find me, they were not to bring me back for trial because I had been weighed by the King himself. As a traitor, I should die immediately, wherever they found me.

Fortunately, as Jonathan genuinely knew nothing about the escape, he was able to convince his father that he had had no part in it. Moreover, he had a very unexpected witness: Abner.

Jonathan had been with him trying to see if there was some way through which the differences between them could be patched up. As others had been present and witnessed their meeting, Abner was a reluctant attestant to Jonathan's innocence. Wisely, at that point, Jonathan did not speak of reconciliation for it was obvious that Saul had become unhinged.

Jonathan's previous words to me, spoken with harrowing sadness, had proved prophetic. "Madness in an ordinary man is tragic, but madness in the great places all in danger."

This echoed through my brain as I sped away, suddenly feeling frightened for those I was leaving behind. As the journey lengthened and I saw no sign of pursuit behind me, I began to think over what had happened. Why had I failed to ease Saul's mood as I had in the past? Was it as Michal had suggested: that the accumulative whisperings of Abner had undermined our former trust, which was now converted it into a terrible indictment of treachery?

I began to feel angry. I had never been disloyal to Saul – not even in my secret soul. My love for Jonathan and Saul, who when himself was a great King, were barriers to any hostile thought. I would still die for them and Israel if called upon to do so. But after risking what I had, I would not have been human if I did not feel that I deserved better from Saul and, naturally,

I began to feel very sorry for myself.

As the enormity of the break between Saul and me became clearer, I could see no way out. There was a hideous vacuum in front of me. If my attempt to serve honestly ended in his attempts to kill me, where could I go? What could I do?

As I rode on, I dared not think of God, whom I began to feel had played me as falsely as He had Saul. In the darkness, I reckoned it safer to halt somewhere lest I lose my way. As if to mock my growing despair, neither the stars nor the moon accompanied me on my desperate flight and I began to feel desolate. Thoughts of life-long exile, or a treacherous death with every man's hand against me, sent me into an almost wild panic. I hated everything. I could take no joy in the stillness of the wilderness. The words of poor Agag came to me. Now I understood his sense of desolation – rejected by all men, alone, betrayed by his God.

My soul silently let fall my tearful prayer.

"My God, my God, why art thou so far from helping me and from the words of my roaring.

Oh my God I cry in the daytime and Thou hearest not and in the night-time I am not silent."

As my soul prayed, my body's fear became my total reality.

"I am a worm and no man: a reproach of men and despised of the people.

All they that see me laugh me to scorn.

I am poured out like water and all my bones are out of joint my heart is like wax, it is melted in the middle of my bowels.

My strength is dried up like a potsherd and my tongue cleaveth to my jaws, thou hast brought me into the dust of death."

Now my soul looked into the chasm of desolation. I was empty. I was nothing. I was blown away like dead grass. I was nothing more than dust in the wind.

Yet, from out of this emptiness came a trickle of hope: a slow inspiration began to buoy up my desperate spirits as, from out of nothingness, came the memory of whom I served. Of He who had held me in His hands and would not desert me as the words were poured into my mind.

"But thou art holy, Oh thou that inhabitest the praises of Israel. Our fathers trusted in thee and thou didst deliver them.

The meek shall eat and be satisfied, they shall praise the Lord that seek Him, your heart shall live for ever."

I again recalled Agag and his dread but magnificent secret: that all the peoples are the Lord's and "there's no difference between us".

"All the ends of the world shall remember and turn unto the Lord and All the Kindreds of the nations shall worship before thee.
For the kingdom is the Lord's and He is governor amongst the nations."

I could not explain how my despair had been eased. I did not seek to analyse it. Perhaps when the depths are reached, then out of the soul's despair, bereft of all humane assistance, it is only to Him one can turn and, in total submission, await the unfolding of His plan.

Though alone, I now felt comforted. In obedience to His will, I slept and awoke at dawn with renewed energy.

I was in Nob late the following day to be greeted by a very anxious looking Amlech, the priest of the Ark. His son, Abathar, was more welcoming but whether Amlech knew of the split between Saul and me, who knows?

He was very suspicious of why I was alone without guards or companions. I told him I was on a secret unexpected mission for the King and that I was going north to meet the elders but, in my haste, I had lost the sack of provisions from my horse.

Amlech said, "Prince David, that is difficult. We cannot help you as we have no food."

I could see his son look askance at this very unhelpful response.

"Amlech the priest, I am claiming your hospitality by right as a traveller, by the right of your priestly duty and my right of being the King's messenger. How can you say you have no food?"

The pompous fool had the audacity to argue that the only food they had had been consecrated for use at the altar and for the priests. I was furious and it showed, but I dared not do a sacrilegious act.

Then I had an idea. "Amlech, it is your time to guard the Ark but what permanent holy object have you here for the glory of God and of Israel?"

"You know well, Prince David. Here hangs the sword of the Philistine, Goliath, whom you slew, as a trophy for all time to show that God is not mocked."

"Exactly – whom I slew. Now, sir priest, I have need of both sword and bread in the name of God, whose holy name I would not mock. So, in His service I claim your hospitality and aid."

"Father, Prince David has more call upon the sword and the consecrated bread than any man in Israel. We should give it to him and tell the King that we acted justly," broke in Abathar.

By this time our words and my presence had aroused the whole compound. Dozens of the priests who attend the Tent of the Ark and its altar were now milling around, curious about what was happening. So, with slightly better grace, Amlech brought out five loaves of consecrated bread and sent Abathar for the sword.

I restrained my keen hunger for a little longer, but took Goliath's sword reverently. It was heavy, magnificent weapon and I drew it from its sheath.

I waved it above my head and cried, "Priests of Nob, guardians of the Tent of the Ark and its altar. See, here is the sword of Goliath, whom I slew in the name of God for the honour of Israel and the King. When I killed the uncircumcised dog I took his sword to Saul, the King. He, in honour of the Lord's assistance at the Battle of Eilah, caused the sword to be hung here as a monument to God's glory. I take it in His name and swear to you to draw it in no unjust cause."

With that, I remounted my weary horse and, to the echoes of their farewells, rode off. This time, I headed north east to Rammah and hopes of safety.

I had some vague idea that, through Samuel's intervention, backed up by the support of Jonathan and Michal, when the dark mood of Saul left him, we could be reconciled. I had decided that I would offer to resign my captaincy, demonstrating that I was not seeking anything from the King but would leave his court and return to Bethlehem.

I smiled ruefully at the thought of Michal living under my father's roof.

As I arrived at Rammah, I began to feel more hopeful. I drew near and I saw Samuel's house.

A priest came running towards me shouting, "Hail, David! The Prophet greets you in the Lord's name. You are to come to him immediately."

After such a journey, I was travel stained but did not think to disobey – or even marvel that the Prophet knew of my approach.

I was ushered in to Samuel. I was saddened to see how frail he looked.

With difficulty, he rose to greet me. "My son, the Lord has sent you in time – whilst my eyes can still delight in your face."

The warmth I felt at his welcome was cooled by the realisation that he could hardly see. I threw myself on the ground and would have appealed for his protection and forgiveness, but he knew my mission already.

His words were loud and resonant, and he spoke formally. "I need not be told. Saul the Benjaminite has forsaken God. In his pride, God has struck him so that he throws away his shield. Saul's enmity to you is his final doom. He has disobeyed God too often. Whatever greatness he has achieved, it has been with the Lord's help. Saul, in his soul's arrogance, has forgotten who raised him up."

I realised that these words were not just for me. They were a re-assertion of the reasons for the division between them, giving the priests and Elders standing there an explanation for Saul's behaviour.

With his usual facility, Samuel could read my thoughts before I had expressed them to myself. "David, why else but to fulfil God's purpose, is Saul rejecting his bard, his champion, his loyal son-in-law and setting at nought the counsels of his eldest son and his daughter, your wife? Come now, we will walk alone awhile. Then you must take on a new responsibility before all the people."

He took my arm. But, this time, he clearly needed my support. My heart filled with pity at the obvious signs of his great age.

I began to feel uncomfortable at what his last words meant.

We walked a small distance without speaking and stopped at his signal. This time he spoke to me with the warmth and gentleness that he used when he put aside his authority.

"Oh David, I am so pleased to see you this last time."

He gestured away my response as to the implications of what he was saying. "Nay, my boy. I am old, weary and long for the bosom of Abraham. I am glad the Lord has used me up and that I can pass on His burden and His joy to others.

"But it does my heart good to see what a fine man you have become. You're still unspoilt, despite the injustice shown to you and the anguish in your soul. Your faith is restored in the Lord."

I was quite melted. He knew and understood everything.

"My only sadness, dear son, is that I must leave you behind. You are not to follow me for many years and have a long journey ahead."

We spoke quietly together. I told him the details of what had happened and began to try to offer such justification for Saul.

I tried to consider a way in which we could all work together. "Father, if Saul is moon-struck, then he cannot help it and his punishment is his madness. As you yourself have inferred, Prince Jonathan and Michal, my wife, have tried to remonstrate and therefore – "

He broke in, his voice gentle but the import terrible. "David my son, your sentiments do you credit. I can see that you still would love Saul, if only for what he has been. I too, as a man grieve for him but, as the Lord's Prophet, I can only condemn. Of course, as to Jonathan and Michal, you love them both. Again, my son, that says much for their discernment as your good heart. But it is to no avail. Your love and brotherhood for Jonathan cannot save him. Neither he nor any of Saul's seed will ever reign in Israel."

His words echoed in my brain as he gave his dreadful pronouncement – not only against Saul, but dooming Jonathan. I felt a frantic panic in my heart. What did it mean?

The Prophet continued. "Yes, Saul has achieved much. He was always outwardly a Son of God."

Samuel's voice rose in thunder. "Does the Lord delight in burnt offerings and sacrifices as much as obeying the voice of the Lord? To obey is better than sacrifice.

"Rebellion is like the sin of divination. Arrogance is like the evil of idolatry. Saul rejected the Word of the Lord. Therefore, God has rejected him as King."

The air crackled with the tension.

I whispered, "What are you saying?" I was dreading his answer.

He replied with great gentleness. "My son, now is the time to take up your burden – the task for which the Lord has been preparing you. Whilst you will not fulfil it for some time, and many vicissitudes lie before you, you cannot escape the destiny that the Lord has planned for you."

I looked at him in total alarm.

Suddenly he stood up, gripped my arm with such intensity and said, "In your heart of hearts, you know you have been called. Your soul recoils from the burden but you know you have no choice. Though you would flee into the desert and live as a hermit, you must obey the Voice. He will give you the strength to fulfil His purpose even though your soul is cast down utterly."

I was spellbound. Of course, he knew of the Voice but he also knew of my despair. I did not want this.

He continued. "You must be anointed. It is no use, I tell you. Jonathan, though a good man, a great man in many ways, can never be King, though you would serve him for he has greatness of heart. He already has some notion of God's plan for you. Do not grieve that he will hate you, for you are both in God's hands. It is decided. Come, my son. You must go and prepare yourself."

He said these last words with such gentle sadness, but with a finality that I knew there was to be no more argument.

We returned to his house and I went to bathe. No one said a word to me. I was given a little wine and bread. When a priest asked me whether I was clean and had not been with women, I almost laughed at his earnestness and the absurdity of his inquiry. I assured him that I could make a sacrifice undefiled and was left alone awhile to pray.

I tried to pray but I felt strangely empty. There were no words. No thoughts! What was happening and what was before me drained me. I felt a sad lethargy. Not from the journey, nor the enforced fasting, but rather from a tired expectancy. I did not know whether I wished to sleep or run.

I was called once again into the presence of Samuel, who was now dressed in his most magnificent Prophet's robes. Apart from four server priests, and two northern Elders, Micah and Jonah – who were most unwilling witnesses – there were no others.

Gone was Samuel's frailty of years. His office uplifted him. His voice, powerful and majestic, held us all in his power. Our thoughts, minds and bodies were his to command.

Samuel's voice rose. Now in a trance, his eyes were blank as his body shook with the ecstasy of the Lord. "The Lord called you, David bar Jesse, of Judah. The Lord makes His face to shine upon you, now and for ever more. You are to walk in the sight of God the whole of your days. You have been chosen to unite His people and to defend them against the Lord's enemies. You are to smite the ungodly and bring light to lighten the gentiles."

He stood over my kneeling form as I looked into his unseeing face. He raised the holy oil above me. I trembled with awesome dread.

He chanted, "In the name of the Lord God of Israel. I, Samuel, His Prophet, declare you to be the Lord's anointed. You are His choice to be King of all Israel.

"All of Israel shall acknowledge this day that you will be King, Father and Shepherd of His people. All the nations of the earth shall know you are His. Amen. Amen."

The holy oil was upon my head. Blood raced through my veins in a fiery fear at his words. Only I knew that, though spoken by Samuel, the words came from Him and that Samuel was but the instrument of the Voice.

My soul quaked before Him and at the terrible blessing that Samuel now gave me.

"This is my beloved son, in whom I am well pleased." With this, he kissed me, drew me up and presented me to the others, who were as spellbound as I was.

I was then inspired. Gone was my lethargy. The words flowed out of me as if He had told me to read His words. My body shook with a fiery ecstasy even greater than in the love I had for Leah.

"God is our refuge and strength, a very present help in trouble.
Therefore we wilt not fear though the earth be removed and though the mountains be carried into the midst of the sea.

Though the waters roar and be troubled – there is a river the streams whereof shall

make glad the City of God,
The holy place of the tabernacles of the most high.
God is in the midst of her, she shall not be moved; God shall help her and that right
early.

The Lord of hosts is with us, the God of Jacob is our refuge.
He maketh wars to cease unto the end of the earth, he breaketh the bow and cutteth
the spear in sunder, He burneth the chariot in the fire.

Be still and know that I am God.

I will be exalted among the heathen, I will be exalted in the earth, the Lord of Hosts
is with us the God of Jacob is our refuge."

My inspiration was ended. My body had slacked itself. I could barely stand and I could not see.

My eyes focused. I saw Samuel, Micah and Jonah, the Elders and the priests looking amazed.

Slowly with great dignity and reverence, Samuel knelt before me!

The others quickly followed them in awed silence.

Samuel was first to speak. "Blessed be the Lord God of Israel and may He show mercy and light upon His chosen one, David bar Jesse. Though Bethlehem be slight in the face of Israel, out of her has come forth greatness – one who shall lead Israel and build Her a City of God."

It was over.

Unlike the euphoria I had felt a moment ago, I now felt an almost childlike fear – as a small child longs for its mother's touch to take control and comfort his aches. I ached to be the David I had been before this day had dawned.

Instead, unlike the child, I knew I had to go away and be a man.

I had no more words. I turned on my heels and walked as fast as I could past the staring people. I looked neither to the left nor right until I was in the wilderness. I threw off the sacred garments, filled with the gentle scent of the holy oil, and stood naked before my God.

I cried and cried for my lost innocence, for my lost freedom, and for my loss of Jonathan. Standing there, before the skies, my nakedness signifying my helplessness, I knew with a terrible certainty that whatever I did from this day on was being marked by an ever vigilant God. I was overwhelmed by this unsought burden of greatness and slowly wept myself to sleep.

Chapter Seventeen

Saul's Prophetic Fury

I stayed with the Prophet for a whole week. Daily, he spoke with me about the responsibilities that were to be mine. He would not or could not give me a time, other than to say it would follow strife and much heartache.

When I asked whether this meant bloodshed he looked hard at me, "David, the Lord's anointed, you will have to fight for God, but always seek to do good and the Lord will never forsake you. Moreover, you must learn to read men's hearts as they are, not always as they seem – as you are already beginning to know."

He was urgent in his "lessons", which for the most time seemed to be reminding me of the duplicity that surrounded power.

He gave a number of thumbnail sketches of the key personalities around Saul, to whom he said he felt no animosity. "It was not all Saul's fault. He was flawed – as we all are. I warned him of his pride, which would undermine his greatness, but he would not listen. I can easily prophesy that when you finally sit in Saul's seat, you will have more sympathy for both him and me."

He saw my look. "My son, of course you must have sometimes doubted me. It was inevitable. You have been forced to choose between loyalties. Saul was a magnificent man and, for a time, a great King. But glory passes from us all. When you reach your great age you, too, will know the sorrow that comes from knowledge. Then, like me, you will yearn to return to the bosom of Abraham – but be of good cheer, that will not be for many years."

Then he startled me by saying, "Tomorrow, Saul will come, but I will not see him. Nor will you, but it might be well to observe what befalls. When he goes, we shall have time to make our final farewells."

Seeing my expression, he added, "Nay, no protestations. Now, leave me, son. I grow weary."

Whether Samuel had previous knowledge, I do not know. Sure enough the outriders of the King approached demanding that Saul see the Prophet. They were told that Samuel was sick and could see no one.

Saul came up riding on a mule. To those who did not know him, the awe he inspired – and the reverence shown to him by his attendants was impressive.

I could see from his grimacing and drawn face that he was not well. I watched him from the edge of the crowd, disguised in the robes of a servant.

He looked alarmed and excited. In his gestures there was a fine tremor. Most surprising was the presence of Amlech, the priest from Nob and guardian of the Ark. He looked most uneasy at finding himself in the middle of all this high politics. Of equal surprise was the absence of Abner and Jonathan. Whatever was to happen was to follow from Saul's deluded purpose.

Saul demanded to see the Prophet. "I have come to warn the old man of the apostasy of his protégé, David bar Jesse, who tried to kill me. He has cast a spell upon me and tried to fill my mind with dark thoughts – to make me doubt that I am the Lord's anointed."

I was furiously indignant and close to rushing out to declaring my innocence. But from his ravaged face, I could see the mood was upon him and that he was not open to reason. So I held back and watched, fascinated.

Then I had a sudden dread. What if the priests, or the Elders, or someone from the crowd told Saul that I had been anointed? I felt sure that the whole of Samuel's household must now know of my anointment, but no one came forward.

Saul sent Amlech in to see the Prophet. The King was in command of himself enough to know that to enter into Samuel's tabernacle uninvited would be a terrible sacrilege.

Poor Amlech went in reluctantly. After about half an hour, she returned, looking even more apprehensive.

He knelt before Saul. "Great King, the Prophet asks what is the commotion about. He knows of no ill report of David, your son and God's bard."

Saul looked as if he would burst. "No ill report?" he hissed through contorted features. "No ill report! I tell you and the world, that David bar Jesse was a snake in my bosom. He has caused black moods to invade my heart. Had not I been alert, he would have speared me to death in my own tent."

The best Amlech could do was to ask the King to come tomorrow when the Prophet might be easier and able to see the King.

Furiously Saul went off to make camp, refusing all offers of hospitality other than those from the Prophet.

At noon the next day, in great ceremony, Saul approached the house of the Prophet. Again, he was refused entry and, again, Amlech was called upon to exchange messages between the two pillars of Israel.

I wished to go to Saul, for I could see his torment and passion was upon him. Yet, as he stood there in the noonday sun I appreciated that there was something new about him. Gone was the terror of the deep blackness of his mood – now there was a feverish excitement about him. My heart feared for him as I saw that he was possessed.

After an hour Amlech returned. Almost crawling upon his knees. "Great King, have I your permission to speak the full words of the Prophet to you the Lord's anointed?"

Poor priest, he had little reason to feel reassured by the curt angry nod from the suffused looking King.

"The words of the Prophet, oh King, are Samuel's words, not mine. He is old and he himself says he has not long for this world so perhaps – "

"Shut up, you prating fool! Give your King the words of Samuel and let's hear no more of thee."

Amlech was terrified. Who wouldn't have been? There was absolute stillness yet there must have been two hundred men present. Slowly the words of doom were pronounced. Oddly, the words, as if had they power themselves, possessed the quavering priest and filled him with a dignity he did not have earlier.

"Hear then, Saul bar Nesh, Benjaminite, sometime King of Israel. Thou liest. David bar Jesse is no apostate but loves and serves the Lord. It is you, King that was, who has turned from God in the sweat of your pride. Your disobedience has washed the holy oil from you. You are no longer the anointed of God – no matter what you claim. God is not mocked and you have hardened your heart against Him."

Barely stopping to draw breath, the priest continued. "These are the words of God's Prophet. In his name, go! Your shadow despoils the sacred place."

No one noticed that Amlech had now fallen to the ground in a faint. All eyes were fixed upon Saul.

This tallest of men grew taller with anger as he screamed a wordless defiance and began to tear his robes from him. "I am Saul bar Nesh, King and servant of Israel. I am the Victor of Jabesh Gilead, of Michmash, of Havilah and of Eilah. I am Saul King of Israel. Destroyer of the Lord's enemies, slayer of the Ammonites, the Moabites, the Amalekites and the Philistines."

He was now naked and his big frame danced with fury. In a fit of extreme ecstasy he raised his arms to the heavens and screamed, "My God, My God, I cry unto thee. Remember Your words unto me."

"The King shall joy in thy strength Oh Lord in Thy salvation how greatly do I rejoice. Thou hast given me my heart delight, Thou settest a crown of gold upon my head. I asked life of thee and Thou gavest it to Me for ever. My glory is Great in Thy salvation and Majesty has Thou laid upon Me."

These last words were hurled into the air. All present felt sorrow and fear at the desperation that he showed. All knew the words were the King's Psalm.

I yearned to go to him, and who knows what may have happened except it was too late. He gave an agonised appealing cry:

"My God, my God, speakest Thou to Me."
He crashed to the ground. Writhing amongst the dust, his mouth foamed and he had a wild look in his eyes. All the onlookers were horrified, yet they could not tear their attention away from the monstrous spectacle in front of them.

I could see people wondering: was this prophecy or possession?

The spell was broken as Eban stepped forward, his face filled with sadness as he mouthed the words, "Oh, my dear Master. What moon-struck grief is this?" He slowly covered the naked and defenceless old man with a cloak, picked up his long frame from which many an enemy had shrank, and, with the gentleness of a mother, carried him away from the sight of the vulgar.

My own eyes were close to being overwhelmed. I could not but regret his fall from greatness and felt disturbed that this man, who wanted nothing more than to serve Israel, had come to this. I agonised whether I should show myself to Eban but thought that, if he knew I had witnessed his master's humiliation, even though he loved me, he might not forgive me. No, this wasn't the time. I crept away and concealed myself until the King's party had left.

I sat quietly outside the door of Samuel. At nightfall, an attendant called me in.

Samuel looked very tired but he had lost none of his acuity.

Reading my heart, he said, "You feel sorry for him, David, even though he has branded you a traitor, a witch and tried to kill you. Well, so do I! Though he denied the Voice and would have ruled God's people according to his own plans rather than God's. Yes, I too weep for him and for Israel, because disobedience in the great is like madness – it has fearful consequences. Yet never forget, David, even at your most desperate, you never sought this quarrel. Once entered into, you cannot but give God your obedience and seek His will in all things."

Samuel waved me towards him. "David, the only time real hurt will come upon you is when you turn your back on what you know is right. Oh, men may damage you, seek to take your life, but your soul is not in danger in those situations. You risk your soul only when you disobey in your heart."

He drew himself up and stretched out his arms. "Come, embrace me, my son. No words, for even an old man's heart can break. David, though you shall never see my face again, I will always be with you."

Then he rose up and spoke in that voice that all Israel knew. "David bar Jesse, you are the Lord's anointed and set to rule one day over God's united people. You shall bring the scattered flock together. You shall cause the Lord's name to be venerated amongst the heathen. You shall found God's City and His people will bless your name for ever in many tongues. In every land upon where God's sun shines, your name will be spoken of as with Abraham, Jacob and Moses. Your inspiration will be such that men shall say, 'we too seek and worship the God of David'.

"Blessed is the Nation whose God is the Lord and People whom He hath chosen for His own inheritance. God is our strength."

He stopped and seemed to shrink back into his frail self. This dear, dear, old man blessed me and sent me on my journey.

Now, truly alone, I wept. I knew that through the whole aeons of time, I would never, never, never see his face again.

Jonathan and the Arrows

I left the Prophet well provisioned but I had no idea where to go. I had asked Samuel, but he admitted that his advice was as good as mine but, yes, a final effort to seek reconciliation with Saul would please me and the people. However, he was hardly encouraging as he doubted anything would come of it. Yet self-evidently I needed to make contact with my friends for I had no doubts that Jonathan, Michal and the Companions would not desert me. So I retraced my steps back to Gilbeah with something like hope.

I came up slowly to the outskirts of the King's place. It was strange approaching it like an enemy but that's how I must think of myself now. It was no good having wishful thinking as hard decisions were required.

It was not too difficult to steal into the camp, I thought with some annoyance. After all, I really might have been an enemy of Israel. It was late, few were about, though the inevitable late revellers were staggering back.

I was close to our tents when, to my delight, I saw young Joab leave with a most beautiful looking woman. The way they clung to each other showed they had both enjoyed themselves and they seemed loath to let each other go.

I called my nightjar call, rapidly, three times. To my satisfaction, I could see Joab stiffen at the third call and, with great presence of mind, he calmed his partner down and sent her on her way.

He could not spy me but I could see he was very alert. I called once more to give him the direction of my hiding place. He pleased me by slowly turning towards me as if he would come over to the dark place and relieve himself.

I thought to myself, He's learning to think, not feel.

He found me quickly and we embraced. He said urgently, "David, you are in danger. The King has proscribed you. The Companions did not know what to do. Beniah suggested we go as a body to plead for you but Jonathan counselled us against that at this time. However, the King has not troubled us so far but clearly he is not himself. All know that the idea that you practised witchcraft on him or tried to kill him is nonsense. That's the sad thing, for it shows to everybody that the King of Israel is stark raving mad."

I smiled in spite of myself. "Joab, your analysis is excellent. Yes, the King is sick but, hopefully, only temporarily. How is Prince Jonathan?"

"You won't like this, David. He was under arrest for almost a week, guarded by Abner's brood. I don't trust Abner, David. I shouldn't wonder if he's behind this whole sorry mess. Anyway, Jonathan has been released. So has your lady wife because, she too, was kept under guard for a while."

It was not altogether encouraging news but at least Jonathan and Michal were out of immediate danger.

Joab agreed to go quietly and let Jonathan know I was here. I told him to tell Jonathan to go to the pool that he knew and I would meet him on the way.

Joab was excellent. He gave me his embrace and a cheery, "Don't you worry, David. With the Companions, the Prince and your wife behind you, the King will have to see sense." Before I could remonstrate at his implied treason, he had melted away.

There was no moon but a few stars. I found my way to the track that ran to what I had thought of as "our pool" though, to be fair, it was known as the Pool of Joshua in memory of our great hero. It seemed a good omen. I walked about half a mile and waited. Sure enough, I could hear the sound of a man hurrying as fast as he could in the dark. But instead of rushing out and greeting my friend, I held myself in check for, after all, it might not be him and I was a declared outlaw.

I need not have worried. His tall shape, which I would have known anywhere, emerged out of the darkness. Before any words were out of my mouth, we were in each other's arms and he was kissing me. I could feel the tears on his cheeks.

"David! David, it is good that you are here. Yet he is even more obdurate and I don't know where all this is going to end."

I tried to cheer him up and said, with confidence I did not feel, "Surely, Jonathan, when the mood has passed, he will know that he has nothing to fear from me. Even Abner's poison won't work when he's himself again. It's just time that we need – to avoid any untoward event."

I could just see Jonathan's face in the starlight and he was smiling a tight smile. "But David, we have had two 'events' as you call them. Did you hear about my father prophesying at Rammah – "

"Jonathan, I was there. I would have given anything to stop it, but he was possessed. I truly think even Samuel's people knew he was ill and felt pity on him. Eban was terrific."

I realised I was not saying quite the right thing.

"Does the King of Israel need the people's pity, especially of your friend, the Old Man?" Jonathan cut in bitterly.

I tensed – he knew! I had totally forgotten about the anointing. The last thing I was thinking of was some distant time. All I yearned for was reconciliation with my King and reunion with the people I loved.

I trusted him completely, and kneeled before him, handing him the handle of Goliath's sword. "Jonathan, Prince of Israel, my captain and my love, take this sword and use it as you think fit. I swear by the Living God that I mean no harm to you or the King, your father. Samuel the Prophet has anointed me as the next King of Israel. I did not seek it and will give my life to see you upon the throne of your Father."

I pleaded with him. "Jonathan, look at me. I beg of you. If you have any doubts of my love and loyalty, use this sword."

Then the enormity of the situation overwhelmed me. I broke down and sobbed. "If you doubt me then I do not wish to live, for no one is dearer to me in this world. I never asked for this bloody curse."

I then started some nonsense about he and I turning our backs on Israel and seeking a new life elsewhere. "Perhaps with Achish, because he had the highest regard for us both."

Jonathan stopped my mouth with his, held me tight and then breathed the words slowly. "I, Jonathan bar Saul, Prince of Israel, have sworn to love and cherish you, David bar Jesse, and put you above all other men. I do not understand how or why – for I do not think that the King my Father is an evil man – but I feel that in the Lord's plan, neither he nor I will continue to reign in Israel."

He stopped my attempted denials. "David, somehow this has been decreed, fated – we are all in God's hands. I, like you, can only play the part He has given us. Yes, I've heard that Samuel had anointed you, so I'm glad you have told me. It hurt when I first heard of it, not because I do not think you are unworthy, but I wondered was this a rejection of our friendship. But now, seeing you, knowing you, I realise this to have been foolish fear. I ask your forgiveness if for a moment I doubted you. So, my dearest friend and brother, now I have to learn to how to serve my Father, Israel, God and you. For when I think of what you have achieved, I can see that the Lord's hand is upon you. Come the time, you will be a great King of Israel."

With these words, this wonderful hero, this most generous of friends and most gracious of princes, knelt before me! Me – who was not fit to tie his shoes! He gave me back Goliath's sword.

He held my hand between his and said, "I, Jonathan bar Saul, Prince of Israel, do swear loyalty to you, David bar Jesse, Prince of Israel, the Lord's anointed. I cry defiance against any who would deny you."

What other men would have killed for, my Jonathan, in love, renounced freely: his birthright. Has there ever been a prince who gave up so much, though he had talents that would have made a thousand kings great? Yet he swore to ensure that the birthright would be passed on as God had willed.

We both swore to each other that we would never do anything to hurt each other or each other's families and that our brotherhood had been renewed with even firmer bonds. We knew that this was part of God's hidden purpose that we must believe was for the ultimate good of Israel.

We arranged that I would hide out at the pool and be supplied by one of the Companions until he found an opportunity to try for a final reconciliation.

We agreed a signal. He would come as if practising archery and, if all were well, he would shout out that the arrows were near and I could come from my hiding place. If there were still danger, however, he would tell the boy the arrows had overshot the mark and I was to remain hidden.

So, we parted as he returned to discover whether there was any chance of my restoration.

Next day, in the late afternoon, Beniah came and, after making sure he had not been followed, I came out. We fell into each other's arms. He assured me of everyone's loyalty and that Joab and Jonathan together had sworn them to secrecy. All were working for a reconciliation with the King,

"But David, we are your Companions and captains. Jonathan has told us of your anointment and we wish to be with you to protect the Lord's anointed."

I did not know how to answer, other than to say that I hoped to return with them soon and serve the King.

Late the next day, I observed other visitors, only, this time, there were two of them. One of them was a woman. Then, to my amazement, I saw that it was Michal. She was being escorted by Hushai. I rushed out to greet them but also to remonstrate with her.

She cut my words short. "Husband, this good man is here to help me. Jonathan and Beniah were willing to come, but I insisted that they would be too easily missed. So, I announced that the Princess was sick and would not be seen for two days – though I'd better return before the morning."

I still could not understand what she was doing here and why she had placed herself in danger.

Again, she took control. "Hushai, I wish to be alone with my husband. Please, go by the tree I showed you and wait for me there until midnight."

There was no gainsaying her. She turned her back on the surprisingly docile Hushai who, after I had returned his embrace, did as he was bid.

She asked to be shown where I secreted myself. I led her to the side of the copse that partially hides the Pool of Joshua. I ushered her to the grassy knoll that, skirted by trees, made it a natural rampart to hide against prying eyes. I was filled with warm concern and love for her. There she stood, wraith-like, her delicate beauty out of place in this wilderness. She was as brave and resourceful as any Companion might have been.

"Michal, I heard from Jonathan how hard it has been for you and this is the first time that I had the chance to say thank you. Not only for saving my life but honouring me with the words you did."

She turned around, her face filled with torment but her arms out-stretched with longing. "Oh David! David, love me."

I took her gently in my arms. In the golden red light that filled the sky above, mirrored in the waters, and that cast a magical orange glow over us, I held her close, close, close. Her hand went to my now bearded face with such gentleness that I was quite over- come. I thought that this amazing woman could never surprise me – but I was wrong.

She began to undress me as she whispered, "If you are to be away from me, I want to see you as you are, so that the long nights won't be so empty."

She, who was usually so modest, began to disrobe. She let her dress fall to the ground, revealing all her wondrous nakedness. I gasped at her beauty.

She stood there, caressing herself for my delight. Coming closer, she slowly kissed my lips – so gently. Then she kissed my throat, my neck and my nipples, as her hand caressed my fiercely erect hardness.

She whispered, "My Lord must be tired. Let Michal, his loving wife, serve him to preserve his energy and his seed."

She led me to lie upon the ground and stretched me out as she knelt by me. I longed to take her but she motioned my compliance, so I lay happy for her to lead. I lay back on the grass my arms outstretched. Her soft hands took oil she had brought. She inflamed my senses as she smoothed the oil, first across my chest, then to my stomach, then to my sack. She cradled each ball in her hands and, with such delicacy, stroked my phallus, which wanted to let fly its pearly stream.

She now lay beside me and gave me her breast. My mouth took it whole and her nipple touching the back of my throat drove me nearly to despair as I drank and suckled at her hillocks of sweetness. My nostrils were filled with her scent.

She parted my legs wide. She left me, pushing aside my appealing arms, and knelt between my legs.

Her eyes were wide open as she stared at my prostrate body. Her eyes full of excitement fired me even more. The sight of her was a vision of delight. I was also thrilled by the realisation of her joy in my body, in its hard difference and firm contours that ached to be embraced by her soft curves.

She raised herself up and, taking the end of my hard, hard manhood, moistened me with her sweet self. Slowly, she speared herself upon to my aching phallus.

I knew I could not hold myself long as I thrust upward deep into he. She held me down as in a wrestling hold, thrusting her whole body over me. She glided her breast over my gleaming chest and held me inside her with a velvety, sinewy grasp. Once, twice, thrice, I thrust myself up to meet her, but on the fourth plunge her mouth filled mine. I fired the hot, sharp, sweet, tingling love into her, as if it would never cease.

She rolled me over and had me rest upon and within her, holding me tight inside. I was filled with love for this dear, dear, brave creature, who had put aside her pride, as she sought to hold every drop of my seed. We lay still together for almost an hour, until she spoke.

"Is My Lord pleased with his Michal?"

I laughed with her. We had never been so close. "Oh yes, my Princess. Your Lord is very pleased, nay captivated, by his Michal. And do I please my dear wife?"

She blushed at this but through her smiles, said, "So much so, it is not seemly to talk about it."

"Oh Michal. Dear, dear, Michal. It is part of us: shepherd boy, Prince and King as it is for shepherd girl and Princess."

I began to be aroused again but she said, "No, my Lord. I do so want to bear you a son. I have your seed now. Let it rest."

What could I say but kiss her gently and mumble, "There is always tomorrow."

But then, I had broken the spell.

She sat upright, alert, her mind thinking hard. "Oh, my Lord. Now you have been anointed."

I was suddenly anxious – if she knew, I wondered whether there was anyone who did not know.

She divined my thoughts. "The King suspects but Abner has dismissed the idea – though many know it. At the moment, whilst you are still outlawed, his anger is growing against the priests, Amlech in particular. Father knows Amlech gave you the sword of Goliath and he is calling you both thieves. Yes, my darling, I know you won it. As you gave it to him for Israel, he is adding this to his lists of grievances. Whilst he dare not move against Samuel, he is patient because he thinks the Old Man cannot live much longer. Whilst a push against Amlech, who is likely to succeed Samuel, would give him more satisfaction."

I was surprised at this news. It was stupid. It put his quarrel with me into a new perspective and gave me natural allies.

She went on, "I said to my father that Samuel, living or dead, will continue to be a power in the land – well beyond us. Indeed, he may be more dangerous when he dies because his legend will have no inconvenient facts to challenge it, such as his stubbornness and the rapacity of his sons. Whereas, Amlech is weak and wants an accommodation, and would happily let the Saul lead if the King ignores the slight he feels."

Again I was filled with admiration at her political acumen.

"Dearest husband, who will be King, hereafter, you remember I told you it was prophesied that I would be the wife of a King? Jonathan, when the time comes, will see you as the Lord's anointed. The House of Saul and David will found a line of Kings that will stretch out for ever."

She said this with such fervour.

"Dearest Princess and wife. If the Lord blesses us, he cannot fail to give us sons."

So, we said our farewells and exchanged hopes for the morrow. I escorted her back to the patiently waiting Hushai.

I have to tell you of events about which I did not know for some time but, to assist the chronology of the story, I have to return to Saul again.

Poor Saul was frantic. His dark moods appeared to have lessened but he was still irritable, uneasy, worried and obviously untrusting of all around. Sadly, throughout, he never doubted his evil genius Abner.

What happened next may not have occurred if the blackest of Saul's moods had been upon him because, when he was so smitten, he had no energy or any ability to take action. Now he had a frantic burst of nervous energy, which alarmed all about him, so that no one dared tell him anything which might provoke his capricious rage that was always bubbling near the surface.

Whether Abner knew of my anointment, it was hard to say. The news was unlike the usual rumour which surrounded the King's camp: this was a whisper, an idea, and, as there had been no calling together of the elders and no message from Samuel, no one knew where the idea was coming from. Furthermore, whilst Saul had probably lost the confidence of the people, Jonathan was rightly very popular and many felt his succession would be good. Hence, people had little reason to concern themselves about me, as I was so much younger than the Prince. Jonathan was the King's son and had already showed himself a great commander and a friend of the poor. So, if Saul were to abdicate or die, people rightly looked to Jonathan as the next King.

Abner, of course, may have had other ideas and, therefore, it was not in his interests to suggest that the succession had already been decided – or it would be outside his influence.

Saul on a number of occasions had asked that I be sent for.

He became moody and angry when Abner told him that his bard had fled. "Great King, you must remember he has shown great ingratitude to you. You have banished him. He is now a proscribed outlaw. However, we know the priests have been hiding him and even gave him your great sword of your mighty victory at Eilah."

Perhaps Abner did not intend what followed. Saul flew into a rage and immediately ordered a battalion of guards to go to Nob and kill the priest Amlech and all with him.

Saul justified this by saying, "They have hidden the outlaw, David. They are all traitors and collude in his practice of witchcraft upon me."

The men went off reluctantly and, to Amlech's great credit, when they arrived he greeted them in the name of God. He reminded them they were near the Tent of the Ark, that I was not amongst them, and that though I may have been ungrateful to the King, I was no traitor. Yes, they had given me the sword of Goliath, but they should remember that it was David who was their champion and single-handedly had slain the giant making the victory of Eilah possible. Neither the men nor the captain could quarrel with this so they returned to the King, hoping for different instructions.

They rode back must faster than they came, but again Saul's bad luck hurt him. He may even have forgotten his earlier order but he was seeing an Edomite, Doeg, who had taken a dislike to Jonathan and me because neither of us would intercede for him in a dispute he had with a Moabite ally.

When the men returned, the captain merely said that Amlech had given good answers so they had not proceeded any further. Saul seemed satisfied with this until Doeg intervened. He quickly elicited the story, which made Saul furious. Doeg said, "Great King, I myself have seen the Prince, your son, in conference with David, the outlaw, and seen them both blessed by Amlech the priest. How dare that arrogant priest set himself up against the Lord's anointed?"

Saul raged and asked whether anybody would ever obey him again. "I should cast off this golden band and the cares that go with it, and return to my father's flocks, rather than endure the insult to me and Israel's majesty. The kings of the nations laugh at Israel. They say there is no order in the land and seek alliances elsewhere."

Doeg, that evil man, said, "Great King, I, Doeg the Edomite, to earn your love and show how highly we Edomites value our alliance, give me but your order and authority and I will bring you this priest's head and silence all his followers."

It was too late. Even Abner tried to intervene at this. But Saul was beside himself and drew his sword. He might even have menaced Abner, who bowed to the inevitable. Perhaps I am being unjust, but Abner watched with satisfaction as Saul perfected his own destruction.

Doeg rode off with twenty Edomites and a small detachment of the King's men to protect the Tent of the Ark while Doeg did his bloody work.

They hit Nob like a whirlwind. Doing terrible damage, Doeg slew Amlech, severing his head as a trophy for the King. Over eighty priests and altar servers died that day in the pillaging of the small town of Nob. The whole of Israel was aghast: no amount of justification from the King could make the killing of the priests of the Ark sound anything but sacrilege and crass, despotic murder.

Men muttered that Israel might expect this from the Philistines but not from the King of Israel.

Amazingly, the only comment from Samuel was devastating in its simplicity, "God is not mocked and He will be avenged."

Two days later, Jonathan, who very nobly had worn mourning for Amlech, gave assistance to his son, Abathar, to flee to Samuel at Rammah. He hoped that the King's excess now done, there might be the possibility of an opportunity to plead my cause. He reasoned that even Abner admitted that Saul had exceeded his authority and created strife in the kingdom. Therefore, reconciliation with me, known as a friend of Samuel, might help to bind the wounds of this damaging action.

It would have made political sense to any other than a disturbed, moon-struck King. Here was terrible evidence that madness in the great is dangerous indeed. Jonathan had even gone to consult Abner, rehearsing the advantages to the King and Abner of my recall.

Jonathan said, "Of course, Lord Abner, David will never be as close to the King again. So we should use him to correct this mistake of the slaughter of the priests."

Jonathan had to endure Abner's sneers and slights. Was Jonathan now a priest lover? He marvelled at Jonathan's perseverance for such a friend who rumour suggested would some day supplant him. Jonathan bore all, for he loved his father and knew that his proposal was the only way to ease the situation. Abner whilst sneering, none the less agreed to support him, such was the seriousness of the situation. "I will support you, Prince Jonathan, but not initiate. You must do that, for I warn you, the King your father is unpredictable which makes him hazardous."

Jonathan went before his father, along with Abner. The two of them together were sufficient for Saul to take notice, for he was under no illusions that there was rivalry between them, though Jonathan never sought it.

Jonathan began quietly reviewing the situation, avoiding all direct criticisms of the King and drawing Abner in to support his analysis.

At first, the King took Jonathan's review well, until he asked what did he suggest.

At the mention of my name, Jonathan hardly got another word out. Saul completely lost control of himself and, almost incoherent with anger and frantic energy, stormed around his room.

He grabbed a spear and hurled it at Jonathan. Fortunately, his fury was so great that he was too unco-ordinated to find his target – otherwise, Jonathan would have died on the spot.

Even Abner was shocked.

Saul threw himself on the floor, raging and crying out for God to strike his enemies and relieve him from disobedient sons.

Jonathan knew it was all over and, making his bow to his father, left.

The next day, he came to me at the Pool of Joshua. Of course, at this time I knew nothing of the tragedy.

I had had another visit from Michal and, being able to see my Companions, I was feeling that my situation was not unbearable. So, when I saw from my lookout Jonathan coming with a boy attendant carrying bows and arrows, I was so confident that I nearly rushed out to meet them.

Fortunately, I did not do so. As Jonathan began shooting in quick succession he shouted at the boy that the wind had taken them too long. "The arrows are over the other side."

As I heard these words, my heart sank. "Over the other side" meant there was to be no recall. Suddenly, I felt panic. What in God's name was I to do now? I had not really thought that I would be cast out in permanent outlawry. After all, I was Saul's kinsman as well as being a respected captain of his army.

Jonathan sounded to be in a peevish mood with the boy. He told him to collect the arrows and return to the camp' whilst he would take some further exercise but alone.

"And remember boy, I said alone. So if anyone asks for me, you are to say I went to the east of the camp, not here in this direction."

I waited until the boy had gone and came out from hiding. Jonathan's face said it all.

I tried to expostulate with Jonathan: surely he'd tried this, said that, flattered his father.

"We all know that men, and powerful men in particular, like flattery." As I babbled on, I realised that I was making a fool of myself as my panic began to unnerve me.

"Look Jonathan, I'll return unarmed. As a suppliant, playing my harp and singing his psalm. I could even suggest I deserve a public whipping ..." As I tailed off incoherently, I could see Jonathan's despair reflected my own sense of desperation. Slowly he shook his head.

Then, I saw in his eyes that something had happened, something already dreadful. I asked half-fearing the tyrant had harmed Michal.

"What has he done, Jonathan? You look white."

Simply, Jonathan told me of the massacre of the priests.

I was dumbstruck, horrified at the slaughter of innocent men and the stupidity of the sacrilege. I did not know what to say to Jonathan though I could see he needed comfort.

He spoke with some resolution. "This settles it. You will be King. This blasphemy has washed the holy oil from his head. He no longer deserves to be King."

I replied angrily, "What has that got to do with it? You must be King now. The people will see he is mad and who better than you to lead Israel?"

He smiled and held out his hand to me, taking mine in his. "Don't you see, David? This time he really has disobeyed and rejected the word of the Lord. You and I both know he did the right thing at Havilah. Not only were the men sick of killing, they and he knew Samuel had got it wrong about the annihilation. Those were not grounds for his being rejected, other than the pride and the stupidity of the Old Man. But this ... this is the crime of a tyrant! To kill God's own priests outside the Tent of the Ark was unforgivable. By this mark, he renounced for ever his, and the House of Saul's, right to be King of Israel."

He looked grim as he took upon himself "the sins of the father". What could I say? We both knew that Saul's actions against the Amalekites was just and, therefore, there was always a chance of some reunion between Saul and the Prophet. But Saul's massacre had made this irrelevant for this deed was beyond the forgiveness of God.

"But Jonathan, I do not want it!"

Jonathan dismissed my desperate remarks somewhat curtly. "David, you have not been asked. It is now obvious that the Lord has been preparing you for this. What matters is how can we preserve the Lord's anointed so that he may lead His people."

I stood aghast at his words.

Jonathan then knelt before me! "David, I have sworn to you already so you no longer need my oath. But I will declare that, though I must protect my father and support his efforts for Israel, I am yours to command. I will make it my sacred duty to atone for the crime done by my father. I will ensure that God's chosen one will lead Israel and to avert God's just vengeance on the House of Saul."

We renewed our oaths to each other: that his kin would be my kin and that my kin would be his. I also prayed that someday the House of Saul and David would be reunited and would lead Israel.

Then the enormity of my situation hit me. Where was I to go to escape Saul? If he could kill innocent priests and try to murder his son, then it was plain I had to flee Israel.

To my surprise, it was Jonathan who suggested that, until other arrangements could be made, I needed a secure refuge where the rite of the King of Israel did not run.

He grasped my shoulders. "Go to your blood brother Achish, now King of Gath."

Jonathan eyed me keenly as he put this to me as I thought of the implications. I hesitantly said, "Do you think I could dare? After all, you and I have done much damage to the Philistines."

As I thought about it, I was overwhelmed by bitterness at the effect of Saul's injustice upon me: to have to seek refuge amongst Israel's most dangerous foes.

Jonathan sensed my feelings. "David, it need only be for a short while. I think that some of the Companions would share your exile. Perhaps you could find a place in the land of the Amalekites until such time as my father relents or ... he dies, because these terrible moods exhaust his strength."

I tried to say that, if this happened, then I would support him as King but he shut me up. "David, I am no seer, but of this I am sure: God's plan for me is already written and, no matter how you and I may struggle against it, my destiny is fixed. Me being King is not part it. I pray only that this sacrilegious crime of my father is not visited upon the heads of my children."

Then he looked straight at me and said, "David, do you realise that this may be our final parting? No, don't deny it – it is a possibility. Come, let's go to the pool and make the best of the time we have. I must return by morning, for I need to be there for Michal, who is an even keener advocate for you than I am. Only she does not spare Father. She has such a clear mind, which he used to respect, but her tongue is still too sharp. I am glad that it has worked well between you."

I found myself blushing and he laughed. "Yes, in that curious woman's logic of hers, she assured me, that after you, she loved me most of all. But as I could not be King then you had to fulfil the prophecy that she would be the wife of a King. She obviously loves you. I must say brother-in-law, I am very pleased for you."

I was happy to respond to Jonathan changing our mood and, arm in arm amidst the gathering gloom, we went towards the Pool of Joshua, which for ever in my mind I think of as the Pool of Jonathan. He stripped off and I watched this man who I loved above all other men, as I followed him into the water which was a glorious balm to our hot bodies and weary souls.

We swam, raced, wrestled – I always lost – until the moon rose and the sky was full of stars. It was an enchanted night. We climbed out of the pool and, without words, began to dry each other and let our fingers run gentle caresses over arms and chests.

I kissed Jonathan first for I knew he would never lead. Our lips entwined as chaste brothers but our manhoods pressed hard against each other's.

My kisses began to go down his body, over the firm muscles, which had a beauty all of their own. We lay side by side and, in the whiteness of the moon, his body looked like alabaster. I could not help but marvel at my feelings for him, which were so like and unlike my desires and love for Leah and Michal.

Then I laughed aloud with delight at the wondrous thought: we men were moulded in the image of God – no wonder I could love his manly frame and he mine.

I whispered to him, "Jonathan you are very beautiful and pleasing to me above women. I have worried about our love because it is not in our tradition. But, Jonathan, when I see you there, under the stars, caressed by the moonlight, it is a confirmation that men are made in the image of God. He too must be beautiful beyond all imaginings. Do you think he is like a perfect youthful man, or will he have an awesome beauty of an aged Samuel?"

Jonathan laughed. "David, I sometimes forget you are a poet, a spinner of words."

His hands caressed my now aching phallus.

He lent over and kissed me. "And my 'youthful' beauty perhaps just a little vain. David, as you are now, my eyes and my senses tell me that God will choose His own shape and that His beauty can be found in everyone who loves."

There was no more time for words as the urgings of our bodies demanded their rites.

His lips traced the lines of my yearning manhood with such exquisite pleasure that I thought I would faint. My mouth closed around his phallus and, with bodies head to toe, our mouths and tongues answered in ever-quickening urgings to our thrusting thighs. My soul erupted a burning delight as I emptied my seed in him and he in me. We re-sealed our love, devotion and loyalty to each other and to God. So that He would be honoured and that justice and mercy would return to Israel.

As the night went on, we shared ecstasy with each other again and again, made more urgent by the fear that this might be the last time.

As the moon went down and the star of the morning appeared, I lay content in the arms of my brother, lover, friend and champion.

He kissed me anew but this time in farewell, so that I clung to him desperately.

I looked at his naked beauty for the last time, to share with him God's inspiration and to ask His protection for this good man. For my Jonathan was gracious, generous and above all other men, before or since.

I looked at the slowly emerging hills and sang.

"I will lift up mine eyes unto the hills from whence cometh my help. My help cometh from the Lord which made heaven and earth."

I prayed with every fibre of my being,

"He will not suffer thy foot to be moved, he that keepeth thee shall not slumber. Behold he that keepeth Israel shall neither slumber or sleep."

If God willed it neither he nor I could come to harm.

"The Lord is thy keeper, the Lord is thy shade upon thy right hand.
The sun shall not smite thee by day nor the moon by nights."

I wanted to protect him against this horror of unreasonableness above all other hurts.

"The Lord preserve thee from all evil and he shall preserve thy soul. The Lord shall preserve thy going out and thy coming in from this time forth and even for evermore."

    We left each other at dawn. I went into an exile whose only certainty was its uncertainty.

    Jonathan returned to a court of duplicity, deceit and doubtful loyalties, which, for this Prince of absolute loyalty, was hell itself.

PART SIX

THE EXILE

Chapter Eighteen

Gath, the City of Doubt

As I journeyed toward Philistia, the city of Gath and Achish, I pondered the range of possibilities of how I would reach him. Should I pretend to an ambassador, or, as a friend of Gath, now I was an enemy of Saul? Should I present myself as a suppliant under the flag of truce, or enter secretly and declare myself to Achish and seek his protection?

On balance, I decided to enter as I was, a suppliant, which was closest to the truth. Also, it would allow Achish greater flexibility in how to respond to my plea. With my straggly beard and no effort to disguise myself that I was an Israelite, I came near to Gath.

I admit that when I saw a small patrol of young Philistine warriors turn towards me, I was filled with fear and trembling. I dismounted from my horse to demonstrate to them that I put myself totally in their power. My hand shook as I held high the flag of truce. They rode around me, snarling insults, wide-eyed with anger at my impertinence.

I called, in a very unsteady voice, "Men of Gath, warriors of King Achish. See, I bring the sign of truce and seek a suppliant's protection that tradition and respect of the gods demand."

They rode around me in a circle. I was blinded and choked by the dust of their horses and felt the air swish as they waved their swords and spears around my head.

I stumbled and fell down amidst the stamping feet of the horses. My bowels churned in anguish, fearing the cruel blow of the iron splitting my skull.

In a frenzy of fear, from my knees I held the tattered flag of truce and cried out, "Men of Gath, do not blaspheme against Dagon, who gives you the rules of war and custom."

Amidst the dust, dirt and stink of the horses a tall warrior alighted with his drawn sword – obviously the leader of the band.

He grabbed my shoulder and shouted above the din, "Silence!"

With the excellent discipline usual amongst the Philistines the men ceased their insults.

The leader addressed me. "Who are you, Israelite, that dares call upon the customs of Philistia? As an uncivilised barbarian, do you dare to seek the benefit of the god's bounty?"

Here was the crunch. Throughout the turmoil I had clung to my mantra, think, not feel, otherwise I would have collapsed into a crying hulk. I began to institute my half-formed plan.

I spoke back, in a calm voice. "I am a Bethlehemite, son of Jesse bar Obiad. I am an unjust outcast from Israel. In a dream I was commanded by the gods to seek the protection of Achish, King of Gath, mirror of courtesy and honour."

I could sense these words found an echo. For I guessed these young men of Achish would be proud of their King and of his reputation.

The young captain spoke with less anger but still with caution in his voice, "Stranger, you are right to speak well of Achish, King of Gath. But are you a criminal? Have you done terrible deeds which all peoples abominate and, thus, have no right to the sanctuary you claim?"

Now I knew I had passed the first barrier, and I could speak with more confidence. "I swear to you, sir captain, by the God of Israel and all the gods, upon the head of my father and my tribe, that I have committed no wickedness. I am a fugitive from injustice and my enemies' slander – I am no criminal. By Dagon and your custom, I can freely call upon your protection."

I was safe for the moment. The captain helped me to my horse and the troop formed into a guard around me. I noted with appreciation that half his troop had been sent to scout against any surprise, taking in the possibility that I might be a decoy. I realised I was still trembling and thought about how Saul sometimes acted. So I continued to show signs of agitation as if I might be moon-struck, relying upon the good manners and customs of Philistia that the captain would not press me any further.

I was greatly impressed with Gath, which was bigger than any city in Israel. As we came closer, I noted that there was a small moat and barricades around the city that were a very effective defence against any attack. I marvelled at the King's palace, which was built half of stone and half of cedar. I saw the great riches of the Philistines that Jonathan had spoken of.

The captain had sent a man ahead. As we approached the King's palace a man of importance came out. He first demanded that I give up my sword and dagger. Then I was stripped to ensure that I had no hidden weapons.

I felt very vulnerable. My nakedness and circumcised phallus caused new laughter and derision, properly silenced by the young captain, who was about my age. My sword aroused comment for it had obviously been made in Philistia.

The King's man, throwing my clothes back to me, said, "I am Janna, counsellor to the King. I am to escort you to the King. But who are you?"

Before I could answer the captain showed Janna my sword, which caused him some agitation. "Israelite, though you come under truce, you are in danger. Where did you get this sword, which I think I know?"

I replied, "Sir Janna, this I promise in the name of all the gods: I have done no crime and come as a suppliant and in truce. I acquired that sword honourably and will declare all to Achish, the King, and tell him of my dream."

As all peoples know, dreams are often the instruments of God and as such are sacred and often need the priests to explain. He reluctantly took me forward, after allowing me to re-dress, but he carried my sword himself.

We entered the portals of the King's palace. I had never seen such wealth. I had grown accustomed to the splendours of Saul's royal tent but this surpassed anything I had seen before.

The palace opened out into a large hall and I could see tables around the walls. This allowed the vast room to be both used for banqueting and as a meeting place. There were window spaces that lit up the hall during the day. In the centre, sitting on a wonderful carved throne of cedar, edged with gold, sat Achish.

I threw myself on the ground and began to crawl towards him crying, "Hail Achish, King of Gath. I come in peace a victim of injustice. I, of Bull Horns ..." I could sense the enthroned sitter go tense as he heard the words "Bull Horns".

"I come as a suppliant as ordered in a dream to claim your protection, in your god's and my God's name, who both instruct us to offer hospitality and succour to the guiltless."

I stopped about a yard before him.

Achish answered, "Janna, this man is as you say. Now I can tell you that I too had a dream, foretelling that such a stranger would seek our protection. I saw that he would do good things for Gath. So withdraw and I will examine this man of lucky omen myself."

This obviously impressed Janna, who answered, "I hear my King and obey, but you should know this man carries a sword which I am convinced was that of Goliath. I trust that you will discover how he came of it."

With that Janna bowed and left us.

Achish waited until we were alone. He raised me up, embraced me warmly and kissing me in greeting. There was no feigning the warmth and sincerity of his welcome.

"David! David, it is you! I would know you anywhere dear brother – even with your beard, which reminds me you are still an uncivilised Israelite, despite your learning the lessons of Philistia."

I looked in his eyes and saw his delight, reflecting my pleasure in seeing him, and knew that, for the time being, I was safe.

He took me into his private chamber and made me tell him everything. The only time he interjected was when I told him how Jonathan had counselled me to come here and how he sent his greeting.

Achish smiled, "And are you now philia?"

I blushed at his question and was amazed at how he had guessed.

He said, "No matter – but I am glad for you. He is an honourable example and worthy to be my brother's philia. It is good to know that there is the beginning of civilisation amongst you hill peoples. It is time they knew that the love between men is the highest love – apart, of course, from reverence to the gods."

He smiled in his gentle, teasing way so that I never knew whether or not he was serious. We spoke as if we had last met only yesterday. He joked about what he called our uncivilised state, which, now I had seen such riches, I at last understood. For the first time, I felt a hint of shame at our relative poverty.

However, my dilemma was how much I should tell Achish who, after all, despite our brotherhood, was a potential enemy and a likely candidate to be High King of Philistia. I felt a sense of real bitterness that Saul's persecution put me at risk of being a traitor – for it could only be good news to hear that there was division in Israel. I told him virtually all, but not that I had been anointed.

Then we complimented each other. First, I remarked on his fame as King of Gath and he on my successes.

"I cannot rejoice in your growing fame amongst my people, David. You and Jonathan have done much harm, but the fact that you are here will please the discerning in Gath. Your name, as the slayer of Goliath, and that of Jonathan as the victorious brothers means we might expect some quiet on our borders. If Saul is afflicted by this madness, I thank Dagon that he protects his people and thankful that he has sent my brother to me who I can delight in giving whatever I can."

I saw immediately his problem: though King, his power was not absolute. He could only go as far as was politically feasible. He explained that our recent victories were a little too fresh. He told me to follow his lead. He would have to call a council before he could give me absolute protection.

416

He suggested that I leave my beard intact, "To remind my council, if they need reminding, of your barbaric status. But I can keep you secure for a week whilst I slowly assemble a Council."

He showed me great courtesy and helped me rid myself of the travel-stained garments. He also paid me the honour of assisting his guest to bathe.

"You have become a fine warrior, David. If all the battles you have been engaged are true, I marvel that your body is so unscathed."

I immediately gave credit to the Living God and he approved.

"It is good that you do not risk hubris, which is to be arrogant before the gods, as that, in our nation, is a great crime. My people, before they came across the Great Sea, as our priests tell us, had great hubris. We ruled a great empire but failed to acknowledge our indebtedness to the gods. So our former land was destroyed by a great fire and the remnants of our people fled. We were wanderers until we carved out the land of Philistia for ourselves."

We talked the first night away and my feelings for Achish were rekindled. Just before he bade me goodnight, the look in his eyes stirred my blood but I felt obligated to Jonathan not to answer his look.

He found time for me every evening until late and our talk ranged widely. I must confess that, apart from Jonathan's conversation, I had never met a man with such a breadth of interest, knowledge and curiosity – no, not even Samuel.

Whether he was being especially polite, he encouraged me to sing him some of my psalms, which he found, "Quite inspiring!"

Seeing my look of surprise his smiling counter was, "Beauty and poetry have no boundaries for those willing to find excellence in unexpected places. These are jewels for every man with a soul. Despite coming from my mountain barbarian, who I love very much."

With such responses, I could not be angry with him.

He was very interested in our people's story and was delighted that, from my conversations with Leah, I had some idea of the origins of the Philistines.

He questioned me about Moses. I explained and recited to him the Lord's Ten Commandments,

Thou shalt have no other Gods but me.
Thou shalt not bow down to any graven image,
Thou shalt not take thy Lord's name in vain.
Thou shalt remember the Lord's Sabbath and keep it holy.
Thou shalt honour thy father and thy mother.

Thou shalt not kill.
Thou shalt not steal.
Thou shalt not bear false witness.
Thou shalt not commit adultery.
Thou shalt not covert thy neighbour's goods.

Achish nodded wisely and said, "That's real genius. Although, of course, your Prophet borrowed from the ancient Sumerians. Also, the Assyrians in the far north have something similar – indeed, most civilised peoples share values which enhance the family, social cohesion, religion and the priests. Though none, I confess, quite so well worked out as those of your Moses."

I was shocked at this. I found our evening discussions about our different faiths stimulating but, at times, alarming.

What follows is a summary of some of the most memorable conversations I had. Achish was always so polite, never asserting his view. He simply asked questions, rather like we are taught to do in the rabbis' school. But later I began to think of Gath as the City of Doubt.

He pointed out that the Commandments, whilst essential for basic living, do not go far enough.

"If I've got it right, eight are prohibitions. True, they are good prohibitions, without which there could be no civil society."

He argued, however, that active, positive commandments – that is, "thou shalts" – were what was required, where each man was honour bound to seek the good of his brother. This was assertive, to enhance the brother, not merely dourly avoid sinning.

He grinned his quite wicked grin. "Such as ... adultery!"

I would have been shocked except he said it with such humour. I did not realise just how dangerous his humour could be.

I tried to describe the nature of God through the Books of Moses. Achish's response was that was typical of descriptions of other gods.

"Jealousy, down right cruelty in face of opposition and a desire to maintain a priestly monopoly. Yet, dear David, all mixed in with inspiring and uplifting ideals. This makes men of god tolerate the less helpful aspects, but which invariably seem to serve the interests of the priests."

His paralleling of Dagon – and Ashtoreth, in particular – with the Lord was alarming.

"But come, David. You yourself said that your Prophet's instruction to annihilate the Amalekites was from your God? Now, either He is a cruel and blind God, as the innocent would be destroyed with the guilty, or, did Samuel have his own agenda? What did you say? 'Samuel must have got the instructions wrong.' Rightly, you, I and most of warriors of any nation cannot kill women and children in cold blood, simply because they belonged to another people. Even killing men in cold blood, unless it is lawful execution, is the abomination of murderers and tyrants. And your Moses said 'thou shalt not kill', as well as giving help to strangers. Surely all his commandments are relevant and none more so than 'thou shalt not kill'."

Achish continued. "No. You and Jonathan were right. I am sure your God could not have meant genocide – though, to be fair to Samuel, it is an interesting policy option. However, when you think about it, it is both impractical and very wasteful. Whilst I can understand some people wanting to be separate, am I a lesser man simply because I am a Philistine, when compared with the ordinary, slow-witted Israelite foot-solider?"

He joked. "Ah, perhaps that's why you are having these troubles: you have a non-Israelite great grandmother!"

He saw me smile weakly and carried on. "No, such a description of God would not be worthy of men of honour. You and Jonathan could never follow such a limited deity. Therefore, there must be more to Him. So your priest got it wrong! I wonder what his reasons were?"

Despite his quizzical smiles, this indirect slur upon Samuel left me speechless. I dare not consider the implications.

He was interested in different kinds of religious experience. Whilst I told him nothing of the Voice, he did press me to speak a little of my inspiration.

He said such experiences, "Were a witness for an ideal – a search, a longing for oneness with the One."

I jumped in. "So, you do believe, despite your cynicism."

Achish smiled and said, "I am a seeker, like every man. Sometimes I face events that I cannot understand – as I did as a child. But what I took to be an all-powerful 'god' was really my father's authority, strength and wisdom. Later, I learned it was just that. Human intelligence! So, when I find I cannot answer a question, rather than assert an external explanation, I am content to say, 'I do not know'. I do not fill the gap with some magical or god-like figure to make up for my ignorance. 'Wonder grows when knowledge fails,' said one of our poets."

He was attacking the religious experiences that coincide with advantage, especially after the event.

To my astonishment, he took the example of Samuel's victory at Mizpah. "David, you say that this was evidence of your God's direct intervention – and you may be right. But Samuel's situation was such that he had nothing left to offer, other than a final appeal. Consider this: what if it was a coincidence, and that the two kings at the battle were fools by not noticing that they had encamped on a riverbed. It is not unknown for summer storms to occur – though they tend to be rare, I grant you. But was there really something miraculous?"

I countered with my victory over Goliath and my inspiration, but I was too polite to mention Bull Horns.

He looked grave. "David, I honour you more than you appreciate. Yet your challenge to Goliath was, in retrospect, absolutely logical and had a measurable chance of success. It rested upon you being able to keep out of his range for an hour in the noon sun. Of course, he would tire quicker than you would, especially when you cleverly left Acrah's armour behind. You saw that for yourself – though others didn't, nor, frankly, did I at the time. He nearly did for you with his discus throw but, apart from that, he could not reach you. It was the heat and his exhaustion that would ultimately work for you."

He placed his hand on my shoulder. "The only miracles were the clarity of your thinking and your God's inspiration for you to take such action. Not even your hero, Jonathan, had worked out what to do. But God's intervention? Who knows?"

He went on. "An equally valid explanation was that it came from your intelligence, of which, perhaps, you are not fully aware. You surprised those who did not think it, including myself. Indeed, my people were so embarrassed that, to save their faces, they are more than happy to put your victory down to witchcraft.

Furthermore, your "'miracle' at Bull Horns, which you are far too gracious to mention, was another example of your own abilities. Yes, let us give your God the credit for your morale, but it was your speed and quicker intelligence that won the day. You took advantage of our mistakes – on the day you were the better solider – and we were lulled by misplaced confidence. Deservedly, we were beaten. As to your inspiration, that's another matter."

I understood his arguments but, I could not allow myself to agree with his conclusions.

He could see my confusion, so he tried another tack. "Your psalms are beautiful and, I promise you, they will echo in men's hearts while ever humans continue to seek understanding and beauty. Here, I begin to think that they truly reflect something of the Divine. But not of a God whose priest urged the annihilation of innocent women and children just because they belonged to another tribe – that was a bad business. No, David, your psalms come from you and your speed of thought. You say that, before you begin, you do not know how they will end. I believe you, truly, but could it not be possible that they come from a human, rather than from an exclusively divine, inspiration?"

He could see this disturbed me, but hastened to say, "I do not know, David. I have never had a religious experience. It might be considered strange by someone like you or Samuel, but most people seldom ever do – certainly, they are very rare for most of us. That they exist cannot be doubted. So let us agree with the words of poor Agag: that we are more alike each other than we realise. We are all seeking to understand our lives. We are all in a search for a greater belonging, which lifts us from the ultimate end, the corruption of our flesh. Let us celebrate our common brotherhood in a joint search, so that each man seeks to leave the world a better place."

No one could disagree with such a sentiment, though I admit I was amazed and deeply shocked at the thought of his unbelief.

Yet, I could see he was honest in his search for understanding but pitied him. As he said, he had no experience of the One and, with his pride in his intellect, he did not realise that he could not understand that spiritual communication comes from being willing to let go: to subjugate the self. It is necessary to allow the Lord to come in, rather than keep Him at bay by sophistry and mental tricks.

We did, however, agree in an unexpected area. I challenged him about the limits of his intellect, observation and experience. I argued that, important as this was, there was no agreed form of measurement. One man's experience, for example, of the taste of wines, was as good as the next. There were few firm measurements say like a yard or a foot.

Furthermore, what were his observations really worth when age and experience made one re-evaluate them?

I said, "If had known at fourteen what I know now, my life would have been very different, so I understand why you place such importance upon your intellect and observation. Yes, I grant you that, apart from Jonathan – and Samuel, but in a different way – you have wisdom and perception far greater than anyone I have ever known."

I could see this pleased him. He roared with laughter and said, "David, be with me for a month and I'll civilise you yet, though I may spoil a simple Israelite."

I ignored his gibe and continued, "Consider Bull Horns as a physical place. What did your 'measurements' tell you. You were there almost three days but each hour of each day was subtly different. Before dawn, Bull Horns is a canopy for stars, strung in a wondrous bow which bends and touches the darker shadows that I know to be the hills. Though I cannot see them, I know they are there. Someone visiting for the first time could not, on the basis of their observation affirm, their existence."

I wasn't sure that Achish was following me, but I continued to make my point all the same. "Then comes a defused light. Like a chord of music, there is an easing of the darkness so that the shapes of the hills and the plain can be seen. There also emerge waving shapes which I know to be sheep though, in that light, they do not look like sheep. Then, suddenly, and there ought to be trumpets, the sky behind begins to glow, rose-petalled. All at once you see delicate clouds appear out of nowhere. Next the first clear sharp golden ray of sunlight breaks the horizon, and those misty insubstantial hills become a grey backdrop for a range of colours. The mountaintops are golden, and as the eye tumbles down they become orange, rose, dark red and plum and light and deep grey. As your eye flows, you see a kaleidoscope of light and colour changing, out of which a sharp definition emerges, the hills and mountain sides, seemingly out of nothing. Now you can clearly see the sharp gullies, scraps and trees, which were merged in blankness of the pre-dawn light now take their true shape in the dawn's clear light. They become a host of radiant greens, yet none of them was available to the observer an hour ago.

"By mid-day, the light can be so fierce everything is washed out by bright sunlight, which hurts the eyes and creates a haze, which shimmers. You see movement on the rock, on the plain, in the air.

"Yet by even-tide, it is as if the sky sucks in its breath and draws all those colours back again, and for a moment, leaves the rocks have their own light which gives an illumination which seems brighter than the sky. In that brief moment they are no longer passive recipients. As the colour drains from the sky, clouds that have been rose, golden, white now become grey and purple black. And, out of nowhere, because the sky still has the vanished suns reflected light, a lone star shines. It shines as bright as a sun, it blazes more until the light fades and other stars, like shy fish peeping through the firmament, confirm that another day is over in Bull Horns.

"All this a man can observe, yet how do you describe my valley? At best you catch but a glimpse of a shimmering rainbow of impressions through God's day. How much more illusive is the Divine Himself."

I stopped suddenly, feeling rather foolish as my enthusiasm triggered a longing for home.

Achish came and kissed me chastely and said, "David, I forgot that you are a poet. That was beautiful because it was true. All those pictures, every minute of that wondrous change you described were valid. But, dear brother, would you kill to assert that the dawn is better than the sunset? Would you ostracise someone who preferred rose to golden clouds? We are in agreement – we can never know enough. We can only catch a glimpse of the beauty that sends echoes to our souls. So let us glory when we find another kindred spirit and cast the dross away. We all journey to oblivion, so we should celebrate the sharing of the world's beauty. Especially if, unlike you, I, like most men, seldom experience such spiritual ecstasies."

He left me deeply disturbed. I had never imagined that one might have to argue for the obvious reality of God. Yet Achish, though a Philistine, was a good and honourable man, so we sought to find a common area where our minds could meet in peace.

He was always attentive, considerate and delicately avoided political questions, which he knew would cause me pain. We needed no words to say that my presence in Gath could not be good for Israel.

On our last night together he clapped his hands and said, "I have a gift for you in gratitude."

Anna his wife entered, bowing low, and leading her maidens to bring us our supper. In reality, it was more like a feast, though only Achish and I shared the meal.

Anna greeted me. "How fares my lord's brother, David? We oft speak of you in gratitude, for you brought his humble servant great happiness."

Achish laughed and said generously, "Anna, for you alone, David merits our protection. You have brought me great joy and for this I am committed to giving you every protection. But you realise that we Philistines are a civilised people – not even the High King rules unconditionally. Even our priest would not claim to speak absolutely for God."

Being the last evening before the Council I thought I should ask serious questions about the morrow.

Achish tried to answer me as honestly as he could. "It is obvious that Janna has guessed who you are. The sword of Goliath was something special as you have nothing like that in Israel. So how will my Council feel about having David the Champion of Israel in their midst?"

He paused and then continued. "If – and I say, 'if' – they had any sense, they would appreciate the value to us because, self-evidently, it bodes ill for Saul to have expelled one of his most successful warriors. But, my friend, Goliath was of Gath and the Battle of Eilah lies heavily upon us. Though our division did well in retreat, we lost heavily and were shocked by Goliath's death. Furthermore, there was some rumour about my visit to you, so I have to be doubly careful. Your exploits at Bull Horns are not unknown, for Acrah, may he rest in Dagon, spoke highly of your valour. Frankly, David, some feel you were very lucky against Goliath and some spoke of witchcraft to ease their shame. Then again, your last two campaigns with Jonathan in the North does not endear you to us."

I valued Achish's frank analysis and I was much heartened when he said, "I say this honestly because you are always my brother and I will do all that is possible to help you. All I can guarantee tomorrow is that, at worst, you will leave Philistia unharmed."

It was out. I had not really thought beyond reaching Achish and his protection. Having had a whole week of his wonderful company, I had forgotten that he might not be able to give me the asylum I desperately needed.

We had a long embrace in case it was a final farewell. We both realised that the morrow was very uncertain and it would be impolitic if he was to be seen too partial to me.

Next morning, the Council was called and Janna immediately "accused" me of being David, the slayer of Goliath. I was expecting this and decided to continue to appear half moon-struck. I rose, with shaking hand and, thinking upon Saul in his darkest and most disturbed moments, darted looks to left and right.

I tried to speak with a wild and distracted voice. "I am David. Yes, yes, yes. I slew Goliath but only with the help of God. I have dreamed that Goliath is with his God and that we have both been forgiven. Do you have dreams? Oh, I have terrible dreams. Do your seers hear the voice of Dagon in dreams? Some of our priests tell of God speaking through dreams to those moon-struck, I sometimes think I am moon-struck."

There was great consternation at this. Achish, as is their custom, waited till last to speak so as to be able to respond to his Council's advice.

The young captain, who had brought me in, obviously represented the younger men as he was clearly too young to be an Elder. I now realised that I half recognised his face: yes, I had met him in battle.

He spoke out in a strong voice. "I am Baalal, nephew of Goliath, and of Ganz. I have met you in battle, David the Israelite. I think we should kill you here and now and send your treacherous headless trunk back to the barbarians."

Then he addressed the Council and Achish directly. "I speak for the warriors of Gath and for the captains. This man is an affront to us. He slew Goliath by treachery. He uses spies and some traitors amongst the Philistines."

This was dangerous stuff indeed.

Baalal continued. "He and the accursed barbarian, Jonathan, have done enough hurt to us. Let us rid ourselves of this pest, thanking Dagon that this man's arrogance and Saul's stupidity has brought him into our hands. Once their lucky charm is dead, let us lead the army and exterminate these mountain pests for ever."

There was much applause and shouting from the young men settled around the hall. My blood froze. I was surrounded by enemies who would defile my body but only after terrible tortures.

To my relief, Janna spoke and argued for giving me some protection. "Consider, men of Gath, if their barbarian King tears off his right arm are we to sorrow? David safe amongst us will encourage their northern tribes to come over to us. We will break up their tenuous unity, without which they are little better than brigands."

The older men agreed with this proposal but then the young firebrand was on his feet again. He was quaking with anger. "How can anyone think of giving my uncle's murderer asylum. It is an absurdity. The other cities of Philistia will think we are the moon-struck ones."

The echoing cries from the assembly told me that I had lost, so I interjected,

"Ganz, yes, yes, I see his ghost frequently. He comes in terrible dreams. He has no head. Is he moon-struck?"

Then I began a silly rhyme about being stone and moon-struck. It was not very good but it gave Achish the opportunity he needed.

The angry shouts my intervention had caused were stilled as he rose from his throne. "Councillors and captains of Gath. I have heard your words and all speakers have much wisdom. Certainly this man has done great harm to us and to Philistia.

"I was inclined to follow the words of Janna and see his sojourn amongst us as an opportunity, but I cannot fail to hear the just words of Baalal. But I tell you truly brothers, this man seems to me to be moon-struck. Why else would he come here, although bearing the flag of truce and claiming the protection of a civilised people?

My decision is that we have no need of any further moon-struck ones in Philistia." There some was laughter at this, but Achish gestured for silence. "Therefore, we should offer him the chance that the gods will restore or take him. We should give him the customary provisions for four weeks and escort him to the Cave of Adallum, where dwells all our other moon-struck. If Dagon wills, they live and return to us in their right minds – if not, they sleep quietly in the wilderness."

I did not quite appreciate what this half banishment meant but realised it was the best compromise Achish could get.

It seemed to unite the Council but Baalal pursued the issue. "But if he live, what then? Do we give him security?"

Achish spoke. "No, if he comes alive from the Cave of Adallum then he is again our enemy. The only time David can enter Gath is if this Council so decrees."

It was over. I was not to die but nor was I to have a refuge against Saul. I had no chance to speak to Achish as I was bundled out.

Janna escorted me to my horse and looked hard at me. "I tell you, David bar Jesse, that this day Dagon has had you in His care. I suspect, therefore, that someday you will return to do us good."

He smiled a knowing smile. "Achish, the King, is as wise as he is valiant. I prophesy that you were never moon-struck and that you will return – but invited by this same Council."

The Cave

So I began my journey into the south-eastern desert.

Two days later, I could see a tall mountain that seemed to jump out of the flat desert and hurl itself into the blue heaven, piercing the clouds. About five miles further, the tall mountain still seemed no nearer but grew taller before our eyes.

Baalal, who insisted on being my escort, pointed. "There, Israelite dog and wizard. Can you see? Beneath the summit of Spear Mountain is the Cave of Adallum. There may you dwell and may death and starvation come upon you."

With that, he struck my horse sharply across its flanks. The poor, tired beast lurched forward, which nearly threw me from his back.

With oaths and laughs, the escort rode away but not without Baalal's dread warning, "If we should find you anywhere but in the Cave of Adallum, we will kill you. But only after cutting off your mutilated prick, removing your arms and legs and splitting your bowels, which we will stuff into your barbarian mouth."

My flesh crawled. I knew he meant every word and that he felt cheated of his revenge.

I came up under the cave. It must have been a thousand feet high and, as there was no shelter anywhere on that desolate plain, the cave was the only refuge.

Everything was arid. The harsh heat of the air burned the throat. Dust bathed everything in a fine sheen that troubled the air as it vibrated in the sun's torrid glare, washing out all colour, turning everything a dross of ash brown.

There was a steep path upwards and my heart sank at the thought of how many desperate men had trudged up its barren sides. There was no place for the horse. So, after letting him drink a little just to slake his thirst and removing my supplies, I smote his side and sent him off to fend for himself.

The sun beat down. It was a suntrap and the rocks threw back its fierce heat threefold.

426

Wearily, holding my screaming thoughts in check, I made two energy-sapping journeys with which I carried everything to the cave.

The cave at least gave cool and shade, for which I was very grateful. The first positive feature was that the slope of the cave opened to allow me to wedge a flat stone. If the wind blew in the right direction, it would send cold air against my rock and condense, thus giving me a few dewy drops to supplement my small supply of water.

The view, if I had bothered to consider it, was magnificent. Beneath me rolled out the desert of El Gid – but, oh, it was so desolate. Due east of here lay Bethlehem but that must be sixty or more miles away. Between my home and this horror lay the rest of the desert.

As the light began to fade, my spirits fell. What had I done? I had placed myself in a trap, for it was obvious that the vengeful Baalal would be patrolling the area to ensure that I did not try to escape. Gloomily, I reflected that he was a resourceful captain and had probably thrown a patrol further east on the offchance that I was mad enough to try to cross that desert alone.

I stopped thinking lest I truly go mad with frustration, anger, fear, despair, loneliness and sheer dread at my situation.

I built on the bitter words Agag:

"My God my God why hast thou forsaken me, why art thou so far from helping me and from the words of my roaring.
O my God, I cry in the daytime and thou hearest not, and in the night-time I am not silent.

I am poured out like water and all my bones are out of joint my heart is like wax, it is melted in the middle of my bowels. My strength is dried up like a potsherd and my tongue cleaveth to my jaws and thou hast brought me into the dust of death."

I was alone. My God had truly deserted me. The doubts of Achish were infectious. Could it all be self-illusion and wishful thinking? I was nothing – nothing!

"I am a worm and no man, a reproach of men and despised of the people. All that see me laugh me to scorn, they shoot out the lip and say, He trusted on the Lord that He would deliver him. Let Him deliver him if He delighteth in him."

All my aspirations through my naive faith in God were in vain. Here was a test to prove that either He did not exist or that He did not care whether I lived or died. I could almost hear the mockery, not of

427

Achish, but of the people of Israel, laughing at my presumption.

I was not sure which held the most horror: the sense of being rejected, the helplessness of the isolation, or the churning vacuum of unbelief.

The next three days were the worst of my life.

All I could do was sit, inert, fearing that if I was too active, the hunger and thirst would increase and then the mean provisions would be quickly exhausted.

I was completely unnerved. My anointing was a mockery. My hopes and ambitions bizarre. All I knew was that I was totally and absolutely alone – deserted.

That night, I did not even have the emotional or spiritual energy to cry or to pray. I lay hoping that death would come quickly and not extend my suffering.

Then, I thought of the sword of Goliath. No – I would not give him the satisfaction of my death. I would use my dagger. Then angrily thought: yes, I would use the sword to show my anger at a God who mocks us for His sport. I would cheat and show my contempt for His unfaithfulness. I prayed that it would be Baalal who would return and find my body, slain by a Philistine sword as a witness to God's unfaithfulness – or worse, the blasphemy that he did not exist.

My mind drifted. Suddenly, I felt cold. Was I dying? Was I dreaming? My soul shrank to nothing. I observed my useless, desolate body lying crouched upon the ground beneath me. I no longer felt the pain of the cold that was consuming the still form below. Yes, this was death – my spirit was leaving my body. But then the cold began to ebb and I felt a warmth, a glow all around my soul. I dare not think. Was I being taken into the bosom of Abraham?

The glow filled the heavens and illuminated everything – only I could see nothing, feel nothing, other than the joy of the sense of freedom. My own words of inspiration for Jonathan came to my soul.

BE STILL AND KNOW THAT I AM GOD.

I lost all sense of body, mind, soul or time. I was filled with a divine languor and happiness. Oh, I yearned that this moment would last, for I knew it could last forever. Then, with total certainty, I knew I was in the presence of God.

The Voice spoke:

DAVID, DAVID, WHY DOUBTEST THOU ME?
DAVID, YOU KNOW THAT I AM HE

THAT I HAVE GIVEN YOU MY WORD
THAT YOU ARE MY ANOINTED.
CONSIDER THE STARS, THE HEAVENS, THE WORK OF MY
FINGERS.
CONSIDER MAN THAT I AM MINDFUL OF HIM
AND THOU ART SPECIAL UNTO ME.
I SEE THE SPARROW FALL.
HOW MUCH MORE DO I CARE FOR YOU?
SO, BE OF GOOD CHEER,
I WILL NOT SUFFER A HAIR OF THY HEAD TO FALL.
DAVID, BE VALIANT.
DAVID, REMEMBER,
THINK, NOT FEEL.

Was the Voice laughing? Was He teasing me as a friend gently chides those he loves?

The Voice was silent. My soul cried aloud for forgiveness for doubting. My being pleaded for His presence to return. I yearned to return to the envelope of the love of God's caress, who for that moment held my mind, soul, body and spirit.

With a jarring crash, I was myself again, alone on the bare cave floor.

I was consumed by guilt and ingratitude, yet I held a longing to return to the Father of all certainty and love. I stood up and went to the mouth of my cave.

I explored my heart and soul.

"O sing unto the Lord a new song, sing unto the Lord all the earth. For he hath done marvellous things.
His right hand and His holy arm hath gotten Him the victory.
Declare his glory amongst the heathen his wonders among all people."

Yes, I visited the heathen and even there God's hand was over me.

"For the Lord is great and greatly to be praised,
He is feared above all other gods, for all the gods of the nations are idols
But the Lord made the heavens."

Yes, the Living God sometimes brings burdens upon us, but never too great to bear. I was ashamed of my weakness and the little strength of my faith. I knew that He saw and that He forgave.

I awoke next day, confident that rescue was at hand. Before the sun had risen to the tenth hour, I saw a figure – no, three figures – approaching.

I ran down from my cave. I did not know who they were but had complete confidence that, whoever they were, they brought succour and rescue. As they came closer, to my absolute joy, I recognised Josh, Eli and Joab leading a spare horse full of supplies. I ran to greet them and our joy was great.

My questions poured over them. How did they find me? How did they know? Joab spoke amidst the ecstatic embraces. "We had a secret message from Achish. He let us know where you were and that we needed as many supplies as we could carry. The Companions are organising a larger rescue, but we three thought that as, without us you always get into trouble, we'd come early."

I wept with joy and admiration. These dear, brave men were willing to risk all for their friend.

Amazingly, because they had brought enough water, we did not need to let the horses go. Also, Baalal and his murdering crew would not be here for two weeks, which gave us time to spare. Frankly, I felt that we four were a match for his ten any time.

They told me how Saul had threatened Jonathan again. This time, however, he had boldly told his father that he was wrong in killing the priests and driving me away. He knew Saul would later regret it and, therefore, for the moment, Jonathan would not obey the King, but be his guardian until he recovered. Oh that he had thought of this earlier! Jonathan had prepared his coup and was accompanied by his guard. Though Abner was present, he and his men were outnumbered, so Abner thought it wisest to let Jonathan have his way.

Somewhat surprisingly, Saul seemed to accept the situation – especially when Jonathan renewed his oath of allegiance and said that he was ready to obey the King in everything, except to go against the King's son, David. Unfortunately, after a week, Jonathan restored his father to his throne.

The next night, Beniah, Hitophel, and Abashi and Ashael, Joab's firebrand younger brothers, arrived. I feared nothing less than a whole division of Philistines to counter us. With the exception of Jonathan, these were the "mighty men of Israel" and were the match of any ten Philistines. However, I could not help but notice that my dear friends were somewhat overly tender of me and were almost deferential in their response.

Then, Beniah said, "I think that the Lord's anointed has had another visitation."

How did he know? Did he know of the Voice?

He saw my surprise and asked to borrow the sword of Goliath. Wondering, I drew if from its sheath and handed it to him.

He gave it a further polish and then handed it to me.

"See," he said.

I saw. Across my head was another whitened band. I realised that a mere man cannot come close to the majesty of God without danger from His divine fire. God, in His care, has to hold Himself afar from His chosen, lest He consume them utterly if they come too near His presence.

I nodded. Though I did not tell them about the Voice, I did speak of my anointment.

I then gave what was to become a political statement for the next ten troubled years. "I am the Lord's anointed. But I and mine are loyal to the House of Saul until such time as God clearly calls me to reign. I am not a rebel. Nor am I a traitor to my oath. I will never attack Saul or his – unless to defend myself."

I saw that I had their rapt attention. "I want you all to swear that you will never raise your hands against Saul unless it is to protect your lives. Jonathan and I have sworn such an oath and you know he is the Prince of All Princes."

The men silently nodded, so I continued. "I do not know the purpose of God, but my prayer is that Jonathan will succeed his father and that I will serve him until God calls me to take up the burden of kingship."

They all looked serious at my passionate earnestness, because I think some of them almost enjoyed the idea of an alternative power. They all swore, and it was oath that we never broke. No matter what others say or what happened.

Then I did something stupid. Without thinking, in that highly charged atmosphere, I said, "Oh Joab, this water is a bit stale. How I have longed for the water of Bethlehem. Whilst alone, I found myself dreaming of its sweet freshness. What I would give to share with you the waters of Bethlehem."

They agreed and we closed the night comparing waters. Although Beniah defended his water, we Bethlehemites knew that there was nothing to compare with the water of Bethlehem.

Next morning, I arose late as the sun was already up.

"Where's Joab, Beniah?" I asked.

He looked a little uncomfortable and mumbled something about, "He's gone on a little errand."

"An errand? What are you talking about?"

Then, suddenly, I saw that the others were also gone. "Where are Josh and Eli?"

Beniah seemed to be keeping something from me. "Don't worry. Abashi, Ashael and I are still here. We can defend this cave against any odds."

Then it emerged: the idiots, drunk with glory, had talked about the waters of Bethlehem and had decided amongst themselves that, if their captain wanted to drink from the well of Bethlehem, they would go and get it!

I was aghast, outraged, astounded and totally guilt-ridden. What a fool I had been! Here indeed was the stupidity of feeling rather than thinking.

I could see the sensible Beniah agreed with me, whereas Joab's brothers were disgruntled that they had been told to remain behind to guard the cave.

I was frantic with worry. I knew I could do nothing but wait. Then, I knew the real terror and burden of command: waiting for others' return whom you have placed in danger. The ordinary soldier seldom thinks of the anxiety that the general endures, apparently safe in the camp.

It was as if I had personally sent these three brave, magnificent, foolish heroes into terrible danger. There was no doubt that the area would be alive with Philistine patrols. Whilst they were mighty indeed, in the open I would not give them much chance if they were attacked by more than ten.

So I sat, irritable, anxious and biting my nails to their end – the beginning of a very bad habit.

Late on the third day, as the evening gilded the western clouds, an armed party approached. After first fears that they might be Philistines, we saw with relief and joy that they heralded the return of Josh, Eli and Joab.

I rushed down from the cave to greet them, leaving Abashi and Beniah struggling in my wake.

Sure enough, they were there as large as life, laughing all over their faces and waving water skins containing the precious waters from Bethlehem.

To my added joy, they were followed by the other Companions, all thirty now re-united.

Amidst shouts of joy and greeting, I was swept over by the tide of my comrades showing me their friendship. No wonder I could hardly speak for tears of thankfulness.

When we were all assembled and they had dismounted, I called Josh, Eli and Joab before the captains.

I asked them where they had been.

Josh, as usual, was the one to speak up. "We had to lead the Companions, so we thought we would go early. When our Captain asks for something, the Companions of David take it as a matter of honour to obey before an order is required."

Those lovely, brave, idiotic, glorious men cheered his nonsense to the skies.

I tried to sound angry, I tried to sound stern, but my voice kept cracking with emotion. "My dear, dear Joab, Eli and Josh. Mighty men of Israel, never, never, never again, risk your lives for the vanity of a mere man. I was a fool."

They laughed at this but they were pleased at the acknowledgement of their deed. There were answers of "Come on, David, have your drink – you know it's the best – get Beniah to try it and learn what good water really tastes like."

I raised my hand for silence, as I tried to steady my voice but with only little success. "My friends, and I am honoured beyond all men to call you my friends."

I had to stop as they applauded. "My friends and Companions. Can any in the whole of time have had such comrades and warriors, who dared all for me and for each other?"

They cheered again, but I continued. "This water of Bethlehem is the very best."

They whooped with delight and roared the praises of Bethlehem.

"But, my brothers, this is not water. By your daring, courage, and glorious bravery, it has been transformed into liquid gold."

They were still. I gathered myself, still fighting to control my bursting heart.

"I am not worthy to drink this sacred water. Such courage has made it holy water. Through the whole aeons of time, men will wonder and speak of such valour and ask were these truly men or giants from the mists of time. No, they are men, men of Israel, who, until the sands of time run out, will be spoken of with awe, you are truly sons of God and of Israel."

There was complete silence as the other Companions appreciated just what The Three had dared.

"I am not worthy to put these holy drops to my lips. Nay, they are too holy for any man to drink. See, I pour this honour-bought gold as a worthy libation to the Almighty Living God of Israel. I call upon Him, Father and maker of all, to see His great handiwork, for here are Men of Israel indeed."

And with those words I offered a prayer unto God. With my heart, I asked Him to bless these, His glorious servants, and accept our renewed vows of service to Him.

As my words came to an end, all fell silent. Upon their knees, they sang a psalm of the Glory of Our God and of Israel, which had been given me to sing before Saul and all the people after Eilah in happier times. But our hearts sang it together in unison because we all knew that we had shared a great benediction and baptism from the waters of the heroes rightly given to God.

433

"Make a joyful noise unto the Lord all ye lands
Serve the Lord with gladness and come before His presence with singing.

Know Ye that the Lord is God and it is Him that hath made us and not we ourselves.

We are His people and the sheep of His pasture.
Enter His gates with thanksgiving and into His courts with praise, be thankful unto Him and bless His name.

For the Lord is good, His mercy everlasting and His truth endureth to all generations."

Chapter Nineteen

The Desert Band

Now began a period that, despite the hardships, I cannot fail but to remember with some satisfaction.   The Thirty, as they became known throughout Israel, led by the Mighty Three, Joab, Eli and Josh, who had been captains of my regiment, added their names to the original Companions.

We took counsel together for I was very mindful of how Achish ruled. First hearing others, he would benefit from their advice before making his decision. This would be seen to be less arbitrary because all that were worthy had spoken. I decided that, like Achish, whilst I might offer an idea, I would encourage discussion before taking on the responsibility.

This proved invaluable in deciding war strategy though, of course, in battle I, as leader, expected and always received immediate obedience.

So I called my first Council and asked what they thought we should do next.

There needed to be little discussion because as all agreed that, though the cave was impregnable to us as we were, it could not be garrisoned with such a force. Therefore, we should seek a place on the borders of the Desert of El Gid from which we could either raid Philistine villages for provisions, or take from the Amalekite lands, or even receive help from friendly Israelites, whom we might defend from any marauding Philistines.

Our morale was high and we felt we were a match for ten times our number. We moved into the borders of the lands which linked that of the Amalekites, Israel and Philistia, living from our small flocks and the help of kinsmen who were not afraid to send us succour.

What we had not thought credible was that Saul would send Israelite soldiers against us. I was angry and astounded but all agreed we had to defend ourselves.

On the first three such occasions, however, no blood was spilt. The first group, comprising a hundred men, when they saw who they were opposing, willingly agreed to a truce. They gave us some of their supplies, wished us God's speed and returned back to Saul – though ten men decided to join us.

The second and third times, they were led by some of Saul's guards, who were intent on making some impression.

By this time, we knew the terrain backwards and were easily able to lead them into a blind ravine. When faced by archers who blocked off their escape, they saw that their position was hopeless and were happy to withdraw. However, on the last occasion, a man called Simeon, who had ambitions to be a general of Saul, treacherously attempted to hurl his spear at me. By the time spear had passed harmlessly over my head, he was riddled with more than twenty arrows. The others could not retreat quickly enough.

The next time, however, Saul came himself, with a thousand men. No matter what his mood or motives were, he was still a very able commander. He almost turned the tables on me as we were locked in a narrow defile, which at both ends he had stationed a hundred men.

Things looked desperate. I suggested that I go to Saul as a suppliant.

Ura, who had been sent to us by Jonathan, spoke for them all. "David, my captain, you are the Lord's anointed. I would rather the Philistines defile my body before I would see you place your life in the hands of that tyrant."

So it was agreed to resist. I decided that ten of us would ride late in the afternoon, just before sunset, as a threat to the men in the west of the ravine. Others would seek to break out and make their way to the Cave of Adallum during the night.

The situation was critical until, without warning, we heard Saul's trumpeters sound the recall. We later learned that Saul had been warned that three regiments of Philistines had gone raiding at his rear, hence his speedy withdrawal.

That was the closest Saul ever came to crushing me. I often wonder whether it was Achish, perhaps influenced by God, who had intuitively sent them out? Undoubtedly, we were within less than half a day of being totally defeated.

Saul did not trouble us for more than a year, but, each month, men came out to join us so that eventually we had six hundred fighting men, all dedicated to protecting the Lord's anointed.

Once we had established ourselves, and you must remember that we Israelites were still a semi-nomadic people, living in the desert and moving our small herds to follow the pasture was no real hardship. Many men had also brought their wives to our camp. Indeed, amongst the

436

Thirty, only Ashael and I had no wives.

Perhaps I would not have done what I did, but the last to join us, Aggar, a Judean, brought me news that turned a knife in me.

Saul, in an act of extreme mean-mindedness, had declared my marriage to Michal ended. This, of course, was against the law as only the husband can declare a divorce. Moreover, he should have returned my dowry, the two hundred Philistine foreskins, so his behaviour was totally illegal.

Worse, he spitefully married her to a nonentity, Pateil. Michal protested but she was in no position to assert my rights and, typical of Saul's advancing tyranny, he did this whilst Jonathan was with an army chastising the Moabites.

I never realised until then how corrosive a poison jealousy can be. I wept with anger and frustration at the thought of another man possessing my Michal. I dared not think of the pain that it would cause her.

Some days later, we came across a Philistine war party returning home. We made short shrift of them and recovered much of their booty, including two young Israelite women who had been seized by them and were being taken into concubinage.

Fortunately, neither had been defiled: that was against Philistine custom because it would reduce their bond price considerably.

Ura and Joab brought up the idea. Joab, on this occasion, was the spokesman.

"David, my captain. We have two fair women of Israel, Annah of Jezreel and Mocha of Gilbeah. Both are comely. You and Ashael are the only bachelors amongst the Companions. Ura and I have sounded out the women and they are willing to become wives to each of you. As captain, if they please you, you should take the first choice."

I could see this entertained the men greatly. On rare occasions, it amused them to remember that I was still one of the youngest of the band, though there must have been at least ten warriors younger than me.

I had inquired of Aggar whether the Princess Michal was with child. When he sorrowfully told me no, I was sad for both of us, as Michal, not having given me a child, left me free. So I confess to a slight stirring of the blood and I went to see the two maidens we had rescued.

Both were very comely. Annah of Jezreel was of a special, rare beauty as she was quite fair and had almost golden hair.

"Lady, would it please you to become my wife?"

She looked surprised at this. Perhaps, at best, she thought I would only offer her to become my concubine. When I repeated my offer, she knelt and made a gracious acceptance speech.

We had one priest amongst us, Abathar, son of Amlech, whose slaughter had washed away Saul's anointment. He readily married me to Annah, and then Ashael, Joab's brother, to Mocha.

We had much sport that night. In the desert, we had little privacy but the men, in decency, allowed us to move far off. For security, Ashael and I stayed on the same side of the camp.

By now, my blood was fully aroused. I suspect that we had a thrilling competition of love that night. From the sound of our climatic delights, we sought to discover who could serve his wife most times.

I had been celibate for months. Whether my six times of ecstasy was one more than Ashael's, or whether he felt it only proper not to exceed his captain, I will never know. But both of us, for the next few weeks, found the days tedious.

We did not know it then, but the next twelve months were to be a very good time. True, it was hard living. We had no luxuries and how our women managed was a daily wonder, but we were young warriors, bound to each other, fit and in our prime.

We had daily drills in which I was included. Though I was Chief Captain, I still had much to learn. It would have been stupid not to use the great talents of Ura.

Dear Ura, he always had a joke but underneath I could tell he pined for Jonathan. I let him know how much I was aware of his sacrifice.

"Well David, I'm only a poor Hittite but my bond is for life. Though I am committed to Prince Jonathan, he said the greatest service I could do for him was to serve you. It's clear you Bethlehemites need all the help you can get. But it's good to know that I'm appreciated and the way you have helped young Uriah to settle in is appreciated too."

We drilled in my shock cavalry tactics and, of course, once the Philistines understood about our simple stirrups they adapted very quickly. They speedily mastered my new way, but they were never as good as slingers as we were. I also I realised that we needed to do something slightly better – not a great invention but having something to surprise them. This worked by mixing archers and slingers. War being war, if it meant bringing down their horses, so be it. Some Philistines thought this cowardly and confirmed for them our barbarism but I think that's because they treated their horses almost as well as their women. For us, a horse was just something to use, though being living creatures some did become special.

What the enemy found difficult was how quickly we were heavy infantry one minute, then cavalry and then back again. This always gave us an advantage if the ground was good and they did not outnumber us too greatly.

I improved my swordsmanship. As I discovered that I was a natural rider, it was reasonable for me to lead the elite group of shock troops.

Ura and Beniah were superb with the men as infantry whilst Joab very quickly showed that he too was a natural commander. Joab, with his brothers, Abashi and young Ashael, were irrepressible. Joab had taken to heart the study of leadership and he watched closely Beniah and Ura. If we split our small army into four, Joab was the obvious commander after Ura, Beniah and myself.

Moreover it was good for all to see that it was merit, not age, that mattered for promotion.

During this time, I first became a father. Annah, of whom I was very fond, was a good wife and never complained, though she lacked the fire of Michal and the imagination and intelligence of my Leah.

But parenthood: it was wonderful. When I was called into the laying-in tent, she was surrounded by the other women. Then, I saw Annah and the child. The look on her face made her the equal of any king's daughter. She had brought life into the world – unlike we men, who seemed destined to take and despoil creation.

I had a slight sense of guilt about Annah. Whilst our lovemaking was good and it eased my mind and body, I had no sense of shared spirit. Whether this was my fault it is hard to say, so when she gave me a son, I let her name him. She called my first born Amnon.

I had never held my child in my arms before. Amnon was so tiny, fragile, barely larger than a rabbit, but the miracle of God was that he was so perfectly formed. Again, I can understand why we do not need graven images to see beauty. Just take the time to stop and look at a child. The Great Pharaoh himself cannot command such beauty to be imitated, unless he has a child of his own.

I would have fought bears and lions single-handed to preserve that little creature. No wonder when the prophets want to express something very intimate they draw upon the image of a child.

Unfortunately, as you will see, one can be too indulgent as a father and Amnon was to cause me much distress though, to be fair, not before confirming upon me the greatest title a man can have, "Father".

The birth of Amnon set me musing on the nature of love. I had been so lucky to have found Leah and perhaps we were so perfect together that it was not possible for it to last. Our love was so intense that our minds, body and spirit would have been consumed.

I might have loved Merab like that, too, because there was a sharing of minds, she had a spiritual dimension and I am sure our bodies would have played in perfect harmony.

Whilst I came to like and admire Annah, who always sought to please me with her body, I never really loved her with my mind. I quickly found that if I shared with her one of my psalms, a blank look slowly came over her face.

With Michal, my first attraction to her was little better than the lust I felt for Mera, of whom I used to shamefully dream. In the end, I grew to love Michal and the root to that harmony was not in the body but from a shared intelligence. And, of course, who could fail to love someone who had saved your life. So, at the end, Michal and I brought the three elements of love together, albeit in a fragile way.

I have mentioned Mera. She taught me about that side of man's nature which he calls love, although if it is purely physical, it can be dangerous. By itself, it is empty. It seeks only its own gratification and can lessen other, more complete, loves. It can also be the source of great violence and sacrilege if a man forgets his humanity and the humanity of others. Boaz, my brother, taught me that and his hideous example never left me.

My love for Jonathan was, like that of Leah, of the perfect kind. We had an integration of mind, body and spirit. Yet the physical side was so different from that of Leah. I did worry that the early Prophets had been so hostile to physical love between men, but that was because I think they were concerned with uncleanliness. Some men use each other physically as they would women. That is obviously unclean and I have never been tempted to follow that route. But with Jonathan and Leah, the merging of our bodies was a celebration of the essence of humanity, of reason and soul.

Jonathan was an echo of the fact that we are made in God's image and that a woman reflects our mother, Eve, who perhaps less so than a man, shares something of the divine shape of God. After all, it is the woman who carries and nurtures the seed, and whose wondrous breasts feed the warrior when he is a child and when he takes her as a man.

In my heart of hearts, I who have heard the Voice, also know that the perfect consummation of two human beings is the nearest we come to that joy and all embracing warmth of the love of God.

Thus, all men – and women, too – if they find delight in the complete surrender and sharing of another's mind, sprit and body, can find the Godhead lies at the heart of every soul.

The time in the Desert of Ziph also gave the Companions an opportunity to learn the value of each other.

It seemed that we fell into two types. There was the pragmatist: down-to-earth, super-competent men, like Ura and Joab. Give them a problem and ask them to solve it, and if anyone could it would be them. They never forgot the practical considerations. Indeed, Ura taught us all that an army needs feeding, watering and mucking out. Those practical organisational issues, when done well, meant that we always had what was necessary, be it weapons, horses, adequate supplies or cleanliness. Hence, we seldom lost men from disease.

Joab, along with his brothers Abashi, and Ashael, seemed to fear nothing. This was also the case with Ura, and even more so his brother, Uriah, even though he was dour.

Other men, and perhaps I am inclined to this side, always seemed to seek for meanings in a situation. Josh for all his gaiety had as much an interest in the spiritual or the inspirational as did Eli.

The surest way the differences showed was if I walked the mountains with Josh, Eli, and Beniah, and, of course, Jonathan. We would notice the blaze of colour at our feet. Then raise our eyes to the hills that threw their sharp peaks against the blue or dark grey of the heavens. We would listen to the music contained in the hills' great silences and know that we were communing with God's great paean of life. Whereas, take Joab and Ura to the same place and they would notice the lie of the land, whether it was good defensive or attacking ground and nod condescendingly if ever I was carried away with what Ura called "your enthusiasms".

Beniah, whilst one of these thinkers, also had a practical side, so he was an ideal second-in-command and was totally reliable. But of course, I loved them all and would have died for them and they for me.

Whilst Jonathan was surely the greatest-ever commander, what a soul he had. He was sheer perfection. If he had been with us, life would have been ideal.

Unfortunately, Saul could not let matters rest. In the second year, he sent out two large columns to "hunt and smoke out these wild beast outlaws and enjoy the sport of ridding Israel of our enemies."

Mercy to Saul

I find the idea of turning war into hunting an abomination. War is necessary and one must kill, but not for pleasure. To describe war between men as hunting is a profanity.

He brought ten thousand into the field and, to our great sorrow, there was some fighting.

Because we knew the country better and had a good supply of information from people sympathetic to me, we caused Saul's men great discomfort. We must have killed nearly 400 in small battles and guerrilla exchanges, and lost barely 20 men ourselves. However, these losses were the more hurtful because we had become warrior brothers. Any loss was felt

441

personally by all in the Band.

There was one incident when the war might have ended in our favour.

Abashi and I had taken a small patrol of ten and had sneaked behind Saul's main column. We recognised that Saul himself was leading a large patrol as he was desperately trying to find where our main strength lay. We followed him discreetly and came up behind them. I left two men with the horses and, splitting the group into two small files, we were able to run along a path on top of the small ravine, into which Saul had blundered.

He was not a very good rider and went on mule, which, whilst fine in hills, are no match for a horse for speed.

Abashi and I were together with the other file on the far side of the ravine, along which a small cleft ran for about twenty yards.

Amazingly, Saul dismounted and gave his mule to an attendant, telling him to go on a little. He would relieve himself and take a drink at the spring further ahead.

Abashi looked at me in sheer delight. There was Saul beneath us, barely ten yards away. He had no idea we were there.

Abashi's eyes gleamed and a hard rage came over him. "David," he hissed. "Let's kill the bastard and rid Israel of its curse. Let's do away with this moon-struck King and restore Israel to the true Lord's anointed."

For a moment, I imagined what was to be done. An arrow would bring him down and, even if he cried out, we were closer to him than his men were. The sword of Goliath would take his head before his men knew what was happening. A call from me would engage our file at the other side of the ravine, Saul's men would feel surrounded and probably run.

There he was. He had struggled up the stony bank and dropped a neck cloth. He was oblivious to all around him. Rapidly, I thought of what the death of Saul would mean. The end of the civil war; Jonathan would be King; Israel would be re-united; I could retrieve Michal; the exile with the Companions would be over. At my side, Abashi was hissing to break my revere. "Do it! Do it!"

For one murderous and sacrilegious moment, I could have done it. Instead, gathering up Saul's fallen neck cloth, I turned to Abashi, shook my head and said,

"How can I, of all men, raise my hands against the Lord's anointed. How can any man of Israel do such a thing? No, Abashi, my friend, we will commit no sacrilege."

Abashi's face fell. He gave me a look, which was a mixture of contempt and incomprehension. He was about to argue. "But – "

"No," I whispered. "He is the Lord's anointed. He is my Father-in-law. He is mistaken and misled, but we do not strike at God's chosen one."

Abashi gave a big sigh and looked completely lost. I had an idea. I beckoned him to follow me. In three strides, we were in line with Saul but above him. He was in the most defenceless position a man can be, squatting – very unking-like.

I called out clearly, "Father. Saul, my King. I have here the neck cloth that you dropped."

He sprung up immediately, looking terrified, but could see there was no escape. Like the brave man he was, he drew his sword.

I laughed. "King Saul, if I had wanted to kill you, you would have been dead even before I took this neck cloth as trophy. Is this not proof indeed that I am not your enemy? I am not a traitor but slandered by those who would hurt you and Israel."

There was shouting from Saul's column when they heard voices around their King.

Saul showed great presence of mind. He called out, "It is all right, Haggar. I am amongst friends. Call the men together and withdraw out of the ravine. I will join you shortly."

Haggar would have protested but Saul curtly ordered, "Go, Haggar! Do as you are bid. I shall join you shortly. Send out messages we are to return to Gilbeah at first light. Now hurry, I don't want the columns to get too far ahead."

As the man left, Saul turned towards us and laid his sword on the ground.

He looked perplexed and sad. "Is it really you, my Son David, my bard, whom I miss more than I can ever say? Is it you my son?"

My heart broke. Dare I go down to him and be reconciled? Though I had spared his life would he, once back amongst his army, be equally just. There were many that had much to lose if I returned.

"Yes, Father. Why do you persecute me? I have never been anything but loyal."

"But David, you know the source of the black moods and you say you are loyal. There are others who say you let the Old Man anoint you as King-to-be. Now, that's hardly loyal."

I could see that he was not convinced, yet I could have slain him.

"Father, I could have slain you. My Companion here could have slain you and he would not have been guilty of parricide."

Swift as a flash, Saul retorted, "No, but he would be guilty of raising his hand against the Lord's anointed. I am glad to see, David my bard, that you still know your duty and try to serve the Lord. You heard me say I return to Gilbeah tomorrow. I will and I swear to leave your people alone for a whole year. But you, who claim loyalty, how is it you have turned my son's heart away from his father. Michal I had to banish because she, too, would exalt you before her duty to me. The band of outlaws gathered around you are not loyal. There can be only one King in Israel."

He had worked himself up into an angry mood.

I tried to answer. "King Saul, whilst you or Jonathan live, there will be no other King in Israel – I swear it. But you have slain the innocent, driven out the loyal and listened to evil counsellors. Can you imagine Abner letting such a chance as this pass today?"

This seemed to get home.

"David, my son, I am tired. Thank you for my neck cloth – aye, and my life. The Lord preserve you. I tell you truly, I wish you were still my bard, but there can only be one anointed voice in Israel. Farewell."

I let him go. Abashi thought I was a fool but, to his credit, he never said it or held it against me.

Saul honoured his word and left us alone for more than a year.

The Battles of the City of Kileah

We decided that our camp was too near to Saul, so we moved further south, back into the desert of El Gid.

Inevitably, it became known that I had spared Saul. To be fair, the majority of the men thought like Abashi: that I had missed a conclusive opportunity to end our exile. A few, however, agreed with me about the sacrilege. Moreover, if I had killed Saul, could Jonathan in all truth welcome home as a friend he who had killed his father? This was the compelling argument.

The question was what to do next, because we seemed to lack purpose.

Now, at the tip of Israel, and bordering upon the lands of the Amalekite and Philistines, was the city of Kileah. Their Elders heard that we were in the vicinity and sent out men seeking our help to drive off some Philistines and a small remnant of Amalekites, who had re-formed and were plaguing them.

We discussed this in Council. We were unsure whether or not to respond to their request for help. It was one of those rare occasions that we adjourned without taking a decision.

That night, I was in a deep sleep when I realised that I was watching my slumbering form peacefully below me.

I knew the warmth of the caress of being in the presence of the Lord and I heard the Voice:

DAVID, DAVID,

I AM PLEASED THAT YOU DID NOT COMMIT THE SACRILEGE THAT
TEMPTED YOU.
DAVID, GO DOWN TO KILEAH.
THEY NEED YOUR HELP AND HAVE CRIED UNTO ME,
BUT BE NOT TOO TRUSTING,
BUT GO TO BRING SUCCOUR TO MY PEOPLE WHO ARE SORE
OPPRESSED.
THIS IS YOUR MISSION.
YOU ARE THE SHEPHERD OF MY PEOPLE.
GO, COMFORT MY PEOPLE.
DAVID, IN YOU I AM PLEASED.

As in each time of experiencing the Voice, my soul longed to stay with Him, to be part of His great whole, to be lost in His Oneness. But, until we are to enter the bosom of Abraham, no living man can enter God's majesty without being all-consumed. So, when I awoke with a start, I knew I had been visited and I knew that our band had a purpose, whose aim was to prepare me for my ultimate role. I was going to be the shepherd of Israel and bring succour to the oppressed. However, I could not help notice that this time I heard the Voice when my soul was not in agony – which suggested He sought me rather than I Him.

Before dawn, I called a Council meeting. They all came running, thinking that Saul had re-invaded.

Though I did not say a word about the Voice, they could see I was inspired.

I called to them. "Companions, you brave Thirty, you asked what was our purpose. It has been with us all the time. In a psalm, that you call my psalm, we are to be the shepherds of Israel, to give protection and succour to any who are oppressed. This is the prime duty of the Lord's anointed."

I sang and they joined with me in what became the Battle Hymn of Israel:

"Make a Joyful noise unto the Lord all ye lands. Serve the Lord with Gladness and come before His presence with singing.
Know ye that the Lord He is God. It is Him that hath made us and not we ourselves, We are His People and the Sheep of His pasture.
Enter His gates with thanksgiving and into His courts with praise, be thankful unto him and bless His name.
For the Lord is good, his mercy everlasting and His truth endureth to all generations."

We rode immediately towards Kileah. As I had learned from Jonathan and Ura, I never send a large body of men into the unknown but always have scouts to see the way ahead.

Within an hour of Kileah, Josh, who had led the scouting party, came back excited. "There is a combined Philistines and Amalekite war party besieging the city. I sent Meran to the east and I scouted to the west. I estimate them to be about 2,000 warriors."

I made a rapid calculation. With 550 effective men, the other 50 to guard our women and camp, we were outnumbered almost four to one. We had surprise on our side, but how effective that would be?

Rapidly, I made inquiries of Josh as to their dispositions.

He said, "They're on three of the four sides of the city."

That decided me. I quickly explained my initial plan but said I needed to go forward before taking a final decision.

I went ahead and found all as Josh had described. I told Ura to take 30 to the east and, if necessary, mount a holding attack. Joab would do the same to the west. I would take the rest and attack their centre.

I estimated that there would be about a 1,000 enemies in front of us. But, as the city was between us, they could not gather all their strength immediately. If our 400 hit their main body, which my dispositions had made their centre, we should do sufficient damage to them to, if not totally defeat them, make them retreat from the city. Moreover, if the men of Kileah had any idea, they would attack from inside and complete the rout.

We hardly needed a word of explanation, such was the excellence of our training. We moved into position as I hurried along to where we could hear the sound of the attacking army.

We were within 200 yards of them. Their backs were towards us as I whispered my final orders. Just for a moment, my feelings got the better of me. I remembered Lev and his hopes of an Israelite cavalry. Well, here was going to be the biggest-ever Israelite cavalry charge.

Suddenly, ahead, I realised there was a commotion amongst the enemy. Had they seen us? Yes, they had – but they thought we were their reinforcements. I signalled the whole line to trot forward and passed the word: no war cries, just cheers. We started to approach them slowly, then trotted, quicker and quicker, and then – at the gallop!

The enemy, half of whom were looking at the City of Kileah, the other half happily waving at us, suddenly saw that we were not help, but avengers. Within 20 yards of them, I slowed the line right down. Almost from a standstill, our arrows flew into their front and backs. Many went down. We followed up with slings at their few horses.

As usual in these situations, my nerves got the better of me. My shouts turned to a piercing scream. "For Israel and the Lord of Hosts. He has delivered them into our hands."

Now we were upon them, there was confusion everywhere. There was a Philistine captain who was splendidly re-organising his troop. I wheeled towards him.

We recognised each other in an instant – it was Baalal of the family of Ganz. In our hate we were ahead of everyone. I could see he had not panicked but was drawing his bow, but I had loosed my arrows earlier. As we closed, I could see his dark eyes screwed up in hate as he took careful aim. I swerved as the arrow caught my breastplate, diverting it harmlessly away. He was drawing his sword. Too late – laying myself along the neck of my horse, I thrust at him with the sword of Goliath out stretched. He parried, but his horse crashed into mine, bringing us both down. We fell together amidst the kicking mayhem.

He was first to recover and threw himself upon me. I could feel his hand on my throat as he raised his other hand to bring down his sword. But it was too long for such close work. I threw up my knee and caught him in his middle. He cried out in pain and anger as I threw a blow across his head. Now I was on him, my legs pinning his and, though he was heavier, I had the advantage. His eyes blazed in hate but his grasp on my dagger hand was vice-like. He was holding me. In his snarling face was a look of triumph as he realised he was the stronger.

Then, slowly, with our muscles cracking in their fierceness, he began to push me back. Oh God, I was losing this deadly wrestling match. So I used my head – and battered it against his face. Once .., twice ..., his visage split with blood and gore. He was choking, he could hardly breathe. As his grip loosened, I forced through his enfeebled hands and sunk my knife deep into the side of his neck.

His mouth opened in agony. His eyes held mine. The look of total hate faded in amazement as death passed over and the light left him.

Just then, a pair of huge arms lifted me up.

It was Ura, convulsed with anxiety, then he gave a great shout. "Hosanna to David, our Captain."

It was over. With their captain down, the rallying group of Philistines broke and fled, turning the whole of the besieging army into a rout. In their desperate fight to get away, they went too close to the city barricade and were caught by the defenders. Those that escaped galloped or ran past the flank guards of Ura and Joab. In their panic, they trampled upon their own men at the other side of the city.

It was an amazing sight: 2,000 men disintegrated. Those who had held the line suddenly peeled away into utter confusion. But the men of Kileah

447

did nothing but cheer us.

I was furious. There should have been no survivors yet at least 600 got away.

Joab came up to me, bleeding from a slight scratch, as Josh galloped up with a particularly grizzly trophy: the head of their general.

I never liked this part of a battle but understood that we needed it for our morale.

"David, he wears the emblem of a full general of the Philistines. We'll send it back with the body count attached."

Men can be bloody in such circumstances. I was still angry with the men of Kileah who, to my further astonishment, had still not opened their gates.

I rode up to their wall and an Elder cried, "Blessing upon your heads, you defenders and savers of Israel. A thousand thanks to our Father Saul who has preserved his people."

Unfortunately, some of my men laughed. One of the Joab brothers, Ashael, called out, "Save your thanks for Saul, old man. Your saviour this day is David bar Jesse, the Lord's anointed. He was sent by God, not King Saul, to succour the oppressed of Israel."

This quite clearly nonplussed the old man.

I felt I ought to take control and called out, "Sir Elder, we do indeed come in the Lord's name. You can see there are no enemies left in the field, though they outnumbered us four to one. God gave us the victory because we were called to defend the city of Kileah – the Lord heard your prayer. But Sir Elder, why did your men not attack the fleeing enemy? If they had, not one would have escaped. Now there are those with extra desire to hurt Kileah. And why, Sir Elder, are your gates still closed to your rescuers?"

There was clear turmoil on the top of the rampart.

The Elder called back. "I am Kildron, son of Kileah, Chief Elder of Kileah. We had been expected King Saul, who promised to come to our aid weeks ago. Are you really David the Rebel?"

This was rapidly descending into a farce. I curtly inquired of Beniah about our losses and whether he had any idea of their body count.

"David, praise God, it has been a great victory but we have lost three brave brothers and ten others have severe injuries. At least 1,400 of the uncircumcised fell under your sword this day."

I could not help but feel elated. Clearly, the Voice had given us a great victory – not that I ever doubted it.

By now I was quite close to the gate. "Kildron, Elder of Kileah, greetings. I am David, slayer of Goliath, champion of King Saul, brother-in-law and friend of Prince Jonathan. I am no rebel. God has shown you this. We have not lost ten men but their dead are more than a thousand. Is this not a great sign that David and his Companions fight for the Lord?"

A younger voice cried out as the gates were rolled back. "Greetings, David and warriors of Israel. I, Caade, captain, greet you in the name of the warriors of Kileah. We would willingly have rendered you more aid but our Elders were nervous. Come into our gates that we may greet you as deliverers and saviours. We trust that you will dwell amongst us as long as you wish."

Our men gave a great cheer at this.

Later, after the burial parties and body count were finalised, the stripping of the dead meant that we had a spare supply of first class iron swords, spears and bows – as well as gold from those vain enough to fight with such ostentation.

So we entered into Kileah.

Beniah, as he was wont to do, sensed the reaction I always felt after conflict and quietly said, "David, my captain, that was the first cavalry battle. Lev would be pleased. And it has delivered your first city."

That night we turned down our glasses in a libation to his and Aaron's memory.

We stayed in Kileah for some months. Ura warned against it because he said it would make the men go soft. On the other hand, for over a year they had dwelt in the wilderness and it was a joy to enjoy the simple pleasures of city living, not least for the women, who could gather round the wells and not have to travel long distances for water of doubtful quality.

Whilst we did not know it, Ura was right. Despite what we had done for the people of Kileah, unbeknown to us, a conspiracy was hatching.

It was obvious that Saul would have had no chance to relieve the city before the Amalekites and Philistines had burnt it to the ground and carried the people off into bondage, yet Kildron, the Elder, was in communication with Saul.

Whilst Caade was our friend, Kildron took it very badly being beholden to me as a captain, not yet in my mid-twenties, as he was a man who placed great emphasis on tradition and age. Once, I mildly asked him how he would feel about serving Jonathan, who was a leader of armies at my age and before.

This posed no problem for him, "But he is a King's son and was born to command."

Try as I might to explain that Jonathan and I were friends, brothers and had jointly commanded armies, nothing would move that old man's acid heart.

After some months, Kildron came to visit me. I ought to have realised something was very wrong but, in my vanity, I thought I had at last won the old fool over. He became kind, calling upon me daily or twice daily, inquiring after Annah and Amnon.

"My, how he grows! Clearly, Amnon will be a great captain like his father."

Of course, we are all vulnerable to flattery through our children. Though again, I was stupid, for even Annah raised doubts about his sincerity and I should have listened to her.

Late that night, I recalled Annah's words and Ura's unease about us being too long in one place. Then, I half-recalled something I had forgotten. Something the Voice had said.

I tried to concentrate, but being in the presence of God is so warming and comforting. I could not remember. Then, suddenly, I sprang out of bed disturbing Annah and Amnon. My hair standing on end with alarm.

I curtly told her to stop the alarmed brat as, at that moment, I had no tender fatherly thoughts.

I knew I had been a total fool and that we were in great danger.

I quickly called the Four together and ordered them to round up the men and their families.

"What? Now? At midnight?"

"Yes, because it is midnight!"

Our activities had disturbed Caade, who came to see what the commotion was about.

I looked hard at him. My instincts told me to have no doubts: I could trust this young man.

"Caade, I believe that my men and I were sent by God as a witness that we are the shepherd of Israel and that we are to defend the oppressed. Our victory at your gates was no less a sign than Joshua's victories. However, our band is in great danger because I believe Kildron has sent to gather our enemies. As we are dwelling amongst you, we are no longer in a position to defend ourselves."

He looked very serious and asked, "What can I do, David, to remove this shame from the people of Kileah? Anything – I swear to you by my Father's head and my children that I would rather die than any ill befall you and your men. Tell me to do absolutely anything – and, if a man can accomplish it, I shall."

I had chosen right. "Go as fast as you can towards the direction of Gilbeah. Find out if there is an army coming from Saul. Also, send men you can trust to the north and south to discover whether any are coming from either direction. For, as the Lord lives, I am sure we are in deadly danger."

Just before dawn, Caade returned, pale and dishevelled. He reported, "David, there were no men coming from the east and Gilbeah. But, less than five miles away, there are two columns: one to the north and the other to the south. They are the men of Israel!"

Now I knew. In the meantime, we had aroused everyone and, of course, could not do so without arousing the whole city, which was now as frantic as an upturned beehive.

Just then, Kildron strode in in his worst pompous mood.

I cut him short and drew my dagger. "Old man, you are not fit to be an Elder of your city. Elders should guard, preserve. Why did you send for Saul? Deny it if you dare!"

For a moment, I thought he might try to bluff it out but Caade went up to him and said, "You despicable old man. You have brought shame upon the men of Kileah for ever. Whenever people speak of David, the Lord's anointed, they will recall that, after bringing us salvation, you betrayed him."

That dreadful old man fell on his knees and moaned for pity. He whined about doing his duty to his rightful King.

Caade cut him short. "Rightful King? Bah! You are seeking a marriage of your granddaughter into the House of Saul. It is for yourself that you did this, not for any sense of justice."

Then, turning to me, Caade asked, "Shall I give him his just desert and execute him to wipe away the stain of our ingratitude?"

Oh, I was tempted! I felt the surging joy of red anger. It would have been very easy – so very easy – just to nod and the ingrate's head would have become a football.

I closed down the temptation and held back. "Let him live to greet King Saul. He can explain his ingratitude after David the bard had done the King's service and relieved a city under oppression from the uncircumcised. One last service, Caade, guard the old fool to make sure he does not do any other mischief. Bind and gag him – but gently – I would not want his miserable death to be on your or my hands."

I rapidly gave orders to leave as quietly as possible through the western gate, towards Philistia. I almost felt it was inevitable.

"Come on, Abashi and Ashael. I've got jobs for you two."

I gave Beniah, Joab and Ura their orders and they started out with the three columns. I wished them God's speed.

"Where the hell are you off to, David. Begging your pardon, but this simple-minded Hittite always thought generals were to be with their troops – not going on some fool errand."

I must confess I enjoyed annoying and surprising Ura, so I just grinned at him and said, "I'm taking these firebrands to a party."

He shrugged and raised his eyes to heaven, but such was his discipline that he went off as bid.

I quickly told the Joab brothers what I wanted. Their faces went wild with delight and excitement – it was the perfect task for them.

"Listen," I said, "not more than five men each and not more than two fire arrows each, and, for God's sake, don't kill anyone. I don't want to be accused of being an arsonist."

They laughed at this.

"As soon as I see your fires, I'll start mine here. Then, away as quickly as you can and join the others. Now, no heroics. I'll need that for later."

Oh, the joy that comes from action – especially after a time of inertia. I took my three men and, as we had more time, we cleared everybody out of the two wooded towers. We saw the lights of fires coming from Saul's camp and heard shouts of, "David, treason, treachery".

I was utterly confident that Saul's columns would be in no fit state to start any pursuit and, with a little luck, we might stampede them.

My fires were burning brightly, to the great consternation of the citizens. I reasoned that they would be far too busy quelling the flames to do us any mischief as we left.

It worked perfectly. Ashael reported that he was not sure which scared Saul's northern column most: the fire arrows or the shouts of "David" and "treachery", but the column simply dissolved into a confused mess.

Abashi reported similar success. "I was quite sure I heard fighting. I think they started attacking each other. Oh, David, we should have charged them. We would have had another Kileah victory."

I loved his enthusiasm and his lack of doubts, but he did not carry the same burden as I had to.

I calmed him down. "We'll save that for another time. I would love to be present when Saul seeks to understand and explain how we all got away though trapped in a walled city. How his two columns were in confusion, all from a mere 600 who had done his work for them at the battle of Kileah."

Perhaps I could be forgiven my exhilaration. After all, it was my foolishness that nearly brought all to disaster. Worse, Saul's entry was not to have a happy conclusion.

Caade, as captain, led the bound Kildron to Saul, who angrily asked how his enemies had been allowed to escape. Caade asked whom did he mean: the Amalekites and Philistines, who had been besieging the city when relieved by David of Israel?

"Your enemies, oh King, kept the gates shut so that I and my men could not add to the glory of your arms. For know this, Great King, David, your son, bard and slayer of Goliath, was here and defeated an enemy ten times his number, whilst we were awaiting succour from you, oh Great King – "

Poor Caade did not finish. Saul, with a cry of fury, struck him down as he knelt. Saul had become a man to whom good deeds and reason were now an anathema unless they fed his passion and prejudice. The only notice he took of the poor man was to step over his congealing pool of blood flowing from his cloven head.

From that day on, the Lord took away any favour from the King. Saul showed no signs of remorse but darkened his days with tyranny, to the distress of those who loved him.

Chapter Twenty

Abigail

Love and the Wise Women

We rode away from Kileah and, for the next year or so, migrated between the deserts of El Gid and Moan, making ourselves useful where we could but mostly living from good husbandry.

Some critics suggested that we became more like bandits than defenders, arguing that we offered to protect villages and towns only in return for some assistance with supplies. The accusation was that this protection was forced upon them and that our presence was more of a threat to people than what we were protecting them from. This was very unfair because we took nothing by force. Although we did invite a contribution to our cause, if they declined, we did not press them.

I received two letters, which proved to be a major influence upon me for years to come.

The first was from the Prophet who sent his greetings and wrote:

"Be resilient and remember that you are the Lord's anointed as Saul has committed the great sacrilege of disobedience. You alone are the only defender of the priesthood now that the tyrant has cast off his obligation to the Lord.

"I have let it be known that Abathar, son of Amlech, who was a martyr for the Lord, will be Chief Priest, though you know he is but a weak bulwark for God's people. Despite Saul killing his father, he would give into Saul's hands the keys of the Lord's kingdom. Therefore, heed my last advice to you.

"You will meet three young priests, whom I know are close to God. You will eventually meet them in Hebron when you become King of Judah. They are Gad, Nathan and Zadok. Though not of the House of Moses, as is Abathar, they already have shown the signs of being chosen to walk with God, which you my son and friend know only too well, is both a burden and a joy.

"We have already said our final farewells and my spirit goes with you. When I am gone to Abraham, remember your oath to God to reunite our peoples, which Saul's folly has split asunder.

"Remember you have my love, my voice and may He who knows all men's hearts keep you in His everlasting care.

"Farewell – your Father, Brother and Friend – Samuel."

A week later we learned of his death. The whole Band mourned with Israel, but I most of all. His death made me feel even more isolated. He alone understood the nature of the Lord's inspiration as he too heard the Voice, so my sense of isolation was even more profound. I was shattered. When would come such another with such authority or one who so clearly walked with God?

Saul's response to Samuel's death was to make a mock of mourning. Everything about him and his court showed great delight in "the passing of the Old Man".

What Saul had failed to appreciate was that, though he was in conflict with Samuel, his authority had reinforced both their efforts to keep Israel united. Now men spoke quietly of "Saul the Benjaminite", for they could not help but notice that, despite his wives from amongst the tribes, virtually all Saul's great men were Benjaminites.

My father and the other Elders of Judah were especially unhappy. My father had so clearly sided with Samuel and the priesthood, and, now Samuel was dead, he along with my brother, Eliab, feared Saul's vengeance. Consequently I, with just two files of Companions, secretly rode into Bethlehem and escorted the family to our cousins amongst the Moabites. I had friendly relations with them and had already deposited some gold and iron with Moab of the Moabites for my family's safety.

My father was unhappy and I had to endure a lecture about the ills I had brought the family. Why could I not keep close to Saul? This after his warnings to the contrary, but then fathers are ever so in their authority. However, he also gave good advice. I was not to forget that I was a man of Judah and there in lay my strength.

We parted kindly, though with sadness. We both thought it unlikely that we would meet again for he was now taken in years. His exile was made more bitter as he was far from the fair water of his beloved Bethlehem.

The second letter came from Jonathan. I poured over every word and line.

He greeted me and renewed our vows of friendship and brotherhood.

"I love no man more than you, little David.

"Though you are now a great warrior and the Lord's anointed, I think of you as at the Pool of Joshua and how we two stood alone before God in total harmony.

"However, whilst our oaths will last until our doom, my duty to Israel and my father means we cannot meet. Despite you sparing his life – and, David, I was so proud of you that you avoided the temptation – there can be no reconciliation with him yet. I tell you in absolute secrecy, despite my efforts, the King's court has become that of Abner and we Benjaminites. This brings ill to the land of Israel.

"I am engaged with a division of the army far from you. I thank God that my father did not confront me with an impossible dilemma, for I would not and could not take arms against you. But, David, my brother, I am sworn to the King my father and cannot, nor will I, desert him.

"I feel in my bones that we will not meet again, though I would have had great joy in serving your Kingship and renewing our love.

"Think kindly on your friend and brother.

"Farewell until we meet in the bosom of Abraham."

I re-read this letter again and again, trying in vain to find some hint of hope of reunion.

I went alone into the hills to weep for Samuel but, most of all, to grieve that I would never again stand at the side of the greatest Prince and friend who ever lived.

Amidst the silence of the hills, I cried in silence to God. To have to endure grief whilst my love lived was intolerable and I felt a despair that would have led me to throw myself upon the mercy of Saul, but realised this was not possible. We were instruments in the hands of a cruel fate. Yes, I admit I cursed God, "take this burden from me", but there was no answering Voice or inspiration.

That night I dreamed and knew I dreamt. I was visited by Jonathan who tearfully said, "We are tempted to fulfil our love and brotherhood. We could flee together, you and I. Many kings would welcome us. Our sons would be come friends and we would grow old together. But David, you are the Lord's anointed and you must put away temptation of normal happiness. You must take up the burden no one else can carry so that God's purpose can be achieved."

I awoke in a cold sweat – here was temptation indeed. Yes, let us flee together! We could carve out a kingdom where I could serve Jonathan, re-create a bastion for the Living God and then take back the people of Israel. But I knew it was but a dream. Jonathan's spirit had called out to me, to urge me to take on the yoke of God, which could not be denied. I might have had great human happiness, but ultimately I knew this would bring bitterness in the knowledge of my betrayal of the Living God.

I wept and mourned for a week, until Beniah led a small deputation to urge me to show myself and take charge, lest my despair undermine all.

So I resumed the role of leader of our band, trying hard to present a positive image. We responded to any requests for help as Saul's inability to protect all of Israel became more obvious and the marauding border tribes became more daring.

I was invited to visit a rich man called Nabal, a Carmelite. He had three huge herds and had been suffering troublesome raids from small bands of Amalekites.

I went to see him and was treated civilly enough, and took a meal with him served by his wife, Abigail.

I should describe her, for she proved to be a very important person in my life. She entered modestly, as one would expect, but had a natural grace that was immediately striking.

At first glance, you would not think she was exceptionally beautiful – until she looked at you with her wondrous dark eyes. They had a depth and intelligence that I had seldom seen in anyone, least of all a woman.

She was slightly built, with a delightful bosom, but it was her grace that showed in her combined pose.

I was drifting away to the sound of her melodic voice when, to my intense embarrassment, Nabal broke in and said, "I am pleased that the Captain finds my wife attractive. Does not the Captain have a wife of his own?"

It was clear I had stumbled badly. I found myself blushing and answering, "Sir Elder, Nabal, forgive me. Yes, indeed I have a wife and a son, Amnon, and, like you, I am blessed. But you must forgive we rough soldiers who live in the field. We seldom meet people of your sophistication."

Whether this pacified him or not, I don't know. We concluded our business. I offered to protect his southern herds and, if possible, recover a small herd he lost a month previously.

He explained, "You will know them by the red dye. Any in this area belong only to Nabal."

As I left, I hoped my ears misled me. There was the sound of blows and a woman's cry. Of course, one cannot intervene between man and wife, but he was an old man, obese and, frankly, crude. Whereas she was but a year or so older than me and any man would have found her pleasing.

We were fortunate as Josh, following a band of Amalekites, came across Nabal's sheep. After slaying most of the raiders, brought the flock back. Unfortunately, he lost a man, while two were seriously wounded and were unlikely to be effective warriors. Hence, Josh's coup had, from our point of view, been rather costly because the fifteen or so dead Amalekites meant little to us, though their fierce fighting capacity reminded one of how formidable they once had been.

Perhaps I should explain. We had not killed every Amalekite after the battle of Havilah – perhaps a few thousand survived – though at least 150,000 men were slain, not counting the women and children. Some had escaped and re-formed somewhere in the far south-east. Later, many women who had been married to Israelites or gone into concubinage had gone back to their lands so there was again a small tribe of Amalekites. However, apart from a local level, they posed no serious threat to any of the major peoples.

I thought it best if Josh returned the sheep to Nabal. He was to ask him for assistance in good hard bread and one-in-ten of the sheep we had recovered. To Josh's amazement, Nabal, instead of being grateful, and despite knowing we had casualties, berated him as a thief. He said the 60 sheep represented only half what had been stolen. We were asking for two rewards after first robbing him of half his goods.

Josh was rightly angry. The stupid man raged at Josh, threatening him with a beating from his men.

Josh simply went up to the ungrateful, obese creature and, despite his bulk, lifted him out of his seat by the scruff of his neck and said, "No one, but no one threatens Joseph, a Companion of David, the Lord's anointed, with a beating. And least of all being called a thief by someone who themselves has no courage. David asked for bread and a small proportion of what we recovered, but I'll leave you to choke on your ingratitude."

He stormed out, leaving Nabal terrified and raging to such an extent that he fell ill.

His wife, upon learning what had happened, ordered the servants to gather bread, fruit and ten sheep and make ready to bring them to our camp. At first, they remonstrated with her. What would the master say?

She was so diplomatic, though inside she must have scorned them. "The master is ill. We have offended honourable men. If I were their captain, I would have come and taken what my husband would have been wise to give. Come, do as I bid and I will hurry after Captain David and intercede with him, lest, in his just anger, he destroy us."

The men suddenly realised that their master had placed them in danger, Though they had not realised that we would not compel where honour and obligation could not prevail.

Josh reported back to me. I must confess that I was pleased at his rough handling of Nabal, though I had a qualm that the wretched man might further abuse his wife in petty spite.

So, I had half-decided to return myself to Nabal, when I received a message that a party had been observed coming from Nabal, but led by a woman. At first, I was totally surprised but then appreciated that it must be Abigail, Nabal's wife, who had the intelligence to do the right thing – though it was highly unconventional.

I rode out to meet her.

Before I could do her courtesy, she had alighted from her mule and in a gentle but thrilling voice that commanded attention said, "Oh great Captain David, the Lord's anointed. We bring, for your mercy and consideration, gifts my husband in his folly refused. But now he has been smitten ill and lies in a stupor. I bring bread, fruit, salt and sheep in the hope that you will forgive our earlier foolishness. Now we have offered the hospitality you merited, my husband may be restored to full health."

She charmed me. I bid her rise and walked with her into my tent.

I asked Annah to bring refreshments, but I could see she was not pleased at behaviour she obviously thought unseemly.

As if Abigail sensed her animosity, she breathed, "Lady, blessed wife of this great Captain, the Lord's anointed. You have been already twice blessed: first in your Lord and then, secondly, in giving him a son. He must take great delight in you."

I found it hard to read Annah's expression, but Abigail continued. "Pardon me if I seem forward, but my husband lies sick and has done your husband a great wrong. In search of the Lord's and your husband's forgiveness, I have brought what was due to your husband. I feel sure that, in my circumstances, you would have acted as I have done. Though, of course, your husband would never break the duties owed to strangers."

Annah was flattered. Though she would never, ever have had the initiative to do such a thing, she had sufficient grace to recognise Abigail's predicament.

I politely inquired of her husband and introduced Josh to her, who immediately fell under her charm. He was courtesy itself and was eager to know that his "excess" had not caused her any difficulties.

She smiled, but a look crossed her face, which made us both decide to move away from such a sensitive issue.

I must confess that I kept her longer than politeness demanded. I found myself asking her questions that I would have normally only asked of a man. She was thoughtful and considered in everything she said. When our fingers touched momentarily when I refilled her cup, I was aroused and eager to know more of her.

She looked me full in the face and deep into my eyes. She was so frank in her appraisal of me. I allowed myself to be inspected and then my eyes followed what my senses wished to discover. I knew I desired her, but it was not her body – rather it was her mind and soul that seemed to call out to mine.

She said, "My Lord, I must return to my husband. This day I account blessed, not just for being graciously received by the Lord's anointed, but also because I have met David, the man whose person far exceeds the high praise that all give of his valour, mercy, duty and comeliness."

I blushed furiously at this. No woman had ever said to my face that I was comely – though I would be lying if I thought myself ugly.

She smiled at my discomfort. "I greet your wife, Annah, in sisterly greetings and tell her that she is blessed amongst women. Now, my Lord, farewell. I will return to my husband."

Whether it was my imagination or whether this was expressed bitterly, I don't know. For a change, I was lost for words. I led her to her mule and attendants.

When I returned, Josh was grinning from ear to ear.

I snapped at him, "What are you looking so pleased at?"

"Well, I'm sure you don't know! I couldn't take my eyes from her. What a woman! David, dear friend, I thought you were going to drool."

What could I say?

I simply threw cushion at him and ruefully admitted that I was taken with her and, "All right, Josh. You've had your laugh, but I can't help but feel sorry that such a wonderful woman is wed to that moronic creature."

I must confess that, as I lay by the side of Annah, in my heart I committed adultery, because I was really thinking of Abigail. For the next few weeks, my thoughts never completely left her.

I was amazed with myself: I had only seen her twice.

It was not as if I was a youth, just discovering the joys of women, which, after his warrior training, occupies most of his mind. Or rather, as I remember, women first and then the training. No, I had had loves. I had a good wife and would never set her aside. This is a cruel custom that dishonours a man when, in her years, he casts off the woman. Moreover, it is an insult to the sons of that wife and can lead to unhappy hours within the family.

No, my preoccupation with Abigail was simply because she was, after Leah, the most complete women I had ever met. In only two meetings, I could see she was a jewel amongst women.

Later that month, Josh came in to see me quietly. He was grinning again and made great mock of trying to control his humour, which was always breaking out at embarrassing moments, "David, my Captain, am I still your friend? I am here to do you good, unless, that is, you give me permission first to take in marriage Abigail, the widow of the Carmelite."

I did not quite take in his meaning. The widow of the Carmelite? I must have looked stupid.

Josh gave me a big hug. "David, old friend, Nabal has died of his angry stroke and I am giving you first chance to refuse his widow. What I am saying to you, dunderhead, is that if you don't want to marry Abigail, the wife of the late Nabal the Carmelite, I will ask her for myself. Never did one do a greater service to his friend than I am doing for you."

I understood. I embraced him. I kissed him on both cheeks. Before he knew it, I was on my horse and was galloping towards Nabal's homestead, praying that some other discerning man or relative of Nabal had not taken her in.

I arrived and, with little politeness, demanded to see the widow Abigail.

The senior attendant, a man who must have studied pomposity at his master's feet, said, "The widow Abigail is not to be a widow much longer. Tubal, Nabal's younger brother, has let it be known that he will be pleased to take her as a third wife, in memory of his brother and to the honour of his family."

I coldly said, "That will not be necessary."

I pushed by the gasping servant aside.

Abigail must have heard the noise I made, for she stood there with only a housedress on. She bowed low and stayed kneeling.

"Abigail! Abigail! Tell me it's not true that you're going to marry that oaf's brother."

Was she laughing or teasing me as she stayed kneeling? "David, it is the custom for good men to take on the widows of their brothers – to give them a home and to be an assistant to the senior wives. It is a kindly custom and ensures that the widow has a place."

I reached for her, pulling her to her feet. "But Abigail, I love you. I want you for my wife."

The words were out. I was behaving like a love-struck boy, but my senses were aroused. I longed to take her in my arms, to talk to her, to hear her sing, to enjoy her laugh – to make love.

She looked at me gravely and, with music in her words, she answered me, "This day, the Lord's handmaiden is blessed beyond all others. From this day forth, generations will call me blessed. I, Abigail, daughter of Ede an Edomite, take you with all my soul, my mind and my body. Only you will I serve until the Lord take me into the bosom of Abraham."

I knelt before her and prayed to her. "Abigail, I believe you have been sent by God to help me with my burden. Long have I laboured alone. My comrades, who I love beyond measure, assist me but even in their midst I am alone. Abigail, sweet Abigail, I must tell you that there is nothing ahead for me – therefore, nothing for you – but turmoil and danger. I can give you no settled home. I am like our forefathers, dwelling in the desert, moving place to place, often from stony to rocky places. If you have any sense, you will take your brother-in-law's offer."

She shook her head in refusal. "Then I, David bar Jesse, promise you my heart, my head, my body and my spirit. I claim you before God as my true help mate."

I took her into my tent that day and Abathar married us.

Annah very sensibly gave place that night and, oh, the rapture.

We first talked and, delight upon delight, I heard her first laugh and she sang for me. It was not flattery, for as she sang the psalm of David, never had it sounded so perfect. As her words drifted off into the night, my mouth closed on hers and our bodies sought the union which our minds and spirits had already decided upon.

I sought to please her with my consideration. I sensed that Nabal, for whom I had conceived a dreadful jealousy, would have had little thought for her.

She relaxed in my arms as my lips sought to evoke passion in her. She lay back in complete surrender as I softly undid the light tassels of her dress.

Oh bliss! Even in the dark, I could see she was beautiful and her smooth, unclothed body had all the grace that her words had. She was dark, like her Edomite ancestors. Her breasts were large, but firm and round, and her nipples were the colour of sweet darkened dates, which yielded to my importunity.

Now she was aroused, her hands were over my body, caressing my nipples, to be followed by her lips. Then, our mouths closed on each other and we grew dizzy with delight. Her hands flowed down my chest. Her fingers rippled over my stomach muscles and, as she did so, she moaned in appreciation.

She kissed my stomach, then my bush and, to my amazement but intense excitement, she gently kissed my thrusting phallus.

My lips fled from her breast and down her silk stomach to her wondrous thighs, as she opened herself for me. I entered her in one glorious lunge, which took me far into her welcome clinging, sinewy, grasping self. Almost without moving her body, her secret place milked my engorged manhood.

I lay deep, deep inside her and felt her body's mouth around me. Then our new ride of union commenced. At first, long and slow, but with gathering intensity as I closed her love cry with my mouth. I breathed her name "Abigail" and filled her with my sweet, hot, sharp, hurtling fiery seed as we clung tight, tight together.

For a moment, I thought of Leah. Had she returned to me in this dear, dear person? Momentarily, I wondered whether Leah would have approved? But, as I felt Abigail's gentle kiss and caress, I knew that, at last, I was complete. The cruel fate that robbed me had relented and that, Leah, from the bosom of Abraham, would be glad.

We did not immediately make love again. Abigail asked if there was a song of mine that might bless this moment. Of course, it was Leah's psalm.

There, with my arms about her, I became aroused and buried myself deep inside her.

I sang to her my marriage song to Leah, as she had indeed been returned to me in Abigail.

"I will bless the Lord at all times; his praise shall be continually in my mouth.
My soul shall make her boast in the Lord; the humble shall hear and be glad.
Oh magnify the Lord with me and let us exalt his name together."

Yes, I was confident that, with Abigail at my side, I could face what was before me.

"I sought the Lord and he delivered me from all my fears
Oh taste and see that the Lord is good, blessed be the man that trusteth in him.
The young lions do lack and suffer hunger but they that shall seek the Lord shall not want any good thing.
Come ye children, harken unto me I will teach you the fear of the Lord.
The righteous cry and the Lord heareth and delivereth them out of all their troubles."

We both sang it again to each other, in praise of God and for our love for each other.

In our love for God, we were blessed with a new ecstasy. We passionately came together and, in a moment, resealed our vows as my seed shot deep into her, which she received with rapturous cries of joy.

We only made love three times that night. But we spoke to each other, as I delighted in her wisdom and quickness to understand. We agreed that we must give respect to Annah but, as she had Amnon, she would be happy for us.

Now I thanked God, whatever the future held. He had restored my helpmate. Feeling renewed, I turned to confront the burden facing me and the people of Israel.

Saul's Farewell

I had hoped that Saul would leave us in peace, but he was constantly reminded by Abner that he would never be fully the King whilst ever I remained at large mocking his majesty. Abner was the evil genius of Saul, which, along with his dark moods, made his poisoned words a deadly brew.

First was the joy, however, of second parenthood, as Abigail gave me another son, Kiliab. I thought the joys of fatherhood were known to me by the birth of Amnon but now, Abigail's son was the fruit of my loins completely in love. The miracle that our ecstasy had been transformed into this perfect babe moved me to an indescribable, humble joy that I never imagined possible. A child of total love, created in perfect harmony of body, mind and soul.

I was, of course, especially considerate to Amnon, who was a delight. But Kiliab had something of his mother's dignity and seriousness. From the first, I felt sure that he would become a priest.

My comrades and I often spoke of the joys of our nomadic life together and how our forefathers must have lived like this. It was not too great a burden and, had Saul left us alone, I think we could have completed our days quite happily.

The local tribes quickly found they were no match for our discipline so we were left well alone by them. In turn, the local Israelites benefited enormously and they were more pleased to be under our protection than that of the King in the distant north.

Yet peace it was not to be. Beggaring belief, Saul split the army of Israel into two.

One half he gave in command of Jonathan to watch the Philistines. Most of the tribes other than that of Benjamin joined him and were happy to serve under Jonathan, who was always a considerate and successful leader.

Saul and Abner, however, led a virtually total Benjaminite army, strengthened with levies from the Ruebenites and the Manassehites, but no man of Judah would serve with him in his obsession to crush us. He had effectively divided Israel for, after all, Judah was the largest tribe. He came at us with no less than 30,000 warriors.

I was frantic. With such an army, however, there was no disguising where he was and we could move fairly easily between his patrolling columns.

Also, he paid us a kind of compliment. There had been clashes and loss of life, but for every man we lost, Saul lost ten or more, so few would venture out in less than bodies of 2,000. The cat and mouse game began again.

I was weary and dispirited, though Abigail was a wonder. Never exceeding her position as a woman, she would quietly observe and watch our councils. Then, she would willingly speak with The Four: Joab, Ura, and Beniah and especially Josh, who clearly loved her so that I was slightly jealous.

Her calmness, dignity and obvious intelligence made her beloved of all. In a strange kind of way, if I was the captain then she was the mother of our band. I would tease her with this but, after some especially thrilling lovemaking, she would ask if this is the conduct of a mother of grown men.

She was present, as was Annah, to serve my Companions at our council. At first, she was not asked to speak but, afterwards, if I raised a matter, she showed such discernment and balance that I began to call her "my wise woman".

At one conference, the question was raised as to whether we should go on to the attack. But how? A number of ideas were put about, but most were too fantastic to take seriously, much to the annoyance of Joab, Abashi and Ashael. They wanted a particular hare-brained scheme to go and sack Gilbeah.

I mentioned this to Abigail and she gently asked, "Would my Lord like to hear what his servant thinks?"

I grinned at her, kissed her passionately and said, "Listen, my wise woman, your lord wants to make love to you – and will do so after you have given him the benefit of your wisdom. Yet, if your advice is not as it should be, I may make love to you twice, so, therefore, dear counsellor, do not be too successful."

"Sweet David, if you have the strength, make love to me three times if my counsel is thought good. Will that content you?"

Perhaps this is irrelevant but I made love to her immediately because she was so delectable. As I rested, I asked her to counsel me.

"Joab, Abashi and Ashael are saying something important. They feel trapped. They feel like the rest of the band. They are reacting rather than controlling events."

I had to agree.

She went on. "It seems that all would, if they could, mount some form of active response to Saul. Yet he commands overwhelming numbers – even

465

too great for Israel's greatest general."

"Ah, there wife, unusually, you're wrong. Jonathan is Israel's greatest general. Therefore, if he were in my shoes, what would Jonathan do?"

"I stand corrected as always," she smiled. "But because you are outnumbered, have you not said that Jonathan taught you the advantage of local superiority."

I started to laugh. In my love and warmth for her, I began to feel aroused once more. "Would my wife now talk strategy? Perhaps I have married a secret warrior who belies her sex."

As always, she was very patient with me and let me babble on. "David, my husband, where lies the weakest link in Saul's army?"

That was a splendid question!

Our eyes met as we both saw at once and said it together, "Saul!"

"Exactly, Abigail. He is their weakest link. If he should die, not that I would strike him, then Abner is but a general from the tribe of Benjamin. Jonathan would become King. In his moods Saul is unstable. Abigail, you've got it! Let us hunt the King."

It was so obvious. Why had I not thought of this before? Then I smiled and we made love again, but with such satisfaction that there was no need for a third time.

Next morning I called a Council and put it to them. We would identify the column in which Saul was travelling and harry it. We would track it and create such an anxiety that, if Saul brought his troops together, they would be too slow and we could move away. If he accepted the challenge, then it made him vulnerable.

"But comrades, you and I have sworn an oath to protect the Lord's anointed – and this includes Saul. If circumstances permit, we will capture him, but he is not to be harmed. If Abner, however, falls into our hands, he is to be condemned as a traitor to Israel and stirrer-up of the people."

So there followed a strange set of manoeuvres in which, to the consternation of Saul's guards, they suddenly found they were not the hunters but the hunted.

The plan was simple. We divided our effective band into six parts, one to guard the baggage and the families, another to create a cavalry screen around them and the other four to alternately harry whichever column Saul was in.

Each in turn would be responsible for two days of aiming specifically at Saul. The rest would lead the other columns out into the desert by just ten horsemen, each with brushwood and scattering debris to make the enemy think they were following a column. Thus, we would seem to be more numerous than we really were.

However, they were now unsure whether they were the pursued or pursuers, as the threat to Saul came from different directions. Josh, Joab, Beniah and I commanded the harrying parties. Saul's columns responded to our thrusts by almost going in circles.

As luck would have it, it was my patrol that was shadowing Saul as night fell. I felt that it was time for us to do something effective. I reasoned to myself that, somehow, we had to bring this to a climax. I wondered about who would best for a special mission – it was obvious: Abashi.

I said, "I am almost certain that Abner is with Saul. Let's go to visit them tonight and, whilst Saul is sacrosanct, Abner's head would go a long way to re-uniting Israel."

Abashi could not have been more willing.

At first, some of the men protested about Abashi and I going by ourselves. But I argued that two amidst a mass could easily escape. What we wanted to was to make a significant impact, not attempt to defeat a whole column, which was unnecessary.

We arranged that it if there were signs that we had been discovered, then they would create a diversion. Five would then enter the King's camp and effect any rescue.

I must confess that I increasingly found a sense of relief in being involved in direct action, though I knew it worried the others and distressed Abigail.

We crept in close to their camp. We decided we would not take out any sentries because, if discovered, this would alert the whole camp. What we would try to do in the moonlight would be to find where the King and Abner lay, and, if possible, execute just Abner.

Abashi was a natural. He crept through the sleeping men as if he were a ghost. Yet, I was always conscious of my foot scraping across a stone. I could never understand how they could not hear my heart pounding in excitement and fear. It was with great difficulty that I kept my breathing under control.

Abashi pointed to a clearing where as custom decreed that generals and the king were given space between them and their men.

I prayed that it was Abner, for I would have no compunction in delivering him his doom. I just hoped that I would reach him before Abashi did.

There must have been a square of about a hundred men laid out sleeping in three lines with Abner in the centre. To our surprise, the two sentries at our side of the square were obviously asleep. I looked at Abashi and nodded. We did not intend to be disturbed now.

I gave Abashi a few minutes to reach his man as I crept up behind mine. I quelled any thoughts that this was an Israelite I was slaying in the night.

With practised stealth, my hand was across his throat as my dagger plunged once, twice, thrice, rapidly into his heart.

Apart from the warm ooze on my hands, nothing appeared to have changed as I lowered his body to the ground.

I crawled forward and saw Abashi coming towards me, a blood-stained knife in his hand. I raised my head to see who was in the middle of the square and to my intense disappointment realised that it was not Abner but Saul.

I slowly inched my way forward, having first put a restraining hand upon Abashi. His face was so contorted with excitement and intent that I was afraid he might forget himself. We reached the sleeping Saul, who had laid his head upon a rich cushion.

I stood there. The moment seemingly extended into for ever as I contemplated the helpless figure of my persecutor.

What thoughts went through my head? Anger, sadness, bitterness – a yearning to be healed? To be at one again with him who had once shown me so much kindness, and to be able to freely return to Jonathan and Israel. No matter how just I knew my cause to be, I was outside Israel and bitterly admitted that we were little better than brigands. Yet one little word from this man, who owed me much, could end all our exile.

As I stood there, I realised that if Abashi perpetrated the sacrilege I might not really object. That thought burnt like fire into my brain and in an almost panic I grabbed Abashi fiercely and mouthed the words "No".

Later, I was convinced he was beginning to guess my mind and his look of obedience was also tinged with cynicism.

I pulled myself together and, looking around, saw that at the side of Saul were his war spear and the King's cup he was wont to give ceremonial toasts with. I nodded to Abashi and, with a broad smile, he picked up both. I cleaned my knife on the King's cloak and gently cut a piece of cloth from it.

Quicker than it takes to tell, we were gone and rejoined one of our bands. At my signal, the call was passed on and we all reassembled north of Saul's camp.

Abashi was beside himself with excitement, "There he was – like a babe. You wouldn't think he was responsible for the deaths of thousands. For a moment, I thought David would come to his senses and finish him off, but you know him." He did not complete what he had to say. Perhaps a little too keenly I told him to shut up. He went to bring his trophies.

He was obviously annoyed, but he knew he had gone too far. He consoled himself with a defiant look at me as much to say, I know how close you came to getting me to do your dirty work.

He eagerly showed our comrades the spear and the cup of the King of Israel.

We retreated up some high ground. I had also brought my own trophy, the King's war horn, and, to the disquiet of his troop, started sending fierce blasts down to the plain beneath.

There was a commotion below. I advanced with Abashi to another small rock a hundred yards from their lines and, with my men stretched out in a line, called out, "What ho! Sleeping Abner! Who deserts King Saul, the Lord's anointed, King of Israel? What ho! What ho! Here stands David, the King's bard, taking care of the King's spear. I will now drink the King's health in the King's cup and wipe my lips with a piece of the King's cloak."

To the front of the line, I saw Saul emerge. He took in the situation in a trice.

"Is that you, my son, David? Have you indeed got my spear and my cup? Is this bloody mark upon my cloak your doing, when you took your trophy?"

"Yes, my Father. How dare men say I wish you harm when I could have killed you as you slept. Again, the great Lord Abner has failed to protect you. But I, David bar Jesse, am true to my oath and protected my Lord, the King, from the dangers of the night."

We both stood silent for a while.

To my amazement Saul called to his men, "All depart."

They looked at him dumbfounded.

He roared again. "Depart, I say! Save you, young sir." He pointed to a warrior close by.

Then Saul came forward, cast his royal cloak from him and, kneeling down, cast dust upon his head. "Give the warrior my spear and cup and let him take them to the Lord Abner. I want to show him the extent of my son's mercy and loyalty, and as a sign that my heart is purged of anger to my bard. Say that the Lord has lifted the darkness from my eyes."

I nodded to Abashi to do as Saul asked. He handed over the trophies with a show of bravado, whilst I watched carefully to ensure that Saul's emissary was harmless. Whether he had thought himself to become a hero, our eyes met and the cold cautious look I gave him banished any idea that he might take us by surprise.

He did obeisance to me and said, "David, the Lord's anointed, my name is Shamma. I would serve the Lord God of Israel. Remember me when you come into your kingdom."

This was a bold spirit to say such things in the presence of Saul.

I nodded curtly and returned his salute.

All the while Saul sat upon the ground in the state of traditional mourning.

His men had gone far off and now I felt secure against any treachery.

I advanced up to Saul. Oh, he was piteous to see. This once magnificent man, the first King of Israel, valiant, his frame above all other men's, looked as ordinary as any other old man, impotent against the fate that God had decreed for him. Without his dark moods, he was as perfect as Jonathan. His real tragedy was that he was too eager to serve God, so that he resented those who were called differently. He would have had God all to himself. He was jealous for God! This is what had corroded his Kingship.

He looked up at me, as he had done so often in the past when my music has soothed him and the dark oppression lifted.

He was crying. "Oh, David, my son. When you left me, my spirit turned to sand. Oh, I have listened to foolishness. In my heart were black angry thoughts, which agitated my mind and spirit, and which found echoes amongst envious men. I believed – truly, I believed – you could wish me harm."

Pitifully, he carried on. "My son! My son! Can you forgive me? My weakness and stupidity have undone Israel. Oh, that I could take back these years that the locust has eaten."

No one listening to that proud man could fail to be moved by his complete surrender.

I ran to him, embraced him and we wept together. He for his lost Kingship, I for my lost youth and innocence. The words of Samuel echoed in my mind about "the purpose of God" and knew that we served a hard taskmaster.

As we clung to each other, I began to wonder about my trial. If or when I fell short of the demands laid upon me, how then would the Lord deal with me?

I tried to comfort my King, friend and master, but he was beyond solace because he said, "David, what have I done? I did not intend to become a tyrant."

There – he had said it! What an admission. I was relieved that Abashi and the others had had the decency to move from us and give us some privacy.

Then, he stood up to his full height and proudly said, "The Lord knoweth my heart was loyal. But He has seen fit to let this moon-struck darkness descend upon my soul. So be it. He has His purpose. But I united Israel. I was the victor of Jabesh Gilead, of Havilah, and shared your victory at Eilah. Most of all, my son, Jonathan, who is a light for all time, is a prince without parallel. He is a model for the men of Israel and for you, dear son, to emulate. It was I who first cherished and loved David bar Jesse and I shall complete the work I started."

These words touched me deeply. Saul, with growing realisation, continued. "My spirit tells me that I must play out my part but that you will be my successor. God has chosen you. Some day, not only will you found a dynasty that will take God's name to the heathen, but you will also build God a wondrous city that will be called the 'City of David' in time to come and for ever."

This was prophecy indeed.

He bade me farewell and to go and serve God. "Other gods, away from those in Israel, who are jealous and envious of your calling. Your commitment to our God is an affront to them and for that they hate you. Do not put yourself in their power. My Son, go with my peace. When you are King and understand the loneliness of my place, think of me kindly."

This devastated me. Though I knew the strife between us had ended, there were others who had been wronged, so I knew the Band and I must withdraw to let the poison consume itself.

I knelt before him. "As I love you my King, my Master and – yes – you once called me your friend. These titles I re-assert before the entire world. Greet and kiss my brother Jonathan for me and tell him I love him. But thou, oh my King, give me your Father's blessing."

With that, we knelt side by side, our tears unashamedly falling.

He blessed me. With his hands upon my head and said, "This is my beloved Son in whom I am well pleased."

Chapter Twenty-one

Mercenary

Achish

It was the usually placid Beniah who come bursting in with great excitement.

"David! David! The patrol has just sent word that Janna of Gath is here under a flag of truce. We are bringing him in. What do you think it means?"

Something that Saul had said came to mind. Was it a warning, a prophecy or both? He had said something about "serving other gods".

Quizzically, I looked towards Abigail but she responded by saying, "If the Captain Beniah is perplexed, I am too. I wonder, does this mean new journeys?"

Beniah looked to us both and slowly said, "Were you expecting this?"

"No, in all truth," I replied. "Only, as I left Gath before being driven to the Cave of Adallum, this same Janna said something unexpected and Saul had almost warned me of 'serving other gods'."

Then I laughed and said, "Well, my friends. We can but wait and see. But, Beniah, I think it would be wise to have the rest of the Four together – no, on reflection call, the Thirty."

I truly had no pre-warning. When Janna was brought before me, his whole demeanour spoke volumes. He entered not in fear, but as someone who is the bearer of good tidings. The fact that it was Janna, Achish's most important counsellor, meant this was momentous.

"Hail, Janna of Gath. I greet you in courtesy under the flag of truce you bring and in the names of my comrades here."

Janna was so smooth. He smiled and said, "David bar Jesse, Champion of Israel, brother of Achish. Hear what words of comfort and succour my Master brings."

He looked around and asked, "But would you rather not hear the words

472

of Achish, King of Gath alone? These are words from brother to brother."

No one amongst the Thirty knew that I had become blood brother to Achish. Though the thought crossed my mind to take the offer of Janna and speak alone, I decided against it.

I replied, "Janna, indeed I am a blood-brother of Achish. But these men give me great glory by being the Companions of David and from whom David can never have any secrets."

This made a very good impression and the tension I had begun to sense disappeared immediately.

I invited Janna to sit and tell us Achish's message.

Janna looked around. He took from his side bag a long scroll and began to read.

"Achish, son of Achish, King of Gath of Philistia, to my brother, David bar Jesse of Judah – greetings.

"I and my Council, hearing of your great valour against many peoples, am mindful to call for a treaty between you, your warriors, their wives and chattels, and us.

"I ask that you join in service with us for two years. During this time, your enemies will my enemies and my enemies will be yours.

"Furthermore, nothing will be asked of you or your warriors which would be against their honour.

"During this time, I will give you every grace, both as my brother, because I love you, and also as a great commander of men.

"I will make the city of Ziklag for the use of you and your people, to dwell in and my people will assist you as neighbours.

"This area is sometimes troubled with brigands and it would be beholden upon you and your warriors to 'keep the peace'.

"During your treaty with us, you, your men may worship your gods freely. Equally, you will not hinder my people in the worship of our gods.

"As a sign of my valuing your friendship, at the end of each year I will give to you and your warriors a thousand shekels of gold and a thousand shekels of iron.

"Furthermore, at the end of our treaty together, it may be renewed for five more years. If, however, my brother should die, the treaty ends within three months of his death and a new treaty may be drawn up between your people and mine.

"Come, my brother, David bar Jesse, and learn to be civilised."

All was going well until this last sentence which, of course, was for my ears alone. The final comment was the joke that Achish and I had shared for

473

almost all the time that we had known each other. I suspected that the remainder of the audience would take the jibe with less humour.

Janna sat calmly, showing no emotion, but I could see his eyes intently upon me.

I rose to address the murmurings. "You have heard the letter from my friend, Achish, King of Gath. First, I note he teases me, as he and his people think we are barbarians."

This clearly had riled them. There were shouts now.

I had to think fast, so I decided to jibe back and demonstrate that I could give as well as I received when it came to teasing. "It was ever thus. The soft plains people use rough words for warriors they cannot subdue!"

There were echoing calls of agreement and some laughter.

With indisputable logic, I cried, "It is the King of Gath who asks us, not we he. Moreover, he would give us tributes of iron and gold, not we him. So, if we are barbarians, we are very prized and highly paid barbarians!"

The men applauded. Crisis over.

I thought that Achish, with God's direction, had pointed the way for us to go. I must confess my heart felt joyful about the prospect of seeing Achish again.

Then, Beniah signified he would speak. "David, Captain of the Companions, you are the Lord's anointed. I can see many advantages this treaty brings to us. At a stroke, it solves the problem of where we lay our heads. Also, to be given a city, albeit one we must obviously defend, is a sign of this king's confidence in you and us."

There was a tense pause. Beniah was known by all to be my greatest supporter but also very wise and thoughtful. "But, our enemies become the king's enemies? Then, frankly, who would dare attack us? The marauding brigands around Ziklag would be our only rent for the city. They are no problem. These men are outlaws and oppress the border people. If God gives us the opportunity to end their pestilence, then it would be for the greater good for all."

Beniah now looked puzzled. "But, his enemies to become our enemies? What if that should be Israel?"

Typical of Beniah: he had got to the core of the problem.

Janna was intent and looked as if he would speak. I decided it safer that he did not.

My thoughts raced on as I quickly interjected. "My brother Beniah, ever the cautious wise one. Have we not all benefited from your wisdom. Indeed, I say here and now that, whilst I owe you all, this man, Beniah, gives me a special gift: wisdom that fears not to offend with difficult questions. Thus his counsel is doubly valuable."

I could see Beniah was pleased and the men reassured.

Of course, I had immediately decided upon hearing the first half of Achish's letter that I wanted to accept, but it was crucial that we should go unanimously.

I had an idea. I gestured to Janna. "But if I recall right – give me the letter, please – the king says in our honour ..., ah, yes, here it is!"

I read out. "'.... and my enemies yours. Furthermore, nothing will be asked of you or your warriors which would be against their honour ...' Companions, have I ever asked more of you? I think King Achish shows us great esteem, for he understands the temper and calibre of our band. Moreover, I promise that if we accept this treaty and live in the city of Ziklag, I will never lead you into battle against any foe unless I have consulted the Thirty."

There was an almost audible sigh of relief. Beniah smiled, nodded his satisfaction and waved an acknowledgement of his acceptance.

I hurried on. "Therefore, my brothers, for each of you is as a brother to me. How many times have we shed our blood together? That makes us all blood brothers a score of times."

Then a wit broke in – it might have been Josh. "Our blood, David. You've yet to have your first wound!"

Oh, I thought. What a dark ominous sign. But the men laughed uproariously. I had forgotten they saw me as much as a lucky omen as a successful captain. The Four had debated this quite seriously as being vital to our morale. Needless to say, I just felt it as another burden.

The issue was decided, so I laughingly replied, "So brothers – blooded and unblooded together – are we for tributes of iron and gold? Do we forge an honourable alliance with a faithful king and the city of Ziklag?"

The cheers and acclamations of approval were deafening.

Janna stood up on his feet, bowed low and was pleased to take my proffered hand.

I wrote immediately to Jonathan, of course I could not bear it if he did not think well of me.

I received a reply some months later expressing his understanding and reminding me that it was an opportunity to study the enemy at close quarters as he had done.

But, he also added, "You are never to forget who you are or what you were chosen for. I would not ask to understand God's mysterious plan but, clearly, He must have you in His purpose. I ask that at each Sabbath you remember me in your prayers as I will for you, thus, beloved, our spirits can be united if we ourselves can not serve together."

Was there ever such a wondrous friend and Prince?

Then began a strange two years, which had both delights and disasters. It was an amazing change. Here I was, the killer of Goliath, and, with Jonathan, a victor over the Philistines every time we had fought them, now invited in as a trusted ally. However, my slaying of Baalal last year showed that there were some that did not favour the alliance. So I made sure that I spent much of my time at Ziklag and did not venture to Gath. I knew I must not allow people to see how close Achish and I were growing, as it is always easy to resent a stranger's influence.

The City of Ziklag was wonderful. Many houses were of stone and cedar and there was room for 5,000 souls. Abigail and Annah were thrilled as they now had rooms for themselves and the children. This made it much easier for one of them to quietly share my bed in a special intimacy.

Both Abigail and Annah delighted me by giving birth to children in Ziklag, even though both babes were girls. Annah must have been very fertile for I did not claim her as often as Abigail, and then more as a gesture of kindness than of love. Whereas Abigail was a delight in all things, not only in our lovemaking, but especially in her counsel.

Her genius was in her ability to listen. She let me explore. With her, I could give way to those frustrations that every leader must suppress lest he offend the over-delicate, who then sulk and are surly in their duties.

Being Captain was not easy and there were times when I ached for someone else to say what should or should not be done. Worst were the occasional quarrels or slights between them – then they were like children. If I smiled on one, then the aggrieved behaved as if I had frowned on him. So if I was gracious to the latter the former felt he had lost my friendship. Much of my time and effort was spent in keeping the peace and maintaining everyone's morale.

The most difficult were the mean-minded. Instead of taking delight in a brother's success, say in cutting out an Amalekite patrol, slaying ten and losing none, such men behaved as if this was a slight on their valour – as if another's success demeaned them.

Abigail was so good at helping me with this and would take the burden of inviting the most recently slighted pair to eat with us. By her smiles and diplomacy she would send them both away as friends. Sadly, she even needed her skills with the Four, for though Josh and Eli were never at odds, they sometimes found Beniah's older gravity trying. Whereas Joab, urged on by his two firebrand brothers Abashi and Ashael, was always ready to claim to be the bluff pragmatist who was never properly appreciated. Although Ura, who had no peer, on occasions felt slighted because he was a Hittite and it was some time before I realised that his frequent jokes against himself were an effort to gain a re-affirming response. Without

Abigail's wisdom I might not have seen this and our band would have been the weaker for it.

There were three troublesome tribal marauders, but the first two we quickly wiped out leaving less than a dozen to escape. Despite having a body count of nearly 1,100, we only lost a dozen men. They really were no match for the Band who were battle hardened and highly disciplined.

The third were the remnants of the Amalekites who had survived Havilah and its aftermath. We reckoned there must be about three to four thousand. They continued to be an intermittent nuisance but, of course, they covered a vast area and they never came into the field together. I felt confident that we could face them at any time with odds of two to one. They wisely realised they had more to lose if they engaged in a major battle, so they sought to regain viable numbers to consider themselves a people again.

My time with Achish was a joy. His mind was so sharp. He was the very soul of honour. Yes, I admit he was a man of rare beauty and I felt blessed by his friendship. We spoke of many things and he taught me much, mainly to open my mind to new ideas. Sometimes this was disturbing but, in our times together, it was not just him being the teacher and me as the student. On occasions, I made Achish look anew at his ideas. In particular, he was fascinated by my psalms. I quickly realised that he was not just pleasing me.

When I said they were inspired by God for the people of Israel, his argument was, "We can argue about the source of beauty and creativity until the end of the world. I cannot deny that they have the power, as does all beauty, of moving my soul. I would have them written down."

I was a little uneasy, not least because I was very flattered. However, he persuaded me with the clinching argument that his wife Anna would also find them inspirational.

"You are not the only man to have such a helpmate as Abigail – my Anna is every bit her intellectual equal," he told me.

At first the riches of the Philistines and their images, which the chief men used to decorate their houses, shocked me. But some of our men, after a time, grew to guardedly enjoy their luxuries.

Late in the first year, I was invited by Achish to visit Gath.

"I am surrounded by boring people in the time of peace. Now you have been so successful in clearing out the vipers, give Beniah or one of the others the experience of command. Come and stay with me," he wrote.

I went like a schoolboy on holiday.

Of course, there are no holidays for kings. Sometimes I would sit at his Council, but being very, very careful not to say anything unless invited to do so. Thus, we only saw each other alone in the evenings when we talked the sun down – and often till early next dawn.

Achish was ten years older than me, thirty-three, so he was at his peak of intellect and physique.

He was interested in everything. Once I appreciated that he was not inquiring of me in a way that could damage to Israel, for both of us knew there was always the possibility, his mind fascinated and thrilled me.

Sometimes he would shock me by his questions, not just about our beliefs and laws. He was very interested in how similar yet different our faiths were. But he had daring questions as to why this? and why that?. When he was given an answer, he would again ask of the answer "why?". So that, rapidly after three questions and answers, one did not have the knowledge to explain the earlier reasoning. This showed just how fragile was our knowledge.

He was right, of course. We Israelites were not as civilised as the Philistines, who lived in cities. We still had echoes of our recent nomadic past and I began to understand their delight in decoration, as well as their psalms, which often were about noble men, or about love and not just the worship of God.

He would ask in a gentle, teasing way, why had God allowed this or that? Indeed, in such a manner that made me wonder whether he really doubted the existence of the Living God.

"Do you not believe in your god Dagon, Achish? I cannot think it possible that any man could doubt the existence of the Living God. Why, the whole of Israel is an example of God's hand in our affairs."

"Oh, David. One could not do other than believe in the gods."

But he said this with such a considerate smile upon his face, that I still thought he was mocking me.

He asked me the simple question, "If the gods do exist, why do they make it so difficult for us to know them? If you or I had their purported powers, could we stand by and watch, say, the mortal fevers of a child without intervening? Sometimes I think the only justification for the non-intervention of the gods is that they may not exist – or they do not have the power we ascribe to them!"

I was shocked. I argued that God required that should man exercise of his free will. We lacked the vision and the time to see the clear purpose of God. Moreover, I believed that if man came too near the divine, we would be consumed. Hence, our understanding of the mind of God is wider than the distance between man and a worm.

Achish perceptively asked, "Is that how you came by your whitened hair?"

I replied, "That is too holy to speak of, Achish – even to you or, indeed, any man."

He looked as if he would press me further but had the great sensitivity not to. He honestly said, "See, David. There is so much to know and I know nothing."

He was, however, more outspoken about what he called our lack of culture. Pointing to the images upon his walls, he asked did I not indeed think them beautiful.

I countered: was anything more beautiful than the originals that the figures represented? What is more beautiful than a real fish, a real bird, the thrill of a real hunt, the beauty of a real women's body or the wonder of a real man's form?

"Ah, David. There you have it. Our images, as you call them, are to remind us of that sublime beauty, the spirit at the core of all physical boundaries. It is a balm for our souls when we cannot have the original to hand. We try to catch the moment before age and decay transforms the wonder of a man's body into corruption."

Then he looked at me in a serious, pleading way. "And you, dear David? You are the origin of beauty. You speak of the wonder of a man's body. Were you thinking of Jonathan, my body, or your own?"

I flushed. We had never spoken before of Jonathan or of our being philia. "I suppose Jonathan's body comes to mind. We believe that man is made in the image of God. I will tell you, Achish, I have seen Jonathan and know that his body is wondrous and in God's image."

We were lying side-by-side on couches, with the drinking cups in our hands. My mouth grew dry with tension.

Achish whispered, "But, David, your body is wondrous. If we are truly made in His image, then you are a glorious ambassador of a God of supreme beauty."

I was a little taken aback at his near blasphemy and I tried to demur.

He smiled. "Come, indulge me. Let us drink a special toast and let me feast my eyes on the beauty that I will cherish for ever."

He stood and I did the same. He linked our arms, we drank from our cups and then, quite naturally, kissed.

His lips were moist from the wine. They touched mine and I was unsure how to respond. Half of me knew but my senses were confused.

"Let me give you a gift that lovers give to each other, sometimes on their first marriage, sometimes on their first philia – and at other times, too, to bring great joy because of thankfulness."

As he said this, he took a delicate jar in which was fragrant oil. He began to take off my shirt. I just stood there with my chest bared as he delicately massaged the oil over my trunk. His hands went to my skirt and loincloth.

He unfastened it and it fell to the ground, revealing me naked.

If he was disappointed that I was not aroused, he did not show it. He stood back a pace, looking at me as if I were indeed one of his images which he was sketching.

He unfastened his upper garment to reveal his broad muscled chest, on which I could see the scars from his wars. He came close to me and kissed me, but this time his arms went around me and the oil on his chest moved silkily over me. He gently untied his long skirt, which fell to the floor, showing me his manhood, uncircumcised. It was long, slender and beginning to thicken in harmony with mine.

He drew more oil onto his hands and put oil on mine. Without a word, his hands explored my body. My hands followed in answer, creating a fiery harmony that blazed beneath our oil glistening fingers. His oiled hands swept fires over me. His lips seemed touched with an urgent need. I closed with him, holding him fast, our two manhoods aligned in a duel-like pose.

Now I wanted to look at him. I pulled away and my eyes drank in his form. This excited him. I caressed his now shining body as the shadows and the light from the flames of the torchlight tumbled over him.

I took his hardness in my hand and he moaned in delight. Our mouths were glued together. His silken hand so smoothly milked my hard, hard, fleshy spear that I thought I would explode.

With smiles, he urged me to the ground and I sank in a delicious inertia. If this had been Abigail or Annah, I would have entered her, but no, this fiery passivity was intoxicating. I lay outstretched, my eyes enjoying the sight of my own oiled body reflecting the flickering light whilst drinking in his beauty.

He lay by me. Placing his leg between mine, his hand found my phallus and started the ancient ritual. But then, I felt his other hand between my legs and his fingers sought to penetrate me. I rolled away in shock and some anger.

He sat up. "Ah, David. I understand. I am sorry. It is our custom not yours."

I was unhappy, hurt, angry and ashamed. I could feel my passion ebbing swiftly.

I was about to rise and Achish motioned me to stay. "David, believe me, I love you above all other men. I honour you above all other men. Let us therefore use our bodies only as men."

I was unsure what he meant but felt soothed by his words.

Then, he smiled a lovely smile. "Come, let's wrestle like boys and see who can gain the other's seed first."

With that he gently closed with me in a mock wrestle and laughingly I responded. Now I was aroused again as I could feel his hard manly body move against mine. Our erect manhoods, loose and engorged, flapped against each other.

I was on top of him, pinning him down, with my phallus hard against his chest. He was slippery in the oil and wriggled clear, but as he did so his mouth came to my hard member.

I gasped and loosed my hold. Quickly, he rolled me back and pinned me. His mouth, holding my erect, straining member firm, slowly milked me, giving me such joy.

I grasped him by the waist and, letting my arms slip over his oiled hardness, turned myself under him and took him in my mouth. Now in harmony, our bodies were hard against each other. Our tongues caressed the other's quivering phallus. His hand came around my back. He took my sack and gently pulled to make my hard, bursting spear even longer. We lay side by side, head to phallus, thrusting, thrusting till we could hold no more and exchanged our seed in a sharp, tingling, fiery sweet explosion.

We lay exhausted for some time, without thought or speech. Then he took me to his greatest luxury: a pool next to his chamber. We began to bathe each other free of the oil. But his hands re-aroused me as we lay beneath the waters. Our bodies curled together and re-enacted the ancient ritual.

I slept that night in Achish's bed but there was no more lovemaking.

Though we did not know it, we were never to come together again as philia.

Doubtful Allies

The whole band, especially the Thirty, and I learned much during our stay amongst the Philistines. Some things we could admire, others less so. Occasionally we were shocked, especially at their disregard for eating unclean things. We wondered how they kept so relatively free from disease.

Into the second year, I was beginning to feel a little apprehensive because life had never been easier. We only needed the occasional patrol to maintain security.

I tried to find time alone – even from Abigail. At night-time I would leave the city barricades and wander, looking in the night sky.

Was I being ungrateful to God, to Achish? At times, however, I was feeling lower than when I was in the Cave of Adallum. For no real reason, I felt miserable. Was it because my companions and I were cut off from the roots that gave us spiritual succour?

The words came at last, bringing tears and ease in equal measure.

"Save me oh God for the waters are come into my soul.
I sink into the deep mire where there is no standing I am come into deep waters where
the flood overflows me.
I am weary of my crying, my throat is dried mine eye falls as I wait for God.
I am become a stranger to my brethren and an alien unto my mother's children."

This was it. I was a stranger and nothing – even the kindness and love of Achish – could make this different. I knew I would have to hold my sadness to myself until the others were ready to leave. But I knew with absolute certainty that I did not want the exile to continue, no matter what the outcome.

We had much free time. Some we enjoyed as guests of noble Philistines with hunting. Others, though rarer, as guests in their homes, where, to our amazement, their wives enjoyed as much conversation as did the men. Although the women were always modest they would nevertheless stand and hold their opinions.

I learned that, whilst Achish was a man above all other men, their nobility had the level of education that we found only amongst our priests. They seemed fascinated in trying to understand the mind of God, in what they called philosophy. They were concerned with the meaning of life. For a few, this was a real passion.

It made for delightful evenings, even though at times we feared we were in the presence of blasphemy. Amongst these men of learning, there seemed to be no idea of what was sacred and secure against challenge.

Reason seemed everything to them. They took little on trust unless they could prove it for themselves.

I pondered this and wondered whether this was a sign of their decline. They had lost their reverence for the gods through their constant questioning. Perhaps this was why the Lord had sent us to Philistia, for now I was convinced that it was part of His plan.

I recalled the comments from when I last saw Saul. He spoke about "other gods". Samuel had said something of travelling to other lands, though he also spoke in his farewell letter of meeting his three priests in Hebron. I did not understand this but was confident that it would be revealed in time.

One issue that troubled me from the first was whether I would declare my being the Lord's anointed to Achish.

In the end, it did not matter. He and his Council already knew of it. So, one day, when I was a guest at the Council, Janna cunningly raised the matter.

"May I ask my Lord's brother, David, about the future when, as we all hope, our treaty together will be extended?"

I answered that whilst two years go quickly we still had much time before a decision was needed. But I too hoped we would all wish to extend it, "if God wishes".

"Ah, Lord David. You have it. As I understand, you are your God's anointed to be the next King of Israel after the House of Saul. Thus, you will be greater even than the King of Gath, as it is foretold you will rule over of all Israel, like our High King."

I could sense the keen alertness of these very able men. What did they want to hear? What did I want to offer?

I suddenly realised that I had been silent and Achish gently chided me.

"Can you answer my councillor, Janna. Or do you not want to? I, too, would be interested in knowing my brother's mind for the future."

I was alone and felt that this discussion was the crux of our time in Gath.

"I shall speak frankly to my brother, the King, and his wise councillors. It is true that I have been chosen to be the next King of Israel. But I pray that day will not come for many, many years. For I tell you frankly, whilst I must accept the burden that will be placed upon me, I would do nothing to bring that day nearer. However, as the Living God has spoken through His prophet, Samuel, I know that I will be King."

I continued. "Our God is a jealous God. When he delivered our people from the Land of Egypt, he was afraid that others would corrupt us. So he laid upon us the need to be a separate people."

There was no movement from these men, as all appreciated the import of our discussion.

I went on. "Some of our people, especially some of our priests, are wholly against any alliance with other peoples, unless they are subject to us." There was a growl at this.

I carried on. "But others believe that we can be confident in our worship because God has established us for all time."

I pretended not to notice one of two sly smiles at these words. "If it is to God's glory and Israel's benefit, we can live at peace with our neighbours, providing they respect all the land that God has promised us. I am not yet King. I think, after enjoying your friendship, I am beginning to favour the later course. Although I would die to defend every yard of the land that God promised us, I can see the benefits of peace with all our neighbours."

Then I got carried away a little. "I know not how or when, but this I do know. I was a shepherd youth and fought Goliath. I was a new commander but garnered more than 200 warriors with my band of ten. God has been my inspiration. I cannot doubt that I am part of His plan. Whilst I may wish peace with you in future times, if you provoke us, then it will be war. So, Janna, wisest of the wise amongst the councillors of my brother and friend, King Achish, it will not be I who choose peace or war, but you yourselves."

This was a compromise. As I was speaking, I realised I was working out the problem as I spoke. Yet it seemed to satisfy them for now. I realised, however, that some of my greatest supporters in Israel, the priesthood, might be very disappointed with my answer.

Later, Achish told me with a smile that Janna had praised my answer as typical of a natural politician. I cannot say I was pleased with this.

Achish grew serious. "David, on the whole it was as good an answer as I could have hoped for. You must remember that I, too, have obligations to our god who can be just as jealous as your irascible old man."

Seeing me shocked at his blasphemy, he was all apologetic. He did it with his customary delicacy so that I could not do anything other than forgive him his "ignorance", as he sometimes pretended to forgive my infelicitous words and manners because I was a barbarian.

Then the blow fell – it had to. There had been three aggressive Benjaminite raiding parties from Saul. Why, I wondered, was he keen to provoke them? Unfortunately, a file of my men had been with the Philistines and, in the mêlée, whilst we had helped to drive off our own people, two of our men died and one was so severely hurt he could not live.

For some reason, this incensed our men and the call I was dreading arrived. With the Four, I was called to visit Achish, who was looking very grave.

"Saul has entered our territory three times. He came mainly with Benjaminites, as the northern tribes rightly are saying, 'why trouble the Philistines who have not broken the peace?'"

Achish spoke with some difficulty. "David, Saul is my enemy. Is he yours? Will you and your men come with me?"

I was at a loss. Could I? Could we go and fight Israel?

Joab interjected. "Great King Achish, you say Saul's army are only Benjaminites. If so, I for one would not shirk our duty to you and to show Israel that Saul of Benjamin is no longer the King of all Israel. He furthers only his tribe's interest to the cost of all."

To my amazement, Beniah, of all people, agreed with Joab, and Josh, and Eli followed suit.

What were they thinking? Did they want to bring to an end the schism, so that we could return?

At that moment, I wanted nothing more than to be part of Israel. I remained silent as Janna pressed Joab more closely as to what help the

Band would offer.

"I think, Janna, that we should be your mounted infantry. We move more quickly than the Benjaminites on horseback and faster than Philistines on foot."

I noticed Joab spoke of Benjaminites not Israelites.

They were right, of course. I remained a spectator as the Four spoke about the dispositions and what our line of march might be.

Suddenly, Achish spoke. "And what says my brother, David? There is no doubt that your cousin Benjaminites are both your and my enemy. It seems that your counsellors, the mightiest warriors in your Band, are for honouring our treaty. Have they spoken for you, too?"

For a moment, I froze. I did not say a word but then nodded acquiescence. I thought Beniah, Janna and, of course, Achish, would have appreciated that I had not spoken a word and had allowed myself just a glimmer of justification if ever this decision had to be justified.

Joab and Beniah quickly persuaded the Thirty in an unusual alliance, for rest of the men were happy to go wherever the Thirty went. Surprisingly, none seemed to notice that I had not added my voice to theirs. I later wondered whether they were part of a conspiracy to protect my conscience?

We said tearful goodbyes to our wives at Ziklag. We left thirty men as guards, mainly those slightly disabled from wounds, who now busied themselves as support troops to their more active warrior brothers.

We left Ziklag early at dawn. Within less than a day, we were with Achish's army.

The following day, as arranged, we were Achish's flank guard for his 20,000. They were magnificent men and had great discipline. Of course, they all had tremendous confidence in Achish, who had proved himself at every level.

I could not help think how alike he and Jonathan were, but quickly suppressed these thoughts. I was secretly thankful that only Saul's name had been mentioned – there was no word of Jonathan's whereabouts.

Two days later, we met up with the King of Eskalon's army, another 20,000 men. Eska and Achish were good friends and, that evening, I and the Four dined with Eska, Achish and their generals.

I had forgotten that whilst I and the Thirty had reverted to shaving in respect to our Gath allies, the majority of our men did not and they were startled at the overt hostility shown by Philistine soldiers, who did not know us as allies. Sadly, there had been skirmishes between our men and Eska's and though we came off best it was not a good sign.

Eska was willing, just, to be assured that our presence was no danger, but when we met with King Agra's army, it was clear there was no trust.

Achish, who had the honourable ambition to become Philistia's High King, and was keenly supported by Eska, began to look very worried. Agra made it plain he wanted no "dubious allies on my flank".

Achish came to a speedy decision. "Frankly, David, I do not think you and you men will be acceptable. Rather than risk any further incidents, I think it best if you withdraw."

I cannot say that I was sorry and perfectly understood how his fellow countrymen, not knowing us, would be concerned to have such a band of warriors on their flank. Perhaps they doubted whether, in the shock of battle, we would be reliable. In my heart of hearts, I did not know either.

So, with a far lighter heart than when I set out, I said farewell to the Philistine host and turned the Band around. We set off back to Ziklag.

To my delight and the salvation of all our souls, Ura came to see me. "Captain David, I honour you and am sworn to you in obedience. David, their host is enormous. They are bringing all the Philistine cities together to march against Saul. I care not for the King, though in the past he showed me many kindnesses, but his soul was lost when he turned against you. But, my Captain, my heart is with Jonathan – as I think yours is also. May I take my company, find Jonathan and take him your greetings and love."

I was heartbroken at his devotion.

My tears and embrace told him everything. "Tell my brother that I wish I was with him and that I pray the Lord will preserve him. My dear Ura, go to him speedily, and tell him all you have seen. Urge him to persuade his father to avoid a battle or seek a truce. At this moment, tell Jonathan I think they are too powerful and I fear for the Lord's anointed. Without the might of all Israel, he is lost. He must avoid a battle."

Everyone in the band knew where Ura was going. All silently wished him well.

We turned our way southward with heavy hearts. No one spoke of what was in their minds but I was grateful that I was partly freed from the responsibility of aiding Israel's enemies. Because, no matter that the men of Gath had become our friends and that Saul was leading a rump of the twelve tribes, we were all of the same blood. Our hearts were with our brothers.

The Fire Storm

Then, as if the Lord wanted to punish us for our infidelity, Nathan, a man no longer fitted for the wars though he had once been a great warrior before losing his shield arm, met us on the way.

He was just able to keep his seat on his horse, but had terrible wounds. He was desperate to reach us and tell us the dreadful news.

What had I been thinking of – leaving Ziklag unprotected!

The Amalekites were a wary foe. They had seen the bulk of our men leave and quickly had worked out that we had gone with the army of Achish. They may even have been encouraged by Saul to attack whilst the Philistines advanced north against him.

Before Nathan died in my arms, he told us that the city had been sacked. All the men, save himself, had been slain. The Amalekites had carried off all the women and children.

I closed his eyes for him and kept my sense of bitterness to myself. I told him that I did not hold him responsible and that his valour would be remembered.

After that, there was no time for grieving or recriminations. Some of the men were so angry that they talked of stoning me. I had to show that I was for immediate action, to head off their wild and mutinous talk. I felt bitter that when things go wrong it is he who leads who must bear the burden of other men's frustration.

I quickly ordered four scouting parties to go quickly, to pick up the trail of the Amalekites and bring the information back to the main body immediately. I chewed my nails in anger and impatience as we returned to Ziklag, where a sorry sight met our eyes.

The barricades were destroyed. A few Philistine stragglers had returned and were staggering about, crying and wailing for their lost ones and their destroyed homes.

Again, I could hear a murmur from some of the men. Why had I led them on a wild goose chase and left their families unprotected? I knew it would be fatal to try to justify my action – which they conveniently forgot had been a joint one. So I made sure that duties occupied them until I could find the real target for their rage.

I took a harsh decision and left only one man to supervise the burial of the dead.

If the Amalekites thought that I would wait to give the dead their rites, they had made a mistake. I barked an order and, without a backward glance, rode grimly on. I cared not whether any followed because my heart ached for Abigail, Annah and the children. But this was no time for feeling – only intense concentration to fuel rapid action.

Josh had found the trail and, like the excellent solider he was, had garnered the other three groups together. As we came up to him, I had almost 600 warriors to deploy.

Josh quickly made his report. "I have found them. They are more than three days ahead. They are going slowly as they have so much plunder."

There was a growl from the men as they heard this. Josh was speaking about their homes.

He continued. "It seems the women and children are all right and are being herded together. I reckon there are about 2,000 warriors and I think they are heading for their stronghold beyond the Besor Ravine, a place which we had never crossed."

It was close to nightfall. We were exhausted. The horses were blown. There was nothing for it but to order a rest and follow them across the ravine at daybreak.

The men threw themselves on the ground to sleep. There was no longer any talk of stoning me – they were too intent on reaching their families to give thought to anything else. I knew that I had prove myself, yet again. My desperate anxiety for Abigail and the children almost unmanned me. I had to fight hard to maintain my concentration.

I gave orders to set guards. I wanted no reconnoitring Amalekite force to turn us from pursuers to the pursued. I rather curtly denied Beniah my company as, finally, the danger we were in almost overwhelmed me.

I went off into a nearby hill and pondered what had I done. How had I allowed Jonathan and Saul to be trapped in deepest danger? My stupidity had risked all against the fiercest enemy, to whom the name Israelite is more hateful than any other. I nearly choked trying to restrain the thoughts of what might be happening to the women.

Then, in stark focus, into my mind came the picture of the crazed Amalekite mother who had first slain her children then herself. She was so real I could hear her screams and curses in my head. I was totally unnerved and I fell to my knees, imploring God to defend our people.

My soul sought to fly to him. He knew I was willing to die to save Abigail or to lose my life to secure Jonathan. I was desperate. I did not know what to do. I was empty of thought – the reason of life itself – so afraid was I for my loved ones.

Then I felt His presence coming closer. I saw my pathetic huddled figure upon the ground. The warmth of His love soothed away all my anxieties.

I was immersed within His great Oneness.

DAVID, DAVID, YOU MUST CROSS THE RAVINE.
YOU MUST SEPARATE THE AMALEKITES FROM MY PEOPLE.
THINK OF HOW THEY WILL BE MOST SURPRISED.
DAVID, I SHALL BE WITH YOU ON THE MORROW.

GATHER OUR PEOPLE, FOR AGAIN THEY WILL SEE THAT THEY ARE
MY PEOPLE.
THEN, DAVID, REMEMBER WHO YOU ARE, YOUR PURPOSE.
WE SHALL MEET IN HEBRON.

As the Voice left me, as if in one of Achish's images, in an instant I saw the whole fearful battle that shocked my very being – but I now knew what to do.

His words echoed in my soul. I again longed to be part of His wholeness now knew how I would complete His purpose.

I ran, refreshed and rejuvenated, back to the men as I mused on His last words, "meet in Hebron". Of course, the meaning of Samuel's letter was now clear. I would scatter the Amalekites and return our people to Hebron in Judah. The exhilaration of knowing, after interminable doubt, lifted my spirits high, high, high! Is there anything that the soul loathes more than doubt and uncertainty? Whatever the morrow brought, I knew my people were to be restored in Judah.

I called the men to arms. My exhilaration showed itself so they became excited at my obvious transformation. We moved on.

We came to the fearsome Ravine of Besor and crossed it in small groups. We re-assembled in the desert beyond and struggled on to follow the retreating Amalekites.

There was one piece of my plan missing: I knew nothing of the Amalekite stronghold at Besor itself. Without that knowledge, how could I deploy my forces successfully against a larger enemy, who would fight all the more desperately to preserve his last refuge?

Eli found the key. An Egyptian slave of an Amalekite chieftain had been left behind because he had fallen sick. He feared we would kill him but when Eli found that he knew Besor, he refreshed and reassured him. Now, he brought him to me.

He proved to be an intelligent man. When I asked him to sketch out a plan of Besor, he did so easily. Then, remarkably, he offered me some advice.

"Great Lord, if you and your small body of men are intent to raid Besor then I think you should wait awhile. In two days' time they have a feast of Baal, after which they will take their captives southward to sell into bondage. Fear not that they will harm the women – they are more valuable whole than ravaged. The Amalekites have learned that shekels of iron and gold bring greater gifts than mere sport."

I told him that I was convinced we would be successful. I said that if he came with us and assisted with his local knowledge, then I would set him free and return him with shekels for himself to the land of the Pharaohs.

My plan was simple but hellish. It was based upon the Egyptian's plan of the stronghold. I prayed that he was not serving us false because we were facing massive odds, even though we would have the advantage of surprise.

Besor was not a city but a huge encampment on a small plain, which was surrounded by high natural ramparts. It was as if some giant had scoured out of the living rock a place in which to lay his head.

There were two stockades. The one where the Amalekites kept their captives and plunder was a little below the real stronghold, which was a hundred or more feet higher. At the entrance to their lair they had built a wooden barrier, behind which they had set up tents and small wooden houses.

I explained the problem to the Four, though it was hardly necessary. "This is not an attack on the Amalekites but a rescue of our families. Frankly, if we can get them away without a single Amalekite casualty, I care not. They are our first priority. So, Beniah, you will take 200 men. You'll need that many to assist the women. You are to steal to the captives' stockade and secure it – without any noise if you can. If our Egyptian is telling the truth, they should be chanting to their heathen god, so your throat-cutting might go unnoticed."

"So," said Beniah, "I get them away and retreat?"

"No, my friend – though that is the main task. We might well get away unnoticed in their revels but in the morning they would discover we have gone. If we were on the road, even with our horses, as we would be transporting the women, they would be upon us before we were out of their range. I have no need to tell you that, in the open desert, our 600 against their host of four or more thousand would overwhelm us. We have to destroy them in their lair."

There was an interruption.

The Egyptian had been listening to our Council and spoke. "Sir King, I have to tell you they have more than 5,000 warriors here in Besor. Last week, their southern group rejoined their people."

There was a groan. These were terrible odds.

It was important that I not let morale fall. "Come, come, my Companions. You forget two things. God has spoken to me and I know they will be delivered unto our hands."

There was an immediate response to this.

I had never ever told all them that I heard the Voice, but now I felt it was necessary. "Last night, I was in His presence. He promised me that, this day, you will see that we are His people and He our God."

The men were not fools. Whilst I did not think they would expect me to blaspheme at such a time, they needed more practical reassurance. "Secondly, as I see it, they are trapped, not defended, in their wooden fortress. A wooden fortress, brothers. Notice which way the wind blows."

Slowly, realisation crossed their faces. Grimly, we knew we had hot work ahead.

I called out, "Right, Beniah. Once the families are secure, your signal is to fire a lighted arrow into the stronghold. I promise you it will burn because I want 40 volunteers to get close to their outer stockade and cover it with pitch. Once we see Beniah's fire arrow, we will light our own."

At the thought of what was to come and the images I had seen, I could not help but say, "and may God have mercy on their souls".

By next evening, we had moved into position. That had been easy as there was a half-moon and the Amalekites' celebration was loud and employed bonfires for their barbaric sacrifices.

I had spread out all our men in a line around the stockade. Their main task would be to slay any who tried to escape from their burning camp. It was going to be terrible.

There was no sound coming from the captives' stockade. I later learned that our women were magnificent, avoiding making any noise and carrying the children gently out of harm's way. Beniah's men escorted them, and I was particularly proud of how Abigail and Annah kept order and made it possible for most of Beniah's men to return to us when we really needed them.

Before Beniah's burning arrow had reached its zenith, our arrows were upon them. We had nearly 400 bows drawn, each with a lit arrow. When we fired them off into the darkness, the night sky became a mass of blazing lines.

At first, the enemy did not appreciate they were under attack but when a number of their men fell pierced with arrows they quickly knew.

There was complete pandemonium. The front barricade was blazing fiercely and many of the houses deeper in the camp were well alight. Cruelly, the wind blew warm upon the flames as if a hand went around and set alight to all it could find.

The noise was deafening. Then, as I feared some men, their clothes and their bodies blazing, broke through the now semi-charred remains of the barricade. They were met without mercy by our avenging swords and spears.

It was a scene from hell: the flames roared and men screamed in terror. The cries were of both triumph and despair as warrior met warrior.

At first, we just killed and killed but we had to fall back because their bodies were becoming a parapet. Now they could see us. The survivors who still greatly outnumbered us.

With a roar, they came forward. My arm ached from dealing blows. Earlier, they were in no fit state to parry our sword thrusts, but now they had armed themselves and now it was we who were battling for our lives. The fire behind them drove them on to our death-dealing weapons, which were becoming blunt through over-use.

One man, taller than the rest, had broken out with his hair on fire. His arm was blackened, but he could still use his hand. He slashed with his evil-looking sword and hacked Aban down at my side. His face was that of a demon. Despite his injuries, he had beyond human strength.

He hacked at me. I parried. He hacked again. I swayed to feint, but he was not fooled. Driven on by desperation, his blows came so fast and heavy upon my arm that I began to despair as my sword began to droop. He came on again, standing on a body of a comrade, screaming at me, his sword upraised. I knew I was too slow. Here was my wound, my death. Suddenly, I was knocked over. Beniah stood on my fallen body and, with his spear, ran through the snarling Amalekite, bringing his guts and mess out at the other side.

It was Beniah bringing reinforcements. Never had help been so welcome. The snarling, screaming men in front saw we were renewed and a wailing howl of despair came from them.

One warrior cried above the others, "To the east! All to the east!"

He led as many as a company at the far eastern side of our line. It buckled as our men were overrun and cruelly slain by the trampling hoard. I saw quickly that we needed to block this flow. I called to Eli, who was at the far west end of the line. I could see the enemy in front of him run across our lines to escape through the gap.

They were flowing out as through a breached dam. But that was their undoing. Whilst the first rush got away, they were now fighting and trampling on each other, as we stood around them adding to the bloody mayhem. More importantly, Beniah's men still had their bows.

I screamed out, "Arrows! Arrows and slings!"

What a fool! Why had I not remembered this earlier? We could fire missiles at them and stay out of reach. It was a massacre.

Soon, all that was left of Besor was a smoking ruin. There were piles of dead men everywhere, and some women too, many hideously burnt. The stench clung to our nostrils for days afterwards. Since that day, after the fiery Battle of Besor. I found burnt offerings difficult to stomach.

The men did not need any orders. We just sat or stood, taking our desperate rest as we saw the enemy melt and crumple before us. After pausing for fifteen minutes, I ordered the only kind thing to do: to advance amongst their fallen and finish their agony.

It was over. I was exhausted. I had nothing left.

I looked around at the charnel house that I had created. I felt so sick.

There was a gentle touch upon my shoulder. It was Abigail. She spoke no words. Her wide, dark eyes were full of pity for all she saw. She led me away.

I paused for a moment, fighting down my tears and revulsion.

I turned to Beniah. "Beniah, thank you for my life. Can you organise a guard? We want no nasty surprises in the morning."

I held Abigail close to me. I had no words. I sobbed on to her shoulder as she softly cooed a lullaby to her frightened boy.

Next day, we could see the terrible effects of what we had achieved. Joab had taken the body count.

He said, "I can't include the burnt ones, who've nothing left. There are 4,200 – so I reckon that only about 400 or so got away." There were times when Joab's harsh insensitivity made me sick.

I nodded. This was the time I hated most. In my soul of souls, I knew I gloried in the battle. I knew I could see the whole, whereas most others simply fought the fight in front of them.

Yes, I admit that I gloried and took pride in seeing the fruits of my plans come to pass. But, at the end of the battle, to see the destruction my gift of war had wrought, I tell you, I wished I had been a priest.

"Thank you, Joab, and what of our losses?" I asked, dully.

I feared the worst because when I was down I saw many a brave brother down with me.

"Not too bad in the circumstances," was his cold reply. "There are thirty-five dead and fifteen others severely wounded."

I felt the beginning of an angry retort. Then, I suddenly appreciated that this was Joab, who loved his men as much as I. It was his way of covering his hurt.

I swallowed. These were the most casualties I had ever had with the Band. I calculated one in twelve of us had been lost.

Then, the Egyptian appeared, as from nowhere. He made hideous obeisance to me, calling out, "Great King, to have slain so many and lost so few – the gods indeed must fight on your behalf."

I could have killed him in my anger and grief.

"But they were my brothers! I am not some tyrant. How dare you! Leave me, you offend my sight."

Eli came up to me and put his arms around me.

He spoke gently. "Great Captain and the Lord's anointed, who can doubt this day that the Lord looks kindly upon you. Yes, we all grieve for our brothers, but they died shouting your name. They took their vengeance of the Lord's enemies. David, come. This is a great victory and, when we have laid our brothers to rest, we must celebrate even greater joy. Not one wife, boy or girl is lost and all our goods are recovered. David, you have an even greater triumph. In the captives' stockhold, it looks like years of plunder."

With that, he led shouts of triumph and hosannas. I had to endure it all, knowing that I had remembered what most forgot: this slaughter was only necessary because I had erred in the first place.

Eli was right, of course. Whilst some of the restored women were now widows, our men generously took them in. As we moved out from that dreadful place, each child and women had their man. The plunder was enormous.

But we did not know of the outcome of Saul's war with the Philistines. I prayed and prayed that Jonathan would be safe.

After travelling a day, I called a general Council of all the men and asked the women to chose 50 of their number to hear our deliberations, whilst the other women looked after the children.

I sent a letter to Achish telling him of what we had achieved; this is what I wrote:

"Brother, friend and protector,

"I know not how it went with you and Saul, though I pray that Jonathan still lives. After him, only you are more beloved.

"What follows may seem like ingratitude, but by now you will have heard of the destruction of Ziklag by the Amalekites. However, the Lord was good and we have recovered all that was lost at the sacking of Ziklag. Less than 500 of the Amalekites remain. We slew more than 4,000. Truly, the Amalekites are no longer a people.

"The Band will return to their people and see what the Lord has in store for me. Though I have found love in Philistia, my mind, my body and my soul long for the tabernacles of my God.

"I will return to Judah. I trust you will think kindly of your brother and that your forgiveness will surely follow, as you understand him.

"Perhaps we shall be allied again. I pray so. Therefore, may the Lord bless and keep you and may his countenance shine upon you and bring you peace. Your brother, David."

What our priest would think of me praying over a Philistine, I can only image. I felt it no blasphemy, for Achish of Gath was a man in whom the Godhead shone bright – aye, even amongst the heathens.

My other message was to the Elders of Judah and went off immediately for I had made up my mind. I recognised that much of the Amalekite plunder came from them. I asked that they send 200 men at once to collect their share of our victory, as my Band and I were dedicated to preserving God's people.

Meanwhile, I had to face the Band. I looked over their familiar faces.

I began to speak to them. "I can see faces that I cherish and respect: some blooded, all looking more battle wise and hardened. Yes, and you may know that I, too, have a wound from Besor."

There was much animated response at this.

"When Beniah saved my life, he did so by kicking me out of the way. I've such an enormous bruise on my backside that it ..."

I knew what would follow: they yelled and roared with laughter, tears rolling down their faces. These heroes at times could be like schoolboys, enjoying shocking the rabbi with some crude joke.

The uproarious words resounded amongst them. They chanted, "bloody big bruise on his backside".

I waited till they ceased and then raised my hands.

"Aye, brothers. I know you all. I know this too: I could go to the end of the world and not meet your match."

They roared again, but with angry delight because they had an idea of what they had achieved.

"But, brothers and sisters, it is time to turn our back on the stranger. The Lord has commanded me to return to Judah – to our own people. God's people need us. I yearn for home."

They moaned in response. I had touched a chord. We had not spoken of it. No one had known my intention.

To soothe them, I took up my harp. Closing my eyes, I let my spirit be guided by the Lord.

He answered me and the words flowed.

"How amiable are thy tabernacles oh Lord of Hosts.
My soul longeth; yea even fainteth for the courts of the Lord.
My heart and my flesh cry out for the living God.
Yea the sparrow hath found a house and the swallow a nest where she may lay her young, even thine altars; O Lord of Hosts my King and my God.
For a day in thy courts is better than a thousand.
I had rather be a door keeper in the house of my God than dwell in the tents of the heathen for ever."

With wild hallelujahs, glad hosannas and copious tears, the men cried out in unison, "To Judah! To Judah! The Lion of Judah returns home!"

This was the last celebration that we would make.

Soon, there began a sorrow which, more than fifty years later, still rends my heart.

PART SEVEN

CATASTROPHE AND KINGSHIP

Chapter Twenty-two

How Are the Mighty Fallen

The Witch of Endor

Saul was obsessed with demonstrating his authority in Israel, but the more he did this the less effective he became. Whilst Jonathan counselled moderation and consultation, Abner sided with Saul's tense agitated moods, which demanded assertive and rigorous action. Abner argued that unless the tribes and the priests saw that "Saul was King indeed", he would become a mere figurehead and his glorious past would be forgotten.

This was made more bitter by the father knowing of his son's excellence but, instead of glorying in his fame, he was resentful of Jonathan's achievements. Fuelled by that most corrosive of all corruptions, the jealousy of old men for the strength of youths prowess, it undermined everything Saul did. Thus, the more Jonathan tried to please his father, the worse things became between them.

As Jonathan urged a milder policy, he seemed to be always at loggerheads with Saul's aim for rigour – encouraged by the ever-flattering Abner. This led Saul into the disastrous decision to re-assert royal authority and bring the northern tribes into closer allegiance. It was argued this would stem the subtle tide of appeasement the northerners were making with the Philistines.

So, when Saul began collecting the levies for a punitive attack, the northern tribes saw this as coercion by Saul, rather than any perceived threat from the Philistines.

Jonathan warned that this would lead to a general war, which even Saul did not want. But, when the wily Abner asked Jonathan why the King should fear such an event, Jonathan was forced to declare that Saul could no longer rely upon the absolute allegiance of some of the tribes. This, of course, simply confirmed Saul's excitable fears of conspiracy. It also gave added weight to Abner's subtle but prolonged suggestion that Jonathan's behaviour showed his loyalty was less than firm.

The enemy, of course, were not unaware of the disarray in the ranks of Israel. At a secret meeting of all the kings of Philistia, called by Baalal of Gaza, their new High King, Achish argued strongly to respond vigorously to Saul's challenge. This surprised some of his fellow kings as they had looked askance upon his alliance with us.

Achish pressed the case. "The great progress the Israelites had made was because they had become united. Now that their unity is weakened, this is the time to strike. Moreover, Saul has wasted his strength against us, has compounded his difficulties by being active in the north, far away from where his natural strength lies. A major attack cutting Saul's links with the rest of Israel is our opportunity to destroy Saul for ever."

Was this a betrayal of us? Not really. If I had been in Achish's position I would have probably urged the same policy.

The strategy was accepted and within days the armies of the kings were on the move.

Everything that Saul did seemed to fall apart in his hands. Instead of over-awing the northerners and bringing them into closer loyalty, they were incensed at the high-handedness of the Benjaminites. Every meeting with the Elders sent more of them away disaffected with Saul. Sadly, Saul forbade the more diplomatic Jonathan to have any public say. It was easy for men of experience to see that Saul's seeming energy and boastfulness was brittle and without substance.

Many Elders quietly expressed the view that when the Lord removes His favour from the mighty, they are destroyed by their own folly.

Jonathan was desperate. When one of his captains cautiously suggested that Jonathan seek an occasion to leave the army "in the capable hands of Abner", Jonathan struck him in anger and asked whether he really advocating desertion? The captain was ashamed, though he marvelled at Jonathan's loyalty. It was a sign of the times. Jonathan later learned that the captain had left to avoid the coming crisis.

Saul began to realise that his position was becoming serious when he found that the rapidly advancing Philistines were disrupting his communications. The arrival of Ura to Jonathan bringing unequivocal news of the rapid mobilisation of the total enemy strength put Saul into a rage. Whilst Abner simply wanted to know what the "rebel David was doing with his paramour Achish". Jonathan had to endure this scurrilous nonsense and Saul dissipated his energies in cursing me and blaming me for the increasing desertions.

Worse was to follow in a furious orgy of self-destruction. Instead of ordering a strategic retreat, he ordered an advance further north in response to some rumour that the city of Jezreel, because of my ties through marriage, was reminding the people that I was the Lord's anointed. So crazily, Jezreel suddenly became Saul's prime objective. Whether in his frenzy he was advancing to separate the northerners from the Philistines, or whether to quell any potential support for me was unknown, but it played right into the hands of the Philistines.

The trap closed as Saul's army drew close to Jezreel. The Philistines coming up behind Saul occupied the strategic places and only Mount Gilboa lay between the armies.

Jonathan was much moved by the arrival of Ura but, typical of his generosity, immediately urged him to return with his greetings of love to the Band to avoid the coming catastrophe. Of course, Ura would not. After reassuring Jonathan of my love and loyalty, which my letter confirmed, he set about trying to raise the morale of men. So serious was the situation that even Jonathan's guard, probably our elite troops, were downcast. But Ura hoped that in the coming struggle they would lead the breakout. If Jonathan was spared, Ura was confident that I would proclaim Jonathan as the next King and reunite the people.

Poor Saul! He longed so much for the presence of God. He exhausted himself with fasts in the hope of hearing the voice of God. He would run off frantically into wilderness seeking inspiration – he really did want to do the Lord's bidding. Tragically, the more sacrifices he ordered and the more he fasted, the more he exhausted himself. In the end, he came to the realisation that he had lost the Lord's favour.

Too late, he tried to seek forgiveness for his destruction of the Lord's priests. I believe this was the real disobedience to God, not the refusal to annihilate the beaten and defenceless Amalekites. But he found the words of Samuel returning to haunt him.

"Does the Lord delight in burnt offerings and sacrifice as much as in obeying the voice of the Lord?"

He now had no priests with him. Those he had at the beginning of the campaign had drifted away. He was now desperate and asked Abner to find whether there were any seers in the land because he would consult God to try to discover what to do. This was total unreason.

If Abner had any doubts about the future, he had none now. Saul and Samuel had banished seers and witches from the land, making it an offence to foretell the future or conjure spirits. Now, in his despair, he was seeking communication with the devil. None the less, ever willing to compound his master's folly, Abner inquired and heard of a woman of Endor who was famed for raising spirits.

Amazingly, Saul set off in disguise to Endor. This meant leaving the army at a critical juncture and he was missing for nearly four days.

Jonathan, who knew nothing about this, was frantic. When he cautiously asked Abner whether, in view of his father's absence, they should try to move the army into a more defensive position, it was as if Saul's madness was infectious. Abner flatly refused, suggesting that Jonathan was showing a lack of faith and loyalty.

When Saul reached the witch at Endor, at first the women refused his request for a seance, reminding him of the law. However, he said the guilt would be upon his head if ever it should be discovered and promptly doubled his price for her services. So she began her seance.

In her frenzy, she screamed out that he was seeking to entrap her, as her spirit had told her that her inquirer was indeed Saul the King who had cleared the land of seers. Saul acknowledged who he was but reassured her that she had nothing to fear. Moreover, her recognising him was evidence of her prowess and encouraged him. So he promised her immunity and then trebled his price.

The blasphemy increased. She asked him whom did he seek, but in her trance she called out, "I know whom ye seek. I see an ancient man arise out of the ground, standing at your shoulder. He holds a great staff and he is clothed in a long sacred gown."

Saul knew it was the spirit of Samuel and his soul cowered.

The seer continued. "Silence, be still. He knows your question."

Saul felt the hair of his head come to life, for he knew he had committed a terrible sin, but his desperation drove him on.

The spirit cried out to him. At last, poor Saul heard a voice speaking directly to him, but it was not the Lord's.

The tortured strangled voice spewed from the writhing form of the witch:

"Who calls and wakes me?
Thou art Saul.
Foolish man who would know the morrow.
You know the answer, you, who were chosen by God, have because of your disobedience, been rejected.
Tomorrow you and your sons will be with me – trouble me no more."

The spirit disappeared and both the woman of Endor and the King were prostrate on the ground losing their senses utterly.

The men who were with Saul trembled and were chilled to the bone. When Saul recovered, he grieved his folly. Of course, no matter how fierce his injunctions to keep the whole affair secret, there was no doubt that the men spoke amongst themselves. They were now convinced that Saul's cause was doomed.

He returned to his army, which had already begun to shrink as the enemy had been growing. When the rumours of Saul's folly went around his men, the desertions increased even more rapidly.

Jonathan's Glory

Too late, Saul agreed with Jonathan to take up a defensive position on Mount Gilboa, dividing the army into two to occupy the two foothills lying west and east of Mount Gilboa. Saul and Jonathan took the western hills where the attack was expected.

Abner would hold the eastern foothills to await the onslaught of the Philistines. At the right time, he was to repeat the tactics of Havilah and take the enemy in the flank. He was to await the full engagement of the armies and then come to the aid of Saul and Jonathan, as well as the two other sons of Saul, who were also there.

Even then, Saul might have retrieved something from their situation as they commanded nearly 60,000 men on a good defensive position and Jonathan urged caution. Abner's army, on equally good defensive ground, commanded another 40,00 men but they were mainly the Benjaminites.

Baalal handled his army of some 200,000 men with great skill. He leaned heavily upon the advice of Achish. It became obvious that the other kings admired Achish. If Achish lived he would certainly be the next High King of Philistia. His alliance with me had done him no harm as the Philistine men of politics saw that it had enhanced the division amongst the Israelites.

Achish argued that they should throw a defensive screen across the valley of 30,000. This would deter Abner from any advance to come to the aid of Saul. The Philistine could then attack the main Israelite army with their vastly superior numbers. He begged the honour of leading his men of Gath, as the spearpoint of their army. He would press up the valley, cutting between the two wings of the Israelites, and then he would swing west to engage Saul and Jonathan directly. With the whole Philistine army present they were enough to assail Saul and Jonathan both front and flank.

The day dawned but in the night Saul had lost another 10,000 warriors and Abner almost the same.

Saul bravely confronted the situation. In stark contrast to the desperate predicament, he had wonderfully recovered his old verve and elan. He threw off his despondency and went around, his host revitalised. He called his captains together to instruct them to remind their men of the many previous victories and how Prince Jonathan had never failed to defeat the Philistines in battle, even against great odds.

The soldiers responded, as he knew they would. With urgent hope in their hearts, as all knew there was no where else to go and recognising the Saul of old, they began to show some optimism.

Saul showed he was still a great commander. With his ringing voice that reached each warrior, he roared, "Remember, I am the Lord's anointed. Prince Jonathan and I are victors over these same uncircumcised dogs, whose uncleanness is an abomination. Could the Lord suffer them to triumph over his chosen people? Never! The victor of Jabesh Gilead, Michmash, Havilah and Eilah speaks and here stands Jonathan of Benjamin, who has never failed to conquer the Philistines whenever he has faced them."

The men cheered him and for a time hope was truly renewed.

Saul sent for Jonathan to gave him his father's blessing. It was as it the strife of all the years had been taken away in their common danger and as Jonathan knelt, Saul cried for all men to see. "This is my beloved son, in whom I am well pleased."

He called his other sons, Abinadab and Malki, to him and the soldiers were greatly heartened to feel that the King and his sons were there with them at the very centre of the danger. Indeed, many recalled that Saul never asked anything of a warrior that he was not prepared to give himself.

Eban, his armour barrer, now grey-haired, was another inspiration. His face was filled with grinning excitement at the coming battle, showing to the men that there were truly mighty men of Israel present on Mount Gilboa.

Jonathan, who was ever loyal, ever true, was uplifted when he saw that his father was himself again. He became ecstatic and laughed as his soul was filled with valour. "My father, great King, ever victor for Israel. Yes, we are in danger but, men, think of the glory we are to win here on Mount Gilboa."

The men roared their appreciation and all in Jonathan's elite guard felt ashamed of their earlier doubts. They knew they would follow their beloved captain to hell and back, if necessary.

Saul urged Jonathan to go speedily, lest our intrepid warriors see the hosts before us and despair. Saul whispered, "Go in God's name."

Now the glory and gallantry of Jonathan was to be demonstrated. He immediately understood the meaning of Achish's manoeuvre. As he watched his battle lines form up. Jonathan realised that he had to break the

Philistine line as they tried to outflank him whilst marching up the slope. He further saw that, as the enemy advanced, they would be confident in their number and would expect the Israelites to shrink and go higher up the mountain to make their lines tighter. He would not wait for this to happen but surprise them and go over to the offensive. He knew with total certainty that if he could break their line with his guard, then with the advantage of the slope, this could be Michmash again and the Philistines would be thrown off balance and vulnerable to a second counter-attack from Abner.

Oh, my brave Jonathan, greatest of all the sons of Israel. If only others had had your heart and his valour.

With a shout Jonathan led the unexpected charge and rolled back Achish's men with great slaughter. With an exalted Ura at his side, men fled from death and dared not stand in front of the two death-dealing heroes.

Their flaying swords brought death, destruction and terrible wounds with every blow.

Achish himself was down. He suffered an injury to his arm and had to be dragged to the rear by his captains.

The Gath line was wavering and Jonathan, like a giant, was leading the charge at the middle of the Philistine line. He had killed at least twelve and he needed a new sword as the one he carried had been blunted upon their heads. He was inspired and raised the strength of his men two or threefold.

Saul, too, with his war cry, fired up his men and crashed down on to the lines of the advancing enemy. Though the Philistines had a three-to-one advantage, they were near fatally halted in their advance. Nothing is more dangerous than when an army is stopped.

This was the crisis of the battle. Saul saw that the Israelite fury had discomforted the enemy. The Philistines were beginning to weaken and some of their men began to fall back.

Jonathan and Ura, virtually exhausted as their breaths seemed to draw in not air but burning iron fumes, had their energy renewed as they saw the elite of the Philistines waver in front and begin to melt away.

For a moment, there was a break in Achish's lines. He was having a wound bound and was desperately trying to rally his men. Jonathan and Achish saw each other and both knew this was the day of doom for one of them.

Achish, urgently trying to hold his men, cried out his challenge to Jonathan, whilst Jonathan saw his enemy's line collapsing and yelled in an exultant voice,

"Men of Israel. See, they break. They break. The uncircumcised dogs break."

It was true. A significant gap in the Philistine ranks had opened up and

Jonathan went through.

Achish, in terror, had killed his man, but two at his side were down. In gathering desperation, he saw his line peeling away in front of the seemingly inexhaustible and irresistible Israelites. Again, he was down, but this time by his own men who bowled him over in the beginning of a retreat that was close to a rout.

In his despair, he called out to Dagon. For a moment, a few rallied to his side, but Jonathan and his men had broken through. The men of Gath were in retreat and Jonathan and Ura were hacking not at enemy faces, but now at men's fleeing backs.

They were uplifted. It was over. Achish's elite captains began to slowly give ground.

Furiously, Achish tried to hold his men. But, to compound their terror, they could see that, along the hill, Saul's men were inexorably pushing back Baalal's line.

Achish was cursing. All was lost. He thought of finding his doom amidst the slaughter rather than live to face the disgrace of defeat. He called up his last reserves of strength before seeking death amongst his ravaging foes and looked up. But all was not lost. As he raised his head in a final appeal to the God in whom he did not believe, he saw a wondrous sight. Surely, this was a miracle!

Suddenly, he knew Dagon was with him. There was Abner's army on the top of the ridge, in their thousands. But they were not coming down upon them like the avenging furies he expected. They were in total flight, even though they had not been engaged.

Abner had fled. Abner had deserted and left the glory of Israel to perish.

Achish, pointing upwards with his sword, lifted his voice to the skies and roared, "They flee. They flee. Their God has deserted them. They are ours for the slaughter."

Every man on that fell plain heard Achish's words.

Achish's voice had reached Jonathan and his men, who looked up and saw the truth.

When the battle was theirs, when they had achieved the impossible, instead of simply marching down to their assistance, Abner's hosts had betrayed and deserted them.

Their strength drained away. Suddenly their arms and legs ran away to sand. The fleeing enemy stood and with spirits renewed began to return to the fight and advanced all along the line.

The gap, which had been created in front of Jonathan and Ura, now disappeared. They quickly found themselves surrounded by 200 or more warriors, who but a moment ago, had been like chaff before their swords.

Now, the weary 50 were facing a rejuvenated host, who sought to wipe out their recent shame upon the bloody bodies of their foes.

Jonathan and Ura took in the situation in an instant. Just in time, they called the men to stand back to back, to parry the blows of the revitalised and more numerous incensed enemy,

Ura's voice cried out in a final farewell. "Oh, men of Jonathan, to die in such glorious company! Thank you, Jonathan, my brother –"

He said no more as a cruel spear thrust severed his throat. Down he went, loyal and true to the last.

Jonathan was filled with an angry grief and slew two more to give his brother's spirit company. But his eyes were filled with bloody tears as a savage blow half-severed his shield hand, which fell useless at his side. But not before his counter-thrust sent the Philistine off to Dagon.

Suddenly, but three of the gallant men of the 50 still stood upright. Even the cruel, vicious Philistines paused at such valour and drew back a while.

Whilst harrowing screams echoed around that terrible mountain, here was a centre of stillness.

Jonathan felt the touch of his comrades but they knew their doom had arrived.

Jonathan raised himself up.

That noble man, still gallant and beautiful amidst his terrible bleeding wounds, cried, "The Lord God of Israel is with us. Who can be against us? Into thy hands I commend my spirit!"

With that, each man went forward. Forward – not backward!

Jonathan called out. "Where are you, Achish, King of Gath? I, Jonathan of Israel, challenge you."

Jonathan's two comrades were down. Now all was complete stillness as the enemy were halted in their fury by such a great heart.

Achish was amazed. Though he was slightly wounded, he had the angry, surging spirit upon him and was buoyed up by certain victory. He strode forward to take up the challenge. Yet he could not but marvel at the figure before him.

Terribly bloodied, bleeding from every limb, but, incredibly, still upright, Jonathan came on.

Achish cried out to his men. "Stay! Leave him! I, Achish of Gath, claim him as my special foe."

The men stood back in awed respect. Then Achish showed a gallantry that we must respect. There could be little doubt of the outcome because Jonathan was so badly wounded and Achish had but one superficial injury.

Achish called upon Jonathan. "I salute you, Prince Jonathan, worthy foe. Our brother, David, greets you and I shall tell him of your new glory."

Jonathan swayed. He leaned a while on his sword. His breath came in fiery gasps and his answering smile was bloody. "Greet him for me. But tell me, was he true?"

"Ever true, Prince Jonathan. He is worthy of you."

Jonathan rose, wiped the blood from his face, and shocked all around. "He is true. Oh, had David been at the line of Abner this day, I tell you King Achish, you would have been but sport for our swords. I tell ye truly all ye men of Philistia, he will revenge us for he will be the Lord's triumph."

He then turned towards him who might have been his brother, rather than his deadliest foe, and cried, "Greet him for me."

He raised his sword and came on in a stumbling charge.

Achish's great heart showed Jonathan even greater respect. He threw away his shield so that both faced each other with swords only. Raising his sword, Achish hurled himself at Jonathan.

Jonathan feinted but slowly. Achish stood his ground and then, parrying Jonathan's final crashing blow, thrust viciously underneath his guard, piercing his ribs. As their bodies clashed with the fury of their blows, Achish's sword riveted Jonathan through. For a moment, they stood together, as if they were friends embracing, but death was in that terrible clasp. With great and gentle dignity, Achish laid the body of Jonathan, his enemy, upon the ground.

Oh, the shout of triumph that filled the heavens with raucous Philistine voices. Some, may God curse them, even hacked at the fallen hero, whom they would not have dared to face when he was alive. They swarmed up the hill exultant to finish off Saul's remnants.

Achish brought some order and instructed Jonathan's body to be carried towards the tent of King Baalal. He sat and tried to compose himself for he knew they had won a great victory.

Saul's line, when seeing the treachery of Abner, had slowly given ground. Now they knew that all was lost, they were desperate to sell their lives dearly.

Saul, despite his years, was inspired and had slain six of the foe. But he, too, was now dreadfully wounded and had retreated up the mountain. The Philistines had drawn back a little, seeing that the battle was won and had little need to risk more.

Saul looked over the Mountain of Gilboa and cursed it. He saw how his brave son, Jonathan, had had a great victory snatched from him when the Philistine line re-formed following the treachery of Abner. With a sinking heart, he could do nothing other than watch from afar as the enemy horde engulfed his son's gallant few.

Oh, the horror of what Saul had to witness. He had already seen one son, Abinadab, die valiantly. He was spared seeing his youngest Malki, who lay dead beneath his foes. But he had to watch the vanguard of Jonathan and Ura melt before his eyes. He was to be a helpless bystander at the slaughter of his son, the last standing of that gallant band.

He was proud, so very proud, of this most noble prince and son. He cried out to the wind, "Jonathan, my son, my son, in whom I am well pleased."

The ever-faithful and valiant Eban urged him to withdraw and try to escape.

Saul smiled at him and shook his head sorrowfully. He could see that they were now surrounded as some of the enemy, who had being screening Abner, had circled round and gained the summit.

"My dear friend, thank you for all you have done. You try to escape. Go to David and tell him to avenge us. I will try to give you a little cover."

A look of disgust came across Eban's face. Saul saw he had been misunderstood. "Oh, my dear Eban. I did not mean to dishonour you. You have shown such valour today. I would not have Israel lose you, too."

Eban laughed. "Aye, Great King. We Benjaminites have done great things today. The glory you have won today will be remembered for ever. Oh, dear master, I am proud to be with you."

And those two gallant men embraced.

The Philistines had now brought up their archers as there were but pockets of our men still standing. They treacherously just shot them down with no hurt to themselves. Slowly, the small, scattered groups fell almost silently, like piles of dead leaves being quietly blown away.

The enemy called upon Saul to surrender but the dishonour was too terrible to contemplate. So instead, he, four others and Eban staggered to the top of a flat rock. There, they vainly tried to shield themselves from the arrows of the Philistines, who were 20 yards away and freely killing with no risk to themselves.

It was clear, the enemy would take Saul whether he willed or not. They were directing their fire at the other men.

Saul recognised what was happening, turned to Eban and asked, "Friend, Eban – for you were ever my friend. Will you do me one last service?"

Eban was surprised, but said, "Anything, Great King."

Saul placed his hand on his old companion's shoulder. "Then take my sword and run me through so that I am not taken alive by the enemies of God."

Eban paused before replying, for this day had not yet seen the end for valour and gallantry.

Eban kissed his master, but quietly said, "I cannot strike the Lord's anointed. But see Master, it is easy!"

With a smile of joy upon his face, that brave, brave man, took his own sword and slowly fell upon it. He kept his eyes upon his Lord until death's darkness took away their light.

Saul was utterly, utterly alone.

Another hideous stillness centred around the tragedy.

Saul called out, "See, such is the valour of Israel. I am Saul bar Nish, the Benjaminite, King of Israel, the Lord's anointed. Into His hands I commend my spirit!"

With that, the noble, aged King, looking up to heaven, fell upon his sword. His gold diadem, worn so proudly, fell away from him and rolled away into the debris of that bloody field of Gilboa.

Because the Lord is both just and merciful, I know that He cradled the soul of that great, but flawed, King and took it to be placed in the bosom of Abraham, to share the Peace of God.

What happened next is almost too terrible to tell, even after 50 tearful years. King Baalal wanted to demonstrate his brutal triumph. So he brought the bodies of Saul and Jonathan and stripped off their battered armour. He had the bodies of men, who in life they all feared, dragged by their feet before his host, naked and exposed. Their manhoods had been defiled and ridiculed. By the time the bodies had gone around the host of that cruel King, those two beautiful countenances were battered and bloodied beyond recognition. He also fetched the bodies of poor Abinadab and Malki, and made a pile of their royal ruined torsos. Their heathen chants mocked God and Israel in a drunken, ecstatic frenzy.

Oh, they well knew how close they had come to a resounding defeat. Achish was acclaimed amongst them, as not only being the architect of victory, but also bearing such a burden of the fight and having slain Jonathan. Thus, dark relief fuelled their celebration. None dare ask how it was that these now despised Israelites, outnumbered more than three to one, had so nearly defeated the full might of all the Philistines kings.

What now occurred, I try to forget. I pray that Achish did not know or did not approve.

It still causes me so much pain that I will tell it quickly.

Those frightened, vengeful infidels cut off the heads of Jonathan and Saul, and sent them as trophies to their cursed cities of Ashod and Gaza. They had their armour hung up in the Temple of Ashtoreth, a god of particular bloodiness and cruelty. The bodies of Abinadab and Malki each went to other Philistine cities. Oh horror, my love's poor trunk and that of my dear Father were dragged and nailed on the walls of Bathshan as a mockery and a warning to all of Israel.

When I think of that King and man, now into his age so that his hair was grizzled-grey, and how often he had been gracious to me, I mourned more than any in Israel.

For Jonathan, the thought of his beautiful body, which I had caressed as being in the image of God, my grief was such that I still cannot speak of it.

The whole of Israel reeled from the catastrophe at Gilboa. There was but one grain of comfort, which brought great honour upon the men who could not tolerate the sacrilegious treatment of the bodies of their King and Prince. When the men of Jabesh Gilead, the scene of Saul's first great victory, heard of his death they were so distressed at what had happened to one to whom they were so indebted, they vowed to rescue him. So 20 of their best and youngest warriors sought to wipe out the shameful sacrilege and, travelling by night, crossed the Jordan. They took down the mutilated bodies from the walls of Bathshan under the noses of the drunken Philistines guards.

They reverently took those mangled bodies and gave them proper rites and buried their bones beneath a wondrous tamarisk tree at Jabesh. The Gileadites had rid themselves of the shame of not being with Saul at Gilboa and had showed Israel that, even in the midst of disaster, the Lord will aid resolute men. Every man of Israel is ever grateful for their daring at such a time.

Later, I was able to thank the men of Jabesh and visit the tamarisk tree. I shed tears on the graves of Jonathan and Saul, and was able to show the whole of Israel's appreciation for the valour of Israel's two fallen heroes.

Lament for Jonathan

As we were preparing to leave Ziklag, we knew nothing of the disaster that had overtaken Saul and Jonathan, though our thoughts and prayers had been with them.

Just two days before we were to depart, the first eagerly awaited messenger arrived. He was Kalib, an Amalekite, who had joined the men of Gath.

He was brought into me and I could tell at once by the grief-stricken face of Josh that the worst had happened.

I asked for news and Kalib showed he did not know the import of what he was saying. "Great Captain David, your enemies are slain. Saul and his three sons are dead. The army of Israel has been slaughtered and scattered to the winds. Your friend King Achish has gained great repute by slaying Jonathan, the son of Saul."

We all fell to our knees and our cries began to show something of the grief and sorrow we felt. Our women came rushing out to us and, when they heard, their sharp keening added to our bitter despair.

We tore our garments and cast dust upon our heads.

My mind would not take it in. Jonathan slain by Achish – a fate I had always feared.

Oh Jonathan, Jonathan!

My heart then became stone – otherwise it would have broken and I would have been added to the list that died at Gilboa.

The stupid Kalib could not grasp our loss and stood upright amidst our grief.

Joab was the first to collect himself and asked, "Is there more to tell?"

With great effort we, turned to the harbinger of death. "Aye, Great Captain. Their heads are smitten and their bodies are trophies in the cities of Philistia."

I raised my head for silence, amidst the shock at this butchery. "Tell us all, Kalib the Amalekite, tell us all – how did they die?"

The creature puffed himself up and said, "Jonathan the Israelite had broken through, but the army of Abner failed to assist them and fled. So they were outnumbered and King Achish slew him in single combat. Saul the King had asked his armour bearer to slay him but he would not. So Saul stabbed himself and fell amongst the Philistines."

Our abhorrence at what was being told and the realisation that there was more to come, held us back from more tears. There was something about Kalib's demeanour that suggested he was saving his best for last.

"Kalib, you seem to have some special news." As I said this I recoiled in horror. There, without a doubt, in that fool's hand was the golden diadem of Saul!

He answered me with smiles and great familiarity. "Yes, oh Great Captain. I did Saul and you great service. When he fell down, his wound was not mortal and he asked for help lest the Philistines abuse him. So, at his request, I took my knife and slit his throat. Look, I've brought you his diadem."

There was outrage and revulsion at this. Slowly, as Kalib looked around, he began to be anxious. He clearly couldn't understand what he had said.

I asked, very quietly, "You say that you slew King Saul? You killed the Lord's anointed and took his diadem?"

"Yes, but only to assist him – and preserve the trophy for you," he said, beginning to be apprehensive.

"You are condemned out of your own mouth. This diadem belongs to Israel and you boast of your sacrilege in killing the anointed of God."

The wretched creature tried to justify his actions. "But, great Captain, he was your enemy. I thought you would be pleased. I–"

I roared. "Take the dog away and execute him. He boasts of killing the Lord's anointed."

As he was being dragged away, he screamed, "I lied! I lied! I did not kill him. He was already dead. I found his diadem and thought you would reward me. I did not kill him."

The shake of my head confirmed his doom and he was slain, there and then.

The fell tidings had spread swiftly and we received new messengers, this time from the Elders of Judah, who wanted to speak with my generals and me. Naturally, I called in the Four, though my mind was wooden in my grief. My heart had died at cursed Gilboa.

Isaac, the Chief Elder of Judah, was escorted by three of Samuel's priests, Gad, Nathan and Zadok. They had brought letters from the Elders, which explained that, after learning of the death of Saul, they feared that the unity of Israel had been broken, at least for the time being.

The three priests were representatives of the whole priesthood and were known to be close to Samuel the Prophet, who had recommended them to the Elders of Judah.

Their message was simple. I was being asked whether the Band and I would return to Judah to help defend the territory, not as captain or general but as King of Judah.

They said that was appropriate, as I was the Lord's anointed and approved of by Samuel, which both Nathan and Zadok claim to have witnessed – though I could not remember seeing them. Furthermore, they had no doubt that there was no one else to whom God had shown his steadfast mercy, both in my anointing by Samuel and the many victories we had gained in the intervening years.

I almost wanted to laugh.

They wanted me, the reprobate, the betrayer of friends, as their King! Perhaps this was another example of the Lord leading people to their destruction by allowing them to exercise their madness.

I could neither laugh nor cry. I wearily took note of the faces of Beniah, Joab, Eli and Josh. The last three, of course, were men of Judah themselves. I dimly wondered how they felt about their former playfellow being offered such a title.

Beniah spoke for them all. "David, this must go before the whole Band. Nevertheless, I believe this is the hand of God and this is the road the Lord's anointed should take."

I looked at them all. It was obvious that the men would agree. But did they know on whom they were buckling this burden? Did they have any idea of his weaknesses, of his treachery, of his betrayal?

It did not seem to matter. I was so weary.

Woodenly, I agreed to the Elders' repeated request, which they asserted was the wish of them all.

I realised that we were soon to leave the land of Gath for ever.

We burned the empty houses of Ziklag as a memorial to our fallen heroes and then each man went alone to his family to mourn privately.

Abigail had some understanding at what I had lost and what I was feeling, so amidst her quiet tears she said, "My Lord, when you require me, I am there. But I will keep from your tent for a while so that you can be alone."

She was as good as her word and kept everyone away from him whom they would make King – yet should have been condemned as a traitor.

I lay alone for nearly three days in an agony of mind. I wished for death. I should have been at Jonathan's side.

The realisation of my sins burned into my soul. I had deserted Jonathan. I should not have stayed with Achish, his slayer. I had allowed subtle ambition to erode my loyalty. I had begun to accept the insidious poison of flatterers and think myself above other men.

I had failed Jonathan by not going in the place of Ura. I put others before my love for him. I had betrayed Jonathan by my love for Achish, his slayer. I had injured Jonathan by not re-joining Saul to demonstrate that they led a united Israel.

I had insulted God by allowing the Band to be dragged along in the army of the mockers of God. I was faithless to my oath, my love, my brother, my people and my God and I lay willing for the Lord to take me.

But no tears would flow. There was no comfort in anything I thought of.

"I am a worm, not a man." I despised myself. I was worthless.

I could not sleep but after two days of bitter despair I knew I must express to the world what they and I had lost.

I had some conception that I needed to acknowledge my unworthiness in contrast to their greatness. I, who knew and loved Jonathan best, might give him his due praise in declaring the sorrow of the whole of Israel.

After three days I came out to find anxious-looking friends and companions. I stifled their inquiries and called for all the people to be assembled.

I had no need to ask for silence. I began:

"Your Glory O Israel, lies slain on your heights.
How are the Mighty fallen?

Tell it not in Gath,
Proclaim it not in the streets of Ashkelon

Lest the daughters of the Philistines be glad,
Lest the daughters of the uncircumcised rejoice.

O mountain of Gilboa,
May you have neither dew nor rain,
Nor fields that yield offering of grain.
For there was the shield of the Mighty defiled.
From the blood of the slain,
From the flesh of the Mighty,
The Bow of Jonathan did not turn back,
The Sword of Saul did not return unsatisfied.

Saul and Jonathan.
In life they were loved and gracious,
And in death they were not parted.
They were swifter than eagles,
They were stronger than lions.

O daughters of Israel,
Weep for Saul,
Who clothed you in scarlet and finery,
Who adorned your garments with gold.

How are the Mighty Fallen in battle.
Jonathan lies slain on your heights.
I grieve for you Jonathan my Brother;
You were very dear to me.
Your love for me was wonderful,
Surpassing that of women.

How are the Mighty fallen,
And the weapons of war have perished."

No one said a word, but the lament was taken to every tribe, city, and village throughout Israel.

I, David bar Jesse, the bard of Saul the King of Israel, did him and Jonathan one last service.

515

Chapter Twenty-three

King of Judah

Achish's Lament

A chish had just completed a fascinating conversation with Janna. Not that Janna's conversation and counsel was ever anything less than considered and sophisticated. However, unusually they had spoken frankly together as men, not just as King and counsellor.

Achish had shown him David's letter. This led to a discussion about David and how he, Achish, saw the future between Philistia and Israel.

Janna purred, "Lord, it would have been a great coup if you could have permanently detached David from Israel."

Achish asked, "Why?"

"Because, Lord King, not only did you have the wisdom to make him your brother, you, who are so discerning, know that he must be one of the most accomplished warriors in the Middle Lands. Only he does not yet know his own strength or talent."

"That's perceptive of you, Janna."

Janna shrugged. He felt that was his function: to observe, analyse, weigh up and be perceptive.

Achish mused. "Yes, he is, I suspect, a military genius. Consider the way he has developed cavalry and the final destruction of the Amalekites at Besor. Ironic, isn't it, that the apparent quarrel between Saul and Samuel was about a so-called 'divine' instruction to wipe them out. David saw the inhumanity and sided with Saul – and now accomplishes the task himself! Yet, all the time he is quite convinced that he is obeying his God."

Janna suggested that was what made David so dangerous: his military ability fuelled by religious fervour.

"Do you have no religious fervour, Janna?" inquired Achish, which was a remarkably personal question in the circumstances.

"No, my Lord, none. I consider excessive fervour, which is often destructive, unworthy of an intelligent man. Worst of all, it is bad manners."

"Janna, you're a cynic?"

"No, my Lord. To be a cynic, one had to be an idealist – like you. I was never either. Your late father once suggested that I was born thin-blooded. I would rather say I passed from childhood to maturity without too many of the inconveniences in between. But as we appear to have imperceptibly crossed a line, may I, in confidence of course, for my own curiosity, ask what would you have done with David if the High King had not sent his Band away? How would you have used him? Do you think he would have fought against Jonathan?"

"Janna, the truth is I don't know."

Here, Achish paused and looked very hard. "Either way, we would have reduced the biggest threat to Philistine domination we have ever faced."

Janna was clearly intrigued and politely motioned Achish to continue.

"I would have used David's shock troops against Jonathan before using ours. So, if he had betrayed us, we would be in a perfect position to get rid of his Band, too. Our archers would have had them in their sights and the ground would have favoured us. Moreover, he would have been impossibly out numbered."

Achish paused to weigh up the other possibility. "Whereas, if he had fought against the Israelites, our victory would have been even more complete. He and Jonathan would have smashed their troops against each other, thus significantly destroying the Israelite elite for 20 years to come."

Janna looked at him with admiration and said, "David might have been killed by his own people. I congratulate you, Achish. Though it is obvious you loved the man, you were willing to risk his destruction – indeed, partly engineer it for the good of Philistia?"

Achish looked troubled and breathed, "Yes, indeed. How can you stay with such an immoral person Janna? One who will, as you say, risk a person he loves just because of politics."

Janna beamed. "Not just politics. What else is there between men of intelligence and sophistication? Shall I tell you something, King Achish, why I stayed with you and did not accept the invitation of Baalal the High King?"

"Please do, Janna, as we are being unusually frank with each other. This has intrigued me for, clearly, you are one of the most able men in Philistia. Any High King would welcome you, even though you might not be of his city."

Janna bowed accepting the compliment and said in a straight matter-of-fact tone, "Because you will be High King one day – unless your foolish brother kings are so stupid and jealous to block you. I believe that you alone in Philistia have the vision to see what must be. My only anxiety is that they may wait too long before giving you the diadem to allow you the time to use it."

Achish appreciated his frankness but returned to David. "You said something earlier about David's religious fervour and about belief. I take it you are not a believer?"

"Achish!" and Achish was quick to notice that Janna in their frankness had dropped his honorific titles. "It would be virtual death for me to acknowledge, both physically and publicly, my agnosticism. Though I don't know a single noble, or indeed many of the priests, who believe the children's stuff that we give the people most of the time. Sufficient to say, I can accommodate myself to custom – which for polite and civilised people is the self-evidently sensible and comfortable thing to do. You, of course, were once a great believer. Why did you lose your faith?"

Achish smiled. "We are being frank. If you can't speak publicly, can you imagine how the priesthood would respond if they knew that I, too, have major doubts? But I'll tell you something that only my father – and my first philian, Ekron – knew."

Janna interjected. "Yes, of course, I remember Ekron. We were the same age. It was a great pity he died, though being such a valiant and active warrior, it seemed almost inevitable."

Achish did not look pleased, "Janna, be careful. I am very jealous of the reputation of Ekron. He was one of the finest men I have ever known and I was very fortunate that he was both my mentor and philia. Were you never a philian?"

"No, my Lord, as much as I tried – especially when in my teens, but it never seemed to happen for me. I, too, had a good mentor, Astron, but whether he or I lacked something, I don't know – we never consummated our affection."

"That's a pity. I know there are men like you and obviously you miss a great deal. Perhaps that's why you cannot understand how I have feel about Ekron, Acrah and David. Yes, in case you ask, David and I were briefly philian."

Janna nodded accepting the confidence. "I am grateful for your trust. But I diverted you. You were going to tell me why you are not, at least in private, an orthodox believer?"

Achish paused. He had not thought about this for a long time. David had disturbed him with his enthusiasm, his passion and, as Achish recognised, David had access to another dimension, another power, which came from his religion. Achish thought ruefully that one of David's attractions was he seemed oblivious to his effect on others and he obviously had a total acceptance of the living reality of his God.

Achish, too, had once sought to understand the mind of the gods – in particular, Dagon, who was the god of warriors.

Though Achish believed that he had the best of the argument with David in their intellectual duels, he recognised that David had something that he lacked – or had lost. He looked at Janna and, with a shudder, realised that he must be careful. Achish, too, could become like Janna, who, despite all his sophistic abilities, appeared to have lost – or never had – a soul.

"Sorry, Janna. I was thinking. No, it's quite a short story. Due to certain circumstances, I carried out an experiment to test whether Dagon existed or not. In effect, I committed an act of sacrilege so great that it would doom me, and the only excuse for Dagon's non-intervention was that he did not exist."

Janna looked astonished. "An experiment? Certain circumstances? I don't understand."

Achish almost felt pleased with himself. To disconcert Janna: now that was something.

"I was seventeen and, as you remember, I was often in the temple seeking to understand Dagon. There is much in the philosophy of Dagon for the honourable warrior that is very attractive – especially to youth. My mentor and philia, Ekron, was going to be away for two months on a dangerous mission. So I visited the temple daily to pray, fast and perform exercises for his safety. My father heartily approved of Ekron and also my interest in religion, as it pleased the people. However, he would have preferred me to be – I remember him saying – 'a little less devout, otherwise the priests become a little too strong'. At the time I did not understand what he meant, though we do now, don't we Janna?"

Janna smiled in agreement but waited for Achish to continue.

"I had my instructor – I won't say his name and I never speak his name. He was almost twice my age and it was quickly obvious he wanted me for his philia. I tried to explain I was devoted to Ekron but on one particular night he was very pressing. Then he told me that he'd had a dream and that Dagon had a message for me. I was a boy. It won't surprise you what the message was but, sure enough, I learned that to become closer to Dagon and gain greater wisdom, prowess and spiritual merit, I had been chosen to be this man's philia – he was Dagon's earthly manifestation."

Achish smiled ruefully. "If I refused and rejected him, I would also be rejecting Dagon. I was still very doubtful because, even then, I had no time for promiscuity, and I doubted whether it was right to have more than one philia at a time."

"Yes, go on," said Janna.

"This priest told me that Ekron already knew of the dream and, knowing of the god's instruction, would be honoured to share me with him. He said that Ekron had told the priest to make himself known to me whilst he was away. 'Therefore,' said the priest, 'both in respect to the god and to Ekron, I should obey, lest just because I was a king's son, it would appear that I was above Dagon, and that I had an overweening pride, which is close to hubris.'

"Reluctantly, I went with him. It was horrible. I felt abused. It was not love he had for me, but an orgy of lust and domination as he used the drive and energy of youth to carry out his vile purpose. This lasted nearly three weeks and I was very unhappy."

"That's terrible," said Janna. "What happened next?"

"Then the priest said that again the god had come to him in a dream. You can guess what's coming – I was not to tell Ekron because Dagon's love was sacred and I would gain even greater spiritual merit by being the secret lover of a priest of Dagon. Of course, when I finally I told Ekron, who could see the change in me, he was horrified. He confirmed my suspicions that it was a pack of lies. He was all for going to see the Chief Priest to expose this man as an abuser and an oath-breaker. I was just seventeen, and we can be very earnest at seventeen. I said that until I avenged both our honours, I was unclean and unfit to be his philia and student."

Janna cocked his head on one side. "Very noble, but a trifle excessive."

"I immediately went to the priest, who at first tried to bluff it out. He was very concerned for I had taken swords with me. I had already killed my man at sixteen but he, as a priest, had done no military service for more than a decade. But I reasoned that, with his age, weight and size advantage, my challenge was fair. At first he told me that, whether or not he had done wrong, to threaten or actually kill a priest of Dagon was such sacrilege that the God would doom my impiety. He brought into play all his priestly dramatics, which, had I not been so singularly minded, might have had their effect. He reminded me that priests, even erring priests, were sacrosanct. Hence, even the King's court could not try priests lest they commit blasphemy against the gods. So I asked him what the worst thing was that I could do to ensure Dagon's everlasting enmity. He was amazed at my question but said, with that wonderful pious conviction that some charlatans have, 'to defile the temple, I suppose. No, the worst of all would be to injure or kill a priest of Dagon.'"

Janna was shocked. "I'd say he was right."

"His mistake, of course, was to appeal to my reason. Every word he uttered was if someone had stripped away a blindfold. Virtually everything I could think of relating to the worship of Dagon now seemed to have but one end: the glory and power of the priesthood. They were far more concerned with offerings and power than the souls of their worshippers – unless it was to manipulate and control them. So I renewed my challenge. At first, he refused to fight. It was simple, I told him. He either defended himself after the count of three or I would kill him anyway."

"So, what happened?"

"I started counting, slowly, and he saw I was serious. At two he came at me screaming curses of Dagon upon my head. He said, 'You are a spoilt, privileged King's brat. Dagon will defame you for your sacrilegious effrontery!' With that, he threw himself upon me, hacking violently with his sword."

Janna moaned, suspecting the inevitable. "Bad move!"

"It was easy. He lunged wildly, four or five times. I backed away to get a feel of his competence before parrying his next thrust and turning my blade into his liver. He fell dying and cursed me in the name of Dagon. I asked him did he really believe that Dagon would do these things to me, because he was the guilty party not I. He still cursed me and hissed that I would go to the Hell of Molach, Dagon's brother. Amidst his curses and before he died, just to make sure that he and his god understood my rejection and abhorrence of the lie, I disembowelled him."

"Oh no! How could you?" The colour had drained from Janna's cheeks.

"And do you know, Janna? I have had not a qualm from that day to this. Though sometimes I do, in extremity, call out to Dagon, but I suspect more from habit and – as you say – culture, than in expectation. I got rid of the body and Father had to say there had been an accident. None the less, I had committed a sacrilege against a priest of Dagon. Everyone, Janna, tells me this would guarantee my doom. Well, I am still here. I am King and likely to be High King – unless, as you say, some of my colleagues are too stupid to elect me."

Janna nodded silently.

"It's all childish nonsense to keep these men in power. True, there are many fine and inspiring sentiments within the worship of Dagon and Astorath, but most of it is to give children bad dreams and make them guilty. That way, they obey the priests, who get fatter on a lifetime of ignorance and superstition."

Janna was astounded. As the story had unfolded he found his blood running cold at such intellectual ruthlessness. He suddenly saw a side to Achish that made him feel afraid. He saw the strength and audacity of this man's pride in his intellect. It was such that he could tempt the Gods, even at seventeen, which, as he showed no remorse, was terrible hubris. And here was the same ruthlessness that could risk his friend today for policy.

Janna felt a shudder and thanked Dagon that he was not gifted with such rigour.

Achish saw something of Janna's discomfort. "Janna, I think I have shocked you. You consider yourself the detached counsellor, weighing up this and that, but I was born to be King. From the first, I knew that I would be responsible for men's lives and the safety of the city. If I fulfil your ambitions for me I might even be the High King of all Philistia. I must learn to be ruthless indeed, in search of what I always hope is the greater good, and not just to please my vanity."

Achish was amused in spite of himself at Janna's hasty departure. Although when alone he felt a sense of ineffable sadness.

David was gone and he already missed him. Yet he had to confront the fact that, if necessary, he would have been willing to risk his friend. He hoped that David would some day understand – perhaps quite soon, now he was going to be a king, too.

He pondered the remarkable change in David. Oh, he still had the enthusiasm, the passions, that glorious certainty in the search for truth. But already the marks of responsibility were showing. Achish thought back to when he first saw David. He had never seen a more beautiful youth, who had an ecstasy, an intelligence and a spirit that matched his physical perfection.

To have planned and taken command of those raids for his barbaric trophies at the age of eighteen was amazing – as was the victory at Bull Horns, he had to admit. Yet Achish knew that it cost David much. He saw it immediately when David first came to Gath. Rather sadly, Achish remembered that whilst David eventually became his philia, at first he had avoided the temptation. He was careful never to succumb to his blandishments again.

But what a difference when David arrived two years later with his band.

Those two strikes of white in his hair! Then again, David's bearing as a commander was quite remarkable considering most of his warriors were older than he was. Indeed, unlike himself, David had not been born into greatness but was that most dangerous phenomenon: a natural leader.

Yet David had not yet lost the endearing freshness of his unbridled excitement of new ideas, the willingness to believe in people and reach out to what was best in them. Though Achish noticed that this had began to be part of the repertoire of the general and ruler. Whilst it still looked spontaneous, Achish, who understood, now saw that David looked into men's hearts in way that he had not done before. Perhaps, like himself, he was beginning to be hardened and saddened by the process.

All these changes were the signs of the corrosion which command inevitably brings through the responsibility that goes with power. But the biggest change, which offset these negative features, was linked to David's physical and spiritual presence.

David was not just the most remarkable poet he had ever met, he was obviously a seer. The question was: what did David see? Was it only that which he wanted? Was it self-delusion or was it truly divine?

Achish gave a great sigh. He had no doubts that David would become High King in Israel – perhaps even sooner than Achish would in Philistia. But, he wondered, at what cost? Most of all he asked himself, was he really serving a God of love that considered the poor, the lame, and the blind? A God who urged his people to seek and enhance the Godhead in every person. Or was it a bid for power, glory and a drive for personal superiority and achievement?

Oh, he yearned for David. Not just for his mind, not for the delight they had shared as philia, not even for those wondrous psalms he had persuaded him to have written down, but he longed for David's inspiration which would inspire others, not only of his own nation, but men of all nations and all times.

Achish wondered whose soul could fail to be lightened by the sublime psalm of David?

"The Lord is my shepherd, I shall not want.
He maketh me to lie down in green pastures, he leadeth me beside the still waters.

He restoreth my soul, he leads me in the paths of righteousness of his name's sake.
Yea though I walk in the valley of the shadow of death I will fear no evil for thou art
with me thy rod and thy staff comfort me.

Thou preparest a table in the presence of mine enemies, thou anointest my head with
oil my cup runneth over – I will dwell in the house of the Lord for ever."

As Achish sang his friend's words he sighed.

From somewhere deep down inside of him, a prayer formulated itself. "Lord, God of David, help my unbelief."

King's Work

So, as God had commanded and Samuel foretold, I and my band moved into Hebron.

I was formally invited by the Elders and the priests of Judah to become Judah's King. As the Elder Isaac put it, rather flatteringly, not only was I the Lord's anointed but I was already known as the Lion of Judah.

We entered Hebron in great style, being warmly welcomed by the people of the city.

Strategically, Hebron was an ideal place to command and defend Judah, as it was virtually at its centre. There was good access to our borders to both the west and south, and it was also in a good position to deal with any hostility from fellow Israelites.

I was just twenty-four and was soon to be formally anointed King.

It was heady stuff for I had come from one of Judah's less important towns, Bethlehem. I would have been inhuman not to have appreciated that I had been especially blessed.

After some months, the sharpness of the pain from Jonathan's death had eased a little, though for a long time it was like an aching burr in my soul. Frankly, as the activity and demands became more hectic, it became a kind of balm for the hurt. All was new learning – after all, I had never been King before. For instance, who knows what a king does? Or needs to do? At that time, I certainly didn't. Apart from the experience of Saul as King of all the Jews, no one else had any idea. Each day was a new exploration, although not all the lessons I learned were enjoyable.

True, I had observed the manipulations around the throne of Saul. But being an observer was one thing, to find oneself at the centre of power was something very different. Power attracts the ambitious, so that everyone seemed to want something from me. Suddenly, I was the one upon whom their manipulations were focused. It was a horrid and daily experience to look into the eyes of a fellow human being and see avarice, ambition, greed, envy, in the rush for place and influence.

There was the stark political question, put in their different ways by Joab and Beniah: was I there to bolster the Elders, the priests, or the Elders and priests together? Was the Band to be the trainers of the army of Judah? Was I to rule Judah and be content with that, or was this to be a preparation for ruling all of Israel?

I also asked the question: to rule for what purpose and to what extent should we be concerned with other parts of Israel and the heathen nations?

I asserted from the beginning, that my idea of Kingship was that first of all the King is the shepherd of his people. Therefore he must to rule for all the people, which meant recognising the implicit rivalries between the priests, Elders, and yes, the King himself.

The first great practical issue was to acknowledge that, despite all the achievements of Saul, Israel was now disunited. Abner, the traitorous

Abner, had established himself as the greatest man in Israel. Though he ostensibly commanded the allegiance of the other eleven tribes, it was effectively only five, but he had considerably more men than we did, if ever it came to war.

Saul had one surviving son, Ishoboth. The fact that I have yet to mention him shows that not only was he not present at cursed Gilboa, but that he also was a huge disappointment to both Saul and Jonathan, despite the latter taking every effort to make a man of him. Michal once brutally said of him that, if he were alone in a room, a passing observer would still have overlooked him.

None the less, Abner made great play that Ishoboth was a legitimate son of Saul. A Benjaminite, of course, and who else should succeed Saul but Saul's son?

Abner made him King of those tribes still actively clinging to the Benjaminite hegemony. These were mainly the tribes of Gilead, Ephraim, Rueben and Simeon.

The remaining tribes had, in effect, made their peace with the Philistines and whilst not denying Ishoboth's claims made through Abner, they showed no practical enthusiasm nor any opposition, either.

Abner, with quite breath-taking effrontery, had made himself a hero of Gilboa! He argued that, without his timely withdrawal – his euphemism for his cowardly betrayal – Israel's losses would have been even greater. Indeed, as more than 40,000 men had got away, they were to be an ample deterrence against any further Philistine incursions. This he claimed was a major achievement and he quietly ignored the new border towns we had lost.

This was a masterful stroke of politics as, of course, there were now 40,000 so-called warriors who preferred his version of events. Oh, he was clever.

Abner paid a large tribute King Baalal, though in the name of Ishoboth, but generally the Philistines left us to our own divided devices.

Basically, Abner was King of half of Israel in all but name, but ruled using Ishoboth's questionable title. Meanwhile, I was King of Judah, which, as it is the largest single tribe of Israel, meant that there was much to do.

Joab was all for going to make an outright and immediate challenge to Abner and Ishoboth, basing my claim as being the only legitimately anointed King.

I had already decided against this. Israel was too bruised and, furthermore, I argued, the Abner–Ishoboth alliance could not last. Yes, I was the anointed King of Israel, but should I make the crown mine on the bodies of fellow Jews? Far better to let time unfold in our favour and, should it come to war, let it not be us who are seen as the aggressors, "the shepherd does not kill his sheep".

"Aye," retorted Joab, "unless they are wolves in sheep's clothing!"

Very early in the first year of my Kingship, I received a letter under truce from Achish. I showed it to no one except Abigail.

It read:

"Achish, King of Gath of Philistia, sends greetings to David, King of Judah of Israel.

"I am your brother and therefore you have my love. As King you have my felicitations upon your burden. Have you found Kingship a burden yet?

"I would have a truce with Judah or a treaty of peace between us for a year, five years or as long as we both shall live.

"Consider this.

"Farewell, Achish."

I pondered hard and long on my reply. Abigail agreed my final version was wisest:

"David, King of Judah, thanks his brother and King of Gath for his love and greetings, which are returned equally.

"As to a truce or treaty of peace, I also have a responsibility to all Israel. My peace with you may mean war for my northern brothers.

"Therefore, I will honour all truces. Whilst I will not seek a quarrel, nor will I shun it – be it against Judah or Israel.

"In love and duty,
"David."

Abigail saw as I did that, if we guaranteed peace on Philistia's Judean border, Achish could threaten the rest of Israel, thus strengthening his bid to become High King. I hated to think like this but I was quickly learning that as King, my personal feelings had to be set aside. I was experiencing the truth about the weight of Kingship.

One of the most difficult of many trials was how to deal with flattery. It was amazing how my every action had become so perfect. When I showed overt annoyance at their smooth words, they became more subtle, so a constant atmosphere of deference surrounded me.

I talked this over with Abigail, Josh, Eli and Beniah and asked them to help me. I was afraid that, if I was not careful, I might be- come accustomed to such undermining courtesy. I asked them to watch for any telltale signs, take me on one side and speak to me firmly.

For two years, there was no internal war. Joab and I took out punitive parties against some of the border tribes, firstly to remind them that Judah was now Kingly and effectively ruled and secondly to begin to train and integrate the younger men in our battle methods.

These raids were enormously successful, often having body counts of three or four hundred while seldom losing ten of our own men. I followed this up by letting the rest of Israel know of our success. I made a point of writing through the priests and Elders to our "brothers", Abner and Ishoboth, at Gilbeah in Benjamin, which was less than a subtle reminder that we were developing an effective army.

There was an official anointing of me as King of Judah by the priest-prophets Gad, Nathan and Zadok, who, of course, were seen to be in direct line from Samuel. This took place in the presence of all the people and Elders of Judah, which gave us the opportunity of showing how well disciplined our men were becoming and let the people see the famous Four and Thirty.

The Band were now formed into an elite guard of the army of Judah. I decided to keep the numbers at 600, but would allow replacements if and as when vacancies occurred. Consequently, there was always the keenest competition for entry. I am pleased to say that we did not need to fill up our numbers too often, such was the success and prowess of our arms.

I had particular pleasure in bringing my family back from our Moabite cousins, where they had been in exile out of the reach of Saul's unpredictability. Typically, my father, now very advanced in years, found something to complain about, but he could not hide his pride in being the father of the first King of Judah.

Josh had volunteered and I was happy for him to go as he knew my father. To his shock, he arrived to find Boaz there.

Without alarming anyone, he called Boaz out, took him one side and, giving him a sword, he told him to defend himself. This was more than he deserved for his rape of Leah. There was a brutal and bloody fight, with Josh receiving a head wound, but Josh slew my brother.

When he kneeled before me and confessed at what he had done, I lifted him up and we shed tears together. "Josh, you know I would have committed the sacrilege of fratricide if I had the opportunity. I cannot condemn you for killing my brother. He was a criminal in the sight of all honourable men and of God. He had laid aside his humanity in his brutality and therefore he stepped outside civilised rules and behaviour. He could make no claim upon me, you or Judah, for there are crimes that can never be forgiven: the murder of a child, the killing of one's parents and rape of the innocent.   Thank you for Leah. I know that justice has been rightly done."

I felt troubled for a week but then dreamed a beautiful dream about Leah and, after that, felt at peace.

During these early days in Judah, Abigail was superb. I quickly realised that being King was different from being a captain or general. We needed to spend many long nights discussing the principles and practicalities together. Sadly, I found that now my companions were companions of a King, there emerged delicate rivalries from personalities and temperaments that must be melded together.

Abigail showed her wisdom. In many ways, we had never been closer but it was as friends and companions rather than just as passionate lovers. This is partly because, once a woman has children, the father must realise that he is no longer the only person she considers – though still, of course, he is the most important. Thus, whilst we were still lovers, it was for more comfort and conciliation. We had sweet, gentle lovemaking, after which, in total satiation, we fell into sleep.

I also had Annah and I felt it only right to take her at least once a week. This suited Abigail because I realised that I had a big appetite. Over the next six years, I took other wives, mainly for political reasons to link my House with those of important Elders and other allies, but this gave Abigail some extra space. It also meant that I seldom lay with the same wife more than once a week, though I always called Abigail to me in the evenings to discuss the day's events. Tacitly, even Annah acknowledged her as the senior wife. On the other hand, Annah was very happy to take a lead with the children. Not only with the boys, Amnon and Kileab, but also with the girls – and the others, as they came along.

Abigail recognised that Joab, by capability and by ambition, rightly expected to be the second man in Judah and, ultimately, in Israel.

"Joab is your Abner. Say what you like, Abner was a very able man," Abigail said. "Though he was neither Jonathan's nor your friend, he more than anyone kept some stability during Saul's worst times."

It was not easy giving acknowledgement to an enemy but she was right. Undoubtedly, Joab was the natural second in command. So I formally announced this a little later to the intense satisfaction of Joab and his brothers.

Beniah, of course, was both counsellor and general and I made him captain of my guard, which suited him perfectly. He did not show the slightest sign of jealousy towards Joab and, if he did feel any, he controlled it marvellously well. I suspect he understood my purpose and, moreover, I think he preferred a less conspicuous role.

Abigail's great wisdom contributed to ensuring that it was the King of

Judah who ruled, though others took important responsibilities and therefore laboured in the best interest of Judah – and, of course, themselves.

All the Four urged me to be more dignified, royal and distant. But I knew I could not. They thought that my youth was a weakness, so no one ever spoke of it now. I used my spontaneity as strength by being available to people, especially if they had an interesting idea to improve the people's lot.

This apparent easy accessibility was, however, balanced with my religious activities. This included joining with the priests at sacrifices and declaiming my psalms, which, all agreed, gave me great gravitas to offset my occasional outbursts of enthusiasm.

I resolved the core question of the Kingdom of Judah. I was chosen by God, was anointed by the priests and was approved of by the Elders. But the King's day-to-day power lay with the army, the Four and the Thirty. For whilst I was unsure where the challenge would come from, it was obvious there would be a challenge before I had re-united Israel, which, of course, was the prime objective of my Kingship.

I called a meeting of all the Elders. There were more than 300, which was an impossible figure to consult frequently, so I suggested that I should seek their advice at least once a year as a whole body. In the meantime, they were to choose from amongst's themselves ten Senior Elders to be part of the King's Council. Unless I was campaigning, they would be expected to meet with me monthly.

I did the same for the priesthood. I also invited Abathar, who was acknowledged Chief Priest in Israel, if only because of how his father died. Perhaps not surprisingly, he declined to come though sent me his blessings. However he stayed with Abner and Ishoboth, and he wrote somewhat disingenuously that they "needed him more". This caused great laughter amongst us, but I gravely commented it showed where Abathar thought the greater power still lay.

So I had ten priests, including Gad, Nathan and Zadok join the Council and they were supplemented by the Thirty, which included the Four, Joab, Josh, Eli and Beniah.

I emphasised this council was consultative and that I wanted to hear their advice but, having God's responsibility, I would have to carry the final burden.

The priests ruled the morals and behaviour of the people by referring to the Law of Moses, though I sometimes was needed to resolve the occasional impasse. Like Saul, I ensured that both Elders and priests were judges in equal number.

I encouraged trade and left this largely to the Elders. I also ensured that there were no brigands in the land. Robbery had become a problem in Saul's later days, and I let it be known that, after a two-month amnesty during which time men would be forgive earlier infringements, brigandage would be a capital offence. I made this a priority and had many patrols throughout the country. After ten or so exemplary gory deaths, merchants could soon cross the whole of Judah without the need of an escort. That was something that could not be said of every tribal land in Israel.

With an eye to the rest of Israel, Abigail advised a reduction in taxation, which was still at Saul's level of twelve parts. I restored it to the traditional ten parts, giving six to the priests and only four for the King's government. If necessary, however, I could always organise a punitive raid to increase my finances. The priests were not too happy about the reduction in their tithes, but they realised they had little choice. However, as the land prospered they began to find they were better off than before.

The army, of course, was my prime responsibility and Joab had become a superb deputy. Almost daily, he continued to improve their effectiveness. He had real ability. We would identify the problem together, I would suggest a solution and Joab would simply get on and do it in the most efficient way.

I decided that neither Judah, nor ultimately Israel, would be able to have large bodies of cavalry because we did not have the spare capacity to feed the horses in the winter, unlike the plain's people. Of course, even then I had the idea that if ever Israel did control better grasslands, then we would have to improve that branch of the army. Until that time, however, in addition to the Band, I kept two cavalry divisions of 1,000 men each, all mounted, who also served as heavy infantry. This maximised their mobility and effectiveness, being highly competent with bow and sling from their horses. When it came to a major battle, these men were my shock troops. Equally, they could be used to give us cover if ever we needed to retreat.

Frankly, if Jonathan had been there to share it, it would have been perfect – even fun. Indeed, if ever I had a particularly awkward problem which taxed even Abigail, I invariably was able to resolve it by asking myself, what would Jonathan have done?

I had a special group that some called the King's Family, though we did not formally meet either all together or at set times. This consisted of the Four, and the Elders, Isaac and Haroth.

I married the latter's daughter, Eglah, not just because he was one of the richest men in Judah, but because it strengthened my lines of kinship and she was very comely.

She was my fourth wife and we had some very spirited lovemaking, not least because she had a wonderful sense of humour. She showed no jealousy at all, a feature I was beginning to appreciate as I increased my wives.

Also included in the Family were Samuel's priest-prophets Gad, Nathan and Zadok. Gad and Nathan were a little older than I was and all had been trained for the priesthood since boyhood, with Zadok being the youngest.

Gad was totally loyal to the idea of complete support to the Lord's anointed. What particularly pleased me was his interest in my psalms, as he also had inspiration and was clearly a seer. I had no doubts about his calling.

Nathan was an enthusiast, bold in his thinking and a handsome man, but to my surprise he walked alone, having neither wife nor lover. On a number of occasions I asked him why, for our priests marry which is not the custom in every land.

His answer was surprising. "I love the Lord, but I recognise that my soul is not as spiritual as some: Gad, Zadok or yours, for example. I'm certainly not like our Master, Samuel the Prophet. I discussed this with Samuel when I was young and he asked me what I thought stood in the way of my knowing the Lord – in other words, what else shared my thoughts?"

I had to restrain myself from smiling for I thought I knew what was coming.

He grinned. "Perhaps I should not say so, but I was always conscious of my body, morning, noon and, especially, at night. That was it, said the Prophet. Some men have no great physical needs, others do and some can think of nothing else. He told me to try celibacy for a time. He said that it would make demands upon me but, if the Lord accepted the gift, he would answer my sacrifice."

So that was it, Nathan was a celibate priest and continued to be. Certainly, it seemed to account for some of his fiery energy, but it seemed a strange notion, all the same.

Zadok was the youngest and an idealist. He would sometimes chide Gad and Nathan, who, in my view, did not need it. I had the idea he was something of a traditionalist and would, if he could, have returned Israel and Judah to priestly rule. Despite his youth, he, like the others, was very able, though I saw he enjoyed being close to the centre of power.

In those early, relatively untroubled days, after supper I would call in my friends or some of the Family. They had all learned to accept the presence of Abigail and valued her intelligence as I did. Though, of course, she seldom spoke unless invited to do so. Such was their regard for her that I was delighted that they sought her counsel almost as much as I did.

The most frequent topic was that of Kingship and the future of Israel. I argued that the Kingship had to be strong at the centre because potential enemies surrounded us.

The second most popular subject was that we should and would be united, whatever happened to us, Judah or Israel.

Third, and this was controversial, was that we should be willing to seek alliances with former enemies. Indeed, I thought we should augment our strength by these alliances. We people in the middle lands, with the Assyrians to the far north and the Egyptians in the south might do far better if we were allied together.

Of course, the worship of the Lord and serving His purpose was central, but we should no longer fear, as Moses had feared, that our faith was so weak that we could not have intercourse with other peoples.

I was asked if I included the Philistines in my plans.

"Especially the Philistines. If, and I stress if, we could establish a better border, they would have to swear to honour our claims to the Land of Canaan. This, of course, would mean they would have to give up territory to us. This may be unlikely, but if it were possible, can you imagine the impact we could have?"

I did not dare say any more as my mind whirled.

Surprisingly, Gad and Nathan agreed, though it was less surprising that it was Zadok who was very dubious about the approach. However, what was useful about these frank discussions was that I showed I could hear contrary opinions in an honest search for the truth. So, more as friends than as counsellors, our conversations were open and wide-ranging.

Usually, I would try to close the evening with a laugh, reminding them that we ruled in Judah not Israel.

My first opportunity at an external alliance came from Talmai, King of Geshur, who wanted to join with us in dealing with some of the troublesome nomads to the far south-east.

This was an important opportunity for us. It was significant that he sought our assistance, not that of Abner. To cement the alliance, he offered me his daughter, Macha, in marriage.

I consulted with Abigail and she was understanding. So, with great festivities, the King of Geshur brought his daughter to the King of Judah.

It made a great impression, but mainly upon me as Macha proved to be the most beautiful of my wives. She was my fifth wife and, when I saw her, I could not wait.

She was ripe for marriage, very slender but with those wondrous curves of a fully new women. She had the most attractive reddish-brown hair, with light brown eyes and had the most perfect skin that glowed with that special vibrancy of youth.

She told me later that she was delighted to come to Judah because I was not yet old and she was just sixteen. Her father had been considering marrying her to an Ammonite king who was sixty, so she was pleased to have a comely consort.

Whether it was her sense of relief at avoiding every maiden's dread, a marriage with an old man, when we were brought to the marriage bed, after all the usual jostlings, she secured the curtains but declined to put out the torch.

At first, I was a little concerned about her lack of modesty. But when I looked at her, I could see that she was just trying to please and I put away my doubts.

As I was disrobing her, she began to undress me and very quickly we were naked before each other.

To begin with, I tried to avoid becoming fully aroused as I did not wish to frighten her, but as she gazed at me I found this very exciting and soon I was standing in quivering, eager anticipation.

I drew her to me and caressed her silken skin. I followed my hands with my mouth. She almost swooned with pleasure.

Then, she gave me a gift, which was the custom of Geshur on the first marriage night. It was a jar of most beautifully scented oil, with which she began to lave over me. As she did so, she glided nearer and nearer to my hardness.

I took some of the oil and massaged her. Sensing her relaxed yielding, I took her up in my arms. I laid her on the bed and, using the oil liberally upon us both, I put my leg gently between hers. I let the oil from my fingers flow over her secret place. With my fingers, I entered her and eased apart her hymen. The tension we both expected was eased and, after a slight shudder, my mouth tasted her sweetness as she relaxed utterly. I withdrew my fingers. Amidst the oil and her exciting moistness, I entered her with a long slow plunge, right up to my hilt, creating that vibrant intoxicating union of man and women.

She was so slight that, with my arms around her, I could feel my hard member almost pressing out of the other side.

The oil drove us both to a frenzy and she cried out in a delirious passion, clawing at my back, urging me onward, faster and faster with long firm strokes until my fiery, sweet sharp seed filled her – and again ... and again.

The silken fire of her glowing skin incensed me so I kept her with me almost a whole month. Our lovemaking became almost all consuming.

Haggeth, the daughter of Isaac the Elders, who was the mother of Adonijah, my third wife, was clearly jealous. Annah appeared not to like her, but Abigail smiled sweetly and said, "Whatever pleases my Lord".

Then we would discuss business and, just to show her how much I loved her, I would lie with her. We would come to those trembling, gentle climaxes that characterise the physical and mental harmony of the perfect union after the first passions subside.

Macha was a delight and, unlike many women, overtly enjoyed love-making as much, if not more than, I did. I was not unreluctant when she persuaded her sisters to give way.

Ten months later, she gave birth to my son Absalom. This doubly proved the alliance and our lovemaking. Because of the delight I had in his mother, I had a special love for the boy, who from the first was beautiful. I showed him much favour, sometimes to the point of folly.

Chapter Twenty-four

The Battle for the Crown

I knew the peace could not last. Abner had been making huge claims on behalf of Ishoboth, and was calling me a rebel and the destroyer of Israel's unity. I was not too concerned as he had not attacked. I was certainly not going to be the first to show any aggression.

Did either of us want a war? Did Abner think he could rule Israel through poor Ishoboth? Was he hoping that I might die or be killed in a raid and then he could claim all without a struggle? Or was his posturing just that and he waiting until people became accustomed to what some had already begun to call North and South Israel?

Certainly, I hoped that nature might take its course. I felt that, as he was nearly sixty, all I had to do was wait.

Yet we both consciously prepared for the clash that might come at any time. It the end, it broke out in an unexpected way.

Joab had taken a division of the army on exercises. Perhaps I ought to have been more aware or perhaps I was careless, but I failed to realise that he was taking them to our border with Benjamin. Whilst it was necessary for us to be seen, and for our men to know the area and complete its mapping, I invariably cautioned Joab not to get into any conflict.

As luck would have it, Abner also had a division in the area and both small armies were close to the Pool of Gibeon.

Apparently, it started in a so-called friendly competition. After all, Abner and Joab knew each other.

Joab asked Abner to send over twelve of his young fighters to meet twelve of ours in a friendly contest of swordsmanship.

It was a stupid thing to do. Joab knew well just how keen young warriors are to show their metal. To be able to do so before two such commanders was an irresistible lure to show off their prowess.

The twelve young men came across. They all carried practice swords, though they did carry their personal knives as was our custom. Again, I blame Joab as much as Abner. Joab should have ensured there were no lethal weapons available.

The twelve paired off and stripped for what should have been a sword competition. But that was not what eventually happened.

There is no dispute about the beginning. The two dozen young men simply looked at each other and took an instant dislike to their opponents. Crying "Abner and Benjamin", they fell upon our boys, who rallied with the cry "David and Judah".

There were no instructors near to take care and their blows, which can hurt at the best of times, began to be lethal. First, one boy went down with a fatally smashed head. Then another. One pulled his knife on a Judean boy who was getting the best of it and treacherously stabbed him to death. Within ten horrendous minutes, every one of those youths was prostrate on the ground, dead or dying from fatal wounds.

Joab claimed, and I do not know the truth, that a Benjaminite warrior then threw a spear. No matter, Joab had called up his division, whom he said had been there "to cheer on our men". In battle order, he crossed over the Pool of Gibeon and, meeting Abner's division marching in the other direction, hit them with his full force using our shock tactics.

Abner claims Joab began the war and pointed out that he was on the Benjamin side. Joab pointed out that Abner's troops were already in battle order and were advancing.

It was short and very brutal.

Despite Abner being a very capable commander, our tactics worked perfectly. Joab's small elite guard of 50 were used in a shock assault. The Benjaminites had never met this before. Abner was bowled over but not killed. The rest of Joab's men came up in line and, quickly, the Benjaminites were in total confusion.

Abner had the presence of mind to call a retreat. They were able to leave the field in some order, but at only at the cost of nearly 400 slain, whilst we lost only eighteen of our men.

Clearly, we had demonstrated our superiority in battle tactics and gained a moral superiority over them from which they never recovered. However, this was an unwanted battle and worse was to follow.

Abner had been separated from his men, having escaped on a mule. Ashael, who of course was at the thick of the fighting, had seen him.

Perhaps if Ashael had given a little time for his horse to recover, what happened next might have been avoided. He had fought and killed his man six times, and this saps even the strongest and youngest warriors. But Ashael was always impetuous and, seeing the fleeing Abner, urged his tired horse after him.

Joab very sensibly called Ashael back. He knew he would be in trouble when he had to report to me, recognising that the war I had wanted to avoid had just begun. But Ashael with a cheerful wave rode on. Joab ought to have been much more active. Unfortunately, he assumed that, as Abner had such a good start and that Ashael's horse had been exhausted in the brunt of the fighting, Ashael would never catch Abner. Even if he did, Abner would probably have sufficient guards around him so that Ashael would have to return.

Oh, Ashael! I loved that lad's spirit. He was irrepressible. Unfortunately, he began to catch up with Abner, who had not been able to rally any of his men to him because he had outpaced them.

However, Abner could see some of his troops about 200 yards to his right up a hill. Abandoning his mule, he began to struggle towards safety.

Ashael saw what was happening. He jumped from his horse and pursued Abner up the hill. Waving with his sword, he called upon Abner to stand and fight.

Abner now turned around. Here, there is no disagreement about what ensued. He was less than 150 yards from his men, who now realised their commander was in trouble, with Ashael less than 50 yards behind him.

Abner had a spear that he was wisely using as a staff to get up the hill. He called out to Ashael to go back, shouting that Ashael had already gained sufficient honour on the dreadful day when Israelite slew Israelite.

Ashael just laughed. He called Abner a foolish old man and that he was proving himself as fearful here as he had at Gilboa.

This taunt angered Abner, but he still sought to avoid fighting and struggled on. He was now within less than 100 yards of his men, who were streaming to his rescue.

Abner turned. To his horror, Ashael had made major efforts and was now within ten yards.

"Go back, you young fool! I do not want your death on my head to start a blood feud with that ambitious brother of yours. Look, you're going to be outnumbered," cried Abner.

But Ashael was a fighter, not a thinker. Abner's remarks had angered him.

"You treacherous dog! How dare you speak of Joab's ambition when it is your scheming that keeps Israel disunited?"

They were now within striking distance of each other. A clash was inevitable.

Ashael struck out a swathing blow, under which Abner ducked. In his anger, Ashael slightly over-balanced. Abner, who was an experienced warrior and had the advantage of height, thrust his spear into the lunging

Ashael's stomach. The tip of the spear passed straight through the youth and came out the other side.

In his exertions, Abner fell over. Ashael rocked back in agony, his hands clutching at his destruction. He could not believe it. He opened his mouth to curse. The dart had extinguished his flame as doom passed over his face. Ashael fell dead.

They brought Ashael's body back to Hebron with the dreadful news that civil war had broken out. Abner was already sending out rallying cries to the rest of Israel, saying that David and his bloody Joab had brought the wrath of God upon the people, for what can be worse than a war between brothers?

Abner tried to claim that, as Joab had been the victor at Gibeon, this proved he was the aggressor because Abner had been unprepared for Joab's treacherous attack.

What could I do? I loved Ashael. His death was tragic – worse, unnecessary. The pain felt by Joab and Abashi at the loss of their brother held me back from any criticism of their impetuous behaviour at Gibeon.

I held a council of war, composed of the Four first and then the Thirty.

I knew what we must do. Whether Joab and Abashi, who were both fired up for revenge for Ashael, would like my plan, we would have to wait and see.

I set out my war objectives: minimum destruction on all sides and diplomacy more important than fighting. We would not go on the attack unless Judah was assaulted, or it became necessary to repel a major combination of forces against us. I was confident that with our superior tactics and discipline, we could demonstrate we were chosen of God. It was also important to make the point that, whilst we had the ability to destroy, we would merciful and seek a healing peace.

I argued fervently that the war was mainly a battle for men's allegiances, rather than body counts. "Brothers, I tell you I did not seek this war. I would have re-united Israel some other way. Still, we are in it now. Yet, I promise you, the more we damage our enemy the more damage we do to Israel. Just think how pleased the Philistines must be at this civil strife."

This point hadn't escaped anyone. I carried on. "Furthermore, brothers, this is a war about wining loyalty. When the people truly consider who should rule in Israel, Ishoboth or I, there will be seen there is no contest. Moreover, Abner, whilst an experienced and capable commander, controls troops who are not with him heart and soul – "

Joab coldly interrupted me, "Why do you praise Abner? He slew my brother!"

I looked hard at him. He should know why I was anointed and not he.

I would broker no disagreement, but wanted to assert my will by rational argument if possible.

I spoke formally and with equal coldness. "First, the greatest mistake in war is not to overestimate your enemy, but underestimate him. Abner is very able and will be a particularly wily enemy. Second, Ashael would have slain Abner. It was a straightforward battle, so it was not a murder."

Joab didn't like that point at all. I waved him to remain silent and continued. "Third, whilst he lives, Abner is the key to a peaceful reunification. If possible, I want no blood feud with Abner's family. Fourth, eventually Israel will need the Benjaminites to be as good as our troops when you, brother Joab, and I lead Israel against the most disciplined foes, the Philistines."

This re-affirmation of Joab's central role in my plans calmed him somewhat. "They are our main target after reunification," I said. "If we defeat them, the middle lands will be ours. When with God's help, my brothers we shall wipe away the shame of Gilboa for ever. These are my war aims. This is what I want. This is what I shall do. Is all understood?" I dismissed them all without waiting for a reply.

Abigail told me later that everyone was astounded at my delivery.

Indeed, Beniah came later and told me, "That was Kingly, David. I am sure they see that the people's shepherd must take a long view. You were graceful enough to Joab – I am sure he will do his part."

Later I took Joab on one side. He did not appear to need reassuring but looked at me quizzically and said, "David, my King, for so you are. You think at so many levels. I was impressed with you this afternoon – truly impressed – not least with your aims to avenge Gilboa."

This excited him and he embraced me, "Oh yes, David. Let us give those bastards a real lesson, you and I. Then, with the Philistines down, all the middle kingdoms are ours."

He saw my look and laughed and then said, "Surely, I am not the only ambitious one? But David, best of all today is that you have got what you wanted. No one can blame you. That's clever, my friend – really clever."

I laughed and put my arms around him. I said that we would drink to our strategy and both of us noticed that I did not respond to his gibe of implied ambition and opportunism.

Over the next two years or so, there were desultory skirmishes. When possible, I was happy for Joab to repel them. On occasions, young Abashi would sometimes grumble that it was always Joab who was fighting for a kingdom, not David.

However, I was to lead and fight the battle that counted. Without doubt, it was strategically and politically the most important of the whole war.

There were very few dead, which was what I intended. I achieved everything I wanted. It was perhaps my most successful battle to date, though few ever speak of it – it proved to be too bloodless for the bloody-minded.

Just prior to the final military confrontation with Abner, there was a delightful interlude when, at Uriah's request, I agreed to see his youngest brother, Uzza. He was the very image of their eldest brother Ura, my old mentor and Jonathan's right-hand man.

Everyone who saw Uzza was compelled to respond to his frank, boyish, friendly looks with an answering smile. He was irrepressible and, with something of a pang, I suddenly realised that dear, dear Ura, whom I had admired and looked up to, must have been like this at seventeen.

I asked him what he wanted.

"To serve you, King David, as Uriah serves and as my brother, Ura, served Prince Jonathan," he said, beaming at me.

Laughingly, I said, "With such sponsors I cannot refuse but are you not a little young, Uzza?"

He looked amazed. "King David, I am hardly younger than you were when you slew Goliath. My brother Ura told me he taught you all you knew. Well, he taught me also!"

Uriah, with his usual seriousness was shocked, "Uzza, you don't know what you are saying. King David commanded armies. Our brother was but a captain to the King and Jonathan."

I could not help myself. "Uzza, your brother, my friend and Companion, Uriah, is too gentle with us. You are right: Ura taught me everything as he, as a modest Hittite, often reminded me. He was my first captain and to be a captain with Prince Jonathan, Israel's greatest general, then Ura was as good as any man. If you are but half of what he was – and your brother, Uriah, is – why then, Uriah, I will be proud to accept Uzza's service. Oh, come, my friend Uriah. Smile, please. For here I see Ura returned. I tell you and all Israel that, after Jonathan, there was no greater soldier for God and Israel's cause."

These last comments pleased even the ever-earnest Uriah, who almost smiled. Uzza just laughed out loud and let go a wild whoop, winning the hearts of all around. We had gained as kind, brave and warm hearted a comrade as any would wish. As I was confident of the coming struggle, I agreed that he should be part of my guard but, of course, under Uriah's watchful eye.

Abner began to realise that we would not disintegrate before his threat. Judah was not going to expel me and he saw that, the longer the war went on indecisively, the weaker his position became. For sometimes, Ishoboth would petulantly complain that he was King and that he was getting tired of being told what to do by Abner.

So Abner rallied the Benjaminites and his active allies for one final last throw. He gathered an army of 70,000, the largest we had seen since Gilboa.

Our troops were not 30,000 but the Four Mighty men of Judah and the Thirty led us.

I referred to Abner's warriors as "our poor brothers" when I addressed the troops.

"Yes, I say 'our poor brothers'. I pity them. They are led by an old man who should be contemplating his last days and by a so-called King who is less than a man. So tomorrow, when we come upon them, let me tell you my plan and how it shall unfold."

Everyone was agog and all craned forward to catch my words. I had never explained a plan before.

"They will come up through the valley of Judah and we will ensure that they come on right down. As the valley narrows when they come to the Judean hills, there we will be waiting, unbeknown to them, just behind the brow of the hills. As they advance, they will be increasingly huddled and packed beneath us as the valley narrows rapidly. We will be above with our bows and slings with all the advantage of the high ground. But until I attack, you will not show yourselves."

Gasps went up. I continued with resolution in my voice. "I will lead the vanguard to break the nose of Abner's Benjaminite guard. When that's broken, the rest will become a rabble. Then, from the top of the hills you will show yourselves for the first time. I prophesy that, when they see that there are surrounded on three sides, their advance guard smashed, you above them, their only way out is it to run back down the valley. Which, brothers, we will earnestly invite them to do."

Then I revealed my masterstroke. "We will urge them towards us with cheers and greetings, not death-dealing iron. This is what will happen tomorrow. We all will be praised for our clemency."

They were experienced warriors. Their morale was high. They could see it as I said. They had confidence in me and cheered and cheered. Moreover, they saw my conviction and, despite any tensions, we all knew we could rely upon each other.

Josh came to me, hugging me in his bear-like arms, grinning with excitement.

"David, my David! I love you when you're in your Captain's mood. Do you know, I think you actually enjoy it! I'm already feeling sorry for Abner and his puppet."

He gave me a big kiss. I grinned back. Yes, this was the exhilaration of generalship. Whilst I stopped myself in time from getting too excited, I knew I had done enough thinking so that, tomorrow, I might let myself enjoy a little feeling.

As predicted, Abner's army came along down the narrowing valley with gently increasing steep-sided hills. He could do nothing else because, as I thought, with such dubious allies, he needed to keep them all together. Otherwise, he feared they might either change sides or simply return home. I was sure that the Abner of old, if he had an army upon which he could rely, would have been a much doughtier opponent.

I had Joab lead a small screening force in front of them to keep him busy and happy. But I strictly ordered him not to do too much damage, rather give them the impression that we were indecisive where to meet them. Then he was to lead them on to the Band and the cavalry, which I was commanding at the end of the valley.

By mid-afternoon, their seventy-or-so thousand were marching but becoming more cramped together in a front barely a quarter of a mile wide.

By this time, Joab had disappeared. As instructed, he took his station up behind the ridge on the right, with Beniah on the left line of hills.

Josh and Eli were with me, along with Uriah. Because I was very confident, I let Uzza stay with us.

I repeated my intention that they were not to charge or take life unless we, the advance guard, were in trouble. "I want the whole of Israel to see how incompetent the great Abner has become and how we are the merciful shepherd of our people by deliberately letting them return home safely. Every man we kill tomorrow will have a family hating our name. Every man who returns home will spread the news that God is on our side and that we are not vengeful."

We were ready when Abner's troops came into view. I gave them no opportunity for parley or time to prepare for battle, but immediately rode to within twenty yards of them.

"For the Lord of Hosts and God's anointed," I screamed.

We hit them hard. My 2,000, riding in a tight oblong shape, took up a front of about 100 yards. When we were within 20 yards, we first attacked with our bows, which must have slain at least 500. My horn stopped our advance and we stood off with swords drawn. I could see they were in total confusion so I only ordered one volley of sling shots.

They became a confused rabble before our eyes. The mayhem of the slain was added to by their few horses bolting, which did terrible damage amongst their men. They were in total confusion and all over the place.

My war horn called out to Joab and Beniah, whose replying trumpets were heard on the hills. The mass in front of us looked up and saw what appeared to be an enormous force. Almost as one man, they turned and ran.

The triumphant warriors from Judah rode quietly after them, calling out to them to go faster, but taking care not to make them feel so desperate as to stand and fight.

My men called out after them, "David could have killed every man, but you are our brothers. We wish you no harm. Go in the peace that David has given you."

They heeded our words for they could see the truth of their situation.

It was a complete success. We lost only one man – and that was by accident because he was thrown from his horse and trampled upon. Sadly, there were nearly 600 new widows, which was more than I wanted, but as we had routed an army twice our size and had clearly got our political message ove, I could not really complain about the outcome of the battle of the Valley of Judah.

The only sword thrusts that were exchanged that day proved to be between one of Abner's guards, whose horse I think bolted towards us, and young Uzza, who killed his man, but showed real quality when Uriah roared for him to return. Without letting his exploit go to his head, he did as he was ordered, which was very impressive.

There was one slight irritant about this battle. Despite its importance, because there were so few killed, seldom do the people, the priests or any of my flatterers mention it, yet it achieved all my war aims. But when there is great slaughter, they sing my praises to the heavens; apparently a battle with little blood is soon forgotten. It is strange.

In the next year, I don't think we killed more than a dozen men, mainly from accidental skirmishes, whilst we lost not a single man.

I knew it was now just a matter of time. My only difficulty was stopping those who wanted a more decisive, but bloody, triumph.

I arranged for Joab and Ashabi to take parties out and raid the south-eastern bandits. This kept both of them out of harm's way and pleased my father-in-law.

Assassins

As I expected, the break between Abner and Ishoboth was not long in coming, but it was over a very unlikely issue considering Abner's age.

Abner fell in love with Rapha, who had been Saul's concubine. Whether or not they had consummated that love, this was technical adultery. Ishoboth, who was Rapha's protector, could not have her for himself as that would have been incest. He was very distressed at such a slight to his and

Saul's honour.

Abner called him a silly fool. "Ishoboth, you are such a fool. You have no idea how foolish you just have been. Tomorrow, I will go to David and your Kingship, for whatever it was worth, will end. I advise you to learn a speech of submission. Your only asset is that David has sworn not to kill any of the family of Saul, so you are secure. You depart from history from this moment."

I received Abner's letter of what was in effect surrender. He greeted me as King of Israel and as the Lord's anointed. He wrote that we were both men of authority and that we knew this war was hurting Israel. So, if I agreed to a number of what he called "arrangements"; he would himself lead me to a meeting of all the tribes to reconfirm my Kingship.

Of course, he knew I would agree. I accepted all his arrangements and demanded one of my own, which was that I wanted my former wife and Saul's daughter, Michal, returned to me.

I reminded Abner, who knew it well, that her dowry had been dearly bought, and, that she was my wife. As she had not given her present husband a child, I could re-claim her according to the law.

Indeed, I wrote that if he did not come with the Princess Michal, then he need not come at all. I asserted that now was the time for the Lord's anointed to come forward and claim the diadem that God had ordained. Therefore, he was either to attend with the Princess or prepare to leave the lands of Israel. Whatever happened, I was coming to claim my rights.

Abner's messenger must have had wings for he returned that afternoon, agreeing to everything. He said that it was hoped Princess Michal, the King's first wife, would be ready in three days.

I could almost hear Michal's hand in his missive – "first wife" indeed.

I had not thought much about Michal. After all, it was more than nine years since I fled Saul. Though she saved my life and I had grown to love her in a way, my demand of her was to repay the past. Though I knew it would please her that, at last, she now was truly the wife of a King.

As she had not given either her second husband or me a child, it may have been that she was barren. Poor Merab had died giving birth to her third child. Sadly, none of her children had survived her.

Indeed, apart from Michal, Ishoboth and Jonathan's lame son, Mephib, there were no direct descendants left of the House of Saul, only cousins.

Cynics may say I took Michal back because she was of royal blood and gave me some spurious legitimacy, but she genuinely was my wife. Saul's act of temper in giving her over to Pateil was unlawful.

However, poor Michal was angry with me for not demanding her return sooner. If it had not been for the skills and diplomacy of Abigail, Michal would had wrought misery in my house, because she insisted upon being the First Wife.

Abigail smoothed it over with Annah, but Michal's return meant that I had now six wives and she insisted that I lie with her after every Sabbath.

She was still very lovely and, in the privacy of our bed, she could be very tender. Though I never recovered my love for her, I felt a warm pity because she still hoped to give me a son. Eventually, she and Abigail became good friends. Abigail, being older, could feel sorry for this poor woman who had been used as a pawn in the affairs of the great. Of course, as Michal was interested in politics and was quite intelligent, she was a good companion for Abigail, though she lacked the depth and wisdom of my dear Abigail.

At this time, I decided that I would also seek out Mephib, Jonathan's boy, and offer him a home. I had learned from Abner that he had not been able to regain Jonathan's property and, being disabled, found himself in serious poverty.

The next time Abner came with the Elders, he brought Mephib and I made time for the lad.

He looked much like Jonathan. His presence brought sadness as well as pleasure at my being able to fulfil my vow to treat Jonathan's family as my own.

Mephib was so grateful, especially when I said that, after my coronation, I would ensure his property would be restored. Also, from henceforth, he would live under my roof as my son – it was what I had promised his father.

"Mephib, your father was the greatest Prince Israel has ever had – or likely to have," I told him. It was a sentiment he happily shared. Being crippled, of course, meant that he could not marry. I said that until he recovered his property, I would find the means for him to procure him two concubines. I realised this must have been hard for him for he was now of age.

All was agreed.

Abner could not have been more charming. Of course, he had been a highly successful courtier to a King as unpredictable as Saul, so I must have appeared like putty in his hands.

When Abner introduced me to the Tribal Elders, all bowed, and he brought a bonus, the Chief Priest Abathar.

There was some discussion about the coronation and whether I should be re-anointed by Abathar. I said I thought not, as being anointed by the Prophet Samuel seemed more than enough, though he should bring the Holy Oil and I would make my own reconfirmation with my own hands.

Abathar could not have been more compliant. I assured him that I did not think it necessary to make any of Samuel's protégés, Gad, Nathan or

Zadok, High Priest just at the moment. I said that, if he were willing, it would please me greatly if he continued as High Priest. Abathar's response was more than enthusiastic and I began to hear how not only did Samuel prophesy I would be King one day, but also his poor father Amlech. He, of course, always knew that I would lead Israel!

Well, he had stood by me at Nob, so his version of history had some validity, but of course his claims about Samuel and Amlech were quite false. But this is typical of what a King must face daily. Oh, I missed Ura's presence to deflate pomposity, both in others and in me.

Abner, who hated me as much as I hated him, knew he was safe and we spent a number of hours going over the time of Saul. He gave me his perspective, which helped me to understand more of the events through which I lived, although that is not always the best view because inevitably one is biased. It also helped to fill in potential gaps in my story.

Abner was completely relaxed. He even went so far as to correct me about the Battle of Gilboa. "My King, you thought it was going to be another Havilah when the similar tactics that defeated King Agag could be used against the Philistines. But at Havilah, we were an army whose morale was high. At Mount Gilboa, all of poor Saul's disasters came to him at once. The witch of Endor was the final disastrous throw of a desperate man and all could see it. I could barely keep those men on the mountain, let alone get them to charge."

Who knows? He might have been right but I still could not forgive him, though I smiled.

Then, as he left, he said with the same irritating air of superiority that I remembered so well, "It was a very good move about Abathar. He's a complete cipher. He will have no ambitions to be 'Samuel' to your 'Saul'. Be careful to watch Samuel's three zealots – but I am sure you are already learning this."

He was just about to leave when he turned. "By the way, taking in young Mephib was such a kindness. I wonder if you would do the same for poor Ishoboth? If you did, then you would have all the sons of Saul's house under your roof."

Then he looked at me, as if for the first time. "David, my King. I seriously under-estimated you and that is the worst mistake a statesman can make. You learned your lessons well. I did not expect you to achieve so much. I congratulate you."

The arrogance of the man, the smooth effrontery! He had wished me dead a hundred times over, but I took a deep breath, accepted the proffered hand and smiled my most winning smile.

I said, "If I have learned it is because I had to learn quickly and from such great teachers – and you, Lord Abner, were amongst the best."

Just as he was leaving, I sighted Joab and Abashi's party returning from a raid. They galloped up and were shouting excitedly about their great plunder.

When Joab saw Abner he went white.

Abner saluted and bowed. I had to intimate to Joab that good manners meant he should return the salute. We had argued fiercely before about what can and cannot be forgiven.

I had reminded my firebrands that we had made truces even with the Philistines and we had to honour them – and we would do so with Abner's party.

What I had not told Joab before he started on this last mission was that Abner was being brought into my council and that he would retain all his dignities and properties. I had meant to and had been looking for the right time to get him used to the idea.

We all exchanged pleasantries, but Abner was looking intently at Joab. "Lord Joab, I take it you approve of our Lord the King's dispositions at this joyful reunion of the people of Israel?"

Joab nodded and boldly said, "Of course, I am second man in Judah and I will be second to the King in Israel. Hence, I can say with confidence that I know the King's mind better than any who brought division to our people."

Abner, ever the courtier, bowed and said, "Lord Joab, those sad days are happily ended and much, may I say, due to your great generalship and valour. Israel is fortunate indeed to have two such outstanding commanders as David and Joab."

I had hoped this flattery would have gone down well with Joab who only replied with a thin smile.

"Lord Abner," I said, eager to make up to Joab for my omission, "your acknowledgements of my brother Joab's genius is well met. Truly sir, you who have much experience of great office are well fitted to judge. I doubt that ever a King had a greater commander than I do in Joab, but I am privileged that he is also my brother, friend and companion."

Joab seemed assuaged by this and bowed low.

All would have been well had Abner not said the fatal words, "And I shall look forward to hearing you in the King's Council? For I am sure all his councillors will value your weighty words."

Joab suddenly smiled warmly at Abner. I ought to have known, for when Joab smiled that particular smile he was at his most dangerous. "Lord Abner, you are too kind. I do look forward to sharing your counsel in the King's chamber for we brethren are young and inexperienced, whereas you will have served three Kings."

Foolishly, I wanted to see them reconciled and I took Joab at his word. We all greeted each other farewell and went our separate ways. Joab ostensibly to cleanse himself, I back to my chamber and Abner returned to Gilbeah.

Ten minutes later, Joab and Abashi mounted on fresh horses, trotted out of Hebron and caught up with Abner at the bridge at the end of the town.

Joab was courtesy itself and said, "Lord Abner, can you spare me a small moment of your time? I have here a parchment from the King and we are both anxious to know that our interpretation of the words matches your own."

Abner, suspecting nothing, alighted from his mule and walked between the two brothers into the shade to study the paper.

Suddenly, he sensed his danger as Joab put his hand upon his shoulder as if he would consult with him. But, as their eyes met, each saw deadly hate. In Joab's hands was a dagger which he, without a word, slowly pushed into the side of Abner, who was being tightly held by Abashi, who then slowly plunged his own dagger into the back of Abner. Still holding him up, they then slit his throat.

Not a word had been said. His attendants came rushing towards their bloody prostrate master, horrified, but too afraid to say or do anything in the presence of his killers.

The two men remounted their horses and, laughing, shouted, "Ashael, you are avenged!" before riding back to Hebron.

They left the wailing attendants by the side of the body of Abner, once commander of the armies of Israel, the second man in the Kingdom, lying slaughtered in a gutter by the hand of Israelites.

Worse was to follow.

I knew nothing of the murder for nearly five days, though the rest of Israel did and were outraged. Of course, many blamed me, suggesting that all my peaceful words hid a vengeful nature now that I was unopposed.

The day after Abner's death, two Benjaminites, Banah and Reccab, famous hunters and swordsmen, visited Saul's surviving son, Ishoboth.

The servants said that the Lord Ishoboth – no one called him King any more – was sleeping.

The two men said, "Oh, the lazy dog! We bring a gift to solve his lethargy and reconcile him to King David."

So the servants, knowing them to have been supporters of the boy's father, did not prevent their entry.

They broke into his sleeping chamber and, without more ado, stabbed him while he lay sleeping. Without waiting to see if he was dead, they cut off his head to bring to me as a trophy!

To my amazement, for I still did not know of these terrible events, a deputation of Elders, along with Abathar, the Chief Priest, came to complain about the murder of Abner.

I was aghast and could say truthfully that I knew nothing about it.

Joab came forward and quite casually said, "True, oh King. We did not tell you because it was a family matter. Abner slew my brother Ashael, a darling of your heart, so I slew Abner."

I was horrified. I tore my garments and called upon all men present to witness, as I called upon God, that I did not know of the murder. I had not wished it. I had not arranged it, and that I and all Israel would go into mourning. Furthermore, I declared that I would fast for five days and walk behind Abner's bier. May the Lord strike me in my weakness if I had known about or planned Abner's murder.

At the same time, I angrily ordered Joab and Abashi to immediately leave Hebron because they offended my sight.

Careful observers noted and whispered slyly that I did not chastise the two further, nor banish them. But how could I? Their claim that it was a family matter carried some weight. Whilst I, as King, would never approve of blood feuds, they were not unknown in Israel. Of course, blood money would have to be paid to Abner's family and I certainly would make sure that happened.

When my attendants hurried Joab and Abashi out of the chamber, another drama unfolded.

Banah and Reccab demanded audience. They were told that David was with the Elders and was involved in weighty business.

"Even better," said Banah. "We have something of importance for all of Israel and for the Lord King that would gladden all present."

Little did I suspect what was to follow. So, asking the Elders whether we should see these insistent men, one Elder said Banah was a distant kinsman of his and was a man of some weight amongst the Benjaminites. All agreed that we should see them.

They entered, swaggering, and hailed me. "King David, now truly King of all Israel. We have here the head of your enemy. One who would usurp your greatness."

With that, they opened their bag and rolled the head of poor Ishoboth at may feet.

Everyone was astounded and horrified. As I was not expecting it, I was almost sick. I had to turn my head away and use a cloth to stop my churning stomach.

There was complete silence. I did not know what to say. So, weakly, I asked what had happened.

"Great King, we heard of the death of Abner, who was your enemy, but we knew of one who was even a greater threat. We came upon this pretended King as he was sleeping. We slew your enemy and brought you his head so that you and all your House can sleep peacefully."

Now the shock had passed and I had the time to think, I was more angry than I can remember. These two blundering, stupid, cruel fools! With Abner and Ishoboth dead it looked as if my reign was beginning with a vengeful and murderous bloodbath, something I had sought to avoid at all cost. Abner understood this clearly and consequently, to his doom, had trusted in my protection.

This time I could let my feelings go. "You wicked, cruel murderers. Ishoboth was the son of my Father, Saul. He was the brother of Michal, my wife. He was my kinsman, and I had taken an oath to defend the family of Saul with my Brother, Jonathan."

I was livid. "You are dogs! Unclean! You have murdered an innocent man. You have besmirched the word of the King and disturbed the peace of Israel. On all these counts you die and your bodies be flung on the dunghill, the fate of all outcasts and murderers. Away with them!"

Their shouts for mercy were stifled by my guards. A little later, their bodies were amongst the dung.

I was as good as my word and followed Abner's bier. I fasted five days to the extent that my friends became concerned for me. Yet, it was vital that all Israel could see that I was guiltless and also mourned the death of this great, if flawed, man.

I called Joab and Abashi to me and demanded that they pay Abner's family a thousand shekels of gold and iron. Joab accused me of being a hypocrite to my face.

I answered him coldly. "Joab, I tell you in truth, whilst I did not love Abner, nor ever could, I did not want him dead. Only our brotherhood and companionship has stood between you and the executioner, so do not tempt me further."

Joab, for the first time, looked concerned as if at last he had seen the stupidity of his act and how it endangered everything. He threw himself upon the floor and refused to get up unless I called him "brother". Yes, he would pay Abner's family not a thousand, but two thousand shekels.

So we made our peace and journeyed towards my coronation.

When asked where the tribes should gather, I had no hesitation – at Gilbeah. This was Saul's home camp, which symbolised continuity, and that David of Judah could go safely to Gilbeah in the land of the Benjaminites.

It was strange being back again after almost ten years. I could not help but be amused at the difference at this entry compared with my last hurried departure.

Night had fallen and I began to feel uneasy. I dismissed everyone, even Abigail, and said I would be alone in preparation for the morrow. I did not sleep as my mind restlessly reviewed what was happening to me.

Here I was, now thirty and a King, but seemingly, only yesterday, a follower of sheep – frightened and lost in this camp. Now my every word was law.

I needed to talk, so I called for Josh and Eli. It was now midnight, so they came hurrying, looking grave with their swords drawn.

At the sight of them I started laughing, they looked very confused.

"My Lord King, are we the cause of your amusement?" asked an embarrassed Josh.

With a stab of horror, I suddenly realised that my casual words were now weighty. The anxious look between them posed the question: "is this the beginning of the tyranny or madness of kings?".

I knelt before them, but with a smile, and craved their pardon. "My comrades and brothers, it is I, David – your playmate and boyhood friend. He pleads with you to put off our glories: you, your generalship, and I, the heaviness of Kingship. Please Josh, Eli, come swimming with me – as a favour to an old friend. I'm not moon-struck but I can't sleep and I am scared."

Something of my predicament and loneliness reached them and Josh said, "David, you always were a queer one! It's not all that warm but, if you can still run, we'll more than keep up with you and get to the Pool of Joshua before you."

I was instantly tempted to rename the pool "Jonathan", but saw that this would confirm the force of power that I was complaining of.

Without another word, we set off. It was not difficult and though there was a half-moon I would have known the way blindfolded. Though the evening air was cool, we kept up such a good pace that when we arrived, we were sweating well. I was pleased to be able to show my oldest friends that I was still the better long-distance runner.

I stripped off and, with a whoop, plunged in. They followed.

Oh, we frolicked and laughed. Josh showed he could still out-wrestle me and nearly half drowned me. We played together as if we were still the boys of our memory who had been given a holiday.

We came out and ran to dry ourselves.

Then, sheltering from the wind, I began, "Josh, Eli, I am so fearful of tomorrow. I long for the yesterdays when we, along with Aaron, could swim at Bull Horns and need only think of that day."

They understood at once. Josh said, "Poor Aaron. He always did find it hard – and he was so modest!"

We laughed and appreciated that we seldom spoke of our dead comrade.

I said, "I'll never forget how quickly he grew up when we were in Bethlehem. He would blush at Josh's never-ending talk of women, yet within a little year he could not think of anything else. Tell me, did he ever...?"

Josh laughed. "Though he had no time to marry, he found a great prostitute called Mera. He must have visited her daily – he was always borrowing shekels to pay her."

I was glad that he had experienced something of manhood. Mind you, I was also grateful that they could not see my blushing face when Mera was mentioned.

"But tomorrow ..., oh, I don't know! What has happened to me? When we first came back into Judah, I was still your friend. But every day afterwards, I felt a growing barrier between us. You are my oldest friends. It was as if you were addressing someone else, not the young, naive youth that – yes, I admit it – at times was rather priggish!"

We all laughed at this.

Eli looked to Josh and said, "David, we too have spoken about that. We have experienced it since we became the Four. Others became cautious of our authority, as we are of yours. But I see a plan – nay, almost a straight line. First, you had to learn and be taught valour and skill as a warrior. You were exposed to the test and killed your man so early."

I wondered what Eli was leading up to.

He continued. "Then you had to learn the ways of the camp and of the great. Always, you had to be seen as belonging to neither the priest nor the King, but to both. You were also known to be inspired by God. Then you needed to campaign and to learn how to succeed as a commander of men – to be sent into the wilderness and into exile. Again, you learned and stored up that wisdom, and all the time you were just and righteous."

Josh nodded in approval. Eli carried on. "Your anointment by Samuel was a clear sign. And, to those who knew you, it was but a step on your road of learning. You learned to command the Band and armies. You learned from the heathens, yes for I will admit we learned much from our time in Gath, and then to complete your apprenticeship, you learned to rule as a King in Judah before taking up your final task."

Eli now seemed moved to tears by what he was about to say. "David, my little friend, schoolfellow and brother, this night will be the last we can speak with such open hearts. I cry for your loneliness but as sure as the Living God lives, I can see his plan for you as a straight line. You are His chosen one and He has tempered you to be His instrument."

None of us spoke. I tried to take in Eli's words, but he had made it plain. I, too, could see the pattern as the Lord had tested every part of me and had been my schoolmaster.

I looked at my two oldest friends. I was overwhelmed with gratitude for their friendship but knew this night was a final farewell to those yesterdays.

Eli's words had brought balm to my soul and joy to my heart. I felt inspired.

Without a word, I stood, indifferent to the chill night air and held out my hands to my friends. We were naked to the world, signifying our common frailty, yet we were all part of God's purpose.

I said, "As Eli's words have traced my path, so too the Lord chose you to walk with me and share the burden."

Then I became truly inspired and knew what God wanted from me.

"Together with the Lord's direction, we will build a City of God for His united people, where justice and righteousness shall be manifested each day. We shall scatter the enemies of God, so that they will marvel at our valour. Kings shall bow down before the representative of the Living Lord and together we shall found an Empire that knows the Lord."

We clasped our hands together and my spirit cried out.

The Lord answered me as I sang:

"The Lord is my rock and my fortress and my deliverer – my buckler and the horn of my salvation and my high tower.
I will call upon the Lord who is worthy to be praised.
In my distress I called upon the Lord,
He heard my voice out of his temple and my cry came before him, even unto his ears.

The earth shook and trembled; the foundations of the hills moved and were shaken because he was wroth.
He brought me forth also into a large place because he delighteth in me.

It is God that girdeth me with strength and maketh my way perfect.
He maketh my feet like hind's feet and setteth me upon my high places.
He teaches my hands to war so that a bow of steel is broken in my arms.
The Lord liveth
Blessed be my rock and let the God of my salvation be exalted."

Coronation

And the day of coronation dawned and there were loud cries, "DAVID! DAVID! LION OF JUDAH! DAVID KING OF ISRAEL! HALLELUJAH! HALLELUJAH!"

The sound was deafening as the people of Israel acclaimed my coronation.

My senses reeled. I was overwhelmed by the crowd's excitement and dazzled by the upraised swords. The waving of palms and the glorious colours of the clothes of the hosts of the Twelve Tribes filled the valley as far as the eye could see.

"DAVID, KING OF THE JEWS. HALLELUJAH! DAVID. KING DAVID, LION OF JUDAH. DAVID. KING OF ISRAEL."

The rolling waves of sound and colour crashed against the hillsides and cascaded back again, each cry building upon the other as the Israelites celebrated their nationhood.

Yes, all the Twelve Tribes were there. All could see that I led a united people. Every face reflected back my delight, forgotten or forgiven was the blood that had been spilt. The years in the wilderness, when Jew had hunted Jew and self-inflicted wounds that threatened to shatter our people for ever, were over. I had staunched the bleeding with victory against our enemies. I had turned our weapons against the foes of the Living God and not on to the people themselves.

Almost in a delirium, I could look around and see what was happening. This had always been the gift of God: that in the turmoil of the stomach-wrenching fear, amidst the fight or desperate flight, I could see clearly. Others were overwhelmed by the events but I rode through them, even though I shared the emotion.

Oh yes, I too feared the spear thrust, the slash of the sharp iron biting deep, deep into my limbs, as I slashed, thrust and cut into his limbs of him who would kill me. I, too, felt the exhilaration as my sword beat through his defence into his quivering and thrashing body. The relief that the despair at the bleakness of death was on his face not mine. My foot placed upon his chest, to cast his falling body aside, and so confirm my triumph and his doom. Then the sharp agony of tired fearfulness, as another warrior stood in his place and the killing or be killed began again.

"DAVID, KING OF ISRAEL! DAVID, KING OF ISRAEL!" had become a rhythm. The Horns of the Rams of the priests blared in unison. The cries of the people, every man and woman, were as one. They acclaimed their King, affirmed they were one people and that this triumph belonged to them.

Every face had become a mouth to give voice to the cry, "DAVID, KING OF ISRAEL!"

Every face seemed to be filled with eyes wide, wide, with excitement, intoxicated with the moment as they chanted, "DAVID, KING OF ISRAEL!"

Even Joab was smiling. Our eyes met. He looked at me with unusual warmth, my dour second in command, who liked to style himself "The Second Man in Israel".

I walked over to him and embraced him. I could feel his excitement and smell his perspiration. I looked into his eyes and, perhaps for the last time, I could see total joy and loyalty. I kissed him and if possible the shouts grew even louder.

He embraced me in his huge bear hug. "David! David! You've done it! You are King! The Tribes are yours. We are one people. You are the Lord's anointed!"

He stood close in his delight but still gave recognition that it was my triumph. Oh yes, he had helped, but here was his admission that I was the chosen one. Through all the doubts and trials, I was the rightful King.

I kissed him again and then raised my hand to salute him. The crowd went wild as he kneeled before me.

I walked over to Abashi who stood amongst the Band of Thirty, my brothers in arms, my Captains over the thousands. I turned to him. He was dauntless and ever true. His face told it all as he, too, kneeled before me. His delight was for me. He had never doubted me. He shared unquestioningly the goal of freeing the people.

He looked up, "David, my King, my general, Chosen of the Living God. David, I am so proud and so humble."

I put my hand gently to his mouth, and raised him up. "No, no, Abashi, my Captain, Companion, friend, and from this day, brother. You and your brothers, along with the captains and the Six Hundred have made this day. You have accomplished all, which the Lord of Hosts demanded of us. Your wounds are marks of honour in the service of God and the people. I am the privileged one. Although God chose me, it was your right arm that slew God's enemies and set the people free."

I had to shout this to make Abashi hear even though I was close to him. The other captains heard what I had said and repeated it to those around as I went and saluted each of them in turn. The noise grew even louder.

The Thirty as one man kneeled and began to sing our battle song, "Hosanna to the God of Israel. Hosanna to David, the Lord's Anointed."

The Six Hundred followed, as did the crowd around, the only people standing were the priests surrounding the Ark of the Covenant.

The people's voices swelled into a glorious choir. The valley echoed with the melody that filled every heart reminding them of our journey together.

I walked towards the Ark, the symbol of God's promise to the seed of Abraham, the first father of all Israel. I was smiling but saw clearly what had to be done.

My smiles were returned as I walked towards the singing priests. Abathar, who I had made Chief Priest. He was loyal because he had no where else to turn. Gad, a prophet and aesthetic, whose only ambition was for the people of Israel. Zadok, young but very able, and dear Nathan who was both support and spur.

I turned first to Abathar. It was he who had led the re-anointing. Only he could administer the rites and go near to the Arc of the Covenant without sacrilege. I looked into his eyes and gently placed my hands upon his shoulders and as if I were to kiss him. I gently pressed him downwards. He knew what I wanted. At first there was tension in his body and he could not look me in the eyes. He was aware of the moment. We seemed fixed in time, he and I, as the King of Israel stood with his hands upon the Chief Priest of Israel. Who would kneel to whom? As if each subtle movement took an age, I was conscious of the smell of the holy oil on Abathar's hands, of his woollen cloak, coloured scarlet, of his blue headband holding fast his hair, which drooped in long curls. His skin was moist, and, at the corner of his mouth, the light caught the spittle lying upon his lips from his singing. Would he never kneel? Or would I have to bow and give way? My arms grew tense. Though my face still held its smile, there was no pretence in my grip as my fingers dug into his flabby shoulders. Suddenly, the tension eased as Abathar slowly bent his knees.

He lowered his head, kneeled upon the ground, threw wide his arms and cried above the singing, "Blessed be David, King of Israel, the Lord's Anointed. Hosanna!"

Now I was King indeed. Amidst the peoples of Israel, no one stood except I.

It was the King who was the Lord's anointed. He led God's people because he was chosen. Though it was the priest and Prophets who confirmed the Lord's Anointed, it was the King who led and united the people of Israel.

With a gesture, I caught the people's attention and suddenly all were silent. This was almost more awe-inspiring than the earlier deafening hallelujahs.

All had become one person as there was a catching of the breath. The moment was an echo of silence, the tension was palpable, unbearable.

I was inspired, terrified and knew that God was about to speak through me in a way He had never done before. But, as before, I felt an emptying of myself, everything fell from me. There was a stillness inside me as I became part of everything. A blade of grass, a stone, a cloud, I was nothing but belonged in everything. I was at Oneness with the One.

"People of Israel," I cried. "People of Israel! Your Lord's anointed speaks to you from the Lord of Hosts. I am commanded to say His words, from the mouth of the Ever Living God. You are my chosen people and through you I will reach the ends of the world. You are my people who will fulfil my purpose for all mankind. As I spoke to your father Abraham and Moses, who brought you out of the land of Egypt, I am still with you."

I paused.

There was utter stillness. Even the breeze was still. I circled, with my hands raised high. Every eye was upon me.

The Spirit possessed me. "Hear what the Lord your God says to you. This day, is a day of renewal of My covenant. You are My people and I am your God. I will make you great in the face of all peoples. The King shall rejoice in the strength of the Lord. I will bless the Lord at all times. In Him do I put my trust. Clap your hands, you people of God. Shout unto Him with the voice of triumph for He is a Great King over all the earth."

I was overcome. I sank to the ground, my arms held out in supplication.

Slowly I stood, dazed and drained by everything that had gone before. Abigail, sweet, sweet Abigail, my wife, had come to me in my faint.

She drew me up and, as she did so, I saluted her. "Daughter of Judah, my succour. I acknowledge you and all the daughters of Judah who gave so much."

I sensed a step behind me and there stood Michal, the daughter of Saul of the tribe of Benjamin, my first wife. She was queenly. This was the high point of her life and our marriage.

"To you, Michal, royal daughter of the Benjaminites," I said, "for your loyalty and devotion to Israel's cause, I salute you also." This reminded the Benjaminites of my direct link with their tribe and Israel's first royal family.

Looking at Michal there could be no doubt that she was indeed royal.

She bowed rather than kneeled. "Oh King, my husband, I am your maidservant, and the daughter of Saul." There, his name was out in the open. "I salute you in obedience, as the Lord's Anointed, and ask for the people's prayer that I may give you a son."

This gave me the opportunity to fulfil my obligation to Abigail and all the women of Israel. "Men of Israel, salute your wives, mothers, sisters who have also born all our tribulations. Hosanna to the women of Israel!"

There was a great answering shout of "Hosanna!" from every man present and then the ululating cry of the women, which we men heard only as we went off for battle. My hair rose on end, as did every man's, reminding us of the separation between being a worker in the fields, a tender of flocks, to becoming a soldier, who goes to kill or be killed.

Stupidly, Michal intervened again. "And I greet you in the name of my brother Jonathan, first Prince of Israel."

At the name of Jonathan, my heart ached. He who should have been King here on this day. He who I had begged to take his rightful place had, in love and obedience, denied his birthright and had knelt before me and proclaimed me King. He whose foot I was not worthy to touch had taught me everything. Oh, but I loved him beyond measure, for he had a mind and body that excelled all, yet loved me when I was but a poor urchin from little Bethlehem. Never a day goes by without me thinking of Jonathan since that bitterest time of his cruel slaying by my friend and brother. Lord God, was all this built on that betrayal? Oh Jonathan, Jonathan, I weep for you.

Suddenly, I realised that I was lost in my thoughts of him, whilst those around me stood and wondered whether I was inspired. I drew myself together.

My glance at Michal was angry and sad. "Aye, Lady. Jonathan, Prince of Israel, was the greatest of all men. All know it and I acknowledge it to the world. I proclaim that I will avenge him and Israel for that bitter day at Gilboa."

Then sheer revelation from Gad, the prophet and priest. "David, King of Israel, you have given us the word of God. Now, give us your word."

I was stunned for a moment. I could hardly think. Then, signalling to the Thirty Captains, they strung out into the tribes, a hundred paces each so that they could hear my voice without too much strain and then pass on my message, as we learned to do with the troops.

This would be my message, my recollection of how it was. "People of Israel, you are now and must always be one people – God's people. You must seek him in justice and love. My ideal will be to be what my love and brother taught me, to be the Shepherd of my people. Together, we proclaim God's greatness to all the lands. When we are prepared and ready to be one, we will avenge Jonathan, Prince of Israel, and his father, Saul, and make us an Empire for the Lord."

I drew breath and said:

"The Lord is My shepherd I shall not want he maketh me to lie down in green pastures."

All the people took up the psalm, which I had written at another time, for another cause, but which the Six Hundred had found an inspiration.

When we came to:

"Yea though I walk through the valley of the shadow of death I will fear no evil."

there was a roar and the chant broke out again.

"DAVID! DAVID! LION OF JUDAH! DAVID, KING OF ISRAEL! HALLELUJAH! HALLELUJAH!"

So David, the shepherd boy, the youthful bard, the young warrior, the Lord's anointed had become King of Israel because he was God's warrior bard.

And tomorrow? He would seek to build the City of God, which would become a byword for a place of justice and truth. He would extol the Lord's name and make His people great throughout the world.

He would indeed be worthy of the greatest prince the world has ever known, Jonathan.